THE MAMMOTH BOOK OF
20TH CENTURY
SCIENCE FICTION

THE MAMMOTH BOOK OF
20TH CENTURY
SCIENCE FICTION

VOLUME TWO

EDITED BY DAVID G. HARTWELL

ROBINSON
London

Constable & Robinson Ltd
3 The Lanchesters
162 Fulham Palace Road
London W6 9ER
www.constablerobinson.com

First published [...] Century

This edition [...] on,
an imprint of Constable & Rob[...] 4

Copyr[...]

A copy of the British Library Cataloguing in
Publication data is available from the British Library

ISBN 1-84119-514-6

Printed and bound in the EU

10 9 8 7 6 5 4 3 2 1

Contents

Copyright Acknowledgments

Acknowledgments

*To Maron Waxman, Susan Ann Protter, Les Pockell, and
Kathryn Cramer, without whom this book would never
have been completed.*

I would like to acknowledge the significant presence of John W.
Campbell, Isaac Asimov, Robert A. Heinlein, and Arthur C. Clarke,
and all the other science fiction writers who are not reprinted in this
book. I used their work to support my argument for the consideration
of science fiction as a worthwhile literature in *The World Treasury of
Science Fiction*. I used many of them again to illuminate and uphold the
value of the hard SF tradition in *The Ascent of Wonder*. In this book, I
chose the work of other major writers, some of them less familiar, some
of them equally famous, so as not to allow my argument to get lost in
the particular aesthetic of SF that is so dominant in their work. But
their presence is here anyway, anyhow, even in the absence of
representative examples of their work.

Rooted as they are in the facts of contemporary life, the phantasies of even a second-rate writer of modern Science Fiction are incomparably richer, bolder, and stranger than the Utopian or Millennial imaginings of the past.

– ALDOUS HUXLEY

Science fiction is no more written for scientists than ghost stories are written for ghosts. Most frequently, the scientific dressing clothes fantasy. As fantasies are as meaningful as science, the phantasms of technology now fittingly embody our hopes and anxieties.

– BRIAN W. ALDISS

Introduction

The twentieth century was the science fiction century. We are now living in the world of the future described by the genre science fiction of the 1930s, 1940s and 1950s – a world of technologies we love and fear, sciences so increasingly complex and steeped in specialized diction and jargon that fewer and fewer of us understand science on what used to be called a "high school level". These are the days, as Paul Simon sings, of miracles and wonder.

Science fiction is a literature for people who value knowledge and who desire to understand how things work in the world and in the universe. In science fiction, knowledge is power and power is technology, and technology is useful in improving the human condition. It is, by extension, a literature of empowerment. The lesson of the genre megatext – that body of genre literature that in aggregate embodies the standard plots, tropes, images, specialized diction and clichés – is that one can solve problems through the application of knowledge of science and technology. By further extension, the SF megatext is an allegory of faith in science. Everyone knows there are science fiction addicts – I am one – and this is why: it expresses, represents, and confirms faith in science and reason.

Life is never so neat that abstract patterns, such as centuries, are more than arbitrary dividers. In the case of science fiction, the twentieth century really began about 1895, with the first stories of H.G. Wells, the greatest writer in a vigorous literary tradition now superseded, called the Scientific Romance. Wells had many contemporaries writing Scientific Romances, such as George Griffith and

M.P. Shiel; predecessors include Jules Verne and Sir Edward Bulwer-Lytton. But the tradition did end in Wells's lifetime, although Brian Stableford, in *Scientific Romance in Britain, 1890–1950* (1985), revives the term, which fell out of usage by World War II, to emphasize the differences between the evolution of American and British science fiction. Olaf Stapledon, S. Fowler Wright, Aldous Huxley and George Orwell, for instance, might properly be considered as having written late examples of Scientific Romance.

But Wells, especially in his works between 1895 and 1911, was the primary model for a variety of other writers, in many languages, to explore the explosion of ideas and technologies that the advent of the new century promised. Not the only model, I hasten to add. I have included a fine story by J.H. Rosny aîné, from the French, in this anthology. And as the genre of science fiction began to coalesce in the teens and twenties of the new century, it became evident that a number of earlier writers, first of all Jules Berne but also many others from Mary Shelley and Edgar Allan Poe to Fitz-James O'Brien and Sir Edward Bulwer-Lytton might provide variant models for science fiction. Wells, however, was that spark that ignited the genre.

The fires of science fiction did not blaze in the United States until April 1926, when editor and publisher Hugo Gernsback launched *Amazing Stories* – the first magazine devoted to the new genre and which provided, as it were, a fireplace. To give examples of the new literature he proposed to support and publish, Gernsback filled parts of his issues with "classic reprints" of Wells and many of the others named above. And in his oft-quoted first editorial, in which he defined *scientifiction* (the term *science fiction* was not coined until 1929), he said it was in the manner of Poe, Verne and Wells: "charming romance intermingled with scientific fact and prophetic vision".

In addition to this relative confusion, Gernsback, an eccentric immigrant and technological visionary, was tone-deaf to the English language, printing barely literate stories, often by enthusiastic teenagers, about new inventions and the promise of a wondrous technological future cheek by jowl with fiction by Wells, Poe, Edgar Rice Burroughs, and a growing number of professional pulp writers who simply wanted to break into the new market. Gernsback was the man who first saw science fiction as the ordinary pleasure reading of the new technological world. But his standards were not the standards of a literary man or a modernist. They were the standards of a publisher of popular entertainment in pulp magazines – low-class, low-paying, low-priced popular entertainment serving the mass market.

So genre science fiction became anti-modernist. It rapidly developed a loyal readership, literary conventions, and a body of specialized writers who, converted by the evangelical pitch of Gernsback and the other early editors – chief among them John W. Campbell, Jr, who took over the helm of *Astounding* in the late 1930s and set higher stylistic standards for the genre (his was for decades the highest-paying market) – set about improving themselves.

Of all the pulp magazine genres, science fiction was the most socially unacceptable for decades, so it attracted the alienated of all stripes, some of them extremely talented writers. By the early 1940s the SF field had come into being. And it decided to rule the world. "Science fiction is the central literature of our time. It is not part of the mainstream. It is the mainstream", says Ray Bradbury, and such grandiose claims are part of the essence of the SF field. Bradbury was a teenager who published a fanzine in the late 1930s and became a writer in the 1940s under the tutelage of such established SF professionals as Leigh Brackett (who co-authored the script for *The Big Sleep* with William Faulkner, and later wrote the screenplay for *The Empire Strikes Back*). Science fiction did not aspire to take over literature, but reality.

The field (an aggregation of people) as opposed to the genre (a body of texts) was originally a closely-knit international group of passionate readers and writers of science fiction in the 1930s and 1940s, people who knew each other for the most part only through correspondence and rarely met. They published fanzines and sent them to one another. They developed and evolved their own practical literary criticism and their own literary standards. Most of them were teenagers at the start – including the writers. Practically speaking, none of them had the benefit of a literary or humanist education. They read a lot. Some of them had technical training, some a scientific education – like Wells. But they were organized, and when the economy and publishing opportunities expanded after World War II, the SF field was ready to expand.

In its own view, science fiction had already grown up; in Campbell's *Astounding*, the 1940s were the Golden Age of SF. But by any sensible calculation the SF field really began to grow up after the war and blossomed with the first publications of genre science fiction in hardback books; the founding of major new magazines, such as *Galaxy* and *Fantasy & Science Fiction* in 1949; and the growth of the mass market paperback publishing industry in the early 1950s, which discovered science fiction right away. Most of the stories in this book are post-

World War II mainly because that was the time at which the idea of
revision took hold in the SF writing community, with a concomitant
improvement in the fiction; it was a time when the money improved,
although not enough for any but five or six of the highest paid writers
to make a living without a "day job"; and most of all it was a time of
optimism in the West after the terrible war.

The international SF field grew with the sudden influx of American
science fiction, and a dialogue began among literatures that grew and
continues to grow today. In Russia in the 1940s, one of the key texts
was a story written in response to a Murray Leinster story in *Astounding*.
In France, Boris Vian translated A.E. van Vogt's uneven English (*The
World of Null-A*) into literate French and launched van Vogt as the most
important SF writer of the period in France. American science fiction,
in translation or in the original, dominated the discourse worldwide. It
still does; even though there have been major writers in other
languages who have made major contributions. American science
fiction is still the dominant partner in all dialogues. I have attempted,
in this anthology, to provide some translations that give evidence of the
growth of other traditions, but the overwhelming evidence is that
American science fiction and the American market place drive the SF
world.

It is a source of both amusement and frustration to SF people,
writers and readers that public consciousness of science fiction has
almost never penetrated beyond the first decade of the field's development. Sure, *Star Wars* is wonderful, but in precisely the same way and
at the same level of consciousness and sophistication that science
fiction from the late twenties and early thirties was: fast, almost plotless
stories of zipping through the ether in spaceships, meeting aliens, using
futuristic devices and fighting the bad guys (and winning). SF people
generally call this sci-fi (affectionately) "skiffy", to distinguish it from
the real, grown-up pure quill.

Science fiction is read throughout the English language-reading
world, and in many other languages for pleasure and entertainment.
But it is not read with much comprehension or pleasure by the dominant literary culture, the writers and academics who, on the whole,
define literary fashions and instruct us in the values and virtues of fashionable literatures. This is understandable given the literary history of
the genre, which has now outlasted all the other counterculture or
outsider literary movements of the twentieth century. I wrote an entire
book, *Age of Wonders* (1984, 1996), devoted to elucidating the nature of
the field and the problems of understanding it and the literature

associated with it, for outsiders, but one particular point needs to be repeated each time the subject arises. Science fiction is read properly, as an experienced reader can, only if the givens of the story are granted as literal, so that if the story is set on Mars in the future, that is the literal time and place. It might secondarily be interpretable as "only" a metaphor for the human condition, or for some abnormal psychological state of the character or characters, but with rare exceptions in science fiction, the literal truth of the time and place and ideas is a necessary precondition to making sense of the story. This is because only through this literality (the real world is pared away and reduced to an imaginable invented world, in which we can focus on things happening that could not happen in the mainstream world of everyday reality) can the emotional significance of totally imaginary times and places and events be felt.

Kingsley Amis, in *New Maps of Hell* (1960), quotes his friend Edmund Crispin as saying, "Where an ordinary novel or short story resembles portraiture or at the widest the domestic interior, science fiction offers the less cosy satisfaction of a landscape with figures; to ask that these distant manikins be shown in as much detail as the subject of the portrait is evidently to ask the impossible"; he then goes on himself to say: "This is perhaps partisan in tone, but it does indicate a scale of priorities which operates throughout the medium and which, of course, is open to objection, though this is not often based on much more than an expectation that science fiction should treat the future as fiction of the main stream treats the present, an expectation bound to be defeated" (p.128).

Tom Shippey, in his introduction to *The Oxford Book of Science Fiction Stories* (1992), comments, " What, then, has science fiction had to offer its human readers? Whatever it is, it has been enough for the genre to make its way into a prominent, if not dominant place in popular literary culture despite every kind of literary misunderstanding or discouragement. A very basic answer must be – truth. Not every science fiction story, of course, can 'come true,' indeed . . . probably none of them do, can, or ever will. Just the same, many of them (perhaps all of them, in some way or another) may be trying to solve a question for which many people this century have had no acceptable answer".

In the end this anthology is a collection of attempts to get at the truth of the human condition during the twentieth century, so contoured and conditioned by science and technology. Overall, perhaps, you can see the big picture, surely a bigger picture than any

other. One might even get some intimations of the scope of the future
– which of course leads us always back to the ground at present. And
perhaps we return illuminated.

David G. Hartwell
Pleasantville, N.Y.

A Work of Art

JAMES BLISH

James Blish (1921–75) was perhaps the most sophisticated of the literary critics grown inside the SF field. Though self-educated, he was respected as a James Joyce scholar and was a music critic as well. Of all SF writers at mid-century, Blish most worshipped the Modernists and most aspired to "high" art.

Blish moved permanently to England in the 1960s, where his writing was taken more seriously as contemporary literature than in the U.S. His major achievements in science fiction are generally regarded as the four-volume *Cities in Flight* (1970) and *A Case of Conscience* (1958), a classic theological SF novel. His short fiction, collected in *The Seedling Stars* (1957), *The Best* of *James Blish* (1979), and several other volumes, is also a major body of work in the modern field. He also edited the first SF anthology about the arts of the future, *New Dreams This Morning* (1966).

Perhaps his most ambitious project began with *A Case of Conscience*, about the discovery of Christian aliens without original sin, which is linked to an even larger literary construct (Blish called it *After Such Knowledge* – essentially an ongoing theological argument) involving an additional non-genre novel about Francis Bacon, *Doctor Mirabilis* (1964), and two fantasy novels about the end of the world, *Black Easter* (1968) and *The Day After Judgement* (1971).

At a time in the 1950s when science fiction as a whole had ignored the arts and artists as subjects for most of its history, Blish published this story. Blish said: "Ostensibly this is a story about the future of serious music." It is of course more broadly about art. Such writers as Brian

Aldiss, Samuel R. Delany, Michael Moorcock, and Bruce Sterling carry on the intellectual tradition of Blish today.

Instantly, he remembered dying. He remembered it, however, as if at two removes – as though he were remembering a memory, rather than an actual event; as though he himself had not really been there when he died.

Yet the memory was all from his own point of view, not that of some detached and disembodied observer which might have been his soul. He had been most conscious of the rasping, unevenly drawn movements of the air in his chest. Blurring rapidly, the doctor's face had bent over him, loomed, come closer, and then had vanished as the doctor's head passed below his cone of vision, turned sideways to listen to his lungs.

It had become rapidly darker, and then, only then, had he realized that these were to be his last minutes. He had tried dutifully to say Pauline's name, but his memory contained no record of the sound – only of the rattling breath and of the film of sootiness thickening in the air, blotting out everything for an instant.

Only an instant, and then the memory was over. The room was bright again, and the ceiling, he noticed with wonder, had turned a soft green. The doctor's head lifted again and looked down at him.

It was a different doctor. This one was a far younger man, with an ascetic face and gleaming, almost fey eyes. There was no doubt about it. One of the last conscious thoughts he had had was that of gratitude that the attending physician, there at the end, had not been the one who secretly hated him for his one-time associations with the Nazi hierarchy. The attending doctor, instead, had worn an expression amusingly proper for that of a Swiss expert called to the deathbed of an eminent man: a mixture of worry at the prospect of losing so eminent a patient, and complacency at the thought that, at the old man's age, nobody could blame this doctor if he died. At eighty-five, pneumonia is a serious matter, with or without penicillin.

"You're all right now," the new doctor said, freeing his patient's head of a whole series of little silver rods which had been clinging to it by a sort of network cap. "Rest a minute and try to be calm. Do you know your name?"

He drew a cautious breath. There seemed to be nothing at all the matter with his lungs now; indeed, he felt positively healthy. "Certainly," he said, a little nettled. "Do you know yours?"

The doctor smiled crookedly. "You're in character, it appears," he said. "My name is Barkun Kris; I am a mind sculptor. Yours?"

"Richard Strauss."

"Very good," Dr. Kris said, and turned away. Strauss, however, had already been diverted by a new singularity. *Strauss* is a word as well as a name in German; it has many meanings – an ostrich, a bouquet; von Wolzogen had had a high old time working all the possible puns into the libretto of *Feuersnot*. And it happened to be the first German word to be spoken either by himself or by Dr. Kris since that twice-removed moment of death. The language was not French or Italian, either. It was most like English, but not the English Strauss knew; nevertheless, he was having no trouble speaking it and even thinking in it.

Well, he thought, *I'll be able to conduct* The Love of Danae, *after all. It isn't every composer who can premier his own opera posthumously.* Still, there was something queer about all this – the queerest part of all being that conviction, which would not go away, that he had actually been dead for just a short time. Of course, medicine was making great strides, but . . .

"Explain all this," he said, lifting himself to one elbow. The bed was different, too, and not nearly as comfortable as the one in which he had died. As for the room, it looked more like a dynamo shed than a sickroom. Had modern medicine taken to reviving its corpses on the floor of the Siemanns-Schukert plant?

"In a moment," Dr. Kris said. He finished rolling some machine back into what Strauss impatiently supposed to be its place, and crossed to the pallet. "Now. There are many things you'll have to take for granted without attempting to understand then, Dr. Strauss. Not everything in the world today is explicable in terms of your assumptions. Please bear that in mind."

"Very well. Proceed."

"The date," Dr. Kris said, "is 2161 by your calendar – or, in other words, it is now two hundred and twelve years after your death. Naturally, you'll realize that by this time nothing remains of your body but the bones. The body you have now was volunteered for your use. Before you look into a mirror to see what it's like, remember that its physical difference from the one you were used to is all in your favor. It's in perfect health, not unpleasant for other people to look at, and its physiological age is about fifty."

A miracle? No, not in this new age, surely. It is simply a work of science. But what a science! This was Nietzsche's eternal recurrence and the immortality of the superman combined into one.

"And where is this?" the composer said.

"In Port York, part of the State of Manhattan, in the United States. You will find the country less changed in some respects than I imagine you anticipate. Other changes, of course, will seem radical to you, but it's hard for me to predict which ones will strike you that way. A certain resilience on your part will bear cultivating."

"I understand," Strauss said, sitting up. "One question, please; is it still possible for a composer to make a living in this century?"

"Indeed it is," Dr. Kris said, smiling. "As we expect you to do. It is one of the purposes for which we've – brought you back."

"I gather, then," Strauss said somewhat dryly, "that there is still a demand for my music. The critics in the old days – "

"That's not quite how it is," Dr. Kris said. "I understand some of your work is still played, but frankly I know very little about your current status. My interest is rather – "

A door opened somewhere, and another man came in. He was older and more ponderous than Kris and had a certain air of academicism, but he, too, was wearing the oddly tailored surgeon's gown and looked upon Kris' patient with the glowing eyes of an artist.

"A success, Kris?" he said. "Congratulations."

"They're not in order yet," Dr. Kris said. "The final proof is what counts. Dr. Strauss, if you feel strong enough, Dr. Seirds and I would like to ask you some questions. We'd like to make sure your memory is clear."

"Certainly. Go ahead."

"According to our records," Kris said, "you once knew a man whose initials were R. K. L.; this was while you were conducting at the Vienna *Staatsoper*." He made the double "a" at least twice too long, as though German were a dead language he was striving to pronounce in some "classical" accent. "What was his name, and who was he?"

"That would be Kurt List – his first name was Richard, but he didn't use it. He was assistant stage manager."

The two doctors looked at each other. "Why did you offer to write a new overture to *The Woman Without a Shadow* and give the manuscript to the city of Vienna?"

"So I wouldn't have to pay the garbage removal tax on the Maria Theresa villa they had given me."

"In the backyard of your house at Garmisch-Partenkirchen there was a tombstone. What was written on it?"

Strauss frowned. That was a question he would be happy to be unable to answer. If one is to play childish jokes upon oneself, it's best not to carve them in stone and put the carving where you can't help seeing it every time you go out to tinker with the Mercedes. "It says," he replied wearily, "'Sacred to the memory of Guntram, Minnesinger, slain in a horrible way by his father's own symphony orchestra.'"

"When was *Guntram* premiered?'"

"In – let me see – 1894, I believe."

"Where?"

"In Weimar."

"Who was the leading lady?"

"Pauline de Ahna."

"What happened to her afterwards?"

"I married her. Is she . . . ," Strauss began anxiously.

"No," Dr. Kris said. "I'm sorry, but we lack the data to reconstruct more or less ordinary people."

The composer sighed. He did not know whether to be worried or not. He had loved Pauline, to be sure; on the other hand, it would be pleasant to be able to live the new life without being forced to take off one's shoes every time one entered the house, so as not to scratch the polished hardwood floors. And also pleasant, perhaps, to have two o'clock in the afternoon come by without hearing Pauline's everlasting, "Richard – *jetzt komponiert!*"

"Next question," he said.

For reasons which Strauss did not understand, but was content to take for granted, he was separated from Drs. Kris and Seirds as soon as both were satisfied that the composer's memory was reliable and his health stable. His estate, he was given to understand, had long since been broken up – a sorry end for what had been one of the principal fortunes of Europe – but he was given sufficient money to set up lodgings and resume an active life. He was provided, too, with introductions which proved valuable.

It took longer than he had expected to adjust to the changes that had taken place in music alone. Music was, he quickly began to suspect, a dying art, which would soon have a status not much above that held by flower arranging back in what he thought of as his own century. Certainly it couldn't be denied that the trend toward fragmentation, already visible back in his own time, had proceeded almost to completion in 2161.

He paid no more attention to American popular tunes than he had bothered to pay in his previous life. Yet it was evident that their assembly-line production methods – all the ballad composers openly used a slide-rule-like device called a Hit Machine – now had their counterparts almost throughout serious music.

The conservatives these days, for instance, were the twelve-tone composers – always, in Strauss' opinion, dryly mechanical but never more so than now. Their gods – Berg, Schoenberg, Webern – were looked upon by the concert-going public as great masters, on the abstruse side perhaps, but as worthy of reverence as any of the Three B's.

There was one wing of the conservatives however, that had gone the twelve-tone procedure one better. These men composed what was called "stochastic music," put together by choosing each individual note by consultation with tables of random numbers. Their bible, their basic text, was a volume called *Operational Aesthetics*, which in turn derived from a discipline called information theory, and not one word of it seemed to touch upon any of the techniques and customs of composition which Strauss knew. The ideal of this group was to produce music which would be "universal" – that is, wholly devoid of any trace of the composer's individuality, wholly a musical expression of the universal Laws of Chance. The Laws of Chance seemed to have a style of their own, all right, but to Strauss it seemed the style of an idiot child being taught to hammer a flat piano, to keep him from getting into trouble.

By far the largest body of work being produced, however, fell into a category misleadingly called science-music. The term reflected nothing but the titles of the works, which dealt with space flight, time travel, and other subjects of a romantic or an unlikely nature. There was nothing in the least scientific about the music, which consisted of a mélange of clichés and imitations of natural sounds, in which Strauss was horrified to see his own time-distorted and diluted image.

The most popular form of science-music was a nine-minute composition called a concerto, though it bore no resemblance at all to the classical concerto form; it was instead a sort of free rhapsody after Rachmaninoff – long after. A typical one – "Song of Deep Space," it was called, by somebody named H. Valerion Krafft – began with a loud assault on the tam-tam, after which all the strings rushed up the scale in unison, followed at a respectful distance by the harp and one clarinet in parallel 6/4's. At the top of the scale cymbals were bashed together, *forte possible*, and the whole orchestra launched itself into a major-minor wailing sort of melody; the whole orchestra, that is, except for the French horns, which were plodding back down the scale again in what was evidently supposed to be a countermelody. The second phrase of the theme was picked up by a solo trumpet with a suggestion of tremolo, the orchestra died back to its roots to await the next cloudburst, and at this point – as any four-year-old could have predicted – the piano entered with the second theme.

Behind the orchestra stood a group of thirty women, ready to come in with a wordless chorus intended to suggest the eeriness of Deep Space – but at this point, too, Strauss had already learned to get up and leave. After a few such experiences he could also count upon meeting in the lobby Sindi Noniss, the agent to whom Dr. Kris had introduced him and who was handling the reborn composer's output – what there was of it thus far. Sindi had come to expect these walk-outs on the part of his client and patiently awaited them, standing beneath a bust of Gian-Carlo Menotti, but he liked them less and less, and lately had been greeting them by turning alternately red and white, like a totipotent barber pole.

"You shouldn't have done it," he burst out after the Krafft incident. "You can't just walk out on a new Krafft composition. The man's the president of the Interplanetary Society for Contemporary Music. How am I ever going to persuade them that you're a contemporary if you keep snubbing them?"

"What does it matter?" Strauss said. "They don't know me by sight."

"You're wrong; they know you very well, and they're watching every move you make. You're the first major composer the mind sculptors ever tackled, and the ISCM would be glad to turn you back with a rejection slip."

"Why?"

"Oh," said Sindi, "there are lots of reasons. The sculptors are snobs; so are the ISCM boys. Each of them wanted to prove to the other that their own art is the king of them all. And then there's the competition; it would be easier to flunk you than to let you into the market. I really think you'd better go back in. I could make up some excuse – "

"No," Strauss said shortly. "I have work to do."

"But that's just the point, Richard. How are we going to get an opera produced without the ISCM? It isn't as though you wrote theremin solos, or something that didn't cost so – "

"I have work to do," he said, and left.

And he did, work which absorbed him as had no other project during the last thirty years of his former life. He had scarcely touched pen to music paper – both had been astonishingly hard to find – when he realized that nothing in his long career had provided him with touchstones by which to judge what music he should write *now*.

The old tricks came swarming back by the thousands, to be sure: the sudden, unexpected key changes at the crest of a melody, the interval stretching, the piling of divided strings, playing in the high harmonics, upon the already tottering top of a climax, the scurry and bustle as phrases were passed like lightning from one choir of the orchestra to another, the flashing runs in the brass, the chuckling in the clarinets, the snarling mixtures of colors to emphasize dramatic tension – all of them.

But none of them satisfied him now. He had been content with them for most of a lifetime and had made them do an astonishing amount of work. But now it was time to strike out afresh. Some of the tricks, indeed, actively repelled him: Where had he gotten the notion, clung to for decades, that violins screaming out in unison somewhere in the stratosphere were a sound interesting enough to be worth repeating inside a single composition, let alone in all of them?

And nobody, he reflected contentedly, ever approached such a new beginning better equipped. In addition to the past lying available in his memory, he had always had a technical armamentarium second to none; even the hostile critics had granted him that. Now that he was, in a sense, composing his first opera – his first after fifteen of them! – he had every opportunity to make it a masterpiece.

And every such intention.

There were of course, many minor distractions. One of them was that search for old-fashioned score paper, and a pen and ink with which to write on it. Very few of the modern composers, it developed, wrote their music at all. A large bloc of them used tape, patching together snippets of tone and sound snipped from other tapes, super-imposing one tape on another, and varying the results by twirling an elaborate array of knobs this way or that. Almost all the composers of 3-V scores, on the other hand, wrote on the sound track itself, rapidly scribbling jagged wiggly lines which, when passed through a photocell-audio circuit, produced a noise reasonably like an orchestra playing music, overtones and all.

The last-ditch conservatives who still wrote notes on paper did so with the aid of a musical typewriter. The device, Strauss had to admit, seemed perfected at last; it had manuals and stops like an organ, but it was not much more than twice as large as a standard letter-writing typewriter and produced a neat page. But he was satisfied with his own spidery, highly legible manuscript and refused to abandon it, badly though the one pen nib he had been able to buy coarsened it. It helped to tie him to his past.

Joining the ISCM had also caused him some bad moments, even after Sindi had worked him around the political roadblocks. The

Society man who examined his qualifications as a member had run through the questions with no more interest than might have been shown by a veterinarian examining his four-thousandth sick calf.

"Had anything published?"

"Yes, nine tone poems, about three hundred songs, an – "

"Not when you were alive," the examiner said, somewhat disquietingly. "I mean since the sculptors turned you out again."

"Since the sculptors – ah, I understand. Yes, a string quartet, two song cycles, a – "

"Good. Alfie, write down, 'Songs.' Play an instrument?"

"Piano."

"Hmmm." The examiner studied his fingernails. "Oh well. Do you read music? Or do you use a Scriber, or tape clips? Or a Machine?"

"I read."

"Here." The examiner sat Strauss down in front of a viewing lectern, over the lit surface of which an endless belt of translucent paper was traveling. On the paper was an immensely magnified sound track. "Whistle me the tune of that, and name the instruments it sounds like."

"I don't read that *Musiksticheln*," Strauss said frostily, "or write it, either. I use standard notation, on music paper.

"Alfie, write down, 'Reads notes only.'" He laid a sheet of grayly printed music on the lectern above the ground glass. "Whistle me that."

"That" proved to be a popular tune called "Vangs, Snifters, and Store-Credit Snooky," which had been written on a Hit Machine in 2159 by a guitar-faking politician who sang it at campaign rallies. (In some respects, Strauss reflected, the United States had indeed not changed very much.) It had become so popular that anybody could have whistled it from the title alone, whether he could read the music or not. Strauss whistled it and, to prove his bona fides, added, "It's in the key of B flat."

The examiner went over to the green-painted upright piano and hit one greasy black key. The instrument was horribly out of tune – the note was much nearer to the standard 440/cps A than it was to B flat – but the examiner said, "So it is. Alfie, write down, 'Also reads flats.' All right, son, you're a member. Nice to have you with us; not many people can read that old-style notation anymore. A lot of them think they're too good for it."

"Thank you," Strauss said.

"My feeling is, if it was good enough for the old masters, it's good enough for us. We don't have people like them with us these days, it seems to me. Except for Dr. Krafft, of course. They were *great* back in the old days – men like Shilkrit, Steiner, Tiomkin, and Pearl . . . and Wilder and Jannsen. Real goffin."

"*Doch gewiss,*" Strauss said politely.

But the work went forward. He was making a little income now, from small works. People seemed to feel a special interest in a composer who had come out of the mind sculptors' laboratories, and in addition the material itself, Strauss was quite certain, had merits of its own to help sell it.

It was the opera that counted, however. That grew and grew under his pen, as fresh and new as his new life, as founded in knowledge and ripeness as his long, full memory. Finding a libretto had been troublesome at first. While it was possible that something existed that might have served among the current scripts for 3-V – though he doubted it – he found himself unable to tell the good from the bad through the fog cast over both by incomprehensibly technical production directions. Eventually, and for only the third time in his whole career, he had fallen back upon a play written in a language other than his own, and – for the first time – decided to set it in that language.

The play was Christopher Fry's *Venus Observed,* in all ways a perfect Strauss opera libretto, as he came gradually to realize. Though nominally a comedy, with a complex farcical plot, it was a verse play with considerable depth to it, and a number of characters who cried out to be brought by music into three dimensions, plus a strong undercurrent of autumnal tragedy, of leaf-fall and apple-fall – precisely the kind of contradictory dramatic mixture which von Hofmannsthal had supplied him with in *The Knight of the Rose,* in *Ariadne at Naxos,* and in *Arabella.*

Alas for von Hofmannsthal, but here was another long-dead playwright who seemed nearly as gifted, and the musical opportunities were immense. There was, for instance, the fire which ended Act II; what a gift for a composer to whom orchestration and counterpoint were as important as air and water! Or take the moment where Perpetua shoots the apple from the Duke's hand; in that one moment a single passing reference could add Rossini's marmoreal *William Tell* to the musical texture as nothing but an ironic footnote! And the Duke's great curtain speech, beginning:

> *Shall I be sorry for myself? In Mortality's name*
> *I'll be sorry for myself. Branches and boughs,*
> *Brown hills, the valleys faint with brume,*
> *A burnish on the lake . . .*

There was a speech for a great tragic comedian in the spirit of Falstaff: the final union of laughter and tears, punctuated by the sleepy comments of Reedbeck, to whose sonorous snore (trombones, no less than five of them, *con sordini?*) the opera would gently end . . .

What could be better? And yet he had come upon the play only by the unlikeliest series of accidents. At first he had planned to do a straight knockabout farce, in the idiom of *The Silent Woman*, just to warm himself up. Remembering that Zweig had adapted that libretto for him, in the old days, from a play by Ben Jonson, Strauss had begun to search out English plays of the period just after Jonson's, and had promptly run aground on an awful specimen in heroic couplets called *Venice Preserv'd*, by one Thomas Otway. The Fry play had directly followed the Otway in the card catalogue, and he had looked at it out of curiosity; why should a twentieth-century playwright be punning on a title from the eighteenth?

After two pages of the Fry play, the minor puzzle of the pun disappeared entirely from his concern. His luck was running again; he had an opera.

Sindi worked miracles in arranging for the performance. The date of the premiere was set even before the score was finished, reminding Strauss pleasantly of those heady days when Fuestner had been snatching the conclusion of *Elektra* off his worktable a page at a time, before the ink was even dry, to rush it to the engraver before publication deadline. The situation now, however, was even more complicated, for some of the score had to be scribed, some of it taped, some of it engraved in the old way, to meet the new techniques of performance; there were moments when Sindi seemed to be turning quite gray.

But *Venus Observed* was, as usual, forthcoming complete from Strauss' pen in plenty of time. Writing the music in first draft had been hellishly hard work, much more like being reborn than had been that confused awakening in Barkun Kris' laboratory, with its overtones of being dead instead, but Strauss found that he still retained all of his old ability to score from the draft almost effortlessly, as undisturbed by Sindi's half-audible worrying in the room with him as he was by the terrifying supersonic bangs of the rockets that bulleted invisibly over the city.

When he was finished, he had two days still to spare before the beginning of rehearsals. With those, furthermore, he would have nothing to do. The techniques of performance in this age were so completely bound up with the electronic arts as to reduce his own experience – he, the master *Kapellmeister* of them all – to the hopelessly primitive.

He did not mind. The music, as written, would speak for itself. In the meantime he found it grateful to forget the months-long pre-occupation with the stage for a while. He went back to the library and browsed lazily through old poems, vaguely seeking texts for a song or two. He knew better than to bother with recent poets; they could not speak to him, and he knew it. The Americans of his own age, he thought, might give him a clue to understanding this America of 2161, and if some such poem gave birth to a song, so much the better.

The search was relaxing, and he gave himself up to enjoying it. Finally he struck a tape that he liked; a tape read in a cracked old voice that twanged of Idaho as that voice had twanged in 1910, in Strauss' own ancient youth. The poet's name was Pound; he said, on the tape:

> ". . . the souls of all men great
> At times pass through us,
> And we are melted into them, and are not
> Save reflexions of their souls.
> Thus I am Dante for a space and am
> One François Villon, a ballad-lord and thief,
> Or am such holy ones I may not write,
> Lest Blasphemy be writ against my name;
> This for an instant and the flame is gone.
> 'Tis as in midmost us there glows a sphere
> Translucent, molten gold, that is the 'I'
> And into this some form projects itself:
> Christus, or John, or eke the Florentine;
> And as the clear space is not if a form's
> Imposed thereon,
> So cease we from all being for the time,
> And these, the masters of the Soul, live on."

He smiled. That lesson had been written again and again from Plato onward. Yet the poem was a history of his own case, a sort of theory for the metempsychosis he had undergone, and in its formal way it was moving. It would be fitting to make a little hymn of it, in honor of his own rebirth, and of the poet's insight.

A series of solemn, breathless chords framed themselves in his inner ear, against which the words might be intoned in a high, gently bending hush at the beginning . . . and then a dramatic passage in which the great names of Dante and Villon would enter ringing like challenges to Time . . . He wrote for a while in his notebook before he returned the spool to its shelf.

These, he thought, are good auspices.

And so the night of the premiere arrived, the audience pouring into the hall, the 3-V cameras riding on no visible supports through the air, aud Sindi calculating his share of his client's earnings by a complicated game he played on his fingers, the basic law of which seemed to be that one plus one equals ten. The hall filled to the roof with people from every class, as though what was to come would be a circus rather than an opera.

There were, surprisingly, nearly fifty of the aloof and aristocratic mind sculptors, clad in formal clothes which were exaggerated black versions of their surgeons' gowns. They had bought a block of seats near the front of the auditorium, where the gigantic 3-V figures which would shortly fill the "stage" before them (the real singers would perform on a small stage in the basement) could not but seem monstrously out of proportion, but Strauss supposed that they had taken this into account and dismissed it.

There was a tide of whispering in the audience as the sculptors began to trickle in, and with it an undercurrent of excitement, the meaning of which was unknown to Strauss. He did not attempt to fathom it, however; he was coping with his own mounting tide of opening-night tension, which, despite all the years, he had never quite been able to shake.

The sourceless, gentle light in the auditorium dimmed, and Strauss mounted the podium. There was a score before him, but he doubted that he would need it. Directly before him, poking up from among the musicians, were the inevitable 3-V snouts, waiting to carry his image to the singers in the basement.

The audience was quiet now. This was the moment. His baton swept up and then decisively down, and the prelude came surging up out of the pit.

For a little while he was deeply immersed in the always tricky business of keeping the enormous orchestra together and sensitive to the flexing of the musical web beneath his hand. As his control firmed and became secure, however, the task became slightly less demanding, and he was able to pay more attention to what the whole sounded like.

There was something decidedly wrong with it. Of course there were the occasional surprises as some bit of orchestral color emerged with a different *Klang* than he had expected; that happened to every composer, even after a lifetime of experience. And there were moments when the singers, entering upon a phrase more difficult to handle than he had calculated, sounded like someone about to fall off a tightrope (although none of them actually fluffed once; they were as fine as troupe of voices as he had ever had to work with).

But these were details. It was the overall impression that was wrong. He was losing not only the excitement of the premiere – after all, that couldn't last at the same pitch all evening – but also his very interest in what was coming from the stage and the pit. He was gradually tiring, his baton arm becoming heavier; as the second act mounted to what should have been an impassioned outpouring of shining tone, he was so bored as to wish he could go back to his desk to work on that song.

Then the act was over; only one more to go. He scarcely heard the applause. The twenty minutes' rest in his dressing room was just barely enough to give him the necessary strength.

And suddenly, in the middle of the last act, he understood.

There was nothing new about the music. It was the old Strauss all over again – but weaker, more dilute than ever. Compared with the output of composers like Krafft, it doubtless sounded like a masterpiece to this audience. But he knew.

The resolutions, the determination to abandon the old clichés and mannerisms, the decision to say something new – they had all come to nothing against the force of habit. Being brought to life again meant bringing to life as well all those deeply graven reflexes of his style. He had only to pick up his pen and they overpowered him with easy automatism, no more under his control than the jerk of a finger away from a flame.

His eyes filled; his body was young, but he was an old man, an old man. Another thirty-five years of this? Never. He had said all this before, centuries before. Nearly a half century condemned to saying it all over again, in a weaker and still weaker voice, aware that even this

debased century would come to recognize in him only the burnt husk
of greatness? – no, never, never.

He was aware, dully, that the opera was over. The audience was
screaming its joy. He knew the sound. They had screamed that way
when *Day of Peace* had been premiered, but they had been cheering the
man he had been, not the man that *Day of Peace* showed with cruel
clarity he had become. Here the sound was even more meaningless:
cheers of ignorance, and that was all.

He turned slowly. With surprise, and with a surprising sense of relief,
he saw that the cheers were not, after all, for him.

They were for Dr. Barkun Kris.

Kris was standing in the middle of the bloc of mind sculptors, bowing
to the audience. The sculptors nearest him were shaking his hand one
after the other. More grasped at it as he made his way to the aisle and
walked forward to the podium. When he mounted the rostrum and
took the composer's limp hand, the cheering became delirious.

Kris lifted his arm. The cheering died instantly to an intent hush.

"Thank you," he said clearly. "Ladies and gentlemen, before we
take leave of Dr. Strauss, let us again tell him what a privilege it has
been for us to hear this fresh example of his mastery. I am sure no
farewell could be more fitting."

The ovation lasted five minutes and would have gone another five if
Kris had not cut it off.

"Dr. Strauss," he said, "in a moment, when I speak a certain formulation to you, you will realize that your name is Jerom Bosch, born in
our century and with a life in it all your own. The superimposed
memories which have made you assume the mask, the *persona*, of a
great composer will be gone. I tell you this so that you may understand
why these people here share your applause with me."

A wave of asserting sound.

"The art of mind sculpture – the creation of artificial personalities
for aesthetic enjoyment – may never reach such a pinnacle again. For
you should understand that as Jerom Bosch you had no talent for
music at all; indeed, we searched a long time to find a man who was
utterly unable to carry even the simplest tune. Yet we were able to
impose upon such unpromising material not only the personality, but
the genius, of a great composer. That genius belongs entirely to you –
to the *persona* that thinks of itself as Richard Strauss. None of the credit
goes to the man who volunteered for the sculpture. That is your
triumph, and we salute you for it."

Now the ovation could no longer be contained. Strauss, with a crooked smile, watched Dr. Kris bow. This mind sculpturing was a suitably sophisticated kind of cruelty for this age, but the impulse, of course, had always existed. It was the same impulse that had made Rembrandt and Leonardo turn cadavers into art works.

It deserved a suitably sophisticated payment under the *lex talionis:* an eye for an eye, a tooth for a tooth – and a failure for a failure.

No, he need not tell Dr. Kris that the "Strauss" he had created was as empty of genius as a hollow gourd. The joke would always be on the sculptor, who was incapable of hearing the hollowness of the music now preserved on the 3-V tapes.

But for an instant a surge of revolt poured through his bloodstream. *I am I*, he thought. *I am Richard Strauss until I die, and will never be Jerom Bosch, who was utterly unable to carry even the simplest tune.* His hand, still holding the baton, came sharply up, through whether to deliver or to ward off a blow he could not tell.

He let it fall again, and instead, at last, bowed – not to the audience, but to Dr. Kris. He was sorry for nothing, as Kris turned to him to say the word that would plunge him back into oblivion, except that he would now have no chance to set that poem to music.

2066: Election Day

MICHAEL SHAARA

Michael Shaara (1929–88) was one of the bright young SF writers of the early 1950s, who left the genre in 1957 after producing a number of fine short stories, and later wrote a boxing novel and the Pulitzer Prize-winning American Civil War novel, *The Killer Angels* (1974). Most of his short stories are collected in *Soldier Boy* (1982), along with an afterword reminiscing about his early days in science fiction, the excitement of selling to John W. Campbell's *Astounding,* the frustrations of dealing with genre markets. Algis Budrys remembers that Robert Sheckley, Michael Shaara and he were the hot new writers of 1952–3.

After the generally positive editorial reaction to *Soldier Boy*, Shaara completed an SF novel, *The Herald* (1981 – actually published before the collection, which was delayed, but not published as a genre novel, since Shaara had won the Pulitzer and his publisher was certain that a genre label would compromise his, and their, reputation). *The Encyclopedia of Science Fiction* praises his writing for its "quick, revelatory ironies about the human condition." I recall joking with him in 1982 that this, of all his stories, was predictive and that it had already come true. It is still coming true.

Early that afternoon Professor Larkin crossed the river into Washington, a thing he always did on Election Day, and sat for a long while in the Polls. It was still called the Polls, in this year A.D. 2066, although what went on inside bore no relation at all to the elections of primitive American history. The Polls was now a single enormous building which rose out of the green fields where the ancient Pentagon had once stood. There was only one of its kind in Washington, only one Polling Place in each of the forty-eight states, but since few visited the Polls nowadays, no more were needed.

In the lobby of the building, a great hall was reserved for visitors. Here you could sit and watch the many-colored lights dancing and flickering on the huge panels above, listen to the weird but strangely soothing hum and click of the vast central machine. Professor Larkin chose a deep soft chair near the long line of booths and sat down. He sat for a long while smoking his pipe, watching the people go in and out of the booths with strained, anxious looks on their faces.

Professor Larkin was a lean, boyish-faced man in his late forties. With the pipe in his hand he looked much more serious and sedate than he normally felt, and it often bothered him that people were able to guess his profession almost instantly. He had a vague idea that it was not becoming to look like a college professor, and he often tried to change his appearance – a loud tie here, a sport coat there – but it never seemed to make any difference. He remained what he was, easily identifiable, Professor Harry L. (Lloyd) Larkin, Ph.D., Dean of the Political Science Department at a small but competent college just outside of Washington.

It was his interest in Political Science which drew him regularly to the Polls at every election. Here he could sit and feel the flow of American history in the making, and recognize, as he did now, perennial candidates for the presidency. Smiling, he watched a little old lady dressed in pink, very tiny and very fussy, flit doggedly from booth to booth. Evidently her test marks had not been very good. She was clutching her papers tightly in a black-gloved hand, and there was a look of prim irritation on her face. But *she* knew how to run this country, by George, and one of these days *she* would be President. Harry Larkin chuckled.

But it did prove one thing. The great American dream was still intact. The tests were open to all. And anyone could still grow up to be President of the United States.

Sitting back in his chair, Harry Larkin remembered his own childhood, how the great battle had started. There were examinations for everything in those days – you could not get a job streetcleaning without taking a civil-service examination – but public office needed no qualification at all. And first the psychologists, then the newspapers, had begun calling it a national disgrace. And, considering the caliber of some of the men who went into public office, it *was* a national disgrace. But then psychological testing came of age, really became an exact science, so that it was possible to test a man thoroughly – his knowledge, his potential, his personality. And from there it was a short but bitterly fought step to – SAM.

SAM. UNCLE SAM, as he had been called originally, the last and greatest of all electronic brains. Harry Larkin peered up in unabashed awe at the vast battery of lights which flickered above him. He knew that there was more to SAM than just this building, more than all the other forty-eight buildings put together, that SAM was actually an incredibly enormous network of electronic cells which had its heart in no one place, but its arms in all. It was an unbelievably complex analytical computer which judged a candidate far more harshly and thoroughly than the American public could ever have judged him. And crammed in its miles of memory banks lay almost every bit of knowledge mankind had yet discovered. It was frightening, many thought of it as a monster, but Harry Larkin was unworried.

The thirty years since the introduction of SAM had been thirty of America's happiest years. In a world torn by continual war and unrest, by dictators, puppet governments, the entire world had come to know and respect the American President for what he was: the best possible man for the job. And there was no doubt that he was the best. He had competed for the job in fair examination against the cream of the country. He had to be a truly remarkable man to come out on top.

The day was long since past when just any man could handle the presidency. A full century before men had begun dying in office, cut down in their prime by the enormous pressures of the job. And that was a hundred years ago. Now the job had become infinitely more complex, and even now President Creighton lay on his bed in the White House, recovering from a stroke, an old, old man after one term of office.

Harry Larkin shuddered to think what might have happened had America not adopted the system of "the best qualified man." All over the world this afternoon men waited for word from America, the calm and trustworthy words of the new President, for there had been no leader in America since President Creighton's stroke. His words would mean more to the people, embroiled as they were in another great crisis, than the words of their own leaders. The leaders of other countries fought for power, bought it, stole it, only rarely earned it. But the American President was known the world over for his honesty, his intelligence, his desire for peace. Had he not those qualities, "old UNCLE SAM" would never have elected him.

Eventually, the afternoon nearly over, Harry Larkin rose to leave. By this time the President was probably already elected. Tomorrow the world would return to peace. Harry Larkin paused in the door once before he left, listened to the reassuring hum from the great machine. Then he went quietly home, walking quickly and briskly toward the most enormous fate on Earth.

"My name is Reddington. You know me?"

Harry Larkin smiled uncertainly into the phone.

"Why . . . yes, I believe so. You are, if I'm not mistaken, general director of the Bureau of Elections."

"Correct," the voice went on quickly, crackling in the receiver, "and you are supposed to be an authority on Political Science, right?"

"Supposed to be?" Larkin bridled. "Well, it's distinctly possible that I –"

"All right, all right," Reddington blurted. "No time for politeness. Listen, Larkin, this is a matter of urgent national security. There will be a car at your door – probably be there when you put this phone down. I want you to get into it and hop on over here. I can't explain further. I know your devotion to the country, and if it wasn't for that I would not have called you. But don't ask questions. Just come. No time. Good-bye."

There was a click. Harry Larkin stood holding the phone for a long shocked moment, then he heard a pounding at the door. The housekeeper was out, but he waited automatically before going to answer it. He didn't like to be rushed, and he was confused. Urgent national security? Now what in blazes –

The man at the door was an Army major. He was accompanied by two young but very large sergeants. They identified Larkin, then escorted him politely but firmly down the steps into a staff car. Larkin could not help feeling abducted, and a completely characteristic rage began to rise in him. But he remembered what Reddington had said about national security and so sat back quietly with nothing more than an occasional grumble.

He was driven back into Washington. They took him downtown to a small but expensive apartment house he could neither identify nor remember, and escorted him briskly into an elevator. When they reached the suite upstairs they opened the door and let him in, but did not follow him. They turned and went quickly away.

Somewhat ruffled, Larkin stood for a long moment in the hall by the hat table, regarding a large rubber plant. There was a long sliding door before him, closed, but he could hear an argument going on behind it. He heard the word "SAM" mentioned many times, and once he heard a clear sentence: ". . . Government by machine. I will not tolerate it!" Before he had time to hear any more, the doors slid back. A small, square man with graying hair came out to meet him. He recognized the man instantly as Reddington.

"Larkin," the small man said, "glad you're here." The tension on his face showed also in his voice. "That makes all of us. Come in and sit down." He turned back into the large living room. Larkin followed.

"Sorry to be so abrupt," Reddington said, "but it was necessary. You will see. Here, let me introduce you around."

Larkin stopped in involuntary awe. He was used to the sight of important men, but not so many at one time, and never so close. There was Secretary Kell, of Agriculture; Wachsmuth, of Commerce; General Vines, Chief of Staff; and a battery of others so imposing that Larkin found his mouth hanging embarrassingly open. He closed it immediately.

Reddington introduced him. The men nodded one by one, but they were all deathly serious, their faces drawn, and there was now no conversation. Reddington waved him to a chair. Most of the others were standing, but Larkin sat.

Reddington sat directly facing him. There was a long moment of silence during which Larkin realized that he was being searchingly examined. He flushed, but sat calmly with his hands folded in his lap. After a while Reddington took a deep breath.

"Dr. Larkin," he said slowly, "what I am about to say to you will die with you. There must be no question of that. We cannot afford to have any word of this meeting, any word at all, reach anyone not in this room. This includes your immediate relatives, your friends, anyone – anyone at all. Before we continue, let me impress you with that fact. This is a matter of the gravest national security. Will you keep what is said here in confidence?"

"If the national interests – " Larkin began, then he said abruptly, "of course."

Reddington smiled slightly.

"Good. I believe you. I might add that just the fact of your being here, Doctor, means that you have already passed the point of no return . . . well, no matter. There is no time. I'll get to the point."

He stopped, looking around the room. Some of the other men were standing and now began to move in closer. Larkin felt increasingly nervous, but the magnitude of the event was too great for him to feel any worry. He gazed intently at Reddington.

"The Polls close tonight at eight o'clock." Reddington glanced at his watch. "It is now six-eighteen. I must be brief. Doctor, do you remember the prime directive that we gave to SAM when he was first built?"

"I think so," said Larkin slowly.

"Good. You remember then that there was one main order. SAM was directed to elect, quote, *the best qualified man.* Unquote. Regardless of any and all circumstances, religion, race, so on. The orders were clear – the best qualified man. The phrase has become world famous. But unfortunately" – he glanced up briefly at the men surrounding him – "the order was a mistake. Just whose mistake does not matter. I think perhaps the fault lies with all of us, but – it doesn't matter. What matters is this: SAM will not elect a president."

Larkin struggled to understand. Reddington leaned forward in his chair.

"Now follow me closely. We learned this only late this afternoon. We are always aware, as you no doubt know, of the relatively few people in this country who have a chance for the presidency. We know not only because they are studying for it, but because such men as these are marked from their childhood to be outstanding. We keep close watch on them, even to assigning the Secret Service to protect them from possible harm. There are only a very few. During this last election we could not find more than fifty. All of those people took the tests this morning. None of them passed."

He paused, waiting for Larkin's reaction. Larkin made no move.

"You begin to see what I'm getting at? *There is no qualified man.*"

Larkin's eyes widened. He sat bolt upright.

"Now it hits you. If none of those people this morning passed, there is no chance at all for any of the others tonight. What is left now is simply crackpots and malcontents. They are privileged to take the tests, but it means nothing. SAM is not going to select anybody. Because sometime during the last four years the presidency passed the final limit, the ultimate end of man's capabilities, and with scientific certainty we know that there is probably no man alive who is, according to SAM's directive, qualified."

"But," Larkin interrupted, "I'm not quite sure I follow. Doesn't the phrase 'elect the best qualified man' mean that we can at least take the best we've got?"

Reddington smiled wanly and shook his head.

"No. And that was our mistake. It was quite probably a psychological block, but none of us ever considered the possibility of the job surpassing human ability. Not then, thirty years ago. And we also never seemed to remember that SAM is, after all, only a machine. He takes the words to mean exactly what they say: Elect the best, comma, *qualified*, comma, man. But do you see, if there is no qualified man, SAM cannot possibly elect the best. So SAM will elect no one at all. Tomorrow this country will be without a president. And the result of that, more than likely, will mean a general war."

Larkin understood. He sat frozen in his chair.

"So you see our position," Reddington went on wearily. "There's nothing we can do. Reelecting President Creighton is out of the question. His stroke was permanent, he may not last the week. And there is no possibility of tampering with SAM, to change the directive. Because, as you know, SAM is foolproof, had to be. The circuits extend through all forty-eight states. To alter the machine at all requires clearing through all forty-eight entrances. We can't do that. For one thing, we haven't time. For another, we can't risk letting the world know there is no qualified man.

"For a while this afternoon, you can understand, we were stumped. What could we do? There was only one answer, we may come back to it yet. Give the presidency itself to SAM – "

A man from across the room, whom Larkin did not recognize, broke in angrily.

"Now Reddington, I told you, that is government by machine! And I will not stand – "

"What else can you *do!*" Reddington whirled, his eyes flashing, his tension exploding now into rage. "Who else knows all the answers? Who else can compute in two seconds the tax rate for Mississippi, the parity levels for wheat, the probable odds on a military engagement? Who else but SAM! And why didn't we do it long ago, just feed the problems to *him*, SAM, and not go on killing man after man, great men, *decent* men like poor Jim Creighton, who's on his back now and dying because people like you – " He broke off suddenly and bowed his head. The room was still. No one looked at Reddington. After a moment he shook his head. His voice, when he spoke, was husky.

"Gentlemen, I'm sorry. This leads nowhere." He turned back to Larkin.

Larkin had begun to feel the pressure. But the presence of these men, of Reddington's obvious profound sincerity, reassured him. Creighton had been a great president, he had surrounded himself with some of the finest men in the country. Larkin felt a surge of hope that such men as these were available for one of the most critical hours in American history. For critical it was, and Larkin knew as clearly as anyone there what the absence of a president in the morning – no deep reassurance, no words of hope – would mean. He sat waiting for Reddington to continue.

"Well, we have a plan. It may work, it may not. We may all be shot. But this is where you come in. I hope for all our sakes you're up to it."

Larkin waited.

"The plan," Reddington went on, slowly, carefully, "is this. SAM has one defect. We can't tamper with it. But we *can* fool it. Because when the brain tests a man, it does not at the same time identify him. We do the identifying ourselves. So if a man named Joe Smith takes the personality tests and another man also named Joe Smith takes the Political Science tests, the machine has no way of telling them apart. Unless our guards supply the difference, SAM will mark up the results of both tests to one Joe Smith. We can clear the guards, no problem there. The first problem was to find the eight men to take the eight tests."

Larkin understood. He nodded.

"Exactly. Eight specialists," Reddington said. "General Vines will take the Military; Burden, Psychology; Wachsmuth, Economics; and so on. You, of course, will take the Political Science. We can only hope that each man will come out with a high enough score in his own field so that the combined scores of our mythical 'candidate' will be enough to qualify him. Do you follow me?"

Larkin nodded dazedly. "I think so. But – "

"It should work. It has to work."

"Yes," Larkin murmured, "I can see that. But who, who will actually wind up – "

"As President?" Reddington smiled very slightly and stood up. "That was the most difficult question of all. At first we thought there was no solution. Because a president must be so many things – consider. A president blossoms instantaneously, from nonentity, into the most important job on earth. Every magazine, every newspaper in the country immediately goes to work on his background, digs out his life story, anecdotes, sayings, and so on. Even a very strong fraud would never survive it. So the first problem was believability. The new president must be absolutely believable. He must be a man of obvious character, of obvious intelligence, but more than that, his former life must fit the facts: he must have had both the time and the personality to prepare himself for the office.

"And you see immediately what all that means. Most businessmen are out. Their lives have been too social, they wouldn't have had the time. For the same reason all government and military personnel are also out, and we need hardly say that anyone from the Bureau of Elections would be immediately suspect. No. You see the problem. For a while we thought that the time was too short, the risk too great. But then the only solution, the only possible chance, finally occurred to us.

"The only believable person would be – a professor. Someone whose life has been serious but unhurried, devoted to learning but at the same time isolated. The only really believable person. And not a scientist, you understand, for a man like that would be much too over-balanced in one direction for our purpose. No, simply a professor, preferably in a field like Political Science, a man whose sole job for many years has been teaching, who can claim to have studied in his spare time, his summers – never really expected to pass the tests and all that, a humble man, you see – "

"Political Science," Larkin said.

Reddington watched him. The other men began to close in on him.

"Yes," Reddington said gently. "Now do you see? It is our only hope. Your name was suggested by several sources, you are young enough, your reputation is well known. We think that you would be believable. And now that I've seen you" – he looked around slowly – "I for one am willing to risk it. Gentlemen, what do you say?"

Larkin, speechless, sat listening in mounting shock while the men agreed solemnly, one by one. In the enormity of the moment he could not think at all. Dimly, he heard Reddington.

"I know. But, Doctor, there is no time. The Polls close at eight. It is now almost seven."

Larkin closed his eyes and rested his head on his hands. Above him, Reddington went on inevitably.

"All right. You are thinking of what happens after. Even if we pull this off and you are accepted without question, what then? Well, it will simply be the old system all over again. You will be at least no worse off than presidents before SAM. Better even, because if worse comes to worst, there is always SAM. You can feed all the bad ones to him. You will have the advice of the cabinet, of the military staff. We will help you in every way we can, some of us will sit with you on all conferences. And you know more about this than most of us, you have studied government all your life.

"But all this, what comes later, is not important. Not now. If we can get through tomorrow, the next few days, all the rest will work itself out. Eventually we can get around to altering SAM. But we must have a president in the morning. You are our only hope. You can do it. We all know you can do it. At any rate there is no other way, no time. Doctor," he reached out and laid his hand on Larkin's shoulder, "shall we go to the Polls?"

It passed, as most great moments in a man's life do, with Larkin not fully understanding what was happening to him. Later he would look back to this night and realize the enormity of the decision he had made, the doubts, the sleeplessness, the responsibility and agony toward which he moved. But in that moment he thought nothing at all. Except that it was Larkin's country, Larkin's America. And Reddington was right. There was nothing else to do. He stood up.

They went to the Polls.

At 9:30 that evening, sitting alone with Reddington back at the apartment, Larkin looked at the face of the announcer on the television screen, and heard himself pronounced President-elect of the United States.

Reddington wilted in front of the screen. For a while neither man moved. They had come home alone, just as they had gone into the Polls one by one in the hope of arousing no comment. Now they sat in silence until Reddington turned off the set. He stood up and straightened his shoulders before turning to Larkin. He stretched out his hand.

"Well, may God help us," he breathed, "we did it."

Larkin took his hand. He felt suddenly weak. He sat down again, but already he could hear the phone ringing in the outer hall. Reddington smiled.

"Only a few of my closest friends are supposed to know about that phone. But every time anything big comes up – " He shrugged. "Well," he said, still smiling, "let's see how it works."

He picked up the phone and with it an entirely different manner. He became amazingly light and cheerful, as if he was feeling nothing more than the normal political goodwill.

"Know him? Of course I know him. Had my eye on the guy for months. Really nice guy, wait'll you meet him . . . yup, college professor, Political Science, written a couple of books . . . must know a hell of a lot more than Poli Sci, though. Probably been knocking himself out in his spare time. But those teachers, you know how it is, they don't get any pay, but all the spare time in the world . . . Married? No, not that I know of – "

Larkin noticed with wry admiration how carefully Reddington had slipped in that bit about spare time, without seeming to be making an explanation. He thought wearily to himself, I hope that I don't have to do any talking myself. I'll have to do a lot of listening before I can chance any talking.

In a few moments Reddington put down the phone and came back. He had on his hat and coat.

"Had to answer a few," he said briefly, "make it seem natural. But you better get dressed."

"Dressed? Why?"

"Have you forgotten?" Reddington smiled patiently. "You're due at the White House. The Secret Service is already tearing the town apart looking for you. We were supposed to alert them. Oh, by the saints, I hope that wasn't too bad a slip."

He pursed his mouth worriedly while Larkin, still dazed, got into his coat. It was beginning now. It had already begun. He was tired but it did not matter. That he was tired would probably never matter again. He took a deep breath. Like Reddington, he straightened his shoulders.

The Secret Service picked them up halfway across town. That they knew where he was, who he was, amazed him and worried Reddington. They went through the gates of the White House and drove up before the door. It was opened for him as he put out his hand, he stepped back in a reflex action, from the sudden blinding flares of the photographers' flashbulbs. Reddington behind him took him firmly by the arm. Larkin went with him gratefully, unable to see, unable to hear anything but the roar of the crowd from behind the gates and the shouted questions of the reporters.

Inside the great front doors it was suddenly peaceful again, very quiet and pleasantly dark. He took off his hat instinctively. Luckily he had been here before, he recognized the lovely hall and felt not awed but at home. He was introduced quickly to several people whose names made no impression on him. A woman smiled. He made an effort to smile back. Reddington took him by the arm again and led him away. There were people all around him, but they were quiet and hung back. He saw the respect on their faces. It sobered him, quickened his mind.

"The President's in the Lincoln Room," Reddington whispered. "He wants to see you. How do you feel?"

"All right."

"Listen."

"Yes."

"You'll be fine. You're doing beautifully. Keep just that look on your face."

"I'm not trying to keep it there."

"You aren't?" Reddington looked at him. "Good. Very good." He paused and looked again at Larkin. Then he smiled.

"It's done it. I thought it would but I wasn't sure. But it does it every time. A man comes in here, no matter what he was before, no matter what he is when he goes out, but he feels it. Don't you feel it?"

"Yes. It's like – "

"What?"

"It's like . . . when you're in here . . . you're *responsible*."

Reddington said nothing. But Larkin felt a warm pressure on his arm.

They paused at the door of the Lincoln Room. Two Secret Service men, standing by the door, opened it respectfully. They went on in, leaving the others outside.

Larkin looked across the room to the great, immortal bed. He felt suddenly very small, very tender. He crossed the soft carpet and looked down at the old man.

"Hi," the old man said. Larkin was startled, but he looked down at the broad weakly smiling face, saw the famous white hair and the still-twinkling eyes, and found himself smiling in return.

"Mr. President," Larkin said.

"I hear your name is Larkin." The old man's voice was surprisingly strong, but as he spoke now Larkin could see that the left side of his face was paralyzed. "Good name for a president. Indicates a certain sense of humor. Need a sense of humor. Reddington, how'd it go?"

"Good as can be expected, sir." He glanced briefly at Larkin. "The President knows. Wouldn't have done it without his okay. Now that I think of it, it was probably he who put the Secret Service on us."

"You're doggone right," the old man said. "They may bother the by-jingo out of you, but those boys are necessary. And also, if I hadn't let them know we knew Larkin was material – " He stopped abruptly and closed his eyes, took a deep breath. After a moment he said: "Mr. Larkin?"

"Yes, sir."

"I have one or two comments. You mind?"

"Of course not, sir."

"I couldn't solve it. I just . . . didn't have time. There were so many other things to do." He stopped and again closed his eyes. "But it will be up to you, son. The presidency . . . must be preserved. What they'll start telling you now is that there's only one way out, let SAM handle it. Reddington, too," the old man opened his eyes and gazed sadly at Reddington, "he'll tell you the same thing, but don't you believe it.

"Sure, SAM knows all the answers. Ask him a question on anything, on levels of parity tax rates, on anything. And right quick SAM will compute you out an answer. So that's what they'll try to do, they'll tell you to take it easy and let SAM do it.

"Well, all right, up to a certain point. But, Mr. Larkin, understand this. SAM is like a book. Like a book, he knows the answers. *But only those answers we've already found out.* We gave SAM those answers. A machine is not creative, neither is a book. Both are only the product of creative minds. Sure, SAM could hold the country together. But growth, man, there'd be no more growth! No new ideas, new solutions, change, progress, development! And America *must* grow, must progress – "

He stopped, exhausted. Reddington bowed his head. Larkin remained idly calm. He felt a remarkable clarity in his head.

"But, Mr. President," he said slowly, "if the office is too much for one man, then all we can do is cut down on his powers – "

"Ah," the old man said faintly, "there's the rub. Cut down on what? If I sign a tax bill, I must know enough about taxes to be certain that the bill is the right one. If I endorse a police action, I must be certain that the strategy involved is militarily sound. If I consider farm prices . . . you see, you see, what will you cut? The office is responsible for its acts. It must remain responsible. You cannot take just someone else's word for things like that, you must make your own decisions. Already we sign things we know nothing about, bills for this, bills for that, on somebody's word."

"What do you suggest?"

The old man cocked an eye toward Larkin, smiled once more with half his mouth, anciently worn, only hours from death, an old, old man with his work not done, never to be done.

"Son, come here. Take my hand. Can't lift it myself."

Larkin came forward, knelt by the side of the bed. He took the cold hand, now gaunt and almost translucent, and held it gently.

"Mr. Larkin," the President said. "God be with you, boy. Do what you can. Delegate authority. Maybe cut the term in half. But keep us human, please, keep us growing, keep us alive." His voice faltered, his eyes closed. "I'm very tired. God be with you."

Larkin laid the hand gently on the bed cover. He stood for a long moment looking down. Then he turned with Reddington and left the room.

Outside, he waited until they were past the Secret Service men and then turned to Reddington.

"Your plans for SAM. What do you think now?"

Reddington winced.

"I couldn't see any way out."

"But what about now? I have to know."

"I don't know. I really don't know. But . . . let me tell you something."

"Yes."

"Whatever I say to you from now on is only advice. You don't have to take it. Because understand this: however you came in here tonight, you're going out the President. You were elected. Not by the people maybe, not even by SAM. But you're President by the grace of God and that's enough for me. From this moment on you'll be President to everybody in the world. We've all agreed. Never think that you're only a fraud, because you aren't. You heard what the President said. You take it from here."

Larkin looked at him for a long while. Then he nodded once, briefly.

"All right," he said.

"One more thing."

"Yes?"

"I've got to say this. Tonight, this afternoon, I didn't really know what I was doing to you. I thought . . . well . . . the crisis came. But you had no time to think. That wasn't right. A man shouldn't be pushed into a thing like this without time to think. The old man just taught me something about making your own decisions. I should have let you make yours."

"It's all right."

"No, it isn't. You remember him in there. Well. That's you four years from tonight. If you live that long."

Now it was Larkin who reached out and patted Reddington on the shoulder.

"That's all right, too," he said.

Reddington said nothing. When he spoke again, Larkin realized he was moved.

"We have the greatest luck, this country," he said tightly. "At all the worst times we always seem to find all the best people."

"Well," Larkin said hurriedly, "we'd better get to work. There's a speech due in the morning. And the problem of SAM. And . . . oh, I've got to be sworn in."

He turned and went off down the hall. Reddington paused a

moment before following him. He was thinking that he could be watching the last human President the United States would ever have. But – once more he straightened his shoulders.

"Yes, sir," he said softly, "Mr. President."

The Rose

CHARLES HARNESS

Charles Harness (1915–   ) wrote one highly regarded SF novel in the 1950s, *Flight into Yesterday (The Paradox Men,* 1953). Damon Knight, in a famous review essay, said, "Harness told me in 1950 that he had spent two years writing the story, and had put into it every fictional idea that occurred to him during the time. He must have studied his model [van Vogt] with painstaking care." But Knight's point is that Harness surpasses van Vogt in SF: "All this, packed even more tightly than the original, symmetrically arranged, the loose ends tucked in, and every outrageous twist of the plot fully justified both in science and in logic." Brian W. Aldiss is also partisan to it: "This novel may be considered as the climax to the billion year spree . . . I call it Wide Screen Baroque . . . Harness's novel has a zing of its own, like whiskey and champagne, the drink of the Nepalese sultans."

After such praise, it is difficult to understand why Harness has suffered such comparative neglect, except that his career as a patent attorney allowed him only occasional time to write. His second novel, *The Ring of Ritornel,* was not published until 1968, and this third, *Wolfhead,* in 1978. Seven more novels followed between 1980 and 1991, altogether a significant body of genre work. Most of his short fiction has never been collected.

His only collection, *The Rose* (1966), was an obscure paperback original, containing the title novella and two other fine stories. Michael Moorcock, though, in an essay about "The Rose," calls it Harness's "greatest novel," and says, "although most of his work is written in the magazine style of the time and at first glance appears to have only the appeal of colorful escapism, reminiscent of A. E. van Vogt or James Blish of the same period, it contains nuances and throw away ideas that show a serious (never earnest) mind operating at a much deeper and broader level than its contemporaries."

Moorcock goes on to say, "'The Rose' [is] crammed with delightful notions – what some SF readers call 'ideas' – but these are essentially icing on the cake of Harness's fiction. [His] stories are what too little science fiction is – true stories of ideas, coming to grips with the big abstract problems of human existence and attempting to throw fresh, philosophical light on them."

"The Rose" was first published in a British SF magazine in 1953, at a time when not a hundred copies of such a publication were seen in the U.S., and not reprinted in America until 1966, long after the dust had settled from *Flight into Yesterday*. Except for the few new readers caught by the sixties paperbacks, the story, which deserves a place on the shelf next to the works of Cordwainer Smith, fell into obscurity. Here it is again, at last, one of the finest examples of "Grand Opera" science fiction.

Chapter One

Her ballet slippers made a soft slapping sound, moody, mournful, as Anna van Tuyl stepped into the annex of her psychiatrical consulting room and walked toward the tall mirror.

Within seconds she would know whether she was ugly.

As she had done half a thousand times in the past two years, the young woman faced the great glass squarely, brought her arms up gracefully and rose upon her tip-toes. And there resemblance to past hours ceased. She did not proceed to an uneasy study of her face and figure. She could not. For her eyes, as though acting with a wisdom and volition of their own, had closed tightly.

Anna van Tuyl was too much the professional psychiatrist not to recognize that her subconscious mind had shrieked its warning. Eyes still shut, and breathing in great gasps, she dropped from her toes as if to turn and leap away. Then gradually she straightened. She must force herself to go through with it. She might not be able to bring herself here, in this mood of candid receptiveness, twice in one lifetime. It must be now.

She trembled in brief, silent premonition, then quietly raised her eyelids.

Sombre eyes looked out at her, a little darker than yesterday: pools ploughed around by furrows that today gouged a little deeper – the result of months of squinting up from the position into which her spinal deformity had thrust her neck and shoulders. The pale lips were pressed together just a little tighter in their defence against unpredictable pain. The cheeks seemed bloodless having been bleached finally and completely by the Unfinished Dream that haunted her sleep, wherein a nightingale fluttered about a white rose.

As if in brooding confirmation, she brought up simultaneously the pearl-translucent fingers of both hands to the upper borders of her forehead, and there pushed back the incongruous masses of newly-grey hair from two tumorous bulges – like incipient horns. As she did this she made a quarter turn, exposing to the mirror the humped grotesquerie of her back.

Then by degrees, like some netherworld Narcissus, she began to sink under the bizarre enchantment of that misshapen image. She could retain no real awareness that this creature was she. That profile, as if seen through witch-opened eyes, might have been that of some enormous toad, and this flickering metaphor paralyzed her first and only forlorn attempt at identification.

In a vague way, she realized that she had discovered what she had set out to discover. She was ugly. She was even very ugly.

The change must have been gradual, too slow to say of any one day: Yesterday I was not ugly. But even eyes that hungered for deception could no longer deny the cumulative evidence.

So slow – and yet so fast. It seemed only yesterday that had found her face down on Matthew Bell's examination table, biting savagely at a little pillow as his gnarled fingertips probed grimly at her upper thoracic vertebrae.

Well, then, she was ugly. But she'd not give in to self-pity. To hell with what she looked like! To hell with mirrors!

On sudden impulse she seized her balancing tripod with both hands, closed her eyes, and swung.

The tinkling of falling mirror glass had hardly ceased when a harsh and gravelly voice hailed her from her office. "Bravo!"

She dropped the practice tripod and whirled, aghast. "Matt!"

"Just thought it was time to come in. But if you want to bawl a little, I'll go back out and wait. No?" Without looking directly at her face or pausing for a reply, he tossed a packet on the table. "There it is. Honey, if I could write a ballet score like your *Nightingale and the Rose*, I wouldn't care if my spine was knotted in a figure eight."

"You're crazy," she muttered stonily, unwilling to admit that she was both pleased and curious. "You don't know what it means to have once been able to pirouette, to balance en *arabesque*. And anyway" – she looked at him from the corner of her eye – "how could anyone tell whether the score's good? There's no Finale as yet. It isn't finished."

"Neither is the Mona Lisa, *Kublai Khan*, or a certain symphony by Schubert."

"But this is different. A plotted ballet requires an integrated sequence of events leading up to a climax – to a Finale. I haven't figured out the ending. Did you notice I left a thirty-eight-beat hiatus just before The Nightingale dies? I still need a death-song for her. She's entitled to die with a flourish." She couldn't tell him about The Dream – that she always awoke just before that death song began.

"No matter. You'll get it eventually. The story's straight out of Oscar Wilde, isn't it? As I recall, The Student needs a Red Rose as admission to the dance, but his garden contains only white roses. A foolish, if sympathetic Nightingale thrusts her heart against a thorn on a white rose stem, and the resultant ill-advised transfusion produces a Red Rose . . . and a dead Nightingale. Isn't that about all there is to it?"

"Almost. But I still need The Nightingale's death song. That's the whole point of the ballet. In a plotted ballet, every chord has to be fitted to the immediate action, blended with it, so that it supplements it, explains it, unifies it, and carries the action toward the climax. That death song will make the difference between a good score and a superior one. Don't smile. I think some of my individual scores are rather good, though of course I've never heard them except on my own piano. But without a proper climax, they'll remain unintegrated. They're all variants of some elusive dominating leitmotiv – some really marvellous theme I haven't the greatness of soul to grasp. I know it's something profound and poignant, like the *liebestod* theme in *Tristan*. It probably states a fundamental musical truth, but I don't think I'll ever find it. The Nightingale dies with her secret."

She paused, opened her lips as though to continue, and then fell moodily silent again. She wanted to go on talking, to lose herself in volubility. But now the reaction of her struggle with the mirror was setting in, and she was suddenly very tired. Had she ever wanted to cry? Now she thought only of sleep. But a furtive glance at her wristwatch told her it was barely ten o'clock.

The man's craggy eyebrows dropped in an imperceptible frown, faint, yet craftily alert. "Anna, the man who read your *Rose* score wants to talk to you about staging it for the Rose Festival – you know, the annual affair in the Via Rosa."

"I – an unknown – write a Festival ballet?" She added with dry incredulity: "The Ballet Committee is in complete agreement with your friend, of course?"

"He *is* the Committee."

"What did you say his name was?"

"I didn't."

She peered up at him suspiciously. "I can play games, too. If he's so anxious to use my music, why doesn't *he* come to see *me*?"

"He isn't that anxious."

"Oh, a big shot, eh?"

"Not exactly. It's just that he's fundamentally indifferent toward the things that fundamentally interest him. Anyway, he's got a complex about the Via Rosa – loves the district and hates to leave it, even for a few hours."

She rubbed her chin thoughtfully. "Will you believe it, I've never been there. That's the rose-walled district where the ars-gratia-artis professionals live, isn't it? Sort-of a plutocratic Rive Gauche?"

The man exhaled in expansive affection. "That's the Via, all right. A six-hundred pound chunk of Carrara marble in every garret, resting most likely on the grand piano. Poppa chips furiously away with an occasional glance at his model, who is momma, posed *au naturel*."

Anna watched his eyes grow dreamy as he continued. "Momma is a little restless, having suddenly recalled that the baby's bottle and that can of caviar should have come out of the atomic warmer at some nebulous period in the past. Daughter sits before the piano keyboard, surreptitiously switching from Czerny to a torrid little number she's going to try on the trap-drummer in Dorran's Via orchestra. Beneath the piano are the baby and mongrel pup. Despite their tender age, this thing is already in their blood. Or at least, their stomachs, for they have just finished an *hors d'oeuvre* of marble chips and now amiably share the *pièce de résistance*, a battered but rewarding tube of Van Dyke brown."

Anna listened to this with widening eyes. Finally she gave a short amazed laugh. "Matt Bell, you really love that life, don't you?"

He smiled. "In some ways the creative life is pretty carefree. I'm just a psychiatrist specializing in psychogenetics. I don't know an arpeggio from a drypoint etching, but I like to be around people that do." He bent forward earnestly. "These artists – these golden people – they're the coming force in society. And you're one of them, Anna, whether you know it or like it. You and your kind are going to inherit the earth – only you'd better hurry if you don't want Martha Jacques and her National Security scientists to get it first. So the battle lines converge in Renaissance II. Art versus Science. Who dies? Who lives?" He looked thoughtful, lonely. He might have been pursuing an introspective monologue in the solitude of his own chambers.

"This Mrs. Jacques," said Anna. "What's she like? You asked me to see her tomorrow about her husband, you know."

"Darn good looking woman. The most valuable mind in history, some say. And if she really works out something concrete from her Sciomnia equation, I guess there won't be any doubt about it. And that's what makes her potentially the most dangerous human being alive: National Security is fully aware of her value, and they'll coddle her tiniest whim – at least until she pulls something tangible out of Sciomnia. Her main whim for the past few years has been her errant husband, Mr. Ruy Jacques."

"Do you think she really loves him?"

"Just between me and you she hates his guts. So naturally she doesn't want any other woman to get him. She has him watched, of course. The Security Bureau cooperate with alacrity, because they don't want foreign agents to approach *her* through *him*. There have been ugly rumors of assassinated models . . . But I'm digressing." He cocked a quizzical eye at her. "Permit me to repeat the invitation of your unknown admirer. Like you, he's another true child of the new Renaissance. The two of you should find much in common – more than you can now guess. I'm very serious about this, Anna. Seek him out immediately – tonight – now. There aren't any mirrors in the Via."

"Please, Matt."

"Honey," he growled, "to a man my age you aren't ugly. And this man's the same. If a woman is pretty, he paints her and forgets her. But if she's some kind of an artist, he talks to her, and he can get rather endless sometimes. If it's any help to your self-assurance, he's about the homeliest creature on the face of the earth. You'll look like De Milo alongside him."

The woman laughed shortly. "I can't get mad at you, can I? Is he married?"

"Sort of." His eyes twinkled. "But don't let that concern you. He's a perfect scoundrel."

"Suppose I decide to look him up. Do I simply run up and down the Via paging all homely friends of Dr. Matthew Bell?"

"Not quite. If I were you I'd start at the entrance – where they have all those queer side-shows and one-man exhibitions. Go on past the vendress of love philters and work down the street until you find a man in a white suit with polka dots."

"How perfectly odd! And then what? How can I introduce myself to a man whose name I don't know? Oh, Matt, this is so silly, so *childish* . . ."

He shook his head in slow denial. "You aren't going to think about names when you see him. And your name won't mean a thing to him, anyway. You'll be lucky if you aren't 'hey you' by midnight. But it isn't going to matter."

"It isn't too clear why you don't offer to escort me." She studied him calculatingly. "And I think you're withholding his name because you know I wouldn't go if you revealed it."

He merely chuckled.

She lashed out: "Damn you, get me a cab."

"I've had one waiting half an hour."

Chapter Two

"Tell ya what the professor's gonna do, ladies and gentlemen. He's gonna defend not just one paradox. Not just two. Not just a dozen. No, ladies and gentlemen, the professor's gonna defend *seventeen,* and all in the space of one short hour, without repeating himself, and including a brand-new one he has just thought up today: 'Music owes its meaning to its ambiguity.' Remember, folks, an axiom is just a paradox the professor's already got hold of. The cost of this dazzling display . . . don't crowd there, mister . . ."

Anna felt a relaxing warmth flowing over her mind, washing at the encrusted strain of the past hour. She smiled and elbowed her way through the throng and on down the street, where a garishly lighted sign, bat-wing doors, and a forlorn cluster of waiting women announced the next attraction:

"FOR MEN ONLY. Daring blindfold exhibitions and variety entertainments continuously."

Inside, a loudspeaker was blaring: "Thus we have seen how to compose the ideal end-game problem in chess. And now, gentlemen, for the small consideration of an additional quarter . . ."

But Anna's attention was now occupied by a harsh cawing from across the street.

"Love philters! Works on male or female! Any age! Never fails!"

She laughed aloud. Good old Matt! He had foreseen what these glaring multifaceted nonsensical stimuli would do for her. Love philters! Just what she needed!

The vendress of love philters was of ancient vintage, perhaps seventy-five years old. Above cheeks of wrinkled leather her eyes glittered speculatively. And how weirdly she was clothed! Her bedraggled dress was a shrieking purple. And under that dress was another of the same hue, though perhaps a little faded. And under *that*, still another.

"That's why they call me Violet," cackled the old woman, catching Anna's stare. "Better come over and let me mix you one."

But Anna shook her head and passed on, eyes shining. Fifteen minutes later, as she neared the central Via area, her receptive reverie was interrupted by the outburst of music ahead.

Good! Watching the street dancers for half an hour would provide a highly pleasant climax to her escapade. Apparently there wasn't going to be any man in a polka dot suit. Matt was going to be disappointed but it certainly wasn't her fault she hadn't found him.

There was something oddly familiar about that music.

She quickened her pace, and then, as recognition came, she began to run as fast as her crouching back would permit. This was *her* music – the prelude to Act III of her ballet!

She burst through the mass of spectators lining the dance square. The music stopped. She stared out into the scattered dancers, and what she saw staggered the twisted frame of her slight body. She fought to get air through her vacuously wide mouth.

In one unearthly instant, a rift had threaded its way through the dancer-packed square, and a pasty white face, altogether spectral, had looked down that open rift into hers. A face over a body that was enveloped in a strange glowing gown of shimmering white. She thought he had also been wearing a white academic mortar board, but the swarming dancers closed in again before she could be sure.

She fought an unreasoning impulse to run.

Then, as quickly as it had come, logic reasserted itself; the shock was over. Odd costumes were no rarity on the Via. There was no cause for alarm.

She was breathing almost normally when the music died away and someone began a harsh harangue over the public address system. 'Ladies and gentlemen, it is our rare good fortune to have with us tonight the genius who composed the music you have been enjoying."

A sudden burst of laughter greeted this, seeming to originate in the direction of the orchestra, and was counterpointed by an uncomplimentary blare from one of the horns.

"Your mockery is misplaced, my friends. It just so happens that this genius is not I, but another. And since she has thus far had no opportunity to join in the revelry, your inimitable friend, as The Student, will take her hand, as The Nightingale, in the final *pas de deux* from Act III. That should delight her, yes?"

The address system clicked off amid clapping and a buzz of excited voices, punctuated by occasional shouts.

She must escape! She must get away!

Anna pressed back into the crowd. There was no longer any question about finding a man in a polka dot suit. *That* creature in white certainly wasn't he. Though how could he have recognized her?

She hesitated. Perhaps he had a message from the other one, if there really was one with polka dots.

No, she'd better go. This was turning out to be more of a nightmare than a lark.

Still –

She peeked back from behind the safety of a woman's sleeve, and after a moment located the man in white.

His pasty-white face with its searching eyes was much closer. But what had happened to his *white* cap and gown? *Now*, they weren't white at all! What optical fantasy was this? She rubbed her eyes and looked again.

The cap and gown seemed to be made up of green and purple polka dots on a white background! So he was her man!

She could see him now as the couples spread out before him, exchanging words she couldn't hear, but which seemed to carry an irresistible laugh response.

Very well, she'd wait.

Now that everything was cleared up and she was safe again behind her armor of objectivity, she studied him with growing curiosity. Since that first time she had never again got a good look at him. Someone always seemed to get in the way. It was almost, she thought, as though he was working his way out toward her, taking every advantage of human cover, like a hunter closing in on wary quarry, until it was too late . . .

He stood before her.

There were harsh clanging sounds as his eyes locked with hers. Under that feral scrutiny the woman maintained her mental balance by the narrowest margin.

The Student.

The Nightingale, for love of The Student, makes a Red Rose. An odious liquid was burning in her throat, but she couldn't swallow.

Gradually she forced herself into awareness of a twisted, sardonic mouth framed between aquiline nose and jutting chin. The face, plastered as it was by white powder, had revealed no distinguishing features beyond its unusual size. Much of the brow was obscured by the many tassels dangling over the front of his travestied mortarboard cap. Perhaps the most striking thing about the man was not his face, but his body. It was evident that he had some physical deformity, to outward appearances not unlike her own. She knew intuitively that he was not a true hunchback. His chest and shoulders were excessively broad, and he seemed, like her, to carry a mass of superfluous tissue on his upper thoracic vertebrae. She surmised that the scapulae would be completely obscured.

His mouth twisted in subtle mockery. "Bell said you'd come." He bowed and held out his right hand.

"It is very difficult for me to dance," she pleaded in a low hurried voice. "I'd humiliate us both."

"I'm no better at this than you, and probably worse. But I'd never give up dancing merely because someone might think I look awkward. Come, we'll use the simplest steps."

There was something harsh and resonant in his voice that reminded her of Matt Bell. Only . . . Bell's voice had never set her stomach churning.

He held out his other hand.

Behind him the dancers had retreated to the edge of the square, leaving the centre empty, and the first beats of her music from the orchestra pavilion floated to her with ecstatic clarity.

Just the two of them, out there . . . before a thousand eyes . . .

Subconsciously she followed the music. There was her cue – the signal for The Nightingale to fly to her fatal assignation with the white rose.

She must reach out both perspiring hands to this stranger, must blend her deformed body into his equally misshapen one. She must, because he was The Student, and she was The Nightingale.

She moved toward him silently and took his hands.

As she danced, the harsh-lit street and faces seemed gradually to vanish. Even The Student faded into the barely perceptible distance, and she gave herself up to The Unfinished Dream.

Chapter Three

She dreamed that she danced alone in the moonlight, that she fluttered in solitary circles in the moonlight, fastened and appalled by the thing she must do to create a Red Rose. She dreamed that she sang a strange and magic song, a wondrous series of chords, the song she had so long sought. Pain buoyed her on excruciating wings, then flung her heavily to earth. The Red Rose was made, and she was dead.

She groaned and struggled to sit up.

Eyes glinted at her out of pasty whiteness. "That was quite a *pas* – only more *de seul* than *de deux*," said The Student.

She looked about in uneasy wonder.

They were sitting together on a marble bench before a fountain. Behind them was a curved walk bounded by a high wall covered with climbing green, dotted here and there with white.

She put her hand to her forehead. "Where are we?"

"This is White Rose Park."

"How did I get here?"

"You danced in on your own two feet through the archway yonder."

"I don't remember . . ."

"I thought perhaps you were trying to lend a bit of realism to the part. But you're early."

"What do you mean?"

"There are only white roses growing in here, and even *they* won't be in full bloom for another month. In late June they'll be a real spectacle. You mean you didn't know about this little park?"

"No. I've never ever been in the Via before. And yet . . ."

"And yet what?"

She hadn't been able to tell anyone – not even Matt Bell – what she was now going to tell this man, an utter stranger, her companion of an hour. He had to be told because, somehow, he too was caught up in the dream ballet.

She began haltingly. "Perhaps I *do* know about this place. Perhaps someone told me about it, and the information got buried in my subconscious mind until I wanted a white rose. There's really something behind my ballet that Dr. Bell didn't tell you. He couldn't, because I'm the only one who knows. *The Rose* comes from my dreams. Only, a better word is nightmares. Every night the score starts from the beginning. In The Dream, I dance. Every night, for months and months, there was a little more music, a little more dancing. I tried to get it out of my head, but I couldn't. I started writing it down, the music and the choreography."

The man's unsmiling eyes were fixed on her face in deep absorption.

Thus encouraged, she continued. "For the past several nights I have dreamed almost the complete ballet, right up to the death of The Nightingale. I suppose I identify myself so completely with The Nightingale that I subconsciously censor her song as she presses her breast against the thorn on the white rose. That's where I always awakened, or at least, always did before tonight. But I think I heard the music tonight. It's a series of chords . . . thirty-eight chords, I believe. The first nineteen were frightful, but the second nineteen were marvellous. Everything was too real to wake up. The Student, The Nightingale, the white roses.

But now the man threw back his head and laughed raucously. "You ought to see a psychiatrist!"

Anna bowed her head humbly.

"Oh, don't take it too hard," he said. "My wife's even after *me* to see a psychiatrist."

"Really?" Anna was suddenly alert. "What seems to be wrong with you? I mean, what does she object to?"

"In general, my laziness. In particular, it seems I've forgotten how to read and write." He gave her widening eyes a sidelong look. "I'm a perfect parasite, too. Haven't done any real work in months. What would *you* call it if you couldn't work until you had the final measures of the *Rose*, and you kept waiting, and nothing happened?"

"Hell."

He was glumly silent.

Anna asked, hesitantly, yet with a growing certainty. "This thing you're waiting for . . . might it have anything to do with the ballet? Or to phrase it from your point of view, do you think the completion of my ballet may help answer your problem?"

"Might. Couldn't say."

She continued quietly. "You're going to have to face it eventually, you know. Your psychiatrist is going to ask you. How will you answer?"

"I won't. I'll tell him to go to the devil."

"How can you be so sure he's a *he*?"

"Oh? Well, if he's a *she*, she might be willing to pose *alfresco* an hour or so. The model shortage is quite grave you know, with all of the little dears trying to be painters."

"But if she doesn't have a good figure?"

"Well, maybe her face has some interesting possibilities. It's a rare woman who's a total physical loss."

Anna's voice was very low. "But what if *all* of her were very ugly? What if your proposed psychiatrist were me, Mr. *Ruy Jacques*?"

His great dark eyes blinked, then his lips pursed and exploded into insane laughter. He stood up suddenly. "Come, my dear, whatever your name is, and let the blind lead the blind."

"Anna van Tuyl," she told him, smiling.

She took his arm. Together they strolled around the arc of the walk toward the entrance arch.

She was filled with a strange contentment.

Over the green-crested wall at her left, day was about to break, and from the Via came the sound of groups of die-hard revellers, breaking up and drifting away, like spectres at cock-crow. The cheerful clatter of milk bottles got mixed up in it somehow.

They paused at the archway while the man kicked at the seat of the pants of a spectre whom dawn had returned to slumber beneath the arch. The sleeper cursed and stumbled to his feet in bleary indignation.

"Excuse us, Willie," said Anna's companion, motioning for her to step through.

She did, and the creature of the night at once dropped into his former sprawl.

Anna cleared her throat. "Where now?"

"At this point I must cease to be a gentleman, *I'm* returning to the studio for some sleep, and *you* can't come. For, if your physical energy is inexhaustible, mine is not." He raised a hand as her startled mouth dropped open. "Please, dear Anna, don't insist. Some other night, perhaps."

"Why, you – "

"Tut tut." He turned a little and kicked again at the sleeping man. "I'm not an utter cad, you know. I would never abandon a weak, frail, unprotected woman in the Via."

She was too amazed now even to splutter.

Ruy Jacques reached down and pulled the drunk up against the wall of the arch, where he held him firmly. "Dr. Anna van Tuyl, may I present Willie the Cork."

The Cork grinned at her in unfocused somnolence.

"Most people call him the Cork because that's what seals in the bottle's contents," said Jacques. "*I* call him the Cork because he's always bobbing up. He looks like a bum, but that's just because he's a good actor. He's really a Security man tailing me at my wife's request, and he'd only be too delighted for a little further conversation with you. A cheery good morning to you both!"

A milk truck wheeled around the corner. Jacques leaped for its running board, and he was gone before the psychiatrist could voice the protest boiling up in her.

A gurgling sigh at her feet drew her eyes down momentarily. The Cork was apparently bobbing once more on his own private alcoholic ocean.

Anna snorted in mingled disgust and amusement, then hailed a cab. As she slammed the door, she took one last look at Willie. Not until the cab rounded the corner and cut off his muffled snores did she realize that people usually don't snore with their eyes half-opened and looking at you, especially with eyes no longer blurred with sleep, but hard and glinting.

Chapter Four

Twelve hours later, in another cab and in a different part of the city, Anna peered absently out at the stream of traffic. Her mind was on the coming conference with Martha Jacques. Only twelve hours ago Mrs. Jacques had been just a bit of necessary case history. Twelve hours ago Anna hadn't really cared whether Mrs. Jacques followed Bell's recommendation and gave her the case. Now it was all different. She wanted the case, and she was going to get it.

Ruy Jacques – how many hours awaited her with this amazing scoundrel, this virtuoso of liberal – nay, loose – arts, who held locked within his remarkable mind the missing pieces of their joint jigsaw puzzle of The Rose?

That jeering, mocking face – what would it look like without makeup? Very ugly, she hoped. Beside his, her own face wasn't too bad.

Only – he was married, and she was en route at this moment to discuss preliminary matters with his wife, who, even if she no longer loved him, at least had prior rights to him. There were considerations of professional ethics even in thinking about him. Not that she could ever fall in love with him or any other patient. Particularly with one who had treated her so cavalierly. Willie the Cork, indeed!

As she waited in the cold silence of the great antechamber adjoining the office of Martha Jacques, Anna sensed that she was being watched. She was quite certain that by now she'd been photographed, x-rayed for hidden weapons, and her fingerprints taken from her professional card. In colossal central police files a thousand miles away, a bored clerk would be leafing through her dossier for the benefit of Colonel Grade's visigraph in the office beyond.

In a moment –

"Dr. van Tuyl to see Mrs. Jacques. Please enter door B-3," said the tinny voice of the intercom.

She followed a guard to the door, which he opened for her.

This room was smaller. At the far end a woman, a very lovely woman, whom she took to be Martha Jacques, sat peering in deep abstraction at something on the desk before her. Beside the desk, and slightly to the rear, a moustached man in plain clothes stood, recon- noitring Anna with hawklike eyes. The description fitted what Anna had heard of Colonel Grade, Chief of the National Security Bureau.

Grade stepped forward and introduced himself curtly, then presented Anna to Mrs. Jacques.

And then the psychiatrist found her eyes fastened to a sheet of paper on Mrs. Jacques' desk. And as she stared, she felt a sharp dagger of ice sinking into her spine, and she grew slowly aware of a background of brooding whispers in her mind, heart-constricting in their suggestions of mental disintegration.

For the thing drawn on the paper, in red ink, was – although warped, incomplete, and misshapen – unmistakably a rose.

"Mrs. Jacques!" cried Grade.

Martha Jacques must have divined simultaneously Anna's great interest in the paper. With an apologetic murmur she turned it face down. "Security regulations, you know. I'm really supposed to keep it locked up in the presence of visitors." Even a murmur could not hide the harsh metallic quality of her voice.

So *that* was why the famous Sciomnia formula was sometimes called the "Jacques Rosette": when traced in an everexpanding wavering red spiral in polar coordinates, it was . . . a Red Rose.

The explanation brought at once a feeling of relief and a sinister deepening of the sense of doom that had overshadowed her for months. So you, too, she thought wonderingly, seek The Rose. Your artist-husband is wretched for want of it, and now you. But do you seek the same rose? Is the rose of the scientist the true rose, and Ruy Jacques' the false? What is The Rose? Will I ever know?

Grade broke in. "Your brilliant reputation is deceptive, Dr. van Tuyl. From Dr. Bell's description, we had pictured you as an older woman."

"Yes," said Martha Jacques, studying her curiously. "We really had in mind an older woman, one less likely to . . . to – "

"To involve your husband emotionally?"

"Exactly," said Grade. "Mrs. Jacques must have her mind completely free from distractions. However" – he turned to the woman scientist – "it is my studied opinion that we need not anticipate difficulty from Dr. van Tuyl on that account."

Anna felt her throat and cheeks going hot as Mrs. Jacques nodded in damning agreement: "I think you're right, Colonel."

"Of course," said Grade, "*Mr.* Jacques may not accept her."

"That remains to be seen," said Martha Jacques. "He might tolerate a fellow artist." To Anna: "Dr. Bell tells us that you compose music, or something like that?"

"Something like that," nodded Anna. She wasn't worried. It was a question of waiting. This woman's murderous jealousy, though it might some day destroy her, at the moment concerned her not a whit.

Colonel Grade said: "Mrs. Jacques has probably warned you that her husband is somewhat eccentric; he may be somewhat difficult to deal with at times. On this account, the Security Bureau is prepared to triple your fee, if we find you acceptable."

Anna nodded gravely. Ruy Jacques and money, too!

"For most of your consultations you'll have to track him down," said Martha Jacques. "He'll never come to you. But considering what we're prepared to pay, this inconvenience should be immaterial."

Anna thought briefly of that fantastic creature who had singled her out of a thousand faces. "That will be satisfactory. And now, Mrs. Jacques, for my preliminary orientation, suppose you describe some of the more striking behaviorisms that you've noted in your husband."

"Certainly. Dr. Bell, I presume, has already told you that Ruy has lost the ability to read and write. Ordinarily that's indicative of advanced dementia praecox, isn't it? However, I think Mr. Jacques' case presents a more complicated picture, and my own guess is schizophrenia rather than dementia. The dominant and most frequently observed psyche is a megalomanic phase, during which he tends to harangue his listeners on various odd subjects. We've picked up some of these speeches on a hidden recorder and made a Zipf analysis of the word-frequencies."

Anna's brows creased dubiously. "A Zipf count is pretty mechanical."

"But scientific, undeniably scientific. I have made a careful study of the method, and can speak authoritatively. Back in the forties Zipf of

Harvard proved that in a representative sample of English, the interval separating the repetition of the same word was inversely proportional to its frequency. He provided a mathematical formula for something previously known only qualitatively: that a too-soon repetition of the same or similar sound is distracting and grating to the cultured mind. If we must say the same thing in the next paragraph, we avoid repetition with an appropriate synonym. But not the schizophrenic. His disease disrupts his higher centres of association, and certain discriminating neural networks are no longer available for his writing and speech. He has no compunction against immediate and continuous tonal repetition."

"A rose is a rose is a rose . . ." murmured Anna.

"Eh? How did you know what this transcription was about? Oh, you were just quoting Gertrude Stein? Well, I've read about her, and she proves my point. She admitted that she wrote under autohypnosis, which we'd call a light case of schizo. But she could be normal, too. My husband never is. He goes on like this all the time. This was transcribed from one of his monologues. Just listen:

"'Behold, Willie, through yonder window the symbol of your mistress' defeat: the rose! The rose, my dear Willie, grows not in murky air. The smoky metropolis of yester-year drove it to the country. But now, with the unsullied skyline of your atomic age, the red rose returns. How mysterious, Willie, that the rose continues to offer herself to us dull, plodding humans. We see nothing in her but a pretty flower. Her regretful thorns forever declare our inept clumsiness, and her lack of honey chides our gross sensuality. Ah, Willie, let us become as birds! For only the winged can eat the fruit of the rose and spread her pollen . . .'"

Mrs. Jacques looked up at Anna. "Did you keep count? He used the word rose' no less than five times, when once or twice was sufficient. He certainly had no lack of mellifluous synonyms at his disposal, such as 'red flower,' 'thorned plant,' and so on. And instead of saying 'the red rose returns' he should have said something like 'it comes back'."

"And lose the triple alliteration?" smiled Anna. "No, Mrs. Jacques, I'd reexamine that diagnosis very critically. Everyone who talks like a poet isn't necessarily insane."

A tiny bell began to jangle on a massive metal door in the right-hand wall.

"A message for me," growled Grade. "Let it wait."

"We don't mind," said Anna, "if you want to have it sent in."

"It isn't *that*. That's my private door, and I'm the only one who knows the combination. But I told them not to interrupt us, unless it dealt with this specific interview."

Anna thought of the eyes of Willie the Cork, hard and glistening. Suddenly she knew that Ruy Jacques had not been joking about the identity of the man. Was The Cork's report just now getting on her dossier? Mrs. Jacques wasn't going to like it. Suppose they turned her down. Would she dare seek out Ruy Jacques under the noses of Grade's trigger men?

"Damn that fool," muttered Grade. "I left strict orders about being disturbed. Excuse me."

He strode angrily toward the door. After a few seconds of dial manipulation, he turned the handle and pulled it inward. A hand thrust something metallic at him. Anna caught whispers. She fought down a feeling of suffocation as Grade opened the cassette and read the message.

The Security officer walked leisurely back toward them. He stroked his moustache coolly, handed the bit of paper to Martha Jacques, then clasped his hands behind his back. For a moment he looked like a glowering bronze statue. "Dr. van Tuyl, you didn't tell us that you were already acquainted with Mr. Jacques. Why?"

"You didn't ask me."

Martha Jacques said harshly: "That answer is hardly satisfactory. How long have you known Mr. Jacques? I want to get to the bottom of this."

"I met him last night for the first time in the Via Rosa. We danced. That's all. The whole thing was purest coincidence."

"You are his lover," accused Martha Jacques.

Anna colored. "You flatter me, Mrs. Jacques."

Grade coughed. "She's right. Mrs. Jacques. I see no sex-based espionage."

"Then maybe it's even subtler," said Martha Jacques. "These platonic females are still worse, because they sail under false colors. She's after Ruy, I tell you."

"I assure you," said Anna, "that your reaction comes as a complete surprise to me. Naturally, I shall withdraw from the case at once."

"But it doesn't end with that," said Grade curtly. "The national safety may depend on Mrs. Jacques' peace of mind during the coming weeks. I *must* ascertain your relation with Mr. Jacques. And I must warn you that if a compromising situation exists, the consequences will be most unpleasant." He picked up the telephone. "Grade. Get me the O.D."

Anna's palms were uncomfortably wet and sticky. She wanted to wipe them on the sides of her dress, but then decided it would be better to conceal all signs of nervousness.

Grade barked into the mouthpiece. "Hello! That you, Packard? Send me – "

Suddenly the room vibrated with the shattering impact of massive metal on metal.

The three whirled toward the sound.

A stooped, loudly dressed figure was walking away from the great and inviolate door of Colonel Grade, drinking in with sardonic amusement the stuporous faces turned to him. It was evident he had just slammed the door behind him with all his strength.

Insistent squeakings from the teleset stirred Grade into a feeble response. "Never mind . . . it's Mr. Jacques . . ."

Chapter Five

The swart ugliness of that face verged on the sublime. Anna observed for the first time the two horn-like protuberances on his forehead, which the man made no effort to conceal. His black woollen beret was cocked jauntily over one horn; the other, the visible one, bulged even more than Anna's horns, and to her fascinated eyes he appeared as some Greek satyr; Silenus with an eternal hangover, or Pan wearying of fruitless pursuit of fleeting nymphs. It was the face of a cynical post-gaol Wilde, of a Rimbaud, of a Goya turning his brush in saturnine glee from Spanish grandees to the horror-world of Ensayos.

Like a phantom voice Matthew Bell's cryptic prediction seemed to float into her ears again: ". . . much in common . . . more than you guess . . ."

There was so little time to think. Ruy Jacques must have recognized her frontal deformities even while that tasselated mortar-board of his Student costume had prevented her from seeing his. He must have identified her as a less advanced case of his own disease. Had he foreseen the turn of events here? Was he here to protect the only person on earth who might help him? That wasn't like him. He just wasn't the sensible type. She got the uneasy impression that he was here solely for his own amusement – simply to make fools of the three of them.

Grade began to sputter. "Now see here, Mr. Jacques. It's impossible to get in through that door. It's my private entrance. I changed the combination myself only this morning." The moustache bristled indignantly. "I must ask the meaning of this."

"Pray do, Colonel, pray do."

"Well, then, what is the meaning of this?"

"None, Colonel. Have you no faith in your own syllogisms? No one can open your private door but you. Q.E.D. No one did. I'm not really here. No smiles? Tsk tsk! Paragraph 6, p. 80 of the Manual of Permissible Military Humor officially recognizes the paradox."

"There's no such publication – " stormed Grade.

But Jacques brushed him aside. He seemed now to notice Anna for the first time, and bowed with exaggerated punctilio. "My profound apologies, madame. You were standing so still, so quiet, that I mistook you for a rose bush." He beamed at each in turn. "Now isn't this delightful? I feel like a literary lion. It's the first time in my life that my admirers ever met for the express purpose of discussing my work."

How could he know that we were discussing his "composition," wondered Anna. *And how did he open the door?*

"If you'd eavesdropped long enough," said Martha Jacques, "you'd have learned we weren't admiring your 'prose poem'. In fact, I think it's pure nonsense."

No, thought Anna, he couldn't have eavesdropped, because we didn't talk about his speech after Grade opened the door. There's something here – in this room – that *tells* him.

"You don't even think it's poetry?" repeated Jacques, wide-eyed. "Martha, coming from one with your scientifically developed poetical sense, this is utterly damning."

"There *are* certain well recognized approaches to the appreciation of poetry," said Martha Jacques doggedly. "You ought to have the autoscanner read you some books on the aesthetic laws of language. It's all there."

The artist blinked in great innocence. "*What's* all there?"

"Scientific rules for analyzing poetry. Take the mood of a poem. You can very easily learn whether it's gay or sombre just by comparing the proportion of low-pitched vowels – *u* and *o*, that is – to the high-pitched vowels – *a, e* and *i*."

"Well, what do you know about that!" He turned a wondering face to Anna. "And she's right! Come to think of it, in Milton's *L'Allegro*, most of the vowels are high-pitched, while in his *Il Penseroso*, they're mostly low-pitched. Folks, I believe we've finally found a yardstick for genuine poetry. No longer must we flounder in poetastical soup. Now let's see." He rubbed his chin in blank-faced thoughtfulness. "Do you

know, for years I've considered Swinburne's lines mourning Charles
Baudelaire to be the distillate of sadness. But that, of course, was before
I had heard of Martha's scientific approach, and had to rely solely on
my unsophisticated, untrained, uninformed feelings. How stupid I was!
For the thing is crammed with high-pitched vowels, and long *e* dominates: 'thee,' 'sea,' 'weave,' 'eve,' 'heat,' 'sweet,' 'feet' . . ." He struck
his brow as if in sudden comprehension. "Why, it's gay! I must set it to
a snappy polka!"

"Drivel," sniffed Martha Jacques. "Science – "

" – is simply a parasitical, adjectival, and useless occupation devoted
to the quantitative restatement of Art," finished the smiling Jacques.
"Science is functionally sterile; it creates nothing; it says nothing new.
The scientist can never be more than a humble camp-follower of the
artist. There exists no scientific truism that hasn't been anticipated by
creative art. The examples are endless. Uccello worked out mathematically the laws of perspective in the fifteenth century; but
Kallicrates applied the same laws two thousand years before in
designing the columns of the Parthenon. The Curies thought they
invented the idea of 'half-life' – of a thing vanishing in proportion to
its residue. The Egyptians tuned their lyre-strings to dampen
according to the same formula. Napier thought he invented logarithms
– entirely overlooking the fact that the Roman brass workers flared
their trumpets to follow a logarithmic curve."

"You're deliberately selecting isolated examples," retorted Martha
Jacques.

"Then suppose you name a few so-called scientific discoveries,"
replied the man. "I'll prove they were scooped by an artist, every
time."

"I certainly shall. How about Boyle's gas law? I suppose you'll say
Praxiteles knew all along that gas pressure runs inversely proportional
to its volume at a given temperature?"

"I expected something more sophisticated. That one's too easy.
Boyle's gas law, Hooke's law of springs, Galileo's law of pendulums,
and a host of similar hogwash simply state that compression, kinetic
energy, or whatever name you give it, is inversely proportional to its
reduced dimensions, and is proportional to the amount of its displacement in the total system. Or, as the artist says, impact results from, and
is proportional to, displacement of an object within its milieu. Could
the final couplet of a Shakespearean sonnet enthral us if our minds
hadn't been conditioned, held in check, and compressed in suspense
by the preceding fourteen lines? Note how cleverly Donne's famous

poem builds up to its crash line, 'It tolls for thee!' By blood, sweat, and genius, the Elizabethans lowered the entropy of their creations in precisely the same manner and with precisely the same result as when Boyle compressed his gases. And the method was long old when *they* were young. It was old when the Ming artists were painting the barest suggestions of landscapes on the disproportionate backgrounds of their vases. The Shah Jahan was aware of it when he designed the long eye-restraining reflecting pool before the Taj Mahal. The Greek tragedians knew it. Sophocles' *Oedipus* is still unparalleled in its suspensive pacing toward climax. Solomon's imported Chaldean arthitects knew the effect to be gained by spacing the Holy of Holies at a distance from the temple pylae, and the Cro-Magnard magicians with malice afore-thought painted their marvellous animal scenes only in the most inaccessible crannies of their limestone caves."

Martha Jacques smiled coldly. "Drivel, drivel, drivel. But never mind. One of these days soon I'll produce evidence you'll be *forced* to admit art can't touch."

"If you're talking about Sciomnia, there's *real* nonsense for you," countered Jacques amiably. "Really, Martha, it's a frightful waste of time to reconcile biological theory with the unified field theory of Einstein, which itself merely reconciles the relativity and quantum theories, a futile gesture in the first place. Before Einstein announced *his* unified theory in 1949, the professors handled the problem very neatly. They taught the quantum theory on Mondays, Wednesdays and Fridays and the relativity theory on Tuesdays, Thursdays and Saturdays. On the Sabbath they rested in front of their television sets. What's the good of Sciomnia, anyway?"

"It's the final summation of all physical and biological knowledge," retorted Martha Jacques. "And as such, Sciomnia represents the highest possible aim of human endeavor. Man's goal in life is to under-stand his environment, to analyze it to the last iota – to know what he controls. The first person to understand Sciomnia may well rule not only this planet, but the whole galaxy – not that he'd want to, but he could. That person may not be me – but will certainly be a scientist, and not an irresponsible artist."

"But Martha," protested Jacques. "Where did you pick up such a weird philosophy? The highest aim of man is *not* to analyze, but to synthesize – to *create*. If you ever solve all of the nineteen sub-equations of Sciomnia, you'll be at a dead end. There'll be nothing left to analyze. As Dr. Bell the psychogeneticist says, overspecialization, be it mental, as in the human scientist, or dental, as in the sabre-tooth tiger, is just a synonym for extinction. But if we continue to create, we shall eventually discover how to transcend – "

Grade coughed, and Martha Jacques cut in tersely: "Never mind what Dr. Bell says. Ruy, have you ever seen this woman before?"

"The rose bush? Hmm." He stepped over to Anna and looked squarely down at her face. She flushed and looked away. He circled her in slow, critical appraisal, like a prospective buyer in a slave market of ancient Baghdad. "Hmm," he repeated doubtfully.

Anna breathed faster; her cheeks were the hue of beets. But she couldn't work up any sense of indignity. On the contrary, there was something illogically delicious about being visually pawed and handled by this strange leering creature.

Then she jerked visibly. What hypnotic insanity was this? This man held her life in the palm of his hand. If he acknowledged her, the vindictive creature who passed as his wife would crush her professionally. If he denied her, they'd know he was lying to save her – and the consequences might prove even less pleasant. And what difference would her ruin make to *him?* She had sensed at once his monumental selfishness. And even if that conceit, that gorgeous self-love, urged him to preserve her for her hypothetical value in finishing up the Rose score, she didn't see how he was going to manage it.

"Do you recognize her, Mr. Jacques," demanded Grade.

"I do," came the solemn reply.

Anna stiffened.

Martha Jacques smiled thinly. "Who is she?"

"Miss Ethel Twinkham, my old spelling teacher. How are you, Miss Twinkham? What brings you out of retirement?"

"I'm not Miss Twinkham," said Anna dryly. "My name is Anna van Tuyl. For your information, we met last night in the Via Rosa."

"Oh! Of course!" He laughed happily. "I seem to remember now, quite indistinctly. And I want to apologize, Miss Twinkham. My behavior was execrable, I suppose. Anyway, if you will just leave the bill for damages with Mrs. Jacques, her lawyer will take care of everything. You can even throw in ten per cent, for mental anguish."

Anna felt like clapping her hands in glee. The whole Security office was no match for this fiend.

"You're getting last night mixed up with the night before," snapped Martha Jacques. "You met Miss van Tuyl last night. You were with her several hours. Don't lie about it."

Again Ruy Jacques peered earnestly into Anna's face. He finally shook his head. "Last night? Well, I can't deny it. Guess you'll have to pay up, Martha. Her face is familiar, but I just can't remember what I did to make her mad. The bucket of paint and the slumming dowager was *last* week, wasn't it?"

Anna smiled. "You didn't injure me. We simply danced together on the square, that's all. I'm here at Mrs. Jacques' request." From the corner of her eye she watched Martha Jacques and the colonel exchange questioning glances, as if to say, "Perhaps there is really nothing between them."

But the scientist was not completely satisfied. She turned her eyes on her husband. "It's a strange coincidence that you should come just at this time. Exactly why *are* you here, if not to becloud the issue of this woman and your future psychiatrical treatment? Why don't you answer? What is the matter with you?"

For Ruy Jacques stood there, swaying like a stricken satyr, his eyes coals of pain in a face of anguished flames. He contorted backward once, as though attempting to placate furious fangs tearing at the hump on his back.

Anna leaped to catch him as he collapsed.

He lay cupped in her lap moaning voicelessly. Something in his hump, which lay against her left breast, seethed and raged like a genie locked in a bottle.

"Colonel Grade," said the psychiatrist quietly, "you will order an ambulance. I must analyze this pain syndrome at the clinic immediately."

Ruy Jacques was hers.

Chapter Six

"Thanks awfully for coming, Matt," said Anna warmly.

"Glad to, honey." He looked down at the prone figure on the clinic cot. "How's our friend?"

"Still unconscious, and under general analgesic. I called you in because I want to air some ideas about this man that scare me when I think about them alone."

The psychogeneticist adjusted his spectacles with elaborate casualness. "Really? Then you think you've found what's wrong with him? Why he can't read or write?"

"Does it have to be something *wrong?*"

"What else would you call it? A . . . *gift?*"

She studied him narrowly. "I might – and you might – if he got something in return for his loss. That would depend on whether there was a net gain, wouldn't it? And don't pretend you don't know what I'm talking about. Let's get out in the open. You've known the Jacques – both of them – for years. You had me put on his case because you think he and I might find in the mind and body of the other a mutual solution to our identical aberrations. Well?"

Bell tapped imperturbably at his cigar. "As you say, the question is, whether he got enough in return – enough to compensate for his lost skills."

She gave him a baffled look. "All right, then, I'll do the talking. Ruy Jacques opened Grade's private door, when Grade alone knew the combination. And when he got in the room with us, he knew what we had been talking about. It was just as though it had all been written out for him, somehow. You'd have thought the lock combination had been pasted on the door, and that he'd looked over a transcript of our conversation."

"Only, he can't read," observed Bell.

"You mean, he can't read . . . *writing*?"

"What else is there?"

"Possibly some sort of thought residuum . . . in *things*. Perhaps some message in the metal of Grade's door, and in certain objects in the room." She watched him closely. "I see you aren't surprised. You've known this all along."

"I admit nothing. You, on the other hand, must admit that your theory of thought-reading is superficially fantastic."

"So would writing be – to a Neanderthal cave dweller. But tell me, Matt, where do our thoughts go after we think them? What is the extra-cranial fate of those feeble, intricate electric oscillations we pick up on the encephalograph? We know they can and do penetrate the skull, that they can pass through bone, like radio waves. Do they go on out into the universe forever? Or do dense substances like Grade's door eventually absorb them all? Do they set up their wispy patterns in metals, which then begin to vibrate in sympathy, like piano wires responding to a noise?"

Bell drew heavily on his cigar. "Seriously, I don't know. But I will say this: your theory is not inconsistent with certain psychogenetic predictions."

"Such as?"

"Eventual telemusical communication of all thought. The encephalograph, you know, looks oddly like a musical sound track. Oh, we can't expect to convert overnight to communication of pure thought by pure music. Naturally, crude transitional forms will intervene. But *any* type of direct idea transmission that involves the sending and receiving of rhythm and modulation as such is a cut higher than communication in a verbal medium, and may be a rudimentary step upward toward true musical communion, just as dawn man presaged true words with allusive, onomatapoeic monosyllables."

"There's your answer, then," said Anna. "Why should Ruy Jacques trouble to read, when every bit of metal around him is an open book?" She continued speculatively. "You might look at it this way. Our ancestors forgot how to swing through the trees when they learned how to walk erect. Their history is recapitulated in our very young. Almost immediately after birth, a human infant can hang by his hands, apelike. And then, after a week or so, he forgets what no human infant ever really needed to know. So now Ruy forgets how to read. A great pity. Perhaps. But if the world were peopled with Ruys, they wouldn't need to know how, for after the first few years of infancy, they'd learn to use their metal-empathic sense. They might even say, 'It's all very nice to be able to read and write and swing about in trees when you're *quite* young, but after all, one matures.'

She pressed a button on the desk slide viewer that sat on a table by the artist's bed. "This is a radiographic slide of Ruy's cerebral hemispheres as viewed from above, probably old stuff to you. It shows that the 'horns' are not mere localized growths in the prefrontal area, but extend as slender tracts around the respective hemispheric peripheries to the visuo-sensory area of the occipital lobes, where they turn and enter the cerebral interior, there to merge in an enlarged ball-like juncture at a point over the cerebellum where the pineal 'eye' is ordinarily found."

"But the pineal is completely missing in the slide," demurred Bell.

"That's the question," countered Anna. "Is the pineal absent – or, are the 'horns' actually the pineal, enormously enlarged and bifurcated? I'm convinced that the latter is the fact. For reasons presently unknown to me, this heretofore small, obscure lobe has grown, bifurcated, and forced its destructive dual limbs not only through the soft cerebral tissue concerned with the ability to read, but also has gone on to skirt half the cerebral circumference to the forehead, where even the hard frontal bone of the skull has softened under its pressure." She looked at Bell closely. "I infer that it's just a question of time before I, too, forget how to read and write."

Bell's eyes drifted evasively to the immobile face of the unconscious artist. "But the number of neurons in a given mammalian brain remains constant after birth," he said. "These cells can throw out numerous dendrites and create increasingly complex neural patterns as the subject grows older, but he can't grow any more of the primary neurons."

"I know. That's the trouble. Ruy can't grow more brain, but he has." She touched her own "horns" wonderingly. "And I guess I have, too. *What – ?*"

Following Bell's glance, she bent over to inspect the artist's face, and started as from a physical blow.

Eyes like anguished talons were clutching hers.

His lips moved, and a harsh whisper swirled about her ears like a desolate wind: ". . . The Nightingale . . . in death . . . greater beauty unbearable . . . *but watch . . . THE ROSE!*"

White-faced, Anna staggered backwards through the door.

Chapter Seven

Bell's hurried footsteps were just behind her as she burst into her office and collapsed on the consultation couch. Her eyes were shut tight, but over her labored breathing she heard the psychogeneticist sit down and leisurely light another cigar.

Finally she opened her eyes. "Even *you* found out something that time. There's no use asking me what he meant."

"Isn't there? Who will dance the part of The Student on opening night?"

"Ruy. Only, he will really do little beyond provide support to the prima ballerina, The Nightingale, that is, at the beginning and end of the ballet."

"And who plays The Nightingale?"

"Ruy hired a professional – La Tanid."

Bell blew a careless cloud of smoke toward the ceiling. "Are you sure *you* aren't going to take the part?"

"The role is strenuous in the extreme. For me, it would be a physical impossibility."

"Now."

"What do you mean – *now?*"

He looked at her sharply. "You know very well what I mean. You know it so well your whole body is quivering. Your ballet premiere is four weeks off – but you know and I know that Ruy has already seen it. Interesting." He tapped coolly at his cigar. *"Almost as interesting as your belief he saw you playing the part of The Nightingale.*"

Anna clenched her fists. This must be faced rationally. She inhaled deeply, and slowly let her breath out. "How can even *he* see things that haven't happened yet?"

"I don't know for sure. But I can guess, and so could you if you'd calm down a bit. We do know that the pineal is a residuum of the single eye that our very remote seagoing ancestors had in the centre of their fishy foreheads. Suppose this fossil eye, now buried deep in the normal brain, were reactivated. What would we be able to see with it? Nothing spatial, nothing dependent on light stimuli. But let us approach the problem inductively. I shut one eye. The other can fix Anna van Tuyl in a depthless visual plane. But with two eyes I can follow you stereoscopically, as you move about in space. Thus, adding an eye adds a dimension. With the pineal as a third eye I should be able to follow you through time. So Ruy's awakened pineal should permit him at least a hazy glimpse of the future."

"What a marvellous – and terrible gift."

"But not without precedent," said Bell. "I suspect that a more or less reactivated pineal lies behind every case of clairvoyance collected in the annals of para-psychology. And I can think of at least one historical instance in which the pineal has actually tried to penetrate the forehead, though evidently only in monolobate form. All Buddhist statues carry a mark on the forehead symbolic of an 'inner eye'. From what we know now, Budda's 'inner eye' was something more than symbolic."

"Granted. But a time-sensitive pineal still doesn't explain the pain in Ruy's hump. Nor the hump itself, for that matter."

"What," said Bell, "makes you think the hump is anything more than what it seems – a spinal disease characterized by a growth of laminated tissue?"

"It's not that simple, and you know it. You're familiar with 'phantom limb' cases, such as where the amputee retains an illusion of sensation or pain in the amputated hand or foot?"

He nodded.

She continued: "But you know, of course, that amputation isn't an absolute prerequisite to a 'phantom'. A child born armless may experience phantom limb sensations for years. Suppose such a child were thrust into some improbable armless society, and their psychiatrists tried to cast his sensory pattern into their own mould. How could the child explain to them the miracle of arms, hands, fingers – things of which he had occasional sensory intimations, but had never seen, and could hardly imagine? Ruy's case is analogous. He is four-limbed and presumably springs from normal stock. Hence the phantom sensations in his hump point toward a *potential* organ – a fore-shadowing of the future, rather than toward memories of a limb once possessed. To use a brutish example, Ruy is like the tadpole rather than the snake. The snake had his legs briefly, during the evolutionary recapitulation of his embryo. The tadpole has yet to shed his tail and develop legs. But one might assume that each has some faint phantom sensoria of legs."

Bell appeared to consider this. "That still doesn't account for Ruy's pain. I wouldn't think the process of growing a tail would be painful for a tadpole, nor a phantom limb for Ruy – if it's inherent in his physical structure. But be that as it may, from all indications he is still going to be in considerable pain when that narcotic wears off. What are you going to do for him *then?* Section the ganglia leading to his hump?"

"Certainly not. Then he would *never* be able to grow that extra organ. Anyhow, even in normal phantom limb cases, cutting nerve tissue doesn't help. Excision of neuromas from limb stumps brings only temporary relief – and may actually aggravate a case of hyperaesthesia. No, phantom pain sensations are central rather then peripheral. However, as a temporary analgesic I shall try a two per cent solution of novocaine near the proper thoracic ganglia." She looked at her watch. "We'd better be getting back to him."

Chapter Eight

Anna withdrew the syringe needle from the man's side and rubbed the last puncture with an alcoholic swab.

"How do you feel, Ruy?" asked Bell.

The woman stooped beside the sterile linens and looked at the face of the prone man. "He doesn't," she said uneasily. "He's out cold again."

"Really?" Bell bent over beside her and reached for the man's pulse. "But it was only two per cent novocaine. Most remarkable."

"I'll order a counter-stimulant," said Anna nervously. "I don't like this."

"Oh, come, girl. Relax. Pulse and respiration normal. In fact, I think you're nearer collapse than he. This is very interesting . . ." His voice trailed off in musing surmise. "Look, Anna, there's nothing to keep both of us here. He's in no danger whatever. I've got to run along. I'm sure you can attend to him."

I know, she thought. You want me to be alone with him.

She acknowledged his suggestion with a reluctant nod of her head, and the door closed behind his chuckle.

For some moments thereafter she studied in deep abstraction the regular rise and fall of the man's chest.

So Ruy Jacques had set another medical precedent. He'd received a local anaesthetic that should have done nothing more than desensitise the deformed growth in his back for an hour or two. But here he lay, in apparent coma, just as though under a general cerebral anaesthetic.

Her frown deepened.

X-ray plates had showed his dorsal growth simply as a compacted mass of cartilaginous laminated tissue (the same as hers) penetrated here and there by neural ganglia. In deadening those ganglia she should have accomplished nothing more than local anaesthetization of that tissue mass, in the same manner that one anaesthetizes an arm or leg by deadening the appropriate spinal ganglion. But the actual result was not local, but general. It was as though one had administered a mild local to the radial nerve of the forearm to deaden pain in the hand, but had instead anaesthetized the cerebrum.

And *that*, of course, was utterly senseless, completely incredible, because anaesthesia works from the higher neural centres down, not vice versa. Deadening a certain area of the parietal lobe could kill sensation in the radial nerve and the hand, but a hypo in the radial nerve wouldn't knock out the parietal lobe of the cerebrum, because the parietal organization was neurally superior. Analogously, anaesthetizing Ruy Jacques' hump shouldn't have deadened his entire cerebrum, because certainly his cerebrum was to be presumed neurally superior to that dorsal malformation.

To be presumed . . .

But with Ruy Jacques, presumptions were – invalid.

So *that* was what Bell had wanted her to discover. Like some sinister reptile of the Mesozoic, Ruy Jacques had *two* neural organizations, one in his skull and one on his back, the latter being superior to, and in some degree controlling, the one in his skull, just as the cerebral cortex in human beings and other higher animals assists and screens the work of the less intricate cerebellum, and just as the cerebellum governs the still more primitive medulla oblongata in the lower vertebrata, such as in frogs and fishes. In anaesthetizing his bump, she had disrupted communications in his highest centres of consciousness, and in anaes-thetizing the higher, dorsal centre, she had apparently simultaneously deactivated his "normal" brain.

As full realization came, she grew aware of a curious numbness in her thighs, and of faint overtones of mingled terror and awe in the giddy throbbing in her forehead. Slowly, she sank into the bedside chair.

For as this man was, so must she become. The day lay ahead when *her* pineal growths must stretch to the point of disrupting the grey matter in her occipital lobes, and destroy her ability to read. And the time must come, too, when *her* dorsal growth would inflame her whole body with its anguished writhing, as it had done his, and try with probable equal futility to burst its bonds.

And all of this must come – soon; before her ballet premiere, certainly. The enigmatic skein of the future would be unravelled to her evolving intellect even as it now was to Ruy Jacques'. She could find all the answers she sought . . . Dream's end . . . The Nightingale's death song . . . The Rose. And she would find them whether she wanted to or not.

She groaned uneasily.

At the sound, the man's eyelids seemed to tremble; his breathing slowed momentarily, then became faster.

She considered this in perplexity. He was unconscious, certainly; yet he made definite responses to aural stimuli. Possibly she had anaesthetized neither member of the hypothetical brain-pair, but had merely cut, temporarily, their lines of intercommunication, just as one might temporarily disorganize the brain of a laboratory animal by anaesthetizing the pons Varolii linking the two cranial hemispheres.

Of one thing she was sure: Ruy Jacques, unconscious, and temporarily mentally disintegrate, was not going to conform to the behavior long standardized for other unconscious and disintegrate mammals. Always one step beyond what she ever expected. Beyond man. Beyond genius.

She arose quietly and tiptoed the short distance to the bed.

When her lips were a few inches from the artist's right ear, she said softly: "What is your name?"

The prone figure stirred uneasily. His eyelids fluttered, but did not open. His wine-colored lips parted, then shut, then opened again. His reply was a harsh, barely intelligible whisper: "Zhak."

"What are you doing?"

"Searching . . ."

"For what?"

"A red rose."

"There are many red roses."

Again his somnolent, metallic whisper: "No, there is but one."

She suddenly realized that her own voice was becoming tense, shrill. She forced it back into a lower pitch. "Think of that rose. Can you see it?"

"Yes . . . yes!"

She cried: *"What is the rose?"*

It seemed that the narrow walls of the room would clamour forever their outraged metallic modesty, if something hadn't frightened away their pain. Ruy Jacques opened his eyes and struggled to rise on one elbow.

On his sweating forehead was a deep frown. But his eyes were apparently focused on nothing in particular, and despite his seemingly purposive motor reaction, she knew that actually her question had but thrown him deeper into his strange spell.

Swaying a little on the dubious support of his right elbow, he muttered: *"You* are not the rose . . . not yet . . . not yet . . ."

She gazed at him in shocked stupor as his eyes closed slowly and he slumped back on the sheet. For a long moment there was no sound in the room but his deep and rhythmic breathing.

Chapter Nine

Without turning from her glum perusal of the clinic grounds framed in her window, Anna threw the statement over her shoulder as Bell entered the office. "Your friend Jacques refuses to return for a check-up. I haven't seen him since he walked out a week ago."

"Is that fatal?"

She turned blood-shot eyes on him. "Not to Ruy."

The man's expression twinkled. "He's your patient, isn't he? It's your duty to make a house call."

"I certainly shall. I was going to call him on the visor to make an appointment."

"He doesn't have a visor. Everybody just walks in. There's something doing in his studio nearly every night. If you're bashful, I'll be glad to take you."

"No thanks. I'll go alone – early."

Bell chuckled. "I'll see you tonight."

Chapter Ten

Number 98 was a sad, ramshackled, four-storey, plaster-front affair, evidently thrown up during the materials shortage of the late forties.

Anna took a deep breath, ignored the unsteadiness of her knees, and climbed the half dozen steps of the front stoop.

There seemed to be no exterior bell. Perhaps it was inside. She pushed the door in and the waning evening light followed her into the hall. From somewhere came a frantic barking, which was immediately silenced.

Anna peered uneasily up the rickety stairs, then whirled as a door opened behind her.

A fuzzy canine muzzle thrust itself out of the crack in the doorway and growled cautiously. And in the same crack, farther up, a dark wrinkled face looked out at her suspiciously. "Whaddaya want?"

Anna retreated half a step. "Does he bite?"

"Who, Mozart? Nah, he couldn't dent a banana." The creature added with anile irrelevance, "Ruy gave him to me because Mozart's dog followed him to the grave.

"Then this is where Mr. Jacques lives?"

"Sure, fourth floor, but you're early." The door opened wider. "Say, haven't I seen you somewhere before?"

Recognition was simultaneous. It was that animated stack of purple dresses, the ancient vendress of love philters.

"Come in, dearie," purred the old one, "and I'll mix you up something special."

"Never mind," said Anna hurriedly. "I've got to see Mr. Jacques." She turned and ran toward the stairway.

A horrid floating cackle whipped and goaded her flight, until she stumbled out on the final landing and set up an insensate skirling on the first door she came to.

From within an irritated voice called: "Aren't you getting a little tired of that? Why don't you come in and rest your knuckles?"

"Oh." She felt faintly foolish. "It's me – Anna van Tuyl."

"Shall I take the door off its hinges, doctor?"

Anna turned the knob and stepped inside.

Ruy Jacques stood with his back to her, palette in hand, facing an easel bathed in the slanting shafts of the setting sun. He was apparently blocking in a caricature of a nude model lying, face averted, on a couch beyond the easel.

Anna felt a sharp pang of disappointment. She'd wanted him to herself a little while. Her glance flicked about the studio.

Framed canvases obscured by dust were stacked willy-nilly about the walls of the big room. Here and there were bits of statuary. Behind a nearby screen the disarray of a cot peeped out at her. Beyond the screen was a wire-phono. In the opposite wall was a door that evidently opened into the model's dressing alcove. In the opposite corner stood a battered electronic piano which she recognized as the Fourier audiosynthesizer type.

She gave an involuntary gasp as the figure of a man suddenly separated from the piano and bowed to her.

Colonel Grade.

So the lovely model with the invisible face must be – Martha Jacques.

There was no possibility of mistake, for now the model had turned her face a little, and acknowledged Anna's faltering stare with complacent mockery.

Of all evenings, why did Martha Jacques have to pick *this* one?

The artist faced the easel again. His harsh jeer floated back to the psychiatrist:

"Behold the perfect female body!"

Perhaps it was the way he said this that saved her. She had a fleeting suspicion that he had recognized her disappointment, had anticipated the depths of her gathering despair, and had deliberately shaken her back into reality.

In a few words he had borne upon her the idea that his enormously complex mind contained neither love nor hate, even for his wife, and that while he found in her a physical perfection suitable for transference to canvas or marble, nevertheless he writhed in a secret torment over this very perfection, as though in essence the woman's physical beauty simply stated a lack he could not name, and might never know.

With a wary, futile motion he lay aside his brushes and palette. "Yes, Martha is perfect, physically and mentally, and knows it." He laughed brutally. "What she doesn't know, is that frozen beauty admits of no plastic play of meaning. There's nothing behind perfection, because it has no meaning but itself."

There was a clamour on the stairs. "Hah!" cried Jacques. "More early-comers. The word must have got around that Martha brought the liquor. School's out, Mart. Better hop into the alcove and get dressed."

Matthew Bell was among the early arrivals. His face lighted up when he saw Anna, then clouded when he picked out Grade and Martha Jacques.

Anna noticed that his mouth was twitching worriedly as he motioned to her.

"What's wrong?" she asked.

"Nothing – yet. But I wouldn't have let you come if I'd known *they'd* be here. Has Martha given you any trouble?"

"No. Why should she? I'm here ostensibly to observe Ruy in my professional capacity."

"You don't believe that, and if you get careless, *she* won't either. So watch your step with Ruy while Martha's around. And even when she's not around. Too many eyes here – Security men – Grade's crew. Just don't let Ruy involve you in anything that might attract attention. So much for that. Been here long?"

"I was the first guest – except for *her* and Grade."

"Hmm. I should have escorted you. Even though you're his psychiatrist, this sort of thing sets her to thinking."

"I can't see the harm of coming alone. It isn't as though Ruy were going to try to make love to me in front of all these people."

"That's exactly what it is as though!" He shook his head and looked about him. "Believe me, I know him better than you. The man is insane . . . unpredictable."

Anna felt a tingle of anticipation . . . or was it of apprehension? "I'll be careful," she said.

"Then come on. If I can get Martha and Ruy into one of their eternal Science-versus-Art arguments, I believe they'll forget about you."

Chapter Eleven

"I repeat," said Bell, "we are watching the germination of another Renaissance. The signs are unmistakable, and should be of great interest to practicing sociologists and policemen." He turned from the little group beginning to gather about him and beamed artlessly at the passing fate of Colonel Grade.

Grade paused. "And just what are the signs of a renaissance?" he demanded.

"Mainly climatic change and enormously increased leisure, Colonel. Either alone can make a big difference, combined, the result is multiplicative rather than additive."

Anna watched Bell's eyes rove the room and join with those of Martha Jacques, as he continued: "Take temperature. In seven thousand B.C. *homo sapiens,* even in the Mediterranean area, was a shivering nomad; fifteen or twenty centuries later a climatic upheaval had turned Mesopotamia, Egypt and the Yangste valley into garden spots, and the first civilizations were born. Another warm period extending over several centuries and ending about twelve hundred A.D. launched the Italian Renaissance and the great Ottoman culture, before the temperature started falling again. Since the middle of the seventeenth century the mean temperature of New York City has been increasing at the rate of about one-tenth of a degree per year. In another century palm trees will be commonplace on Fifth Avenue." He broke off and bowed benignantly. "Hello, Mrs. Jacques. I was just mentioning that in past renaissances, mild climates and bounteous crops gave man leisure to think, and to create."

When the woman shrugged her shoulders and made a gesture as though to walk on, Bell continued hurriedly: "Yes, *those* renaissances gave us the Parthenon, *The Last Supper,* the Taj Mahal. *Then,* the *artist* was supreme. But this time it might not happen that way, because we face a simultaneous technologic and climatic optimum. Atomic energy has virtually abolished labor as such, but without the international leavening of common art that united the first Egyptian, Sumerian, Chinese and Greek cities. Without pausing to consolidate his gains, the scientist rushes on to greater things, to Sciomnia, and to a Sciomnic power source" – he exchanged a sidelong look with the woman scientist – "a machine which, we are informed, may overnight fling man toward the nearer stars. When that day comes, the artist is through . . . unless . . ."

"Unless what?" asked Martha Jacques coldly.

"Unless this Renaissance, sharpened and intensified as it has been by its double maxima of climate and science, is able to force a response comparable to that of the Aurignacean Renaissance of twenty-five thousand B.C., to wit, the flowering of the Cro-Magnon, the first of the modern men. Wouldn't it be ironic if our greatest scientist solved Sciomnia, only to come a cropper at the hands of what may prove to be one of the first primitive specimens of *homo superior* – her husband?"

Anna watched with interest as the psychogeneticist smiled engagingly at Martha Jacques' frowning face, while at the same time he looked beyond her to catch the eye of Ruy Jacques, who was plinking in apparent aimlessness at the keyboard of the Fourier piano.

Martha Jacques said curtly: "I'm afraid, Dr. Bell, that I can't get too excited about your Renaissance. When you come right down to it, local humanity, whether dominated by art or science, is nothing but a temporary surface scum on a primitive backwoods planet."

Bell nodded blandly. "To most scientists Earth is admittedly commonplace. Psychogeneticists, on the other hand, consider this planet and its people one of the wonders of the universe."

"Really?" asked Grade. "And just what have we got here that they don't have on Betelgeuse?"

"Three things," replied Bell. "One – Earth's atmosphere has enough carbon dioxide to grow the forest-spawning grounds of man's primate ancestors, thereby ensuring an unspecialized, quasi-erect, manually-activated species capable of indefinite psychophysical development. It might take the saurian life of a desert planet another billion years to evolve an equal physical and mental structure. Two – that same atmosphere had a surface pressure of 760 mm. of mercury and a mean temperature of about 25 degrees Centigrade – excellent conditions for the transmission of sound, speech, and song; and those early men took to it like a duck to water. Compare the difficulty of communication by direct touching of antennae, as the arthropodic pseudo-homindal citizens of certain airless worlds must do. Three – the solar spectrum within its very short frequency range of 760 to 390 millimicrons offers seven colors of remarkable variety and contrast, which our ancestors quickly made their own. From the beginning, they could see that they moved in multichrome beauty. Consider the ultra-sophisticate dwelling in a dying sun system – and pity him for he can see only red and a little infra red."

"If that's the only difference," snorted Grade, "I'd say you psychogeneticists were getting worked up over nothing."

Bell smiled past him at the approaching figure of Ruy Jacques. "You may be right, of course, Colonel, but I think you're missing the point. To the psychogeneticist it appears that terrestrial environment is promoting the evolution of a most extraordinary being – a type of *homo* whose energies beyond the barest necessities are devoted to strange, unproductive activities. And to what end? We don't know – yet. But we can guess. Give a psychogeneticist Eohippus and the grassy plains, and he'd predict the modern horse. Give him archeopteryx and a dense atmosphere, and he could imagine the swan. Give him *h. sapiens* and a two-day work week, or better yet, Ruy Jacques and a no-day work week, and what will he predict?"

"The poorhouse?" asked Jacques, sorrowfully.

Bell laughed. "Not quite. An evolutionary spurt, rather. As *sapiens* turns more and more into his abstract world of the arts, music in particular, the psychogeneticist foresees increased communication in terms of music. This might require certain cerebral realignments in *sapiens,* and perhaps the development of special membranous neural organs – which in turn might lead to completely new mental and physical abilities, and the conquest of new dimensions – just as the human tongue eventually developed from a tasting organ into a means of long distance vocal communication."

"Not even in Ruy's Science/Art diatribes," said Mrs. Jacques, "have I heard greater nonsense. If this planet is to have any future worthy of the name, you can be sure it will be through the leadership of her scientists."

"I wouldn't be too sure," countered Bell. "The artist's place in society has advanced tremendously in the past half-century. And I mean the minor artist – who is identified simply by his profession and not by any exceptional reputation. In our own time we have seen the financier forced to extend social equality to the scientist. And today the palette and musical sketch pad are gradually toppling the test tube and the cyclotron from their pedestals. In the first Renaissance the merchant and soldier inherited the ruins of church and feudal empire; in this one we peer through the crumbling walls of capitalism and nationalism and see the artist . . . or the scientist . . . ready to emerge as the cream of society. The question is, *which one?*"

"For the sake of law and order," declared Colonel Grade, "it must be the scientist, working in the defence of his country. Think of the military insecurity of an art-dominated society. If – "

Ruy Jacques broke in: "There is only one point on which I must disagree with you." He turned a disarming smile on his wife. "I really don't see how the scientist fits into the picture at all. Do you, Martha? For the artist is *already* supreme. He dominates the scientist, and if he likes, he is perfectly able to draw upon his more sensitive intuition for those various restatements of artistic principles that the scientists are forever trying to fob off on a decreasingly gullible public under the guise of novel scientific laws. I say that the artist is aware of those 'new' laws long before the scientist, and has the option of presenting them to the public in a pleasing art form or as a dry, abstruse equation. He may, like da Vinci, express his discovery of a beautiful curve in the form of a breathtaking spiral staircase in a *château* at Blois, or, like Dürer, he may analyze the curve mathematically and announce its logarithmic formula. In either event he anticipates Descartes, who was the first mathematician to rediscover the logarithmic spiral."

The woman laughed grimly. "All right. *You're* an artist. Just what scientific law have *you* discovered?"

"I have discovered," answered the artist with calm pride, "what will go down in history as 'Jacques' Law of Stellar Radiation'."

Anna and Bell exchanged glances. The older man's look of relief said plainly: "The battle is joined, they'll forget you."

Martha Jacques peered at the artist suspiciously. Anna could see that the woman was genuinely curious but caught between her desire to crush, to damn any such amateurish "discovery" and her fear that she was being led into a trap. Anna herself, after studying the exaggerated innocence of the man's wide, unblinking eyes knew immediately that he was subtly enticing the woman out on the rotten limb of her own dry perfection.

In near-hypnosis Anna watched the man draw a sheet of paper from his pocket. She marvelled at the superb blend of diffidence and braggadocio with which he unfolded it and handed it to the woman scientist.

"Since I can't write, I had one of the fellows write it down for me, but I think he got it right," he explained. "As you see, it boils down to seven prime equations."

Anna watched a puzzled frown steal over the woman's brow. "But each of these equations expands into hundreds more, especially the seventh, which is the longest of them all." The frown deepened. "Very interesting. Already I see hints of the Russell diagram . . ."

The man started. "What! H. N. Russell, who classified stars into spectral classes? You mean he scooped me?"

"Only if your work is accurate, which I doubt."

The artist stammered: "But – "

"And here," she continued in crisp condemnation, "is nothing more than a restatement of the law of light-pencil wavering, which explains why stars twinkle and planets don't, and which has been known for two hundred years."

Ruy Jacques' face lengthened lugubriously.

The woman smiled grimly and pointed. "These parameters are just a poor approximation of the Bethe law of nuclear fission in stars – old since the thirties."

The man stared at the scathing finger. "Old . . . ?"

"I fear so. But still not bad for an amateur. If you kept at this sort of thing all your life, you might eventually develop something novel. But this is a mere hodge-podge, a rehash of material any real scientist learned in his teens."

"But Martha," pleaded the artist, "surely it isn't *all* old?"

"I can't say with certainty, of course," returned the woman with malice-edged pleasure, "until I examine every sub-equation. I can only say that, fundamentally, scientists long ago anticipated the artist, represented by the great Ruy Jacques. In the aggregate, your amazing Law of Stellar Radiation has been known for two hundred years or more."

Even as the man stood there, as though momentarily stunned by the enormity of his defeat, Anna began to pity his wife.

The artist shrugged his shoulders wistfully. "Science versus Art. So the artist has given his all, and lost. Jacques' Law must sing its swan song, then be forever forgotten." He lifted a resigned face toward the scientist. "Would you, my dear, administer the *coup de grâce* by setting up the proper co-ordinates in the Fourier audiosynthesizer?"

Anna wanted to lift a warning hand, cry out to the man that he was going too far, that the humiliation he was preparing for his wife was unnecessary, unjust, and would but thicken the wall of hatred that cemented their antipodal souls together.

But it was too late. Martha Jacques was already walking toward the Fourier piano, and within seconds had set up the polar-defined data and had flipped the toggle switch. The psychiatrist found her mind and tongue to be literally paralyzed by the swift movement of this unwitting drama, which was now toppling over the brink of its tragicomic climax.

A deep silence fell over the room.

Anna caught an impression of avid faces, most of whom – Jacques' most intimate friends – would understand the nature of his little playlet and would rub salt into the abraded wound he was delivering his wife.

Then in the space of three seconds, it was over.

The Fourier piano had synthesized the seven equations, six short, one long, into their tonal equivalents, and it was over.

Dorran, the orchestra leader, broke the uneasy stillness that followed. "I say, Ruy old chap," he blurted, "just what is the difference in 'Jacques' Law of Stellar Radiation' and 'Twinkle, twinkle, little star'?"

Anna, in mingled amusement and sympathy, watched the face of Martha Jacques slowly turn crimson.

The artist replied in amazement. "Why, now that you mention it, there does seem to be a little resemblance."

"It's a dead ringer!" cried a voice.

"'Twinkle, twinkle' is an old continental folk tune," volunteered another. "I once traced it from Haydn's 'Surprise Symphony' back to the fourteenth century."

"Oh, but that's quite impossible," protested Jacques. "Martha has just stated that science discovered it first, only two hundred years ago."

The woman's voice dripped *aqua regia*. "You planned this deliberately, just to humiliate me in front of these . . . these clowns."

"Martha, I assure you . . . !"

"I'm warning you for the last time, Ruy. If you ever again humiliate me, I'll probably kill you!"

Jacques backed away in mock alarm until he was swallowed up in a swirl of laughter.

The group broke up, leaving the two women alone. Suddenly aware of Martha Jacques' bitter scrutiny, Anna flushed and turned toward her.

Martha Jacques said: "Why can't you make him come to his senses? I'm paying you enough."

Anna gave her a slow wry smile. "Then I'll need your help. And you aren't helping when you deprecate his sense of values – odd though they may seem to you.

"But Art is really so *foolish!* Science – "

Anna laughed shortly. "You see? Do you wonder he avoids you?"

"What would *you* do?"

"*I?*" Anna swallowed dryly.

Martha Jacques was watching her with narrowed eyes. "Yes, you. *If you wanted him?*"

Anna hesitated, breathing uneasily. Then gradually her eyes widened, became dreamy and full, like moons rising over the edge of some unknown, exotic land. Her lips opened with a nerveless fatalism. She didn't care what she said:

"I'd forget that I want, above all things, to be beautiful. I would think only of him. I'd wonder what he's thinking, and I'd forsake my mental integrity and try to think as he thinks. I'd learn to see through his eyes, and to hear through his ears. I'd sing over his successes, and hold my tongue when he failed. When he's moody and depressed, I wouldn't probe or insist that-I-could-help-you-if-you'd-only-let-me. Then – "

Martha Jacques snorted. "In short, you'd be nothing but a selfless shadow, devoid of personality or any mind or individuality of your own. That might be all right for one of your type. But for a scientist, the very thought is ridiculous!"

The psychiatrist lifted her shoulders delicately. "I agree. It *is* ridiculous. What *sane* woman at the peak of her profession would suddenly toss up her career to merge – you'd say 'submerge' – her identity, her very existence, with that of an utterly alien male mentality?"

"What woman, indeed?"

Anna mused to herself, and did not answer. Finally she said: "And yet, that's the price; take it or leave it, they say. What's a girl to do?"

"Stick up for her rights!" declared Martha Jacques spiritedly.

"All hail to unrewarding perseverance!" Ruy Jacques was back, swaying slightly. He pointed his half-filled glass toward the ceiling and shouted: "Friends! A toast! Let us drink to the two charter members of the Knights of the Crimson Grail." He bowed in saturnine mockery to his glowering wife. "To Martha! May she soon solve the Jacques Rosette and blast humanity into the heavens!"

Simultaneously he drank and held up a hand to silence the sudden spate of jeers and laughter. Then, turning toward the now apprehensive psychiatrist, he essayed a second bow of such sweeping grandiosity that his glass was upset. As he straightened, however, he calmly traded glasses with her. "To my old schoolteacher, Dr. van Tuyl. A nightingale whose secret ambition is to become as beautiful as a red red red rose. May Allah grant her prayers." He blinked at her beatifically in a sudden silence. "What was that comment, doctor?"

"I said you were a drunken idiot," replied Anna. "But let it pass." She was panting, her head whirling. She raised her voice to the growing cluster of faces. "Ladies and gentlemen, I offer you the third seeker of the grail! A truly great artist. Ruy Jacques, a child of the coming epoch, whose sole aim is not aimlessness, as he would like you to think, but a certain marvellous rose. Her curling petals shall be of subtle texture, yet firm withal, and brilliant red. It is this rose that he must find, to save his mind and body, and to put a soul in him."

"She's right!" cried the artist in dark glee. "To Ruy Jacques, then! Join in, everybody. The party's on Martha!"

He downed his glass, then turned a suddenly grave face to his audience. "But it's really such a pity in Anna's case, isn't it? Because her cure is so simple."

The psychiatrist listened; her head was throbbing dizzily.

"As any *competent* psychiatrist could tell her," continued the artist mercilessly, "she has identified herself with the nightingale in her ballet. The nightingale isn't much to look at. On top it's a dirty brown; at bottom, you might say it's a drab grey. But ah! The soul of this plain little bird! Look into my soul, she pleads. Hold me in your strong arms, look into my soul, and think me as lovely as a red rose."

Even before he put his wineglass down on the table, Anna knew what was coming. She didn't need to watch the stiffening cheeks and flaring nostrils of Martha Jacques, nor the sudden flash of fear in Bell's eyes, to know what was going to happen next.

He held out his arms to her, his swart satyr-face nearly impassive save for its eternal suggestion of sardonic mockery.

"You're right," she whispered, half to him, half to some other part of her, listening, watching. "I *do* want you to hold me in your arms and think me beautiful. But you can't, because you don't love me. It won't work. Not yet. Here, I'll prove it."

As from miles and centuries away, she heard Grade's horrified gurgle.

But her trance held. She entered the embrace of Ruy Jacques, and held her face up to his as much as her spine would permit, and closed her eyes.

He kissed her quickly on the forehead and released her. "There! Cured!"

She stood back and surveyed him thoughtfully. "I wanted you to see for yourself, that nothing can be beautiful to you – at least not until you learn to regard someone else as highly as you do Ruy Jacques."

Bell had drawn close. His face was wet, grey. He whispered: "Are you two insane? Couldn't you save this sort of thing for a less crowded occasion?"

But Anna was rolling rudderless in a fatalistic calm. "I had to show him something. Here. Now. He might never have tried it if he hadn't had an audience. Can you take me home now?"

"Worst thing possible," replied Bell agitatedly. "That'd just confirm Martha's suspicions." He looked around nervously. "She's gone. Don't know whether that's good or bad. But Grade's watching us. Ruy, if you've got the faintest intimations of decency, you'll wander over to that group of ladies and kiss a few of them. May throw Martha off the scent. Anna, you stay here. Keep talking. Try to toss it off as an amusing incident." He gave a short strained laugh. "Otherwise you're going to wind up as the First Martyr in the Cause of Art."

"I beg your pardon, Dr. van Tuyl."

It was Grade. His voice was brutally cold, and the syllables were clipped from his lips with a spine-tingling finality.

"Yes, Colonel?" said Anna nervously.

"The Security Bureau would like to ask you a few questions."

"Yes?"

Grade turned and stared icily at Bell. "It is preferred that the interrogation be conducted in private. It should not take long. If the lady would kindly step into the model's dressing room, my assistant will take over from there."

"Dr. van Tuyl was just leaving," said Bell huskily. "Did you have a coat, Anna?"

With a smooth unobtrusive motion Grade unsnapped the guard on his hip holster. "If Dr. van Tuyl leaves the dressing room within ten minutes, alone, she may depart from the studio in any manner she pleases."

Anna watched her friend's face become even paler. He wet his lips, then whispered, "I think you'd better go, Anna. Be careful."

Chapter Twelve

The room was small and nearly bare. Its sole furnishings were an ancient calendar, a clothes tree, a few stacks of dusty books, a table (bare save for a roll of canvas patching tape) and three chairs.

In one of the chairs, across the table, sat Martha Jacques.

She seemed almost to smile at Anna; but the amused curl of her beautiful lips was totally belied by her eyes, which pulsed hate with the paralyzing force of physical blows.

In the other chair sat Willie the Cork, almost unrecognizable in his groomed neatness.

The psychiatrist brought her hand to her throat as though to restore her voice, and at the movement, she saw from the corner of her eye that Willie, in a lightning motion, had simultaneously thrust his hand into his coat pocket, invisible below the table. She slowly understood that he held a gun on her.

The man was the first to speak, and his voice was so crisp and incisive that she doubted her first intuitive recognition. "Obviously, I shall kill you if you attempt any unwise action. So please sit down, Dr. van Tuyl. Let us put our cards on the table."

It was too incredible, too unreal, to arouse any immediate sense of fear. In numb amazement she pulled out the chair and sat down.

"As you may have suspected for some time," continued the man curtly, "I am a Security agent."

Anna found her voice. "I know only that I am being forcibly detained. What do you want?"

"Information, doctor. What government do you represent?"

"None."

The man fairly purred. "Don't you realize, doctor, that as soon as you cease to answer responsively, I shall kill you?"

Anna van Tuyl looked from the man to the woman. She thought of circling hawks, and felt the intimations of terror. What could she have done to attract such wrathful attention? She didn't know. But then, *they* couldn't be sure about *her,* either. This man didn't want to kill her until he found out more. And by that time surely he'd see that it was all a mistake.

She said: "Either I am a psychiatrist attending a special case, or I am not. I am in no position to prove the positive. Yet, by syllogistic law, you must accept it as a possibility until you prove the negative. Therefore, until you have given me an opportunity to explain or disprove any evidence to the contrary, you can never be certain in your own mind that I am other than what I claim to be."

The man smiled, almost genially. "Well put, doctor. I hope they've been paying you what you are worth." He bent forward suddenly. "Why are you trying to make Ruy Jacques fall in love with you?"

She stared back with widening eyes. "What did you say?"

"Why are you trying to make Ruy Jacques fall in love with you?"

She could meet his eyes squarely enough, but her voice was now very faint: "I didn't understand you at first. You said . . . that I'm trying to make him fall in love with me." She pondered this for a long wondering moment, as though the idea were utterly new. "And I guess . . . it's true."

The man looked blank, then smiled with sudden appreciation. "You *are* clever. Certainly, you're the first to try *that* line. Though I don't know what you expect to gain with your false candour."

"False? Didn't you mean it yourself? No, I see you didn't. But Mrs. Jacques does. And she hates me for it. But I'm just part of the bigger hate she keeps for *him.* Even her Sciomnia equation is just part of that hate. She isn't working on a biophysical weapon just because she's a patriot, but more to spite him, to show him that her science is superior to – "

Martha Jacques' hand lashed viciously across the little table and struck Anna in the mouth.

The man merely murmured: "Please control yourself a bit longer, Mrs. Jacques. Interruptions from outside would be most inconvenient at this point." His humorless eyes returned to Anna. "One evening a week ago, when Mr. Jacques was under your care at the clinic, you left stylus and paper-with him."

Anna nodded. "I wanted him to attempt automatic writing."

"What is 'automatic writing'?"

"Simply writing done while the conscious mind is absorbed in a completely extraneous activity, such as music. Mr. Jacques was to focus his attention on certain music composed by me while holding stylus and paper in his lap. If his recent inability to read and write was caused by some psychic block, it was quite possible that his subconscious mind might bypass the block, and he would write – just as one 'doodles' unconsciously when talking over the visor."

He thrust a sheet of paper at her. "Can you identify this?"

What was he driving at? She examined the sheet hesitantly. "It's just a blank sheet from my private monogrammed stationery. Where did you get it?"

"From the pad you left with Mr. Jacques."

"So?"

"We also found another sheet from the same pad under Mr. Jacques' bed. It had some interesting writing on it."

"But Mr. Jacques personally reported nil results."

"He was probably right."

"But you said he wrote something?" she insisted; momentarily her personal danger faded before her professional interest.

"I didn't say *he* wrote anything."

"Wasn't it written with that same stylus?"

"It was. But I don't think he wrote it. It wasn't in his handwriting."

"That's often the case in automatic writing. The script is modified according to the personality of the dissociated subconscious unit. The alteration is sometimes so great as to be unrecognizable as the handwriting of the subject."

He peered at her keenly. "This script was perfectly recognizable, Dr. van Tuyl. I'm afraid you've made a grave blunder. Now, shall I tell you in *whose* handwriting?"

She listened to her own whisper: "Mine?"

"Yes."

"What does it say?"

"You know very well."

"But I don't." Her underclothing was sticking to her body with a damp clammy feeling. "At least you ought to give me a chance to explain it. May I see it?"

He regarded her thoughtfully for a moment, then reached into his pocket sheaf. "Here's an electrostat. The paper, texture, ink, everything, is a perfect copy of your original."

She studied the sheet with a puzzled frown. There were a few lines of scribblings in purple. But it *wasn't* in her handwriting. In fact, it wasn't even handwriting – just a mass of illegible scrawls!

Anna felt a thrill of fear. She stammered: "What are you trying to do?"

"You don't deny you wrote it?"

"Of course I deny it." She could no longer control the quaver in her voice. Her lips were leaden masses, her tongue a stone slab. "It's – unrecognizable . . ."

The Cork floated with sinister patience. "In the upper left hand corner is your monogram: 'A. vT.', the same as on the first sheet. You will admit that, at least?"

For the first time, Anna really examined the presumed trio of initials enclosed in the familiar ellipse. The ellipse was there. But the print within it was – gibberish. She seized again at the first sheet – the blank one. The feel of the paper, even the smell, stamped it as genuine. It had been hers. But the monogram! "Oh no!" she whispered.

Her panic-stricken eyes flailed about the room. The calendar . . . same picture of the same cow . . . *but the rest* . . . ! A stack of books in the corner . . . titled in gold leaf . . . gathering dust for months . . . the label on the roll of patching tape on the table . . . even the watch on her wrist.

Gibberish. She could no longer read. She had forgotten how. Her ironic gods had chosen this critical moment to blind her with their brilliant bounty.

Then take it! And play for time!

She wet trembling lips. "I'm unable to read. My reading glasses are in my bag, outside." She returned the script. "If *you'd* read it, I might recognize the contents."

The man said: "I thought you might try this, just to get my eyes off you. If you don't mind, I'll quote from memory:

"' – what a queer climax for The Dream! Yet, inevitable. Art versus Science decrees that one of us must destroy the Sciomniac weapon; but that could wait until we become more numerous. So, what I do is for him alone, and his future depends on appreciating it. Thus, Science bows to Art, but even Art isn't all. The Student must know the one greater thing when he sees The Nightingale dead, for only then will he recognize . . .'"

He paused.

"Is that all?" asked Anna.

"That's all."

"Nothing about a . . . rose?"

"No. What is 'rose' a code word for?"

Death? mused Anna. Was the rose a cryptolalic synonym for the grave? She closed her eyes and shivered. Were those really *her* thoughts, impressed into the mind and wrist of Ruy Jacques from some grandstand seat at her own ballet three weeks hence? But after all, why was it so impossible? Coleridge claimed *Kublai Khan* had been dictated to him through automatic writing. And that English mystic, William Blake, freely acknowledged being the frequent amanuensis for an unseen personality. And there were numerous other cases. So, from some unseen time and place, the mind of Anna van Tuyl had been attuned to that of Ruy Jacques, and his mind had momentarily forgotten that both of them could no longer write, and had recorded a strange reverie.

It was then that she noticed the – whispers.

No – not whispers – not exactly. More like rippling vibrations, mingling, rising, falling. Her heart beats quickened when she realized that their eerie pattern was soundless. It was as though something in her mind was suddenly vibrating *en rapport* with a subetheric world. Messages were beating at her for which she had no tongue or ear; they were beyond sound – beyond knowledge, and they swarmed dizzily around her from all directions. From the ring she wore. From the bronze buttons of her jacket. From the vertical steam piping in the corner. From the metal reflector of the ceiling light.

And the strongest and most meaningful of all showered steadily from the invisible weapon. The Cork grasped in his coat pocket. Just as surely as though she had seen it done, she knew that the weapon had killed in the past. And not just once. She found herself attempting to unravel those thought residues of death – once – twice – three times . . . beyond which they faded away into steady, indecipherable time-muted violence.

And now that gun began to scream: "Kill! Kill! Kill!"

She passed her palm over her forehead. Her whole face was cold and wet. She swallowed noisily.

Chapter Thirteen

Ruy Jacques sat before the metal illuminator near his easel, apparently absorbed in the profound contemplation of his goatish features, and oblivious to the mounting gaiety about him. In reality he was almost completely lost in a soundless, sardonic glee over the triangular death-struggle that was nearing its climax beyond the inner wall of his studio, and which was magnified in his remarkable mind to an incredible degree by the paraboloid mirror of the illuminator.

Bell's low urgent voice began hacking at him again. "Her blood will be on your head. All you need to do is to go in there. Your wife wouldn't permit any shooting with you around."

The artist twitched his misshapen shoulders irritably. "*Maybe*. But why should I risk my skin for a silly little nightingale?"

"Can it be that your growth beyond *sapiens* has served simply to sharpen your objectivity, to accentuate your inherent egregious want to identity with even the best of your fellow creatures? Is the indifference that has driven Martha nearly insane in a bare decade now too ingrained to respond to the first known female of your own unique breed?" Bell sighed heavily. "You don't have to answer. The very senselessness of her impending murder amuses you. Your nightingale is about to be impaled on her thorn – for nothing – as always. Your sole regret at the moment is that you can't twit her with the assurance that you will study her corpse diligently to find there the rose you seek."

"Such unfeeling heartlessness," said Jacques in regretful agreement, "is only to be expected in one of Martha's blunderings. I mean The Cork, of course. Doesn't he realize that Anna hasn't finished the score of her ballet? Evidently has no musical sense at all. I'll bet he was even turned down for the policemen's charity quarter. You're right, as usual, doc. We must punish such philistinism." He tugged at his chin, then rose from the folding stool.

"What are you going to do?" demanded the other sharply.

The artist weaved toward the phono cabinet. "Play a certain selection from Tchaikovsky's *Sixth*. If Anna's half the girl you think, she and Peter Ilyitch will soon have Mart eating out of their hands."

Bell watching him in anxious, yet half-trusting frustration as the other selected a spool from his library of electronic recordings and inserted it into the playback sprocket. In mounting mystification, he saw Jacques turn up the volume control as far as it would go.

Chapter Fourteen

Murder, a one-act play directed by Mrs. Jacques, thought Anna. With sound effects by Mr. Jacques. But the facts didn't fit. It was unthinkable that Ruy would do anything to accommodate his wife. If anything, he would try to thwart Martha. But what was his purpose in starting off in the finale of the first movement of the *Sixth*? Was there some message there that he was trying to get across to her?

There was. She had it. She was going to live. If –

"In a moment," she told The Cork in a tight voice, "you are going to snap off the safety catch of your pistol, revise slightly your estimated line of fire, and squeeze the trigger. Ordinarily you could accomplish all three acts in almost instantaneous sequence. At the present moment, if I tried to turn the table over on you, you could put a bullet in my head before I could get well started. But in another sixty seconds you will no longer have that advantage, because your motor nervous system will be laboring under the superimposed pattern of the extraordinary Second Movement of the symphony that we now hear from the studio."

The Cork started to smile, then he frowned faintly. "What do you mean?"

"All motor acts are carried out in simple rhythmic patterns. We walk in the two-four time of the march. We waltz, use a pickaxe, and manually grasp or replace objects in three-four rhythm."

"This nonsense is purely a play for time," interjected Martha Jacques. "Kill her."

"It is a fact," continued Anna hurriedly. (Would that Second Movement never begin?) "A decade ago, when there were still a few factories using hand-assembly methods, the workmen speeded their work by breaking down the task into these same elemental rhythms, aided by appropriate music." (There! It was beginning! The immortal genius of that suicidal Russian was reaching across a century to save her!) "It so happens that the music you are hearing *now* is the Second Movement that I mentioned, and it's neither two-four nor three-four but *five*-four, an oriental rhythm that gives difficulty even to skilled occidental musicians and dancers. Subconsciously you are going to try to break it down into the only rhythms to which your motor nervous system is attuned. But you can't. Nor can *any* occidental, even a professional dancer, unless he has had special training" – her voice wobbled slightly – "in Delcrozian eurhythmics."

She crashed into the table.

Even though she had known that this must happen, her success was so complete, so overwhelming, that it momentarily appalled her.

Martha Jacques and The Cork had moved with anxious, rapid jerks, like puppets in a nightmare. But their rhythm was all wrong. With their ingrained four-time motor responses strangely modulated by a five-time pattern, the result was inevitably the arithmetical composite of the two: a neural beat, which could activate muscle tissue only when the two rhythms were in phase.

The Cork had hardly begun his frantic, spasmodic squeeze of the trigger when the careening table knocked him backward to the floor, stunned, beside Martha Jacques. It required but an instant for Anna to scurry around and extract the pistol from his numbed fist.

Then she pointed the trembling gun in the general direction of the carnage she had wrought and fought an urge to collapse against the wall.

She waited for the room to stop spinning, for the white, glass-eyed face of Martha Jacques to come into focus against the fuzzy background of the cheap paint-daubed rug. And then the eyes of the woman scientists flickered and closed.

With a wary glance at the weapon muzzle, The Cork gingerly pulled a leg from beneath the table edge: "You have the gun," he said softly. "You can't object if I assist Mrs. Jacques?"

"I *do* object," said Anna faintly. "She's merely unconscious . . . feels nothing. I want her to stay that way for a few minutes. If you approach her or make any unnecessary noise, I will probably kill you. So – both of you must stay here until Grade investigates. I know you have a pair of handcuffs. I'll give you ten seconds to lock yourself to that steam pipe in the corner – hands *behind* you, please."

She retrieved the roll of adhesive patching tape from the floor and fixed several strips across the agent's lips, following with a few swift loops around the ankles to prevent him stamping his feet.

A moment later, her face a damp mask, she closed the door leisurely behind her and stood there, breathing deeply and searching the room for Grade.

He was standing by the studio entrance, staring at her fixedly. When she favored him with a glassy smile, he simply shrugged his shoulders and began walking slowly toward her.

In growing panic her eyes darted about the room. Bell and Ruy Jacques were leaning over the phono, apparently deeply absorbed in the racing clangor of the music. She saw Bell nod a covert signal in her direction, but without looking directly at her. She tried not to seem hurried as she strolled over to join them. She knew that Grade was now walking toward them and was but a few steps away when Bell lifted his head and smiled.

"Everything all right?" said the psychogeneticist loudly.

She replied clearly: "Fine. Mrs. Jacques and a Security man just wanted to ask some questions." She drew in closer. Her lips framed a question to Bell: "Can Grade hear?"

Bell's lips formed a soft, nervous guttural: "No. He's moving off toward the dressing room door. If what I suspect happened behind that door is true, you have about ten seconds to get out of here. And then you've got to hide." He turned abruptly to the artist. "Ruy, you've got to take her down into the Via. Right now – *immediately*. Watch your opportunity and lose her when no one is looking. It shouldn't be too hard in that mob."

Jacques shook his head doubtfully. "Martha isn't going to like this. You know how strict she is on etiquette. I think there's a very firm statement in Emily Post that the host should never, never, *never* walk out on his guests before locking up the liquor and silverware. Oh, well, if you insist."

Chapter Fifteen

"Tell ya what the professor's gonna do, ladies and gentlemen. He's gonna defend not just one paradox. Not just two. But seventeen! In the space of one short hour, and without repeating himself, and including one he just thought up five minutes ago: 'Security is dangerous.'"

Ruy frowned, then whispered to Anna: "That was for us. He means Security men are circulating. Let's move on. Next door. They won't look for a woman there."

Already he was pulling her away toward the chess parlor. They both ducked under the For Men Only sign (which she could no longer read), pushed through the bat-wing doors, and walked unobtrusively down between the wall and a row of players. One man looked up briefly out of the corner of his eyes as they passed.

The woman paused uneasily. She had sensed the nervousness of the barker even before Ruy, and now still fainter impressions were beginning to ripple over the straining surface of her mind. They were coming from that chess player: from the coins in his pocket; from the lead weights of his chess pieces; and especially from the weapon concealed somewhere on him. The resonant histories of the chess pieces and coins she ignored. They held the encephalographic residua of too many minds. The invisible gun was clearer. There was something abrupt and violent, alternating with a more subtle, restrained rhythm. She put her hand to her throat as she considered one interpretation: *Kill – but wait*. Obviously, he'd dare not fire with Ruy so close.

"Rather warm here, too," murmured the artist. "Out we go."

As they stepped out into the street again, she looked behind her and saw that the man's chair was empty.

She held the artist's hand and pushed and jabbed after him, deeper into the revelling sea of humanity.

She ought to be thinking of ways to hide, of ways to use her new sensory gift. But another, more imperative train of thought continually clamored at her, until finally she yielded to a gloomy brooding.

Well, it was true. She wanted to be loved, and she wanted Ruy to love her. And he knew it. Every bit of metal on her shrieked her need for his love.

But – was she ready to love him? No! How could she love a man who lived only to paint that mysterious unpaintable scene of the nightingale's death, and who loved only himself? He was fascinating, but what sensible woman would wreck her career for such unilateral fascination? Perhaps Martha Jacques was right, after all.

"So you got him, after all!"

Anna whirled toward the crazy crackle, nearly jerking her hand from Ruy's grasp.

The vendress of love-philters stood leaning against the front centre pole of her tent, grinning toothily at Anna.

While the young woman stared dazedly at her, Jacques spoke up crisply: "Any strange men been around, Violet?"

"Why, Ruy," she replied archly, "I think you're jealous. What kind of men?"

"Not the kind that haul you off to the alcoholic ward on Saturday nights. Not city dicks. Security men – quiet – seem slow, but really fast – see everybody – everything."

"Oh, *them*. Three went down the street two minutes ahead of you."

He rubbed his chin. "That's not so good. They'll start at that end of the Via and work up toward us until they meet the patrol behind us."

"Like grains of wheat between the millstones," cackled the crone. "*I knew* you'd turn to crime, sooner or later, Ruy. You were the only tenant I had who paid the rent regular."

"Mart's lawyer did that."

"Just the same, it looked mighty suspicious. You want to try the alley behind the tent?"

"Where does it lead?"

"Cuts back into the Via, at White Rose Park."

Anna started. "White rose?"

"We were there that first night," said Jacques. "You remember it –

big rose-walled cul-de-sac. Fountain. Pretty, but not for us, not now. Has only one entrance. We'll have to try something else."

The psychiatrist said hesitantly: "No, wait."

For some moments she had been struck by the sinister contrast in this second descent into the Via and the irresponsible gaiety of that first night. The street, the booths, the laughter seemed the same, but really weren't. It was like a familiar musical score, subtly altered by some demoniac hand, raised into some harsh and fatalistic minor key. It was like the second movement of Tchaikovsky's *Romeo and Juliet:* all the bright promises of the first movement were here, but repetition had transfigured them into frightful premonitions.

She shivered. That second movement, that echo of destiny, was sweeping through her in ever faster tempo, as though impatient to consummate its assignation with her. Come safety, come death, she must yield to the pattern of repetition.

Her voice had a dream-like quality: "Take me again to the White Rose Park."

"What! Talk sense! Out here in the open you may have a chance."

"But I *must* go there. Please, Ruy. I think it's something about a white rose. Don't look at me as though I were crazy. Of course I'm crazy. If you don't want to take me, I'll go alone. But I'm going."

His hard eyes studied her in speculative silence, then he looked away. As the stillness grew, his face mirrored his deepening introspection. "At that, the possibilities are intriguing. Martha's stooges are sure to look in on you. But will they be able to see you? Is the hand that wields the pistol equally skilled with the brush and palette? Unlikely. Art and Science again. Pointillist school versus police school. A good one on Martha – if it works. Anna's dress is green. Complement of green is purple. Violet's dress should do it."

"My dress?" cried the old woman. "What are you up to, Ruy?"

"Nothing. Luscious. I just want you to take off one of your dresses. The outer one will do."

"Sir!" Violet began to splutter in barely audible gasps.

Anna had watched all this in vague detachment, accepting it as one of the man's daily insanities. She had no idea what he wanted with a dirty old purple dress, but she thought she knew how she could get it for him, while simultaneously introducing another repetitive theme into this second movement of her hypothetical symphony.

She said: "He's willing to make you a fair trade, Violet."

The spluttering stopped. The old woman eyed them both suspiciously. "Meaning what?"

"He'll drink one of your love potions."

The leathery lips parted in amazement. "*I'm* agreeable, if *he* is, but I know he isn't. Why, that scamp doesn't love any creature in the whole world, except maybe himself."

"And yet he's ready to make a pledge to his beloved," said Anna.

The artist squirmed. "I like you, Anna, but I won't be trapped. Anyway, it's all nonsense. What's a glass of acidified water between friends?"

"The pledge isn't to me, Ruy. It's to a Red Rose." He peered at her curiously. "Oh? Well, if it will please you . . . All right, Violet, but off with that dress before you pour up."

Why, wondered Anna, do I keep thinking his declaration of love to a red rose is my death sentence? It's moving too fast. Who, what – is The Red Rose? The Nightingale dies in making the white rose red. So *she* – or I – can't be The Red Rose. Anyway, The Nightingale is ugly, and The Rose is beautiful. And why must The Student have a Red Rose? How will it admit him to his mysterious dance?

"Ah, Madame De Medici is back." Jacques took the glass and purple bundle the old woman put on the table. "What are the proper words?" he asked Anna.

"Whatever you want to say."

His eyes, suddenly grave, looked into hers. He said quietly: "If ever The Red Rose presents herself to me, I shall love her forever."

Anna trembled as he upended the glass.

Chapter Sixteen

A little later they slipped into the Park of the White Roses. The buds were just beginning to open, and thousands of white floreate eyes blinked at them in the harsh artificial light. As before, the enclosure was empty, and silent, save for the chattering splashing of its single fountain.

Anna abandoned a disconnected attempt to analyze the urge that had brought her here a second time. It's all too fatalistic, she thought, too involved. If I've entrapped myself, I can't feel bitter about it. "Just think," she murmured aloud, "in less than ten minutes it will all be over, one way or the other."

"Really? But where's my red rose?"

How could she even *consider* loving this jeering beast? She said coldly: "I think you'd better go. It may be rather messy in here soon."

She thought of how her body would look, sprawling, misshapen, uglier than ever. She couldn't let him see her that way.

"Oh, we've plenty of time. No red rose, eh? Hmm. It seems to me, Anna, that you're composing yourself for death prematurely. There really is that little matter of the rose to be taken care of first, you know. As The Student, I must insist on my rights."

What made him be this way? "Ruy, please . . ." Her voice was trembling, and she was suddenly very near to tears.

"There, dear, don't apologize. Even the best of us are thoughtless at times. Though I must admit, I never expected such lack of considera-tion, such poor manners, in *you*. But then, at heart, you aren't really an artist. You've no appreciation of form." He began to untie thc bundled purple dress, and his voice took on the argumentative dogmatism of a platform lecturer. "The perfection of form, of technique, is the highest achievement possible to the artist. When he subordinates form to subject matter, he degenerates eventually into a boot-lick, a scientist, or, worst of all, a Man with a Message. Here, catch!" He tossed the gaudy garment at Anna, who accepted it in rebellious wonder.

Critically, the artist eyed the nauseating contrast of the purple and green dresses, glanced momentarily toward the semi-circle of white-budded wall beyond, and then continued: "There's nothing like a school-within-a-school to squeeze dry the dregs of form. And whatever their faults, the pointillists of the impressionist movement could depict color with magnificent depth of chroma. Their palettes held only the spectral colors, and they never mixed them. Do you know why the Seines of Seurat are so brilliant and luminous? It's because the water is made of dots of pure green, blue, red and yellow, alternating with white in the proper proportion." He motioned with his hand, and she followed as he walked slowly on around the semi-circular gravel path. "What a pity Martha isn't here to observe our little experiment in tricolor stimulus. Yes, the scientific psychologists finally gave arithmetical vent to what the pointillists knew long before them – that a mass of points of any three spectral colors – or of one color and its complementary color – can be made to give any imaginable hue simply by varying their relative proportion."

Anna thought back to that first night of the street dancers. So *that* was why his green and purple polka dot academic gown had first seemed white!

At his gesture, she stopped and stood with her humped back barely touching the mass of scented buds. The arched entrance was a scant hundred yards to her right. Out in the Via an ominous silence seemed to be gathering. The Security men were probably roping off the area, certain of their quarry. In a minute or two, perhaps sooner, they would be at the archway, guns drawn.

She inhaled deeply and wet her lips.

The man smiled. "You hope I know what I'm doing, don't you? So do I."

"I think I understand your theory," said Anna, "but I don't think it has much chance of working."

"Tush, child." He studied the vigorous play of the fountain speculatively. "The pigment should never harangue the artist. You're forgetting that there isn't really such a color as white. The pointillists knew how to simulate white with alternating dots of primary colors long before the scientists learned to spin the same colors on a disc. And those old masters could even make white from just two colors: a primary and its complementary color. Your green dress is our primary; Violet's purple dress is its complementary. Funny, mix 'em as pigments into a homogeneous mass, and you get brown. But daub 'em on the canvas side by side, stand back the right distance, and they blend into white. All you have to do is hold Vi's dress at arm's length, at your side, with a strip of rosebuds and green leaves looking out between, and you'll have that white rose you came here in search of."

She demurred: "But the angle of visual interruption won't be small enough to blend the colors into white, even if the police don't come any nearer than the archway. The eye sees two objects as one only when the visual angle between the two is less than sixty seconds of arc."

"That old canard doesn't apply too strictly to colors. The artist relies more on the suggestibility of the mind rather than on the mechanical limitations of the retina. Admittedly, if our lean-jawed friends stared in your direction for more than a fraction of a second, they'd see you not as a whitish blur, but as a woman in green holding out a mass of something purple. But they aren't going to give your section of the park more than a passing glance." He pointed past the fountain toward the opposite horn of the semi-circular path. "I'm going to stand over *there*, and the instant someone sticks his head in through the archway, I'm going to start walking. Now, as every artist knows, normal people in western cultures absorb pictures from left to right, because they're laevo-dextro readers. So our agent's first glance will be toward you, and then his attention will be momentarily distracted by the fountain in the centre. And before he can get back to you, I'll start walking, and his eyes will have to come on to me. His attentive transition, of course, must be sweeping and imperative, yet so smooth, so subtle, that he will suspect no control. Something like Alexander's painting, *Lady on a Couch*, where the converging stripes of the lady's robe carry the eye forcibly from the lower left margin to her face at the upper right."

Anna glanced nervously toward the garden entrance, then whispered entreatingly, "Then you'd better go. You've got to be beyond the fountain when they look in.

He sniffed. "All right, I know when I'm not wanted. That's the gratitude I get for making you into a rose."

"I don't care a tinker's damn for a *white* rose. Scat!"

He laughed, then turned and started on around the path.

As Anna followed the graceful stride of his long legs, her face began to writhe in alternate bitterness and admiration. She groaned softly. "You – *fiend!* You gorgeous, egotistical, insufferable, unattainable *FIEND!* You aren't elated because you're saving my life; *I* am just a blotch of pigment in your latest masterpiece. *I hate you!*"

He was past the fountain now, and nearing the position he had earlier indicated.

She could see that he was looking toward the archway. She was afraid to look there.

Now he must stop and wait for his audience.

Only he didn't. His steps actually hastened.

That meant . . .

The woman trembled, closed her eyes, and froze into a paralytic stupor through which the crunch of the man's sandals filtered as from a great distance, muffled, mocking.

And then, from the direction of the archway, came the quiet scraping of more footsteps.

In the next split second she would know life or death.

But even now, even as she was sounding the iciest depths of her terror, her lips were moving with the clear insight of imminent death. "No, I don't hate you. I love you, Ruy. I have loved you from the first."

At that instant a blue-hot ball of pain began crawling slowly up within her body, along her spine, and then outward between her shoulder blades, into her spinal hump. The intensity of that pain forced her slowly to her knees and pulled her head back in an invitation to scream.

But no sound came from her convulsing throat.

It was unendurable, and she was fainting.

The sound of footsteps died away down the Via. At least Ruy's ruse had worked.

And as the mounting anguish spread over her back, she understood that all sound had vanished with those retreating footsteps, forever, because she could no longer hear, nor use, her vocal chords. She had forgotten how, but she didn't care.

For her hump had split open, and something had flopped clumsily out of it, and she was drifting gently outward into blackness.

Chapter Seventeen

The glum face of Ruy Jacques peered out through the studio window into the night-awakening Via.

Before I met you, he brooded, loneliness was a magic, ecstatic blade drawn across my heart strings; it healed the severed strands with every beat, and I had all that I wanted save what I had to have – the Red Rose. My search for that Rose alone matters! I must believe this. I must not swerve, even for the memory of you, Anna, the first of my own kind I have ever met. I must not wonder if they killed you, nor even care. They must have killed you . . . It's been three weeks.

Now I can seek The Rose again. Onward into loneliness.

He sensed the nearness of familiar metal behind him. "Hello, Martha," he said, without turning. "Just get here?"

"Yes. How's the party going?" Her voice seemed carefully expressionless.

"Fair. You'll know more when you get the liquor bill."

"Your ballet opens tonight, doesn't it?" Still that studied toneless-ness.

"You know damn well it doesn't." His voice held no rancour. "La Tanid took your bribe and left for Mexico. It's just as well. I can't abide a prima ballerina who'd rather eat than dance." He frowned slightly. Every bit of metal on the woman was singing in secret elation. She was thinking of a great triumph – something far beyond her petty victory in wrecking his opening night. His searching mind caught hints of something intricate, but integrated, completed – and deadly. Nineteen equations. The Jacques Rosette. Sciomnia.

"So you've finished your toy," he murmured. "You've got what you wanted, and you think you've destroyed what I wanted."

Her reply was harsh, suspicious. "How did you know, when not even Grade is sure? Yes, my weapon is finished. I can hold in one hand a thing that can obliterate your whole Via in an instant. A city, even a continent would take but a little longer. Science versus Art! Bah! This concrete embodiment of biophysics is the answer to your puerile

Renaissance – your precious feather-bed world of music and painting!
You and your kind are helpless when I and my kind choose to act. In
the final analysis Science means *force* – the ability to control the minds
and bodies of men.

The shimmering surface of his mind was now catching the faintest
wisps of strange, extraneous impressions, vague and disturbing, and
which did not seem to originate from metal within the room. In fact,
he could not be sure they originated from metal at all.

He turned to face her. "How can Science control all men when it
can't even control individuals – Anna van Tuyl, for example?"

She shrugged her shoulders. "You're only partly right. They failed to
find her, but her escape was pure accident. In any event, she no longer
represents any danger to me or to the political group that I control.
Security has actually dropped her from their shoot-on-sight docket."

He cocked his head slightly and seemed to listen. "*You* haven't, I
gather."

"You flatter her. She was never more than a pawn in our little game
of Science versus Art. Now that she's off the board, and I've
announced checkmate against you, I can't see that she matters."

"So Science announces checkmate? Isn't that a bit premature?
Suppose Anna shows up again, with or without the conclusion of her
ballet score? Suppose we find another prima? What's to keep us from
holding *The Nightingale and the Rose* tonight, as scheduled?"

"Nothing," replied Martha Jacques coolly. "Nothing at all, except
that Anna van Tuyl has probably joined your former prima at the
South Pole by this time, and anyway, a new ballerina couldn't learn
the score in the space of two hours, even if you found one. If this
wishful thinking comforts you, why, pile it on!"

Very slowly Jacques put his wine glass on the nearby table. He
washed his mind clear with a shake of his satyrish head, and strained
every sense into receptivity. Something was being etched against that
slurred background of laughter and clinking glassware. Then he sensed
– or heard – something that brought tiny beads of sweat to his forehead and made him tremble.

"What's the matter with you?" demanded the woman.

As quickly as it had come, the chill was gone.

Without replying, he strode quickly into the centre of the studio.

"Fellow revellers!" he cried. "Let us prepare to double, nay, re-
double our merriment!" With sardonic satisfaction he watched the
troubled silence spread away from him, faster and faster, like ripples
around a plague spot.

When the stillness was complete, he lowered his head, stretched out his hand as if in horrible warning, and spoke in the tense spectral whisper of Poe's Roderick Usher:

"Madmen! I tell you that she now stands without the door!"

Heads turned; eyes bulged toward the entrance.

There, the door knob was turning slowly.

The door swung in, and left a cloaked figure framed in the doorway.

The artist started. He had been certain that this must be Anna.

It *must* be Anna, yet it could not be. The once frail, cruelly bent body now stood superbly erect beneath the shelter of the cloak. There was no hint of spinal deformity in this woman, and there were no marring lines of pain about her faintly smiling mouth and eyes, which were fixed on his. In one graceful motion her hands reached up beneath the cloak and set it back on her shoulders. Then, after an almost instantaneous *demi-plié*, she floated twice, like some fragile flower dancing in a summer breeze, and stood before him *sur les pointes*, with her cape billowing and fluttering behind her in mute encore.

Jacques looked down into eyes that were dark fires. But her continued silence was beginning to disturb and irritate him. He responded to it almost by reflex, refusing to admit to himself his sudden enormous happiness: "A woman without a tongue! By the gods! Her sting is drawn!" He shook her by the shoulders, roughly, as though to punish this fault in her that had drawn the familiar acid to his mouth.

Her arms moved up, cross-fashioned, and her hands covered his. She smiled, and a harp-arpeggio seemed to wing across his mind, and the tones rearranged themselves into words, like images on water suddenly smooth:

"Hello again, darling. Thanks for being glad to see me."

Something in him collapsed. His arms dropped and he turned his head away. "It's no good, Anna. Why'd you come back? Everything's falling apart. Even our ballet. Martha bought out our prima."

Again that lilting cascade of tones in his brain: "I know, dear, but it doesn't matter. I'll sub beautifully for La Tanid. I know the part perfectly. And I know The Nightingale's death song, too."

"Hah!" he laughed harshly, annoyed at his exhibition of discouragement and her ready sympathy. He stretched his right leg into a mocking *pointe tendue*. "Marvellous! You have the exact amount of drab clumsiness that we need in a Nightingale. And as for the death song, why of course you and you alone know how that ugly little bird feels when" – his eyes were fixed on her mouth in sudden, startled suspicion, and he finished the rest of the sentence inattentively, with no real awareness of its meaning – "when she dies on the thorn."

As he waited, the melody formed, vanished, and reformed and resolved into the strangest thing he had ever known: "What you are thinking is true. My lips do not move. I cannot talk. I've forgotten how, just as we both forgot how to read and write. But even the plainest nightingale can sing, and make the white rose red."

This was Anna transfigured. Three weeks ago he had turned his back and left a diffident disciple to an uncertain fate. Confronting him now was this dark angel bearing on her face the luminous stamp of death. In some manner that he might never learn, the gods had touched her heart and body, and she had borne them straightway to him.

He stood, musing in alternate wonder and scorn. The old urge to jeer at her suddenly rose in his gorge. His lips contorted, then gradually relaxed, as an indescribable elation began to grow within him.

He could thwart Martha yet!

He leaped to the table and shouted: "Your attention, friends! In case you didn't get all this, we've found a ballerina! The curtain rises tonight on our première performance, as scheduled!"

Over the clapping and cheering, Dorran, the orchestra conductor, shouted: "Did I understand that Dr. van Tuyl has finished The Nightingale's death song? We'll have to omit that tonight, won't we? No chance to rehearse . . ."

Jacques looked down at Anna for a moment. His eyes were very thoughtful when he replied: "She says it won't be omitted. What I mean is, keep that thirty-eight rest sequence in the death scene. Yes, do that, and we shall see . . . what we shall see . . ."

"Thirty-eight rests as presently scored, then?"

"Yes. All right, boys and girls. Let's be on our way. Anna and I will follow shortly."

Chapter Eighteen

Now it was a mild evening in late June, in the time of the full blooming of the roses, and the Via floated in a heady, irresistible tide of attar. It got into the tongues of the children and lifted their laughter and shouts an octave. It stained the palettes of the artists along the sidewalks, so that, despite the bluish glare of the artificial lights, they could paint only in delicate crimsons, pinks, yellows and whites. The petalled current swirled through the side-shows and eternally new exhibits and gave them a veneer of perfection; it eddied through the canvas flap of the vendress of love philters and erased twenty years from her face. It brushed a scented message across the responsive mouths of innumerable pairs of lovers, blinding them to the appreciative gaze of those who stopped to watch them.

And the lovely dead petals kept fluttering through the introspective mind of Ruy Jacques, clutching and whispering. He brushed their skittering dance aside and considered the situation with growing apprehension. In her recurrent Dreams he thought, Anna had always awakened just as the Nightingale began her death song. But now she knew the death song. So she knew the Dream's end. Well, it must not be so bad, or she wouldn't have returned. Nothing was going to happen, not really. He shot the question at her: There was no danger any more, was there? Surely the ballet would be a superb success? She'd be enrolled with the immortals.

Her reply was grave, yet it seemed to amuse her. It gave him a little trouble; there were no words for its exact meaning. It was something like "Immortality begins with death."

He glanced at her face uneasily. "Are you looking for trouble?"

"Everything will go smoothly."

After all, he thought, she believes she has looked into the future and has seen what will happen.

"The Nightingale will not fail The Student," she added with a queer smile. "You'll get your Red Rose."

"You can be plainer than that," he muttered. "Secrets . . . secrets . . . why all this you're-too-young-to-know business?"

But she laughed in his mind, and the enchantment of that laughter took his breath away. Finally he said: "I admit I don't know what you're talking about. But if you're about to get involved in anything on my account, forget it. I won't have it."

"Each does the thing that makes him happy. The Student will never be happy until he finds The Rose that will admit him to his Dance. The Nightingale will never be happy until The Student holds her in his arms and thinks her as lovely as a Red Rose. I think we may both get what we want."

He growled: "You haven't the faintest idea what you're talking about."

"Yes I have, especially right now. For ten years I've urged people not to inhibit their healthy inclinations. At the moment I don't have any inhibitions at all. It's a wonderful feeling. I've never been so happy, I think. For the first and last time in my life, I'm going to kiss you."

Her hand tugged at his sleeve. As he looked down into that enchanted face, he knew that this night was hers, that she was privileged in all things, and that whatever she willed must yield to her.

They had stopped at the temporarily-erected stage-door. She rose *sur les pointes*, took his face in her palms, and like a hummingbird drinking her first nectar, kissed him on the mouth.

A moment later she led him into the dressing-room corridor.

He stifled a confused impulse to wipe the back of his hand across his lips. "Well . . . well, just remember to take it easy. Don't try to be spectacular. The artificial wings won't take it. Canvas stretched on duralite and piano wire calls for adagio. A fast pirouette, and they're ripped off. Besides, you're out of practice. Control your enthusiasm in Act I or you'll collapse in Act II. Now, run on to your dressing room. Cue in five minutes!"

Chapter Nineteen

There is a faint, yet distinct anatomical difference in the foot of the man and that of the woman, which keeps him earthbound, while permitting her, after long and arduous training, to soar *sur les pointes*. Owing to the great and varied beauty of the arabesques open to the ballerina poised on her extended toes, the male danseur at one time existed solely as a shadowy *porteur*, and was needed only to supply unobtrusive support and assistance in the exquisite *enchaînements* of the ballerina. Iron muscles in leg and torso are vital in the danseur, who must help maintain the illusion that his whirling partner is made of fairy gossamer, seeking to wing skyward from his restraining arms.

All this flashed through the incredulous mind of Ruy Jacques as he whirled in a double *fouetté* and followed from the corner of his eye the grey figure of Anna van Tuyl, as, wings and arms aflutter, she pirouetted in the second *enchaînement* of Act I, away from him and toward the *maître de ballet*.

It was all well enough to give the illusion of flying, of alighting apparently weightless, in his arms – that was what the audience loved. But that it could ever *really* happen – that was simply impossible. Stage wings – things of grey canvas and duralite frames – couldn't subtract a hundred pounds from one hundred and twenty.

And yet . . . it had seemed to him that she had actually flown.

He tried to pierce her mind – to extract the truth from the bits of metal about her. In a gust of fury he dug at the metal outline of those remarkable wings.

In the space of seconds his forehead was drenched in cold sweat, and his hands were trembling. Only the fall of the curtain on the first act saved him as he stumbled through his exit *entrechat.*

What had Matt Bell said? "To communicate in his new language of music, one may expect our man of the future to develop specialized membranous organs, which, of course, like the tongue, will have dual functional uses, possibly leading to the conquest of time as the tongue has conquered space."

Those wings were not wire and metal, but flesh and blood.

He was so absorbed in his ratiocination that he failed to become aware of an acutely unpleasant metal radiation behind him until it was almost upon him. It was an intricate conglomeration of matter, mostly metal, resting perhaps a dozen feet behind his back, showering the lethal presence of his wife.

He turned with nonchalant grace to face the first tangible spawn of the Sciomnia formula.

It was simply a black metal box with a few dials and buttons. The scientist held it lightly in her lap as she sat at the side of the table.

His eyes passed slowly from it to her face, and he knew that in a matter of minutes Anna van Tuyl – and all Via Rosa beyond her – would be soot floating in the night wind.

Martha Jacques' face was sublime with hate. "Sit down," she said quietly.

He felt the blood leaving his cheeks. Yet he grinned with a fair show of geniality as he dropped into the chair. "Certainly. I've got to kill time somehow until the end of Act I."

She pressed a button on the box surface.

His volition vanished. His muscles were locked, immobile. He could not breathe.

Just as he was convinced that she planned to suffocate him, her finger made another swift motion toward the box, and he sucked in a great gulp of air. His eyes could move a little, but his larnyx was still paralyzed.

Then the moments began to pass, endlessly, it seemed to him.

The table at which they sat was on the right wing of the stage. The woman sat facing into the stage, while his back was to it. She followed the preparations of the troupe for Act II with moody, silent eyes, he with straining ears and metal-empathic sense.

Only when he heard the curtain sweeping across the street-stage to open the second act did the woman speak.

"She *is* beautiful. And so graceful with those piano-wire wings, just as if they were part of her. I don't wonder she's the first woman who ever really interested you. Not that you really *love* her. You'll never love anyone.

From the depths of his paralysis he studied the etched bitterness of the face across the table. His lips were parched, and his throat a desert.

She thrust a sheet of paper at him, and her lip curled. "Are you still looking for that rose? Search no further, my ignorant friend. There it is – Sciomnia, complete, with its nineteen sub-equations."

The lines of unreadable symbols dug like nineteen relentless harpoons ever deeper into his twisting, racing mind.

The woman's face grimaced in fleeting despair. "Your own wife solves Sciomnia and you condescend to keep her company until you go on again at the end of Act III. I wish I had a sense of humor. All I knew was to paralyze your spinal column. Oh, don't worry. It's purely temporary. I just didn't want you to warn her. And I know what torture it is for you not to be able to talk." She bent over and turned a knurled knob on the side of the black steel box. "There, at least you can whisper. You'll be completely free after the weapon fires."

His lips moved in a rapid slur. "Let us bargain, Martha. Don't kill her. I swear never to see her again."

She laughed, almost gaily.

He pressed on. "But you have all you really want. Total fame, total power, total knowledge, the body perfect. What can her death and the destruction of the Via give you?"

"Everything."

"Martha, for the sake of all humanity to come, don't do this thing! I know something about Anna van Tuyl that perhaps even Bell doesn't – something she has concealed very adroitly. That girl is the most precious creature on earth!"

"It's precisely because of that opinion – which I do not necessarily share – that I shall include her in my general destruction of the Via." Her mouth slashed at him: "Oh, but it's wonderful to see you squirm. For the first time in your miserable thirty years of life you really want something. You've got to crawl down from that ivory tower of indifference and actually plead with me, whom you've never even taken the trouble to despise. You and your damned art. Let's see it save her now!"

The man closed his eyes and breathed deeply. In one rapid,

complex surmise, he visualized an *enchaînement* of postures, a *pas de deux* to be played with his wife as an unwitting partner. Like a skilled chess player, he had analyzed various variations of her probable responses to his gambit, and he had every expectation of a successful climax. And therein lay his hesitation, for success meant his own death.

Yes, he could not eradicate the idea from his mind. Even at this moment he believed himself intrigued more by the novel, if macabre, possibilities inherent in the theme rather than its superficial altruism. While seeming to lead Martha through an artistic approach to the murder of Anna and the Via, he could, in a startling, off key climax, force her to kill him instead. It amused him enormously to think that afterward, she would try to reduce the little comedy to charts and graph paper in an effort to discover how she had been hypnotized.

It was the first time in his life that he had courted physical injury. The emotional sequence was new, a little heady. He could do it; he need only be careful about his timing.

After hurling her challenge at him, the woman had again turned morose eyes downstage, and was apparently absorbed in a grudging admiration of the second act. But that couldn't last long. The curtain on Act II would be her signal.

And there it was, followed by a muffled roar of applause. He must stall her through most of Act III, and then . . .

He said quickly: "We still have a couple of minutes before the last act begins, where The Nightingale dies on the thorn. There's no hurry. You ought to take time to do this thing properly. Even the best assassinations are not purely a matter of science. I'll wager you never read Dc Quincey's little essay on murder as a fine art. No? You see, you're a neophyte, and could do with a few tips from an old hand. You must keep in mind your objects: to destroy both the Via and Anna. But mere killing won't be enough. You've got to make *me* suffer too. Suppose you shoot Anna when she comes on at the beginning of Act III. Only fair. The difficulty is that Anna and the others will never know what hit them. You don't give them the opportunity to bow to you as their conqueror."

He regarded her animatedly. "You see, can't you, my dear, that some extraordinarily difficult problems in composition are involved?"

She glared at him, and seemed about to speak.

He continued hastily: "Not that I'm trying to dissuade you. You have the basic concept, and despite your lack of experience, I don't think you'll find the problem of technique insuperable. Your prelude was rather well done: freezing me *in situ*, as it were, to state your theme simply and without adornment, followed immediately by variations of dynamic and suggestive portent. The finale is already implicit; yet it is kept at a disciplined arm's length while the necessary structure is formed to support it and develop its stern message."

She listened intently to him, and her eyes were narrow. The expression on her face said: "Talk all you like. This time, you won't win."

Somewhere beyond the flimsy building-board stage wing he heard Dorran's musicians tuning up for Act III.

His dark features seemed to grow even more earnest, but his voice contained a perceptible burble. "So you've blocked in the introduction and the climax. A beginning and an end. The *real* problem comes now: how much, and what kind – of a middle? Most beginning murderesses would simply give up in frustrated bafflement. A few would shoot the moment Anna floats into the white rose garden. In my opinion, however, considering the wealth of material inherent in your composition, such abbreviation would be inexcusably primitive and garish – if not actually vulgar."

Martha Jacques blinked, as though trying to break through some indescribable spell that was being woven about her. Then she laughed shortly. "Go on. I wouldn't miss this for anything. Just when *should* I destroy the Via?"

The artist sighed. "You see? Your only concern is the *result*. You completely ignore the *manner* of its accomplishment. Really, Mart, I should think you'd show more insight into your first attempt at serious art. Now please don't misunderstand me, dear. I have the warmest regard for your spontaneity and enthusiasm: to be sure, they're quite indispensable when dealing with hackneyed themes, but headlong eagerness is not a substitute for method, or for art. We must search out and exploit subsidiary themes, intertwine them in subtle counterpoint with the major motifs. The most obvious minor theme is the ballet itself. That ballet is the loveliest thing I've ever seen or heard. Nevertheless, *you* can give it a power, a dimension, that even Anna wouldn't suspect possible, simply by blending it contrapuntally into your own work. It's all a matter of firing at the proper instant." He smiled engagingly. "I see that you're beginning to appreciate the potentialities of such unwitting collaboration."

The woman studied him through heavy-lidded eyes. She said slowly: "You *are* a great artist – and a loathsome beast."

He smiled still more amiably. "Kindly restrict your appraisals to your fields of competence. You haven't, as yet, sufficient background to evaluate me as an artist. But let us return to your composition. Thematically, it's rather pleasing. The form, pacing, and orchestration are irreproachable. It is adequate. And its very adequacy condemns it. One detects a certain amount of diffident imitation and over-attention to technique common to artists working in a new medium. The overcautious sparks of genius aren't setting us aflame. The artist isn't getting enough of his own personality into the work. And the remedy is as simple as the diagnosis: the artist must penetrate his work, wrap it around him, give it the distilled, unique essence of his heart and mind, so that it will blaze up and reveal his soul even through the veil of unidiomatic technique."

He listened a moment to the music outside. "As Anna wrote her musical score, a hiatus of thirty-eight rests precedes the moment The Nightingale drops dying from the thorn. At the start of that silence, you could start to run off your nineteen sub-equations in your little tin box, audio-Fourier style. You might even route the equations into the loudspeaker system, if our gadget is capable of remote control."

For a long time she appraised him calculatingly. "I finally think I understand you. You hoped to unnerve me with your savage, over-accentuated satire, and make me change my mind. So you aren't a beast, and even though I see through you, you're even a greater artist than I at first imagined."

He watched as the woman made a number of adjustments on the control panel of the black box. When she looked up again, her lips were drawn into hard purple ridges.

She said: "But it would be too great a pity to let such art go to waste, especially when supplied by the author of 'Twinkle, twinkle, little star'. And you will indulge an amateur musician's vanity if I play *my* first Fourier composition *fortissimo*."

He answered her smile with a fleeting one of his own. "An artist should never apologize for self-admiration. But watch your cueing. Anna should be clasping the white rose thorn to her breast in thirty seconds, and that will be your signal to fill in the first half of the thirty-eight rest hiatus. Can you see her?"

The woman did not answer, but he knew that her eyes were following the ballet on the invisible stage and Dorran's baton, beyond, with fevered intensity.

The music glided to a halt.

"Now!" hissed Jacques.

She flicked a switch on the box.

They listened, frozen, as the multi-throated public address system blared into life up and down the two miles of the Via Rosa.

The sound of Sciomnia was chill, metallic, like the cruel crackle of ice heard suddenly in the intimate warmth of an enchanted garden, and it seemed to chatter derisively, well aware of the magic that it shattered.

As it clattered and skirled up its harsh tonal staircase, it seemed to shriek:

"Fools! Leave this childish nonsense and follow me! I am Science! I AM ALL!"

And Ruy Jacques, watching the face of the prophetess of the God of Knowledge, was for the first time in his life aware of the possibility of utter defeat.

As he stared in mounting horror, her eyes rolled slightly upward, as though buoyed by some irresistible inner flame, which the pale translucent cheeks let through.

But as suddenly as they had come, the nineteen chords were over, and then, as though to accentuate the finality of that mocking manifesto, a ghastly aural afterimage of silence began building up around his world.

For a near eternity it seemed to him that he and this woman were alone in the world, that, like some wicked witch, she had, through her cacophonic creation, immutably frozen the thousands of invisible watchers beyond the thin walls of the stage wings.

It was a strange, yet simple thing that broke the appalling silence and restored sanity, confidence, and the will to resist to the man: from somewhere far away, a child whimpered.

Breathing as deeply as his near paralysis would permit, the artist murmured: "Now, Martha, in a moment I think you will hear why I suggested your Fourier broadcast. I fear Science has been had once mo – "

He never finished, and her eyes, which were crystallising into question marks, never fired their barbs.

A towering tidal wave of tone was engulfing the Via, apparently of no human source and from no human instrument.

Even he, who had suspected in some small degree what was coming, now found his paralysis once more complete. Like the woman scientist opposite him, he could only sit in motionless awe, with eyes glazing, jaw dropping, and tongue cleaving to the roof of his mouth.

He knew that the heart strings of Anna van Tuyl were one with this mighty sea of song, and that it took its ecstatic timbre from the reverberating volutes of that godlike mind.

And as the magnificent chords poured out in exquisite consonantal sequence, now with a sudden reedy delicacy, now with the radiant gladness of cymbals, he knew that his plan must succeed.

For, chord for chord, tone for tone, and measure for measure, The Nightingale was repeating in her death song the nineteen chords of Martha Jacques' Sciomnia equations.

Only now those chords were transfigured, as though some Parnassian composer were compassionately correcting and magically transmuting the work of a dull pupil.

The melody spiralled heavenward on wings. It demanded no allegiance; it hurled no pronunciamento. It held a message, but one almost too glorious to be grasped. It was steeped in boundless aspiration, but it was at peace with man and his universe. It sparkled humility, and in its abnegation there was grandeur. Its very incompleteness served to hint at its boundlessness.

And then it, too, was over. The death song was done.

Yes, thought Ruy Jacques, it is the Sciomnia, rewritten, recast, and breathed through the blazing soul of a goddess. And when Martha realizes this, when she sees how I tricked her into broadcasting her trifling, inconsequential effort, she is going to fire her weapon – at *me*.

He watched the woman's face go livid, her mouth work in speechless hate.

"You *knew*!" she screamed. "You did it to humiliate me!"

Jacques began to laugh. It was a nearly silent laughter, rhythmic with mounting ridicule, pitiless in its mockery.

"Stop that!"

But his abdomen was convulsing in rigid helplessness, and tears began to stream down his cheeks.

"I warned you once before!" yelled the woman. Her hand darted toward the black box and turned its long axis toward the man.

Like a period punctuating the rambling, aimless sentence of his life, a ball of blue light burst from a cylindrical hole in the side of the box.

His laughter stopped suddenly. He looked from the box to the woman with growing amazement. He could bend his neck. His paralysis was gone.

She stared back, equally startled. She gasped: "Something went wrong! *You should be dead!*"

The artist didn't linger to argue.

In his mind was the increasingly urgent call of Anna van Tuyl.

Chapter Twenty

Dorran waved back the awed mass of spectators as Jacques knelt and transferred the faerie body from Bell's arms into his own.

"I'll carry you to your dressing room," he whispered. "I might have known you'd over-exert yourself."

Her eyes opened in the general direction of his face; in his mind came the tinkling of bells: "No . . . don't move me."

He looked up at Bell. "I think she's hurt! Take a look here!" He ran his hands over the seething surface of the wing folded along her side and breast: It was fevered fire.

"I can do nothing," replied the latter in a low voice. "She will tell you that I can do nothing."

"Anna!" cried Jacques. "What's wrong? What happened?"

Her musical reply formed in his mind. "Happened? Sciomnia was quite a thorn. Too much energy for one mind to disperse. Need two . . . three. Three could dematerialize weapon itself. Use wave formula of matter. Tell the others."

"*Others?* What are you talking about?" His thoughts whirled incoherently.

"Others like us. Coming soon. Bakine, dancing in streets of Leningrad. In Mexico City . . . the poetess Orteza. Many . . . this generation. *The Golden People.* Matt Bell guessed. Look!"

An image took fleeting form in his mind. First it was music, and then it was pure thought, and then it was a crisp strange air in his throat and the twang of something marvellous in his mouth. Then it was gone. "What was that?" he gasped.

"The Zhak symposium, seated at wine one April evening in the year 2437. Probability world. May . . . not occur. Did you recognize yourself?"

"Twenty-four thirty-seven?" His mind was fumbling.

"Yes. Couldn't you differentiate your individual mental contour from the whole? I thought you might. The group was still somewhat immature in the twenty-hundreds. By the fourteenth millennium . . ."

His head reeled under the impact of something titanic.

". . . your associated mental mass . . . creating a star of the M spectral class . . . galaxy now two-thirds terrestrialized . . ."

In his arms her wings stirred uneasily; all unconsciously he stroked the hot membranous surface and rubbed the marvellous bony framework with his fingers. "But Anna," he stammered, "I do not understand how this can be."

Her mind murmured in his. "Listen carefully, Ruy. Your pain . . . when your wings tried to open and couldn't . . . you needed certain psychoglandular stimulus. When you learn how to" – here a phrase he could not translate " – afterwards, they open . . ."

"When I learn – *what*?" he demanded. "What did you say I had to know, to open my wings?"

"One thing. The one thing . . . must have. . . to see the Rose."

"Rose-rose-*rose*!" he cried in near exasperation. "All right, then, my dutiful Nightingale, how long must I wait for you to make this remarkable Red Rose? I ask you, where is it?"

"Please . . . not just yet . . . in your arms just a little longer . . . while we finish ballet. Forget yourself, Ruy.Unless . . . leave prison . . . own heart . . . never find The Rose. Wings never unfold . . . remain a mortal. Science . . . isn't all. Art isn't . . . one thing greater . . . Ruy! I can't prolong . . ."

He looked up wildly at Bell.

The psychogeneticist turned his eyes away heavily. "Don't you understand? She has been dying ever since she absorbed that Sciomniac blast."

A faint murmur reached the artist's mind. "So you couldn't learn . . . poor . . . poor Nightingale . . ."

As he stared stuporously, her dun-colored wings began to shudder like leaves in an October wind.

From the depths of his shock he watched the fluttering of the wings give way to a sudden convulsive straining of her legs and thighs. It surged upward through her blanching body, through her abdomen and chest, pushing her blood before it and out into her wings, which now appeared more purple than grey.

To the old woman standing at his side, Bell observed quietly: "Even *homo superior* has his death struggle . . ."

The vendress of love philters nodded with anile sadness. "And she knew the answer . . . lost . . . lost . . ."

And still the blood came, making the wing membranes thick and taut.

"Anna!" shrieked Ruy Jacques. "You *can't* die. I won't let you! I love you! *I love you!*"

He had no expectation that she could still sense the images in his mind, nor even that she was still alive.

But suddenly, like stars shining their brief brilliance through a rift in storm clouds, her lips parted in a gay smile. Her eyes opened and seemed to bathe him in an intimate flow of light. It was during this momentary illumination, just before the lips solidified into their final enigmatic mask, that he thought he heard, as from a great distance, the opening measures of Weber's *Invitation to the Dance*.

At this moment the conviction formed in his numbed understanding that her loveliness was now supernal, that greater beauty could not be conceived or endured.

But even as he gazed in stricken wonder, the blood-gorged wings curled slowly up and out, enfolding the ivory breast and shoulders in blinding scarlet, like the petals of some magnificent rose.

The Time Machine

DINO BUZZATI

Dino Buzzati (1906–72) was one of the important Italian writers to emerge after the second world war. His principal modes were the absurd and the fantastic. He first came to international attention with his contemporary novel *The Tartar Steppe* (1945). His only SF novel, *Larger Than Life* (1960), a big computer story (a mainframe computer is programmed with the personality of a woman), is undistinguished. Critics agree, however, that his major work was in his short stories.

"The effectiveness of a fantastic story will depend on its being told in the most simple and practical terms . . . fantasy should be as close as possible to journalism," Buzzati said. He wrote a number of SF stories but has never been published or recognized as a writer of the genre in English. A collection of his fantasy and SF is, it seems to me, overdue. This story is a small, graceful piece on a classic SF idea.

The first great installation to slow down time was built near Grosseto, in Mariscano. In fact, the inventor, the famous Aldo Cristofari, was a native of Grosseto. This Cristofari, a professor at the University of Pisa, had been interested in the problem for at least twenty years and had conducted marvelous experiments in his laboratory, especially on the germination of legumes. In the academic world, however, he was thought a visionary. Until, under the aegis of his supporter, the financier Alfredo Lopez, the society for the construction of Diacosia was created. From then on Aldo Cristofari was regarded as a genius, a benefactor to humanity.

His invention consisted of a special electrostatic field called "Field C," within which natural phenomena required an abnormally longer period of time to complete their life cycles. In the first decisive experiments, this delay did not exceed five or six units per thousand; in practice, that is to say, it was almost unnoticeable. Yet once Cristofari had discovered the principle, he made very rapid progress. With the installation at Mariscano the rate of retardation was increased to nearly half. This meant that an organism with an average life span of ten years could be inserted in Field C and reach an age of twenty years.

The installation was built in a hilly zone, and it was not effective beyond a range of 800 meters. In a circle with a diameter of one and a half kilometers, animals and plants would grow and age half as quickly as those on the rest of the earth. Man could now hope to live for two centuries. And so – from the Greek for two hundred – the name Diacosia was chosen.

The zone was practically uninhabited. The few peasants who lived there were given the choice of staying or relocating elsewhere with a sizeable settlement. They preferred to clear out. The area was entirely enclosed within an insurmountable fence. There was only one entrance, and it was carefully guarded. In a short time there rose immense skyscrapers, a gigantic nursing home (for terminally ill patients who desired to prolong the little life they had left), movie houses, and theaters, all amid a forest of villas. And in the middle, at a height of forty meters, stood a circular antenna similar to those used for radar; this constituted the center of Field C. The power plant was completely underground.

Once the installation was finished, the entire world was informed that within three months the city would open its doors. To gain admission, and above all to reside there, cost an enormous sum. All the same, thousands of people from every corner of the globe were tempted. The subscriptions quickly exhausted the available housing. But then the fear began, and the flow of applicants was slower than anticipated.

What was there to fear? First of all, anyone who had settled in the city for any appreciable length of time could not leave without injury. Imagine an organism accustomed to the new, slower pace of physical existence. Suddenly transplant it from Field C to an area where life moves twice as fast; the function of every organ would have to accelerate immediately. And if it is easy for a runner to slow down, it is not so easy for someone moving slowly to bolt into a mad dash. The violent disequilibrium could have harmful or simply fatal consequences.

As a result, anyone who was born in the city was strictly forbidden to leave it. It was only logical to expect that an organism created in that slower speed could not be shifted to an environment that ran, we might say, in double time without risking destruction. In anticipation of this problem, special booths for acceleration and retardation were to be constructed on the perimeter of Field C so that anyone who left or entered it might gradually acclimate himself to the new pace and avoid the trauma of an abrupt change (they were similar to decompression chambers for deep-sea divers). But these booths were delicate devices, still in the planning stage. They would not be in service for many years.

In short, the citizens of Diacosia would live much longer than other men and women, but in exile. They were forced to give up their country, old friends, travel. They could no longer have a variety of lovers and acquaintances. It was as if they had been sentenced to life imprisonment, although they enjoyed every imaginable luxury and convenience.

But there was more. The danger posed by an escape could also be caused by any damage to the installation. It is true that there were two generators in the power plant, and that if one stopped, the other began to operate automatically. But what if both malfunctioned? What if there was a blackout? What if a cyclone or lightning struck the antenna? What if there was a war, or some outrage?

Diacosia was inaugurated at a celebration for its first group of citizens, who numbered 11,365. For the most part, they were people over fifty. Cristofari, who did not intend to settle in the city, was absent. He was represented by one Stoermer, a Swiss who was the director of the installation. There was a simple ceremony.

At the foot of the transmitting antenna that rose in the public garden, precisely at noon, Stoermer announced that from that moment on in Diacosia men and women would age exactly one-half as slowly as before. The antenna emitted a very soft hum, which was, moreover, pleasing to the ear. In the beginning, no one noticed the altered conditions. Only toward evening did some people feel a kind of lethargy, as if they were being held back. Very soon they started to talk, walk, chew with their usual composure. The tension of life subsided. Everything required greater effort.

About one month later, in *Technical Monthly*, a magazine based in Buffalo, the Nobel laureate Edwin Mediner published an article that proved to be the death knell for Diacosia. Mediner maintained that Cristofari's installation carried a grave threat. Time – we here present a synthesis of his argument in plain words – tends to rush headlong, and if it does not encounter the resistance of any matter, it will assume a progressively accelerated pace, with a tendency to increase to infinity. Thus any retardation of the flow of time requires immense effort, while it is nothing at all to augment its speed – just as in a river it is difficult to go against the current, but easy to follow it. From this observation Mediner formulated the following law: If one wishes to slow down natural phenomena, the necessary energy is directly proportional to the square of the retardation to be obtained; if one wishes to speed them up, on the other hand, the acceleration is directly proportional to the cube of the necessary energy. For example, ten units of energy are enough to achieve an acceleration of one thousand units; but the same ten units of energy applied to achieve the opposite purpose hardly produce a retardation of three units. In the first case, in fact, the human intervention operates in the same direction as time, which expects as much, so to speak. Mediner argued that Field C was such that it could operate in both directions; and an error in maintenance or a breakdown of some minor mechanism was sufficient to reverse the effect of the emission. In this case, instead of extending life to twice its average length, the machine would devour it precipitously. In the space of a few minutes, the citizens of Diacosia would age decades. And there followed the mathematical proof.

After Edwin Mediner's revelation, a wave of panic swept through the city of longevity. A few people, overlooking the risk of abruptly reentering an "accelerated environment," took flight. But Cristofari's assurances about the efficiency of the installation and the very fact that nothing had happened placated the anxieties. Life in Diacosia continued its monotonous succession of identical, placid, colorless days. Pleasures were weak and insipid, the throbbing delirium of love lacked the overpowering force it once had, news, voices, even the music that came from the outside world were now unpleasant because of their great speed. In a word, life was less interesting, despite the constant distractions. And yet this boredom was slight when compared to the thought that tomorrow, when one by one their contemporaries would pass away, the citizens of Diacosia would still be young and strong; and then their contemporaries' children would gradually die off, but the Diacosians would be full of vigor; and even their contemporaries' grandchildren and great-grandchildren would leave the world, and they who were still alive, with decades of good years ahead of them, would read the obituary notices. This was the thought that dominated the community, that calmed restless spirits, that resolved jealousies and quarrels; this was why they were not agonized as before by the passage of time and the future presented itself as a vast land-scape and when confronted by disappointment men and women told themselves: Why worry about it? I'll think about it tomorrow, there isn't any hurry.

After two years, the population had climbed to 52,000, and already the first generation of Diacosians had been born. They would reach full maturity at forty. After ten years, more than 120,000 creatures swarmed over that square kilometer, and slowly, much more slowly than in other cities where time galloped, the skyline rose to dizzying heights. Diacosia had now become the greatest wonder of the world. Caravans of tourists lined the periphery, observing through the gates those people who were so different, who moved with the slowness of MS victims succumbing to paralysis.

The phenomenon lasted twenty years. And a few seconds were enough to destroy it. How did the tragedy occur? Was it caused by a man's will? Or was it chance? Perhaps one of the technicians, anguished by love or illness, wanted to abbreviate his torment and set the catastrophe in motion. Or was he maddened simply from exasper-ation with that empty, egocentric life, concerned only with self-preser-vation? And so he purposely reversed the effect of the machine, freeing the vandal forces of time.

It was May 17th, a warm, sunny day. In the fields, along the fence that ran around the perimeter, hundreds of curious observers were stationed, their eyes riveted to people just like them, whose life passed twice as slowly. From within the city came the thin, harmonious voice of the antenna. It had a bell-like resonance. The present writer was there that day and he observed a group of four children playing with a ball. "How old are you?" I asked the oldest one. "Last month I was twenty," she answered politely, but with exaggerated slowness. And their way of running was strange: all soft, viscous movements, like a film shot in slow motion. Even the ball had less bounce for them.

Beyond the fence were the lawns and paths of a garden; the barrier surrounding the buildings began at about fifty meters. A breeze moved the leaves in the trees, yet languidly, it seemed, as if they were leaden. Suddenly, about three in the afternoon, the remote hum of antenna grew more intense and rose like a siren, an unbearable piercing whistle. I will never forget what happened. Even today, at a distance of years, I awake in the dead of night with a start, confronting that horrible vision.

Before my eyes the four children stretched monstrously. I saw them grow, fatten, become adults. Beards sprouted from male chins.

Transformed this way and half naked, their childhood clothes having split under the pressure of the lightning growth, they were seized with terror. They opened their mouths to speak, but what came out was a strange noise I had never heard before. In the vortex of unleashed time, the syllables all ran together, like a record played at a higher, mad speed. That gurgling quickly turned into a wheeze, then a desperate shout.

The four children looked around for help, saw us and rushed toward the railing. But life burned inside them; at the railing, a matter of seven or eight seconds, four old people arrived, with white hair and beards, flaccid and bony. One managed to seize the fence with his skeletal hands. He collapsed at once, together with his companions. They were dead. And the decrepit bodies of those poor children immediately gave off a foul odor. They were decomposing, flesh fell away, bones appeared, even the bones – before my very eyes – dissolved into a whitish dust.

Only then did the fatal scream of the machine subside and finally fall silent. Mediner's prophecy came true. For reasons that will forever remain unknown, the time machine had reversed its operation, and a few seconds were enough to swallow three or four centuries of life.

Now a gloomy, sepulchral silence has frozen the city. The shadow of abject old age has fallen over the skyscrapers, which had just been resplendent with glory and hope. The walls are wrinkled; ominous lines and creases have appeared, oozing black liquids amid a fringe of rotting spider webs. And there is dust everywhere. Dust, stillness, silence. Of the two hundred thousand wealthy, fortunate people who had wanted to live for centuries there remained nothing but white dust, collecting here and there, as on millennial tombs.

Mother

PHILIP JOSÉ FARMER

Philip José Farmer (1918–   ) is a powerful and energetic writer of fantasy and SF who has published over fifty novels and hundreds of short stories. His most famous novels and stories are the Riverworld series, beginning with *To Your Scattered Bodies Go* (1971), which feature such historical personages as Richard Francis Burton, Mark Twain, and Jack London as central characters. He entered the genre with a powerful short story, "The Lovers" (1952), a mixture of alien biology and sex that earned him a not-undeserved reputation as a taboo-breaker and a somewhat shocking writer, if not downright disgusting. He has written most often about psychology, sex, and race, often all three at once.

Leslie A. Fiedler called him the best living science fiction writer. *The Encyclopedia of Science Fiction* says, "Farmer is governed by an instinct for extremity. Of all science fiction writers of the first or second rank, he is perhaps the most threateningly impish, and the most anarchic."

Farmer was so underpaid and underappreciated for so long in his career that when Kurt Vonnegut wrote of a fictional hack SF writer Kilgore Trout, who was psychologically and philosophically profound while writing of absurd things, Farmer identified with Trout and ultimately obtained Vonnegut's permission to write an SF novel under that name – even though Vonnegut had really been thinking of himself.

Farmer's chief mode is a startling confrontation with psychological states and symbols made literal and manifest. This story certainly does that. It is Freudian science fiction.

I

"Look, Mother. The clock is running backward."

Eddie Fetts pointed to the hands on the pilot room dial.

Dr. Paula Fetts said, "The crash must have reversed it."

"How could it do that?"

"I can't tell you. I don't know everything, Son."

"Oh!"

"Well, don't look at me so disappointedly. I'm a pathologist, not an electronician."

"Don't be so cross, Mother. I can't stand it. Not now."

He walked out of the pilot room. Anxiously, she followed him. The burial of the crew and her fellow scientists had been very trying for him. Spilled blood had always made him dizzy and sick; he could scarcely control his hands enough to help her sack the scattered bones and entrails.

He had wanted to put the corpses in the nuclear furnace, but she had forbidden that. The Geigers amidships were ticking loudly, warning that there was invisible death in the stern.

The meteor that struck the moment the ship came out of Translation into normal space had probably wrecked the engine room. So she had understood from the incoherent high-pitched phrases of a colleague before he fled to the pilot room. She had hurried to find Eddie. She feared his cabin door would still be locked, as he had been making a tape of the aria "Heavy Hangs the Albatross" from Gianelli's *Ancient Mariner*.

Fortunately, the emergency system had automatically thrown out the locking circuits. Entering, she had called out his name in fear he'd been hurt. He was lying half unconscious on the floor, but it was not the accident that had thrown him there. The reason lay in the corner, released from his lax hand; a quart free-fall Thermos, rubber-nippled. From Eddie's open mouth charged a breath of rye that not even Nodor pills had been able to conceal.

Sharply she had commanded him to get up and onto the bed. Her voice, the first he had ever heard, pierced through the phalanx of Old Red Star. He struggled up, and she, though smaller, had thrown every ounce of her weight into getting him up and onto the bed.

There she had lain down with him and strapped them both in. She understood that the lifeboat had been wrecked also, and that it was up to the captain to bring the yacht down safely to the surface of this charted but unexplored planet, Baudelaire. Everybody else had gone to sit behind the captain, strapped in crash-chairs, unable to help except with their silent backing.

Moral support had not been enough. The ship had come in on a shallow slant. Too fast. The wounded motors had not been able to hold her up. The prow had taken the brunt of the punishment. So had those seated in the nose.

Dr. Fetts had held her son's head on her bosom and prayed out loud to her God. Eddie had snored and muttered. Then there was a sound like the clashing of the gates of doom – a tremendous bong as if the ship were a clapper in a gargantuan bell tolling the most frightening message human ears may hear – a blinding blast of light – and darkness and silence.

A few moments later Eddie began crying out in a childish voice, "Don't leave me to die, Mother! Come back! Come back!"

Mother was unconscious by his side, but he did not know that. He wept for a while, then he lapsed back into his rye-fogged stupor – if he had ever been out of it – and slept. Again, darkness and silence.

It was the second day since the crash, if "day" could describe that twilight state on Baudelaire. Dr. Fetts followed her son wherever he went. She knew he was very sensitive and easily upset. All his life she had known it and had tried to get between him and anything that would cause trouble. She had succeeded, she thought, fairly well until three months ago when Eddie had eloped.

The girl was Polina Fameux, the ash-blond long-legged actress whose tridi image, taped, had been shipped to frontier stars where a small acting talent meant little and a large and shapely bosom much. Since Eddie was a well-known Metro tenor, the marriage made a big splash whose ripples ran around the civilized Galaxy.

Dr. Fetts had felt very bad about the elopement, but she had, she hoped, hidden her grief very well beneath a smiling mask. She didn't regret having to give him up; after all, he was a full-grown man, no longer her little boy. But, really, aside from the seasons at the Met and his tours, he had not been parted from her since he was eight.

That was when she went on a honeymoon with her second husband. And then she and Eddie had not been separated long, for Eddie had gotten very sick, and she'd had to hurry back and take care of him, as he had insisted she was the only one who could make him well.

Moreover, you couldn't count his days at the opera as a total loss, for he vised her every noon and they had a long talk – no matter how high the vise bills ran.

The ripples caused by her son's marriage were scarcely a week old before they were followed by even bigger ones. They bore the news of the separation of Eddie and his wife. A fortnight later, Polina applied for divorce on grounds of incompatibility. Eddie was handed the papers in his mother's apartment. He had come back to her the day he and Polina had agreed they "couldn't make a go of it," or, as he phrased it to his mother, "couldn't get together."

Dr. Fetts was, of course, very curious about the reason for their parting, but, as she explained to her friends, she "respected" his silence. What she didn't say was that she had told herself the time would come when he would tell her all.

Eddie's "nervous breakdown" started shortly afterward. He had been very irritable, moody, and depressed, but he got worse the day a so-called friend told Eddie that whenever Polina heard his name mentioned, she laughed loud and long. The friend added that Polina had promised to tell some day the true story of their brief merger.

That night his mother had to call in a doctor.

In the days that followed, she thought of giving up her position as research pathologist at De Kruif and taking all her time to help him "get back on his feet." It was a sign of the struggle going on in her mind that she had not been able to decide within a week's time. Ordinarily given to swift consideration and resolution of a problem, she could not agree to surrender her beloved quest into tissue regeneration.

Just as she was on the verge of doing what was for her the incredible and the shameful, tossing a coin, she had been vised by her superior. He told her she had been chosen to go with a group of biologists on a research cruise to ten preselected planetary systems.

Joyfully, she had thrown away the papers that would turn Eddie over to a sanatorium. And, since he was quite famous, she had used her influence to get the government to allow him to go along. Ostensibly, he was to make a survey of the development of opera on planets colonized by Terrans. That the yacht was not visiting any colonized globes seemed to have been missed by the bureaus concerned. But it was not the first time in the history of a government that its left hand knew not what its right was doing.

Actually, he was to be "rebuilt" by his mother, who thought herself much more capable of curing him than any of the prevalent A, F, J, R, S, K, or H therapies. True, some of her friends reported amazing results with some of the symbol-chasing techniques. On the other hand, two of her close companions had tried them all and had gotten no benefits from any of them. She was his mother; she could do more for him than any of those "alphabatties"; he was flesh of her flesh, blood of her blood. Besides, he wasn't so sick. He just got awfully blue sometimes and made theatrical but insincere threats of suicide or else just sat and stared into space. But she could handle him.

II

So now it was that she followed him from the backward-running clock to his room. And saw him step inside, look for a second, and then turn to her with a twisted face.

"Neddie is ruined, Mother. Absolutely ruined."

She glanced at the piano. It had torn from the wall-racks at the moment of impact and smashed itself against the opposite wall. To Eddie it wasn't just a piano; it was Neddie. He had a pet name for everything he contacted for more than a brief time. It was as if he hopped from one appellation to the next, like an ancient sailor who felt lost unless he was close to the familiar and designated points of the shoreline. Otherwise, Eddie seemed to be drifting helplessly in a chaotic ocean, one that was anonymous and amorphous.

Or, analogy more typical of him, he was like the nightclubber who feels submerged, drowning, unless he hops from table to table, going from one well-known group of faces to the next, avoiding the featureless and unnamed dummies at the strangers' tables.

He did not cry over Neddie. She wished he would. He had been so apathetic during the voyage. Nothing, not even the unparalleled splendor of the naked stars nor the inexpressible alienness of strange planets, had seemed to lift him very long. If he would only weep or laugh loudly or display some sign that he was reacting violently to what was happening. She would even have welcomed his striking her in anger or calling her "bad" names.

But no, not even during the gathering of the mangled corpses, when he looked for a while as if he were going to vomit, would he give way to his body's demand for expression. She understood that if he were to throw up, he would be much better for it, would have gotten rid of much of the psychic disturbance along with the physical.

He would not. He had kept on raking flesh and bones into the large plastic bags and kept a fixed look of resentment and sullenness.

She hoped now that the loss of his piano would bring tears and shaking shoulders. Then she could take him in her arms and give him sympathy. He would be her little boy again, afraid of the dark, afraid of the dog killed by a car, seeking her arms for the sure safety, the sure love.

"Never mind, Baby," she said. "When we're rescued, we'll get you a new one."

"When – !"

He lifted his eyebrows and sat down on the bed's edge.

"What do we do now?"

She became very brisk and efficient.

"The ultrad automatically started working the moment the meteor struck. If it's survived the crash, it's still sending SOSs. If not, then there's nothing we can do about it. Neither of us knows how to repair it.

"However, it's possible that in the last five years since this planet was located, other expeditions may have landed here. Not from Earth but from some of the colonies. Or from nonhuman globes. Who knows? It's worth taking a chance. Let's see."

A single glance was enough to wreck their hopes. The ultrad had been twisted and broken until it was no longer recognizable as the machine that sent swifter-than-light waves through the no-ether.

Dr. Fetts said with false cheeriness, "Well, that's that! So what? It makes things too easy. Let's go into the storeroom and see what we can see."

Eddie shrugged and followed her. There she insisted that each take a panrad. If they had to separate for any reason, they could always communicate and also, using the DFs – the built-in direction finders – locate each other. Having used them before, they knew the instruments' capabilities and how essential they were on scouting or camping trips.

The panrads were lightweight cylinders about two feet high and eight inches in diameter. Crampacked, they held the mechanisms of two dozen different utilities. Their batteries lasted a year without recharging, they were practically indestructible and worked under almost any conditions.

Keeping away from the side of the ship that had the huge hole in it, they took the panrads outside. The long wave bands were searched by Eddie while his mother moved the dial that ranged up and down the shortwaves. Neither really expected to hear anything, but to search was better than doing nothing.

Finding the modulated wave-frequencies empty of any significant noises, he switched to the continuous waves. He was startled by a dot-dashing.

"Hey, Mom! Something in the 1000 kilocycles! Unmodulated!"

"Naturally, Son," she said with some exasperation in the midst of her elation. "What would you expect from a radio-telegraphic signal?"

She found the band on her own cylinder. He looked blankly at her. "I know nothing about radio, but that's not Morse."

"What? You must be mistaken!"

"I – I don't think so."

"Is it or isn't it? Good God, Son, can't you be certain of *anything*!"

She turned the amplifier up. As both of them had learned Galacto-Morse through sleeplearn techniques, she checked him at once.

"You're right. What do you make of it?"

His quick ear sorted out the pulses.

"No simple dot and dash. Four different time-lengths."

He listened some more.

"They've got a certain rhythm, all right. I can make out definite groupings. Ah! That's the sixth time I've caught that particular one. And there's another. And another."

Dr. Fetts shook her ash-blond head. She could make out nothing but a series of zzt-zzt-zzt's.

Eddie glanced at the DF needle.

"Coming from NE by E. Should we try to locate?"

"Naturally," she replied. "But we'd better eat first. We don't know how far away it is, or what we'll find there. While I fix a hot meal, you get our field trip stuff ready."

"O.K.," he said with more enthusiasm than he had shown for a long time.

When he came back he ate everything in the large dish his mother had prepared on the unwrecked galley stove.

"You always did make the best stew," he said.

"Thank you. I'm glad you're eating again, Son. I am surprised. I thought you'd be sick about all this."

He waved vaguely but energetically.

"The challenge of the unknown. I have a sort of feeling this is going to turn out much better than we thought. Much better."

She came close and sniffed his breath. It was clean, innocent even of stew. That meant he'd taken Nodor, which probably meant he'd been sampling some hidden rye. Otherwise, how to explain his reckless disregard of the possible dangers? It wasn't like him.

She said nothing, for she knew that if he tried to hide a bottle in his clothes or field sack while they were tracking down the radio signals, she would soon find it. And take it away. He wouldn't even protest, merely let her lift it from his limp hand while his lips swelled with resentment.

III

They set out. Both wore knapsacks and carried the panrads. He carried a gun over his shoulder, and she had snapped onto her sack her small black bag of medical and lab supplies.

High noon of late autumn was topped by a weak red sun that barely managed to make itself seen through the eternal double layer of clouds. Its companion, an even smaller blob of lilac, was setting on the north-western horizon. They walked in a sort of bright twilight, the best that Baudelaire ever achieved. Yet, despite the lack of light, the air was warm. It was a phenomenon common to certain planets behind the Horsehead Nebula, one being investigated but as yet unexplained.

The country was hilly, with many deep ravines. Here and there were prominences high enough and steep-sided enough to be called embryo mountains. Considering the roughness of the land however, there was a surprising amount of vegetation. Pale green, red, and yellow bushes, vines, and little trees clung to every bit of ground, horizontal or vertical. All had comparatively broad leaves that turned with the sun to catch the light.

From time to time, as the two Terrans strode noisily through the forest, small multicolored insect-like and mammal-like creatures scuttled from hiding place to hiding place. Eddie decided to carry his gun in the crook of his arm. Then, after they were forced to scramble up and down ravines and hills and fight their way through thickets that became unexpectedly tangled, he put it back over his shoulder, where it hung from a strap.

Despite their exertions, they did not tire quickly. They weighed about twenty pounds less than they would have on Earth and, though the air was thinner, it was richer in oxygen.

Dr. Fetts kept up with Eddie. Thirty years the senior of the twenty-three-year-old, she passed even at close inspection for his older sister. Longevity pills took care of that. However, he treated her with all the courtesy and chivalry that one gave one's mother and helped her up the steep inclines, even though the climbs did not appreciably cause her deep chest to demand more air.

They paused once by a creek bank to get their bearings.

"The signals have stopped," he said.

"Obviously," she replied.

At that moment the radar-detector built into the panrad began to ping. Both of them automatically looked upward.

"There's no ship in the air."

"It can't be coming from either of those hills," she pointed out. "There's nothing but a boulder on top of each one. Tremendous rocks."

"Nevertheless, it's coming from there, I think. Oh! Oh! Did you see what I saw? Looked like a tall stalk of some kind being pulled down behind that big rock."

She peered through the dim light. "I think you were imagining things, Son. I saw nothing."

Then, even as the pinging kept up, the zzting started again. But after a burst of noise, both stopped.

"Let's go up and see what we shall see," she said.

"Something screwy," he commented. She did not answer.

They forded the creek and began the ascent. Halfway up, they stopped to sniff in puzzlement at a gust of some heavy odor coming downwind.

"Smells like a cageful of monkeys," he said.

"In heat," she added. If his was the keener ear, hers was the sharper nose.

They went on up. The RD began sounding its tiny hysterical gonging. Nonplused, Eddie stopped. The DF indicated the radar pulses were not coming from the top of the hill they were climbing, as formerly, but from the other hill across the valley. Abruptly, the panrad fell silent.

"What do we do now?"

"Finish what we started. This hill. Then we go to the other one."

He shrugged and then hastened after her tall slim body in its long-legged coveralls. She was hot on the scent, literally, and nothing could stop her. Just before she reached the bungalow-sized boulder topping the hill, he caught up with her. She had stopped to gaze intently at the DF needle, which swung wildly before it stopped at neutral. The monkey-cage odor was very strong.

"Do you suppose it could be some sort of radio-generating mineral?" she asked, disappointedly.

"No. Those groupings were semantic. And that smell . . ."

"Then what – ?"

He didn't know whether to feel pleased or not that she had so obviously and suddenly thrust the burden of responsibility and action on him. Both pride and a curious shrinking affected him. But he did feel exhilarated. Almost, he thought, he felt as if he were on the verge of discovering what he had been looking for for a long time. What the object of his search had been, he could not say. But he was excited and not very much afraid.

He unslung his weapon, a two-barreled combination shotgun and rifle. The panrad was still quiet.

"Maybe the boulder is camouflage for a spy outfit," he said. He sounded silly, even to himself.

Behind him, his mother gasped and screamed. He whirled and raised his gun, but there was nothing to shoot. She was pointing at the hilltop across the valley, shaking, and saying something incoherent.

He could make out a long slim antenna seemingly projecting from the monstrous boulder crouched there. At the same time, two thoughts struggled for first place in his mind: one, that it was more than a coincidence that both hills had almost identical stone structures on their brows, and, two, that the antenna must have been recently stuck out, for he was sure he had not seen it the last time he looked.

He never got to tell her his conclusions, for something thin and flexible and irresistible seized him from behind. Lifted into the air, he was borne backward. He dropped the gun and tried to grab the bands or tentacles around him and tear them off with his bare hands. No use.

He caught one last glimpse of his mother running off down the hillside. Then a curtain snapped down, and he was in total darkness.

IV

Eddie sensed himself, still suspended, twirled around. He could not know for sure, of course, but he thought he was facing in exactly the opposite direction. Simultaneously, the tentacles binding his legs and arms were released. Only his waist was still gripped. It was pressed so tightly that he cried out with pain.

Then, boot-toes bumping on some resilient substance, he was carried forward. Halted, facing he knew not what horrible monster, he was suddenly assailed – not by a sharp beak or tooth or knife or some other cutting or mangling instrument – but by a dense cloud of that same monkey perfume.

In other circumstances, he might have vomited. Now his stomach was not given the time to consider whether it should clean house or not. The tentacle lifted him higher and thrust him against something soft and yielding – something fleshlike and womanly – almost breast-like in texture and smoothness and warmth and in its hint of gentle curving.

He put his hands and feet out to brace himself, for he thought for a moment he was going to sink in and be covered up – enfolded – ingested. The idea of a gargantuan amoeba-thing hiding within a hollow rock – or a rock-like shell – made him writhe and yell and shove at the protoplasmic substance.

But nothing of the kind happened. He was not plunged into a smothering and slimy jelly that would strip him of his skin and then his flesh and then dissolve his bones. He was merely shoved repeatedly against the soft swelling. Each time, he pushed or kicked or struck at it. After a dozen of these seemingly purposeless acts, he was held away, as if whatever was doing it was puzzled by his behavior.

He had quit screaming. The only sounds were his harsh breathing and the zzts and pings from the panrad. Even as he became aware of them, the zzts changed tempo and settled into a recognizable pattern of bursts – three units that crackled out again and again.

"Who are you? Who are you?"

Of course, it could just as easily had been, "What are you?" or "What the hell!" or "Nov smoz ka pop?"

Or nothing – semantically speaking.

But he didn't think the latter. And when he was gently lowered to the floor, and the tentacle went off to only-God-knew-where in the dark, he was sure that the creature was communicating – or trying to – with him.

It was this thought that kept him from screaming and running around in the lightless and fetid chamber, brainlessly seeking an outlet. He mastered his panic and snapped open a little shutter in the panrad's side and thrust in his righthand index finger. There he poised it above the key and in a moment, when the thing paused in transmitting, he sent back, as best he could, the pulses he had received. It was not necessary for him to turn on the light and spin the dial that would put him on the 1000 kc band. The instrument would automatically key that frequency in with the one he had just received.

The oddest part of the whole procedure was that his whole body was trembling almost uncontrollably – one part excepted. That was his index finger, his one unit that seemed to him to have a definite function in this otherwise meaningless situation. It was the section of him that was helping him to survive – the only part that knew how – at that moment. Even his brain seemed to have no connection with his finger. That digit was himself, and the rest just happened to he linked to it.

When he paused, the transmitter began again. This time the units were unrecognizable. There was a certain rhythm to them, but he could not know what they meant. Meanwhile, the RD was pinging. Something somewhere in the dark hole had a beam held tightly on him.

He pressed a button on the panrad's top, and the built-in flashlight illuminated the area just in front of him. He saw a wall of reddish-gray rubbery substance. On the wall was a roughly circular, light gray swelling about four feet in diameter. Around it, giving it a Medusa appearance, were coiled twelve very long, very thin tentacles.

Though he was afraid that if he turned his back to them the tentacles would seize him once more, his curiosity forced him to wheel about and examine his surroundings with the bright beam. He was in an egg-shaped chamber about thirty feet long, twelve wide, and eight to ten high in the middle. It was formed of a reddish-gray material, smooth except for irregular intervals of blue or red pipes. Veins and arteries?

A door-sized portion of the wall had a vertical slit running down it. Tentacles fringed it. He guessed it was a sort of iris and that it had opened to drag him inside. Starfish-shaped groupings of tentacles were scattered on the walls or hung from the ceiling. On the wall opposite the iris was a long and flexible stalk with a cartilaginous ruff around its free end. When Eddie moved, it moved, its blind point following him as a radar antenna tracks the thing it is locating. That was what it was. And unless he was wrong, the stalk was also a C.W. transmitter-receiver.

He shot the light round. When it reached the end farthest from him, he gasped. Ten creatures were huddled together facing him! About the size of half-grown pigs, they looked like nothing so much as unshelled snails; they were eyeless, and the stalk growing from the forehead of each was a tiny duplicate of that on the wall. They didn't look dangerous. Their open mouths were little and toothless, and their rate of locomotion must be slow, for they moved like snails, on a large pedestal of flesh – a foot-muscle.

Nevertheless, if he were to fall asleep they could overcome him by force of numbers, and those mouths might drip an acid to digest him, or they might carry a concealed poisonous sting.

His speculations were interrupted violently. He was seized, lifted, and passed on to another group of tentacles. He was carried beyond the antenna-stalk and toward the snail-beings. Just before he reached them, he was halted, facing the wall. An iris, hitherto invisible, opened. His light shone into it, but he could see nothing but convolutions of flesh.

His panrad gave off a new pattern of dit-dot-deet-dats. The iris widened until it was large enough to admit his body, if he were shoved in head first. Or feet first. It didn't matter. The convolutions straightened out and became a tunnel. Or a throat. From thousands of little pits emerged thousands of tiny, razor sharp teeth. They flashed out and sank back in, and before they had disappeared thousands of other wicked little spears darted out and past the receding fangs.

Meat-grinder.

Beyond the murderous array, at the end of the throat, was a huge pouch of wafer. Steam came from it, and with it an odor like that of his mother's stew. Dark bits, presumably meat, and pieces of vegetables floated on the seething surface.

Then the iris closed, and he was turned around to face the slugs. Gently, but unmistakably, a tentacle spanked his buttocks. And the panrad zzzted a warning.

Eddie was not stupid. He knew now that the ten creatures were not dangerous unless he molested them. In which case he had just seen where he would go if he did not behave.

Again he was lifted and carried along the wall until he was shoved against the light gray spot. The monkey-cage odor, which had died out, became strong again. Eddie identified its source with a very small hole which appeared in the wall.

When he did not respond – he had no idea yet how he was supposed to act – the tentacles dropped him so unexpectedly that he fell on his back. Unhurt by the yielding flesh, he rose.

What was the next step? Exploration of his resources. Itemization: The panrad. A sleeping-bag, which he wouldn't need as long as the present too-warm temperature kept up. A bottle of Old Red Star capsules. A free-fall Thermos with attached nipple. A box of A-2-Z rations. A Foldstove. Cartridges for his double-barrel, now lying outside the creature's boulderish shell. A roll of toilet paper. Toothbrush. Paste. Soap. Towel. Pills: Nodor, hormone, vitamin, longevity, reflex, and sleeping. And a thread-thin wire, a hundred feet long when uncoiled, that held prisoner in its molecular structure a hundred symphonies, eighty operas, a thousand different types of musical pieces, and two thousand great books ranging from Sophocles and Dostoyevsky to the latest bestseller. It could be played inside the panrad.

He inserted it, pushed a button, and spoke, "Eddie Feffs's recording of Puccini's '*Che gelida manina*,' please."

And while he listened approvingly to his own magnificent voice, he zipped open a can he had found in the bottom of the sack. His mother had put into it the stew left over from their last meal in the ship.

Not knowing what was happening, yet for some reason sure he was for the present safe, he munched meat and vegetables with a contented jaw. Transition from abhorrence to appetite sometimes came easily for Eddie.

He cleaned out the can and finished with some crackers and a chocolate bar. Rationing was out. As long as the food lasted, he would eat well. Then, if nothing turned up, he would . . . But then, he reassured himself as he licked his fingers, his mother, who was free, would find some way to get him out of his trouble.

She always had.

V

The panrad, silent for a while, began signaling. Eddie spotlighted the antenna and saw it was pointing at the snail-beings, which he had, in accordance with his custom, dubbed familiarly. Sluggos he called them.

The Sluggos crept toward the wall and stopped close to it. Their mouths, placed on the tops of their heads, gaped like so many hungry young birds. The iris opened, and two lips formed into a spout. Out of it streamed steaming-hot water and chunks of meat and vegetables. Stew! Stew that fell exactly into each waiting mouth.

That was how Eddie learned the second phrase of Mother Polyphema's language. The first message had been, "What are you?" This was, "Come and get it!"

He experimented. He tapped out a repetition of what he'd last heard. As one, the Sluggos – except the one then being fed – turned to him and crept a few feet before halting, puzzled.

Inasmuch as Eddie was broadcasting, the Sluggos must have had some sort of built-in DF. Otherwise they wouldn't have been able to distinguish between his pulses and their Mother's.

Immediately after, a tentacle smote Eddie across the shoulders and knocked him down. The panrad zzzted its third intelligible message: "Don't ever do that!"

And then a fourth, to which the ten young obeyed by wheeling and resuming their former positions.

"This way, children."

Yes, they were the offspring, living, eating, sleeping, playing, and learning to communicate in the womb of their mother – the Mother. They were the mobile brood of this vast immobile entity that had scooped up Eddie as a frog scoops up a fly. This Mother. She who had once been just such a Sluggo until she had grown hog-sized and had been pushed out of her Mother's womb. And who, rolled into a tight ball, had free-wheeled down her natal hill, straightened out at the bottom, inched her way up the next hill, rolled down, and so on. Until she found the empty shell of an adult who had died. Or, if she wanted to be a first class citizen in her society and not a prestigeless *occupée,* she found the bare top of a tall hill – or any eminence that commanded a big sweep of territory – and there squatted.

And there she put out many thread-thin tendrils into the soil and into the cracks in the rocks, tendrils that drew sustenance from the fat of her body and grew and extended downward and ramified into other tendrils. Deep underground the rootlets worked their instinctive chemistry; searched for and found the water, the calcium, the iron, the copper, the nitrogen, the carbons, fondled earthworms and grubs and larvae, teasing them for the secrets of their fats and proteins; broke down the wanted substance into shadowy colloidal particles; sucked them up the thready pipes of the tendrils and back to the pale and slimming body crouching on a flat space atop a ridge, a hill, a peak.

There, using the blueprints stored in the molecules of the cerebellum, her body took the building blocks of elements and fashioned them into a very thin shell of the most available material, a shield large enough so she could expand to fit it while her natural enemies – the keen and hungry predators that prowled twilighted Baudelaire – nosed and clawed it in vain.

Then, her evergrowing bulk cramped, she would resorb the hard covering. And if no sharp tooth found her during that process of a few days, she would cast another and a larger. And so on through a dozen or more.

Until she had become the monstrous and much reformed body of an adult and virgin female. Outside would be the stuff that so much resembled a boulder, that was, actually, rock: either granite, diorite, marble, basalt, or maybe just plain limestone. Or sometimes iron, glass, or cellulose.

Within was the centrally located brain, probably as large as a man's. Surrounding it, the tons of organs: the nervous system, the mighty heart, or hearts, the four stomachs, the microwave and longwave generators, the kidneys, bowels, tracheae, scent and taste organs, the perfume factory which made odors to attract animals and birds close enough to be seized, and the huge womb. And the antennae – the small one inside for teaching and scanning the young, and a long and powerful stalk on the outside, projecting from the shelltop, retractable if danger came.

The next step was from virgin to Mother, lower-case to upper-case as designated in her pulse-language by a longer pause before a word. Not until she was deflowered could she take a high place in her society. Immodest, unblushing, she herself made the advances, the proposals, and the surrender.

After which, she ate her mate.

The clock in the panrad told Eddie he was in his thirtieth day of imprisonment when he found out that little bit of information. He was shocked, not because it offended his ethics, but because he himself had been intended to be the mate. And the dinner.

His finger tapped, "Tell me, Mother, what you mean."

He had not wondered before how a species that lacked males could reproduce. Now he found that, to the Mothers, all creatures except themselves were male. Mothers were immobile and female. Mobiles were male. Eddie had been mobile. He was, therefore, a male.

He had approached this particular Mother during the mating season, that is, midway through raising a litter of young. She had scanned him as he came along the creekbanks at the valley bottom. When he was at the foot of the hill, she had detected his odor. It was new to her. The closest she could come to it in her memorybanks was that of a beast similar to him. From her description, he guessed it to be an ape. So she had released from her repertoire its rut stench. When he seemingly fell into the trap, she had caught him.

He was supposed to attack the conception-spot, that light gray swelling on the wall. After he had ripped and torn it enough to begin the mysterious workings of pregnancy, he would have been popped into her stomach-iris.

Fortunately, he had lacked the sharp beak, the fang, the claw. And she had received her own signals back from the panrad.

Eddie did not understand why it was necessary to use a mobile for mating. A Mother was intelligent enough to pick up a sharp stone and mangle the spot herself.

He was given to understand that conception would not start unless it was accompanied by a certain titillation of the nerves – a frenzy and its satisfaction. Why this emotional state was needed, Mother did not know.

Eddie tried to explain about such things as genes and chromosomes and why they had to be present in highly developed species.

Mother did not understand.

Eddie wondered if the number of slashes and rips in the spot corresponded to the number of young. Or if there were a large number of potentialities in the heredity-ribbons spread out under the conception-skin. And if the haphazard irritation and consequent stimulation of the genes paralleled the chance combining of genes in human male-female mating. Thus resulting in offspring with traits that were combinations of their parents.

Or did the inevitable devouring of the mobile after the act indicate more than an emotional and nutritional reflex? Did it hint that the mobile caught up scattered gene-nodes, like hard seeds, along with the torn skin, in its claws and tusks, that these genes survived the boiling in the stew-stomach, and were later passed out in the faeces? Where animals and birds picked them up in beak, tooth, or foot, and then, seized by other Mothers in this oblique rape, transmitted the heredity-carrying agents to the conception-spots while attacking them, the nodules being scraped off and implanted in the skin and blood of the swelling even as others were harvested? Later, the mobiles were eaten, digested, and ejected in the obscure but ingenious and never-ending cycle? Thus ensuring the continual, if haphazard, recombining of genes, chances for variations in offspring, opportunities for mutations, and so on?

Mother pulsed that she was nonplused.

Eddie gave up. He'd never know. After all, did it matter?

He decided not, and rose from his prone position to request water. She pursed up her iris and spouted a tepid quartful into his Thermos. He dropped in a pill, swished it around till it dissolved, and drank a reasonable facsimile of Old Red Star. He preferred the harsh and powerful rye, though he could have afforded the smoothest. Quick results were what he wanted. Taste didn't matter, as he disliked all liquor tastes. Thus he drank what the Skid Row bums drank and shuddered even as they did, renaming it Old Rotten Tar and cursing the fate that had brought them so low they had to gag such stuff down.

The rye glowed in his belly and spread quickly through his limbs and up to his head, chilled only by the increasing scarcity of the capsules. When he ran out – then what? It was at times like this that he most missed his mother.

Thinking about her brought a few large tears. He snuffled and drank some more and when the biggest of the Sluggos nudged him for a back-scratching, he gave it instead a shot of Old Red Star. A slug for Sluggo. Idly, he wondered what effect a taste for rye would have on the future of the race when these virgins became Mothers.

At that moment he was shaken by what seemed a lifesaving idea. These creatures could suck up the required elements from the earth and with them duplicate quite complex molecular structures. Provided, of course, they had a sample of the desired substance to brood over in some cryptic organ.

Well, what easier to do than give her one of the cherished capsules? One could become any number. Those, plus the abundance of water pumped up through hollow underground tendrils from the nearby creek, would give enough to make a master-distiller green!

He smacked his lips and was about to key her his request when what she was transmitting penetrated his mind.

Rather cattily, she remarked that her neighbor across the valley was putting on airs because she, too, held prisoner a communicating mobile.

VI

The Mothers had a society as hierarchical as table-protocol in Washington or peck-order in a barnyard. Prestige was what counted, and prestige was determined by the broadcasting power, the height of the eminence on which the Mother sat, which governed the extent of her radar-territory, and the abundance and novelty and wittiness of her gossip. The creature that had snapped Eddie up was a queen. She had precedence over thirty-odd of her kind; they all had to let her broadcast first, and none dared start pulsing until she quit. Then, the next in order began, and so on down the line. Any of them could be interrupted at any time by Number One, and if any of the lower echelon had something interesting to transmit, she could break in on the one then speaking and get permission from the queen to tell her tale.

Eddie knew this, but he could not listen in directly to the hilltop-gabble. The thick pseudo-granite shell barred him from that and made him dependent upon her womb-stalk for relayed information.

Now and then Mother opened the door and allowed her young to crawl out. There they practiced beaming and broadcasting at the Sluggos of the Mother across the valley. Occasionally that Mother deigned herself to pulse the young, and Eddie's keeper reciprocated to her offspring.

Turnabout.

The first time the children had inched through the exit-iris, Eddie had tried, Ulysses-like, to pass himself off as one of them and crawl out in the midst of the flock. Eyeless, but no Polyphemus, Mother had picked him out with her tentacles and hauled him back in.

It was following that incident that he had named her Polyphema.

He knew she had increased her own already powerful prestige tremendously by possession of that unique thing – a transmitting mobile. So much had her importance grown that the Mothers on the fringes of her area passed on the news to others. Before he had learned her language, the entire continent was hooked up. Polyphema had become a veritable gossip columnist; tens of thousands of hillcrouchers listened in eagerly to her accounts of her dealings with the walking paradox: a semantic male.

That had been fine. Then, very recently, the Mother across the valley had captured a similar creature. And in one bound she had become Number Two in the area and would, at the slightest weakness on Polyphema's part, wrest the top position away.

Eddie became wildly excited at the news. He had often daydreamed about his mother and wondered what she was doing. Curiously enough, he ended many of his fantasies with lip-mutterings, reproaching her almost audibly for having left him and for making no try to rescue him. When he became aware of his attitude, he was ashamed. Nevertheless, the sense of desertion colored his thoughts.

Now that he knew she was alive and had been caught, probably while trying to get him out, he rose from the lethargy that had lately been making him doze the clock around. He asked Polyphema if she would open the entrance so he could talk directly with the other captive. She said yes. Eager to listen in on a conversation between two mobiles, she was very cooperative. There would be a mountain of gossip in what they would have to say. The only thing that dented her joy was that the other Mother would also have access.

Then, remembering she was still Number One and would broadcast the details first, she trembled so with pride and ecstasy that Eddie felt the floor shaking.

Iris open, he walked through it and looked across the valley. The hillsides were still green, red, and yellow, as the plants on Baudelaire did not lose their leaves during winter. But a few white patches showed that winter had begun. Eddie shivered from the bite of cold air on his naked skin. Long ago he had taken off his clothes. The womb-warmth had made garments too uncomfortable; moreover, Eddie, being human, had had to get rid of waste products. And Polyphema, being a Mother, had had periodically to flush out the dirt with warm water from one of her stomachs. Every time the tracheae-vents exploded streams that swept the undesirahie elements out through her door-iris, Eddie had become soaked. When he abandoned dress, his clothes had gone floating out. Only by sitting on his pack did he keep it from a like fate.

Afterward, he and the Sluggos had been dried off by warm air pumped through the same vents and originating from the mighty battery of lungs. Eddie was comfortable enough – he'd always liked showers – but the loss of his garments had been one more thing that kept him from escaping. He would soon freeze to death outside unless he found the yacht quickly. And he wasn't sure he remembered the path back.

So now, when he stepped outside, he retreated a pace or two and let the warm air from Polyphema flow like a cloak from his shoulders.

Then he peered across the half-mile that separated him from his mother, but he could not see her. The twilight state and the dark of the unlit interior of her captor hid her.

He tapped in Morse, "Switch to the talkie, same frequency." Paula Fetts did so. She began asking him frantically if he were all right.

He replied he was fine.

"Have you missed me terribly, Son?"

"Oh, very much."

Even as he said this he wondered vaguely why his voice sounded so hollow. Despair at never again being able to see her, probably.

"I've almost gone crazy, Eddie. When you were caught I ran away as fast as I could. I had no idea what horrible monster it was that was attacking us. And then, halfway down the hill, I fell and broke my leg . . ."

"Oh, no, Mother!"

"Yes. But I managed to crawl back to the ship. And there, after I'd set it myself, I gave myself B.K. shots. Only, my system didn't react like it's supposed to. There are people that way, you know, and the healing took twice as long.

"But when I was able to walk, I got a gun and a box of dynamite. I was going to blow up what I thought was a kind of rock-fortress, an outpost for some kind of extee. I'd no idea of the true nature of these beasts. First, though, I decided to reconnoiter. I was going to spy on the boulder from across the valley. But I was trapped by this thing.

"Listen, Son. Before I'm cut off, let me tell you not to give up hope. I'll be out of here before long and over to rescue you."

"How?"

"If you remember, my lab kit holds a number of carcinogens for field work. Well, you know that sometimes a Mother's conception-spot when it is torn up during mating, instead of begetting young, goes into cancer – the opposite of pregnancy. I've injected a carcinogen into the spot and a beautiful carcinoma has developed. She'll be dead in a few days."

"Mom! You'll be buried in that rotting mass!"

"No. This creature has told me that when one of her species dies, a reflex opens the labia. That's to permit their young – if any – to escape. Listen, I'll – "

A tentacle coiled about him and pulled him back through the iris, which shut.

When he switched back to C.W., he heard, "Why didn't you communicate? What were you doing? Tell me! Tell me!"

Eddie told her. There was a silence that could only be interpreted as astonishment. After Mother had recovered her wits, she said, "From now on, you will talk to the other male through me."

Obviously, she envied and hated his ability to change wave-bands and, perhaps, had a struggle to accept the idea.

"Please," he persisted, not knowing how dangerous were the waters he was wading in, "please let me talk to my mother di – "

For the first time, he heard her stutter.

"Wha-wha-what? Your Mo-Mo-Mother?"

"Yes. Of course."

The floor heaved violently beneath his feet. He cried out and braced himself to keep from falling and then flashed on the light. The walls were pulsating like shaken jelly, and the vascular columns had turned from red and blue to gray. The entrance-iris sagged open, like a lax mouth, and the air cooled. He could feel the drop in temperature in her flesh with the soles of his feet.

It was some time before he caught on.

Polyphema was in a state of shock.

What might have happened had she stayed in it, he never knew. She might have died and thus forced him out into the winter before his mother could escape. If so, and he couldn't find the ship, he would die. Huddled in the warmest corner of the egg-shaped chamber, Eddie contemplated that idea and shivered to a degree for which the outside air couldn't account.

VII

However, Polyphema had her own method of recovery. It consisted of spewing out the contents of her stew-stomach, which had doubtless become filled with poisons draining out of her system from the blow. Her ejection of the stuff was the physical manifestation of the psychical catharsis. So furious was the flood that her foster son was almost swept out in the hot tide, but she, reacting instinctively, had coiled tentacles about him and the Sluggos. Then she followed the first upchucking by emptying her other three water-pouches, the second hot and the third lukewarm and the fourth, just filled, cold.

Eddie yelped as the icy water doused him.

Polyphema's irises closed again. The floor and walls gradually quit quaking; the temperature rose; and her veins and arteries regained their red and blue. She was well again. Or so she seemed.

But when, after waiting twenty-four hours, he cautiously approached the subject, he found she not only would not talk about it, she refused to acknowledge the existence of the other mobile.

Eddie, giving up hope of conversation, thought for quite a while. The only conclusion he could come to, and he was sure he'd grasped enough of her psychology to make it valid, was that the concept of a mobile female was utterly unacceptable.

Her world was split into two: mobile and her kind, the immobile. Mobile meant food and mating. Mobile meant – male. The Mothers were – female.

How the mobiles reproduced had probably never entered the hillcrouchers' minds. Their science and philosophy were on the instinctive body-level. Whether they had some notion of spontaneous generation or amoeba-like fission being responsible for the continued population of mobiles, or they'd just taken for granted they "growed," like Topsy, Eddie never found out. To them, they were female and the rest of the protoplasmic cosmos was male.

That was that. Any other idea was more than foul and obscene and blasphemous. It was – unthinkable.

Polyphema had received a deep trauma from his words. And though she seemed to have recovered, somewhere in those tons of unimaginably complicated flesh a bruise was buried. Like a hidden flower, dark purple, it bloomed, and the shadow it cast was one that cut off a certain memory, a certain tract, from the light of consciousness. That bruise-stained shadow covered that time and event which the Mother, for reasons unfathomable to the human being, found necessary to mark KEEP OFF.

Thus, though Eddie did not word it, he understood in the cells of his body, he felt and knew, as if his bones were prophesying and his brain did not hear, what came to pass.

Sixty-six hours later by the panrad clock, Polyphema's entrance-lips opened. Her tentacles darted out. They came back in, carrying his helpless and struggling mother.

Eddie, roused out of a doze, horrified, paralyzed, saw her toss her lab kit at him and heard an inarticulate cry from her. And saw her plunged, headforemost, into the stomach-iris.

Polyphema had taken the one sure way of burying the evidence.

Eddie lay face down, nose mashed against the warm and faintly throbbing flesh of the floor. Now and then his hands clutched spasmodically as if he were reaching for something that someone kept putting just within his reach and then moving away.

How long he was there he didn't know, for he never again looked at the clock.

Finally, in the darkness, he sat up and giggled inanely, "Mother always did make good stew."

That set him off. He leaned back on his hands and threw his head back and howled like a wolf under a full moon.

Polyphema, of course, was dead-deaf, but she could radar his posture, and her keen nostrils deduced from his body-scent that he was in terrible fear and anguish.

A tentacle glided out and gently enfolded him.

"What is the matter?" zzted the panrad.

He stuck his finger in the keyhole.

"I have lost my mother!"

"?".

"She's gone away, and she'll never come back."

"I don't understand. *Here I am.*"

Eddie quit weeping and cocked his head as if he were listening to some inner voice. He snuffled a few times and wiped away the tears, slowly disengaged the tentacle, patted it, walked over to his pack in a corner, and took out the bottle of Old Red Star capsules. One he popped into the Thermos; the other he gave to her with the request she duplicate it, if possible. Then he stretched out on his side, propped on one elbow like a Roman in his sensualities, sucked the rye through the nipple, and listened to a medley of Beethoven, Mussorgsky, Verdi, Strauss, Porter, Feinstein, and Waxworth.

So the time – if there were such a thing there – flowed around

Eddie. When he was tired of music or plays or books, he listened in on the area hookup. Hungry, he rose and walked – or often just crawled – to the stew-iris. Cans of rations lay in his pack; he had planned to eat those until he was sure that – what was it he was forbidden to eat? Poison? Something had been devoured by Polyphema and the Sluggos. But sometime during the music-rye orgy, he had forgotten. He now ate quite hungrily and with thought for nothing but the satisfaction of his wants.

Sometimes the door-iris opened, and Billy Greengrocer hopped in. Billy looked like a cross between a cricket and a kangaroo. He was the size of a collie, and he bore in a marsupialian pouch vegetables and fruit and nuts. These he extracted with shiny green, chitinous claws and gave to Mother in return for meals of stew. Happy symbiote, he chirruped merrily while his many-faceted eyes, revolving independently of each other, looked one at the Sluggos and the other at Eddie.

Eddie, on impulse, abandoned the 1000 kc band and roved the frequencies until he found that both Polyphema and Billy were emitting a 108 wave. That, apparently, was their natural signal. When Billy had his groceries to deliver, he broadcast. Polyphema, in turn, when she needed them, sent back to him. There was nothing intelligent on Billy's part; it was just his instinct to transmit. And the Mother was, aside from the "semantic" frequency, limited to that one band. But it worked out fine.

VIII

Everything was fine. What more could a man want? Free food, unlimited liquor, soft bed, air-conditioning, shower-baths, music, intellectual works (on the tape), interesting conversation (much of it was about him), privacy, and security.

If he had not already named her, he would have called her Mother Gratis.

Nor were creature comforts all. She had given him the answers to all his questions, all . . .

Except one.

That was never expressed vocally by him. Indeed, he would have been incapable of doing so. He was probably unaware that he had such a question.

But Polyphema voiced it one day when she asked him to do her a favor.

Eddie reacted as if outraged.

"One does not – ! One does not – !"

He choked, and then he thought, How ridiculous! She is not – and looked puzzled, and said, "But she is."

He rose and opened the lab kit. While he was looking for a scalpel, he came across the carcinogens. He threw them through the half-opened labia far out and down the hillside.

Then he turned and, scalpel in hand, leaped at the light gray swelling on the wall. And stopped, staring at it, while the instrument fell from his hand. And picked it up and stabbed feebly and did not even scratch the skin. And again let it drop.

"What is it? What is it?" crackled the panrad hanging from his wrist.

Suddenly, a heavy cloud of human odor – mansweat – was puffed in his face from a nearby vent.

"????"

And he stood, bent in a half-crouch, seemingly paralyzed. Until tentacles seized him in fury and dragged him toward the stomach-iris, yawning man-sized.

Eddie screamed and writhed and plunged his finger in the panrad and tapped, "All right! All right!"

And once back before the spot, he lunged with a sudden and wild joy; he slashed savagely; he yelled. "Take that! And that, P . . ." and the rest was lost in a mindless shout.

He did not stop cutting, and he might have gone on and on until he had quite excised the spot had not Polyphema interfered by dragging him toward her stomach-iris again. For ten seconds he hung there, helpless and sobbing with a mixture of fear and glory.

Polyphema's reflexes had almost overcome her brain. Fortunately, a cold spark of reason lit up a corner of the vast, dark, and hot chapel of her frenzy.

The convolutions leading to the steaming, meat-laden pouch closed and the foldings of flesh rearranged themselves. Eddie was suddenly hosed with warm water from what he called the "sanitation" stomach. The iris closed. He was put down. The scalpel was put back in the bag.

For a long time Mother seemed to be shaken by the thought of what she might have done to Eddie. She did not trust herself to transmit until her nerves were settled. When they were, she did not refer to his narrow escape. Nor did he.

He was happy. He felt as if a spring, tight-coiled against his bowels since he and his wife had parted, was now, for some reason, released. The dull vague pain of loss and discontent, the slight fever and cramp in his entrails, and the apathy that sometimes afflicted him, were gone. He felt fine.

Meanwhile, something akin to deep affection had been lighted, like a tiny candle under the drafty and overtowering roof of a cathedral. Mother's shell housed more than Eddie; it now curved over an emotion new to her kind. This was evident by the next event that filled him with terror.

For the wounds in the spot healed and the swelling increased into a large bag. Then the bag burst and ten mouse-sized Sluggos struck the floor. The impact had the same effect as a doctor spanking a newborn baby's bottom; they drew in their first breath with shock and pain; their uncontrolled and feeble pulses filled the ether with shapeless SOSs.

When Eddie was not talking with Polyphema or listening in or drinking or sleeping or eating or bathing or running off the tape, he played with the Sluggos. He was, in a sense, their father. Indeed, as they grew to hog-size, it was hard for their female parent to distinguish him from her young. As he seldom walked any more, and was often to be found on hands and knees in their midst, she could not scan him too well. Moreover, something in the heavywet air or in the diet had caused every hair on his body to drop off. He grew very fat. Generally speaking, he was one with the pale, soft, round, and bald offspring. A family likeness.

There was one difference. When the time came for the virgins to be expelled, Eddie crept to one end, whimpering, and stayed there until he was sure Mother was not going to thrust him out into the cold, dark, and hungry world.

The final crisis over, he came back to the center of the floor. The panic in his breast had died out, but his nerves were still quivering. He filled his Thermos and then listened for a while to his own tenor singing the "Sea Things" aria from his favorite opera, Gianelli's *Ancient Mariner*. Suddenly, he burst out and accompanied himself, finding himself thrilled as never before by the concluding words.

> *And from my neck so free*
> *The Albatross fell off, and sank*
> *Like lead into the sea.*

Afterward, voice silent but heart singing, he switched off the wire and cut in on Polyphema's broadcast.

Mother was having trouble. She could not precisely describe to the continent-wide hookup this new and almost inexpressible emotion she felt about the mobile. It was a concept her language was not prepared for. Nor was she helped any by the gallons of Old Red Star in her bloodstream.

Eddie sucked at the plastic nipple and nodded sympathetically and drowsily at her search for words. Presently, the Thermos rolled out of his hand.

He slept on his side, curled in a ball, knees on his chest and arms crossed, neck bent forward. Like the pilot room chronometer whose hands reversed after the crash, the clock of his body was ticking backward, ticking backward . . .

In the darkness, in the moistness, safe and warm, well fed, much loved.

Veritas

JAMES MORROW

James Morrow (1947–   ) is one of the leading literary satirists today, who chooses to work in the science fiction and fantasy mode. He is particularly notable for his willingness to take on large intellectual and metaphysical challenges, and for his accomplished prose style. He has often, and with some justice, been compared to Kurt Vonnegut, Jr. He is a moralist and an allegorist. He has never been comfortable with the conventions and literary habits of the SF field, and occasionally breaks them, sometimes to good effect. *The Encyclopedia of Science Fiction* says Morrow "has great difficulty giving credence to the artifices of fiction. This may be the price paid for passion and clarity of mind; and it may be a price worth paying." His major novels include *Only Begotten Daughter* (1990), in which God's daughter is born in New Jersey in the closing years of this century. *Towing Jehovah* (1994), in which God is dead and his corpse, about the size of a small city, is found floating in the Atlantic Ocean and must be towed to the Antarctic to be preserved; and its sequel, *Blameless in Abaddon* (1996), in which the corpse is sold.

"Veritas" is a satirical utopia. kathryn Cramer, in "Sincerity and Doom," her long essay on Morrow and science fiction, says, "Beyond defrocking utopia, the story hits you in the face with the uncomfortable relationship between Art (particularly fiction) and the Lie." She also suggests that this story may be in opposition to Orson Scott Card's popular Ender series of SF novels, which aspire to a utopia in which everyone tells the truth. Morrow addresses the question: Will the truth set you free?

Pigs have wings . . .

Rats chase cats . . .

Snow is hot . . .

Even now the old lies ring through the charred interior of my skull. I cannot speak them. I shall never be able to speak them – not without being dropped from here to hell in a bucket of pain. But they still inhabit me, just as they did on that momentous day when the city began to fall.

Grass is purple . . .

Two and two make five . . .

I awoke aggressively that morning, tearing the blankets away as if they were all that stood between myself and total alertness. Yawning vigorously, I charged into the shower, where warm water poured forth the instant the sensors detected me. I'd been with Overt Intelligence for over five years, and this was the first time I'd drawn an assignment that might be termed a plum. Spread your nostrils, Orville. Sniff her out. Sherry Urquist: some name! It sounded more like a mixed drink than like what she allegedly was, a purveyor of falsehoods, an enemy of the city, a member of the Dissemblage. The day could not begin soon enough.

The Dissemblage was like a deity. Not much tangible evidence, but people still had faith in it. Veritas, they reasoned, must harbor its normal share of those who believe the status quo is ipso facto wrong. Paradise will have its dissidents. The real question was not, Do subversives live in our city? The real question was, How do they tell lies without going mad?

My in-shower cablevision receiver winked on. Grimacing under the studio lights, our Assistant Secretary of Imperialism discussed Veritas's growing involvement in the Lethean civil war. "So far, over four thousand of our soldiers have died," the interviewer noted. "A senseless loss," the secretary conceded. "Our policy is impossible to justify on logical grounds, which is why we've started invoking national security and other shibboleths."

Have no illusions. The Sherry Urquist assignment did not fall into my lap because somebody at Overt Intelligence liked me. It was simply this: I am a roué. If any agent had a prayer of planting this particular Dissembler, that agent was me. It's the eyebrows that do it, great bushy extrusions suggesting a predatory mammal of unusual prowess, though I must admit they draw copious support from my straight nose and full, pillowlike lips. Am I handsome as a god? Metaphorically speaking, yes.

The picture tube had fogged over, so I activated the wiper. On the screen, a seedy-looking terrier scratched its fleas. "We seriously hope you'll consider Byproduct Brand Dog Food," said the voice-over. "Yes, we do tie up an enormous amount of protein that might conceivably be used in relieving worldwide starvation. However, if you'll consider the supposed benefits of dogs, we believe you may wish to patronize us."

On the surface, Ms. Urquist looked innocent enough. The dossier pegged her a writer, a former newspaper reporter with several popular self-help books under her belt. She had some other commodities under her belt, too, mainly fat, unless the accompanying OIA photos exaggerated. The case against her consisted primarily of rumor. Last week a neighbor, or possibly a sanitation engineer – the dossier contradicted itself on this point – had gone through her garbage. The yield was largely what you'd expect from someone in Ms. Urquist's profession: vodka bottles, outdated caffeine tablets, computer disk boxes, an early draft of her last bestseller, *How to Find a Certain Amount of Inner Peace Some of the Time If You Are Lucky*. Then came the kicker. The figurative smoking gun. The nonliteral forbidden fruit. At the bottom of the heap, the report asserted, lay "a torn and crumpled page" from what was "almost certainly a work of fiction."

Two hundred and thirty-nine words of it, to be precise. A story, a yarn, a legend. Something made up.

ART IS A LIE, the electric posters in Washington Park reminded us. Truth was beauty, but it simply didn't work the other way around.

I left the shower, which instantly shut itself down, and padded naked into my bedroom. Clothes per se were deceitful, of course, but this was the middle of winter, so I threw on some underwear and a gray suit with the lapels cut off – no integrity in freezing to death. My apartment was peeled to a core of rectitude. Most of my friends had curtains, wall hangings, and rugs, but not I. Why take chances with one's own sanity?

The odor of stale urine hit me as I rushed down the hall toward the lobby. How unfortunate that some people translated the ban on sexually segregated restrooms – PRIVACY IS A LIE, the posters reminded us – into a general fear of toilets. Hadn't they heard of public health? Public health was guileless.

Wrapped in dew, my Plymouth Adequate glistened on the far side of Probity Street. In the old days, I'd heard, you never knew for sure that your car would be unmolested, or even there, when you left it overnight. Twenty-eight degrees Fahrenheit, yet the thing started smoothly. I took off, zooming past the wonderfully functional cinderblocks that constituted city hall and heading toward the shopping district. My interview with Sherry Urquist was scheduled for ten, so I still had time to buy a gift for my nephew's brainburn party, which would happen around two-thirty that afternoon, right after he recovered. "Yes, I did take quite a few bribes during the Wheatstone Tariff affair," a thin-voiced senatorial candidate squeaked from out of my radio, "but you have to understand . . ." His voice faded, pushed aside by the pressure of my thoughts. Today my nephew would learn to hate a lie. Today we would rescue him from deceit's boundless sea, tossing out our lifelines and hauling him aboard the ark called Veritas. So to speak.

Money grows on trees . . .

Horses have six legs . . .

And suddenly you're a citizen.

What could life have been like before the cure? How did the mind tolerate a world where politicians misled, advertisers overstated, women wore makeup, and people professed love for each other at the nonliteral drop of a hat? I shivered. Did the Dissemblers know what they were playing with? How I relished the thought of advancing their doom, how badly I wanted Sherry Urquist's bulky ass hanging figuratively over the mantel of my fireplace.

I was armed for the fight. Two days earlier, the clever doctors down at the agency's Medical Division had done a bit of minor surgery, and now one of my seminal vesicles contained not only its usual cargo but also a microscopic radio transmitter. My imagination showed it to me, poised in the duct like the Greek infantry waiting for the wooden horse to arrive inside Troy.

What will they think of next?

The problem was the itch. Not a literal itch – the transmitter was one thousandth the size of a pinhead. My discomfort was philosophical. Did the beeper lie or didn't it? That was the question. It purported to be only itself, a thing, a microtransmitter, and yet some variation of duplicity seemed afoot here.

I didn't like it.

MOLLY'S RATHER EXPENSIVE TOY STORE, the sign said. Expensive: that was okay. Christmas came every year, but a kid got cured only once.

"My, aren't *you* a pretty fellow?" a female citizen sang out as I strode through the door. Marionettes dangled from the ceiling like victims of a mass lynching. Stuffed animals stampeded gently toward me from all directions.

"Your body is desirable enough," I said, casting a candid eye up and down the sales clerk. A tattered wool sweater molded itself around her emphatic breasts. Grimy white slacks encased her tight thighs. "But that nose," I added forlornly. A demanding business, citizenship.

"What brings you here?" She had one of those rare brands in which every digit is the same. 9999W, her forehead said. "You playboys are never responsible enough for parenthood."

"A fair assessment. You have kids?"

"I'm not married."

"It figures. My nephew's getting burned today."

"And you're waiting till the last minute to buy him a gift?"

"Right."

"Electric trains are popular. We sold eleven sets last week. Two were returned as defective."

She led me to a raised platform overrun by a kind of Veritas in miniature and kicked up the juice on the power-pack. A streamlined locomotive whisked a string of gleaming coaches past a factory belching an impressive facsimile of smoke.

"I wonder – is this thing a lie?" I opened the throttle, and the loco-motive nearly jumped the track.

"What do you mean?"

"It claims to be a train. But it's not."

"It claims to be a *model* of a train, which it is."

I eased the locomotive into the station. "Is your price as good as anybody else's?"

"You can get the same thing for six dollars less at Marquand's."

"Don't have the time. Can you gift-wrap it?"

"Not skillfully."

"Anything will do. I'm in a hurry."

The downtown traffic was light, the lull before lunch hour, so I arrived early at Sherry Urquist's Washington Park apartment, a crum-bling glass-and-steel ziggurat surmounted by a billboard that said, ASSUMING THAT GOD EXISTS, JESUS MAY HAVE BEEN HIS SON. I rode the elevator to the twentieth floor, exiting into a foyer where a handsome display of old military recruitment posters covered the fissured plaster. It was nice when somebody took the trouble to decorate a place. One could never use paint, of course. Paint was a lie. But with a little imagination . . .

I rang the bell. Nothing. Had I gotten the time wrong? CHANNEL

YOUR VIOLENT IMPULSES IN A SALUTARY DIRECTION, the nearest poster said. BECOME A MARINE.

The door swung open, and there stood our presumed subversive, a figurative cloud of confusion hovering about her heavy face, darkening her soft-boiled eyes and pulpy lips, features somewhat more attractive than the agency's photos suggested. "Did I wake you?" I asked. Her thermal pajamas barely managed to hold their contents in check, and I gave her an honest ogle. "I'm two minutes early."

"You woke me," she said. Frankness. A truth-teller, then? No, if there was one thing a Dissembler could do, it was deceive.

"Sorry," I said. I remembered the old documentary films of the oil paintings being burned. Rubens, that was the kind of sensual plumpness Sherry had going for her. Good old Peter Paul Rubens. Sneaking the Greek army inside Troy might be more entertaining than I'd thought.

She frowned, stretching her forehead brand into El Greco numerals. No one down at headquarters doubted its authenticity. Ditto her cerebroscan, voicegram, fingerprints . . .

A citizen, and yet she had written fiction.

Maybe.

"Who are you?" Her voice was wet and deep.

"Orville Prawn," I said. A permanent truth. "I work for *Tolerable Distortions*." A more transient one; the agency had arranged for the magazine to hire me – payroll, medical plan, pension fund, the works – for the next forty-eight hours. "Our interview . . ." I took out a pad and pencil.

Her pained expression seemed like the real thing. "Oh, damn, I'm *sorry*." She snapped her fingers. "It's on my calendar, but I've been up against a dozen deadlines, and I – "

"Forgot?"

"Yeah." She patted my forearm and guided me into her sparsely appointed living room. "Excuse me. These pajamas are probably driving you crazy."

"Not the pajamas per se."

She disappeared, returning shortly in a dingy yellow blouse and a red skirt circumscribed by a cracked and blistered leather belt.

The interview went well, which is to say she never asked whether I worked for Overt Intelligence, whereupon the whole show would have abruptly ended. She did not wish to discuss her old books, only her current project, a popular explanation of psychoanalytic theory to be called *From Misery to Unhappiness*. My shame was like a fever, threading my body with sharp, chilled wires. A toy train was not a lie, that clerk believed. Then maybe my little transmitter wasn't one either . . .

And maybe wishes were horses.

And maybe pigs had wings.

There was also this: Sherry Urquist was charming me. No doubt about it. A manufacturer of bestsellers is naturally stuffed with vapid thoughts and ready-made opinions, right? But instead I found myself sitting next to a first-rate mind (oh, the premier eroticism of intellect intersecting Rubens), one that could be severe with Freud for his lapses of integrity while still grasping his essential genius.

"You seem to love your work, Ms. Urquist."

"Writing is my life."

"Tell me, honestly – do you ever get any ideas for . . . fiction?"

"Fiction?"

"Short stories. Novels."

"That would be suicidal, wouldn't it?"

A blind alley, but I expected as much.

The diciest moment occurred when Sherry asked in which issue the interview would be published, and I replied that I didn't know. True enough, I told myself. Since the thing would never see print at all, it was accurate to profess ignorance of the corresponding date. Still, there came a sudden, mercifully brief surge of unease, the tides of an ancient nausea . . .

"All this sexual tension," I said, returning the pad and pencil to my suit jacket. "Alone with a sensually plump woman in her apartment, and your face is appealing too, now that I see the logic of it. You probably even have a bedroom. I can hardly stand it."

"Sensually plump, Mr. Prawn? I'm fat."

"Eye of the beholder."

"You'd have to go through a lot of beholders in my case."

"I find you very attractive." I did.

She raised her eyebrows, corrugating her brand. "It's only fair to give warning – you try anything funny, I'll knock you flat."

I cupped her left breast, full employment for any hand, and asked, "Is this funny?"

"On one level, your action offends me deeply." She brushed my knee. "I find it presumptuous, adolescent, and symptomatic of the worst kind of male arrogance." If faking her candor, she was certainly doing a good job. "On another level . . . well, you *are* quite handsome."

"An Adonis analogue."

We kissed. She went for my belt buckle. Reaching under her blouse, I sent her bra on a well-deserved sabbatical.

"Any sexually-transmittable diseases?" she asked.

"None." I stroked her dry, stringy hair. The Trojan horse was poised to change history. "You?"

"No," she said.

The truth? I couldn't know.

To bed, then. Time to plant her and, concomitantly, the transmitter. Nice work if you can get it. I slowed myself down with irrelevant thoughts – dogs can talk, rain is red – and left her a satisfied woman.

Full of Greeks.

I had promised Gloria that I wouldn't just come to the party, I would attend the burn as well. Normally both parents were present, but Dixon's tropological scum-bucket of a father couldn't be bothered. It will only take an hour, Gloria had told me. I'd rather not, I replied. He's your nephew, for Christ's sake, she pointed out. All right, I said.

Burn hospitals were in practically every neighborhood, but Gloria insisted on the best, Veteran's Shock Institute. Taking Dixon's badly wrapped gift from the back seat, I started toward the building, a smoke-stained pile of bricks overlooking the Thomas More Bridge. I paused. Business first. In theory the transmitter was part of Sherry now, forever fixed to her uterine wall. Snug as a bug in a . . . I went back to my Adequate and slid the sensorchart out of the dash. Yes, there she was, my fine Dissembler, a flashing red dot floating near Washington Park. I wished for greater detail, so I could know exactly when she was in her kitchen, her bathroom, her bedroom. Peeping Tom goes high tech. No matter. The thing worked. We could stalk her from here to Satan's backyard. As it were.

Inside the hospital, the day's collection of burn patients was everywhere, hugging dads, clinging tearfully to moms' skirts. I'd never understood this child-worship nonsense our culture wallows in, but, even so, the whole thing started getting to me. Every eight-year-old had to do it, of course, and the disease was certainly worse than the cure. Still . . .

I punished myself by biting my inner cheeks. Sympathy was fine, but sentimentality was wasteful. If I wanted to pity somebody, I should go up to Ward Six. Cystic fibrosis. Cancer. Am I going to die, Mommy?

Yes, dear.

Soon?

Yes, dear.

Will I see you in heaven?

Nobody knows.

I went to the front desk, where I learned that Dixon had been admitted half an hour earlier. "Room one-forty-five," said the nurse, a rotund man with a warty face. "The party will be in one-seventeen."

My nephew was already in the glass cubicle, dressed in a green smock and bound to the chair via leather thongs, one electrode strapped to his left arm, another to his right leg. Black wires trailed from the copper terminals like threads spun by a carnivorous spider. He welcomed me with a brave smile, and I held up his gift, hefting it to show that it had substance, it wasn't clothes. A nice enough kid – what I knew of him. Cute freckles, a wide, apple face. I remembered that for somebody his age, Dixon understood a great deal of symbolic logic.

A young, willowy, female nurse entered the cubicle and began snugging the helmet over his cranium. I gave Dixon a thumbs-up signal. (Soon it will be over, kid. Pigs have wings, rats chase cats, all of it.)

"Thanks for coming." Drifting out of her chair, Gloria took my arm. She was an attractive woman – same genes as me – but today she looked lousy: the anticipation, the fear. Sweat collected in her forehead brand. I had stopped proposing incest years ago. Not her game. "You're his favorite uncle, you know."

Uncle Orville. God help me. I was actually present when Gloria's marriage collapsed. The three of us were sitting in a Reconstituted Burgers when suddenly she said, I sometimes worry that you're having an affair – are you? And Tom said, yes, he was. And Gloria said, you fucker. And Tom said, right. And Gloria asked how many. And Tom said lots. And Gloria asked why. Did he do it to strengthen the marriage? And Tom said no, he just liked to screw other women.

Clipboard in hand, a small, homely doctor with MERRICK affixed to his tunic waddled into the room. "Good afternoon, folks," he said, his cheer a precarious mix of the genuine and the forced. "Bitter cold day out, huh? How are we doing here?"

"Do you care?" my sister asked.

"Hard to say." Dr. Merrick fanned me with his clipboard. "Friend of the family?"

"My brother," Gloria explained.

"He has halitosis. Glad there are two of you." Merrick smiled at the boy in the cubicle. "With just one, the kid'll sometimes go into clinical depression on us." He pressed the clipboard toward Gloria. "Informed consent, right?"

"They told me all the possibilities." She studied the clipboard. "Cardiac – "

"Cardiac arrest, cerebral hemorrhage, respiratory failure, kidney damage," Merrick recited.

"When was the last time anything like that happened?"

"They killed a little girl down at Mount Sinai on Tuesday. A freak thing, but now and then we really screw up."

After patting Dixon on his straw-colored bangs, the nurse left the cubicle and told Dr. Merrick that she was going to get some coffee.

"Be back in ten minutes," he ordered.

"Oh, but of course." Such sarcasm from one so young. "We mustn't have a *doctor* cleaning up, not when we can get some underpaid nurse to do it."

Gloria scrawled her signature.

The nurse edged out of the room.

Dr. Merrick went to the control panel.

And then it began. This bar mitzvah of the human conscience, this electroconvulsive rite of passage. A hallowed tradition. An unvarying text. Today I am a man . . . We believe in one Lord, Jesus Christ . . . I pledge allegiance to the flag . . . Why is this night different from all other nights . . . Dogs can talk . . . Pigs have wings. To tell you the truth, I was not really thinking about Dixon's cure just then. My mind was abloom with Sherry Urquist.

Merrick pushed a button, and PIGS HAVE WINGS appeared before my nephew on a lucite tachistoscope screen. "Can you hear me, lad?" the doctor called into the microphone.

Dixon opened his mouth, and a feeble "Yes" dribbled out of the loudspeaker.

"You see those words?" Merrick asked. The lurid red characters hovered in the air like lethargic butterflies.

"Y-yes."

"When I give the order, read them aloud. Okay?"

"Is it going to hurt?" my nephew quavered.

"It's going to hurt a lot. Will you read the words when I say so?"

"I'm scared. Do I have to?"

"You have to." Merrick rested a pudgy finger on the switch. "Now!"

"P-pigs have wings." The volts ripped through Dixon. He yelped and burst into tears. "But they don't," he moaned. "Pigs don't . . ."

My own burn flooded back. The pain. The anger.

"You're right, lad – they don't." Merrick gave the voltage regulator a subtle twist, and Gloria flinched. "You did reasonably well, boy," the doctor continued. "We're not yet disappointed in you." He handed the mike to Gloria.

"Oh, yes, Dixon," she said. "Keep up the awfully good work."

"It's not fair." Sweat speckled Dixon's forehead. "I want to go home."

As Gloria surrendered the mike, TWO AND TWO MAKE FIVE materialized.

"Now, lad! Read it!"

"T-t-two and two make . . . f-five." Lightning struck. The boy shuddered, howled. Blood rolled over his lower lip. During my own burn, I had practically bitten my tongue off. "I don't want this any more," he wailed.

"It's not a choice, lad."

"Two and two make *four*." Tears threaded Dixon's freckles together. "Please stop hurting me."

"Four. Right. Smart lad." Merrick cranked up the voltage. "Ready, Dixon? Here it comes."

HORSES HAVE SIX LEGS.

"Why do I have to do this? *Why?*"

"Everybody does it. All your friends."

"H-h-horses have . . . have . . . They have *four* legs, Dr. Merrick."

"Read the words, Dixon!"

"I hate you! I hate all of you!"

"Dixon!"

He raced through it. Zap. Two hundred volts. The boy began to cough and retch, and a string of white mucus shot from his mouth like a lizard's tongue. Nothing followed: burn patients fasted for sixteen hours prior to therapy.

"Too much!" cried Gloria. "Isn't that too much?"

"The goal is five hundred," said Merrick. "It's all been worked out. You want the treatment to take, don't you?"

"Mommy! Where's my Mommy?"

Gloria tore the mike away. "Right here, dear!"

"Mommy, make them stop!"

"I can't, dear. You must try to be brave."

The fourth lie appeared. Merrick upped the voltage. "Read it, lad!"

"No!"

"Read it!"

"Uncle Orville! I want Uncle Orville!"

My throat constricted, my stomach went sour. Uncle: such a strange sound. I really was one, wasn't I? "You're doing pretty swell, Dixon," I said, taking the mike. "I think you'll like your present."

"Uncle Orville, I want to go home!"

"I got you a fine toy."

"What is it?"

"Here's a hint. It has – "

"Dixon!" Merrick grabbed the mike. "Dixon, if you don't do this, you'll never get well. They'll take you away from your mother." A threat, but wholly accurate. "Understand? They'll take you away."

Dixon balled his face into a mass of wrinkles. "Grass!" he screamed, spitting blood. "Is!" he persisted. "Purple!" He jerked like a gaffed flounder, spasm after spasm. A broad urine stain blossomed on his crotch, and despite the obligatory enema a brown fluid dripped from the hem of his smock.

"Excellent!" Merrick increased the punishment to four hundred volts. "Your cure's in sight, lad!"

"No! Please! Please! Enough!" Sweat encased Dixon's face. Foam leaked from his mouth.

"You're almost halfway there!"

"Please!"

The war continued, five more pain-tipped rockets shooting through Dixon's nerves and veins, detonating inside his mind. He asserted that rats chase cats. He lied about money, saying that it grew on trees. Worms taste like honey, he said. Snow is hot. Rain is red.

He fainted just as the final lie arrived. Even before Gloria could scream, Merrick was inside the cubicle, checking the boy's heartbeat. A begrudging admiration seeped through me. The doctor had a job, and he did it.

A single dose of smelling salts brought Dixon around.

Guiding the boy's face toward the screen, Merrick turned to me. "Ready with the switch?"

"Huh? You want me – " Ridiculous.

"Let's just get it over with. Hit the switch when I tell you."

"I'd rather not." But already my finger rested on the damn thing. Doctor's orders.

"Read, Dixon," muttered Merrick.

"I c-can't."

"One more, Dixon. Just one more and you'll be a citizen."

Blood and spittle mingled on Dixon's chin. "You all hate me! Mommy hates me!"

"I love you as much as myself," said Gloria, leaning over my shoulder. "You're going to have a wonderful party. Almost certainly."

"Really?"

"Highly likely."

"Presumably wonderful," I said. The switch burned my finger. "I love you too."

"Dogs can talk," said Dixon.

And it truly was a wonderful party. All four of Dixon's grandparents showed up, along with his teacher and twelve of his friends, half of whom had been cured in recent months, one on the previous day. Dixon marched around Room 117 displaying the evidence of his burn like war medals. The brand, of course – performed under local anesthesia immediately after his cure – plus copies of his initial cerebroscan, voicegram, and fingerprint set.

Brand, scan, gram, prints: Sherry Urquist's had all been in perfect order. She had definitely been burned. And yet there was fiction in her garbage.

The gift-opening ceremony contained one bleak moment. Pulling the train from its wrapping, Dixon blanched, garroted by panic, and Gloria had to rush him into the bathroom, where he spent several minutes throwing up. I felt like a fool. To a boy who's just been through a brainburn, an electric train has gruesome connotations.

"Thanks for coming," said Gloria. She meant it.

"I *do* like my present," Dixon averred. "A freight train would have been nicer," he added. A citizen now.

I apologized for leaving early. A big case, I explained. Very hot, very political. "Good-bye, Uncle Orville."

Uncle. Great stuff.

I spent the rest of the day tracking my adorable Dissembler, never letting her get more than a mile from me or closer than two blocks. What agonizing hopes that dot on the map inspired, what rampant expectations. With each flash my longing intensified. Oh, Sherry, Sherry, you pulsing red angel, you stroboscope of my desire. No mere adolescent infatuation this. I dared to speak its name. "Neurotic obsession," I gushed, kissing the dot as it crossed Aquinas Avenue. "Mixed with bald romantic fantasy ·and lust," I added. The radio shouted at me: a hot-blooded evangelist no less enraptured than I. "Does faith tempt you, my friends? Fear not! Look into your metaphoric hearts, and you will discover how subconscious human needs project themselves onto putative revelations!"

For someone facing a wide variety of deadlines, my quarry didn't push herself particularly hard. Sherry spent the hour from four to five at the Museum of Secondary Fossil Finds. From five to six she did the Imprisoned Animals Garden. From six to seven she treated herself to dinner at Danny's Digestibles, after which she went down to the waterfront.

I cruised along Third Street, twenty yards from the Pathogen River. This was the city's frankest district, a gray mass of warehouses and abandoned stores jammed together like dead cells waiting to be sloughed off. Sherry walked slowly, aimlessly, as if . . . could it be? Yes, damn, as if arm-in-arm with another person, as if meshing her movements with those of a second, intertwined body. Probably she had met the guy at Danny's, a conceited pile of muscles named Guido or something, and now they were having a cozy stroll along the Pathogen. I pressed the dot, as if to draw Sherry away. What if she spent the night in another apartment? That would pretty much cinch it. I wondered how their passion would register. I pictured the dot going wild, love's red fibrillation.

After pausing for several seconds on the bank, the dot suddenly began prancing across the river. Odd. I fixed on the map. The Saint Joan Tunnel was half a mile away, the Thomas More Bridge even farther. I doubted that she was swimming – not in this weather, and not in the Pathogen, where the diseases of the future were born. Flying, then? The dot moved too slowly to signify an airplane. A hot-air balloon? Probably she was in a boat. Sherry and Guido, off on a romantic cruise.

I hung a left on Beach Street and sped down to the docks. Moonlight coated the Pathogen, settling into the waves, figuratively bronzing a lone, swiftly moving tugboat. I checked the map. The dot placed Sherry at least ten yards from the tug, in the exact middle of the river and heading for the opposite shore. I studied her presumed location. Nothing. Submerged, then? I knew she hadn't committed suicide; the dot's progress was too resolute. Was she in scuba gear?

I abandoned the car and attempted to find where she had entered the water, a quest that took me down concrete steps to a pier hemmed by pylons smeared with gull dung. Jagged odors shot from the dead and rotting river; water lapped over the landing with a harsh sucking sound, as if a pride of invisible lions was drinking here. My gaze settled on a metal grate, barred like the ribcage of some promethean robot. It seemed slightly askew . . . Oh, great, Orville, let's go traipsing through the sewers, with rats nipping at our heels and slugs the size of bagels falling on our shoulders. Terrific idea.

The grate yielded readily to my reluctant hands. Had she truly gone down there? Should I follow? A demented notion, but duty called, using its shrillest voice, and, besides, this was Sherry Urquist, this was irrational need. I secured a flashlight from the car and proceeded down the ladder. It was like entering a lung. Steamy, warm. The flashlight blazed through the blackness. A weapon, I decided. Look out, all you rats and slugs. Make way. Here comes Orville Prawn, the fastest flashlight in Veritas.

I moved through a multilayered maze of soggy holes and dripping catacombs. So many ways to descend: ladders, sloping tunnels, crooked little stairways – I used them all, soon moving beyond the riverbed into other territories, places not on the OIA map.

All around me Veritas's guts were spread: its concrete intestines, gushing lead veins, buzzing nerves of steel and gutta-percha. Much to my surprise, the city even had its parasites – shacks of corrugated tin leaned against the wet brick walls, sucking secretly on the power cables and water mains. This would not do. No, to live below Veritas like this, appropriating its juices, was little more than piracy. Overt Intelligence would hear of it.

My astonishment deepened as I advanced. I could understand a few hobos setting up a shantytown down here, but how might I explain these odd chunks of civilization? These blazing streetlamps, these freshly painted picket fences, these tidy grids of rose bushes, these fountains with their stone dolphins spewing water? Paint, flowers, sculpture: so many lies in one place! Peel back the streets of any city and do you find its warped reflection, its doppelgänger mirrored in distorting glass? Or did Veritas alone harbor such anarchy, this tumor spreading beneath her unsuspecting flesh?

A sleek white cat shot out of the rose bushes and disappeared down an open manhole. At first I thought that its pursuer was a dog, but no. Wrong shape. And that tail.

The shudder began in my lower spine and expanded.

A rat.

A rat the size of an armadillo.

Chasing a cat.

I moved on. Vegetable gardens now. Two bright yellow privies. Cottages defaced with gardenia plots and strings of clematis scurrying up trellises. A building that looked suspiciously like a chapel. A park of some kind, with flagstone paths and a duck pond. Ruddy puffs of vapor bumped against the treetops.

Rain is red . . .

I entered the park.

A pig glided over my head like a miniature dirigible, wheeling across the sky on cherub wings. At first I assumed it was a machine, but its squeal was disconcertingly organic.

"You!"

A low, liquid voice. I dropped my gaze.

Sherry shared the bench with an enormous dog, some grotesque variation on the malamute, his chin snugged into her lap. "You!" she said again, erecting the word like a barrier, a spiked vocable stopping my approach. The dog lifted his head and growled.

"Correct," I said, stock still.

"You followed me?"

"I cannot tell a lie." I examined the nearest tree. No fruit, of course, only worms and paper money.

"Dirty spy."

"Half true. I am not dirty."

She wore a buttercup dress, decorated with lace. Her thick braid lay on her shoulder like a loaf of challah. Her eyes had become cartoons of themselves, starkly outlined and richly shaded. "If you try to return" – she patted the malamute – "Max will eat you alive."

"You bet your sweet ass," said the dog.

She massaged Max's head, as if searching for the trigger that would release his attack. "I expected better of you, Mr. Prawn."

We were in a contest. Who could act the more betrayed, the more disgusted? "I'd always assumed the Dissemblage was just a group." Spit dripped off my words. "I didn't know it was . . . all this."

"Two cities," muttered Sherry, launching her index finger upward. "Truth above, dignity below." The finger descended. Her nails, I noticed, were a fluorescent green.

"Her father built it," explained the dog.

"His life's work," added Sherry.

"Are there many of you?" I asked.

"I'm the first to reach adulthood," said Sherry.

"The prototype liar?"

Her sneer evolved into a grin. "Others are hatching."

"How can you betray your city like this?" I drilled her with my stare. "Veritas, who nurtured you, suckled you?"

"Shall I kill him now?" asked the dog.

Sherry chucked Max under the chin, told him to be patient. "Veritas did not suckle me." Her gesture encompassed the entire park and, by extension, the whole of Veritas's twisted double. "*This* was my cradle – my nursery." She took a lipstick from her purse. "It's not hard to make a lie. The money trees are props. The rats and pigs trace to avant-garde microbiology."

"All I needed were vocal cords," said the dog.

She began touching up her lips. "Thanks to my father, I reached my eighth birthday knowing that pigs had wings, that snow was hot, that two and two equaled five, that worms tasted like honey . . . all of it. So when my burn came – "

"You were incurable," I said. "You walked away from the hospital ready to swindle and cheat and – "

"Write fiction. Four novels so far. Maybe you'd like to read them. You might be a bureaucratic drudge, but I'm fond of you, Orville."

"How do I know you're telling the truth?"

"You don't. And when my cadre takes over and the burn ends – it won't be hard, we'll lie our way to the top – when that happens, you won't know when *anybody's* telling the truth."

"Right," said the dog, leaping off the bench.

"Truth is beauty," I said.

Sherry winced. "My father did not mind telling the truth." Here she became an actress, that consummate species of liar, dragging out her lines. "But he hated his inability to do otherwise. Honesty without choice, he said, is slavery with a smile."

A glorious adolescent girl rode through the park astride a six-legged horse, her skin dark despite her troglodytic upbringing, her eyes alive with deceit. The *gift* of deceit, as Sherry would have it. I wondered whether Dixon was playing with his electric train just then. Probably not. Past his bedtime. I kept envisioning his cerebrum, brocaded with necessary scars.

Sherry patted the spot where the dog had been, and I sat down cautiously. "Care for one?" she asked, plucking a worm off a money tree.

"No."

"Go ahead. Try it."

"Well . . ."

"Open your mouth and close your eyes."

The creature wriggled on my tongue, and I bit down. Pure honey. Sweet, smooth, but I did not enjoy it.

Truth above, dignity below. My index finger throbbed, prickly with that irrevocable little tug of the switch in Room 145. Five hundred volts was a lot, but what was the alternative? To restore the age of thievery and fraud?

History has it I joined Sherry's city that very night. A lie, but what do you expect – all the books are written by Dissemblers. True, sometime before dawn I did push my car into the river, the better to elude Overt Intelligence. But fully a week went by before I told Sherry about her internal transmitter. She was furious. She vowed to have the thing cut out. Go ahead, I told her, do it – but don't expect my blessing. That's another thing the historians got wrong. They say I paid for the surgery.

Call me a traitor. Call me a coward. Call me love's captive. I have called myself all these things. But – really – I did not join Sherry's city that night. That night I merely sat on a park bench staring into her exotically adorned eyes, fixing on her bright lips, holding her fluorescent fingertips.

"I want to believe whatever you tell me," I said.

"Then you'll need to have faith in me," she said.

"It's raining," noted the dog, and then he launched into a talking-dog joke.

"My cottage is over there." Sherry replaced her lipstick in her purse. She tossed her wondrous braid over her shoulder.

We rose and started across the park, hand in hand, lost in the sweet uncertainty of the moment, oblivious to the chattering dog and the lashing wind and bright red rain dancing on the purple grass.

Enchanted Village

A. E. VAN VOGT

A. E. van Vogt (1912–   ) is one of the giants of the Golden Age of science fiction, specifically, the flowering of modern science fiction in John W. Campbell, Jr.'s magazine, *Astounding*, between 1939 and 1949. A Canadian writer, he moved to the U.S. after World War II and spent the 1950s deeply involved in his friend L. Ron Hubbard's Dianetics (later Scientology). He is one of the most influential SF writers of that period, in some ways the dominant SF writer of the 1940s. His novel, *Slan* (1946, appearing first as a serial in *Astounding* in 1940) metaphorically repre- sented the previously unarticulated attitude in the SF field that SF readers and writers were somehow the next stage in human evolution. "Fans are Slans" became a motto of 1940s science fiction, and van Vogt was a hero of the evolution and his influence on the next generation of SF writers, including Philip José Farmer, Philip K. Dick, and Charles Harness, was profound. *The World of Null-A* (1948) was the first work of modern science fiction to be published by a respectable hardcover house and it was a worldwide success. His fiction is filled with powerful imagery and strange ideas, often presented in dreamlike sequence, not a rational flow. His crit- ical reputation was demolished in the U.S. in the the 1950s by Damon Knight's essay, "Cosmic Jerrybuilder: A. E. van Vogt." But van Vogt's popularity did not decrease for decades. In the 1980s Leslie A. Fiedler (in his essay "The Criticism of Science Fiction," 1983) put it succinctly: "Any bright high school sophomore can identify all the things that are wrong about van Vogt . . . But the challenge to criticism which pretends to do justice to science fiction is to say what is right about him: to identify his mythopoeic power, his ability to evoke primordial images, his gift for redeeming the marvelous in a world in which technology has preempted the province of magic and God is dead."

This story is one of his most memorable. Ray Bradbury's later stories of the desert planet Mars, with its hidden survivals of a once-great technological civilization, are strikingly similar in atmosphere. This is van Vogt's "Martian chronicle." In this case it is easy to understand van Vogt's appeal.

"Explorers of a new frontier" they had been called before they left for Mars.

For a while, after the ship crashed into a Martian desert, killing all on board except – miraculously – this one man, Bill Jenner spat the words occasionally into the constant, sand-laden wind. He despised himself for the pride he had felt when he first heard them.

His fury faded with each mile that he walked, and his black grief for his friends became a gray ache. Slowly he realized that he had made a ruinous misjudgment.

He had underestimated the speed at which the rocketship had been traveling. He'd guessed that he would have to walk three hundred miles to reach the shallow, polar sea he and the others had observed as they glided in from outer space. Actually, the ship must have flashed an immensely greater distance before it hurtled down out of control.

The days stretched behind him, seemingly as numberless as the hot, red, alien sand that scorched through his tattered clothes. A huge scarecrow of a man, he kept moving across the endless, arid waste – he would not give up.

By the time he came to the mountain, his food had long been gone. Of his four water bags, only one remained, and that was so close to being empty that he merely wet his cracked lips and swollen tongue whenever his thirst became unbearable.

Jenner climbed high before he realized that it was not just another dune that had barred his way. He paused, and as he gazed up at the mountain that towered above him, he cringed a little. For an instant he felt the hopelessness of this mad race he was making to nowhere – but he reached the top. He saw that below him was a depression surrounded by hills as high as, or higher than, the one on which he stood. Nestled in the valley they made was a village.

He could see trees and the marble floor of a courtyard. A score of buildings was clustered around what seemed to be a central square. They were mostly low-constructed, but there were four towers pointing gracefully into the sky. They shone in the sunlight with a marble luster.

Faintly, there came to Jenner's ears a thin, high-pitched whistling sound. It rose, fell, faded completely, then came up again clearly and unpleasantly. Even as Jenner ran toward it, the noise grated on his ears, eerie and unnatural.

He kept slipping on smooth rock, and bruised himself when he fell. He rolled halfway down into the valley. The buildings remained new and bright when seen from nearby. Their walls flashed with reflections. On every side was vegetation – reddish-green shrubbery, yellow-green trees laden with purple and red fruit.

With ravenous intent, Jenner headed for the nearest fruit tree. Close up, the tree looked dry and brittle. The large red fruit he tore from the lowest branch, however, was plump and juicy.

As he lifted it to his mouth, he remembered that he had been warned during his training period to taste nothing on Mars until it had been chemically examined. But that was meaningless advice to a man whose only chemical equipment was in his own body.

Nevertheless, the possibility of danger made him cautious. He took his first bite gingerly. It was bitter to his tongue, and he spat it out hastily. Some of the juice which remained in his mouth seared his gums. He felt the fire on it, and he reeled from nausea. His muscles began to jerk, and he lay down on the marble to keep himself from falling. After what seemed like hours to Jenner, the awful trembling finally went out of his body and he could see again. He looked up despisingly at the tree.

The pain finally left him, and slowly he relaxed. A soft breeze rustled the dry leaves. Nearby trees took up that gentle clamor, and it struck Jenner that the wind here in the valley was only a whisper of what it had been on the flat desert beyond the mountain.

There was no other sound now. Jenner abruptly remembered the high-pitched, ever-changing whistle he had heard. He lay very still, listening intently, but there was only the rustling of the leaves. The noisy shrilling had stopped. He wondered if it had been an alarm, to warn the villagers of his approach.

Anxiously he climbed to his feet and fumbled for his gun. A sense of disaster shocked through him. It wasn't there. His mind was a blank, and then he vaguely recalled that he had first missed the weapon more than a week before. He looked around him uneasily, but there was not a sign of creature life. He braced himself. He couldn't leave, as there was nowhere to go. If necessary, he would fight to the death to remain in the village.

Carefully Jenner took a sip from his water bag, moistening his cracked lips and his swollen tongue. Then he replaced the cap and started through a double line of trees toward the nearest building. He made a wide circle to observe it from several vantage points. On one side a low, broad archway opened into the interior. Through it, he could dimly make out the polished gleam of a marble floor.

Jenner explored the buildings from the outside, always keeping a respectful distance between him and any of the entrances. He saw no sign of animal life. He reached the far side of the marble platform on which the village was built, and turned back decisively. It was time to explore interiors.

He chose one of the four tower buildings. As he came within a dozen feet of it, he saw that he would have to stoop low to get inside.

Momentarily, the implications of that stopped him. These buildings had been constructed for a life form that must be very different from human beings.

He went forward again, bent down, and entered reluctantly, every muscle tensed.

He found himself in a room without furniture. However, there were several low marble fences projecting from one marble wall. They formed what looked like a group of four wide, low stalls. Each stall had an open trough carved out of the floor.

The second chamber was fitted with four inclined planes of marble, each of which slanted up to a dais. Altogether there were four rooms on the lower floor. From one of them a circular ramp mounted up, apparently to a tower room.

Jenner didn't investigate the upstairs. The earlier fear that he would find alien life was yielding to the deadly conviction that he wouldn't. No life meant no food or chance of getting any. In frantic haste he hurried from building to building, peering into the silent rooms, pausing now and then to shout hoarsely.

Finally there was no doubt. He was alone in a deserted village on a lifeless planet, without food, without water – except for the pitiful supply in his bag – and without hope.

He was in the fourth and smallest room of one of the tower buildings when he realized that he had come to the end of his search. The room had a single stall jutting out from one wall. Jenner lay down wearily in it. He must have fallen asleep instantly.

When he awoke he became aware of two things, one right after the other. The first realization occurred before he opened his eyes – the whistling sound was back; high and shrill, it wavered at the threshold of audibility.

The other was that a fine spray of liquid was being directed down at him from the ceiling. It had an odor, of which technician Jenner took a single whiff. Quickly he scrambled out of the room, coughing, tears in his eyes, his face already burning from chemical reaction.

He snatched his handkerchief and hastily wiped the exposed parts of his body and face.

He reached the outside and there paused, striving to understand what had happened.

The village seemed unchanged.

Leaves trembled in a gentle breeze. The sun was poised on a mountain peak. Jenner guessed from its position that it was morning again and that he had slept at least a dozen hours. The glaring white light suffused the valley. Half hidden by trees and shrubbery, the buildings flashed and shimmered.

He seemed to be in an oasis in a vast desert. It was an oasis, all right, Jenner reflected grimly, but not for a human being. For him, with its poisonous fruit, it was more like a tantalizing mirage.

He went back inside the building and cautiously peered into the room where he had slept. The spray of gas had stopped, not a bit of odor lingered, and the air was fresh and clean.

He edged over the threshold, half inclined to make a test. He had a picture in his mind of a long-dead Martian creature lazing on the floor in the stall while a soothing chemical sprayed down on its body. The fact that the chemical was deadly to human beings merely emphasized how alien to man was the life that had spawned on Mars. But there seemed little doubt of the reason for the gas. The creature was accustomed to taking a morning shower.

Inside the "bathroom," Jenner eased himself feet first into the stall. As his hips came level with the stall entrance, the solid ceiling sprayed a jet of yellowish gas straight down upon his legs. Hastily Jenner pulled himself clear of the stall. The gas stopped as suddenly as it had started.

He tried it again, to make sure it was merely an automatic process. It turned on, then shut off.

Jenner's thirst-puffed lips parted with excitement. He thought, "If there can be one automatic process, there may be others."

Breathing heavily, he raced into the outer room. Carefully he shoved his legs into one of the two stalls. The moment his hips were in, a steaming gruel filled the trough beside the wall.

He stared at the greasy-looking stuff with a horrified fascination –

food – and drink. He remembered the poison fruit and felt repelled, but he forced himself to bend down and put his finger into the hot, wet substance. He brought it up, dripping, to his mouth.

It tasted flat and pulpy, like boiled wood fiber. It trickled viscously into his throat. His eyes began to water and his lips drew back convulsively. He realized he was going to be sick, and ran for the outer door – but didn't quite make it.

When he finally got outside, he felt limp and unutterably listless. In that depressed state of mind, he grew aware again of the shrill sound.

He felt amazed that he could have ignored its rasping even for a few minutes. Sharply he glanced about, trying to determine its source, but it seemed to have none. Whenever he approached a point where it appeared to be loudest, then it would fade or shift, perhaps to the far side of the village.

He tried to imagine what an alien culture would want with a mind-shattering noise – although, of course, it would not necessarily have been unpleasant to them.

He stopped and snapped his fingers as a wild but nevertheless plausible notion entered his mind. Could this be music?

He toyed with the idea, trying to visualize the village as it had been long ago. Here a music-loving people had possibly gone about their daily tasks to the accompaniment of what was to them beautiful strains of melody.

The hideous whistling went on and on, waxing and waning. Jenner tried to put buildings between himself and the sound. He sought refuge in various rooms, hoping that at least one would be soundproof. None were. The whistle followed him wherever he went.

He retreated into the desert, and had to climb halfway up one of the slopes before the noise was low enough not to disturb him. Finally, breathless but immeasurably relieved, he sank down on the sand and thought blankly:

What now?

The scene that spread before him had in it qualities of both heaven and hell. It was all too familiar now – the red sands, the stony dunes, the small, alien village promising so much and fulfilling so little.

Jenner looked down at it with his feverish eyes and ran his parched tongue over his cracked, dry lips. He knew that he was a dead man unless he could alter the automatic food-making machines that must be hidden somewhere in the walls and under the floors of the buildings.

In ancient days, a remnant of Martian civilization had survived here in this village. The inhabitants had died off, but the village lived on, keeping itself clean of sand, able to provide refuge for any Martian who might come along. But there were no Martians. There was only Bill Jenner, pilot of the first rocketship ever to land on Mars.

He had to make the village turn out food and drink that he could take. Without tools, except his hands, with scarcely any knowledge of chemistry, he must force it to change its habits.

Tensely he hefted his water bag. He took another sip and fought the same grim fight to prevent himself from guzzling it down to the last drop. And, when he had won the battle once more, he stood up and started down the slope.

He could last, he estimated, not more than three days. In that time he must conquer the village.

He was already among the trees when it suddenly struck him that the music had stopped. Relieved, he bent over a small shrub, took a good firm hold of it – and pulled.

It came up easily, and there was a slab of marble attached to it. Jenner stared at it, noting with surprise that he had been mistaken in thinking the stalk came up through a hole in the marble. It was merely stuck to the surface. Then he noticed something else – the shrub had no roots. Almost instinctively, Jenner looked down at the spot from which he had torn the slab of marble along with the plant. There was sand there.

He dropped the shrub, slipped to his knees, and plunged his fingers into the sand. Loose sand trickled through them. He reached deep, using all his strength to force his arm and hand down; sand – nothing but sand.

He stood up and frantically tore up another shrub. It also came up easily, bringing with it a slab of marble. It had no roots, and where it had been was sand.

With a kind of mindless disbelief, Jenner rushed over to a fruit tree and shoved at it. There was a momentary resistance, and then the marble on which it stood split and lifted slowly into the air. The tree fell over with a swish and a crackle as its dry branches and leaves broke and crumbled into a thousand pieces. Underneath where it had been was sand.

Sand everywhere. A city built on sand. Mars, planet of sand. That was not completely true, of course. Seasonal vegetation had been observed near the polar ice caps. All but the hardiest of it died with the coming of summer. It had been intended that the rocketship land near one of those shallow, tideless seas.

By coming down out of control, the ship had wrecked more than itself. It had wrecked the chances for life of the only survivor of the voyage.

Jenner came slowly out of his daze. He had a thought then. He picked up one of the shrubs he had already torn loose, braced his foot against the marble to which it was attached, and tugged, gently at first, then with increasing strength.

It came loose finally, but there was no doubt that the two were part of a whole. The shrub was growing out of the marble.

Marble? Jenner knelt beside one of the holes from which he had torn a slab, and bent over an adjoining section. It was quite porous – calciferous rock, most likely, but not true marble at all. As he reached toward it, intending to break off a piece, it changed color. Astounded, Jenner drew back. Around the break, the stone was turning a bright orange-yellow. He studied it uncertainly, then tentatively he touched it.

It was as if he had dipped his fingers into searing acid. There was a sharp, biting, burning pain. With a gasp, Jenner jerked his hand clear.

The continuing anguish made him feel faint. He swayed and moaned, clutching the bruised members to his body. When the agony finally faded and he could look at the injury, he saw that the skin had peeled and that blood blisters had formed already. Grimly Jenner looked down at the break in the stone. The edges remained bright orange-yellow.

The village was alert, ready to defend itself from further attacks.

Suddenly weary, he crawled into the shade of a tree. There was only one possible conclusion to draw from what had happened, and it almost defied common sense. This lonely village was alive.

As he lay there, Jenner tried to imagine a great mass of living substance growing into the shape of buildings, adjusting itself to suit another life form, accepting the role of servant in the widest meaning of the term.

If it would serve one race, why not another? If it could adjust to Martians, why not to human beings?

There would be difficulties, of course. He guessed wearily that essential elements would not be available. The oxygen for water could come from the air . . . thousands of compounds could be made from sand . . . Though it meant death if he failed to find a solution, he fell asleep even as he started to think about what they might be.

When he awoke it was quite dark.

Jenner climbed heavily to his feet. There was a drag to his muscles that alarmed him. He wet his mouth from his water bag and staggered toward the entrance of the nearest building. Except for the scraping of his shoes on the "marble," the silence was intense.

He stopped short, listened, and looked. The wind had died away. He couldn't see the mountains that rimmed the valley, but the buildings were still dimly visible, black shadows in a shadow world.

For the first time, it seemed to him that, in spite of his new hope, it might be better if he died. Even if he survived, what had he to look forward to? Only too well he recalled how hard it had been to rouse interest in the trip and to raise the large amount of money required. He remembered the colossal problems that had had to be solved in building the ship, and some of the men who had solved them were buried somewhere in the Martian desert.

It might be twenty years before another ship from Earth would try to reach the only other planet in the Solar System that had shown signs of being able to support life.

During those uncountable days and nights, those years, he would be here alone. That was the most he could hope for – if he lived. As he fumbled his way to a dais in one of the rooms, Jenner considered another problem: How did one let a living village know that it must alter its processes? In a way, it must already have grasped that it had a new tenant. How could he make it realize he needed food in a different chemical combination than that which it had served in the past; that he liked music, but on a different scale system; and that he could use a shower each morning – of water, not of poison gas?

He dozed fitfully, like a man who is sick rather than sleepy. Twice he wakened, his lips on fire, his eyes burning, his body bathed in perspiration. Several times he was startled into consciousness by the sound of his own harsh voice crying out in anger and fear at the night.

He guessed, then, that he was dying.

He spent the long hours of darkness tossing, turning, twisting, befuddled by waves of heat. As the light of morning came, he was vaguely surprised to realize that he was still alive. Restlessly he climbed off the dais and went to the door.

A bitingly cold wind blew, but it felt good to his hot face. He wondered if there were enough pneumococci in his blood for him to catch pneumonia. He decided not.

In a few moments he was shivering. He retreated back into the house, and for the first time noticed that, despite the doorless doorway, the wind did not come into the building at all. The rooms were cold but not draughty.

That started an association: Where had his terrible body heat come from? He teetered over to the dais where he spent the night. Within seconds he was sweltering in a temperature of about one hundred and thirty.

He climbed off the dais, shaken by his own stupidity. He estimated that he had sweated at least two quarts of moisture out of his dried-up body on that furnace of a bed.

This village was not for human beings. Here even the beds were heated for creatures who needed temperatures far beyond the heat comfortable for men.

Jenner spent most of the day in the shade of a large tree. He felt exhausted, and only occasionally did he even remember that he had a problem. When the whistling started, it bothered him at first, but he was too tired to move away from it. There were long periods when he hardly heard it, so dulled were his senses.

Late in the afternoon he remembered the shrubs and the trees he had torn up the day before and wondered what had happened to them. He wet his swollen tongue with the last few drops of water in his bag, climbed lackadaisically to his feet, and went to look for the dried-up remains.

There weren't any. He couldn't even find the holes where he had torn them out. The living village had absorbed the dead tissue into itself and had repaired the breaks in its "body."

That galvanized Jenner. He began to think again . . . about mutations, genetic readjustments, life forms adapting to new environments. There'd been lectures on that before the ship left Earth, rather generalized talks designed to acquaint the explorers with the problems men might face on an alien planet. The important principle was quite simple: adjust or die.

The village had to adjust to him. He doubted if he could seriously damage it, but he could try. His own need to survive must be placed on as sharp and hostile a basis as that.

Frantically Jenner began to search his pockets. Before leaving the rocket he had loaded himself with odds and ends of small equipment. A jackknife, a folding metal cup, a printed radio, a tiny superbattery that could be charged by spinning an attached wheel – and for which he had brought along, among other things, a powerful electric fire lighter.

Jenner plugged the lighter into the battery and deliberately scraped the red-hot end along the surface of the "marble." The reaction was swift. The substance turned an angry purple this time. When an entire section of the floor had changed color, Jenner headed for the nearest stall trough, entering far enough to activate it.

There was a noticeable delay. When the food finally flowed into the trough, it was clear that the living village had realized the reason for what he had done. The food was a pale, creamy color, where earlier it had been a murky gray.

Jenner put his finger into it but withdrew it with a yell and wiped his finger. It continued to sting for several moments. The vital question was: Had it deliberately offered him food that would damage him, or was it trying to appease him without knowing what he could eat?

He decided to give it another chance, and entered the adjoining stall. The gritty stuff that flooded up this time was yellower. It didn't burn his finger, but Jenner took one taste and spat it out. He had the feeling that he had been offered a soup made of a greasy mixture of clay and gasoline.

He was thirsty now with a need heightened by the unpleasant taste in his mouth. Desperately he rushed outside and tore open the water bag, seeking the wetness inside. In his fumbling eagerness, he spilled a few precious drops onto the courtyard. Down he went on his face and licked them up.

Half a minute later, he was still licking, and there was still water.

The fact penetrated suddenly. He raised himself and gazed wonderingly at the droplets of water that sparkled on the smooth stone. As he watched, another one squeezed up from the apparently solid surface and shimmered in the light of the sinking sun.

He bent, and with the tip of his tongue sponged up each visible drop. For a long time he lay with his mouth pressed to the "marble," sucking up the tiny bits of water that the village doled out to him.

The glowing white sun disappeared behind a hill. Night fell, like the dropping of a black screen. The air turned cold, then icy. He shivered as the wind keened through his ragged clothes. But what finally stopped him was the collapse of the surface from which he had been drinking.

Jenner lifted himself in surprise, and in the darkness gingerly felt over the stone. It had genuinely crumbled. Evidently the substance had yielded up its available water and had disintegrated in the process. Jenner estimated that he had drunk altogether an ounce of water.

It was a convincing demonstration of the willingness of the village to please him, but there was another, less satisfying, implication. If the village had to destroy a part of itself every time it gave him a drink, then clearly the supply was not unlimited.

Jenner hurried inside the nearest building, climbed onto a dais – and climbed off again hastily, as the heat blazed up at him. He waited, to give the Intelligence a chance to realize he wanted a change, then lay down once more. The heat was as great as ever.

He gave that up because he was too tired to persist and too sleepy to think of a method that might let the village know he needed a different bedroom temperature. He slept on the floor with an uneasy conviction that it could *not* sustain him for long. He woke up many times during the night and thought, "Not enough water. No matter how hard it tries – " Then he would sleep again, only to wake once more, tense and unhappy.

Nevertheless, morning found him briefly alert; and all his steely determination was back – that iron will power that had brought him at least five hundred miles across an unknown desert.

He headed for the nearest trough. This time, after he had activated it, there was a pause of more than a minute; and then about a thimbleful of water made a wet splotch at the bottom.

Jenner licked it dry, then waited hopefully for more. When none came he reflected gloomily that somewhere in the village an entire group of cells had broken down and released their water for him.

Then and there he decided that it was up to the human being, who could move around, to find a new source of water for the village, which could not move.

In the interim, of course, the village would have to keep him alive, until he had investigated the possibilities. That meant, above everything else, he must have some food to sustain him while he looked around.

He began to search his pockets. Toward the end of his food supply, he had carried scraps and pieces wrapped in small bits of cloth. Crumbs had broken off into the pocket, and he had searched for them often during those long days in the desert. Now, by actually ripping the seams, he discovered tiny particles of meat and bread, little bits of grease and other unidentifiable substances.

Carefully he leaned over the adjoining stall and placed the scrapings in the trough there. The village would not be able to offer him more than a reasonable facsimile. If the spilling of a few drops on the courtyard could make it aware of his need for water, then a similar offering might give it the clue it needed as to the chemical nature of the food he could eat.

Jenner waited, then entered the second stall and activated it. About a pint of thick, creamy substance trickled into the bottom of the trough. The smallness of the quantity seemed evidence that perhaps it contained water.

He tasted it. It had a sharp, musty flavor and a stale odor. It was almost as dry as flour – but his stomach did not reject it.

Jenner ate slowly, acutely aware that at such moments as this the village had him at its mercy. He could never be sure that one of the food ingredients was not a slow-acting poison.

When he had finished the meal he went to a food trough in another building. He refused to eat the food that came up, but activated still another trough. This time he received a few drops of water.

He had come purposefully to one of the tower buildings. Now he started up the ramp that led to the upper floor. He paused only briefly in the room he came to, as he had already discovered that they seemed to be additional bedrooms. The familiar dais was there in a group of three.

What interested him was that the circular ramp continued to wind on upward. First to another, smaller room that seemed to have no particular reason for being. Then it wound on up to the top of the tower, some seventy feet above the ground. It was high enough for him to see beyond the rim of all the surrounding hilltops. He had thought it might be, but he had been too weak to make the climb before. Now he looked out to every horizon. Almost immediately the hope that had brought him up faded.

The view was immeasurably desolate. As far as he could see was an arid waste, and every horizon was hidden in a mist of wind-blown sand.

Jenner gazed with a sense of despair. If there were a Martian sea out there somewhere, it was beyond his reach.

Abruptly he clenched his hands in anger against his fate, which seemed inevitable now. At the very worst, he had hoped he would find himself in a mountainous region. Seas and mountains were generally the two main sources of water. He should have known, of course, that there were very few mountains on Mars. It would have been a wild coincidence if he had actually run into a mountain range.

His fury faded because he lacked the strength to sustain any emotion. Numbly he went down the ramp.

His vague plan to help the village ended as swiftly and finally as that.

The days drifted by, but as to how many he had no idea. Each time he went to eat, a smaller amount of water was doled out to him. Jenner kept telling himself that each meal would have to be his last. It was unreasonable for him to expect the village to destroy itself when his fate was certain now.

What was worse, it became increasingly clear that the food was not good for him. He had misled the village as to his needs by giving it stale, perhaps even tainted, samples, and prolonged the agony for himself. At times after he had eaten, Jenner felt dizzy for hours. All too frequently his head ached and his body shivered with fever.

The village was doing what it could. The rest was up to him, and he couldn't even adjust to an approximation of Earth food.

For two days he was too sick to drag himself to one of the troughs. Hour after hour he lay on the floor. Some time during the second night the pain in his body grew so terrible that he finally made up his mind.

"If I can get to a dais," he told himself, "the heat alone will kill me, and in absorbing my body, the village will get back some of its lost water."

He spent at least an hour crawling laboriously up the ramp of the nearest dais, and when he finally made it, he lay as one already dead. His last waking thought was: "Beloved friends, I'm coming."

The hallucination was so complete that momentarily he seemed to be back in the control room of the rocketship, and all around him were his former companions.

With a sigh of relief Jenner sank into a dreamless sleep.

He woke to the sound of a violin. It was a sad-sweet music that told of the rise and fall of a race long dead.

Jenner listened for a while and then, with abrupt excitement, realized the truth. This was a substitute for the whistling – the village had adjusted its music to him!

Other sensory phenomena stole in upon him. The dais felt comfortably warm, not hot at all. He had a feeling of wonderful physical well-being.

Eagerly he scrambled down the ramp to the nearest food stall. As he crawled forward, his nose close to the floor, the trough filled with a steamy mixture. The odor was so rich and pleasant that he plunged his face into it and slopped it up greedily. It had the flavor of thick, meaty soup and was warm and soothing to his lips and mouth. When he had eaten it all, for the first time he did not need a drink of water.

"I've won!" thought Jenner. "The village has found a way!"

After a while he remembered something and crawled to the bathroom. Cautiously, watching the ceiling, he eased himself backward into the shower stall. The yellowish spray came down, cool and delightful.

Ecstatically Jenner wriggled his four-foot-tail and lifted his long snout to let the thin streams of liquid wash away the food impurities that clung to his sharp teeth.

Then he waddled out to bask in the sun and listen to the timeless music.

The King and the Dollmaker

WOLFGANG JESCHKE

Wolfgang Jeschke (1936–) is one of the central figures in contemporary German science fiction. He began to write science fiction in 1959, but became more involved by becoming an editor in 1969. He has edited more than 100 SF anthologies since 1970, bringing much of the best science fiction in the world into print in German in the last three decades. Since 1972 he has been the editor of the largest and most successful SF publishing line on the continent, for Heyne Verlag. Most especially, he has been a crucial force in upholding literary standards in German science fiction and for maintaining links with the SF movement in other cultures. He is a commanding presence in international science fiction.

Although he has only published two novels, both have appeared in English: *The Last Day of Creation* (1981; 1984 U.S.) and *Midas* (1987; 1990 UK). He has written a number of stories, of which this one, the centerpiece of his collection, *Der Zeiter,* may be his best. Franz Rottensteiner, in *Science Fiction Writers,* calls it "a virtuoso performance, so complex and well constructed that it can stand beside the best time travel stories, a tour-de-force that turns artifice into high art." Two forces play a complex and perhaps deadly game of domination in the past and future. It is an interesting comparison to John Crowley's "Great Work of Time," and contrast to Connie Willis's "Fire Watch."

"Stay where you are, Collins! Every move now could mean a fracture."

"Yes, Your Majesty," said Collins, and stayed where he was.

"Keep your eyes upon us!" commanded the king.

"Yes, Your Majesty," said Collins, and kept his eyes on His Majesty.

Time was slipping by. There was a deadly silence in the hall. The king was perched nervously on the edge of his throne and stared anxiously at the flickering mirror on the wall. Every time a patrol officer stepped out of the mirror, the king gave a start and leveled his gun at the man. Collins could see that the barrel trembled and that beads of sweat had formed on His Majesty's brow. The intervals grew shorter, and the guards could hardly avoid stumbling over one another. The patrol now had the room under constant control. The mirror twitched every time a man was discharged from or reabsorbed into its field. One guard stepped out into the room, looked attentively about him, and returned with a backward step into the mirror. But there was nothing special to observe. The room was empty. The walls still showed the light spots where the valuable paintings had once hung. Generations of sovereigns who had once peered morosely, critically, or solemnly from the walls upon the most recent offspring of their lineage now peered morosely, critically, or solemnly into some dark corner of the palace cellar which they had never seen during their lifetime. Even the nails had been taken out of the walls, the tapestries removed, the curtains, the furniture, everything. There was only the throne, His Majesty, the patrol's time mirror, which occasionally disgorged and reswallowed a guard, and a man standing at the triply barred and shielded window – Collins, His Majesty's Minister of Personal Security and Futurology.

The throne room was hermetically sealed, doors and windows safe-guarded by energy screens. Not an insect, not even a dust particle, could have penetrated the shield, not to mention a minibattleship or a remote-controlled needle grenade.

"Tell us how long this is to continue, Collins. We cannot bear it much longer!" The king gave his minister a beseeching look. He was trembling.

Collins tossed back his cape, unclasped the purse on his belt, and drew from it a temporal strip. He held it at arm's length, as he was a bit farsighted, and examined it scrupulously. He was calm and composed; only the corners of his mouth curled ever so slightly in scorn. He had seen through more ticklish situations than this. "By Your Majesty's leave," he said, "Your Majesty's alarm is really groundless. The patrol knows that it will all turn out for the best. We have twenty-seven more minutes, during which Your Majesty is constantly supervised, before the arrival of this impenetrable ten-second time seal. From the very second that we regain access to the mirror from the timeline, this room will once again be under control."

Collins's finger ran down the temporal strip, tracing the dots indicating the guards' positions, and compared them with the date and time printed continuously along the margin. He had even jotted down the guards' names on the strip. They were his best men. One could not do more. With the exception of one short interruption, the dots lay so close to one another that they formed a solid line. Collins looked at his watch. Everything was running according to schedule.

"What is the latest report?" demanded the king. His voice was hoarse, fear gripped his throat.

"Nothing precise, I'm afraid, in spite of all our efforts. Your Majesty is aware of the fact that WHITE has undertaken transformations which reach far into the future. The seals are fluid, and the impenetrable time block is constantly shifting position. Our investigations are valid for but a few hours, then the temporal strips are worth no more than the paper they are printed on. Yesterday we could still supervise four days into the future; at present, this period is reduced to a scant two hours, and the block continues to grow toward us. But according to our calculations it will soon come to a standstill, so that we will eventually have thirty minutes left to supervise. But all this can of course change, should WHITE undertake a fracture."

"That's just it. That is the problem," whimpered the king. "Do something! How can you loiter about idly when I am in danger?"

"Your Majesty is not in danger," sighed Collins. "That is practically the only thing about which we are certain. After the critical moment is past, Your Majesty will be sitting upon the throne just as Your Majesty does now. Of course . . ."

"Of course what?"

"Now, Your Majesty, we have discussed it often enough. By Your Majesty's leave, should we really bring this up again now, when the moment is nearing?"

The king slouched in his seat and chewed his fingernails.

"Are you certain that I am the one who will be sitting here after the critical moment?" he asked suspiciously.

"But, Your Majesty, who else?"

"Yes, who else," muttered the king, and looked at Collins.

The minister inspected his temporal strip. The stream of dots discontinued, reappeared, only eventually to disappear altogether. Here was the seal, there the block began. What took place at these inaccessible points? Why had WHITE placed them there? Was this some kind of a trap or ruse? He had spent a great deal of time on the problem, had assigned his best men to it, but he had found no solution in spite of the innumerable facts that had been compiled. He was tired. A holiday would do him good. He looked around him at the dreary room, examined its bare walls. Got to get out of here, he thought. Choose any other time. How about dinosaur hunting in the Mesozoic era? He had grown out of that age. And he detested hunting expeditions. Too loud, too much excitement, too much drinking, and for the last few decades terribly overcrowded. They went and killed off the beasts in less than no time with their laser guns. And what if they did? Ugly creatures they were anyway. A minimal fracture. A couple of bone-collecting scientists of some later age would probably be astonished that the animals had disappeared so quickly. They would certainly find an explanation, that was what they were scientists for. The Tertiary period – yes, that would be better. It had been nice and warm then in this region. A couple of weeks of Tertiary. The patrol had a holiday center there. Plenty of rest, excellent food, saber-toothed-tiger steaks. Once, though, he had chosen a year when he himself had been there. Not that it made much difference to him if he was constantly crossing his own path – that had happened to him before, one got used to it. One had a few drinks with oneself, talked about old times, complimented oneself on how good one had still looked then and how on the other hand one had hardly aged at all since; one bored oneself to tears, felt a certain envy appear which could grow to hatred when one saw the bad habits that one had already had then and had long since wanted to get rid of but still had years later. Youth and experience stood face to face, and in between were all those years that one circled about and avoided mentioning but still could not ignore. Everyone knew that this could bring on disastrous time fractures if one were not careful, irreparable damage, intervention by the Committee, at best deportation to an ice age or to one of the first three millennia, at worst eradication from the timeline, condemnation to nonexistence, unless amnesty were granted by means of a special dispensation from the Supreme Council on the Future.

"You just stand about and say nothing!" The king's voice snapped him out of thoughts. "We asked you a question."

"I beg Your Majesty's pardon."

"What exactly is going to happen?" demanded the king peevishly. "Explain it again, step by step."

"Certainly, Your Majesty. Our guards are in control of all of the timeline which is accessible to us and are closely observing the particular area around the palace. There is absolutely no action. That is, as Your Majesty already knows, apart from the doll . . ."

"Nonsense! Always this damned doll! How often do I have to hear that ridiculous story? What am I paying you for? Always repeating the same foolishness!"

"A small mechanical figure appears," continued Collins, unmoved, "a sort of miniature robot, with which Your Majesty deigns to play."

"Rubbish! How often must I repeat it? What on earth would I be doing with a doll? Have you ever seen me play with dolls? This is utterly absurd!"

"But by Your Majesty's leave, according to the reports of the guards, Your Majesty seems to be quite taken with this small mechanical object."

"But that is just what I don't understand! What am I to do with a doll? Am I a child? Once and for all, enough of this doll! It is beginning to get on my nerves."

The minister shrugged his shoulders and looked at his watch. "I am reporting nothing but the facts when I say that Your Majesty takes pleasure in playing with this figure, actually lays his weapon aside and gives the impression of being relieved of a burden and in extreme good humor, not to say . . ."

"Not to say what?"

"Not to say, well – like a new man."

The king leaned back with a sigh, then shook his head in annoyance and slid nervously forward again to the edge of the throne. "Doll, doll, what the devil does this doll mean?" he brooded. Then, turning and launching into Collins, "For weeks now we have heard nothing from you but reports about dolls and other such nonsense. Collins, you have failed. As Minister for the Personal Security of Our Person you have failed miserably. That can cost you your head; you are well aware of that?"

"By Your Majesty's leave, we have done everything within our means to get hold of the producer of this doll and to find and destroy the doll itself. The research has cost hundreds of years of work by our best specialists in ancient history, time manipulation, and causal coordination. Let me assure Your Majesty without exaggeration that we have done everything, absolutely everything within our power."

"You had orders to cause a fracture in order to avoid this dreadful moment, and what did you do? Nothing! You had orders to find this man in the seventeenth century and to have him disposed of, and was this corrective measure taken? No! And you babble on about your specialists and their hundreds of years of work! It does not interest us in the slightest. Did you hear? Not in the slightest! You have failed!" The king trembled with anger; his fingers tightened around the handle of his weapon. It was aimed at Collins.

"I – I most humbly beg Your Majesty's forgiveness, but as I said, we have done everything within our power."

"Did you have the doll destroyed? Yes or no! If you did, why does it keep reappearing?"

"We did destroy it – at least we destroyed one doll, but an infinite number of such dolls could exist."

"Don't talk nonsense! This simple craftsman can't have made an infinite number of dolls."

"Of course not, Your Majesty, but perhaps two or three of this type."

"And why haven't they been destroyed? Because you failed!"

"As Your Majesty already knows, and as I have allowed myself to emphasize repeatedly, this is in all probability – and in my own humble opinion – not at all where the basic problem lies. This question of the doll is certainly peculiar, but it is clearly just as unimportant as is the craftsman in the seventeenth century. We are dealing with an intervention by WHITE in which this man in the distant past plays either no part or a very subordinate one, in which his function is to lure us onto the wrong track. Your Majesty knows that I have never considered this a very promising lead. How much of a chance could a man in the pretechnical age have had? I personally am convinced that at that time man did not even have electrical energy; they were still experimenting with frogs' legs."

"One can build mechanical automats, Collins, which if they are preserved in museums or private collections can survive several thousand years. But we have other grounds to find this man dangerous. You should have had him eliminated. You had explicit instructions to do so."

"WHITE prevented it," answered Collins with a shrug of his shoulders.

" WHITE, WHITE, WHITE! Let WHITE be damned!"

They were silent. Time was slipping by.

The guards came and went. They now registered every second.

"How long is this to continue, Collins?"

"Exactly eleven minutes and thirty seconds, Your Majesty," answered the minister. He now held his watch in the palm of his hand. After this period the time mirror would blank out and be impenetrable to the patrol for a span of ten seconds.

"What is the purpose of this seal, Collins? Can you explain why WHITE had the seal placed here? What is hidden behind it? Something is happening behind it, but what?"

The king's voice trembled. The tension in the room grew.

"We don't know, Your Majesty," said the minister. "Perhaps it is just a ruse – we will know soon. But Your Majesty need have no fears, there will be no change."

"That is what your guards say. They are dolts," said the king. He coughed and gasped for breath and tugged at the collar of his black cape as if it was too tight. The handkerchief with which he wiped his brow was soaked with perspiration.

"Have you given all the orders? Is everything sealed off?"

"Exactly as Your Majesty commanded. The entire palace has been thoroughly inspected several times, the throne room especially carefully of course. There is not a single square inch that hasn't been meticulously checked. All dolls, toys, and similar objects which we were able to seize in the vicinity of this time-space point have been destroyed. The palace is locked and bolted inside and out. Nothing can penetrate this room unnoticed. Any particle, even a speck of dust, would immediately disintegrate in the energy fields. The doll must either come through the mirror or materialize in a manner unknown us; it is not in the palace now, unless it has taken on a form of energy of which we have no knowledge."

The king looked about suspiciously, as if he could discover some clue that had escaped the attention of the minister's guards, but his weapon found no target. The room was bare, there were only His Majesty upon the throne, the minister, the mirror, and the stream of guards who formed the observation chain.

"I cannot bear to see these faces any longer, Collins."

"Your Majesty has given explicit orders . . ."

"Yes, yes, I know. Are these men absolutely reliable?"

"Absolutely."

"What do you know about this dollmaker?"

"It is an odd story, Your Majesty. A relatively large part of his life seems to contain important historical facts which WHITE does not wish to have changed. As Your Majesty knows, he appears in the year 1623 in a small city in what was then Europe – now our Operations Base 7 – buys a house and apparently earns a living as a simple craftsman, makes few demands on others, mingles little with the townspeople but is respected by all. On August 17, 1629, the period suddenly becomes inaccessible, closed off by a seal which severely handicaps our operations. This seal extends as far as February 2, 1655, covering almost three decades. Nevertheless, we set several of our best specialists to the task of living through the time behind the seal. Your Majesty can hardly conceive of what this meant for those men. But in spite of all our efforts the venture failed; the men were never heard of again. We could find them in neither the fifth nor the sixth decade of that century. Times then were particularly hard, wars were raging, and morale was very low. In short, by the time we could operate again we discovered that our craftsman was dead. We questioned people who knew him. Naturally we cannot examine the validity of the information they gave us, as there are no written records, but this is what we were told: One night he went into a fit of raving madness, and from that moment on he was like a different person. Formerly he had been a respected man whose advice was sought by all, but after this attack he let himself go, fell into the habit of swearing, jabbered incoherently, neglected his work, took to drink, picked quarrels, and proved himself to be generally arrogant and overbearing. For instance, he demanded that his neighbors address him as His Majesty, for which the fellows soundly thrashed him. He had apparently gone mad. He went from bad to worse, living on alms and on what he could occasionally beg or steal. One day he was found hanging by a rope in a barn, where he had apparently been for several weeks. He himself had put an end to his miserable existence. He must have been hastily buried somewhere, for we could not find his grave. We were told that this is commonly done to victims of suicide. We can fix the date of his death with relative certainty to the autumn of the year 1650. As Your Majesty can see, it is all in all nothing remarkable, perhaps not a daily occurrence in those centuries, but by no means an unusual one."

"But this doll, Collins. What about the doll?"

"We succeeded in destroying one doll. Our men blasted it and it exploded. We were not able to reconstruct it completely, hut the parts that we were able to gather up in our haste in the dark give evidence of an extremely simple spring-driven mechanism, such as one finds in the clocks and music boxes of that time. There doesn't seem to be anything special about the doll either."

"Did you find anything in the following centuries?"

"We have inspected innumerable mechanical toys, only sporadically, to be sure, from the mid-twentieth century on, as there are such vast quantities of them, but we never came across anything unusual. Occasionally we found in literature evidences of more highly developed mechanisms such as we were searching for, but all our attempts to test the validity of these allusions failed. The mechanical doll was a well-loved fiction at that time, a sort of fairy-tale figure, the forerunner of the robot, I surmise. But the technical basis necessary to develop it is lacking."

"Nothing! Absolutely nothing!"

The minister shrugged his shoulders regretfully.

"How many minutes, Collins?"

"Five, Your Majesty."

"It is enough to drive one mad! Can't a stop be put to this running about?"

"I am sorry, Your Majesty, but it is Your Majesty's own command that the room be under constant supervision. This supervision cannot be countermanded without causing delicate fractures which might have dire consequences for Your Majesty's safety."

The minister kept his eye on his watch and compared the time with the temporal strips in his hand. In four minutes and thirty seconds the stream of dots indicating the guards' positions would cease for a brief period.

"Collins, have you absolutely no idea what is going to happen in the next four minutes?"

"I am afraid we know nothing for certain, Your Majesty, but . . ."

"But what?"

"But, by Your Majesty's leave, I have my suspicions."

"It is your damned duty to give thought to the situation and to express your thoughts. So go on and express them!"

"Let us assume that Your Majesty himself, on the basis of experience which Your Majesty will have gained in the future and on the basis of further development of time-travel technique, makes certain points and periods of the time-line which seem important to Your Majesty inaccessible by means of this seal."

"We see. Collins, why did you not mention such an important aspect earlier? That is a very plausible possibility; one can hardly consider it seriously enough." The king smiled in relief. He clung to this thought as to a straw. The idea that he himself could be WHITE clearly flattered him. He snapped his fingers energetically and feverishly concentrated upon the thought. Then his face clouded over again.

"But we would at least have transmitted some kind of explanatory message to ourselves in order to make this horrid situation more bearable."

"Perhaps that is impossible for reasons of security," interjected Collins.

The king shook his head. "But this doll. Where does this confounded doll fit into the picture?"

"Perhaps it is supposed to bring Your Majesty some important piece of information."

"And the dollmaker? No, no, it doesn't fit in."

"Perhaps he has nothing to do with the whole affair, perhaps he is just a secondary figure; but, on the other hand, perhaps he is the source of information."

"Perhaps, perhaps! Is that all you have to say? What do you think you are here for – to reel off vague suspicions? We can do that ourselves. You are responsible for our security. Is that clear? Such nonsense! A primitive tinsmith from twelve thousand years ago has information for us, the ruler of four planet systems and all their moons – how ridiculous! Just empty speculation and foolish twaddle!"

The king was provoked. The barrel of his weapon roamed back and forth, and Collins tried to keep out of firing range.

"Then it was a blind alley, by Your Majesty's leave, which our best forces have wasted centuries in exploring."

The king stamped his foot. "Time doesn't interest us! We want information. We want absolute security for our person, even if your people need thousands of years to guarantee it. If you go down blind alleys, it's your problem, Collins, not ours! You are a miserable failure! We are holding you responsible for the consequences. You understand what that means."

"At Your Majesty's command."

"Our command was: bring information and more information about the present sphere of time and everything connected with it; and you dare to enter this room with your suspicions! You can go to the devil with your crazy notions! We want facts and nothing but facts."

"Very well, Your Majesty, but don't forget the seal on Operations Base 7, an intervention by WHITE which made our work extremely difficult and thwarted our action in the decisive years."

"That may very well be. Perhaps there was at that moment a historical event of great importance. As you said, there was a war at the time. Perhaps our intervention would have endangered a politician or scientist of top-ranking future valence, or the great-grandfather of a politician or scientist, or heaven knows who. But that is all irrelevant. What is going to happen here and now in a few seconds? That is the only thing that matters."

Time was slipping by.

The guards came and went, came and went, dots on the temporal strip.

The king leaned back, breathing heavily. He was as white as chalk and dripped with sweat.

"Thirty more seconds, Your Majesty."

"Collins!" The king's eyes were fixed upon him beseechingly; they were filled with tears. "Collins! Keep your eyes on me! Do you hear? Don't lose sight of me for a single moment! Take note of everything, everything!"

He was leaning far forward, and his eyes swept panic-stricken across the room. He began to see dolls everywhere. They crept out from beneath his throne, came out of the walls, slipped down from the ceiling on threads. Everywhere he saw dangling limbs, expressionless plastic faces, beady glass eyes that glared maliciously at him, tiny fists that brandished daggers as big as needles or aimed minute laser pistols at him.

The king trembled and gnawed incessantly at his lower lip. Fear had complete mastery over him now. It was suffocating him. He felt as if he must either crawl off into a hole somewhere or else scream and shoot about him in blind rage.

The minister gave him a worried look.

"I can't bear this any longer, Collins!" shrieked His Majesty. "Don't just stand idly about – do something!"

His shrill voice burst into thousands of tiny splinter-sharp fragments.

Collins followed the second hand of his watch as it ticked nearer and nearer to the critical moment.

"Now."

The mirror went blank.

The minister looked carefully about the room, then fixed his gaze upon the king. The king suddenly leaned back, crossed his legs, and put aside his pistol so that both hands were free to straighten out the clothing of a small plain doll which he was holding.

The minister blinked and shook his head to dispel the optical illusion, but the doll was still there. It hadn't been there before and now it was there. He tried without success to cope with this new situation. The brain refused to accept what the eyes clearly saw. His Majesty was sitting comfortably on the throne, smoothing out the dress of this small mechanical figure, and smiling delightedly.

"Come, Collins, why are you staring so aghast at us? Have you never seen a doll before? A pretty little toy, don't you think? A doll-maker's masterpiece."

The ten seconds were over. The mirror glowed once again and the first guard stepped out into the room.

"Hello, how are you? Have a nice trip?" the king asked him in good humor.

"He-hello," stammered the bewildered man, and fled back into the mirror.

"Good morning," the king greeted the next guard who appeared.

"G-good morning, Your Majesty," he managed to stutter, and stumbled over his feet in his haste to find the mirror and disappear into it.

"This is quite an amazing doll, Collins. Go ahead and take a closer look at it."

The minister approached hesitantly.

"Would Your Majesty deign . . . an explanation . . . the rapid transformation I mean, I beg Your Majesty's pardon, but I find it incomprehensible that all of a sudden Your Majesty is . . ."

". . . Like a new man, you wanted to say?"

"Yes, Your Majesty."

"You will get your explanation soon enough, in a half hour or so, when this spying finally stops." He pointed to the mirror.

"But, Your Majesty, time is running out. Your Majesty's only chance is to explain the whole situation to me immediately, so that we can undertake a fracture and take all other necessary measures, so that all may still turn out for the best. I beseech Your Majesty, this is possible for only a few minutes longer."

The king let out a peal of laughter.

"What for, Collins? Everything is turning out for the best. Why are you so nervous? Fetch a chair and sit down! Aren't there any chairs here?"

"But certainly Your Majesty will explain . . ."

"All in good time, Collins, all in good time. Not now. Let us first take a look at this doll. It seems to be an old piece, doesn't it, perhaps thousands of years old, but still in quite good shape. I believe it even can dance. It has probably made a long trip, we should say a very long trip, but it is still fully intact. Hard to believe what can fit into this little head, if one only knows how to go about filling it properly!" He held the small metal head of the doll between thumb and forefinger and smiled pensively.

"But, Your Majesty, I don't understand. What does this all mean?"

"Be patient, Collins, be patient. You will find out. There are just twenty minutes left. In the meantime, let us watch the review of your troops. Then we will tell you a story, a very ordinary story, but we think it will interest you nevertheless. We would wager on it."

"I am breathless with anticipation, Your Majesty."

Meanwhile, the king continued to greet with a gracious wave of the hand the guards who appeared and disappeared, as if he were holding an audience. The men gave the minister a questioning look, which he answered with a regretful shrug of his shoulders and a resigned sigh. His Majesty continued to play with the doll and seemed to be in unusually high spirits, as if all this was great fun.

Now it was Collins's turn to become nervous. He found that he had torn the temporal strip in his hand to shreds. The king said to his minister, as if he too had noticed this, "That doesn't matter, Collins. We don't need it anymore. In a quarter of an hour the stream of dots will stop anyway."

"Well, that's that, Collins. Your guards can't penetrate the mirror anymore."

The mirror was not blank. It continued to flicker, but no one stepped out from it. The minister stared in astonishment first at the instrument, then at His Majesty.

"Surprises you, doesn't it?" laughed the king.

"Indeed it does," admitted Collins. "But how is it possible?"

"Let us not anticipate."

"As Your Majesty wishes. But it has always been my task to anticipate."

"You are right. Very well, then let us begin." The king settled comfortably into his throne and cleared his throat. "Collins, you are a clever man."

"Your Majesty honors me."

"But you have made several mistakes."

"I beg Your Majesty's pardon, but what mistakes?"

"First of all, you shouldn't have taken your eyes off the mirror for one single instant, for then you would have noticed that it wasn't blank for the entire ten seconds. Not that there was anything you could have done, but you might have gained some information which would have led you to make certain further considerations. And at times you were damned close to having the answer. You almost beat us in our little game."

"Perhaps, Your Majesty. It is not clear to me – what could I have done?"

"You should have thought out the problem more carefully.

Fortunately for us, you didn't. You could for instance have given more consideration to the meaning of this seal and the intervention of WHITE."

"I considered the seal a protection of important timeline intersections, where a fracture could have devastating consequences."

"All of which is true, Collins. And WHITE has to intervene, because sometimes time fissures spread underneath the seals, as a result of imprudent operations, and make repairs necessary, in order to guarantee the safety of the future, our universe, and thereby the very existence of WHITE itself."

"I understand, but why didn't WHITE seal off the entire timeline and cut off all operations of the patrol?"

"A good question. Why not? Think hard, Collins. You have a good head on your shoulders."

"Of course. Your Majesty is right. That would mean cutting off all time travel, which would in turn mean no invention of time travel, as there could be no experiments, and then the existence of WHITE would be impossible."

"Very good! Therefore, WHITE interferes only when its existence is at stake."

"But what about my mistakes, Your Majesty?"

"Without this future power, which we call WHITE, the course of our planet would speedily deteriorate into a state of hopeless confusion. WHITE was actually your opponent, Collins, but you were always looking for an opponent elsewhere. And you didn't know where to look."

"At times I suspected it, but I thought it more probable that certain political-interest groups in the empire, perhaps operating from a base in the future, were giving us trouble. But Your Majesty spoke of several mistakes."

"That is all part of the story which we are about to tell you. You must pay especially close attention to it for reasons which will also be made clear. But we want to anticipate a bit. You were hunting down this dollmaker – "

"Indeed."

" – And at times you made life difficult for him."

"As Your Majesty commanded."

"Hmm," smiled the king.

"Although without much success, I must admit, because WHITE intervened with a seal."

"Why didn't you study the past history of this person more closely, at the very time and place in which it occurred?"

"We didn't think it necessary. We already knew something of the man, though it was second- and third-hand information. The question didn't seem to be worth going into more thoroughly. It was my opinion that we had already spent too much time on him. What we had found out about him didn't seem to be helpful enough . . ."

"Then you know that this man was born in 1594, first learned the blacksmith's trade, then became apprenticed to a watchmaker, and afterward traveled about for five years as a journeyman. During this time war broke out and he was captured by recruiting officers and forced to serve in the army; he spent the next two years with a band of men who had joined Tilly's troops . . ."

"Yes, Your Majesty, and settled down in the town which is now our Operations Base 7; he acquired money somehow, bought himself a cottage, set up a workshop, and devoted himself entirely to his hobby of making watches and mechanical toys. He became a respected citizen of the town but refused all public offices which were offered to him; he escaped the snares of all the spinsters in the neighborhood, having decided upon a bachelor life in order to have his evenings free to pore over blueprints and tinker with mechanical instruments. He engaged a housekeeper who cooked and cleaned the house but was not allowed into the workshop. The watchmaker became more and more withdrawn, hardly leaving his house. Finally he became mentally deranged and in 1650 hung himself. As Your Majesty can see, we know quite a bit about him, but nothing which appears noteworthy to me."

"Nothing noteworthy. You are quite right, Collins. But do you also know that this man was killed in action, near Heidelberg in the year 1621? Tilly's crowd murdered and plundered its way through the countryside. He was killed either by farmers or by one of his fellow cutthroats, who probably fought with him over his booty or some woman."

"I beg Your Majesty's pardon?"

"You heard correctly, Collins. The man whom you supposedly investigated so carefully was no longer alive at the time Operations Base 7 was established."

"That would have been an inexcusable error. But how does Your Majesty know this?"

"More about that later. And your third error was that you failed to have photographs taken of this man in order to examine him more closely. You would perhaps have had quite a surprise. But you and your people had eyes only for the mechanical toys. Fortunately."

There was a crafty smile on the king's face.

"I considered his appearance fully irrelevant in this case, especially as I could never rid myself of the feeling that we were on the wrong track and had wasted much too much time on the man."

"So you yourself have never seen this Weisslinger."

"No, Your Majesty. Why should I have seen him?"

The king shook his head in disapproval. Collins felt more and more uncertain.

"What a pity. Weisslinger is an extremely interesting man. You should have become acquainted with him; you would certainly have learned a great deal from him. He had much to tell, for he had been through much in his life. Perhaps you would have noticed that he wore an ingenious mask, though it was no more ingenious than masks could be in that age. You know us well, Collins, and you have a good head on your shoulders."

"I am beginning to doubt that seriously, Your Majesty."

"Now, now, Collins. It is never too late. Perhaps you will yet meet him."

"How is that possible, Your Majesty? I don't understand . . ."

"Patience, patience! Wait until you have heard our story. Then you will have to admit that you let yourself be checkmated too easily."

"By Your Majesty's leave, I am burning with eagerness to hear the story, for I see more and more clearly that I accomplished my task much more poorly than I had originally thought."

"Indeed you did, Collins. You played miserably and recklessly."

"I most humbly beg Your Majesty's pardon."

"On the other hand, you were pitted against no mean opponent. But everything in its turn. BLACK had the victory as good as in its pocket – the situation was grim. Then it was WHITE's turn, WHITE would have to be damned tricky . . . But where shall we begin? Ah yes, on the day when . . . Now pay strict attention! One evening . . ."

It was evening. The night watchman had just sung out the eleventh hour and had gone down the street, when a carriage drawn by two magnificent horses rounded the corner, rumbled over the cobblestones of the market square, and pulled up in front of the Red Ox Inn, directly across from the house of the dollmaker Weisslinger. The dollmaker went to his window and opened the shutters a tiny crack. He peered out in order to inspect the travelers who were arriving so late at night. He saw two men alight from the vehicle and converse with the proprietor of the Red Ox, who had come out to greet the distinguished guests and escort them into the house. The strangers apparently did not intend to enter and partake of his board and lodging, as they involved him in a conversation on the doorstep. They had a number of questions and seemed to be looking for someone in the town, for the innkeeper nodded his head several times and pointed to Weisslinger's house across the street. The strangers' eyes followed the innkeeper's finger, they carefully surveyed the market square and the neighborhood. Then they took leave of the innkeeper, pressing a gold coin into his hand, and strode toward Weisslinger's house.

"Aha," said the dollmaker knowingly to himself, and cautiously closed the shutters. "The time has come."

He quickly cleared away his mechanical instruments, drew forth several large drawings, and spread them out upon table and work-bench. Then he sat down and waited. As he heard the knock on his door he hesitated, then went to the window and spoke quietly out into the darkness: "Who is there?"

"We beg your forgiveness, Master, for disturbing you at this late hour. The roads are bad and we have made very slow progress. On our travels we heard of a famous watchmaker in this area by the name of Weisslinger. Are you this man?"

"I am Weisslinger, but you honor me, I am certainly not famous. Come in."

Their thick accents indicated that they were foreigners. Weisslinger unbolted the door.

"Please forgive us for disturbing you. But we have little time and must speak with you."

"Come in, gentlemen. You aren't disturbing me at all, I was still up and working. Please excuse the disorderly room. I seldom clean it up and my housekeeper isn't allowed to come in here, she is too careless and always breaks something. Please take a seat. What brings you to this town?"

"We heard of your fame as a maker of highly ingenious dolls."

"That is not my main occupation. By trade I am actually a smith, and I have learned the watchmaker's arts as well. It is true that I have spent much of my – well – spare time making small mechanical toys such as music boxes and dancing dolls – although, I must admit, with little success, due to my insufficient craftsmanship. Please forgive me, gentlemen, I am neglecting my duties as host. But I never expect visitors and have nothing in the house to offer you. I can recommend the Red Ox across the road. You will certainly be pleased with the service there. I often have my meals there myself. The food is good and the wine cellar even better."

"That is not necessary. We have already had our evening meal."

Weisslinger took a closer look at the strangers. Their clothing was simple but elegant: black capes of fine material, close-fitting, well-cut trousers, and low boots fashioned of supple leather. They were examining the room which served both as living room and workshop. They seemed to be particularly interested in his machines, tools, and measuring instruments, which hung on the wall or lay on the workbench; it was not difficult to read from the disappointment on their faces that they had expected more.

"Would you be so kind as to demonstrate one of your models for us?" asked one of the men, trying without success to hide his discontent.

"Of course," answered Weisslinger. He carefully put away his drawings and cleared the workbench, then placed upon it one of his carved music boxes. He wound it up and let it play, then wound up a second and a third music box; the tinny tones of their simple melodies made an odd jingle-jangle. He then took up a small dancing doll with movable limbs, wound it up, and placed it on the bench with the music boxes. The springs whirred, and the doll made stiff, jerky pirouettes on the tabletop.

The gentlemen did not seem to take great interest in the demonstration; they continued to look about the room, glanced at each other and shrugged their shoulders, but pretended to be extremely interested whenever Weisslinger gave them a questioning look. Then one gentleman's eyes fell upon a grandfather clock which was standing in a corner of the room. It was an extraordinary piece with painted face, beautiful case carved out of valuable dark wood, decorated porcelain weights suspended from delicate chains, and a finely chased pendulum on which the astronomic tables and the allegorical figures of the horoscope were engraved.

"Is this clock also a work of yours?"

"Yes, sir. Does it please you?"

"It is a beautiful piece, but it doesn't keep accurate time."

"This is a curious point. You may find it hard to believe, but the clock is not supposed to keep accurate time."

"How can that be?"

"It is a long story, which I am afraid would bore you."

"Not at all!"

"Very well, if you really want to hear it. Please be seated. One day a man came to see me, a Polish count who had spent a good part of his life in Seville and Zaragoza. He was returning to his home in Poland;

on his travels he had heard of me and sought me out. He inspected my clocks and toys, my tools and measuring instruments as well, and seemed to know quite a bit about the craft, as I could judge from his questions. But he denied having any extensive knowledge about such things. In any case, he was apparently satisfied with what he saw and commissioned me to build a clock for him. Nothing simpler, I thought to myself, but I was soon to change my mind. In fact, this man showed me very detailed drawings according to which the clock was to be constructed; these he had bought for a high price from a Jew in Seville. At first everything seemed simple, but I soon ran into difficulties. The more closely I investigated the drawings, the more complicated the works appeared, and I began to doubt seriously that this instrument which I was to build would function at all. The drawings were accompanied by instructions written in Arabic. The count, who could not read Arabic, had had the text translated into Spanish; this he had translated into his mother tongue and had scrawled along the margins of the old parchment documents. We spent several days trying to translate this text into German, but neither of us was capable of making enough sense out of these descriptions so that they might serve me as instructions, which they were obviously intended to be. They were more confusing than the drawings themselves, especially as they were worded in a figurative language which spoke of flowers, fragrant perfumes, and unknown spices, of strange oceans and distant lands, angels and demons, when there should have been nothing but metals and weights, screws and springs, coils and tractive forces, balances and swings of the pendulum. I was utterly bewildered and wanted to refuse the commission, but the count promised me a princely sum for my efforts, even if they should fail. In addition, he placed at my disposal a considerable percentage of this sum in cash, with which I was to procure the necessary materials and tools. I still hesitated, then he raised the sum, imploring me to at least try it. Finally I gave in and set to work. It took me weeks in these troubled times to gather the materials, as only the best would do. I had the face of the clock drawn up according to specifications; it was to be divided into sixteen hours, as if it were to measure some foreign time. I canvassed the countryside to find a cabinetmaker who could build and ornament the case according to the instructions; then we both traveled about selecting and buying the different types of wood out of which he was to construct the case – all of this in wartime, when we never knew at night if we were to see the sun the next morning. But God, all praise be His, held His shielding hand over me and my work, and in spite of all the difficulties the clock eventually took its present form, as it stands before you. It cost me three years' work. When it was finally finished, the clock actually ran, which was the last thing I expected. But the way it ran! According to the drawings, the clock was to have five hands, each of which was to trace its circle with varying speed and direction. The clock could tell the most improbable intervals and constellations of the heavenly bodies, but not the hours of the day. This must have been the invention of some insane infidel who wanted to measure the ages his damned soul would have to spend in Purgatory. It is the unchristian work of the devil which measures the eternity of Hell. Every chime of the evening bell sends its hands spinning in a different direction . . . But I see that my story bores you, gentlemen. Please pardon my prattling on so. I don't have visitors often."

"Who gave you this commission?" inquired one of the strangers.

"A Polish count, as I already mentioned. I never did know his name. He came back once to see me, when the clock was almost finished. He spent hours studying the drawings, measured the positions of the hands, listened to the ticking of the works, made notes in a small book, sighed and shook his head, seemed at times to be discontented with the clock, then again pleasantly surprised, then once again dissatisfied; his eyes followed the pendulum as it swung back and forth, his ears noticed every change in rhythm of the buzzing and whirring mechanism, which sometimes ticked as slowly as drops of water falling from the ceiling of a cave, then again as rapidly as the hoofbeats of a herd of galloping horses – but the man never uttered a word. When I questioned him he cut me off with a wave of the hand, put his finger to his lips, and listened with such concentration to the ticking and whirring of the clock that – I hope you will pardon this severe judgment – I slowly began to question his sanity. As he departed he left me a sack of gold coins. I thanked him profusely, for this was a much greater sum than he had promised me. He smiled and promised to return soon to pick up the clock, but I never saw him again. Heaven knows why he didn't come back; perhaps he was not satisfied with my work, perhaps he had been expecting too much. Who knows? He never spoke a word of praise, which I must admit I would have been glad to hear after all the effort I put into the making of the clock; after all, I did my very best to carry out the order to his satisfaction. But perhaps he perished in that terrible war, God save his poor straying soul. These are frightful times. But you know as well as I, gentlemen, what it is to live in these times. God be merciful to us and let there at last be peace.

Please blame it on my advancing age if I have gone prattling on again."

"Do you still have the drawings?"

"No, the Pole took them with him when he left this workshop for the last time. The clock was finished, I didn't need the drawings anymore. And I didn't want to keep them any longer, as they were quite valuable."

"So you know nothing more of the background or the whereabouts of your client?" inquired the strangers.

"I'm afraid not; otherwise I would have tried to find him myself. The clock has been standing in that corner now for two years. It takes up too much space in my workshop, but I can neither sell it nor give it away, much less take it apart or destroy it, because it doesn't belong to me. I am beginning to develop a passionate dislike for it; I usually cover it with a cloth and let it run down, but the silence that then fills the room is even more unbearable than the crazy ticking, so I wind it up again. But I removed three of the hands and replaced the face with a normal one; it was the only way I could bear the situation . . ."

"Tell us if that isn't a good story, Collins!"

"It certainly is, Your Majesty. But I know it all too well. I fell for it from beginning to end."

"Why didn't you follow up that business about the clock?"

"I held this insane instrument to be the product of a sick mind, not worth our time and attention."

"We assure you, you would have had a surprise. You and your people have been standing a whisker away from the secret of the time seal. If you had only held out a little longer . . . but we expect Weisslinger would have had something to say about that."

"Your Majesty, I am an idiot."

"Dear Collins!" laughed the king. "We judged you right! You have no use for metaphysics and unsound logic, for secrets and mysterious strangers. By the way, that Polish count was an invention of ours, but he was rather good, wasn't he?"

"Yes, indeed, Your Majesty."

"And something else, Collins. Do you know that the pendulum clock was not invented before 1657 by Huygens and was patented in the same year in the States General?"

"My God." Collins was embarrassed.

"Your idiots have missed the anachronism – but not Weiss, who thereupon traced down the dollmaker and let him have some part to assemble a machine, in order to move the time seals."

"I am deeply ashamed, Your Majesty."

"Very good. Now let us continue. We haven't finished yet."

"I am curious to hear how these events untangle themselves."

"Perhaps you will be disappointed. Don't set your hopes too high. It is all very simple. Now, these two gentlemen, who had come to see Weisslinger so late at night and had listened with more and more evident boredom to his story, finally purchased one of the mechanical dolls and two other toys, paid the dollmaker well, and took their leave politely but without concealing their disappointment, exhaustion, and ill humor. After refreshing themselves at the Red Ox, they traveled on, although it was well past midnight. Weisslinger watched the coach as it rounded the corner and rumbled out of the city. He closed the shutters again and rubbed his hands with delight, as if he had just made an excellent bargain. Then he blew out the light and went to bed."

"Do you still have the doll, Collins?"

"Of course, Your Majesty, but if I may say so, it is of little value to us. We have examined it carefully. By means of a simple spring mechanism the figure rotates about a fixed point."

"Collins, you are judging things only by their source of power and mobility potential. In a way you are right; the doll isn't worth much, but it is a nice toy, one that would make many a little girl happy, even nowadays. And it is all handmade, every screw is hand-threaded."

"It is no doubt interesting, Your Majesty, but by far not as interesting as the doll Your Majesty is holding now.

"There you are right, Collins. Technique has a way of improving on the product."

"Is this doll also one of Weisslinger's creations?"

The king gave no answer, but leaning down from his throne he carefully set the doll on the floor. It took a few cautious steps to test the smoothness of the surface, then made two or three elaborate pirouettes, sprang nimbly into the air, turned a somersault, landed lightly on its feet, and ended its performance with a courteous bow. The minister applauded in admiration; the king was sunk deep in thought, but suddenly he turned to Collins.

"Where did we leave off?"

"The dollmaker, Your Majesty."

"Oh yes, we remember. Now then, listen carefully!"

It was evening. The night watchman had just sung out the eleventh hour and had gone down the street, when a carriage drawn by two magnificent horses rounded the corner, rumbled over the cobblestones of the market square, and pulled up in front of the Red Ox Inn, directly across from the house of the dollmaker Weisslinger. The doll-maker went to his window and opened the shutters a tiny crack. He peered out in order to inspect the travelers who were arriving so late at night. The innkeeper came to the door to greet the distinguished guests and escort them into the house. Much to his astonishment, nobody descended from the carriage. The coachman made no move to climb down from his box. Upon being questioned by the innkeeper, he explained by means of gestures that he was mute. The innkeeper looked about him uncertainly, then turned with a shrug of the shoulders and went back into the house, closing the door behind him. But Weisslinger remained at his post and continued to gaze in fascina-tion at the carriage. The carriage curtains were closed, but as his eyes became more and more accustomed to the darkness, he noticed that someone had pulled one of the curtains aside and was examining his house with great interest. Time passed by, and neither observer gave up his station. At last the stranger in the carriage lit a cigarette.

"Bungler," muttered Weisslinger contemptuously, and closed the shutters. He did not bother to look again as the carriage rumbled out of the city an hour later. He was already sound asleep.

"What do you think of this version, Collins?"

"Inexcusable, Your Majesty. A cigarette in the seventeenth century! Such a mistake should never have been made by a patrolman. I give up."

"Not so fast, not so fast, Collins! Let us think. Where did we leave off?"

"The dollmaker, Your Majesty, had that evening . . ."

"Oh yes, we remember. Now pay attention!"

It was evening. The night watchman had just sung out the eleventh hour and had gone down the street, when a carriage drawn by two magnificent horses rounded the corner, rumbled over the cobblestones of the market square, and pulled up in front of the Red Ox Inn, directly across from the house of the dollmaker Weisslinger. The doll-maker went to his window and opened the shutters a tiny crack. He peered out in order to inspect the travelers who were arriving so late at night. He saw two men alight from the vehicle and converse with the innkeeper, who had come out to greet the distinguished guests and escort them into the house. The two strangers apparently did not intend to enter and partake of his board and lodging, as they involved him in a conversation on the doorstep. They had a number of questions and seemed to be looking for someone in the town, for the innkeeper nodded his head and pointed repeatedly to Weisslinger's house across the street. The strangers' eyes followed the innkeeper's finger, they carefully surveyed the market square and the neighborhood. Then they took leave of the innkeeper, pressing a gold coin into his hand, and strode toward Weisslinger's house.

At this very moment the dollmaker wound up one of his dolls and set it on the windowsill. The doll hopped nimbly to the ground and began to run. One of the men noticed it and called out to the other. They searched the square, trying to pierce the darkness with their eyes. Suddenly one of them took a leap and threw himself at the running figure, but it escaped him. The second man drew a small pistol and, aiming it, sent a spitting stream of fire whizzing toward the doll. But the tiny doll zigzagged agilely across the square and disappeared unscathed.

The long blue tongues of flame that came whipping out of the weapon licked up over the housetops, leaving glowing streaks behind them. Flashes of ghostly light lit up the market place, and the spitting, hissing, and roaring resounded so that the nearby streets fairly rattled with the echoes.

Weisslinger watched all the commotion in front of his house with amusement. In fact, he had to laugh so hard that his ribs ached.

"You miserable farmers!" he roared. "You louts! Idiots! You heroes of the laser pistols! Just take a look at that! Isn't this a marvelous joke?"

The disturbance outside had developed into a regular street fight. Fearful cries were heard as the people in the houses on the market square were awakened by the uproar. Shutters were thrown open on all sides and slammed shut again in panic as the shooting grew wilder. The townsmen suspected bold thieves or even enemy troops of causing the tumult, but in the general excitement and by the dim light they could not make out the target of the shooting.

In the meantime, something very odd had happened. Out of the carriage, which was built for four and could hold six at the very most, had swarmed fifteen or twenty shadow forms, which set about madly chasing the doll. Their chase gave off a fireworks display of constantly flickering pale streaks of flame, and in their robes they fluttered about the square and the fountain like an eerie swarm of giant moths. This frightful sight caused the inhabitants of the town who had been disturbed by the commotion to bar their doors and windows and to hide their valuables hastily in every niche and cranny they could find.

Master Weisslinger, however, remained at his window and watched the scuffle with growing amusement. He even goaded on the scufflers, but his laughing, jeering cries were drowned in the general uproar. At last one of the armed figures succeeded in hitting the fleeing doll. It exploded with a dull boom and the parts of its mechanism were scattered in the street. The dark-clad, shadowy forms feverishly searched for these fragments. They threw themselves upon the pavement, lights flared up and died out again, and the men crawled about in the street until they had convinced themselves that not a single screw or spring had escaped them. They were like a pack of hounds fighting over a few bones thrown into their midst.

At last every inch of pavement had been inspected and the men began to climb back into the carriage. There was a great rush and pushing; the carriage swayed on its wheels until at last all twenty men had managed to squeeze into it. It had taken four men to hold the horses, which had been frightened by the shooting and would not stop rearing and kicking. Held no longer, they set off at a gallop, and sparks flew from the wheels as the carriage, skidding and rocking, sped around the corner and out of the town.

As soon as the air had cleared and all was quiet outside, a few stout-hearted citizens dared to peek out of their doors and windows to see if body and soul were still in danger. Some courageously left their houses – carrying weapons – and after taking a rapid look about the square began to strut about fearlessly. Loud debates were carried on about the nocturnal raid, who the bold raiders could have been, whom the attack was intended for, what damage had been done, and what kind of an odd burning smell was still in the air. It turned out that nobody had suffered any harm, and nobody's property or possessions had been damaged or stolen. For the time being, no other conclusion could be reached than that at least one hundred heavily armed men had caused the tumult. They had appeared out of nowhere and disappeared again like lightning into thin air, because the appearance and intervention of so many valiant citizens had put dread fear into their hearts.

The night watchman reported that he had intended to throw himself resolutely before the galloping horses, but then thought better of it and decided to avoid meaningless sacrifice – not to mention the town's loss of his valuable services. Therefore, he had moved out of the path of the madly careening beasts and had contented himself with a loud and distinct "Stop!" which the coachman, however, who brutally whipped the horses and looked like the Old Nick himself, had insolently disregarded.

The discussions were carried on by torchlight long into the night and were not given up until the dawn appeared and the innkeeper was too tired to continue filling beermugs and carrying them across the square to sell to those thirsty citizens who stood about the fountain celebrating their victory.

After several days and many all-night debates in the inns, the townsmen came to the agreement, after having consulted the priest, who had shown a great interest in the speculations, that it must have been a devilish apparition which had come to haunt the town. Some surmised that it was an evil omen, others went so far as to interpret it as a warning to the innkeeper of the Red Ox, who had developed the bad habit of filling his mugs less and less full, and whose beer and wine tasted more and more watered down. The rumor spread about town and came in time to the innkeeper's hearing. The evil omen before his very house gave him grounds for reflection, and soon it could be noticed, to the satisfaction of all, that he had taken his lesson to heart and no longer gave his customers any reason to complain in this respect, at least for a time.

The dollmaker meanwhile had nothing to report about the nocturnal incident. He claimed to have slept so soundly that he hadn't heard the uproar at all, although it had taken place directly outside his window. The innkeeper, who wanted to hush the nasty rumors which were damaging his business, declared that the strangers had actually wanted to talk to Weisslinger. The dollmaker laughed and replied that the innkeeper was just looking for someone else to put the blame on and that he himself had and would have nothing to do with any of these brawlers, be it the Devil Himself. After all, the rowdies had given the innkeeper and not himself the first honors of a visit, which everybody well knew and which the innkeeper had already admitted. Everybody laughed along with Weisslinger, because he knew how to use his cleverness and wit to drive his opponent into a corner. The innkeeper said no more about the matter from that time on.

"What do you say to this version, Collins?"

"Bad work, Your Majesty. Very bad work."

"Like a whole herd of bulls in a china shop. Why this large-scale action? You sent a whole regiment in there! You were lucky that the people of this period are rather superstitious. Imagine that taking place in the twentieth or twenty-first century. Interventions of such dimensions could easily start a war, if you have bad luck. Did it at least help you?"

"Not much, Your Majesty. The doll was much more complex than the ones we had bought from Weisslinger, one could say unbelievably complex by the technical standards of that time, which of course increased our suspicion. But on the other hand, there was nothing mysterious about its mechanism. We couldn't completely reconstruct it from the pieces we had collected, but there was no indication of any electronic instruments – it was certainly a purely mechanical construction. But it seems to me now almost as if the dollmaker wanted to play a trick on us, and we promptly fell for it. He probably already knew that we came from a different age. But by Your Majesty's leave, how can such an idea occur to a man in the seventeenth century?"

The king laughed.

"Don't underestimate the human imagination! The concept that man can travel in time is much older than you think."

"That may be so. We'd have to look into it," said the minister.

"Now look at that! A simple seventeenth-century mechanic has played a trick on our Collins. Shall we give you an early pension?"

"I most humbly beg Your Majesty's forgiveness. We wanted to eliminate this fracture, but it was not possible."

The minister stared at the floor in shame.

The doll now tried to walk on its hands. It succeeded on the first try. The king smirked.

"It didn't work? Well, well. Think of that! It didn't work!"

"No, Your Majesty. It was our last chance to intervene successfully, WHITE had made everything else impossible. The seal started suddenly to move. We even had to leave important instruments at Operations Base 7 . . ."

"Time mirrors too?"

"Time mirrors too. We had to evacuate the station in a great hurry. The seal grew with threatening speed in our direction, as members of the patrol reported."

"Hmm. Does that surprise you? That could have caused a nasty fracture. Imagine the results if in this wild shooting someone had been seriously wounded or even killed. It would have put our entire history in a complete muddle. WHITE was forced to intervene, or else your people would have made more irreparable blunders."

"I beg Your Majesty's pardon, but it was an extremely important matter. For the first time one of these mysterious dolls appeared, time was pressing, and I had strictest orders . . ."

"But you are in charge of security and must certainly be aware of the consequences of intervening along the timeline. That's what you had special training for."

Collins stared contritely at the toes of his shoes.

"Your Majesty is right. It was careless of me."

"Now then, don't make such a face about it. Nothing really serious happened," laughed the king.

"Your Majesty deigns to laugh?"

"Yes, we were just imagining the twenty men squeezing into the coach. We assume that you had an instrument installed in the coach."

"Yes, Your Majesty, one of the time mirrors from Operations Base 7."

The conversation ceased, and both men silently watched the doll. It was dancing now on its hands, now on its feet. One somersault followed another.

"Where were we?"

"The dollmaker, Your Majesty, had on that evening . . ."

"Oh yes, we remember. Now, listen carefully!"

It was evening. The night watchman had just sung out the eleventh hour and had gone down the street, when a carriage drawn by two magnificent horses rounded the corner, rumbled over the cobblestones of the market square, and pulled up in front of the Red Ox Inn, directly across from the house of the dollmaker Weisslinger. The dollmaker went to his window and opened the shutters a tiny crack. He peered out in order to inspect the travelers who were arriving so late at night. The innkeeper had come out to greet the distinguished guests and escort them into the house. To his astonishment, no one got out of the carriage. The coachman made no preparation to climb down from his box. In answer to a question from the innkeeper, he indicated by gestures that he did not understand the language. But the innkeeper did not give up so easily. In sign language he asked again if the coachman was hungry or thirsty. After a moment's hesitation the coachman nodded, pulled the brake, knotted the reins, and climbed down from the box. The innkeeper wanted to lead him into the house, but the coachman preferred first to walk up and down a bit to stretch his legs, then to see to the horses and take another look at the carriage. He then took off his dark cape and shook it out, as if to leave the dust of long journeys on bad roads behind him, hung it about his shoulders with the pale lining to the outside, and at last was ready to follow the innkeeper into the house. Master Weisslinger, at first alarmed and then pleased, had watched the whole scene with breathless interest. The coachman had not taken a deep breath inside the inn before Weisslinger was hard at work. He did something rather odd. Using special tools, he opened the enormous grandfather clock, removed the hands, loosened and pried off the face, replaced some of the works with other pieces, and tightened wires and made new connections. He then put in a new face, fastened on five hands and set them according to the new face, measured the angles they formed, reset them, measured again, wound up the clock, tightened a screw here and loosened one there, listened carefully to the irregular ticking of the clock, checked the movement of the hands, and made new adjustments until a high chirping could be heard above the ticking. Weisslinger cautiously touched some of the wire connections, and they were warm and began to glow – the wires were live then; he had tapped the timeline. The air began to crackle, and sparks flitted along the wires and bathed the room in an eerie light. The chirping had now become so loud that it drowned out the ticking of the works. Weisslinger put down his tools, wiped the sweat from his forehead, and leaned back with a sigh of relief.

"I've done it," he said. "At least it looks like it."

Then he blew out the light and went to the window again. He had to wait over an hour before the stranger finally left the inn. The latter seemed to have refreshed himself liberally, for he swayed slightly as he walked and the innkeeper escorted him to the door.

"Hallooooo there!" he called out, and waved in the direction of Weisslinger's house.

The dollmaker shook his head and said, "Just you wait!"

The innkeeper was helping the coachman to store away the horses' feedbags and to climb up onto the box again.

"Halloo!" called the stranger again. Receiving no reply, he grunted and gave his whip a jerk, but so clumsily that it nearly hit the innkeeper. The carriage started up and rumbled at a leisurely pace out of the town, although it was well past midnight.

Weisslinger watched it disappear. Then he took a small, delicate doll out of its hiding place, took one last careful look at it, and wound it up. The doll woke up and stretched its legs. He held its little smooth head between thumb and forefinger and murmured, "You can do it. You will penetrate thousands of years and will bring me a sign. I know it now."

He put the doll on the windowsill. The little creature cautiously examined the market square.

"Run!" said the dollmaker, and gave the figure a push. With one spring the doll was on the street, whisked over the square like a shadow, and was gone. Weisslinger closed and barred the shutters and retired to bed.

"What do you think of this version, Collins?"

"I hadn't heard that one before, Your Majesty."

"We believe that, Collins, but you will get to know it well."

"How is that, Your Majesty?"

"Just wait. We are not finished yet. We are going to have to act it out together in order to round off the story."

"Your Majesty said 'together'?"

"Yes, Collins, you heard quite rightly. We are going to have to act it out together, the two of us."

"How am I to understand this?"

"It is very simple, and you will understand it clearly, as clearly as we are sitting here."

"Does Your Majesty permit me to ask a question?"

"Naturally."

"Was this doll that Weisslinger sent off that evening the same one with which Your Majesty is now playing?"

"The very same one, Collins. A few thousand years old and still fully intact. Go ahead and take a good look at it."

As if it had understood the conversation, the doll hopped upon the minister's arm, held on to his shoulder, and looked him in the eye.

"By Your Majesty's leave, it is really a marvel."

"Yes, isn't it! But where had we left off, Collins?"

"The dollmaker, Your Majesty, had on that evening . . ."

"Oh yes, now we remember. Now listen carefully!"

It was evening. The night watchman had just sung out the eleventh hour and had gone down the street, when a carriage drawn by two magnificent horses rounded the corner, rumbled over the cobblestones of the market square, and pulled up in front of the Red Ox Inn, directly across from the house of the dollmaker Weisslinger. The dollmaker went to his window and opened the shutters a tiny crack. He peered out in order to inspect the travelers who were arriving so late at night. The innkeeper had come out to greet the distinguished guests and escort them into the house. To his astonishment, no one got out of the carriage. The coachman made no move to climb down from his box, and, in answer to a question from the innkeeper, explained by means of gestures that he did not understand the language. The innkeeper looked uncertainly about him for a while, then shrugging his shoulders returned into the house and closed the door. But Weisslinger continued to stare in fascination at the carriage. The curtains of the carriage windows were drawn, but now that his eyes had become accustomed to the darkness be could see that the interior of the coach was illuminated by a pale and flickering light. Weisslinger gave a small sigh of relief, but for a while absolutely nothing happened. The coachman sat motionless and lost in thought upon his box; the reins were tied up and the brakes drawn. The horses snorted, chafed against the shaft of the carriage, and shook their harnesses. Time slipped by. At last the man climbed down, walked up and down to stretch his legs, saw to the horses, then took off his dark cape and shook it out, as if to leave the dust of long journeys on bad roads behind him, and hung it about his shoulders with the pale lining to the outside. He stepped up to the carriage and opened the door a crack. A small figure hopped out, flitted like a shadow across the square directly to the dollmaker's house, with a single spring bound to the windowsill, raised its little metallic face to Weisslinger, and made a courteous bow.

The master closed the window and unbolted the door. He cautiously peered about the market square, listened to hear if anyone might he passing by at so late an hour or if the night watchman might be approaching on his rounds, but there was no one in sight. Muffled noises drifted across from the Red Ox, where a few townsmen were drinking beer and whiling away the time with politics and card games. For the rest, all was quiet. The fountain in the market square splashed, and the horses snorted and pawed the paving stones. There was not a soul in sight. The stillness of the night lay peacefully over the town. The war was far away.

Weisslinger gave the coachman a sign.

The coachman immediately ripped open the carriage door, leaned far in and hauled out a long and obviously heavy bundle, got it with difficulty onto his shoulder, and staggered over to the dollmaker's house. The dollmaker hurried to help him carry the burden.

"Who are you, stranger?" asked the master in a whisper.

"WHITE," answered the man just as quietly. "Thank you for helping me carry him. He is damned heavy."

The bundle was a body. They carried it into the house and laid it carefully on the bed.

"Is he dead?" asked Weisslinger anxiously.

"No, he's only unconscious. He'll wake up soon."

The stranger breathed heavily.

"Damned heavy, that – uh . . . I beg your pardon . . . that fellow. Got me worked into a good sweat. I'm getting old."

"Did everything go off all right?" Weisslinger wanted to know.

"You can see that it did."

"How did it go?"

"More about that later."

The stranger did not want to waste time. Weisslinger turned to the person on the bed and took a good look at his face.

"He has gotten fat," he laughed. Then he began to transform himself. He took off his wig, removed the clipped gray beard, and with a few clever strokes completely transformed his face, so that he looked like the mirror image of the unconscious man on the bed.

"Finished?" asked the coachman.

"Just one more minute," said Weisslinger. He rolled up the plans which hung on the walls and lay on the table, ripped them up, and threw the scraps into the fire. Then he took a hammer from the workbench and approached the grandfather clock.

"But – " interrupted the stranger, and added hesitantly, "Excuse my meddling, but shouldn't he have a chance?"

"How big were my chances?" replied Weisslinger, and gave the stranger a searching look. He swung the heavy hammer and let it smash into the clock. Glass flew, the valuable case splintered. With the second blow there was a crunching of metal, the pendulum began to clatter, and the hands whirred with increasing speed. The third blow brought the works to a standstill. He took another swing but did not finish it.

"You are right. It is a pity to destroy the clock. It cost me hours of work. With luck and skill it could be repaired. We'll leave him the tools. He can sell them, if he can find somebody to buy them. The materials alone that went into that clock are worth a pretty penny. But if he sells it all he'll be sorry. In any case, he'll get less for it than it is worth. If he can get it back into salable condition at all."

"If," said the stranger.

"I am ready," said Weisslinger.

"Take my cape." And the coachman removed his cape from his shoulders. The dollmaker drew it about himself.

"Not like that – the pale side to the inside."

Weisslinger turned it inside out. The other side was dark.

"Come quickly! He is waking up," urged the coachman.

The figure on the bed rolled over and groaned. Weisslinger took one last look around the room which had been his home for years and in which he had spent many an anxious hour between hope and desperation, many a night, half awake, half dreaming, pondering over and developing fantastic projects. Bent over his workbench, working all night through, summer and winter, he had drawn up plans, with primitive tools had turned and filed and fashioned mechanisms the precision of which his colleagues could not begin to copy. All the while he was on the lookout, constantly stepping to the window and peering out in fear, whenever strangers came to the town and stopped at the Red Ox Inn, that they were already on his trail and wanted to kidnap him or kill him or at least destroy his work.

Weisslinger turned away. He motioned to the doll, which sprang onto his shoulder, and followed the stranger, who was already impatiently waiting at the carriage and holding open the door.

"I'll climb up on the box next to you. I am curious to hear how it all went."

"All right," said the coachman, and helped him up to his perch. The carriage started up, and rumbled at a leisurely pace over the market square and out of the town.

"Now listen carefully," said the coachman. "You must put yourself into the situation and play the exact part which I am now going to describe to you. Pay very close attention, every detail is of the utmost importance."

The stranger then proceeded to give Weisslinger specific instructions on how he was to behave, what he had to say, what gestures he should make. The dollmaker had many questions, and to all of them the coachman had exact answers. He concluded all the descriptions and explanations as the carriage drew up to a dark, secluded farm, which lay deep in a vast forest through which the carriage had been driving for over an hour along narrow and overgrown tracks. They stopped. The moon had risen high in the sky and poured its cold light over the collapsing roofs of barn and sheds, over the muddy barnyard whose deep ruts were filled with water that glittered in the light, over the gardens that had run to seed, in which the weeds had grown high above the crooked fences. Everything looked dirty and dilapidated.

"Is this Operations Base 7?" asked Weisslinger.

"Yes," answered the coachman.

"It is a pigsty."

"That is the best camouflage for it. If anyone wanders into this deserted area, he should not have the impression that there is anything here worth stealing. We are fairly certain that nobody has been snuffling around here. But of course now it doesn't make any difference anymore."

The coachman took the bridle and reins off the horses, let them loose, and chased them out of the farmyard with cries and cracks of the whip.

"It's a pity. They were beautiful beasts," said Weisslinger.

"They'll find another master. First they should enjoy their freedom for a while."

They ransacked the house and sheds, destroyed all the instruments, and set fire to the farmstead. The dry wood of the old building burned like tinder; the flame shot up and in no time had reached the rooftree. The thatched roofs of the sheds blazed like torches in the night and scattered a shower of dark red sparks into the forest.

"A devilishly dangerous business we're doing," commented Weisslinger.

"But it's fun," laughed the coachman, and threw more fuel onto the fire. The heat was tremendous, and the two men withdrew into the carriage. The built-in mirror flickered and quivered in a milky light. The dollmaker smiled.

"Ready?" asked the stranger.

"Ready," said Weisslinger, and picked up the doll. Then they stepped, one after the other, through the mirror.

They had just disappeared when the rooftree of the farmhouse fell in with a great crash and a splash of sparks. The farmyard was strewn with burning shingles and splinters of wood. The fire now blazed several hundred feet into the sky and gave an eerie light far into the night. A few minutes later, a violent explosion demolished the carriage.

"What do you think of this version of the story, Collins?"

"It too is completely new to me, Your Majesty. Not only that, it is inexplicable. But still, the picture seems complete. All the pieces of the puzzle fit together. There seem to be a few pieces still missing however. Am I right, Your Majesty?"

"Quite right, Collins. But those pieces will turn up. Just have a little patience. We haven't finished the story yet."

"So WHITE intervened . . ."

The king smirked.

"We couldn't do anything about that."

"Not anymore, Collins. Not anymore."

"Right, Your Majesty, not anymore. I have to admit defeat."

"Nothing doing, Collins! There will be no giving up now. The story isn't complete. You have to keep playing. We insist on it, even if we have to order you to play. Don't disappoint us. Maybe you can make one more important move."

"I wouldn't know where to . . ."

"We have to fit all the pieces of the puzzle together to get the complete picture. Something is missing."

"Yes – for instance, why this substitution and with whom? . . . and what information did this Weisslinger receive from WHITE? That is, if – and I am not so sure of this – the coachman is in fact WHITE. What did Weisslinger find out from this stranger?"

"He was told the very same story that you just heard. But the doll-maker also heard the end of the story, which you will find out in a moment too. Then you will understand the substitution."

"I already have an idea, Your Majesty. Please carry on with the story."

"Patience, Collins. We have time, plenty of time. Limitless time is at our disposal. You will hear everything."

"I am very eager to hear it all, Your Majesty."

"Very well then. This part of the story is quite different. It takes place much earlier than all the rest that we have already told you."

The king reflected a moment before continuing.

In the meantime, the doll had begun to include double flips in its dance and whirled across the room.

"As you perhaps know, Collins, we once had a brother."

"Your Majesty has strictly forbidden any mention or even knowledge of this fact. I believe he met with a fatal accident many years ago while making some rash experiment in physics."

"That is quite right. He was killed in a time-travel experiment. How that came about, you are now about to hear. Once upon a time . . ."

Once upon a time there was a king, who was very rich and whose power extended over four solar systems and all celestial bodies within a radius of twenty light-years. This king had two sons who were very close to each other in age. When the sons were still children there lived in the palace an eccentric old man, of whom nobody at the court took any real notice. He was a mathematician and physicist and it was his responsibility to look after the electronic systems and computer center of the palace. His entire life was devoted solely to his profession, and he never participated in the social life of the court. His wife had died at an early age and since then he had lived like a recluse, eating and sleeping amid his scientific apparatus and computers and seeing and being seen by nobody for weeks on end, unless he was needed to repair a defective stereo tele-wall or one of the transmitters. He had been born on one of the most godforsaken planets of the kingdom, on which his ancestors, of ancient colonial settler stock, had settled. They had adapted themselves to the climate of the planet and could even exist out of doors in the open air. We believe his father was even a farmer.

He was sent to school, proved to be very bright, studied electronic sciences, and made quite a name for himself in his field. One day his young wife was killed in a transfer ship accident. He must have taken that very hard. He gave up physics and lived like a hermit. His resources were soon exhausted and he suffered bitter want. So he started writing stories, fairy tales full of profound and hidden meaning. He was very gifted at this but good fortune evaded him. His colleagues laughed at him because they did not understand his stories, and many people said that his great misfortune had driven him out of his senses. He was soon forgotten – no one read his works – and he led a wretched and lonely existence in a poor hut outside the city. One day the king heard of his tragic fate and commanded him to come to the palace. After much hesitation he finally accepted a position at the court. He was kept busy with occasional repairs and with the supervision of the automatic central control station and the computer installations, an occupation which did not demand much time or effort. He continued to write his fairy tales and to be derided for doing so. No one took him very seriously. But that did not seem to bother him very much. He only smiled enigmatically whenever he was asked to tell one of his stories, and his listeners turned away shaking their heads. And so he came to be known at the court as an eccentric old man whose thoughts were bewildering and whose logic was peculiar, but he seemed to be harmless, so people left him alone. Only the two princes were genuinely fond of him and considered him to be their good friend. He in turn loved them dearly, but not because he expected to gain anything by it – he had never thought of such a thing. He loved them because they were his most patient listeners and would listen for hours on end and still beg for more, delighted with his stories and never tired of hearing them. He would tell of the past and the future, of distant unknown kingdoms and their strange inhabitants; he could describe in detail the cities, the streets and squares, the palaces and markets, he could give such a clear picture of the clothing and language and the customs and habits of their inhabitants, that it seemed as if he had been to all these marvelous places and had seen them all with his own eyes. And yet he seldom left the windowless rooms of the royal computer control station, passing his days amid computers and field generators, matter transmitters and receiving sets.

Although the princes did not always understand everything he told them, it was always exciting. They liked him because he could tell fascinating stories without constantly putting in flattering phrases or wagging a moralizing finger, as the others always did.

More and more often they found the old man in his laboratory bent over technical drawings or bustling about complicated instruments. He seemed to have rediscovered his profession, but he always rolled up his drawings or wiped his hands and had time for them when they came to see him. Sometimes they watched him at work. The computers were at work day and night, figuring out integral equations which he fed into them. He fitted together tiny parts and wired electrical connections, ordered raw materials and new parts which often had to be sent in from great distances. The princes enjoyed the tingling feeling when he opened one of the small packages which had traveled through half the galaxy and now lay on his workbench, and tiny glittering instruments appeared which specialists in another part of the inhabited universe several thousand light-years away had carefully put together and packed.

One day the two boys noticed that their friend had aged visibly. He had always been in excellent health but was now suddenly declining rapidly. From one week to the next, from one day to the next, he seemed to age several years. His hair turned gray, his face became wrinkled, his eyes grew tired and red-rimmed. He became forgetful and absent-minded and often had difficulty remembering the events and conversations of the previous day. His mind and body disintegrated with terrifying rapidity.

It wasn't until much later that the two boys found out the reason for this startling transformation. The old man had developed an instrument by means of which he could travel in time, and he had been spending months and years at other points on the timeline. In order not to awaken any suspicion, he always returned to the point in time from which he had departed, so that nobody noticed that he was gone and started unpleasant investigations. He had succeeded masterfully in avoiding this. No one had had the slightest notion of his excursions.

And so the years passed. The princes grew into young men and had to study a great deal, but whenever they had time they went to see their friend. One day they found him ill. His hair had turned snow-white and his cheeks were hollow and sunken. He knew that he would not live much longer but he seemed happy, as if he could look back with satisfaction on a fulfilled life. He motioned the two princes to his bedside and in a faint voice initiated them into his secret. He had used his last ounce of strength to destroy his wonderful machine, for some unknown reason, but he left behind drawings, plans, and descriptions, which would enable someone with a clever mind to reconstruct the instrument.

A few days later he died and his body was blasted after a short ceremony which few people attended. Nobody missed him at court; only the two young princes mourned their old friend.

Then they went through his legacy, rummaged through the drawers, drained all the information from the data banks, and set about puzzling out the complicated plans and drawings. The remains of the instrument were painstakingly examined and classified. The princes applied themselves with the greatest zeal to the problem, but it proved to be extraordinarily difficult. The old man's descriptions were as strange and paradoxical as his stories had been. But now the fact that they had so carefully listened to his tales proved to be a great advantage, for they had little trouble in fathoming his odd and apparently illogical way of thinking. Still, the work progressed very slowly, although they spent days and months in the laboratory of the computer control station, brooding over sketches. The king gave them complete freedom to pursue their own interests, in order that their abilities might develop more fully, and no one else paid any attention to how they spent their time.

Soon the princes quarreled, because each one had developed his own theory as to how the problem was best to be approached. Nevertheless, they managed to cooperate to such an extent that one day the mirror of the instrument began to flicker, as the descriptions indicated that it should. But what a disappointment! Its surface proved to be impenetrable. Something was missing.

Despondency seized them. Could it be that their friend had really just played a trick on them, fooled them as he had so often done with his stories? He was entirely capable of having done just that, although in this case much spoke against it. However, after more intensive study of the plans they found that the person who wished to step through the mirror had to take with him a particular instrument which would allow him to penetrate the energy field behind the mirror. This energy field would then transport him along the timeline until the poles of the instrument were reversed, at which point the person would be ejected from the energy field onto a given point on the timeline. Here he would materialize and move with normal speed in time. This mechanism had the form of an attractive brooch the size of a ten Solar piece and consisted of tiny silver leaves and innumerable microscopic crystals in which very fine copper wires were fixed; these were interconnected according to an extremely intricate circuit diagram. The reconstruction of this diagram turned out to be the knottiest problem of all.

The elder of the two princes, who was especially talented in handling tiny mechanical parts, succeeded one day in assembling this extremely complex mechanism. His brother watched as he disappeared and reappeared, only to slip off and return again through the mirror, but he could report little more than that behind the mirror he was swept away by an indefinable current, had a slight feeling of giddiness, and after a few moments was ejected from the instrument again. One could see nothing. The space behind the mirror was immersed in an impermeable milky WHITE, which surrounded one like a heavy fog through which one couldn't see one's hand before one's face. It was impossible to land in another time or even take a peek into another period; one was always thrown out of the field at the same point at which one had entered. The puzzle was still to be solved. Much later the prince discovered that this part of the timeline had been sealed off and that the seal had made travel there impossible. The inventor himself had placed this seal and many others along the timeline, in order to protect its network from careless, unintentional, or even malicious interference.

As soon as the seal was behind them, the brooch functioned perfectly, and the brothers traveled up and down and back and forth along the timeline. They got into extremely confusing situations, since they had absolutely no experience and did not know how to handle the brooch properly. They could set themselves in motion in the machine's time field but had no influence over the time and place at which they were ejected again. Fortunately, this always occurred after a very few minutes. They cautiously increased the field energy and found that they could manage stretches of a day or two, but they still could neither predict nor influence the point at which they were forced out of the field. One of the two disappeared once for six days, and his brother had trouble concealing his absence at court, but the great similarity in their appearance came to his aid.

Then came – this was all many, many years ago – the problem of the succession to the throne, which the king wanted to have settled before his death. He wanted his kingdom to remain undivided, and, according to the ancient right of the firstborn, granted the older son the crown. The second son was to be so well provided for that he could devote himself for the rest of his life to his interests, be they of an artistic or a scientific nature.

Now misfortune had it that the younger son was filled with ambition to rule the kingdom, whereas the designated heir apparent was much more inclined to the sciences than to power. It was he who had contributed the most to the construction of the instrument.

Ill-will and dissension grew and estranged the two brothers, who had once been inseparable. The heir apparent would have preferred to give up his claim to the throne in order to put an end to the wretched and disgraceful quarrel, but the king stubbornly clung to his decision, to conform to tradition and to satisfy the strong conservative elements in the kingdom. He wanted to avoid outbreaks of violence, which would only have shaken the country and awakened the avidity of greedy and jealous neighbors.

The younger brother felt slighted and sank deeper and deeper into malevolent envy. Evil courtiers encouraged him, giving him dubious advice and finally bringing him to the conclusion that he in some way or other had to have his brother eliminated. He succeeded magnificently in doing so, in a cunning manner of which no one would have thought him capable. He used the time-travel machine. The older brother could not rest until he had figured out how to materialize in times where there was no mirror and how to place and remove the seals. As he once again stepped through the mirror, his brother crept up and turned the energy of the time field up to full strength. He himself was horrified as some of the mechanisms suddenly broke down, wired connections burned out, and finally the mirror exploded. The field collapsed and the older brother, who had been carried by the ultra-high-powered transporter to some remote part of the timeline, was thrown out and landed in that distant age. What age it was nobody knew, least of all he himself, but it had to be in the past, since that was the direction in which he had set out to travel.

The court was in an uproar as the terrible accident was discovered. It was feared that the frightful event could have political consequences. Now everyone found out what the two princes had been up to for years and they cursed the dangerous games and fateful legacy of the crazy old physicist – and waited. The days turned into weeks, the weeks lengthened into months, finally an entire year had passed, but there was no sign or trace of the heir to the throne. The king ordered court mourning, for no one could imagine how or where the young man could reappear. Except his brother, of course, who from then on had an exceedingly bad conscience and lived in the constant fear that the victim of his malicious deed could reappear someday and call him to account. He could sleep only when the room was brightly lighted, awoke bathed in sweat out of a sleep troubled by uneasy dreams, started convulsively at every unaccustomed sound, grew more and more nervous and impatient, was convinced he was being pursued, treated his inferiors unjustly, and trusted no one.

"Didn't you have that impression, Collins?"

"Indeed, Your Majesty."

"As the old king died and the younger son acceded to the throne, he could not rest until he had rebuilt the time instrument, to ensure himself against all eventualities. He built up a police corps, which had to travel about in time, searching for suspicious signs along the time-line. The guards had to follow up and report on every trace which could possibly be construed as endangering His Majesty. Their supreme duty was to guarantee the security of the king under all conditions and at all times. Carelessness on the part of the patrol caused innumerable fractures, especially in the first period, and an army of scientists and mechanics was required to repair them. No great damage was done to past history, thanks to the seals, which the patrol came across in many places and which they called WHITE because the area behind the mirror within the sealed time spaces was white and permitted neither takeoff nor landing. But it was no future power which had made these points inaccessible; it was the old man, who in his wise foresight — or perhaps I should say in his better judgment — had placed the seals there. He had accomplished an enormous amount of work, both in the future and in the past; that must have cost him decades, by the way. But back to the patrol. They put in much time and effort learning ancient languages, they studied the customs of bygone civilizations, practiced using primitive weapons and instruments, learned how to handle animals, sleep in the open atmosphere and tolerate vermin and poisoned air, and accustomed their stomachs to barbaric foods, but their success was only moderate. They hunted phantoms and waylaid mechanical dolls. That is the funniest part of the whole story. They hunted a doll which they could not catch and in fact never even saw until it was too late. But why are we telling this to you? You know this part best, don't you, Collins? After all, you directed the operation."

"Quite right, Your Majesty."

"But we must tell you the rest of the story too — it is the ugliest and most distressing part. Let us tell you the fate of the prince whose bitter lot it was to be banned to a distant and obscure century, and how he fared there."

The prince had stepped through the mirror and had directed his path toward the past, in order to examine the seal which had given him trouble at the beginning of his experiments. He let himself be carried through the glimmering darkness by a slight current, then noticed suddenly that his speed was accelerating rapidly. He felt himself being whirled about, as if he were being drawn into a vortex, and nearly lost consciousness. All at once the motion ceased, the field ejected him, and it was light.

Until then he had had no idea how one could materialize without a mirror, what field energy was necessary to accomplish this, and what precautionary measures had to be taken. Now he learned it through personal experience. He materialized at about fifteen feet in the air and fell heavily to the ground. There was a stabbing pain in his right hip and he rolled over onto his face. At the same time, he realized that his hair was singed and his clothing had caught fire. He wallowed in the damp soil and smothered the flames. Exhausted, filthy, and tormented by pains, he lay immobile and tried to overcome the shock. He had to fight back tears, but after a few minutes he was able to pull himself together and attempt to sort out what had happened to him. He had not the slightest notion in which era he was stranded. His first impression was that he must be in an extremely remote area of the past, for there was still agriculture, as he could clearly see by the furrows in the ground, with which he had so painfully become acquainted. Cautiously he looked about him. He lay in the middle of an open field. There was no human settlement in the vicinity. The area was hilly, with a few isolated clumps of trees here and there. A row of scraggly bushes lined a brook which meandered down a wide valley. The countryside seemed ugly and unkempt. There was wild undergrowth everywhere, the plants were neither symmetrical nor genetically refined, and the trees appeared to be authentic and natural. Someone must have recently watered the land absurdly heavily, as the ground was damp and there were great puddles in the overgrown fields and meadows. The sky was so hazy that he could hardly tell where the sun was, but he figured that it must be near midday.

In all his misfortune he had still had the good luck not to materialize amid a thickly populated area. The pressure wave that he must have caused would certainly have torn to pieces the lungs of all living beings within a radius of a hundred yards. And if he had materialized within a solid body, the effect would have been like that of a medium-sized atom bomb, and there would have been nothing left of him. He looked about for a hiding place. He was as clearly visible to air reconnaissance here in the middle of the field as if he were lying on a silver platter. He could not stay here. His clothing, strange and in addition singed, his sudden appearance literally out of the nowhere, and his ignorance of the native language would all make him a suspicious character, and if he were picked up he would certainly be in for severe cross-examination. But nobody would believe him if he told the truth. He searched the sky but there was, fortunately, no helicopter in the area. The best thing would be to seek cover in a wood and wait there until dark. Then he would keep a lookout for lights and try to find a house or small village where he could perhaps get native clothing, food, and a minimum of equipment. After that he would see.

He got up. At once a sharp pang ran through his right hip. He must have injured himself in the unexpected fall. I hope nothing is broken, he thought, that would be a catastrophe. He limped across the fields to the nearest clump of trees, making slow and painful progress. He cursed the meteorologists who had watered the area too heavily. They must not have gotten far in developing their climate regulators. The damp earth clung in heavy clods to his soles and he often had to retrieve his shoes from the sodden field, where they stuck in the mud. He was very inadequately equipped and too lightly clothed, but it could have been worse – he could have landed in an icy winter. The trees that he was heading for stood on the far side of the narrow brook. He would have to wade the brook; jumping over it was out of the question. Every step was torture to him. As he finally reached the bank he suddenly stopped short. In the bed of the stream, washed by the shallow water, lay the mutilated corpses of two men. They were only half clothed, obviously plundered, and must have lain there for many days, for the bodies were bloated and deformed and gave off a nauseating smell. Both of them had ghastly wounds on the head and throat. They had been barbarously murdered and thrown into the brook. He had never seen anything so abhorrent before, and turned away revolted. Was this a crime? That was all he needed! There was nothing worse than getting involved in such business. He must leave the area as quickly as possible. He walked on faster, following the stream down the valley. Three hundred yards farther he came upon a caved-in bridge of rotting wood, over which a narrow road had crossed the stream. He could see that it had been destroyed by force. Here he found a third body, this time of a woman. It lay near an overturned vehicle which had been plundered and destroyed. Apparently the culprits had intended to steal the belongings of the woman, for baskets and crates that had been broken open lay trampled in the fields on either side of the road and in the stream; articles of clothing and pieces of cloth, shoes of various sizes, and objects whose function he could not make out were strewn about. The vehicle appeared to have been a sort of supply wagon. The woman must have defended herself to the very last, for even in death she still clutched some of her belongings. She had apparently been shot through the head with a large-caliber weapon; the shot had ripped away part of her skull. He turned away, nauseated, and gathered up a few pieces of cloth, with which he covered the body. Then he collected everything that could be of use to him. He found an odd piece of clothing whose two tubelike appendages were apparently intended to encase legs, and a jacket of heavy material, torn and wet but still quite serviceable. He tried on this and that until he had outfitted himself like a native. He had more trouble with footwear but finally found two different foot containers made of animal skin which did not fit too badly. He overcame his disgust at wearing the skin of a dead being next to his skin and put them on.

He had reached his first goal, and although he did not fancy himself a looter of corpses, at least he was not so conspicuous in his new clothing. He was aware of the danger of his undertaking, for if he was found near the scene of the crime, he would not have to worry much about his future. As far as he could see, a man's life was not worth much here, and short work was made of it. He had to be on his guard, but fortunately there was not a human being in sight. The region must be very thinly populated and seemed to be completely inaccessible by any means of transport – otherwise, the dead would have been found long ago.

He took a closer look at the destroyed vehicle. It was made entirely of genuine wood held together by bolts and strips and rings of iron, and had the most primitive steering system imaginable. It had no means of propulsion but seemed to have been pulled by some mechanism or even animals, which had been detached and removed from the wagon. This disconcerted him greatly. This sort of vehicle had not been in existence for many thousand years. In which age had he landed? He searched his mind for historical dates. How long had there been automobiles? Their development lay just before the discovery of atomic energy and electronics. That was the end of the second and the beginning of the third millennium. All the horror stories and gruesome reports of those barbaric centuries which he had heard as a child now came to mind again. Had he landed in the twentieth century or even earlier? The transport field couldn't have carried him that far; its energy was too low. Unless . . . That couldn't be! Just keep calm, he told himself. No hasty conclusions. First think it all over. It was surely possible that in an electronic civilization there were people who delighted in imitating the ancients and even had vehicles drawn by animals. Still, the dead woman hadn't looked as if she had been traveling about on a pleasure outing. He examined the articles of clothing – no synthetics, all were made of organic substances. All observations led to the same conclusion. He must be in a pretechnical age. If that were the case, his position was hopeless. Without great sources of electrical energy, without electronics, precision instruments, and high-quality raw materials, he could not help himself out of the situation. He could only wait until help came from the future. They would search for him – his brother would do everything in his power to find him and get him out. But how would he find him, if he had no idea where he was? Keep calm, he repeated to himself. There are several possibilities. He would have to find a way to send information into the future, so that they would take notice of him. He could for instance paint cryptic paintings or write enigmatic books whose anachronisms and precognition would be striking and could be interpreted as a message. But was he a painter or a writer? Would his works survive thousands of years of changing intellectual tendencies, wars and barbarianism, fire and anarchy, vandalism and the condemnation of purist sects – would they even survive him? And if so, would they be understood at the right moment as a message from him? Would anyone consider them worthy of keeping in a library or museum? Would they even be discovered among the thousands of testimonies of the art of clairvoyance and astrology, alchemy and obscure speculative philosophy, black and white magic, science fiction and fairy tales of the distant past? And after all, did his brother – the terrible suspicion which he had been constantly pushing out of his mind took clear form – did his brother have any interest at all in finding him again?

No useless speculations, he warned himself. He would find out. There was plenty of time. Perhaps he could build mechanisms which if well protected could survive several civilizations, ticking like time bombs through the ages, and at a given point attract attention to themselves and to him. If time travel were possible, then they would certainly look into his case again, whether they received a message or not. The important point was for him to establish contact, then perhaps they would find a way to him. He had to be on the alert not to overlook any signs or signals. If they really wanted to help him out of this mess, there would be no problem. It was just better for him to be a bit wary, because if it were in their interest to leave him here, then it would be up to him to make the decisive move. He must be very careful not to cause any contradictions or anachronisms; no camouflage was perfect. But this meant that he would have to know the age perfectly, would have to study it thoroughly and adapt himself completely as a contemporary, no matter how difficult this might be. He would have to gain a firm footing in this involuntary exile, and circumstances dictated that he must do so immediately. At first he was concerned only with pure survival: food, weapons, money, a relatively safe place to live, and information. All the rest he would take care of later. He was perhaps inferior to the natives in physical resistance and hardiness, but his scientific and technical knowledge would stand him in good stead. He just had to make the best use he could of the primitive resources.

He left the scene of horror behind him and scrambled over the remains of the bridge across the stream, turned off from the road, and sought a relatively dry place among the trees and bushes where he would be hidden from the eyes of any natives who might come along. It was warm and he spread out the captured clothing to dry, then examined his injured leg. The injury was painful but there was apparently no break, only a bone bruise. A few hours of rest would do him good. He let himself down upon the ground and had a more leisurely look at his surroundings. The native plants which grew on all sides of him were indescribably ugly. Birds twittered in the branches above him, but he did not have the impression that they were the diverting artificial mechanisms that he was accustomed to, for they behaved in a shy and strange manner. They must be organic beings, but he had to admit that they sang just as nicely as the artificial ones he knew. Every place he set his eyes on was swarming with life. On the ground, in the grass, on the leaves, in the bark of the trees, everywhere tiny animals were creeping and crawling, chirping and rustling. He was somewhat nauseated by so much organic life. He had been brought up in the sterile world of the plastic region, into which every few weeks a stray animal found its way, an odd insect like a fly or moth, which – if it had in some inexplicable manner penetrated the energy screen without being burned – was immediately traced by infrared searchers and chased out of the airspace or killed. I will have to get used to it, he thought. Overcoming his aversion, he let one of the quick, black, six-footed animals run across the back of his hand. It did not hurt and the animal seemed not to be poisonous.

He looked at the sky. It was empty; there were no condensation trails of departing or landing transfer ships to be seen, no observation platforms on invisible gravitation anchors, no programmed control floater in the complex network of directive beams of a ground station for surface inspection, no reflex of an energy halo which surrounded the planet and protected it from extraterrestrial attacks. The sun broke through the thin cloud layer and scattered the clouds. Its warmth and beams of energy pierced the atmosphere and gave the skin a prickling sensation.

He listened. Something had been irritating him all this time, and now he knew what it was. The environment was so quiet. Although there were birds twittering and leaves rustling, it was so unbelievably quiet that he could hear his own pulse. His ears were accustomed to a great jumble of constant sounds caused by the innumerable transport craft, the control and service mechanisms, and other useful apparatus in the palace which he had never really noticed before, as he had heard them all since birth. Now this stillness seemed like a constant dull sound to him, one that lies just under the threshold of hearing and is perceived rather than heard. The sun dried his clothing and lay with calming warmth on his face, and afternoon dozed peacefully over the countryside. The prince felt that he was tired and before he knew it he was fast asleep.

When he awoke, night had come and he saw the stars. He had never seen the inhabited universe with such clarity from the surface of the earth. With his bare eyes he could recognize two of the solar systems which belonged to his father's kingdom. Nonsense, he told himself, in this era not all of that space was settled. It gave him an odd feeling to see that the remote suns formed almost the same constellations that he knew. He shivered. In the distance he heard a strange noise. It sounded like the rumbling of thunder, and flashes of lightning blazed on the horizon, but the sky was completely clear. It looked like a bombardment with explosive chemical weapons. Could it be . . . ? Of course! That was the explanation for the signs of destruction and the bodies that he had found. It was wartime! What he saw on the horizon was the reflection of discharged explosive weapons. There must be a battle raging there. The sky grew red, probably from great fires.

That was all he had needed, to land in the middle of a period of war. Still, he thought, there might be advantages to this situation. In the general confusion it would be easier for him to mingle with the natives, to get money and weapons somehow, and to settle down somewhere. At times like this no one was going to ask many questions about his identity and background. That simplified many matters, but at the same time his situation was much more dangerous, as he might easily land between the two fronts. If he was found he might be put to the sword. He would have to trust to his good fortune.

He got up. His hip ached but he could walk. He dressed himself, tied his possessions together in a bundle, and headed off in the direction of the shooting. There must be a larger settlement there. He would cautiously approach and at first remain withdrawn but observe and gather information. After that he would decide on the further steps to be taken.

Walking across the fields and meadows turned out to be harder than he had thought. The footwork of animal skin was stiff and rubbed him so that his feet were soon in great pain. After an hour he was completely exhausted and had to rest. In addition, hunger began to gnaw at his insides. He pulled himself together and set out again, making a great detour around a forest that frightened him because he did not know how wild plants and animals reacted at night. He plodded through swamps, waded streams, and made very slow progress, because he had to stop more and more often to rest.

Emerging from a large wooded area, he heard loud cries and explosions and saw the glare of a fire. There was a farmstead in front of him. A barn was blazing in flames. He heard more explosions, laughter and piercing screams, and saw figures running and falling to the ground. He limped faster, thinking that he could perhaps help, but as he came closer he saw that even with the best intentions there was nothing he could do. He was witness to an atrocity of war. Hidden behind a hedge, he watched the actions of these people at first with astonishment and then with growing horror. They had built up a great fire, onto which they threw household utensils and furniture. The rain of sparks had set the thatched roof of the barn on fire, and the fire threatened to spread to the other buildings, but this did not seem to disturb anyone. In the flickering firelight he was presented with a grotesque and macabre scene. Several men, who were strangely clothed and who wore on their heads gigantic headgear onto which they had fixed bushes of some fluffy material, staggered about with some sort of container in their hands, from which they occasionally drank. They all appeared to be under the influence of a drug, as they could hardly stay on their feet, vomited, slipped, fell down, and tried in vain to regain their footing. Some of them lay motionless on the ground, either dead or sleeping where they had fallen. They had killed a large animal, lopped off its head, ripped out its intestines, driven a spit in barbaric manner from the hind quarters through to the neck, and hung it over the fire. Others were occupied with forcing open boxes and barrels and rummaging through their contents, over which they fought in the wildest manner, striking one another with fists and weapons and screaming curses at one another. Yet others had captured several women and girls. They formed a ring about them and, roaring with laughter, ripped their clothes from their bodies. Then they threw the poor creatures to the ground and mounted them so brutally that his breath caught in his throat. The women, also partly under the influence of the drug which they had been forced to drink, half numbed from blows on the head, weakly let themselves be mishandled and whimpered with fear, pain, and terror, while the rest of the men followed the doings of their companions and egged them on with loud cries until it was their turn. Horrified and trembling with loathing, the prince felt a great powerless rage surge up in him. If he had only had his laser gun at hand he would have blasted that rabble into the dirt until the water exploded out of their miserable skins. He shook with anger and realized with alarm that he was tending toward more aggression than he had ever thought himself capable of feeling. Had this world already drawn him into its ways, was he beginning to act like a wild man? In what frightful age had he landed?

He fled into the forest and squatted all night long under a tree, his teeth chattering, shivering with cold and horror, watching the glare of the fire and hearing the loathsome cries of the wild men in the distance.

The temperature sank lower and lower. That must be due to the missing energy halo; at night the surface of the earth gave off unhampered into space all the warmth which it had stored up during the day, causing these variations in temperature. He looked into the starlit sky. Even the distant suns looked cold and uninviting; they were still wild and uncolonized systems.

He crouched tightly, in order to gather his own body heat, but his legs grew stiff and he had to stand up and walk up and down. He was grateful to see the gray of dawn and then the sun slowly rising, and the temperature of the atmosphere soon began also to rise to a tolerable warmth. In the course of the morning the disorderly band of debauched soldiers who had afflicted the whole region with their looting and murdering finally moved on, but not until they had set fire to all that was left of the farm. They took a number of animals with them, on the backs of which they had fixed seats. Some of the men had climbed onto these seats and let themselves be carried by the patient beasts. An ingenious arrangement of cords and chains fixed about the mouth of the animal enabled the rider seated on its back to direct the organic vehicle. The prince found it most astonishing that the big strong animals submitted to such treatment.

When the band had disappeared, the prince dared to come out from his hiding place and examine the scene of devastation once again. Perhaps someone had been left behind who needed help, but basically it was hunger that drove him forward. Perhaps he could capture something edible, perhaps he could even find more information on this age, some papers or a calendar.

A gruesome sight met his eye. The charred corpses of men and women who had been shot or beaten to death lay strewn about among the smashed and smoldering remains of buildings and household goods. The women and girls had been massacred in the most grisly manner and left lying in their own blood. They were hardly distinguishable from the ravaged ground onto which they had been thrown and trampled.

The buildings of the farmstead had long since fallen in, and the flames had destroyed what remained of them. Broken vessels and smashed furniture lay in the flattened grass and in food which had been trampled into the dirt. Driven by hunger, he searched about and finally found two or three pieces of some vegetable substance which had been roasted in the fire and which seemed edible. With aversion he bit into one. It was almost tasteless but after much chewing the saliva rendered it rather sweet. He choked it down, and every bite seemed tastier than the last. Searching for something to drink, be came across the dregs of a sour, spicy liquid in the drinking vessels. He smelled it. This must be the drug. Perhaps it is alcohol, he thought, but was not quite certain. He continued the search and found a hole in the ground that was lined with stones and equipped with an instrument by means of which a container could be let down and drawn up again. He tried it out and drew up a bucket of water. Examining it carefully, he found it to be rather clean and drank in great greedy gulps. I am already a regular wild man, he told himself. I drink water out of the ground, which must be teeming with pathogenic agents, and eat dirty food in the company of corpses and surrounded by the stench of half-burnt animals and people. I may already have poisoned myself, but what can I do. I have the alternative of either dying of hunger and thirst or of being killed by the poisons and bacteria of this barbaric food. The problem was purely academic. He had no choice but to take the risk.

He examined the clothing of the corpses, which were stiff with indescribable filth, and discovered two letters in the pocket of a dead soldier. He couldn't read the handwriting, but the numbers were Arabic. They were obviously dated; both bore the figures 1619.

According to this, he was approximately twelve thousand years in the past, or, more precisely, in the first half of the seventeenth century (old calendar), if the dates were accurate. At any rate, the papers appeared not to be very old. The energy of the time field had been far from high enough at the time of his departure to transport him this far. Could the machine have had a breakdown? But then it would have been impossible for the field energy to increase. Someone must have had his hand in the matter, and who could it have been but his brother? He wouldn't have thought it possible, but he had to get used to the idea.

He put both letters in his pocket. They were addressed to a certain Weisslinger, as he found out later when he had learned to decipher the handwriting, and were written by the priest of a small town, who begged the man to return home immediately, as his wife was dangerously ill, the household going to ruin, and his children suffering bitter want. In the second letter the priest informed him that in the meantime his wife had died and had been buried at the costs of the community, his workshop had been demolished, and his five children were being seen after by various families, where they had to work for bed and board. They were cared for well enough but the stern hand of a father was obviously lacking, as they had been occasionally caught thieving. Their father was an unscrupulous vagabond whom God would one day punish for his sins and his disgraceful life by allotting him a base and unworthy death. The man had met his fate; he had died of a slit throat.

The prince also found near the dead man one of those primitive firearms which function on the basis of the rapid expansion of gases which develop from the ignition of certain chemical substances, whereby a small piece of metal is set into rapid motion and is aimed at its target through a pipe in which the explosion takes place. He also found a stock of the burning substance and of the little pieces of metal, which fit exactly into the pipe of the weapon. Outfitted with these, he was no longer defenseless and faced the future more calmly.

Then he dragged all the bodies to one spot and piled wood over them. He set the wood on fire and quickly left the site of horror. He hoped to find a larger settlement. But he was to find even more gruesome scenes of devastation.

"Yes, Collins, and so his life went on. That was the beginning of a period of the most varied adventures and dangers. He struggled along, a prey to good and bad fortune, and learned how to use the cut-and-thrust weapon as well as pistols, muskets, and heavier explosive weapons. He learned many different languages. From the first he attracted no attention to himself, because soldiers from all corners of the earth served in the armies. He learned their coarse and savage customs, learned how to fight and how to kill. It is amazing and frightening, Collins, how quickly one can learn such things. He had soon become so well adapted that he could behave like a man of the seventeenth century in all situations without being the least bit conspicuous. He traveled through many lands in which the war was raging – and God knows there were plenty of them. He was witness to nameless misery and himself bore unspeakable adversity; he was often desperate and sometimes happy, but above all he survived. And he had learned. He had learned how to plunder, how to prepare trick-playing dice, how to protect his property with cunning and spite, force and coldbloodedness. At last he had amassed enough money to insure himself of a carefree existence, and he withdrew from the tradings of war, much to the dismay of his generals, for his knowledge of mechanics and ballistics had made him one of the most sought-after artillerymen and he could have easily earned military distinctions as cannoneer or pyrotechnician, cannonsmith or rocket launcher. But this was not his goal; he had in the true sense of the word more far-reaching plans. One thing had always sustained him and helped him overcome all dangers – his brooch. He often slipped his hand into his pocket to reassure himself that he wasn't simply dreaming of returning, but then he felt the crystal screen vibrate and come alive in the time stream, and as long as there was life in this mechanism there was activity on the timeline in the section where he was helplessly floating along, there were time travelers and there was hope for him. He was cut off, for without a mirror he could not construct a time field. Help must come from outside, even if unwillingly or unwittingly; he was clever enough to know that there was at least one man who considered the present solution to be the better one – his opponent in the little game that he wanted to chance. First he needed a permanent location which could satisfy all the requirements of offering relative safety, raw materials, and tools. Then he would have to wait until someone appeared from the future with a mirror.

"After months and years of restless wandering he found a small town in the south which was fortified and pleased him and was far from all battlefronts. Here he decided to settle down. With his gold he bought a small house on the market square and installed a workshop in it. He took advantage of his technical knowledge and established a modest mechanic's shop. At first he made hinges and handles and repaired locks; later he constructed all manner of clever toys, which he sold or gave away to travelers or citizens of the town. He was friendly and open to everyone, always considerate and ready to help, and he soon came to enjoy the reputation of being the most upright member of the community. Nevertheless, he led a secluded life and was seldom seen in the Red Ox Inn, although it stood directly across from his house.

"He waited. No traveler who entered the town and stopped at the Red Ox escaped his eye. Every evening he put out the lamp and peered for hours through the crack in the shutters at the market place, in case anything suspicious should happen. He spent every free moment which his numerous contracts left him pondering over sketches and plans for solving his problem with only the most primitive means which were available to him and with no source of electrical energy. There were two possibilities which seemed feasible. He could build a mechanism that would survive the twelve thousand years and would bring help by means of some clever trick. This would cause a fracture, but it would be a small one. He would be taking no chances, as this solution worked, if at all, only with complete success. When the mechanism gave him a sign, that would mean at the same time that he had won the move, for that was the prerequisite of the help; he would have to return sooner or later to the future. The second possibility was to build an apparatus which would allow him directly to tap the energy of the time field. With its help he could set up a primitive electronic system which would localize activities on the timeline. He could then establish the position of the seal and perhaps even shift it, for on this subject his research was far more advanced than his brother imagined. He decided to try both possibilities and set to work. Then there was nothing to do but wait. He soon had proof that his work would bring results. The first spies soon showed up, and he could quickly tell by their behavior that they were the wrong ones and had no intention of helping Weisslinger out of his predicament. Are we right, Collins?"

"To be sure, Your Majesty, that was not our intention."

"Now, Weisslinger had expected that and had long since taken it into account. He had even made some preparations. His appearance had changed no small amount during his life in this time period. He had grown older, his features were harder and his body stronger. And he had contributed to the effect somewhat too; he looked older than he actually was, his hair was streaked with gray and reached to his shoulders. He wanted to take no risks, for this move was far too important to him.

"Soon the guests from the future were arriving by the dozen. He registered one fracture and anachronism after another. Obviously they had found him. The visitors gave Weisslinger many an evening's entertainment. But we already told you about that. Then the master started his counterattack. Now it was his move. Who the better player was would soon be seen.

"What do you say now, Collins?"

"I almost know it, Your Majesty. It is not difficult to infer, from Your Majesty's manner of choosing his words and reporting out of the distant past, that it was Your Majesty who outwitted me. Your Majesty must have spent much time in that age, otherwise Your Majesty would not have gained such deep knowledge of it. To think that I didn't realize it earlier!" The minister struck his forehead with the flat of his hand. "Many things are becoming clear to me now, Your Majesty. But there is still something missing in the story."

"You are right there, Collins, something is still missing. The last piece of the puzzle, the decisive move."

"By Your Majesty's leave, who is WHITE in reality?"

"That is unfair, Collins. That means giving up the game. Just try and think back! We have told you everything. You have a good head on your shoulders."

Collins pondered and stared in absorption at the doll, which was making a whirlwind chain of pirouettes.

"It could be the inventor, Your Majesty, the old man who devised the time machine and who appeared as the Polish count – "

"He was a pure figment of the imagination, as we already mentioned," interjected the king.

" – to whom Your Majesty or I tell the story," continued the minister without interruption. "He brings the information to Weisslinger. And Weisslinger in turn, by Your Majesty's leave, exchanges . . ."

"Just wait a minute, Collins! What are you trying to do? Your imagination is running away with you. Take things in their turn! Why try to bring another figure into our game? The old man left all questions unanswered. So let us leave him out of the game. He played neither for WHITE nor for BLACK. He was, let us say, GRAY. Perhaps he knows the whole game, has seen all the moves, but is keeping out of it himself. Perhaps he is playing an entirely different game, which requires all his attention. Anything is possible. The future is vast. Perhaps thousands have watched our moves, in order to learn from them for their own games. We don't need any additional figures. Try it from another angle. How would it be if we finished the story together, gave it a happy end, so to speak?"

"Does Your Majesty mean that . . . that *I* am to play WHITE?"

"What else did you expect, Collins? You've been on our side for a long time, otherwise you would long ago have put an end to Weisslinger and we wouldn't be sitting here. After all, you are our best man. Now, pay close attention! You will take our cloak here and at the appropriate time turn it so that the pale lining is on the outside. The contrast of BLACK and WHITE will be noticed. But you will also give Weisslinger another sign. Upon receiving it he will set the seal in motion and put to rout the crew of Operations Base 7. Later you will get Weisslinger out of the affair. Off with you now! Do exactly what we told you to do. And have a good time!"

"A good time or a good age, Your Majesty?"

"However you prefer to take it, Collins."

"With pleasure, Your Majesty. I am honored to be allowed to finish the game together with Your Majesty."

The minister stepped through the mirror and returned again. He swayed slightly.

"Finished?" asked the king.

"Finished," answered Collins, and rubbed his eyes.

"You took advantage of the occasion to stop in at the Red Ox, we see," laughed the king. "That is our fault, we suppose. We made your mouth water long enough, and you had to stand here over two hours and listen to our stories. We could stand a cool drink too, but first we'll finish the game. The decisive move is still ahead of us. Will you manage, Collins?"

"No question about it, Your Majesty. The long ride through the forest and the cool night air have sobered me up again."

"Very well," said the king. "Now we're going to checkmate you, brother of ours! Collins! Get going now and appear at the critical moment in the throne room, exactly under the seal that is ten seconds long. You will have to make very careful adjustments to accomplish this. You won't be able to see yourself, as you will be working in Zerotime, that is, in complete darkness. This is something which only the seals permit. Here is the equipment you need to get through the mirror. This is an improved model of the brooch. You will cautiously feel your way over to the throne and hoist our brother onto your shoulders. That won't be easy, because he is heavy and of course during Zerotime as stiff as a board. If you were to drop him, you would break all his bones. He won't feel a thing and will think he is still sitting on his little throne. Then you will calmly carry him through the mirror into the carriage and let him smell this excellent essence, which will send him into a deep and beneficial sleep." He handed the minister a small vial. "All the rest you know as well as we do. You did pay extremely close attention to our story, didn't you? A silly question, we see."

"Yes indeed, Your Majesty – that is – I meant, not the question but about the story."

"Then tell it exactly like that to Weisslinger. Teach him how to sit on the throne properly, how to behave – and he had better not make any mistakes! That goes for you too, Collins!"

"Just as Your Majesty commands. But what would happen if I did make a mistake, if I forgot a part of the story or told it incorrectly?"

"We are sure you won't make any mistakes, otherwise we couldn't retell the story to you. How do you think we know it if not from you?"

"But what if I – by Your Majesty's leave, it is just a thought – what if I intentionally twisted the story or told Weisslinger something completely different, which would cause a fracture at the last moment?"

"That, dear Collins, would be damned unfair of you. That would mean changing the rules of the game. That would mean starting all over again from the beginning, and an entirely different story would develop. Neither we two nor anyone else would ever know our story. It would all have been invented in vain. The situation would look like this: you would return to find our brother here and would have no explanation for your absence. The whole game would start again from scratch but you would have a trick card up your sleeve. That could easily cost you your head. But we will take the risk. We trust you. Now, let's get on to the last move! Checkmate the king!"

His Majesty smiled in delight. The doll stopped dancing, sprang into Collins's arms, and clung fast to his cape.

"Checkmate the king!" said the minister, who disappeared into the mirror and stepped out from it again. He was a bit out of breath.

"It all went off as planned, we see."

"At Your Majesty's command. Together we put on pretty fireworks at Operations Base 7, as Your Majesty remembers. Not a stick remained."

"Yes, we remember. And now, how did you like the whole story, Collins?"

"One can imagine it all very well, Your Majesty."

"Quite right, especially as we never did have a brother." The king winked at his minister.

"Especially as Your Majesty never had a brother, as Your Majesty expressly decreed," returned Collins with a smile.

The king stood up and gave his minister a friendly slap on the shoulder.

"We have made a good job of it, the two of us. We have taken many points into consideration, discarded this one, improved that one, added yet another one. Now the picture is complete. The last piece of the puzzle has been fitted in. We think it is rather good. What do you say, Collins?"

"Oh yes, good, Your Majesty, very good. When I think of Weisslinger – he was killed plundering a farmhouse, turns into a doll-maker, and becomes a respected citizen of the town . . ."

"We can afford that fracture. It is insignificant. He had no children, as far as he knew."

". . . One day, that is, one night he awakes with a splitting headache and from that time on is like a different person. He can't put together the simplest clock, is prey to fits of delirium, becomes addicted to the bottle, gets a thrashing at the Red Ox by the young men of the town because of his sudden overbearing behavior, becomes more and more depraved, and all of this, mind you, he can foresee, including the bitter end: one day he will have his fill of it, will put a noose around his neck and will make an end to it all."

"Rather cruel, don't you think?" put in the king doubtfully.

"Hmm," said Collins and nodded. "Hideous."

"But we insist on the sound thrashing at the Red Ox!"

"That he richly deserved, Your Majesty!" smirked the minister.

"We can still grant the poor devil a better fate. But let's let him struggle for a while before we intervene. Do you see, Collins, that is the best part of our story; we can still change any piece of it, if something better occurs to us. But now it is BLACK's move. We shouldn't under-estimate him. After all, he went through the same apprenticeship we did. Let us wait and see. It would be a pity if the game were already

over. At our leisure we will think through all of the possibilities he has
in his position. Agreed, Collins?"

"Agreed, Your Majesty."

They both fell silent and watched the doll as it started an elaborate
new dance and tried out the first steps.

"Does Your Majesty permit one last question?"

"But of course, Collins. And we know what is going to come. You
are going to say, there is one piece left over."

"Yes, Your Majesty. The picture is complete, but where does the
doll fit in? It is useless; I mean, it has absolutely no purpose in our story
as it now stands. It was entirely unnecessary."

The king gave a resigned sigh.

"Yes, Collins. You have a good head on your shoulders, but why
can't you see that not everything must have a purpose?"

"But, Your Majesty, the question is justified. Why did Weisslinger
go to the trouble of making a doll, if he knew from the start that it
would have no – "

"Good God, Collins! You and your frightful utilitarian reasoning!
You still haven't understood. Do you think we are setting our minds
together to solve the problems of the universe when we make up
these stories of ours? All day long we have to grapple with this
problem. At least a few hours should remain for us to paint our
fantasies in the air and do cerebral gymnastics. And we often get
a good idea out of it, for free, so to speak, if you are so intent on
utility!"

The king glared at him and the minister hastened to appease him:
"Certainly, Your Majesty."

"For instance, why do you suppose we made up this story?"

"Out of boredom, perhaps, if I may allow myself to say so, and
because Your Majesty delights in the play of thoughts," suggested the
minister doubtfully.

"One could put it that way. Isn't it wonderful that in our world,
which is so entirely oriented to purpose and utility, profit and efficiency, there are still things which seem to have no purpose or usefulness, because their meaning lies only in the fact that they exist, like the
doll in our story? And yet this little doll is delightful – or perhaps it is
so for that very reason."

Collins nodded.

"I find it quite nice," he ventured, and pointed to the doll.

"One ought to be able to invent better ones," answered the king
disparagingly. "Let us think of something new, Collins."

The king brooded and stared at the empty walls as if he were lost in the contemplation of a picture.

The minister looked pensively at the delicate mechanical figure as it accomplished its last spin and then with a courteous bow announced the end of the performance.

Drunkboat

CORDWAINER SMITH

Cordwainer Smith was the pseudonym of Paul M. A. Linebarger
(1913–66), who wrote the first text on psychological warfare and was
involved in sensitive government work while a professor of Asiatic politics
from 1946 to 1966 in Washington, D.C. His pseudonym was kept a close
secret during his lifetime. He went to college with L. Ron Hubbard, the
famous pulp SF writer who invented Dianetics (later Scientology), and
they published in the same literary magazine. There was apparently some
real competitiveness in Linebarger, for he wrote an entire book manuscript (never published) in the late 1940s, at the same time his first SF
story was published, on the science of mental health.

His science fiction was nearly all published between 1959 and 1963,
and first collected in paperback between 1963 and 1968, then reassembled in 1975 and reissued, at which time serious interest in Smith began
to grow. He is now considered a major figure in science fiction. Nearly all
of Smith's science fiction takes place in a consistent future history, The
Instrumentality of Mankind, comprising many stories *(The Rediscovery of
Man* [1993] collects his complete short fiction) and one novel, *Norstrilia
(1975).* The series chronicles events in the millennia-long struggle
between the human Instrumentality and the Underpeople, intelligent
animals biologically transformed into humanlike forms. A devout Christian,
Smith built complex levels of religious allegory into his series.

The title of "Drunkboat" is an allusion to Arthur Rimbaud. It is a work that
shows Cordwainer Smith's distinctive and unusual voice in science fiction.

Perhaps it is the saddest, maddest, wildest story in the whole long history of space. It is true that no one else had ever done anything like it before, to travel at such a distance, and at such speeds, and by such means. The hero looked like such an ordinary man – when people looked at him for the first time. The second time, ah! that was different.

And the heroine. Small she was, and ash-blonde, intelligent, perky, and hurt. Hurt – yes, that's the right word. She looked as though she needed comforting or helping, even when she was perfectly all right. Men felt more like men when she was near. Her name was Elizabeth.

Who would have thought that her name would ring loud and clear in the wild vomiting nothing which made up space$_3$?

He took an old, old rocket, of an ancient design. With it he outflew, outfled, outjumped all the machines which had ever existed before. You might almost think that he went so fast that he shocked the great vaults of the sky, so that the ancient poem might have been written for him alone. "All the stars threw down their spears and watered heaven with their tears."

Go he did, so fast, so far that people simply did not believe it at first. They thought it was a joke told by men, a farce spun forth by rumor, a wild story to while away the summer afternoon.

We know his name now.

And our children and their children will know it for always.

Rambo. Artyr Rambo of Earth Four.

But he followed his Elizabeth where no space was. He went where men could not go, had not been, did not dare, would not think.

He did all this of his own free will.

Of course people thought it was a joke at first, and got to making up silly songs about the reported trip.

"Dig me a hole for that reeling feeling . . . !" sang one.

"Push me the call for the umber number . . . !" sang another.

"Where is the ship of the ochre joker . . . ?" sang a third.

Then people everywhere found it was true. Some stood stock still and got gooseflesh. Others turned quickly to everyday things. Space$_3$ had been found, and it had been pierced. Their world would never be the same again. The solid rock had become an open door.

Space itself, so clean, so empty, so tidy, now looked like a million million light-years of tapioca pudding – gummy, mushy, sticky, not fit to breathe, not fit to swim in.

How did it happen?

Everybody took the credit, each in his own different way.

"He came for me," said Elizabeth. "I died and he came for me because the machines were making a mess of my life when they tried to heal my terrible, useless death."

"I went myself," said Rambo. "They tricked me and lied to me and fooled me, but I took the boat and I became the boat and I got there. Nobody made me do it. I was angry, but I went. And I came back, didn't I?"

He too was right, even when he twisted and whined on the green grass of earth, his ship lost in a space so terribly far and strange that it might have been beneath his living hand, or might have been half a galaxy away.

How can anybody tell, with space$_3$?

It was Rambo who got back, looking for his Elizabeth. He loved her. So the trip was his, and the credit his.

But the Lord Crudelta said, many years later, when he spoke in a soft voice and talked confidentially among friends, "The experiment was mine. I designed it, I picked Rambo. I drove the selectors mad, trying to find a man who would meet those specifications. And I had that rocket built to the old, old plans. It was the sort of thing which human beings first used when they jumped out of the air a little bit, leaping like flying fish from one wave to the next and already thinking that they were eagles. If I had used one of the regular planoform ships, it would have disappeared with a sort of reverse gurgle, leaving space milky for a little bit while it faded into nastiness and obliteration. But I did not risk that. I put the rocket on a launching pad. *And the launching pad itself was an interstellar ship!* Since we were using an ancient rocket, we did it up right, with the old, old writing, mysterious letters printed all over the machine. We even had the name of our Organization – I and O and M – for 'the Instrumentality of Mankind' written on it good and sharp.

"How would I know," went on the Lord Crudelta, "that we would succeed more than we wanted to succeed, that Rambo would tear space itself loose from its hinges and leave that ship behind, just because he loved Elizabeth so sharply much, so fiercely much?"

Crudelta sighed.

"I know it and I don't know it. I'm like that ancient man who tried to take a water boat the wrong way around the planet Earth and found a new world instead. Columbus, he was called. And the land, that was Australia or America or something like that. That's what I did. I sent

Rambo out in that ancient rocket and he found a way through space$_3$. Now none of us will ever know who might come bulking through the floor or take shape out of the air in front of us."

Crudelta added, almost wistfully: "What's the use of telling the story? Everybody knows it, anyhow. My part in it isn't very glorious. Now the end of it, that's pretty. The bungalow by the waterfall and all the wonderful children that other people gave to them, you could write a poem about that. But the next to the end, how he showed up at the hospital helpless and insane, looking for his own Elizabeth. That was sad and eerie, that was frightening. I'm glad it all came to the happy ending with the bungalow by the waterfall, but it took a crashing long time to get there. And there are parts of it that we will never quite understand, the naked skin against naked space, the eyeballs riding something much faster than light ever was. Do you know what an *aoudad* is? It's an ancient sheep that used to live on Old Earth, and here we are, thousands of years later, with a children's nonsense rhyme about it. The animals are gone but the rhyme remains. It'll be like that with Rambo someday. Everybody will know his name and all about his drunkboat, but they will forget the scientific milestone that he crossed, hunting for Elizabeth in an ancient rocket that couldn't fly from peetle to pootle . . . Oh, the rhyme? Don't you know that? It's a silly thing. It goes,

> '*Point your gun at a murky lurky.*
> (Now you're talking ham or turkey!)
> *Shoot a shot at a dying aoudad.*
> (Don't ask the lady why or how, dad!)'

"Don't ask me what 'ham' and 'turkey' are. Probably parts of ancient animals, like beefsteak or sirloin. But the children still say the words. They'll do that with Rambo and his drunken boat some day. They may even tell the story of Elizabeth. But they will never tell the part about how he got to the hospital. That part is too terrible, too real, too sad and wonderful at the end. They found him on the grass. Mind you, naked on the grass, and nobody knew where he had come from!"

They found him naked on the grass and nobody knew where he had come from. They did not even know about the ancient rocket which the Lord Crudelta had sent beyond the end of nowhere with the letters I, O and M written on it. They did not know that this was Rambo, who had gone through space$_3$. The robots noticed him first and brought him in, photographing everything that they did. They had been programmed that way, to make sure that anything unusual was kept in the records.

Then the nurses found him in an outside room.

They assumed that he was alive, since he was not dead, but they could not prove that he was alive, either.

That heightened the puzzle.

The doctors were called in. Real doctors, not machines. They were very important men. Citizen Doctor Timofeyev, Citizen Doctor Grosbeck and the director himself, Sir and Doctor Vomact. They took the case.

(Over on the other side of the hospital Elizabeth waited, unconscious, and nobody knew it at all. Elizabeth, for whom he had jumped space, and pierced the stars, but nobody knew it yet!)

The young man could not speak. When they ran eye-prints and fingerprints through the Population Machine, they found that he had been bred on Earth itself, but had been shipped out as a frozen and unborn baby to Earth Four. At tremendous cost, they queried Earth Four with an "instant message," only to discover that the young man who lay before them in the hospital had been lost from an experimental ship on an intergalactic trip.

Lost.

No ship and no sign of ship.

And here he was.

They stood at the edge of space, and did not know what they were looking at. They were doctors and it was their business to repair or rebuild people, not to ship them around. How should such men know about space$_3$ when they did not even know about space$_2$, except for the fact that people got on the planoform ships and made trips through it? They were looking for sickness when their eyes saw engineering. They treated him when he was well.

All he needed was time, to get over the shock of the most tremendous trip ever made by a human being, but the doctors did not know that and they tried to rush his recovery.

When they put clothes on him, he moved from coma to a kind of mechanical spasm and tore the clothing off. Once again stripped, he lay himself roughly on the floor and refused food or speech.

They fed him with needles while the whole energy of space, had they only known it, was radiating out of his body in new forms.

They put him all by himself in a locked room and watched him through the peephole.

He was a nice-looking young man, even though his mind was blank and his body was rigid and unconscious. His hair was very fair and his eyes were light blue but his face showed character – a square chin; a handsome, resolute sullen mouth; old lines in the face which looked as though, when conscious, he must have lived many days or months on the edge of rage.

When they studied him the third day in the hospital, their patient had not changed at all.

He had torn off his pajamas again and lay naked, face down, on the floor.

His body was as immobile and tense as it had been on the day before.

(One year later, this room was going to be a museum with a bronze sign reading, "Here lay Rambo after he left the Old Rocket for space₃," but the doctors still had no idea of what they were dealing with.)

His face was turned so sharply to the left that the neck muscles showed. His right arm stuck out straight from the body. The left arm formed an exact right angle from the body, with the left forearm and hand pointing rigidly upward at 90° from the upper arm. The legs were in the grotesque parody of a running position.

Doctor Grosbeck said, "It looks to me like he's swimming. Let's drop him in a tank of water and see if he moves." Grosbeck sometimes went in for drastic solutions to problems.

Timofeyev took his place at the peephole. "Spasm, still," he murmured. "I hope the poor fellow is not feeling pain when his cortical defenses are down. How can a man fight pain if he does not even know what he is experiencing?"

"And you, sir and doctor," said Grosbeck to Vomact, "what do you see?"

Vomact did not need to look. He had come early and had looked long and quietly at the patient through the peephole before the other doctors arrived. Vomact was a wise man, with good insight and rich intuitions. He could guess in an hour more than a machine could diagnose in a year; he was already beginning to understand that this was a sickness which no man had ever had before. Still, there were remedies waiting.

The three doctors tried them.

They tried hypnosis, electrotherapy, massage, subsonies, atropine, surgital, a whole family of the digitalinids, and some quasi-narcotic viruses which had been grown in orbit where they mutated fast. They got the beginning of a response when they tried gas hypnosis combined with an electronically amplied telepath; this showed that something still went on inside the patient's mind. Otherwise the brain might have seemed to be mere fatty tissue, without a nerve in it. The other attempts had shown nothing. The gas showed a faint stirring away from fear and pain. The telepath reported glimpses of unknown skies. (The doctors turned the telepath over to the Space Police promptly, so they could try to code the star patterns which he had seen in a patient's mind, but the patterns did not fit. The telepath, though a keen-witted man, could not remember them in enough detail for them to be scanned against the samples of piloting sheets.)

The doctors went back to their drugs and tried ancient, simple remedies – morphine and caffeine to counteract each other, and a rough massage to make him dream again, so that the telepath could pick it up.

There was no further result that day, or the next.

Meanwhile the Earth authorities were getting restless. They thought, quite rightly, that the hospital had done a good job of proving that the patient had not been on Earth until a few moments before the robots found him on the grass. How had he gotten on the grass?

The airspace of Earth reported no intrusion at all, no vehicle marking a blazing arc of air incandescing against metal, no whisper of the great forces which drove a planoform ship through space₂.

(Crudelta, using faster-than-light ships, was creeping slow as a snail back toward Earth, racing his best to see if Rambo had gotten there first.)

On the fifth day, there was the beginning of a breakthrough.

Elizabeth had passed.

This was found out only much later, by a careful check of the hospital records. The doctors only knew this much: Patients had been moved down the corridor, sheet-covered figures immobile on wheeled beds.

Suddenly the beds stopped rolling.

A nurse screamed.

The heavy steel-and-plastic wall was bending inward. Some slow, silent force was pushing the wall into the corridor itself.

The wall ripped.

A human hand emerged.

One of the quick-witted nurses screamed, "*Push* those beds! *Push* them out of the way."

The nurses and robots obeyed.

The beds rocked like a group of boats crossing a wave when they came to the place where the floor, bonded to the wall, had bent upward to meet the wall as it tore inward. The peace-colored glow of the lights flicked. Robots appeared.

A second human hand came through the wall. Pushing in opposite directions, the hands tore the wall as though it had been wet paper.

The patient from the grass put his head through.

He looked blindly up and down the corridor, his eyes not quite focusing, his skin glowing a strange red-brown from the burns of open space.

"No," he said. Just that one word.

But that "No" was heard. Though the volume was not loud, it carried throughout the hospital. The internal telecommunications system relayed it. Every switch in the place went negative. Frantic nurses and robots, with even the doctors helping them, rushed to turn all the machines back on – the pumps, the ventilators, the artificial kidneys, the brain re-recorders, even the simple air engines which kept the atmosphere clean.

Far overhead an aircraft spun giddily. Its "off" switch, surrounded by triple safeguards, had suddenly been thrown into the negative position. Fortunately the robot-pilot got it going again before crashing into Earth.

The patient did not seem to know that his word had this effect.

(Later the world knew that this was part of the "drunkboat effect." The man himself had developed the capacity for using his neuro physical system as a machine control.)

In the corridor, the machine robot who served as policeman arrived. He wore sterile, padded velvet gloves with a grip of sixty metric tons inside his hands. He approached the patient. The robot had been carefully trained to recognize all kinds of danger from delirious or psychotic humans; later he reported that he had an input of "danger, extreme" on every band of sensation. He had been expecting to seize the prisoner with irreversible firmness and to return him to his bed, but with this kind of danger sizzling in the air, the robot took no chances. His wrist itself contained a hypodermic pistol which operated on compressed argon.

He reached out toward the unknown, naked man who stood in the big torn gap of the wall. The wrist-weapon hissed and a sizeable injection of condamine, the most powerful narcotic in the known universe, spat its way through the skin of Rambo's neck. The patient collapsed.

The robot picked him up gently and tenderly, lifted him through the torn wall, pushed the door open with a kick which broke the lock and put the patient back on his bed. The robot could hear doctors coming, so he used his enormous hands to pat the steel wall back into its proper shape. Work-robots or under-people could finish the job later, but meanwhile it looked better to have that part of the building set at right angles again.

Doctor Vomact arrived, followed closely by Grosbeck.

"What happened?" he yelled, shaken out of a lifelong calm. The robot pointed at the ripped wall.

"He tore it open. I put it back," said the robot.

The doctors turned to look at the patient. He had crawled off his bed again and was on the floor, but his breathing was light and natural.

"What did you give him?" cried Vomact to the robot.

"Condamine," said the robot, "according to rule 47-B. The drug is not to be mentioned outside the hospital."

"I know that," said Vomact absentmindedly and a little crossly. "You can go along now. Thank you."

"It is not usual to thank robots," said the robot, "but you can read a commendation into my record if you want to."

"Get the blazes out of here!" shouted Vomact at the officious robot.

The robot blinked. "There are no blazes but I have the impression you mean me. I shall leave, with your permission." He jumped with odd gracefulness around the two doctors, fingered the broken doorlock absentmindedly, as though be might have wished to repair it; and then, seeing Vomact glare at him, left the room completely.

A moment later soft muted thuds began. Both doctors listened a moment and then gave up. The robot was out in the corridor, gently patting the steel floor back into shape. He was a tidy robot, probably animated by an amplified chicken-brain, and when he got tidy he became obstinate.

"Two questions, Grosbeck," said the sir and doctor Vomact.

"Your service, sir!"

"Where was the patient standing when he pushed the wall into the corridor, and how did he get the leverage to do it?"

Grosbeck narrowed his eyes in puzzlement. "Now that you mention it, I have no idea of how he did it. In fact, he could not have done it. But he has. And the other question?"

"What do you think of condamine?"

"Dangerous, of course, as always. Addiction can – "

"Can you have addiction with no cortical activity?" interrupted Vomact.

"Of course," said Grosbeck promptly. "Tissue addiction."

"Look for it, then," said Vomact.

Grosbeck knelt beside the patient and felt with his fingertips for the muscle endings. He felt where they knotted themselves into the base of the skull, the tips of the shoulders, the striped area of the back.

When he stood up there was a look of puzzlement on his face. "I never felt a human body like this one before. I am not even sure that it *is* human any longer."

Vomact said nothing. The two doctors confronted one another. Grosbeck fidgeted under the calm stare of the senior man. Finally he blurted out,

"Sir and doctor, I know what we *could* do."

"And that," said Vomact levelly, without the faintest hint of encouragement or of warning, "is what?"

"It wouldn't be the first time that it's been done in a hospital."

"What?" said Vomact, his eyes – those dreaded eyes! – making Grosbeck say what he did not want to say.

Grosbeck flushed. He leaned toward Vomact so as to whisper, even though there was no one standing near them. His words, when they came, had the hasty indecency of a lover's improper suggestion:

"Kill the patient, sir and doctor. Kill him. We have plenty of records of him. We can get a cadaver out of the basement and make it into a good simulacrum. Who knows what we will turn loose among mankind if we let him get well?"

"Who knows?" said Vomact without tone or quality to his voice. "But citizen and doctor, what is the twelfth duty of a physician?"

"'Not to take the law into his own hands, keeping healing for the healers and giving to the state or the Instrumentality whatever properly belongs to the state or the Instrumentality.'" Grosbeck sighed as he retracted his own suggestion. "Sir and doctor, I take it back. It wasn't medicine which I was talking about. It was government and politics which were really in my mind."

"And now . . . ?" asked Vomact.

"Heal him, or let him be until he heals himself."

"And which would you do?"

"I'd try to heal him."

"How?" said Vomact.

"Sir and doctor," cried Grosbeck, "do not ride my weaknesses in this case! I know that you like me because I am a bold, confident sort of man. Do not ask me to be myself when we do not even know where this body came from. If I were bold as usual, I would give him typhoid and condamine, stationing telepaths nearby. But this is something new in the history of man. We are people and perhaps he is not a person any more. Perhaps he represents the combination of people with some kind of a new force. How did he get here from the far side of nowhere? How many million times has he been enlarged or reduced? We do not know what he is or what has happened to him. How can we treat a man when we are treating the cold of space, the heat of suns, the frigidity of distance? We know what to do with flesh, but this is not quite flesh any more. Feel him yourself, sir and doctor! You will touch something which nobody has ever touched before."

"I have," Vomact declared, "already felt him. You are right. We will try typhoid and condamine for half a day. Twelve hours from now let us meet each other at this place. I will tell the nurses and the robots what to do in the interim."

They both gave the red-tanned spread-eagled figure on the floor a parting glance. Grosbeck looked at the body with something like distaste mingled with fear; Vomact was expressionless, save for a wry wan smile of pity.

At the door the head nurse awaited them. Grosbeck was surprised at his chief's orders.

"Ma'am and nurse, do you have a weapon-proof vault in this hospital?"

"Yes, sir," she said. "We used to keep our records in it until we telemetered all our records into Computer Orbit. Now it is dirty and empty."

"Clean it out. Run a ventilator tube into it. Who is your military protector?"

"My what?" she cried, in surprise.

"Everyone on Earth has military protection. Where are the forces, the soldiers, who protect this hospital of yours?"

"My sir and doctor!" she called out. "My sir and doctor! I'm an old woman and I have been allowed to work here for three hundred years, but I never thought of that idea before. Why would I need soldiers?"

"Find who they are and ask them to stand by. They are specialists too, with a different kind of art from ours. Let them stand by. They may be needed before this day is out. Give my name as authority to their lieutenant or sergeant. Now here is the medication which I want you to apply to this patient."

Her eyes widened as he went on talking, but she was a disciplined woman and she nodded as she heard him out, point by point. Her eyes looked very sad and weary at the end but she was a trained expert herself and she had enormous respect for the skill and wisdom of the Sir and Doctor Vomact. She also had a warm, feminine pity for the motionless young male figure on the floor, swimming forever on the heavy floor, swimming between archipelagoes of which no man living had ever dreamed before.

Crisis came that night.

The patient had worn handprints into the inner wall of the vault, but he had not escaped.

The soldiers, looking oddly alert with their weapons gleaming in the bright corridor of the hospital, were really very bored, as soldiers always become when they are on duty with no action.

Their lieutenant was keyed up. The wirepoint in his hand buzzed like a dangerous insect. Sir and Doctor Vomact, who knew more about weapons than the soldiers thought he knew, saw that the wirepoint was set to HIGH, with a capacity of paralyzing people five stories up, five stories down or a kilometer sideways. He said nothing. He merely thanked the lieutenant and entered the vault, closely followed by Grosbeck and Timofeyev.

The patient swam here too.

He had changed to an arm-over-arm motion, kicking his legs against the floor. It was as though he had swum on the other floor with the sole purpose of staying afloat, and had now discovered some direction in which to go, albeit very slowly. His motions were deliberate, tense, rigid, and so reduced in time that it seemed as though he hardly moved at all. The ripped pajamas lay on the floor beside him.

Vomact glanced around, wondering what forces the man could have used to make those handprints on the steel wall. He remembered Grosbeck's warning that the patient should die, rather than subject all mankind to new and unthought risks, but though he shared the feeling, he could not condone the recommendation.

Almost irritably, the great doctor thought to himself – where could the man be going?

(To Elizabeth, the truth was, to Elizabeth, now only sixty meters away. Not till much later did people understand what Rambo had been trying to do – crossing sixty mere meters to reach his Elizabeth when he had already jumped an un-count of light-years to return to her. To his own, his dear, his well-beloved who needed him !)

The condamine did not leave its characteristic mark of deep lassitude and glowing skin: perhaps the typhoid was successfully contradicting it. Rambo did seem more lively than before. The name had come through on the regular message system, but it still did not mean anything to the Sir and Doctor Vomact. It would. It would.

Meanwhile the other two doctors, briefed ahead of time, got busy with the apparatus which the robots and the nurses had installed.

Vomact murmured to the others, "I think he's better off. Looser all around. I'll try shouting."

So busy were they that they just nodded.

Vomact screamed at the patient, "Who are you? What are you? Where do you come from?"

The sad blue eyes of the man on the floor glanced at him with a surprisingly quick glance, but there was no other real sign of communication. The limbs kept up their swim against the rough concrete floor of the vault. Two of the bandages which the hospital staff had put on him had worn off again. The right knee, scraped and bruised, deposited a sixty-centimeter trail of blood – some old and black and coagulated, some fresh, new and liquid – on the floor as it moved back and forth.

Vomact stood up and spoke to Grosbeck and Timofeyev. "Now," he said, "let us see what happens when we apply the pain."

The two stepped back without being told to do so.

Timofeyev waved his hand at a small white-enameled orderly-robot who stood in the doorway.

The pain net, a fragile cage of wires, dropped down from the ceiling.

It was Vomact's duty, as senior doctor, to take the greatest risk. The patient was wholly encased by the net of wires, but Vomact dropped to his hands and knees, lifted the net at one corner with his right hand, thrust his own head into it next to the head of the patient. Doctor Vomact's robe trailed on the clean concrete, touching the black old stains of blood left from the patient's swim throughout the night.

Now Vomact's mouth was centimeters from the patient's ear.

Said Vomact, "Oh."

The net hummed.

The patient stopped his slow motion, arched his back, looked steadfastly at the doctor.

Doctors Grosbeck and Timofeyev could see Vomact's face go white with the impact of the pain machine, but Vomact kept his voice under control and said evenly and loudly to the patient, "*Who – are – you?*"

The patient said flatly, "Elizabeth."

The answer was foolish but the tone was rational.

Vomact pulled his head out from under the net, shouting again at the patient, "*Who – are – you?*"

The naked man replied, speaking very clearly:

> *"Chwinkle, chwinkle, little chweeble*
> *I am feeling very feeble!"*

Vomact frowned and murmured to the robot, "More pain. Turn it up to pain ultimate."

The body threshed under the net, trying to resume its swim on the concrete. A loud wild braying cry came from the victim under the net. It sounded like a screamed distortion of the name Elizabeth, echoing out from endless remoteness.

It did not make sense.

Vomact screamed back, *"Who — are — you?"*

With unexpected clarity and resonance, the voice came back to the three doctors from the twisting body under the net of pain:

"I'm the shipped man, the ripped man, the gypped man, the dipped man, the hipped man, the tripped man, the tipped man, the slipped man, the flipped man, the nipped man, the ripped man, the clipped man — aah!" His voice choked off with a cry and he went back to swimming on the floor, despite the intensity of the pain net immediately above him.

The doctor lifted his hand. The pain net stopped buzzing and lifted high into the air.

He felt the patient's pulse. It was quick. He lifted an eyelid. The reactions were much closer to normal.

"Stand back," he said to the others.

"Pain on both of us," he said to the robot.

The net came down on the two of them.

"Who are you?" shrieked Vomact, right into the patient's ear, holding the man halfway off the floor and not quite knowing whether the body which tore steel walls might not, somehow, tear both of them apart as they stood.

The man babbled back at him: "I'm the most man, the post man, the host man, the ghost man, the coast man, the boast man, the dosed man, the grossed man, the toast man, the roast man, no! no! no!"

He struggled in Vomact's arms. Grosbeck and Timofeyev stepped forward to rescue their chief when the patient added, very calmly and clearly:

"Your procedure is all right, doctor, whoever you are. More fever, please. More pain, please. Some of that dope to fight the pain. You're pulling me back. I know I am on Earth. Elizabeth is near. For the love of God, get me Elizabeth! But don't rush me. I need days and days to get well."

The rationality was so startling that Grosbeck, without waiting for orders from Vomact, as chief doctor, ordered the pain net lifted.

The patient began babbling again: "I'm the three man, the he man, the tree man, the me man, the three man, the three man . . ." His voice faded and he slumped unconscious.

Vomact walked out of the vault. He was a little unsteady.

His colleagues took him by the elbows.

He smiled wanly at them: "I wish it were lawful . . . I could use some of that condamine myself. No wonder the pain nets wake the patients up and even make dead people do twitches! Get me some liquor. My heart is old."

Grosbeck sat him down while Timofeyev ran down the corridor in search of medicinal liquor.

Vomact murmured, "How are we going to find *his* Elizabeth? There must be millions of them. And he's from Earth Four too."

"Sir and doctor, you have worked wonders," said Grosbeck. "To go under the net. To take those chances. To bring him to speech. I will never see anything like it again. It's enough for any one lifetime, to have seen this day."

"But what do we do next?" asked Vomact wearily, almost in confusion.

That particular question needed no answer.

The Lord Crudelta had reached Earth.

His pilot landed the craft and fainted at the controls with sheer exhaustion.

Of the escort cats, who had ridden alongside the space craft in the miniature spaceships, three were dead, one was comatose and the fifth was spitting and raving.

When the port authorities tried to slow the Lord Crudelta down to ascertain his authority, he invoked Top Emergency, took over the command of troops in the name of the Instrumentality, arrested everyone in sight but the troop commander, and requisitioned the troop commander to take him to the hospital. The computers at the port had told him that one Rambo, "sans origine," had arrived mysteriously on the grass of a designated hospital.

Outside the hospital, the Lord Crudelta invoked Top Emergency again, placed all armed men under his own command, ordered a recording monitor to cover all his actions if he should later be channeled into a court-martial, and arrested everyone in sight.

The tramp of heavily armed men, marching in combat order, overtook Timofeyev as he hurried back to Vomact with a drink. The men were jogging along on the double. All of them had live helmets and their wirepoints were buzzing.

Nurses ran forward to drive the intruders out, ran backward when the sting of the stun-rays brushed cruelly over them. The whole hospital was in an uproar.

The Lord Crudelta later admitted that he had made a serious mistake.

The Two Minutes' War broke out immediately.

You have to understand the pattern of the Instrumentality to see how it happened. The Instrumentality was a self-perpetuating body of men with enormous powers and a strict code. Each was a plenum of the low, the middle and the high justice. Each could do anything he found necessary or proper to maintain the Instrumentality and to keep the peace between the worlds. But if he made a mistake or committed a wrong – ah, then, it was suddenly different. Any Lord could put another Lord to death in an emergency, but he was assured of death and disgrace himself if he assumed this responsibility. The only difference between ratification and repudiation came in the fact that Lords who killed in an emergency and were proved wrong were marked down on a very shameful list, while those who killed other Lords rightly (as later examination might prove) were listed on a very honorable list, but still killed.

With three Lords, the situation was different. Three Lords made an emergency court; if they acted together, acted in good faith, and reported to the computers of the Instrumentality, they were exempt from punishment, though not from blame or even reduction to citizen status. Seven Lords, or all the Lords on a given planet at a given moment, were beyond any criticism except that of a dignified reversal of their actions should a later ruling prove them wrong.

This was all the business of the Instrumentality. The Instrumentality had the perpetual slogan: "Watch, but do not govern; stop war, but do not wage it; protect, but do not control; and first, survive!"

The Lord Crudelta had seized the troops – not his troops, but the light regular troops of Manhome Government – because he feared that the greatest danger in the history of man might come from the person whom he himself had sent through space$_3$.

He never expected that the troops would be plucked out from his command – an overriding power reinforced by robotic telepathy and the incomparable communications net, both open and secret, reinforced by thousands of years in trickery, defeat, secrecy, victory, and sheer experience, which the Instrumentality had perfected since it emerged from the Ancient Wars.

Overriding, overridden!

These were the commands which the Instrumentality had used before recorded time began. Sometimes they suspended their antagonists on points of law, sometimes by the deft and deadly insertion of weapons, most often by cutting in on other peoples' mechanical and social controls and doing their will, only to drop the controls as suddenly as they had taken them.

But not Crudelta's hastily called troops.

The war broke out with a change of pace.

Two squads of men were moving into that part of the hospital where Elizabeth lay, waiting the endless returns to the jelly baths which would rebuild her poor ruined body.

The squads changed pace.

The survivors could not account for what happened.

They all admitted to great mental confusion – afterward.

At the time it seemed that they had received a clear, logical command to turn and to defend the women's section by counterattacking their own main battalion right in their rear.

The hospital was a very strong building. Otherwise it would have melted to the ground or shot up in flame.

The leading soldiers suddenly turned around, dropped for cover and blazed their wirepoints at the comrades who followed them. The wirepoints were cued to organic material, though fairly harmless to inorganic. They were powered by the power relays which every soldier wore on his back.

In the first ten seconds of the turnaround, twenty-seven soldiers, two nurses, three patients and one orderly were killed. One hundred and nine other people were wounded in that first exchange of fire.

The troop commander had never seen battle, but he had been well trained. He immediately deployed his reserves around the external exits of the building and sent his favorite squad, commanded by a Sergeant Lansdale whom he trusted well, down into the basement, so that it could rise vertically from the basement into the women's quarters and find out who the enemy was.

As yet, he had no idea that it was his own leading troops turning and fighting their comrades.

He testified later, at the trial, that he personally had no sensations of eerie interference with his own mind. He merely knew that his men had unexpectedly come upon armed resistance from antagonists – identity unknown! – who had weapons identical with theirs. Since the Lord Crudelta had brought them along in case there might be a fight with unspecified antagonists, he felt right in assuming that a Lord of the Instrumentality knew what he was doing. This was the enemy all right.

In less than a minute, the two sides had balanced out. The line of fire had moved right into his own force. The lead men, some of whom were wounded, simply turned around and began defending themselves against the men immediately behind them. It was as though an invisible line, moving rapidly, had parted the two sections of the military force.

The oily black smoke of dissolving bodies began to glut the ventilators.

Patients were screaming, doctors cursing, robots stamping around and nurses trying to call each other.

The war ended when the troop commander saw Sergeant Lansdale, whom he himself had sent upstairs, leading a charge out of the women's quarters – directly at his own commander!

The officer kept his head.

He dropped to the floor and rolled sidewise as the air chittered at him, the emanations of Lansdale's wirepoint killing all the tiny bacteria in the air. On his helmet phone he pushed the manual controls to TOP VOLUME and to NONCOMS ONLY, and he commanded, with a sudden flash of brilliant mother-wit, "Good job, Lansdale!"

Lansdale's voice came back as weak as if it had been off-planet, "We'll keep them out of this section yet, sir!"

The troop commander called back very loudly but calmly, not letting on that he thought his sergeant was psychotic.

"Easy now. Hold on. I'll be with you."

He changed to the other channel and said to his nearby men, "Cease fire. Take cover and wait."

A wild scream came to him from the phones.

It was Lansdale. "Sir! Sir! I'm fighting *you*, sir. I just caught on. It's getting me again. Watch out."

The buzz and burr of the weapons suddenly stopped.

The wild human uproar of the hospital continued.

A tall doctor, with the insignia of high seniority, came gently to the troop commander and said, "You can stand up and take your soldiers out now, young fellow. The fight was a mistake."

"I'm not under your orders," snapped the young officer. "I'm under the Lord Crudelta. He requisitioned this force from the Manhome Government. Who are you?"

"You may salute me, captain," said the doctor, "I am Colonel General Vomact of the Earth Medical Reserve. But you had better not wait for the Lord Crudelta."

"But *where* is he?"

"In my bed," said Vomact.

"Your *bed?*" cried the young officer in complete amazement.

"In bed. Doped to the teeth. I fixed him up. He was excited. Take your men out. We'll treat the wounded on the lawn. You can see the dead in the refrigerators downstairs in a few minutes, except for the ones that went smoky from direct hits."

"But the fight . . . ?"

"A mistake, young man, or else – "

"Or else what?" shouted the young officer, horrified at the utter mess of his own combat experience.

"Or else a weapon no man has ever seen before. Your troops fought each other. Your command was intercepted."

"I could see that," snapped the officer, "as soon as I saw Lansdale coming at me."

"But do you know what took him over?" said Vomact gently, while taking the officer by the arm and beginning to lead him out of the hospital. The captain went willingly, not noticing where he was going, so eagerly did he watch for the other man's words.

"I think I know," said Vomact. "Another man's dreams. Dreams which have learned how to turn themselves into electricity or plastic or stone. Or anything else. Dreams coming to us out of $space_3$."

The young officer nodded dumbly. This was too much. "$Space_3$?" he murmured. It was like being told that the really alien invaders, whom men had been expecting for thirteen thousand years and had never met, were waiting for him on the grass. Until now $space_3$ had been a mathematical idea, a romancer's daydream, but not a fact.

The sir and doctor Vomact did not even ask the young officer. He brushed the young man gently at the nape of the neck and shot him through with tranquilizer. Vomact then led him out to the grass. The young captain stood alone and whistled happily at the stars in the sky. Behind him, his sergeants and corporals were sorting out the survivors and getting treatment for the wounded.

The Two Minutes' War was over.

Rambo had stopped dreaming that his Elizabeth was in danger. He had recognized, even in his deep sick sleep, that the tramping in the corridor was the movement of armed men. His mind had set up defenses to protect Elizabeth. He took over command of the forward troops and set them to stopping the main body. The powers which space$_3$ had worked into him made this easy for him to do, even though he did not know that he was doing it.

"How many dead?" said Vomact to Grosbeck and Timofeyev.

"About two hundred."

"And how many irrecoverable dead?"

"The ones that got turned into smoke. A dozen, maybe fourteen. The other dead can be fixed up, but most of them will have to get new personality prints."

"Do you know what happened?" asked Vomact.

"No, sir and doctor," they both chorused.

"I do. I think I do. No, I *know* I do. It's the wildest story in the history of man. Our patient did it – Rambo. He took over the troops and set them against each other. That Lord of the Instrumentality who came charging in – Crudelta. I've known him for a long, long time. He's behind this case. He thought that troops would help, not sensing that troops would invite attack upon themselves. And there is something else."

"Yes?" they said, in unison.

"Rambo's woman – the one he's looking for. She must be here."

"Why?" said Timofeyev.

"Because *he's* here."

"You're assuming that he came here because of his own will, sir and doctor."

Vomact smiled the wise crafty smile of his family; it was almost a trademark of the Vomact house.

"I am assuming all the things which I cannot otherwise prove.

"First, I assume that he came here naked out of space itself, driven by some kind of force of which we cannot even guess.

"Second, I assume he came *here* because he wanted something. A woman named Elizabeth, who must already be here. In a moment we can go inventory all our Elizabeths.

"Third, I assume that the Lord Crudelta knew something about it. He has led troops into the building. He began raving when he saw me. I know hysterical fatigue, as do you, my brothers, so I condamined him for a night's sleep.

"Fourth, let's leave our man alone. There'll be hearings and trials enough, Space knows, when all these events get scrambled out."

Vomact was right.

He usually was.

Trials did follow.

It was lucky that Old Earth no longer permitted newspapers or television news. The population would have been frothed up to riot and terror if they had ever found out what happened at the Old Main Hospital just to the west of Meeya Meefla.

Twenty-one days later, Vomact, Timofeyev and Grosbeck were summoned to the trial of the Lord Crudelta. A full panel of seven Lords of the Instrumentality were there to give Crudelta an ample hearing and, if required, a sudden death. The doctors were present both as doctors for Elizabeth and Rambo and as witnesses for the Investigating Lord.

Elizabeth, fresh up from being dead, was as beautiful as a newborn baby in exquisite, adult feminine form. Rambo could not take his eyes off her, but a look of bewilderment went over his face every time she gave him a friendly, calm remote little smile. (She had been told that she was his girl, and she was prepared to believe it, but she had no memory of him or of anything else more than sixty hours back, when speech had been reinstalled in her mind; and he, for his part, was still thick of speech and subject to strains which the doctors could not quite figure out.)

The Investigating Lord was a man named Starmount.

He asked the panel to rise.

They did so.

He faced the Lord Crudelta with great solemnity. "You are obliged, my Lord Crudelta, to speak quickly and clearly to this court."

"Yes, my Lord," he answered.

"We have the summary power."

"You have the summary power. I recognize it."

"You will tell the truth or else you will lie."

"I shall tell the truth or I will lie."

"You may lie, if you wish, about matters of fact and opinion, but you will in no case lie about human relationships. If you do lie, nevertheless, you will ask that your name be entered in the Roster of Dishonor."

"I understand the panel and the rights of this panel. I will lie if I wish – though I don't think I will need to do so" – and here Crudelta flashed a weary intelligent smile at all of them – "but I will not lie about matters of relationship. If I do, I will ask for dishonor."

"You have yourself been well trained as a Lord of the Instrumentality?"

"I have been so trained and I love the Instrumentality well. In fact, I am myself the Instrumentality, as are you, and as are the honorable Lords beside you. I shall behave well, for as long as I live this afternoon."

"Do you credit him, my Lords?" asked Starmount.

The members of the panel nodded their mitered heads. They had dressed ceremonially for the occasion.

"Do you have a relationship to the woman Elizabeth?"

The members of the trial panel caught their breath as they saw Crudelta turn white: "My Lords!" he cried, and answered no further.

"It is the custom," said Starmount firmly, "that you answer promptly or that you die."

The Lord Crudelta got control of himself. "I am answering. I did not know who she was, except for the fact that Rambo loved her. I sent her to Earth from Earth Four, where I then was. Then I told Rambo that she had been murdered and hung desperately at the edge of death, wanting only his help to return to the green fields of life."

Said Starmount: "Was that the truth?"

"My Lord and Lords, it was a lie."

"Why did you tell it?"

"To induce rage in Rambo and to give him an overriding reason for wanting to come to Earth faster than any man has ever come before."

"A-a-ah! A-a-ah!" Two wild cries came from Rambo, more like the call of an animal than like the sound of a man.

Vomact looked at his patient, felt himself beginning to growl with a deep internal rage. Rambo's powers, generated in the depths of space$_3$, had begun to operate again. Vomact made a sign. The robot behind Rambo had been coded to keep Rambo calm. Though the robot had been enameled to look like a white gleaming hospital orderly, he was actually a police robot of high powers, built up with an electronic cortex based on the frozen midbrain of an old wolf. (A wolf was a rare animal, something like a dog.) The robot touched Rambo, who dropped off to sleep. Doctor Vomact felt the anger in his own mind fade away. He lifted his hand gently; the robot caught the signal and stopped applying the narcoleptic radiation. Rambo slept normally; Elizabeth looked worriedly at the man whom she had been told was her own.

The Lords turned back from the glances at Rambo.

Said Starmount, icily: "And why did you do that?"

"Because I wanted him to travel through space."

"Why?"

"To show it could be done."

"And do you, my Lord Crudelta, affirm that this man has in fact traveled through space₃?"

"I do."

"Are you lying?"

"I have the right to lie, but I have no wish to do so. In the name of the Instrumentality itself, I tell you that this is the truth."

The panel members gasped. Now there was no way out. Either the Lord Crudelta was telling the truth, *which meant that all former times had come to an end and that a new age had begun for all the kinds of mankind,* or else he was lying in the face of the most powerful form of affirmation which any of them knew.

Even Starmount himself took a different tone. His teasing, restless, intelligent voice took on a new timbre of kindness.

"You do therefore assert that this man has come back from outside our galaxy with nothing more than his own natural skin to cover him? No instruments? No power?"

"I did not say that," said Crudelta. "Other people have begun to pretend I used such words. I tell you, my Lords, that I planoformed for twelve consecutive Earth days and nights. Some of you may remember where Outpost Baiter Gator is. Well, I had a good Go-captain, and he took me four long jumps beyond there, out into intergalactic space. I left this man there. When I reached Earth, he had been here twelve days, more or less. I have assumed, therefore, that his trip was more or less instantaneous. I was on my way back to Baiter Gator, counting by Earth time, when the doctor here found this man on the grass outside the hospital."

Vomact raised his hand. The Lord Starmount gave him the right to speak. "My sirs and Lords, we did not find this man on the grass. The robots did, and made a record. But even the robots did not see or photograph his arrival."

"We know that," said Starmount angrily, "and we know that we have been told that nothing came to Earth by any means whatever, in that particular quarter hour. Go on, my Lord Crudelta. What relation are you to Rambo?"

"He is my victim."

"Explain yourself!"

"I computed him out. I asked the machines where I would be most apt to find a man with a tremendous lot of rage in him, and was informed that on Earth Four the rage level had been left high because that particular planet had a considerable need for explorers and adventurers, in whom rage was a strong survival trait. When I got to Earth Four, I commanded the authorities to find out which border cases had exceeded the limits of allowable rage. They gave me four men. One was much too large. Two were old. This man was the only candidate for my excitement. I chose him."

"What did you tell him?"

"Tell him? I told him his sweetheart was dead or dying."

"No, no," said Starmount. "Not at the moment of crisis. What did you tell him to make him cooperate in the first place?"

"I told him," said the Lord Crudelta evenly, "that I was myself a Lord of the Instrumentality and that I would kill him myself if he did not obey, and obey promptly."

"And under what custom or law did you act?"

"Reserved material," said the Lord Crudelta promptly. "There are telepaths here who are not a part of the Instrumentality. I beg leave to defer until we have a shielded place."

Several members of the panel nodded and Starmount agreed with them. He changed the line of questioning.

"You forced this man, therefore, to do something which he did not wish to do?"

"That is right," said the Lord Crudelta.

"Why didn't you go yourself, if it is that dangerous?"

"My Lords and honorables, it was the nature of the experiment that the experimenter himself should not be expended in the first try. Artyr Rambo has indeed traveled through space$_3$. I shall follow him myself, in due course." (How the Lord Crudelta did do so is another tale, told about another time.) "If I had gone and if I had been lost, that would have been the end of the space$_3$ trials. At least for our time."

"Tell us the exact circumstances under which you last saw Artyr Rambo before you met after the battle in the Old Main Hospital."

"We had put him in a rocket of the most ancient style. We also wrote writing on the outside of it, just the way the Ancients did when they first ventured into space. Ah, that was a beautiful piece of engineering and archaeology! We copied everything right down to the correct models of fourteen thousand years ago, when the Paroskii and Murkins were racing each other into space. The rocket was white, with a red and white gantry beside it. The letters IOM were on the rocket, not that the words mattered. The rocket has gone into nowhere, but the passenger sits here. It rose on a stool of fire. The stool became a column. Then the landing field disappeared."

"And the landing field," said Starmount quietly, "what was that?"

"A modified planoform ship. We have had ships go milky in space because they faded molecule by molecule. We have had others disappear utterly. The engineers had changed this around. We took out all the machinery needed for circumnavigation, for survival or for comfort. The landing field was to last three or four seconds, no more. Instead, we put in fourteen planoform devices, all operating in tandem, so that the ship would do what other ships do when they planoform – namely, drop one of our familiar dimensions and pick up a new dimension from some unknown category of space – but do it with such force as to get out of what people call space$_2$ and move over into space$_3$.

"And space$_3$, what did you expect of that?"

"I thought that it was universal and instantaneous, in relation to our universe. That everything was equally distant from everything else. That Rambo, wanting to see his girl again, would move in a thousandth of a second from the empty space beyond Outpost Baiter Gator into the hospital where she was."

"And, my Lord Crudelta, what made you think so?"

"A hunch, my Lord, for which you are welcome to kill me."

Starmount turned to the panel. "I suspect, my Lords, that you are more likely to doom him to long life, great responsibility, immense rewards, and the fatigue of being his own difficult and complicated self."

The miters moved gently and the members of the panel rose.

"You, my Lord Crudelta, will sleep till the trial is finished."

A robot stroked him and he fell asleep.

"Next witness," said the Lord Starmount, "in five minutes."

Vomact tried to keep Rambo from being heard as a witness. He argued fiercely with the Lord Starmount in the intermission. "You Lords have shot up my hospital, abducted two of my patients, and now you are going to torment both Rambo and Elizabeth. Can't you leave them alone? Rambo is in no condition to give coherent answers and Elizabeth may be damaged if she sees him suffer."

The Lord Starmount said to him, "You have your rules, doctor, and we have ours. This trial is being recorded, inch by inch and moment by moment. Nothing is going to be done to Rambo unless we find that he has planet-killing powers. If that is true, of course, we will ask you to take him back to the hospital and to put him to death very pleasantly. But I don't think it will happen. We want his story so that we can judge my colleague Crudelta. Do you think that the Instrumentality would survive if it did not have fierce internal discipline?"

Vomact nodded sadly; he went back to Grosbeck and Timofeyev, murmuring sadly to them, "Rambo's in for it. There's nothing we could do."

The panel reassembled. They put on their judicial miters. The lights of the room darkened and the weird blue light of justice was turned on.

The robot orderly helped Rambo to the witness chair.

"You are obliged," said Starmount, "to speak quickly and clearly to this court."

"You're not Elizabeth," said Rambo.

"I am the Lord Starmount," said the investigating Lord, quickly deciding to dispense with the formalities. "Do you know me?"

"No," said Rambo.

"Do you know where you are?"

"Earth," said Rambo.

"Do you wish to lie or to tell the truth?"

"A lie," said Rambo, "is the only truth which men can share with each other, so I will tell you lies, the way we always do."

"Can you report your trip?"

"No."

"Why not, citizen Rambo?"

"Words won't describe it."

"Do you remember your trip?"

"Do you remember your pulse of two minutes ago?" countered Rambo.

"I am not playing with you," said Starmount. "We think you have been in space$_3$ and we want you to testify about the Lord Crudelta."

"Oh!" said Rambo. "I don't like him. I never did like him."

"Will you nevertheless try to tell us what happened to you?"

"Should I, Elizabeth?" asked Rambo of the girl, who sat in the audience.

She did not stammer. "Yes," she said, in a clear voice which rang through the big room. "Tell them, so that we can find our lives again."

"I will tell you," said Rambo.

"When did you last see the Lord Crudelta?"

"When I was stripped and fitted to the rocket, four jumps out beyond Outpost Baiter Gator. He was on the ground. He waved good-bye to me."

"And then what happened?"

"The rocket rose. It felt very strange, like no craft I had ever been in before. I weighed many, many gravities."

"And then?"

"The engines went on. I was thrown out of space itself."

"What did it seem like?"

"Behind me I left the working ships, the cloth and the food which goes through space. I went down rivers which did not exist. I felt people around me though I could not see them, red people shooting arrows at live bodies."

"*Where* were you?" asked a panel member.

"In the wintertime where there is no summer. In an emptiness like a child's mind. In peninsulas which had torn loose from the land. And I *was* the ship."

"You were what?" asked the same panel member.

"The rocket nose. The cone. The boat. I was drunk. It was drunk. I was the drunkboat myself," said Rambo.

"And where did you go?" resumed Starmount.

"Where crazy lanterns stared with idiot eyes. Where the waves washed back and forth with the dead of all the ages. Where the stars became a pool, and I swam in it. Where blue turns to liquor, stronger than alcohol, wilder than music, fermented with the *red red reds* of love. I saw all the things that men have ever thought they saw, but it was me who really saw them. I've heard phosphorescence singing and tides that seemed like crazy cattle clawing their way out of the ocean, their hooves beating the reefs. You will not believe me, but I found Floridas wilder than this, where the flowers had human skins and eyes like big cats."

"What are you talking about?" asked the Lord Starmount.

"What I found in space₃," snapped Artyr Rambo. "Believe it or not. This is what I now remember. Maybe it's a dream, but it's all I have. It was years and years and it was the blink of an eye. I dreamed green nights. I felt places where the whole horizon became one big waterfall. The boat that was me met children and I showed them El Dorado, where the gold men live. The people drowned in space washed gently past me. I was a boat where all the lost spaceships lay drowned and still. Seahorses which were not real ran beside me. The summer month came and hammered down the sun. I went past archipelagoes of stars, where the delirious skies opened up for wanderers. I cried for me. I wept for man. I wanted to be the drunkboat sinking. I sank. I fell. It seemed to me that the grass was a lake, where a sad child, on hands and knees, sailed a toy boat as fragile as a butterfly in spring. I can't forget the pride of unremembered flags, the arrogance of prisons which I suspected, the swimming of the businessmen! Then I was on the grass."

"This may have scientific value," said the Lord Starmount, "but it is not of judicial importance. Do you have any comment on what you did during the battle in the hospital?"

Rambo was quick and looked sane: "What I did, I did not do. What I did not do, I cannot tell. Let me go, because I am tired of you and space, big men and big things. Let me sleep and let me get well."

Starmount lifted his hand for silence.

The panel members stared at him.

Only the few telepaths present knew that they had all said, *"Aye. Let the man go. Let the girl go. Let the doctors go.* But bring back the Lord Crudelta later on. He has many troubles ahead of him, and we wish to add to them."

Between the Instrumentality, the Manhome Government and the authorities at the Old Main Hospital, everyone wished to give Rambo and Elizabeth happiness.

As Rambo got well, much of his Earth Four memory returned. The trip faded from his mind.

When he came to know Elizabeth, he hated the girl.

This was not his girl – his bold, saucy, Elizabeth of the markets and the valleys, of the snowy hills and the long boat rides. This was somebody meek, sweet, sad and hopelessly loving.

Vomact cured that.

He sent Rambo to the Pleasure City of the Herperides, where bold and talkative women pursued him because he was rich and famous.

In a few weeks – a very few indeed – he wanted *his* Elizabeth, this strange shy girl who had been cooked back from the dead while he rode space with his own fragile bones.

"Tell the truth, darling." He spoke to her once gravely and seriously. "The Lord Crudelta did not arrange the accident which killed you?"

"They say he wasn't there," said Elizabeth. "They say it was an actual accident. I don't know. I will never know."

"It doesn't matter now," said Rambo. "Crudelta's off among the stars, looking for trouble and finding it. We have our bungalow, and our waterfall, and each other."

"Yes, my darling," she said, "each other. And no fantastic Floridas for us."

He blinked at this reference to the past, but he said nothing. A man who has been through space$_3$ needs very little in life, outside of *not* going back to space$_3$. Sometimes he dreamed he was the rocket again, the old rocket taking off on an impossible trip. Let other men follow! he thought. Let other men go! I have Elizabeth and I am here.

Another World

J. H. ROSNY AÎNÉ
Translated by Damon Knight

J. H. Rosny *aîné* was the pseudonym of the important French (Belgian) writer Joseph-Henri Boëx (1856–1940). He was the author of 107 novels, essays, plays, memoirs, etc., a friend of Alphonse Daudet, and a President of the Académie Goncourt. He wrote a small number of SF works, including prehistoric romances such as *The Giant Cat* (1918; translated 1924) and *The Quest for Fire* (1901; translated 1967), from which the film *Quest for Fire* (1981) was made. Only three of his important SF stories have been translated into English, but he is the most important French SF writer between Jules Verne and the contemporary period. This story has only appeared once before in English, in an early 1960s anthology. So his influence on the evolution of the genre in English has thus far been indirect.

Damon Knight, the well-known SF critic and the translator of this piece, said that while only a few of Rosny's works were science fiction, "those few were precedent-making, germinal works. Rosny, not Verne, is considered the father of French science fiction." Knight goes on to say, "I love this story for its human warmth, and for what it has to tell us, not only about one superman, but about the adolescence of all gifted, 'different' human beings. I admire it for many reasons, but chiefly for the absolute, circumstantial conviction with which it describes an imaginary order of living creatures. Few writers have even attempted this most difficult kind of fictional invention: fewer still have succeeded so brilliantly."

This is both a unique "fourth dimension" story and a superman story, set in a small village in France where the events have no impact on the

outside world. It is the earliest story in this anthology, published the same
year as Wells's *The Time Machine,* 1895. It is every bit as powerfully imaginative as Wells, and gives evidence of the substantial trend in literature
in the 1890s toward the themes and ideas of science fiction in works that
later coalesced into the founding documents of the genre in a work by an
early Modern writer.

I

I was born in Gelderland, where our family holdings had dwindled to
a few acres of heath and yellow water. Along the boundary grew pine
trees that rustled with a metallic sound. The farmhouse had only a few
habitable rooms left and was falling apart stone by stone in the solitude. Ours was an old family of herdsmen, once numerous, now
reduced to my parents, my sister and myself.

My fate, dismal enough at the beginning, became the happiest I
could imagine: I met the one who understands me; he will teach those
things that formerly I alone knew among men. But for many years I
suffered and despaired, a prey to doubt and the loneliness of the soul,
which nearly ended by eating away my absolute faith.

I came into the world with a unique constitution, and from the very
beginning I was the object of wonder. Not that I seemed ill-formed; I was,
I am told, more shapely in face and body than is customary in newborn
infants. But my color was most unusual, a sort of pale violet – very pale,
but quite distinct. By lamplight, especially by the light of oil lamps, this
tint grew paler still, turned to a curious whiteness, like that of a lily
submerged in water. That, at least, was how I appeared to others (for I saw
myself differently, as I saw everything in the world differently). To this
first peculiarity others were added which only revealed themselves later.

Though born with a healthy appearance, I developed poorly. I was
thin, and I cried incessantly; at the age of eight months, I had never
been seen to smile. Soon my life was despaired of. The doctor from
Zwartendam declared I was suffering from congenital weakness; he
could think of no remedy but a strict regimen. Nonetheless I continued
to waste away; the family expected me to disappear altogether from
one day to the next. My father, I think, was resigned to it, his pride –
the Hollander's pride in regularity and order – little soothed by the
grotesque appearance of his child. My mother, on the contrary, loved
me all the more for my strangeness, having made up her mind that the
color of my skin was pleasing.

So matters stood, when a very simple thing came to my rescue. Since everything concerning me must be out of the ordinary, this event was the cause of scandal and apprehension.

A servant having left us, her place was given to a vigorous girl from Friesland, honest and willing, but inclined to drink. I was placed in her care. Seeing me so feeble, she took it into her head to give me secretly a little beer and water mixed with Schiedam – remedies, according to her, sovereign against all ills.

The curious thing was that I began immediately to regain my strength and from then on showed a remarkable predilection for alcohol. The good girl rejoiced in secret, not without drawing some pleasure from the bafflement of my parents and the doctor. At last, driven into a corner, she revealed the secret. My father flew into a violent passion; the doctor inveighed against superstition and ignorance. Strict orders were given to the servants; I was taken out of the Frieslander's care.

I began to grow thin again, to waste away, until my mother, forgetting everything but her fondness for me, put me back on a diet of beer and Schiedam. I promptly grew strong and lively again. The experiment was conclusive: alcohol was seen to be necessary to my health. My father was humiliated. The doctor got out of the affair by prescribing medicinal wines; and from that time on my health was excellent – but no one hesitated to prophesy a life of drunkenness and debauch for me.

Shortly after this incident, a new oddity grew apparent to the household. My eyes, which had seemed normal at the beginning, grew strangely opaque, took on a horny appearance, like the wing cases of certain beetles. The doctor concluded from this that I was losing my sight, but he confessed that the ailment was absolutely strange to him, of such a nature that he had never had the opportunity to study a like case. Shortly the pupils of my eyes so fused into the irises that it was impossible to tell one from the other. It was remarked, moreover, that I could stare at the sun without showing any discomfort. In truth, I was not blind in the least, and in the end they had to admit that I saw very well.

So I arrived at the age of three. I was then, in the opinion of the neighborhood, a little monster. The violet color of my skin had undergone little change. My eyes were completely opaque. I spoke awkwardly, and with incredible swiftness. I was dextrous with my hands, and well formed for all activities which called for more quickness than strength. It was not denied that I might have been graceful

and handsome if my coloring had been normal and my pupils transparent. I showed some intelligence, but with deficiencies which my
family did not fully appreciate, since, except for my mother and the
Frieslander, they did not care much for me. I was an object of curiosity
to strangers, and to my father a continual mortification.

If, moreover, he had clung to any hope of seeing me become like
other people, time took ample pains to disabuse him of it. I grew more
and more strange, in my tastes, habits and aptitudes. At the age of six
I lived almost entirely on alcohol. Only very seldom did I take a few
bites of vegetables or fruit. I grew with prodigious swiftness; I became
incredibly thin and light. I mean "light" even in its specific sense,
which is just the opposite of thinness. Thus, I swam without the
slightest difficulty; I floated like a plank of poplar. My head hardly sank
deeper than the rest of my body.

I was nimble in proportion to that lightness. I ran like a deer; I easily
leaped over ditches and barriers which no man would even have
attempted. Quick as a wink, I could be in the crown of a beech tree; or,
what caused even more astonishment, I could leap over the roof of our
farmhouse. In compensation, the slightest burden was too much for me.

All these things added together were nothing but phenomena
indicative of a special nature, which by themselves would have done
no more than single me out and make me unwelcome; no one would
have classified me outside humanity. No doubt I was a monster, but
certainly not to the same degree as those who were born with the ears
or horns of animals; a head like a calf's or horse's; fins; no eyes or an
extra one; four arms; four legs; or without arms and legs. My skin, in
spite of its startling color, was little different from a sun-tanned skin;
there was nothing repugnant about my eyes, opaque as they were. My
extreme agility was a gift, my need for alcohol might pass for a mere
vice, an inheritance of drunkenness; however, the rustics, like our
Frieslander servant, viewed it as no more than a confirmation of their
ideas about the "strength" of Schiedam, a rather lively demonstration
of the excellence of their tastes.

As for the swiftness and volubility of my speech, which made it
impossible to follow, this seemed to be confounded with the defects of
pronunciation – stammering, lisping, stuttering – common to so many
small children. Thus, properly speaking, I had none of the marked
characteristics of monstrosity, however extraordinary my general
effect might be. The fact was that the most curious aspect of my nature
escaped my family's notice, for no one realized that my vision was
strangely different from ordinary vision.

If I saw certain things less well than others did, I could see a great many things that no one else could see at all. This difference showed itself especially in relation to colors. All that was termed red, orange, yellow, green, blue or indigo appeared to me as a more or less blackish gray, whereas I could perceive violet, and a series of colors beyond it – colors which were nothing but blackness to normal men. Later I realized that I could distinguish in this way among some fifteen colors as dissimilar as, for instance, yellow and green – with, of course, an infinite range of gradations in between.

In the second place, my eye does not perceive transparency in the ordinary way. I see poorly through glass or water; glass is highly colored for me, water perceptibly so, even at a slight depth. Many crystals said to be clear are more or less opaque, while, on the other hand, a very great number of bodies called opaque do not interfere with my vision. In general, I see through objects much more frequently than you do; and translucence, clouded transparency, occurs so often that I might say it is for my eye the rule of nature, while complete opacity is the exception. In this way I can make out objects through wood, paper, the petals of flowers, magnetized iron, coal, etc. Nevertheless, at variable thicknesses these substances create an obstacle – as a big tree, a meter's depth of water, a thick block of coal or quartz. Gold, platinum and mercury are black and opaque; ice is grayish black. Air and water vapor are transparent and yet tinted, as are certain specimens of steel, certain very pure clays. Clouds do not hinder me from seeing the sun or the stars. On the other hand, I can clearly see these same clouds hanging in the air.

As I have said, this difference between my vision and that of others was very little remarked by those around me. My color perception was thought to be poor, that was all; the infirmity is too common to attract much attention. It had no importance in the small daily acts of my life, for I saw the shapes of objects in the same manner as most people, and perhaps even more accurately. Designating an object by its color, when it was necessary to distinguish it from another of the same shape, troubled me only when the two objects were new. If someone called one waistcoat blue and another red, it made little difference in what colors these waistcoats really appeared to me; blue and red became purely mnemonic terms.

From this you might conclude that there was a system of correspondence between my colors and those of other people, and therefore that it came to the same thing as if I had seen their colors. But, as I have already written, red, green, yellow, blue, etc., *when they are pure,* as the colors of a prism are pure, appear to me as a more or less blackish gray; they are not colors to me at all. In nature, where no color is simple, it is not the same thing. A given substance termed green, for instance, is for me of a certain mixed color;* but another substance called green, which to you is identically the same shade as the first, is not at all the same color to me. You see, therefore, that my range of colors has no correspondence with yours: when I agree to call both brass and gold yellow, it is a little as if you should agree to call both a cornflower and a corn poppy blue.

II

Were this the extent of the difference between my vision and normal vision, certainly it would appear extraordinary enough. Nevertheless, it is but little compared with that which I have yet to tell you. The differently colored world, differently transparent and opaque, the ability to see through clouds, to perceive the stars on the most overcast nights, to see through a wooden wall what is happening in the next room or on the outside of a house – what is all this, compared with the perception of a *living world*, a world of animate Beings, moving around and beside man without man's being aware of them, without his being warned by any sort of immediate contact?

What is all this, compared with the revelation that there exists on this earth another fauna than our fauna, and one without any resemblance to our own in form, or in organization, or in habits, or in manner of growth, birth and death? A fauna which lives beside and in the midst of ours, influences the elements which surround us, and is influenced, vivified, by these elements, without our suspecting its presence. A fauna which, as I have demonstrated, is as unaware of us as we of it, and which has evolved in ignorance of us, as we in ignorance of it. A living world as varied as ours, as puissant as ours – perhaps more so – in its effect on the face of the planet! A kingdom, in short, moving upon the water, in the atmosphere, on the earth, modifying that water, that atmosphere and that earth entirely otherwise than we, but certainly with formidable strength, and in that way acting indirectly upon us and our destiny, as we indirectly act upon it!

Nevertheless, this is what I have seen, what I alone among men and animals still see; this is what I have *studied* ardently for five years, after having spent my childhood and adolescence merely *observing* it.

*And this mixture naturally does not include green, since green, for me, belongs *to* the realm of darkness.

III

Observing it! As far back as I can remember, I instinctively felt the seductiveness of that creation so foreign to ours. In the beginning, I confounded it with other living things. Seeing that no one took any notice of its presence, that everyone, on the contrary, appeared indifferent to it, I hardly felt the need to point out its peculiarities. At six, I understood perfectly its difference from the plants of the fields, the animals of the farmyard and the stable; but I confused it somewhat with such nonliving phenomena as rays of light, the movement of water, and clouds. That was because these creatures were intangible: when they touched me I felt no sensation of contact. Their shapes, otherwise widely variant, nevertheless had this singularity, that they were so thin, in one of their three dimensions, that they might be compared to drawings, to surfaces, geometric lines that moved. They passed through all organic bodies; on the other hand, they sometimes appeared to be halted, entangled by invisible obstacles.

But I shall describe them later. At present I only wish to draw attention to them, to affirm their variety of contours and lines, their quasi-absence of thickness, their *impalpability*, combined with the autonomy of their movements.

At about my eighth year, I became perfectly sure that they were as distinct from atmospheric phenomena as from the members of our animal kingdom. In the delight this discovery afforded me, I tried to communicate it to others. I never succeeded in doing so. Aside from the fact that my speech was almost entirely incomprehensible, as I have said, the extraordinary nature of my vision rendered it suspect. No one thought of pausing to unravel my gestures and my phrases, any more than to admit that I could see through wooden walls, even though I had given proof of this on many occasions. Between me and the others there was an almost insurmountable barrier.

I fell into discouragement and daydreams; I became a sort of little recluse; I caused uneasiness, and felt it myself, among children of my own age. I was not exactly an underdog, for my swiftness put me beyond the reach of childish tricks and gave me the means of avenging myself easily. At the slightest threat, I was off at a distance – I mocked all pursuit. No matter how many of them there were, children never succeeded in surrounding me, much less in holding me prisoner. It was not worthwhile even to try to seize me by a trick. Weak as I might be at carrying burdens, my leaps were irresistible and freed me at once. I could return at will, overcome my adversary, even more than one, with swift, sure blows. Accordingly I was left in peace. I was looked on as innocent and at the same time a bit magical; but it was a feeble magic, which they scorned.

By degrees I made a life for myself outdoors, wild, meditative, not without its pleasures. Only the affection of my mother humanized me, even though, busy all day long, she found little time for caresses.

IV

I shall try to describe briefly a few scenes from my tenth year, in order to give substance to the explanations which have gone before.

It is morning. A bright glow illuminates the kitchen – a pale yellow glow to my parents and the servants, richly various to me. The first breakfast is being served: bread and tea. But I do not take tea. I have been given a glass of Schiedam with a raw egg. My mother is hovering over me tenderly; my father questions me. I try to answer him, I slow down my speech; he understands only a syllable here and there. He shrugs. "He'll never learn to talk!"

My mother looks at me with compassion, convinced that I am a bit simple. The servants and laborers no longer even feel any curiosity about the little violet monster; the Frieslander has long ago gone back to her country. As for my sister, who is two years old, she is playing near me, and I feel a deep affection for her.

Breakfast over, my father goes off to the fields with the laborers; my mother begins to busy herself with her daily tasks. I follow her into the farmyard. The animals come up to her. I watch them with interest; I like them. But, all around, the other Kingdom is in motion, and it attracts me still more; it is the mysterious domain which only I know.

On the brown earth a few shapes are sprawled out; they move, they pause, they palpitate on the surface of the ground. They belong to several species, different in contours, in movement, and above all in the arrangement, design and shadings of the lines which run through them. Taken together, these lines constitute the essential part of their being, and, child though I am, I know it very well. Whereas the mass of their bodies is dull, grayish, the lines are almost always brilliant. They form highly complicated networks, radiating from centers, spreading out until they fade and lose their identity. Their tints and curves are innumerable. These colors vary within a single line, as the form does also, but to a lesser extent. The creature as a whole is distinguished by a rather irregular but very distinct outline; by the radiant centers; by the multicolored lines which intermingle freely. When it moves, the lines tremble, oscillate; the centers contract and dilate, while the outline changes little.

All this I see very well already, though I may be unable to define it; a delightful spell falls over me when I watch the *Moedigen*.* One of them, a colossus ten meters long and almost as wide, passes slowly across the farmyard and disappears. This one, with some bands the size of cables, and centers as big as eagles' wings, greatly interests and almost frightens me. I pause for a moment, about to follow it, but then others attract my attention. They are of all sizes: some are no larger than our tiniest insects, while I have seen others more than thirty meters long. They advance on the ground itself, as if attached to solid surfaces. When they meet a material obstacle – a wall, or a house – they cross it by molding themselves to its surface, always without any significant change in their outlines. But when the obstacle is of living or once-living matter, they pass directly through it; thus I have seen them appear thousands of times out of trees and beneath the feet of animals and men. They can pass through water also, but prefer to remain on the surface.

These land *Moedigen* are not the only intangible creatures. There is an aerial population of a marvelous splendor, of an incomparable subtlety, variety and brilliance, beside which the most beautiful birds are dull, slow and heavy. Here again there are internal lines and an outline. But the background is not grayish, it is strangely luminous; it sparkles like sunlight, and the lines stand out from it in trembling veins; the centers palpitate violently. The *Vuren*, as I call them, are of a more irregular form than the land *Moedigen* and commonly propel themselves by means of rhythmic dispositions, intertwinings and untwinings which, in my ignorance, I cannot make out and which baffle my imagination.

Meanwhile I am making my way across a recently mowed meadow; the battle of a *Moedig* with another one has drawn my attention. These battles are frequent, and they excite me tremendously. Sometimes the battles are equal; more often an attack is made by the stronger upon the weaker. (The weaker is not necessarily the smaller.) In the present case, the weaker one, after a short defense, takes to flight, hotly pursued by the aggressor. Despite the swiftness of their motions, I follow them and succeed in keeping them in view until the struggle begins again. They fling themselves on each other – firmly, even

---

*This is the name which I gave them spontaneously in my childhood and which I have retained, though it corresponds to no quality or form of these creatures.

rigidly, solid to each other. At the shock, their lines phosphoresce, moving toward the point of contact; their centers grow smaller and paler.

At first the struggle remains more or less equal; the weaker puts forth a more intense energy and even succeeds in gaining a truce from its adversary. It profits by this to flee once more, but is rapidly overtaken, strongly attacked and at last seized – that is to say, held fast in a hollow in the outline of the other. This is exactly what it has been trying to avoid, as it counters the stronger one's buffets with blows that are weaker but swifter. Now I see all its lines shudder, its centers throb desperately; and the lines gradually thin out, grow pale; the centers blur. After a few minutes, it is set free: it withdraws slowly, dull, debilitated. Its antagonist, on the contrary, glows more brightly; its lines are more vivid, its centers clearer and livelier.

This fight has moved me profoundly. I think about it and compare it with the fights I sometimes see between our animals. I realize confusedly that the *Moedigen,* as a group, do not kill, or rarely kill, that the victor contents itself with *increasing its strength* at the expense of the vanquished.

The morning wears on; it is nearly eight o'clock; the Zwartendam school is about to open. I gain the house in one leap, seize my books, and here I am among my fellows, where no one guesses what profound mysteries palpitate around him, where no one has the least idea of the living things through which all humanity passes and which pass through humanity, leaving no mark of that mutual penetration.

I am a very poor scholar. My writing is nothing but a hasty scrawl, unformed, illegible; my speech remains uncomprehended; my absence of mind is manifest. The master calls out continually, "Karel Ondereet, have you done with watching the flies?"

Alas, my dear master! It is true that I watch the flies in the air, but how much more does my mind accompany the mysterious *Vuren* that pass through the room! And what strange feelings obsess my childish mind, to note everyone's blindness and above all your own, grave shepherd of intellects!

V

The most painful period of my life was that which ran from my twelfth to my eighteenth year.

To begin with, my parents tried to send me to the academy. I knew nothing there but misery and frustration. At the price of exhausting struggles, I succeeded in expressing the most ordinary things in a partially comprehensible manner: slowing my syllables with great effort, I uttered them awkwardly and with the intonations of the deaf. But as soon as I had to do with anything complicated, my speech regained its fatal swiftness; no one could follow me any longer. Therefore I could not register my progress orally. Moreover, my writing was atrocious, my letters piled up one on the other, and in my impatience I forgot whole syllables and words; it was a monstrous hodgepodge. Besides, writing was a torment to me, perhaps even more intolerable than speech – of an asphyxiating slowness, heaviness! If occasionally, by taking much pain and sweating great drops, I succeeded in beginning an exercise, at once I was at the end of my energy and patience; I felt about to faint. Accordingly I preferred the masters remonstrances, the anger of my father, punishments, privations, scorn, to this horrible labor.

Thus I was almost totally deprived of the means of expression. Already an object of ridicule for my thinness and my strange color, my odd eyes, once more I passed for a kind of idiot. It was necessary for my parents to withdraw me from school and resign themselves to making a peasant of me.

The day my father decided to give up all hope, he said to me with unaccustomed gentleness, "My poor boy, you see I have done my duty – my whole duty. Never reproach me for your fate."

I was strongly moved. I shed warm tears; never had I felt more bitterly my isolation in the midst of men. I dared to embrace my father tenderly; I muttered, "Just the same, it's not true that I'm a halfwit!" And, in fact, I felt myself superior to those who had been my fellow pupils. Some time ago my intelligence had undergone a remarkable development. I read, I understood, I divined; and I had enormous matter for reflection, beyond that of other men, in that universe visible to me alone.

My father could not make out my words, but he softened to my embrace. "Poor boy!" he said.

I looked at him; I was in terrible distress, knowing too well that the gap between us would never be bridged. My mother, through love's intuition, saw in that moment that I was not inferior to the other boys of my age. She gazed at me tenderly, she spoke artless love words that came from the depths of her being. Nonetheless, I was condemned to give up my studies.

Because of my lack of muscular strength, I was given the care of the horses and the cattle. In this I acquitted myself admirably; I needed no dog to guard the herds, in which no colt or stallion was as agile as I.

Thus, from my fourteenth to my seventeenth year I lived the solitary life of the herdsman. It suited me better than any other. Given over to observation and contemplation, together with some reading, my mind never stopped growing. Incessantly I compared the two orders of creation which lay before my eyes; I drew from them ideas about the constitution of the universe; vaguely I sketched out hypotheses and systems. If it be true that in that period my thoughts were not perfectly ordered, did not make a lucid synthesis – for they were adolescent thoughts, uncoordinated, impatient, enthusiastic – nevertheless they were original, and fruitful. That their value may have depended above all upon my unique constitution, I would be the last to deny. But they did not draw all their strength from that source. I think I may say without pride that in subtlety as in logic they notably surpassed those of ordinary young men.

They alone brought consolation to my melancholy half-pariah's life, without companions, without any real communication with the rest of my household, even my adorable mother.

At the age of seventeen, life became definitely unsupportable to me. I was weary of dreaming, weary of vegetating on a desert island of thought. I fell into languor and boredom. I rested immobile for long hours, indifferent to the whole world, inattentive to anything that happened in my family. What mattered it that I knew of more marvelous things than other men, since in any case this knowledge must die with me? What was the mystery of living things to me, or even the duality of the two living systems crossing through each other without awareness of each other? These things might have intoxicated me, filled me with enthusiasm and ardor, if I could have taught them or shared them in any way. But what would you! Vain and sterile, absurd and miserable, they contributed rather to my perpetual psychic quarantine.

Many times I dreamed of setting down, recording, in spite of everything, by dint of continuous effort, some of my observations But since leaving school I had completely abandoned the pen, and, already so wretched a scribbler, it was all I could do, with the utmost application, to trace the twenty-six letters of the alphabet. If I had still entertained any hope, perhaps I should have persisted. But who would have taken my miserable lucubrations seriously? Where was the reader who would not think me mad? Where the sage who would not show me the door with irony or disdain?

To what end, therefore, should I consecrate myself to that vain task, that exasperating torment, almost comparable to the requirement, for an ordinary man, to grave his thoughts upon tablets of marble with a huge chisel and a Cyclopean hammer? My penmanship would have had to be stenographic – and yet more: of a superswift stenography! Thus I had no courage at all to write, and at the same time I fervently hoped for I know not what unforeseen event, what happy and singular destiny. It seemed to me that there must exist, in some corner of the earth, impartial minds, lucid, searching, qualified to study me, to understand me, to extract my great secret from me and communicate it to others. But where were these men? What hope had I of ever meeting them?

And I fell once more into a vast melancholy, into the desire for immobility and extinction. During one whole autumn, I despaired of the universe. I languished in a vegetative state, from which I emerged only to give way to long groans, followed by painful rebellions of conscience.

I grew thinner still, thin to a fantastic degree. The villagers called me, ironically, "*den Heyligen Gheest,*" the Holy Ghost. My silhouette was tremulous as that of the young poplars, faint as a shadow; and with all this, I grew to a giant's stature.

Slowly, a project was born. Since my life had been thrown into the discard, since my days were without joy and all was darkness and bitterness to me, why wallow in sloth? Supposing that no mind existed which could respond to my own – at least it would be worth the effort to convince myself of that fact. At least it would be worthwhile to leave this gloomy countryside, to go and search for scientists and philosophers in the great cities. Was I not in myself an object of curiosity? Before calling attention to my extrahuman knowledge, could I not arouse a desire to study my person? Were not the mere physical aspects of my being worthy of analysis – and my sight, and the extreme swiftness of my movements, and the peculiarity of my diet?

The more I thought of it, the more it seemed reasonable to me to hope, and the more my resolution hardened. The day came when it was unshakable, when I confided it to my parents. Neither one nor the other understood much of it, but in the end both gave in to repeated entreaties: I obtained permission to go to Amsterdam, free to return if fortune should not favor me.

One morning, I left.

VI

From Zwartendam to Amsterdam is a matter of a hundred kilometers or thereabouts. I covered that distance easily in two hours, without any other adventure than the extreme surprise of those going and coming to see me run so swiftly, and a few crowds at the edges of the villages and towns I skirted. To make sure of my direction, I spoke two or three times to solitary old people. My sense of orientation, which is excellent, did the rest.

It was about nine o'clock when I reached Amsterdam. I entered the great city resolutely and walked along its beautiful, dreaming canals, where quiet merchant fleets dwell. I did not attract as much attention as I had feared. I walked quickly, among busy people, enduring here and there the gibes of some young street Arabs. Nevertheless, I did not decide to stop. I wandered here and there through the city, until at last I resolved to enter a tavern on one of the quays of the Heerengracht. It was a peaceful spot; the magnificent canal stretched, full of life, between cool rows of trees; and among the *Moedigen* which I saw moving about on its banks it seemed to me that I perceived a new species. After some hesitation, I crossed the sill of the tavern, and addressing myself to the publican as slowly as I could, I begged him to be kind enough to direct me to a hospital.

The landlord looked at me with amazement, suspicion and curiosity; took his huge pipe out of his mouth, put it back in after several attempts, and at last said, "You're from the colonies, I suppose?"

Since it was perfectly useless to contradict him, I answered, "Just so!"

He seemed delighted at his own shrewdness. He asked me another question: "Maybe you come from that part of Borneo where no one has ever been?"

"Exactly right!"

I had spoken too swiftly: his eyes grew round.

"Exactly right," I repeated more slowly.

The landlord smiled with satisfaction. "You can hardly speak Dutch, can you? So, it's a hospital you want. No doubt you're sick?"

"Yes."

Patrons were gathering around. It was whispered already that I was an anthropophagus from Borneo; nevertheless, they looked at me with much more curiosity than aversion. People were running in from the street. I became nervous and uneasy. I kept my composure nonetheless and said, coughing, "I am very sick!"

"Just like the monkeys from that country," said a very fat man benevolently. "The Netherlands kills them!"

"What a funny skin!" added another.

"And how does he see?" asked a third, pointing to my eyes.

The ring moved closer, encircling me with a hundred curious stares, and still newcomers were crowding into the room.

"How tall he is!"

In truth, I was a full head taller than the biggest of them.

"And thin!"

"This anthropophagy doesn't seem to nourish them very well!"

Not all the voices were spiteful. A few sympathetic persons protected me:

"Don't crowd so – he's sick!"

"Come, friend, courage!" said the fat man, remarking my nervousness. "I'll lead you to a hospital myself."

He took me by the arm and set about elbowing the crowd aside, calling, "Way for an invalid!"

Dutch crowds are not very fierce. They let us pass, but they went with us. We walked along the canal, followed by a compact multitude, and people cried out, "It's a cannibal from Borneo!"

At length we reached a hospital. It was the visiting hour. I was taken to an intern, a young man with blue spectacles, who greeted me peevishly. My companion said to him, "He's a savage from the colonies."

"What, a savage!" cried the other.

He took off his spectacles to look at me. Surprise held him motionless for a moment. He asked me brusquely, "Can you see?"

"I see very well."

I had spoken too swiftly.

"It's his accent," said the fat man proudly. "Once more, friend."

I repeated it and made myself understood.

"Those aren't human eyes," murmured the student. "And the color! Is that the color of your race?"

Then I said, with a terrible effort to slow myself down, "I have come to show myself to a scientist."

"Then you're not ill?"

"No."

"And you come from Borneo?"

"No."

"Where are you from, then?"

"From Zwartendam, near Duisburg."

"Why, then, does this man claim you're from Borneo?"

"I didn't want to contradict him."

"And you wish to see a scientist?"

"Yes."

"Why?"

"To be studied."

"So as to earn money?"

"No, for nothing."

"You're not a pauper? A beggar?"

"No!"

"What makes you want to be studied?"

"My constitution – "

But again, in spite of my efforts, I had spoken too swiftly. I had to repeat myself.

"Are you sure you can see me?" he asked, staring at me. "Your eyes are like horn."

"I see very well."

And, moving to left and right, I snatched things up, put them down, threw them in the air and caught them again.

"Extraordinary!" said the young man.

His softened voice, almost friendly, filled me with hope. "See here," he said at last, "I really think Dr. van den Heuvel might be interested in your case. I'll go and inform him. Wait in the next room. And, by the way – I forgot – you're not ill, after all?"

"Not in the least."

"Good. Wait – go in there. The doctor won't be long."

I found myself seated among monsters preserved in alcohol: fetuses, infants with bestial shapes, colossal batrachians, vaguely anthropomorphic saurians.

This is well chosen for my waiting room, I thought. Am I not a candidate for one of these brandy-filled sepulchers?

VII

When Dr. van den Heuvel appeared, emotion overcame me. I had the thrill of the Promised Land – the joy of reaching it, the dread of being banished. The doctor, with his great bald forehead, the analyst's penetrating look, the mouth soft and yet stubborn, examined me in silence. As always, my excessive thinness, my great stature, my horny eyes, my violet color, caused him astonishment.

"You say you wish to be studied?" he asked at length.

I answered forcefully, almost violently, "Yes!"

He smiled with an approving air and asked me the usual question: "Do you see all right, with those eyes?"

"Very well. I can even see through wood, clouds – "

But I had spoken too fast. He glanced at me uneasily. I began again, sweating great drops: "I can even see through wood, clouds – "

"Really! That would be extraordinary. Well, then! What do you see through the door there?" He pointed to a closed door.

"A big library with windows . . . a carved table . . ."

"Really!" he repeated, stunned.

My breast swelled; a deep stillness entered my soul.

The scientist remained silent for a few seconds. Then: "You speak with some difficulty."

"Otherwise I should speak too rapidly! I cannot speak slowly."

"Well, then, speak a little as you do naturally."

Accordingly I told him the story of my entry into Amsterdam. He listened to me with an extreme attention, an air of intelligent observation, which I had never before encountered among my fellows. He understood nothing of what I said, but he showed the keenness of his intellect.

"If I am not mistaken, you speak fifteen to twenty syllables a second, that is to say three or four times more than the human ear can distinguish. Your voice, in addition, is much higher than anything I have ever heard in the way of human voices. Your excessively rapid gestures are well suited to your speech. Your whole constitution is probably more rapid than ours."

"I run," I said, "faster than a greyhound. I write – "

"Ah!" he interrupted. "Let us see your writing."

I scrawled some words on a tablet which he offered me, the first few fairly legible, the rest more and more scrambled, abbreviated.

"Perfect!" he said, and a certain pleasure was mingled with his surprise. "I really think I must congratulate myself on this meeting. Certainly it should be very interesting to study you."

"It is my dearest, my only, desire!"

"And mine, naturally. Science . . ."

He seemed preoccupied, musing. He finished by saying, "If only we could find an easy way of communication."

He walked back and forth, his brows knotted. Suddenly: "What a dolt I am! You must learn shorthand, of course! Hm! . . . Hm!" A cheerful expression spread over his face. "And I've forgotten the phonograph – the perfect confidant! All that's needed is to revolve it more slowly in the reproduction than in the recording. It's agreed: you shall stay with me while you are in Amsterdam!"

The joy of a fulfilled vocation, the delight of ceasing to spend vain and sterile days! Aware of the intelligent personality of the doctor, against this scientific background, I felt a delicious well-being; the melancholy of my spiritual solitude, the sorrow for my lost talents, the pariah's long misery that had weighed me down for so many years, all vanished, evaporated in the sensation of a new life, a real life, a saved destiny!

VIII

Beginning the following day, the doctor made all the necessary arrangements. He wrote to my parents; he sent me to a professor of stenography and obtained some phonographs. As he was quite rich and entirely devoted to science, there was no experiment which he could not undertake, and my vision, my hearing, my musculature, the color of my skin, were submitted to scrupulous investigations, from which he drew more and more enthusiasm, crying, "This verges on the miraculous!"

I very well understood, after the first few days, how important it was to go about things methodically – from the simple to the complex, from the slightly abnormal to the wonderfully abnormal. Thus I had recourse to a little legerdemain, of which I made no secret to the doctor: that is, I revealed my abilities to him only one at a time.

The quickness of my perceptions and movements drew his attention first. He was able to convince himself that the subtlety of my hearing was in proportion to the swiftness of my speech. Graduated trials of the most fugitive sounds, which I imitated with ease, and the words of ten or fifteen persons all talking at once, which I distinguished perfectly, demonstrated this point beyond question. My vision proved no less swift; comparative tests between my ability to resolve the movement of a galloping horse, or an insect in flight, and the same ability of an apparatus for taking instantaneous photographs, proved all in favor of my eye.

As for perceptions of ordinary things, simultaneous movements of a group of people, of children playing, the motion of machines, bits of rubble thrown in the air or little balls tossed into an alley, to be counted in flight – they amazed the doctor's family and friends.

My running in the big garden, my twenty-meter jumps, my

instantaneous swiftness to pick up objects or put them back, were admired still more, not by the doctor, but by those around him. And it was an ever renewed pleasure for the wife and children of my host, while walking in the fields, to see me outstrip a horseman at full gallop or follow the flight of any swallow; in truth, there was no thoroughbred but I could give it a start of two-thirds the distance, whatever it might be, nor any bird I could not easily overtake.

As for the doctor, more and more satisfied with the results of his experiments, he described me thus: "A human being, endowed in all his movements with a swiftness incomparably superior, not merely to that of other humans, but also to that of all known animals. This swiftness, found in the most minute constituents of his body as well as in the whole organism, makes him an entity so distinct from the remainder of creation that he merits a special place in the animal kingdom for himself alone. As for the curious structure of his eyes, as well as the skin's violet color, these must be considered simply the earmarks of this special condition."

Tests being made of my muscular system, it proved in no way remarkable, unless for its excessive leanness. Neither did my ears yield any particular information; nor, for that matter, did my skin – except, of course, for its pigmentation. As for my dark hair, a purplish black in color, it was fine as spiderweb, and the doctor made a minute examination of it.

"One would need to dissect you!" he often told me, laughing.

Thus time passed easily. I had quickly learned to write in shorthand, thanks to my intense desire and to the natural aptitude I showed for this method of rapid transcription, into which, by the way, I introduced several new abbreviations. I began to make notes, which my stenographer transcribed; for the rest, we had phonographs built, according to the doctor's special design, which proved perfectly suited to reproduce my voice at a lower speed.

At length my host's confidence in me became complete. During the first few weeks he had not been able to avoid the suspicion – a very natural one – that my peculiar abilities might be accompanied by some mental abnormality, some cerebral derangement. This anxiety once put aside, our relations became perfectly cordial, and I think, as fascinating for one as for the other.

We made analytic tests of my ability to see through a great number of "opaque" substances; and of the dark coloration which water, glass or quartz takes on for me at certain thicknesses. It will be recalled that I can see clearly through wood, leaves, clouds and many other substances; that I can barely make out the bottom of a pool of water half a meter deep; and that a window, though transparent, is less so to me than to the average person and has a rather dark color. A thick piece of glass appears blackish to me. The doctor convinced himself at leisure of all these singularities – astonished above all to see me make out the stars on cloudy nights.

Only then did I begin to tell him that colors too present themselves differently to me. Experience established beyond doubt that red, orange, yellow, green, blue and indigo are perfectly invisible to me, like infrared or ultraviolet to a normal eye. On the other hand, I was able to show that I perceive violet, and beyond violet a range of colors – a spectrum at least double that which extends from the red to the violet.*

This amazed the doctor more than all the rest. His study of it was long and painstaking; it was conducted, besides, with enormous cunning. In this accomplished experimenter's hands, it became the source of subtle discoveries in the order of sciences as they are ranked by humanity; it gave him the key to far-ranging phenomena of magnetism, of chemical affinities, of induction; it guided him toward new conceptions of physiology. To know that a given metal shows a series of unknown tints, variable according to the pressure, the temperature, the electric charge, that the most rarefied gases have distinct colors, even at small depths; to learn of the infinite tonal richness of objects which appear more or less black, whereas they present a more magnificent spectrum in the ultraviolet than that of all known colors; to know, finally, the possible variations in unknown hues of an electric circuit, the bark of a tree, the skin of a man, in a day, an hour, a minute – the use that an ingenious scientist might make of such ideas can readily be imagined.

We worked patiently for a whole year without my mentioning the *Moedigen*. I wished to convince my host absolutely, give him countless proofs of my visual faculties, before daring the supreme confidence. At length, the time came when I felt I could reveal everything.

IX

It happened in a mild autumn full of clouds, which rolled across the vault of the sky for a week without shedding a drop of rain. One

---

*Quartz gives me a spectrum of about eight colors: the longest violet and the seven succeeding colors in the ultraviolet. But there remain about eight more colors which are not refracted by quartz, and which are refracted more or less by other substances.

morning van den Heuvel and I were walking in the garden. The doctor was silent, completely absorbed in his speculations, of which I was the principal subject. At the far end, he began to speak:

"It's a nice thing to dream about, anyhow: to see through clouds, pierce through to the ether, whereas we, blind as we are . . ."

"If the sky were all I saw!" I answered.

"Oh, yes – the whole world, so different . . ."

"Much more different even than I've told you!"

"How's that?" he cried with an avid curiosity. "Have you been hiding something from me?"

"The most important thing!"

He stood facing me, staring at me fixedly, in real distress, in which some element of the mystical seemed to be blended.

"Yes, the most important thing!"

We had come near the house, and I dashed in to ask for a phonograph. The instrument that was brought to me was an advanced model, highly perfected by my friend, and could record a long speech; the servant put it down on the stone table where the doctor and his family took coffee on mild summer evenings. A miracle of exact, fine construction, the device lent itself admirably to recording casual talks. Our dialogue went on, therefore, almost like an ordinary conversation.

"Yes, I've hidden the main thing from you, because I wanted your complete confidence first – and even now, after all the discoveries you've made about my organism, I am afraid you won't find it easy to believe me, at least to begin with."

I stopped to let the machine repeat this sentence. I saw the doctor grow pale, with the pallor of a great scientist in the presence of a new aspect of matter. His hands were trembling.

"I shall believe you!" he said, with a certain solemnity.

"Even if I try to tell you that our order of creation – I mean our animal and vegetable world – isn't the only life on earth, that there is another, as vast, as numerous, as varied, invisible to your eyes?"

He scented occultism and could not refrain from saying, "The world of the fourth state of matter – departed souls, the phantoms of the spiritualists."

"No, no, nothing like that. A world of living creatures, doomed like us to a short life, to organic needs – birth, growth, struggle. A world as weak and ephemeral as ours, a world governed by laws equally rigid, if not identical, a world equally imprisoned by the earth, equally vulnerable to accident, but otherwise completely different from ours, without any influence on ours, as we have no influence on it – except through the changes it makes in our common ground, the earth, or through the parallel changes that we create in the same ground."

I do not know if van den Heuvel believed me, but certainly he was in the grip of strong emotion. "They are fluid, in short?" he asked.

"That's what I don't know how to answer, for their properties are too contradictory to fit into our ideas of matter. The earth is as resistant to them as to us, and the same with most minerals, although they can penetrate a little way into a humus. Also, they are totally impermeable and solid with respect to each other. But they can pass through plants, animals, organic tissues, although sometimes with a certain difficulty; and we ourselves pass through them the same way. If one of them could be aware of us, we should perhaps seem fluid with respect to them, as they seem fluid with respect to us; but probably he could no more *decide* about it than I can – he would be struck by similar contradictions. There is one peculiarity about their shape: they have hardly any thickness. They are of all sizes. I've known some to reach a hundred meters in length, and others are as tiny as our smallest insects. Some of them feed on earth and air, others on air and on their own kind – without killing as we do, however, because it's enough for the stronger to draw strength from the weaker, and because this strength can be extracted without draining the springs of life."

The doctor said brusquely, "Have you seen them ever since childhood?"

I guessed that he was imagining some more or less recent disorder in my body. "Since childhood," I answered vigorously. "I'll give you all the proofs you like."

"Do you see them now?"

"I see them. There are a great many in the garden."

"Where?"

"On the path, the lawns, on the walls, in the air. For there are terrestrial and aerial ones – and aquatic ones too, but those hardly ever leave the surface of the water."

"Are they numerous everywhere?"

"Yes, and hardly less so in town than in the country, in houses than in the street. Those that like the indoors are smaller, though, no doubt because of the difficulty of getting in and out, even though they find a wooden door no obstacle."

"And iron . . . glass . . . brick?"

"All impermeable to them."

"Will you describe one of them, a fairly large one?"

"I see one near that tree. Its shape is extremely elongated, and rather irregular. It is convex toward the right, concave toward the left, with swellings and hollows: it looks something like an enlarged photograph of a big, fat larva. But its structure is not typical of the Kingdom, because structure varies a great deal from one species (if I may use that word) to another. Its extreme thinness, on the other hand, is a common characteristic: it can hardly be more than a tenth of a millimeter in thickness, whereas it's one hundred and fifty centimeters long and forty centimeters across at its widest.

"What distinguishes this, and the whole Kingdom, above all are the lines that cross it in nearly every direction, ending in networks that fan out between two systems of lines. Each system has a center, a kind of spot that is slightly raised above the mass of the body, or occasionally hollowed out. These centers have no fixed form; sometimes they are almost circular or elliptical, sometimes twisted or helical, sometimes divided by many narrow throats. They are astonishingly mobile, and their size varies from hour to hour. Their borders palpitate strongly, in a sort of transverse undulation. In general, the lines that emerge from them are big, although there are also very fine ones; they diverge, and end in an infinity of delicate traceries which gradually fade away. However, certain lines, much paler than the others, are not produced by the centers; they stay isolated in the system and grow without changing their color. These lines have the faculty of moving within the body, and of varying their curves, while the centers and their connected lines remain stable.

"As for the colors of my *Moedig*, I must forego any attempt to describe them to you; none of them falls within the spectrum perceptible to your eye, and none has a name in your vocabulary. They are extremely brilliant in the networks, weaker in the centers, very much faded in the independent lines, which, however, have a very high brilliance – an ultraviolet metallic effect, so to speak . . . I have some observations on the habits, the diet and the range of the *Moedigen*, but I don't wish to submit them to you just now."

I fell silent. The doctor listened twice to the words recorded by our faultless interpreter; then for a long time he was silent. Never had I seen him in such a state: his face was rigid, stony, his eyes glassy and cataleptic; a heavy film of sweat covered his temples and dampened his hair. He tried to speak and failed. Trembling, he walked all around the garden; and when he reappeared, his eyes and mouth expressed a violent passion, fervent, religious; he seemed more like the disciple of some new faith than like a peaceful investigator.

At last he muttered, "I'm overwhelmed! Everything you have just said seems terribly lucid – and have I the right to doubt, considering all the wonders you've already shown me?"

"Doubt!" I said warmly. "Doubt as hard as you can! Your experiments will be all the more fruitful for it."

"Ah," he said in a dreaming voice, "it's the pure stuff of wonder, and so magnificently superior to the pointless marvels of fairy tales! My poor human intelligence is so tiny before such knowledge! I feel an enormous enthusiasm. Yet something in me doubts . . ."

"Let's work to dispel your doubt – our efforts will pay for themselves ten times over!"

X

We worked; and it took the doctor only a few weeks to clear up all his uncertainties. Several ingenious experiments, together with the undeniable consistency of all the statements I had made, and two or three lucky discoveries about the *Moedigen*'s influence on atmospheric phenomena, left no question in his mind. When we were joined by the doctor's elder son, a young man of great scientific aptitude, the fruitfulness of our work and the conclusiveness of our findings were again increased.

Thanks to my companions' methodical habits of mind, and their experience in study and classification – qualities which I was absorbing little by little – whatever was uncoordinated or confused in my knowledge of the *Moedigen* rapidly became transformed. Our discoveries multiplied; rigorous experiments gave firm results, in circumstances which in ancient times and even up to the last century would have suggested at most a few trifling diversions.

It is now five years since we began our researches. They are far, very far from completion. Even a preliminary report of our work can hardly appear in the near future. In any case, we have made it a rule to do nothing in haste; our discoveries are too immanent a kind not to be set forth in the most minute detail, with the most sovereign patience and the finest precision. We have no other investigator to forestall, no patent to take out or ambition to satisfy. We stand at a height where vanity and pride fade away. How can there be any comparison between the joys of our work and the wretched lure of human fame? Besides, do not all these things flow from the single accident of my physical organization? What a petty thing it would be, then, for us to boast about them!

No; we live excitedly, always on the verge of wonders, and yet we live in immutable serenity.

I have had an adventure which adds to the interest of my life, and which fills me with infinite joy during my leisure hours. You know how ugly I am; my bizarre appearance is fit only to horrify young women. All the same, I have found a companion who not only can put up with my show of affection, but even takes pleasure in it.

She is a poor girl, hysterical and nervous, whom we met one day in a hospital in Amsterdam. Others find her wretched-looking, plaster-white, hollow-cheeked, with wild eyes. But to me her appearance is pleasant, her company charming. From the very beginning my presence, far from alarming her like all the rest, seemed to please and comfort her. I was touched; I wanted to see her again.

It was quickly discovered that I had a beneficial influence on her health and well-being. On examination, it appeared that I influenced her by animal magnetism: my nearness, and above all the touch of my hands, gave her a really curative gaiety, serenity, and calmness of spirit. In turn, I took pleasure in being near her. Her face seemed lovely to me; her pallor and slenderness were no more than signs of delicacy; for me her eyes, able to perceive the glow of magnets, like those of many hyperesthesiacs, had none at all of the distracted quality that others criticized.

In short, I felt an attraction for her, and she returned it with passion. From that time, I resolved to marry her. I gained my end readily, thanks to the good will of my friends.

This union has been a happy one. My wife's health was re-established, although she remained extremely sensitive and frail. I tasted the joy of being like other men in the essential part of life. But my happiness was crowned six months ago: a child was born to us, and in this child are combined all the faculties of my constitution. Color, vision, hearing, extreme rapidity of movement, diet – he promises to be an exact copy of my physiology.

The doctor watches him grow with delight. A wonderful hope has come to us – that the study of the *Moedig* World, of the Kingdom parallel to our own, this study which demands so much time and patience, will not end when I cease to be. My son will pursue it, undoubtedly, in his turn. Why may he not find collaborators of genius, able to raise it to a new power? Why may he also not give life to seers of the invisible world?

As for myself, may I not look forward to other children, may I not hope that my dear wife may give birth to other sons of my flesh, like unto their father? As I think of it, my heart trembles, I am filled with an infinite beatitude; and I know myself blessed among men.

If the Stars Are Gods

GORDON EKLUND & GREGORY BENFORD

Gregory Benford (1941–) and Gordon Eklund (1945–) were some-time collaborators in the 1970s. At the start, Eklund was "the writer," producing many other stories and novels on his own, and Benford was "the scientist," a full-time physicist who occasionally published science fiction. But by the end of the decade, Benford had become one of the leading younger writers, producing two significant works, *In the Ocean of Night* (1977) and *The Stars in Shroud* (1978) and then the classic *Timescape* (1980), and Eklund, who had published many short stories and nine novels by 1976 – *If the Stars Are Gods* (1977) was his tenth – stopped writing for long periods of time after 1979. Of all their works, this one (1975), later developed into the novel of the same title, is the best. It was to a large extent written by Eklund and revised by Benford.

Benford in his later works is the first among the hard SF writers to have mastered and integrated Modernist techniques of characterization and use of metaphor, and some of this may have been assimilated through his early collaboration with Eklund. The tension between the daily work of science and the avocation of writing in Benford's life has led him to write some of the finest science fiction of recent decades. Brian W. Aldiss says:

"If he takes the close and narrow view of his characters – an all-too-human view, of illness, work and marital problems – his vision of the universe in which such frail beings exist is one of vast perspectives, rather in the tradition of Stapledon and Clarke."

"If the Stars Are Gods" is an intrusion of the metaphysical into the ordinary world of science fiction. It is very much in the tradition of Clarke, in the mode of *2001: A Space Odyssey.*

> *A dog cannot be a hypocrite, but neither can he be sincere.*
> *— Ludwig Wittgenstein*

It was deceptively huge and massive, this alien starship, and somehow seemed as if it belonged almost anywhere else in the universe but here.

Reynolds stepped carefully down the narrow corridor of the ship, still replaying in his mind's eye the approach to the air lock, the act of being swallowed. The ceilings were high, the light poor, the walls made of some dull, burnished metal.

These aspects and others flitted through his mind as he walked. Reynolds was a man who appreciated the fine interlacing pleasures of careful thought, but more than that, thinking so closely of these things kept his mind occupied and drove away the smell. It was an odd thick odor, and something about it upset his careful equilibrium. It clung to him like Pacific fog. Vintage manure, Reynolds had decided the moment he passed through the air lock. Turning, he had glared at Kelly firmly encased inside her suit. He told her about the smell. "Everybody stinks," she had said, evenly, perhaps joking, perhaps not, and pushed him away in the light centrifugal gravity. Away, into a maze of tight passages that would lead him eventually to look the first certified intelligent alien beings straight in the eye. If they happened to have eyes, that is.

It amused him that this privilege should be his. More rightly, the honor should have gone to another, someone younger whose tiny paragraph in the future histories of the human race had not already been enacted. At fifty-eight, Reynolds had long since lived a full and intricate lifetime. Too full, he sometimes thought, for any one man. So then, what about this day now? What about today? It did nothing really, only succeeded in forcing the fullness of his lifetime past the point of all reasonableness into a realm of positive absurdity.

The corridor branched again. He wondered precisely where he was inside the sculpted and twisted skin of the ship. He had tried to memorize everything he saw but there was nothing, absolutely nothing but metal with thin seams, places where he had to stoop or crawl, and the same awful smell. He realized now what it was about the ship that had bothered him the first time he had seen it, through a telescope from the moon. It reminded him, both in size and shape, of a building where he had once lived not so many years ago, during the brief term of his most recent retirement, 1987 and '88, in São Paulo, Brazil: a huge ultra-modern lifting apartment complex of a distinctly radical design. There was nothing like it on Earth, the advertising posters had proclaimed; and seeing it, hating it instantly, he had agreed. Now here was something else truly like it, but not on Earth.

The building had certainly not resembled a starship, but then, neither did this thing. At one end was an intricately designed portion, a cylinder with interesting modifications. Then came a long, plain tube and at the end of that something truly absurd: a cone, opening outward away from the rest of the ship and absolutely empty. Absurd, until you realized what it was.

The starship's propulsion source was, literally, hydrogen bombs. The central tube evidently held a vast number of fusion devices. One by one the bombs were released, drifted to the mouth of the cone and were detonated. The cone was a huge shock absorber; the kick from the bomb pushed the ship forward. A Rube Goldberg star drive.

Directly ahead of him, the corridor neatly stopped and split, like the twin prongs of a roasting fork. It jogged his memory: roasting fork, yes, from the days when he still ate meat. Turning left, he followed the proper prong. His directions had been quite clear.

He still felt very ill at ease. Maybe it was the way he was dressed that made everything seem so totally wrong. It didn't seem quite right, walking through an alien maze in his shirtsleeves and plain trousers. Pedestrian.

But the air was breathable, as promised. Did they breathe this particular oxygen-nitrogen balance, too? And like the smell?

Ahead, the corridor parted, branching once more. The odor was horribly powerful at this spot, and he ducked his head low, almost choking, and dashed through a round opening.

This was a big room. Like the corridor, the ceiling was a good seven meters above the floor, but the walls were subdued pastel shades of red, orange and yellow. The colors were mixed on all the walls in random, patternless designs. It was very pretty, Reynolds thought, and not at all strange. Also, standing neatly balanced near the back wall, there were two aliens.

When he saw the creatures, Reynolds stopped and stood tall. Raising his eyes, he stretched to reach the level of their eyes. While he did this, he also reacted. His first reaction was shock. This gave way to the tickling sensation of surprise. Then pleasure and relief. He liked the looks of these two creatures. They were certainly far kinder toward the eyes than what he had expected to find.

Stepping forward, Reynolds stood before both aliens, shifting his gaze from one to the other. Which was the leader? Or were both leaders? Or neither? He decided to wait. But neither alien made a sound or a move. So Reynolds kept waiting.

What had he expected to find? Men? Something like a man, that is, with two arms and two legs and a properly positioned head, with a nose, two eyes and a pair of floppy ears? This was what Kelly had expected him to find – she would be disappointed now – but Reynolds had never believed it for a moment. Kelly thought anything that spoke English had to be a man, but Reynolds was more imaginative. He knew better; he had not expected to find a man, not even a man with four arms and three legs and fourteen fingers or five ears. What he had expected to find was something truly alien. A blob, if worst came to worst, but at best something more like a shark or snake or wolf than a man. As soon as Kelly had told him that the aliens wanted to meet him – "Your man who best knows your star" – he had known this.

Now he said, "I am the man you wished to see. The one who knows the stars."

As he spoke, he carefully shared his gaze with both aliens, still searching for a leader, favoring neither over the other. One – the smaller one – twitched a nostril when Reynolds said, ". . . the stars"; the other remained motionless.

There was one Earth animal that did resemble these creatures, and this was why Reynolds felt happy and relieved. The aliens were sufficiently alien, yes. And they were surely not men. But neither did they resemble blobs or wolves or sharks or snakes. They were giraffes. Nice, kind, friendly, pleasant, smiling, silent giraffes. There were some differences, of course. The aliens' skin was a rainbow collage of pastel purples, greens, reds and yellows, similar in its random design to the colorfully painted walls. Their trunks stood higher off the ground, their necks were stouter than that of a normal giraffe. They did not have tails. Nor hooves. Instead, at the bottom of each of their four legs, they had five blunt short fingers and a single wide thick off-setting thumb.

"My name is Bradley Reynolds," he said. "I know the stars." Despite himself, their continued silence made him nervous. "Is something wrong?" he asked.

The shorter alien bowed its neck toward him. Then, in a shrill high-pitched voice that reminded him of a child, it said, "No." An excited nervous child. "That is no," it said.

"This?" Reynolds lifted his hand, having almost forgotten what was in it. Kelly had ordered him to carry the tape recorder, but now he could truthfully say, "I haven't activated it yet."

"Break it, please," the alien said.

Reynolds did not protest or argue. He let the machine fall to the floor. Then he jumped, landing on the tape recorder with both feet. The light aluminum case split wide open like the hide of a squashed apple. Once more, Reynolds jumped. Then, standing calmly, he kicked the broken bits of glass and metal toward an unoccupied corner of the room. "All right?" he asked.

Now for the first time the second alien moved. Its nostrils twitched daintily, then its legs shifted, lifting and falling. "Welcome," it said, abruptly, stopping all motion. "My name is Jonathon."

"Your name?" asked Reynolds.

"And this is Richard."

"Oh," said Reynolds, not contradicting. He understood now. Having learned the language of man, these creatures had learned his names as well.

"We wish to know your star," Jonathon said respectfully. His voice was a duplicate of the other's. Did the fact that he had not spoken until after the destruction of the tape recorder indicate that he was the leader of the two? Reynolds almost laughed, listening to the words of his own thoughts. Not *he*, he reminded himself: *it*.

"I am willing to tell you whatever you wish to know," Reynolds said.

"You are a . . . priest . . . a reverend of the sun?"

"An astronomer," Reynolds corrected.

"We would like to know everything you know. And then we would like to visit and converse with your star."

"Of course. I will gladly help you in any way I can." Kelly had cautioned him in advance that the aliens were interested in the sun, so none of this came as any surprise to him. But nobody knew what it was in particular that they wanted to know, or why, and Kelly hoped that he might be able to find out. At the moment he could think of only two possible conversational avenues to take; both were questions. He tried the first. "What is it you wish to know? Is our star greatly different from others of its type? If it is, we are unaware of this fact."

"No two stars are the same," the alien said. This was Jonathon again. Its voice began to rise in excitement. "What is it? Do you not wish to speak here? Is our craft an unsatisfactory place?"

"No, this is fine," Reynolds said, wondering if it was wise to continue concealing his puzzlement. "I will tell you what I know. Later, I can bring books."

"No!" The alien did not shout, but from the way its legs quivered and nostrils trembled, Reynolds gathered he had said something very improper indeed.

"I will tell you," he said. "In my own words."

Jonathon stood quietly rigid. "Fine."

Now it was time for Reynolds to ask his second question. He let it fall within the long silence which had followed Jonathon's last statement. "Why do you wish to know about our star?"

"It is the reason why we have come here. On our travels, we have visited many stars. But it is yours we have sought the longest. It is so powerful. And benevolent. A rare combination, as you must know."

"Very rare," Reynolds said, thinking that this wasn't making any sense. But then, why should it? At least he had learned something of the nature of the aliens' mission, and that alone was more than anyone else had managed to learn during the months the aliens had slowly approached the moon, exploding their hydrogen bombs to decelerate.

A sudden burst of confidence surprised Reynolds. He had not felt this sure of himself in years, and just like before, there was no logical reason for his certainty. "Would you be willing to answer some questions for me? About *your* star?"

"Certainly, Bradley Reynolds."

"Can you tell me our name for your star? Its coordinates?"

"No," Jonathon said, dipping its neck. "I cannot." It blinked its right eye in a furious fashion. "Our galaxy is not this one. It is a galaxy too distant for your instruments."

"I see," said Reynolds, because he could not very well call the alien a liar, even if it was. But Jonathon's hesitancy to reveal the location of its homeworld was not unexpected; Reynolds would have acted the same in similar circumstances.

Richard spoke. "May I pay obeisance?"

Jonathon, turning to Richard, spoke in a series of shrill chirping noises. Then Richard replied in kind.

Turning back to Reynolds, Richard again asked, "May I pay obeisance?"

Reynolds could only say, "Yes." Why not?

Richard acted immediately. Its legs abruptly shot out from beneath its trunk at an angle no giraffe could have managed. Richard sat on its belly, legs spread, and its neck came down, the snout gently scraping the floor.

"Thank you," Reynolds said, bowing slightly at the waist. "But there is much we can learn from you, too." He spoke to hide his embarrassment, directing his words at Jonathon while hoping that they might serve to bring Richard back to its feet as well. When this failed to work, Reynolds launched into the speech he had been sent here to deliver. Knowing what he had to say, he ran through the words as hurriedly as possible. "We are a backward people. Compared to you, we are children in the universe. Our travels have carried us no farther than our sister planets, while you have seen stars whose light takes years to reach your home. We realize you have much to teach us, and we approach you as pupils before a grand philosopher. We are gratified at the chance to share our meager knowledge with you and wish only to be granted the privilege of listening to you in return."

"You wish to know deeply of our star?" Jonathon asked.

"Of many things," Reynolds said. "Your spacecraft for instance. It is far beyond our meager knowledge."

Jonathon began to blink its right eye furiously. As it spoke, the speed of the blinking increased. "You wish to know that?"

"Yes, if you are willing to share your knowledge. We, too, would like to visit the stars."

Its eye moved faster than ever now. It said, "Sadly, there is nothing we can tell you of this ship. Unfortunately, we know nothing ourselves."

"Nothing?"

"The ship was a gift."

"You mean that you did not make it yourself. No. But you must have mechanics, individuals capable of repairing the craft in the event of some emergency."

"But that has never happened. I do not think the ship could fail."

"Would you explain?"

"Our race, our world, was once visited by another race of creatures. It was they who presented us with this ship. They had come to us from a distant star in order to make this gift. In return, we have used the ship only to increase the wisdom of our people."

"What can you tell me about this other race?" Reynolds asked.

"Very little, I am afraid. They came from a most ancient star near the true center of the universe."

"And were they like you? Physically?"

"No, more like you. Like people. But – please – may we be excused to converse about that which is essential? Our time is short."

Reynolds nodded, and the moment he did, Jonathon ceased to

blink. Reynolds gathered that it had grown tired of lying, which wasn't surprising; Jonathon was a poor liar. Not only were the lies incredible in themselves, but every time it told a lie it blinked like a madman with an ash in his eye.

"If I tell you about our star," Jonathon said, "will you consent to tell of yours in return?" The alien tilted its head forward, long neck swaying gently from side to side. It was plain that Jonathon attached great significance to Reynolds' reply.

So Reynolds said, "Yes, gladly," though he found he could not conceive of any information about the sun which might come as a surprise to these creatures. Still, he had been sent here to discover as much about the aliens as possible without revealing anything important about mankind. This sharing of information about stars seemed a safe enough course to pursue.

"I will begin," Jonathon said, "and you must excuse my impreciseness of expression. My knowledge of your language is limited. I imagine you have a special vocabulary for the subject."

"A technical vocabulary, yes."

The alien said, "Our star is a brother to yours. Or would it be sister? During periods of the most intense communion, his wisdom – or hers? – is faultless. At times he is angry – unlike your star – but these moments are not frequent. Nor do they last for longer than a few fleeting moments. Twice he has prophesied the termination of our civilization during times of great personal anger, but never has he felt it necessary to carry out his prediction. I would say that he is more kind than raging, more gentle than brutal. I believe he loves our people most truly and fully. Among the stars of the universe, his place is not great, but as our home star, we must revere him. And, of course, we do."

"Would you go on?" Reynolds asked.

Jonathon went on. Reynolds listened. The alien spoke of its personal relationship with the star, how the star had helped it during times of individual darkness. Once, the star had assisted it in choosing a proper mate; the choice proved not only perfect but divine. Throughout, Jonathon spoke of the star as a reverent Jewish tribesman might have spoken of the Old Testament God. For the first time, Reynolds regretted having had to dispose of the tape recorder. When he tried to tell Kelly about this conversation, she would never believe a word of it. As it spoke, the alien did not blink, not once, even briefly, for Reynolds watched carefully.

At last the alien was done. It said, "But this is only a beginning. We have so much to share, Bradley Reynolds. Once I am conversant with your technical vocabulary. Communication between separate entities – the great barriers of language . . ."

"I understand," said Reynolds.

"We knew you would. But now – it is your turn. Tell me about your star."

"We call it the sun," Reynolds said. Saying, this, he felt more than mildly foolish – but what else? How could he tell Jonathon what it wished to know when he did not know himself? All he knew about the sun was facts. He knew how hot it was and how old it was and he knew its size and mass and magnitude. He knew about sunspots and solar winds and solar atmosphere. But that was all he knew. Was the sun a benevolent star? Was it constantly enraged? Did all mankind revere it with the proper quantity of love and dedication? "That is its common name. More properly, in an ancient language adopted by science, it is Sol. It lies approximately eight – "

"Oh," said Jonathon. "All of this, yes, we know. But its demeanor. Its attitudes, both normal and abnormal. You play with us, Bradley Reynolds. You joke. We understand your amusement – but, please, we are simple souls and have traveled far. We must know these other things before daring to make our personal approach to the star. Can you tell us in what fashion it has most often affected your individual life? This would help us immensely."

Although his room was totally dark, Reynolds, entering, did not bother with the light. He knew every inch of this room, knew it as well in the dark as the light. For the past four years, he had spent an average of twelve hours a day here. He knew the four walls, the desk, the bed, the bookshelves and the books, knew them more intimately than he had ever known another person. Reaching the cot without once stubbing his toe or tripping over an open book or stumbling across an unfurled map, he sat down and covered his face with his hands, feeling the wrinkles on his forehead like great wide welts. Alone, he played a game with the wrinkles, pretending that each one represented some event or facet of his life. This one here – the big one above his left eyebrow – that was Mars. And this other one – way over here almost by his right ear – that was a girl named Melissa whom he had known back in the 1970s. But he wasn't in the proper mood for the game now. He lowered his hands. He knew the wrinkles for exactly what they really were: age, purely and simply and honestly age. Each one meant nothing without the others. They represented impersonal and unavoidable erosion. On the outside, they reflected the death that was occurring on the inside.

Still, he was happy to be back here in this room. He never realized how important these familiar surroundings were to his state of mind until he was forcefully deprived of them for a length of time. Inside the alien starship, it hadn't been so bad. The time had passed quickly then; he hadn't been allowed to get homesick. It was afterward when it had got bad. With Kelly and the others in her dank, ugly impersonal hole of an office. Those had been the unbearable hours.

But now he was home, and he would not have to leave again until they told him. He had been appointed official emissary to the aliens, though this did not fool him for a moment. He had been given the appointment only because Jonathon had refused to see anyone else. It wasn't because anyone liked him or respected him or thought him competent enough to handle the mission. He was different from them, and that made all the difference. When they were still kids, they had seen his face on the old TV networks every night of the week. Kelly wanted someone like herself to handle the aliens. Someone who knew how to take orders, someone ultimately competent, some computer facsimile of a human being. Like herself. Someone who, when given a job, performed it in the most efficient manner in the least possible time.

Kelly was the director of the moon base. She had come here two years ago, replacing Bill Newton, a contemporary of Reynolds', a friend of his. Kelly was the protégé of some U.S. Senator, some powerful idiot from the Midwest, a leader of the anti-NASA faction in the Congress. Kelly's appointment had been part of a wild attempt to subdue the senator with favors and special attention. It had worked after a fashion. There were still Americans on the moon. Even the Russians had left two years ago.

Leaving the alien starship, he had met Kelly the instant he reached the air lock. He had managed to slip past her and pull on his suit before she could question him. He had known she wouldn't dare try to converse over the radio; too great a chance of being overheard. She would never trust him to say only the right things.

But that little game had done nothing except delay matters a few minutes. The tug had returned to the moon base and then everyone had gone straight to Kelly's office. Then the interrogation had begun. Reynolds had sat near the back of the room while the rest of them flocked around Kelly like pet sheep.

Kelly asked the first question. "What do they want?" He knew her well enough to understand exactly what she meant: What do they want from us in return for what we want from them?

Reynolds told her: They wanted to know about the sun.

"We gathered that much," Kelly said. "But what kind of information do they want? Specifically, what are they after?"

With great difficulty, he tried to explain this too.

Kelly interrupted him quickly. "And what did you tell them?"

"Nothing," he said.

"Why?"

"Because I didn't know what to tell them."

"Didn't you ever happen to think the best thing to tell them might have been whatever it was they wished to hear?"

"I couldn't do that either," he said, "because I didn't know. You tell me: Is the sun benevolent? How does it inspire your daily life? does it constantly rage? I don't know, and you don't know either, and it's not a thing we can risk lying about, because they may very well know themselves. To them, a star is a living entity. It's a god, but more than our gods, because they can see a star and feel its heat and never doubt that it's always there."

"Will they want you back?" she asked.

"I think so. They liked me. Or he liked me. It. I only talked to one of them."

"I thought you told us two."

So he went over the whole story for her once more, from beginning to end, hoping this time she might realize that alien beings are not human beings and should not be expected to respond in familiar ways. When he came to the part about the presence of the two aliens, he said, "Look. There are six men in this room right now besides us. But they are here only for show. The whole time, none of them will say a word or think a thought or decide a point. The other alien was in the room with Jonathon and me the whole time. But if it had not been there, nothing would have been changed. I don't know why it was there and I don't expect I ever will. But neither do I understand why you feel you have to have all these men here with you."

She utterly ignored the point. "Then that is all they are interested in? They're pilgrims and they think the sun is Mecca?"

"More or less," he said, with the emphasis on "less."

"Then they won't want to talk to me – or any of us. You're the one who knows the sun. Is that correct?" She jotted a note on a pad, shaking her elbow briskly.

"That is correct."

"Reynolds," she said, looking up from her pad, "I sure as hell hope you know what you're doing."

He said, "Why?"

She did not bother to attempt to disguise her contempt. Few of them did any more and especially not Kelly. It was her opinion that Reynolds should not be here at all. Put him in a rest home back on Earth, she would say. The other astronauts – they were considerate enough to retire when life got too complicated for them. What makes this one man, Bradley Reynolds, why is he so special? All right – she would admit – ten years, twenty years ago, he was a great brave man struggling to conquer the unknown. When I was sixteen years old, I couldn't walk a dozen feet without tripping over his name or face. But what about now? What is he? I'll tell you what he is: a broken-down, wrinkled relic of an old man. So what if he's an astronomer as well as an astronaut? So what if he's the best possible man for the Lunar observatory? I still say he's more trouble than he's worth. He walks around the moon base like a dog having a dream. Nobody can communicate with him. He hasn't attended a single psychological expansion session since he's been here, and that goes back well before my time. He's a morale problem; nobody can stand the sight of him any more. And, as far as doing his job goes, he does it, yes – but that's all. His heart isn't in it. Look, he didn't even know about the aliens being in orbit until I called him in and told him they wanted to see him.

That last part was not true, of course. Reynolds, like everyone, had known about the aliens, but he did not have to admit that their approach had not overly concerned him. He had not shared the hysteria which had gripped the whole of the Earth when the announcement was made that an alien starship had entered the system. The authorities had known about it for months before ever releasing the news. By the time anything was said publicly, it had been clearly determined that the aliens offered Earth no clear or present danger. But that was about all anyone had learned. Then the starship had gone into orbit around the moon, an action intended to confirm their lack of harmful intent toward Earth, and the entire problem had landed with a thud in Kelly's lap. The aliens said they wanted to meet a man who knew something about the sun, and that had turned out to be Reynolds. Then – and only then – had he had a real reason to become interested in the aliens. That day, for the first time in a half-dozen years, he had actually listened to the daily news broadcasts from Earth. He discovered – and it didn't particularly surprise him – that everyone else had long since got over their initial interest in the aliens. He gathered that war was brewing again. In Africa this time, which was a change in place if not in substance. The aliens were mentioned once, about halfway through the program, but Reynolds could tell they were no longer considered real news. A meeting between a representative of the American moon base and the aliens was being arranged, the newscaster said. It would take place aboard the aliens' ship in orbit around the moon, he added. The name Bradley Reynolds was not mentioned. *I wonder if they remember me*, he had thought.

"It seems to me that you could get more out of them than some babble about stars being gods," Kelly said, getting up and pacing around the room, one hand on hip. She shook her head in mock disbelief and the brown curls swirled downward, flowing like dark honey in the light gravity.

"Oh, I did," he said casually.

"What?" There was a rustling of interest in the room.

"A few facts about their planet. Some bits of detail I think fit together. It may even explain their theology."

"Explain theology with astronomy?" Kelly said sharply. "There's no mystery to sun worship. It was one of our primitive religions." A man next to her nodded.

"Not quite. Our star is relatively mild-mannered, as Jonathon would say. And our planet has a nice, comfortable orbit, nearly circular."

"Theirs doesn't?"

"No. The planet has a pronounced axial inclination, too, nothing ordinary like Earth's twenty-three degrees. Their world must be tilted at forty degrees or so to give the effects Jonathon mentioned."

"Hot summers?" one of the men he didn't know said, and Reynolds looked up in mild surprise. So the underlings were not just spear-carriers, as he had thought. Well enough.

"Right. The axial tilt causes each hemisphere to alternately slant toward and then away from their star. They have colder winters and hotter summers than we do. But there's something more, as far as I can figure it out. Jonathon says its world 'does not move in the perfect path' and that ours, on the other hand, very nearly does."

"Perfect path?" Kelly said, frowning. "An eight-fold way? The path of enlightenment?"

"More theology," said the man who had spoken.

"Not quite," Reynolds said. "Pythagoras believed the circle was a perfect form, the most beautiful of all figures. I don't see why Jonathon shouldn't."

"Astronomical bodies look like circles. Pythagoras could see the moon," Kelly said.

"And the sun," Reynolds said. "I don't know whether Jonathon's world has a moon or not. But they can see their star, and in profile it's a circle."

"So a circular orbit is a perfect orbit."

"Q.E.D. Jonathon says its planet doesn't have one, though."

"It's an ellipse."

"A very eccentric ellipse. That's my guess, anyway. Jonathon used the terms 'path-summer' and 'pole-summer,' so they do distinguish between the two effects."

"I don't get it," the man said.

"An ellipse alone gives alternate summers and winters, but in both hemispheres at the same time," Kelly said brusquely, her mouth turning slightly downward. "A 'pole-summer' must be the kind Earth has."

"Oh," the man said weakly.

"You left out the 'great-summer', my dear," Reynolds said with a thin smile.

"What's that?" Kelly said carefully.

"When the 'pole-summer' coincides with the 'path-summer' – which it will, every so often. I wouldn't want to be around when that happens. Evidently neither do the members of Jonathon's race."

"How do they get away?" Kelly said intently.

"Migrate. One hemisphere is having a barely tolerable summer while the other is being fried alive, so they go there. The whole race."

"Nomads," Kelly said. "An entire culture born with a pack on its back," she said distantly. Reynolds raised an eyebrow. It was the first time he had ever heard her say anything that wasn't crisp, efficient and uninteresting.

"I think that's why they're grazing animals, to make it easy – even necessary – to keep on the move. A 'great-summer' wilts all the vegetation; a 'great-winter' – they must have those, too – freezes a continent solid."

"God," Kelly said quietly.

"Jonathon mentioned huge storms, winds that knocked it down, sand that buried it overnight in dunes. The drastic changes in the climate must stir up hurricanes and tornadoes."

"Which they have to migrate through," Kelly said. Reynolds noticed that the room was strangely quiet.

"Jonathon seems to have been born on one of the Treks. They don't have much shelter because of the winds and the winters that erode away the rock. It must be hard to build up any sort of technology in an environment like that. I suppose it's pretty inevitable that they turned out to believe in astrology."

"What?" Kelly said, surprised.

"Of course." Reynolds looked at her, completely deadpan. "What else should I call it? With such a premium on reading the stars correctly, so that they know the precise time of year and when the next 'great-summer' is coming – what else would they believe in? Astrology would be the obvious, unchallengeable religion – because it worked!" Reynolds smiled to himself, imagining a flock of atheist giraffes vainly fighting their way through a sandstorm.

"I see," Kelly said, clearly at a loss. The men stood around them awkwardly, not knowing quite what to say to such a barrage of unlikely ideas. Reynolds felt a surge of joy. Some lost capacity of his youth had returned: to see himself as the center of things, as the only actor onstage who moved of his own volition, spoke his own unscripted lines. *This is the way the world feels when you are winning*, he thought. This was what he had lost, what Mars had taken from him during the long trip back in utter deep silence and loneliness. He had tested himself there and found some inner core, had come to think he did not need people and the fine edge of competition with them. Work and cramped rooms had warped him.

"I think that's why they are technologically retarded, despite their age. They don't really have the feel of machines, they've never gotten used to them. When they needed a starship for their religion, they built the most awkward one imaginable that would work." Reynolds paused, feeling lightheaded. "They live inside that machine, but they don't like it. They stink it up and make it feel like a corral. They mistrusted that tape recorder of mine. They must want to know the stars very badly, to depart so much from their nature just to reach them."

Kelly's lip stiffened and her eyes narrowed. Her face, Reynolds thought, was returning to its usual expression. "This is all very well, Dr. Reynolds," she said, and it was the old Kelly, the one he knew; the Kelly who always came out on top. "But it is speculation. We need facts. Their starship is crude, but it *works*. They must have data and photographs of stars. They know things we don't. There are innumerable details we could only find by making the trip ourselves, and even using their ship, that will take centuries – Houston tells me that bomb-thrower of theirs can't go above one percent of light velocity. I want – "

"I'll try," he said. "But I'm afraid it won't be easy. Whenever I try to approach a subject it does not want to discuss, the alien begins telling me the most fantastic lies."

"Oh?" Kelly said suspiciously, and he was sorry he had mentioned that, because it had taken him another quarter hour of explaining before she had allowed him to escape the confines of her office.

Now he was back home again – in his room. Rolling over, he lay flat on his back in the bed, eyes wide open and staring straight ahead at the emptiness of the darkness. He would have liked to go out and visit the observatory, but Kelly had said he was excused from all duties until the alien situation was resolved. He gathered she meant that as an order. She must have. One thing about Kelly: she seldom said a word unless it was meant as an order.

They came and woke him up. He had not intended to sleep. His room was still pitch-black, and far away there was a fist pounding furiously upon a door. Getting up, taking his time, he went and let the man inside. Then he turned on the light.

"Hurry and see the director," the man said breathlessly.

"What does she want now?" Reynolds asked.

"How should I know?"

Reynolds shrugged and turned to go. He knew what she wanted anyway. It had to be the aliens; Jonathon was ready to see him again. Well, that was fine, he thought, entering Kelly's office. From the turn of her expression, he saw that he had guessed correctly. And I know exactly what I'm going to tell them, he thought.

Somewhere in his sleep, Reynolds had made an important decision. He had decided he was going to tell Jonathon the truth.

Approaching the alien starship, Reynolds discovered he was no longer so strongly reminded of his old home in São Paulo. Now that he had actually been inside the ship and had met the creatures who resided there, his feelings had changed. This time he was struck by how remarkably this strange twisted chunk of metal resembled what a real starship ought to look like.

The tug banged against the side of the ship. Without having to be told, Reynolds removed his suit and went to the air lock. Kelly jumped out of her seat and dashed after him. She grabbed the camera off the deck and forced it into his hands. She wanted him to photograph the aliens. He had to admit her logic was quite impeccable. If the aliens were as unfearsome as Reynolds claimed, then a clear and honest photograph could only reassure the population of Earth; hysteria was still a worry to many politicians back home. Many people still claimed that a spaceship full of green monsters was up here orbiting the moon only a few hours' flight from New York and Moscow. One click of the camera and this fear would be ended.

Reynolds had told her Jonathon would never permit a photograph to be taken, but Kelly had remained adamant. "Who cares?" he'd asked her.

"Everyone cares," she'd insisted.

"Oh, really? I listened to the news yesterday and the aliens weren't even mentioned. Is that hysteria?"

"That's because of Africa. Wait till the war's over, then listen."

He hadn't argued with her then and he didn't intend to argue with her now. He accepted the camera without a word, her voice burning his ears with last-minute instructions, and plunged ahead.

The smell assaulted him immediately. As he entered the spaceship, the odor seemed to rise up from nowhere and surround him. He made himself push forward. Last time, the odor had been a problem only for a short time. He was sure he could overcome it again this time.

It was cold in the ship. He wore only light pants and a light shirt without underwear, because last time it had been rather warm. Had Jonathon, noticing his discomfort, lowered the ship's temperature accordingly?

He turned the first corner and glanced briefly at the distant ceiling. He called out, "Hello!" but there was only a slight echo. He spoke again and the echo was the same, flat and hard.

Another turn. He was moving much faster than before. The tight passages no longer caused him to pause and think. He simply plunged ahead, trusting his own knowledge. At Kelly's urging he was wearing a radio attached to his belt. He noticed that it was beeping furiously at him. Apparently Kelly had neglected some important last-minute direction. He didn't mind. He already had enough orders to ignore; one less would make little difference.

Here was the place. Pausing in the doorway, he removed the radio, turning it off. Then he placed the camera on the floor beside it, and stepped into the room.

Despite the chill in the air, the room was not otherwise different from before. There were two aliens standing against the farthest wall. Reynolds went straight toward them, holding his hands over his head in greeting. One was taller than the other. Reynolds spoke to it. "Are you Jonathon?"

"Yes," Jonathon said, in its child's piping voice. "And this is Richard."

"May I pay obeisance?" Richard asked eagerly.

Reynolds nodded. "If you wish."

Jonathon waited until Richard had regained its feet, then said, "We wish to discuss your star now."

"All right," Reynolds said. "But there's something I have to tell you first." Saying this, for the first time since he made his decision, he wasn't sure. Was the truth really the best solution in this situation? Kelly wanted him to lie: tell them whatever they wanted to hear, making certain he didn't tell them quite everything. Kelly was afraid the aliens might go sailing off to the sun once they had learned what they had come here to learn. She wanted a chance to get engineers and scientists inside their ship before the aliens left. And wasn't this a real possibility? What if Kelly was right and the aliens went away? Then what would he say?

"You want to tell us that your sun is not a conscious being," Jonathon said. "Am I correct?"

The problem was instantly solved. Reynolds felt no more compulsion to lie. He said, "Yes."

"I am afraid that you are wrong," said Jonathon.

"We live here, don't we? Wouldn't we know? You asked for me because I know our sun, and I do. But there are other men on our homeworld who know far more than I do. But no one has ever discovered the least shred of evidence to support your theory."

"A theory is a guess," Jonathon said. "We do not guess; we know."

"Then," Reynolds said, "explain it to me. Because I don't know." He watched the alien's eyes carefully, waiting for the first indication of a blinking fit.

But Jonathon's gaze remained steady and certain. "Would you like to hear of our journey?" it asked.

"Yes."

"We left our homeworld a great many of your years ago. I cannot tell you exactly when, for reasons I'm certain you can understand, but I will reveal that it was more than a century ago. In that time we have visited nine stars. The ones we would visit were chosen for us beforehand. Our priests – our leaders – determined the stars that were within our reach and also able to help in our quest. You see, we have journeyed here in order to ask certain questions."

"Questions of the stars?"

"Yes, of course. The questions we have are questions only a star may answer."

"And what are they?" Reynolds asked.

"We have discovered the existence of other universes parallel with our own. Certain creatures – devils and demons – have come from these universes in order to attack and capture our stars. We feel we must – "

"Oh, yes," Reynolds said. "I understand. We've run across several of these creatures recently." And he blinked, matching the twitching of Jonathon's eye. "They are awfully fearsome, aren't they?" When Jonathon stopped, he stopped too. He said, "You don't have to tell me everything. But can you tell me this: these other stars you have visited, have they been able to answer any of your questions?"

"Oh, yes. We have learned much from them. These stars were very great – very different from our own."

"But they weren't able to answer all your questions?"

"If they had, we would not be here now."

"And you believe our star may be able to help you?"

"All may help, but the one we seek is the one that can save us."

"When do you plan to go to the sun?"

"At once," Jonathon said. "As soon as you leave. I am afraid there is little else you can tell us."

"I'd like to ask you to stay," Reynolds said. And he forced himself to go ahead. He knew he could not convince Jonathon without revealing everything, yet, by doing so, he might also be putting an end to all his hopes. Still, he told the alien about Kelly and, more generally, he told it what the attitude of man was toward their visit. He told it what man wished to know from them, and why.

Jonathon seemed amazed. It moved about the floor as Reynolds spoke, its feet clanking dully. Then it stopped and stood, its feet only a few inches apart, a position that impressed Reynolds as one of incredulous amazement. "Your people wish to travel farther into space? You want to visit the stars? But why, Reynolds? Your people do not believe. Why?"

Reynolds smiled. Each time Jonathon said something to him, he felt he knew these people – and how they thought and reacted – a little better than he had before. There was another question he would very much have liked to ask Jonathon. How long have your people possessed the means of visiting the stars? A very long time, he imagined. Perhaps a longer time than the whole life-span of the human race. And why hadn't they gone before now? Reynolds thought he knew: because, until now, they had had no reason for going.

Now Reynolds tried to answer Jonathon's question. If anyone could, it should be he. "We wish to go to the stars because we are a dissatis-fied people. Because we do not live a very long time as individuals, we feel we must place an important part of our lives into the human race as a whole. In a sense, we surrender a portion of our individual person in return for a sense of greater immortality. What is an accomplish-ment for man as a race is also an accomplishment for each individual man. And what are these accomplishments? Basically this: anything a man does that no other man has done before – whether it is good or evil or neither one or both – is considered by us to be a great accom-plishment."

And – to add emphasis to the point – he blinked once.

Then, holding his eyes steady, he said, "I want you to teach me to talk to the stars. I want you to stay here around the moon long enough to do that."

Instantly Jonathon said, "No."

There was an added force to the way it said it, an emphasis its voice had not previously possessed. Then Reynolds realized what that was: at the same moment Jonathon had spoken, Richard too had said, "No."

"Then you may be doomed to fail," Reynolds said. "Didn't I tell you? I know our star better than any man available to you. Teach me to talk to the stars and I may be able to help you with this one. Or would you prefer to continue wandering the galaxy forever, failing to find what you seek wherever you go?"

"You are a sensible man, Reynolds. You may be correct. We will ask our home star and see."

"Do that. And if it says yes and I promise to do what you wish, then I must ask you to promise me something in return. I want you to allow a team of our scientists and technicians to enter and inspect your ship. You will answer their questions to the best of your ability. And that means truthfully."

"We always tell the truth," Jonathon said, blinking savagely.

The moon had made one full circuit of the Earth since Reynolds' initial meeting with the aliens, and he was quite satisfied with the progress he had made up to now, especially during the past ten days after Kelly had stopped accompanying him in his daily shuttles to and from the orbiting starship. As a matter of fact, in all that time, he had not had a single face-to-face meeting with her and they had talked on the phone only once. And she wasn't here now either, which was strange, since it was noon and she always ate here with the others.

Reynolds had a table to himself in the cafeteria. The food was poor, but it always was, and he was used to that by now. What did bother him, now that he was thinking about it, was Kelly's absence. Most days he skipped lunch himself. He tried to remember the last time he had come here. It was more than a week ago, he remembered – more than ten days ago. He didn't like the sound of that answer.

Leaning over, he attracted the attention of a girl at an adjoining table. He knew her vaguely. Her father had been an important wheel in NASA when Reynolds was still a star astronaut. He couldn't remember the man's name. His daughter had a tiny cute face and a billowing body about two sizes too big for the head. Also, she had a brain that was much too limited for much of anything. She worked in the administrative section, which meant she slept with most of the men on the base at one time or another.

"Have you seen Kelly?" he asked her.

"Must be in her office."

"No, I mean when was the last time you saw her here?"

"In here? Oh – " The girl thought for a moment. "Doesn't she eat with the other chiefs?"

Kelly never ate with the other chiefs. She always ate in the cafeteria – for morale purposes – and the fact that the girl did not remember having seen her meant that it had been several days at least since Kelly had last put in an appearance. Leaving his lunch where it lay, Reynolds got up, nodded politely at the girl, who stared at him as if he were a freak, and hurried away.

It wasn't a long walk, but he ran. He had no intention of going to see Kelly. He knew that would prove useless. Instead, he was going to see John Sims. At fifty-two, Sims was the second oldest man in the base. Like Reynolds, he was a former astronaut. In 1987, when Reynolds, then a famous man, was living in São Paulo, Sims had commanded the first (and only) truly successful Mars expedition. During those few months, the world had heard his name, but people forgot quickly, and Sims was one of the things they forgot. He had never done more than what he was expected to do; the threat of death had never come near Sims' expedition. Reynolds, on the other hand, had failed. On Mars with him, three men had died. Yet it was he – Reynolds, the failure – who had been the hero, not Sims.

And maybe I'm a hero again, he thought, as he knocked evenly on the door to Sims' office. Maybe down there the world is once more reading about me daily. He hadn't listened to a news broadcast since the night before his first trip to the ship. Had the story been released to the public yet? He couldn't see any reason why it should be suppressed, but that seldom was important. He would ask Sims. Sims would know.

The door opened and Reynolds went inside. Sims was a huge man who wore his black hair in a crewcut. The style had been out of fashion for thirty or forty years; Reynolds doubted there was another crewcut man in the universe. But he could not imagine Sims any other way.

"What's wrong?" Sims asked, guessing accurately the first time. He led Reynolds to a chair and sat him down. The office was big but empty. A local phone sat upon the desk along with a couple of daily status reports. Sims was assistant administrative chief, whatever that meant. Reynolds had never understood the functions of the position, if any. But there was one thing that was clear: Sims knew more about the inner workings of the moon base than any other man. And that included the director as well.

"I want to know about Vonda," Reynolds said. With Sims, everything stood on a first-name basis. Vonda was Vonda Kelly. The name tasted strangely upon Reynolds' lips. "Why isn't she eating at the cafeteria?"

Sims answered unhesitantly. "Because she's afraid to leave her desk."

"It has something to do with the aliens?"

"It does, but I shouldn't tell you what. She doesn't want you to know."

"Tell me. Please." His desperation cleared the smile from Sims' lips. And he had almost added: for old times' sake. He was glad he had controlled himself.

"The main reason is the war," Sims said. "If it starts, she wants to know at once."

"Will it?"

Sims shook his head. "I'm smart but I'm not God. As usual, I imagine everything will work out as long as no one makes a stupid mistake. The worst will be a small local war lasting maybe a month. But how long can you depend upon politicians to act intelligently? It goes against the grain with them."

"But what about the aliens?"

"Well, as I said, that's part of it too." Sims stuck his pipe in his mouth. Reynolds had never seen it lit, never seen him smoking it, but the pipe was invariably there between his teeth. "A group of men are coming here from Washington, arriving tomorrow. They want to talk with your pets. It seems nobody – least of all Vonda – is very happy with your progress."

"I am."

Sims shrugged, as if to say: that is of no significance.

"The aliens will never agree to see them," Reynolds said.

"How are they going to stop them? Withdraw the welcome mat? Turn out the lights? That won't work."

"But that will ruin everything. All my work up until now."

"What work?" Sims got up and walked around his desk until he stood hovering above Reynolds. "As far as anybody can see, you haven't accomplished a damn thing since you went up there. People want results, Bradley, not a lot of noise. All you've given anyone is the noise. This isn't a private game of yours. This is one of the most significant events in the history of the human race. If anyone ought to know that, it's you. Christ." And he wandered back to his chair again, jiggling his pipe.

"What is it they want from me?" Reynolds said. "Look – I got them what they asked for. The aliens have agreed to let a team of scientists study their ship."

"We want more than that now. Among other things, we want an alien to come down and visit Washington. Think of the propaganda value of that, and right now is a time when we damn well need something like that. Here we are, the only country with sense enough to stay on the moon. And being here has finally paid off in a way the politicians can understand. They've given you a month in which to play around – after all, you're a hero and the publicity is good – but how much longer do you expect them to wait? No, they want action and I'm afraid they want it now."

Reynolds was ready to go. He had found out as much as he was apt to find here. And he already knew what he was going to have to do. He would go and find Kelly and tell her she had to keep the men from Earth away from the aliens. If she wouldn't agree, then he would go up and tell the aliens and they would leave for the sun. But what if Kelly wouldn't let him go? He had to consider that. He knew; he would tell her this: If you don't let me see them, if you try to keep me away, they'll know something is wrong and they'll leave without a backward glance. Maybe he could tell her the aliens were telepaths; he doubted she would know any better.

He had the plan all worked out so that it could not fail.

He had his hand on the doorknob when Sims called him back. "There's another thing I better tell you, Bradley."

"All right. What's that?"

"Vonda. She's on your side. She told them to stay away, but it wasn't enough. She's been relieved of duty. A replacement is coming with the others."

"Oh," said Reynolds.

Properly suited, Reynolds sat in the cockpit of the shuttle tug, watching the pilot beside him going through the ritual of a final inspection prior to takeoff. The dead desolate surface of the moon stretched briefly away from where the tug sat, the horizon so near that it almost looked touchable. Reynolds liked the moon. If he had not, he would never have elected to return here to stay. It was the Earth he hated. Better than the moon was space itself, the dark endless void beyond the reach of man's ugly grasping hands. That was where Reynolds was going now. Up. Out. Into the void. He was impatient to leave.

The pilot's voice came to him softly through the suit radio, a low murmur, not loud enough for him to understand what the man was saying. The pilot was talking to himself as he worked, using the rumble of his own voice as a way of patterning his mind so that it would not lose concentration. The pilot was a young man in his middle twenties, probably on loan from the Air Force, a lieutenant or, at most, a junior Air Force captain. He was barely old enough to remember when space had really been a frontier. Mankind had decided to go out, and Reynolds had been one of the men chosen to take the giant steps, but now it was late – the giant steps of twenty years ago were mere tentative contusions in the dust of the centuries – and man was coming back. From where he sat, looking out, Reynolds could see exactly 50 percent of the present American space program: the protruding bubble of the moon base. The other half was the orbiting space lab that circled the Earth itself, a battered relic of the expansive seventies. Well beyond the nearby horizon – maybe a hundred miles away – there had once been another bubble, but it was gone now. The brave men who had lived and worked and struggled and died and survived there – they were all gone too. Where? The Russians still maintained an orbiting space station, so some of their former moon colonists were undoubtedly there, but where were the rest? In Siberia? Working there? Hadn't the Russians decided that Siberia – the old barless prison state of the czars and early Communists – was a more practical frontier than the moon?

And weren't they maybe right? Reynolds did not like to think so, for he had poured his life into this – into the moon and the void beyond.

But at times, like now, peering through the artificial window of his suit, seeing the bare bubble of the base clinging to the edge of this dead world like a wart on an old woman's face, starkly vulnerable, he found it hard to see the point of it. He was an old enough man to recall the first time he had ever been moved by the spirit of conquest. As a schoolboy, he remembered the first time men conquered Mount Everest – it was around 1956 or '57 – and he had religiously followed the newspaper reports. Afterward, a movie had been made, and watching that film, seeing the shadows of pale mountaineers clinging to the edge of that white god, he had decided that was what he wanted to be. And he had never been taught otherwise; only by the time he was old enough to act, all the mountains had long since been conquered. And he had ended up as an astronomer, able if nothing else to gaze outward at the distant shining peaks of the void, and from there he had been pointed toward space. So he had gone to Mars and become famous, but fame had turned him inward, so that now, without the brilliance of his past, he would have been nobody but another of those anonymous old men who dot the cities of the world, inhabiting identically bleak book-lined rooms, eating daily in bad restaurants, their minds always a billion miles away from the dead shells of their bodies.

"We can go now, Dr. Reynolds," the pilot was saying.

Reynolds grunted in reply, his mind several miles distant from his waiting body. He was thinking that there was something, after all. How could he think in terms of pointlessness and futility when he alone had actually seen them with his own eyes? Creatures, intelligent beings, born far away, light-years from the insignificant world of man? Didn't that in itself prove something? Yes. He was sure that it did. But what?

The tug lifted with a murmur from the surface of the moon. Crouched deeply within his seat, Reynolds thought that it wouldn't be long now.

And they found us, he thought, we did not find them. And when had they gone into space? Late. Very late. At a moment in their history comparable to man a hundred thousand years from now. They had avoided space until a pressing reason had come for venturing out, and then they had gone. He remembered that he had been unable to explain to Jonathon why man wanted to visit the stars when he did not believe in the divinity of the suns. Was there a reason? And, if so, did it make sense?

The journey was not long.

It didn't smell. The air ran clean and sharp and sweet through the corridors, and if there was any odor to it, the odor was one of purity and freshness, almost pine needles or mint. The air was good for his spirits. As soon as Reynolds came aboard the starship, his depression and melancholy were forgotten. Perhaps he was only letting the apparent grimness of the situation get the better of him. It had been too long a time since he'd last had to fight. Jonathon would know what to do. The alien was more than three hundred years old, a product of a civilization and culture that had reached its maturity at a time when man was not yet man, when he was barely a skinny undersized ape, a carrion eater upon the hot plains of Africa.

When Reynolds reached the meeting room, he saw that Jonathon and Richard were not alone this time. The third alien – Reynolds sensed it was someone important – was introduced as Vergnan. No adopted Earth name for it.

"This is ours who best knows the stars," Jonathon said. "It has spoken with yours and hopes it may be able to assist you."

Reynolds had almost forgotten that part. The sudden pressures of the past few hours had driven everything else from his mind. His training. His unsuccessful attempts to speak to the stars. He had failed. Jonathon had been unable to teach him, but he thought that was probably because he simply did not believe.

"Now we shall leave you," Jonathon said.

"But – " said Reynolds.

"We are not permitted to stay."

"But there's something I must tell you."

It was too late. Jonathon and Richard headed for the corridor, walking with surprising gracefulness. Their long necks bobbed, their skinny legs shook, but they still managed to move as swiftly and sleekly as any cat, almost rippling as they went.

Reynolds turned toward Vergnan. Should he tell this one about the visitors from Earth? He did not think so. Vergnan was old, his skin much paler than the others, almost totally hairless. His eyes were wrinkled and one ear was torn.

Vergnan's eyes were closed.

Remembering his lessons, Reynolds too closed his eyes.

And kept them closed. In the dark, time passed more quickly than it seemed, but he was positive that five minutes went by.

Then the alien began to speak. No – he did not speak, he simply sang, his voice trilling with the high searching notes of a well-tuned violin, dashing up and down the scale, a pleasant sound, soothing, cool. Reynolds tried desperately to concentrate upon the song, ignoring the existence of all other sensations, recognizing nothing and no one but Vergnan. Reynolds ignored the taste and smell of the air and the distant throbbing of the ship's machinery. The alien sang deeper and clearer, his voice rising higher and higher, directed now at the stars. Jonathon, too, had sung, but never like this. When Jonathon sang, its voice had dashed away in a frightened search, shifting and darting wildly about, seeking vainly a place to land. Vergnan sang without doubt. It – *he* – was certain. Reynolds sensed the overwhelming maleness of this being, his patriarchal strength and dignity. His voice and song never struggled or wavered. He knew always exactly where he was going.

Had he felt something? Reynolds did not know. If so, then what? No, no, he thought, and concentrated more fully upon the voice, too intently to allow for the logic of thought. Within, he felt strong, alive, renewed, resurrected. *I am a new man. Reynolds is dead. He is another.* These thoughts came to him like the whispering words of another. *Go, Reynolds. Fly. Leave. Fly.*

Then he realized that he was singing too. He could not imitate Vergnan, for his voice was too alien, but he tried and heard his own voice coming frighteningly near, almost fading into and being lost within the constant tones of the other. The two voices suddenly became one – mingling indiscriminately – merging – and that one voice rose higher, floating, then higher again, rising, farther, going farther out – farther and deeper.

Then he felt it. Reynolds. And he knew it for what it was.

The Sun.

More ancient than the whole of the Earth itself. A greater, vaster being, more powerful and knowing. Divinity as a ball of heat and energy.

Reynolds spoke to the stars.

And, knowing this, balking at the concept, he drew back instinctively in fear, his voice faltering, dwindling, collapsing. Reynolds scurried back, seeking the Earth, but, grasping, pulling, Vergnan drew him on. Beyond the shallow exterior light of the sun, he witnessed the totality of that which lay hidden within. The core. The impenetrable darkness within. Fear gripped him once more. He begged to be allowed to flee. Tears streaking his face with the heat of fire, he pleaded. Vergnan benignly drew him on. *Come forward – come – see – know.* Forces coiled to a point.

And he saw.

Could he describe it as evil? Thought was an absurdity. Not thinking, instead sensing and feeling, he experienced the wholeness of this entity – a star – the sun – and saw that it was not evil. He sensed the sheer totality of its opening nothingness. Sensation was absent. Colder than cold, more terrifying than hate, more sordid than fear, blacker than evil. The vast inner whole nothingness of everything that was anything, of all.

I have seen enough. No!

Yes, cried Vergnan, agreeing.

To stay a moment longer would mean never returning again. Vergnan knew this too, and he released Reynolds, allowed him to go.

And still he sang. The song was different from before. Struggling within himself, Reynolds sang too, trying to match his voice to that of the alien. It was easier this time. The two voices merged, mingled, became one.

And then Reynolds awoke.

He was lying on the floor in the starship, the rainbow walls swirling brightly around him.

Vergnan stepped over him. He saw the alien's protruding belly as he passed. He did not look down or back, but continued onward, out the door, gone, as quick and cold as the inner soul of the sun itself. For a brief moment, he hated Vergnan more deeply than he had ever hated anything in his life. Then he sat up, gripping himself, forcing a return to sanity. I am all right now, he insisted. I am back. I am alive. The walls ceased spinning. At his back the floor shed its clinging coat of roughness. The shadows in the corners of his eyes dispersed.

Jonathon entered the room alone. "Now you have been," it said, crossing the room and assuming its usual place beside the wall.

"Yes," said Reynolds, not attempting to stand.

"And now you know why we search. For centuries our star was kind to us, loving, but now it too – like yours – is changed."

"You are looking for a new home?"

"True."

"And?"

"And we find nothing. All are alike. We have seen nine, visiting all. They are nothing."

"Then you leave here too?"

"We must, but first we will approach your star. Not until we have drawn so close that we have seen everything, not until then can we dare admit our failure. This time we thought we had succeeded. When we met you, this is what we thought, for you are unlike your star. We felt that the star could not produce you – or your race – without the presence of benevolence. But it is gone now. We meet only the blackness. We struggle to penetrate to a deeper core. And fail."

"I am not typical of my race," Reynolds said.

"We shall see."

He remained with Jonathon until he felt strong enough to stand. The floor hummed. Feeling it with moist palms, he planted a kiss upon the creased cold metal. A wind swept through the room, carrying a hint of returned life. Jonathon faded, rippled, returned to a sharp outline of crisp reality. Reynolds was suddenly hungry and the oily taste of meat swirled up through his nostrils. The cords in his neck stood out with the strain until, gradually, the tension passed from him.

He left and went to the tug. During the great fall to the silver moon he said not a word, thought not a thought. The trip was long.

Reynolds lay on his back in the dark room, staring upward at the faint shadow of a ceiling, refusing to see.

Hypnosis? Or a more powerful alien equivalent of the same? Wasn't that, as an explanation, more likely than admitting that he had indeed communicated with the sun, discovering a force greater than evil, blacker than black. Or – here was another theory: wasn't it possible that these aliens, because of the conditions of their own world, so thoroughly accepted the consciousness of the stars that they could make him believe as well? Similar things had happened on Earth. Religious miracles, the curing of diseases through faith, men who claimed to have spoken with God. What about flying saucers and little green men and all the other incidents of mass hysteria? Wasn't that the answer here? Hysteria? Hypnosis? Perhaps even a drug of some sort: a drug released into the air. Reynolds had plenty of possible solutions – he could choose one or all – but he decided that he did not really care.

He had gone into this thing knowing exactly what he was doing and now that it had happened he did not regret the experience. He had found a way of fulfilling his required mission while at the same time experiencing something personal that no other man would ever know. Whether he had actually seen the sun was immaterial; the experience, as such, was still his own. Nobody could ever take that away from him.

It was some time after this when he realized that a fist was pounding on the door. He decided he might as well ignore that, because sometimes when you ignored things, they went away. But the knocking did not go away – it only got louder. Finally Reynolds got up. He opened the door.

Kelly glared at his nakedness and said, "Did I wake you?"

"No."

"May I come in?"

"No."

"I've got something to tell you." She forced her way past him, sliding into the room. Then Reynolds saw that she wasn't alone. A big, red-faced beefy man followed, forcing his way into the room too.

Reynolds shut the door, cutting off the corridor light, but the big man went over and turned on the overhead light. "All right," he said, as though it were an order.

"Who the hell are you?" Reynolds said.

"Forget him," Kelly said. "I'll talk."

"Talk," said Reynolds.

"The committee is here. The men from Washington. They arrived an hour ago and I've kept them busy since. You may not believe this, but I'm on your side."

"Sims told me.

"He told me he told you."

"I knew he would. Mind telling me why? He didn't know."

"Because I'm not an idiot," Kelly said. "I've known enough petty bureaucrats in my life. Those things up there are alien beings. You can't send these fools up there to go stomping all over their toes."

Reynolds gathered this would not be over soon. He put on his pants.

"This is George O'Hara," Kelly said. "He's the new director."

"I want to offer my resignation," Reynolds said casually, fixing the snaps of his shirt.

"You have to accompany us to the starship," O'Hara said.

"I want you to," Kelly said. "You owe this to someone. If not me, then the aliens. If you had told me the truth, this might never have happened. If anyone is to blame for this mess, it's you, Reynolds. Why won't you tell me what's been going on up there the last month? It has to be something."

"It is," Reynolds said. "Don't laugh, but I was trying to talk to the sun. I told you that's why the aliens came here. They're taking a cruise of the galaxy, pausing here and there to chat with the stars."

"Don't be frivolous. And, yes, you told me all that."

"I have to be frivolous. Otherwise, it sounds too ridiculous. I made an agreement with them. I wanted to learn to talk to the sun. I told them, since I lived here, I could find out what they wanted to know better than they could. I could tell they were doubtful, but they let me go ahead. In return for my favor, when I was done, whether I succeeded or failed, they would give us what we wanted. A team of men could go and freely examine their ship.

They would describe their voyage to us – where they had been, what they had found. They promised cooperation in return for my chat with the sun."

"So, then nothing happened?"

"I didn't say that. I talked with the sun today. And saw it. And now I'm not going to do anything except sit on my hands. You can take it from here."

"What are you talking about?"

He knew he could not answer that. "I failed," he said. "I didn't find out anything they didn't know."

"Well, will you go with us or not? That's all I want to know right now." She was losing her patience, but there was also more than a minor note of pleading in her voice. He knew he ought to feel satisfied hearing that, but he didn't.

"Oh, hell," Reynolds said. "Yes – all right – I will go. But don't ask me why. Just give me an hour to get ready."

"Good man," O'Hara said, beaming happily.

Ignoring him, Reynolds opened his closets and began tossing clothes and other belongings into various boxes and crates.

"What do you think you'll need all that for?" Kelly asked him.

"I don't think I'm coming back," Reynolds said.

"They won't hurt you," she said.

"No. I won't be coming back because I won't be wanting to come back."

"You can't do that," O'Hara said.

"Sure I can," said Reynolds.

It took the base's entire fleet of seven shuttle tugs to ferry the delegation from Washington up to the starship. At that, a good quarter of the group had to be left behind for lack of room. Reynolds had requested and received permission to call the starship prior to departure, so the aliens were aware of what was coming up to meet them. They had not protested, but Reynolds knew they wouldn't, at least not over the radio. Like almost all mechanical or electronic gadgets, a radio was a fearsome object to them.

Kelly and Reynolds arrived with the first group and entered the air lock. At intervals of a minute or two, the others arrived. When the entire party was clustered in the lock, the last tug holding to the hull in preparation for the return trip, Reynolds signaled that it was time to move out.

"Wait a minute," one of the men called. "We're not all here. Acton and Dodd went back to the tug to get suits."

"Then they'll have to stay there," Reynolds said. "The air is pure here – nobody needs a suit."

"But," said another man, pinching his nose. "This smell. It's awful."

Reynolds smiled. He had barely noticed the odor. Compared to the stench of the first few days, this was nothing today. "The aliens won't talk if you're wearing suits. They have a taboo against artificial communication. The smell gets better as you go farther inside. Until then, hold your nose, breathe through your mouth."

"It's making me almost sick," confided a man at Reynolds' elbow. "You're sure what you say is true, Doctor?"

"Cross my heart," Reynolds said. The two men who had left to fetch the suits returned. Reynolds wasted another minute lecturing them.

"Stop enjoying yourself so much," Kelly whispered when they were at last under way.

Before they reached the first of the tight passages where crawling was necessary, three men had dropped away, dashing back toward the tug. Working from a hasty map given him by the aliens, he was leading the party toward a section of the ship where he had never been before. The walk was less difficult than usual. In most places a man could walk comfortably and the ceilings were high enough to accommodate the aliens themselves. Reynolds ignored the occasional shouted exclamation from the men behind. He steered a silent course toward his destination.

The room, when they reached it, was huge, big as a basketball gymnasium, the ceiling lost in the deep shadows above. Turning, Reynolds counted the aliens present: fifteen . . . twenty . . . thirty . . . forty . . . forty-five . . . forty-six. That had to be about all. He wondered if this was the full crew.

Then he counted his own people: twenty-two. Better than he had expected – only six lost en route, victims of the smell.

He spoke directly to the alien who stood in front of the others. "Greetings," he said. The alien wasn't Vergnan, but it could have been Jonathon.

From behind, he heard, "They're just like giraffes."

"And they even seem intelligent," said another.

"Exceedingly so. Their eyes."

"And friendly too."

"Hello, Reynolds," the alien said. "Are these the ones?"

"Jonathon?" asked Reynolds.

"Yes."

"These are the ones."

"They are your leaders – they wish to question my people?"

"They do."

"May I serve as our spokesman in order to save time?"

"Of course," Reynolds said. He turned and faced his party, looking from face to face, hoping to spot a single glimmer of intelligence, no matter how minute. But he found nothing. "Gentlemen?" he said. "You heard?"

"His name is Jonathon?" said one.

"It is a convenient expression. Do you have a real question?"

"Yes," the man said. He continued speaking to Reynolds. "Where is your homeworld located?"

Jonathon ignored the man's rudeness and promptly named a star.

"Where is that?" the man asked, speaking directly to the alien now.

Reynolds told him it lay some thirty light-years from Earth. As a star, it was very much like the sun, though somewhat larger.

"Exactly how many miles in a light-year?" a man wanted to know.

Reynolds tried to explain. The man claimed he understood, though Reynolds remained skeptical.

It was time for another question.

"Why have you come to our world?"

"Our mission is purely one of exploration and discovery," Jonathon said.

"Have you discovered any other intelligent races besides our own?"

"Yes. Several."

This answer elicited a murmur of surprise from the men. Reynolds wondered who they were, how they had been chosen for this mission. Not what they were, but who. What made them tick. He knew what they were: politicians, NASA bureaucrats, a sprinkling of real scientists. But who?

"Are any of these people aggressive?" asked a man, almost certainly a politician. "Do they pose a threat to you – or – or to us?"

"No," Jonathon said. "None."

Reynolds was barely hearing the questions and answers now. His attention was focused upon Jonathon's eyes. He had stopped blinking now. The last two questions – the ones dealing with intelligent life forms – he had told the truth. Reynolds thought he was beginning to understand. He had underestimated these creatures. Plainly, they had encountered other races during their travels before coming to Earth. They were experienced. Jonathon was lying – yes – but unlike before, he was lying well, only when the truth would not suffice.

"How long do you intend to remain in orbit about our moon?"

"Until the moment you and your friends leave our craft. Then we shall depart."

This set up an immediate clamor among the men. Waving his arms furiously, Reynolds attempted to silence them. The man who had been unfamiliar with the term "light-year" shouted out an invitation for Jonathon to visit Earth.

This did what Reynolds himself could not do. The others fell silent in order to hear Jonathon's reply.

"It is impossible," Jonathon said. "Our established schedule requires us to depart immediately."

"Is it this man's fault?" demanded a voice. "He should have asked you himself long before now."

"No," Jonathon said. "I could not have come – or any of my people – because we were uncertain of your peaceful intentions. Not until we came to know Reynolds well did we fully comprehend the benevolence of your race." The alien blinked rapidly now.

He stopped during the technical questions. The politicians and bureaucrats stepped back to speak among themselves and the scientists came forward. Reynolds was amazed at the intelligence of their questions. To this extent at least, the expedition had not been wholly a farce.

Then the questions were over and all the men came forward to listen to Jonathon's last words.

"We will soon return to our homeworld and when we do we shall tell the leaders of our race of the greatness and glory of the human race. In passing here, we have come to know your star and through it you people who live beneath its soothing rays. I consider your visit here a personal honor to me as an individual. I am sure my brothers share my pride and only regret an inability to utter their gratitude."

Then Jonathon ceased blinking and looked hard at Reynolds. "Will you be going too?"

"No," Reynolds said. "I'd like to talk to you alone if I can."

"Certainly," Jonathon said.

Several of the men in the party protested to Kelly or O'Hara, but there was nothing they could do. One by one they left the chamber to wait in the corridor. Kelly was the last to leave. "Don't be a fool," she cautioned.

"I won't," he said.

When the men had gone, Jonathon took Reynolds away from the central room. It was only a brief walk to the old room where they had always met before. As if practicing a routine, Jonathon promptly marched to the farthest wall and stood there waiting. Reynolds smiled. "Thank you," he said.

"You are welcome."

"For lying to them. I was afraid they would offend you with their stupidity. I thought you would show your contempt by lying badly, offending them in return. I underestimated you. You handled them very well."

"But you have something you wish to ask of me?"

"Yes," Reynolds said. "I want you to take me away with you."

As always, Jonathon remained expressionless. Still, for a long time, it said nothing. Then, "Why do you wish this? We shall never return here."

"I don't care. I told you before: I am not typical of my race. I can never be happy here."

"But are you typical of my race? Would you not be unhappy with us?"

"I don't know. But I'd like to try."

"It is impossible," Jonathon said.

"But – but – why?"

"Because we have neither the time nor the abilities to care for you. Our mission is a most desperate one. Already, during our absence, our homeworld may have gone mad. We must hurry. Our time is growing brief. And you will not be of any help to us. I am sorry, but you know that is true."

"I can talk to the stars."

"No," Jonathon said. "You cannot."

"But I did."

"Vergnan did. Without him, you could not."

"Your answer is final? There's no one else I can ask? The captain?"

"I am the captain."

Reynolds nodded. He had carried his suitcases and crates all this way and now he would have to haul them home again. Home? No, not home. Only the moon. "Could you find out if they left a tug for me?" he asked.

"Yes. One moment."

Jonathon rippled lightly away, disappearing into the corridor. Reynolds turned and looked at the walls. Again, as he stared, the rainbow patterns appeared to shift and dance and swirl of their own volition. Watching this, he felt sad, but his sadness was not that of grief. It was the sadness of emptiness and aloneness. This emptiness had so long been a part of him that he sometimes forgot it was there. He knew it now. He knew, whether consciously aware of it or not, that he had spent the past ten years of his life searching vainly for a way of filling this void. Perhaps even more than that: perhaps his whole life had been nothing more than a search for that one moment of real completion. Only twice had he ever really come close. The first time had been on Mars. When he had lived and watched while the others had died. Then he had not been alone or empty. And the other time had been right here in this very room – with Vergnan. Only twice in his life had he been allowed to approach the edge of true meaning. Twice in fifty-eight long and endless years. Would it ever happen again? When? How?

Jonathon returned, pausing in the doorway. "A pilot is there," it said.

Reynolds went toward the door, ready to leave. "Are you still planning to visit our sun?" he asked.

"Oh, yes. We shall continue trying, searching. We know nothing else. You do not believe – even after what Vergnan showed you – do you, Reynolds?"

"No, I do not believe."

"I understand," Jonathon said. "And I sympathize. All of us – even I – sometimes we have doubts."

Reynolds continued forward into the corridor. Behind, he heard a heavy clipping noise and turned to see Jonathon coming after him. He waited for the alien to join him and then they walked together. In the narrow corridor, there was barely room for both.

Reynolds did not try to talk. As far as he could see, there was nothing left to be said that might possibly be said in so short a time as that which remained. Better to say nothing, he thought, than to say too little.

The air lock was open. Past it, Reynolds glimpsed the squat bulk of the shuttle tug clinging to the creased skin of the starship.

There was nothing left to say. Turning to Jonathon, he said, "Goodbye," and as he said it, for the first time he wondered about what he was going back to. More than likely, he would find himself a hero once again. A celebrity. But that was all right: fame was fleeting; it was bearable. Two hundred forty thousand miles was still a great distance. He would be all right.

As if reading his thoughts, Jonathon asked, "Will you be remaining here or will you return to your homeworld?"

The question surprised Reynolds; it was the first time the alien had ever evidenced a personal interest in him. "I'll stay here. I'm happier."

"And there will be a new director?"

"Yes. How did you know that? But I think I'm going to be famous again. I can get Kelly retained."

"You could have the job yourself," Jonathon said.

"But I don't want it. How do you know all this? About Kelly and so on?"

"I listen to the stars," Jonathon said in its high warbling voice.

"They are alive, aren't they?" Reynolds said suddenly.

"Of course. We are permitted to see them for what they are. You do not. But you are young."

"They are balls of ionized gas. Thermonuclear reactions."

The alien moved, shifting its neck as though a joint lay in the middle of it. Reynolds did not understand the gesture. Nor would he ever. Time had run out at last.

Jonathon said, "When they come to you, they assume a disguise you can see. That is how they spend their time in this universe. Think of them as doorways."

"Through which I cannot pass."

"Yes."

Reynolds smiled, nodded and passed into the lock. It contracted behind him, engulfing the image of his friend. A few moments of drifting silence, then the other end of the lock furled open.

The pilot was a stranger. Ignoring the man, Reynolds dressed, strapped himself down and thought about Jonathon. What was it that it had said? I listen to the stars. Yes, and the stars had told it that Kelly had been fired?

He did not like that part. But the part he liked even less was this: when it said it, Jonathon had not blinked.

(1) It had been telling the truth. (2) It could lie without flicking a lash. Choose one.

Reynolds did, and the tug fell toward the moon.

I Still Call Australia Home

GEORGE TURNER

George Turner (1916–   ) is the most influential Australian SF writer and critic. From the 1960s onward he was a leading contemporary Australian novelist who also wrote SF criticism. It wasn't until the mid 1970s that he turned to writing science fiction. His first SF novel, *Beloved Son* (1978), published when he was in his early sixties, was recognized as an important debut, and he has gone on to write a number of first-rate SF novels, including *The Sea and Summer* (1987, published as *Drowning Towers* in the U.S.), which won the Arthur C. Clarke Award. *Beloved Son* involves interstellar travel, a post-holocaust civilization in the 21st century, and genetic engineering – this last has remained one of the principal concerns of his fiction, in recent works such as *Brain Child* (1991), *The Destiny Makers* (1993), and *Genetic Soldier* (1994).

Turner's literary execution is contoured by deeply held moral convictions and his life as a contemporary novelist. "I prefer to maintain a low key in my own work," says Turner. "To this end I have concentrated on simple, staple SF ideas, mostly those which have become conventions in the genre, injected without background or discussion into stories on the understanding that readers know all they need to know about such things. My SF method remains the same as for my mainstream novels – set characters in motion in speculative situations and let them work out their destinies with a minimum of auctorial interference."

His future societies have a satisfying complexity, portraying class conflict and economic disparities in a gritty, realistic fashion absent from most American science fiction. While American science fiction generally sees space as simply the new frontier, Turner, the Australian, envisions it as an alien place with a strange and different culture, one with its own moral imperatives and structures – as he envisions the future on Earth as operating under other moral structures different from ours today.

He has written comparatively few short SF stories, less than a dozen to date. This one is about the conflict of values between cultures in the future, and has intriguing resonances with James Tiptree, Jr.'s "Beam Us Home."

The past is another country; they do things differently there.
– L. P. Hartley

1

The complement of *Starfarer* had no idea, when they started out, of how long they might be gone. They searched the sky, the three hundred of them, men and women, black and brown and white and yellow, and in thirty years landed on forty planets whose life-support parameters appeared – from distant observation – close to those of Earth.

Man, they discovered, might fit his own terrestrial niche perfectly, but those parameters for his existence were tight and inelastic. There were planets where they could have dwelt in sealed environments, venturing out only in special suits, even one planet where they could have existed comfortably through half its year but been burned and suffocated in the other half. They found not one where they could establish a colony of mankind.

In thirty years they achieved nothing but an expectable increase in their numbers and this was a factor in their decision to return home. The ship was becoming crowded and, in the way of crowded tenements, something of a slum.

So they headed for Earth; and, at the end of the thirty-first year, took up a precessing north-south orbit allowing them a leisurely overview, day by day, of the entire planet.

This was wise. They had spent thirty years in space, travelling between solar systems at relativistic speeds, and reckoned that about six hundred local years had passed since they set out. They did not know what manner of world they might find.

They found, with their instruments, that the greenhouse effect had subsided slowly during the centuries, aided by the first wisps of galactic cloud heralding the new ice age, but that the world was still warmer than the interregnal norm. The ozone layer seemed to have healed itself, but the desert areas were still formidably large although the spread of new pasture and forest was heartening.

What they did not see from orbit was the lights of cities by night and this did not greatly surprise them. The world they had left in a desperate search for new habitat, had been an ant heap of ungovernable, unsupportable billions whose numbers were destined to shrink drastically if any were to survive at all. The absence of lights suggested that the population problem had solved itself in grim fashion.

They dropped the ship into a lower orbit just outside the atmosphere and brought in the spy cameras.

There were people down there, all kinds of people. The northern hemisphere was home to nomadic tribes, in numbers like migratory nations; the northern temperate zone had become a corn belt, heavily farmed and guarded by soldiers in dispersed forts, with a few towns and many villages; the equatorial jungles were, no doubt, home to hunter-gatherers but their traces were difficult to see; there were signs of urban communities, probably trading centres, around the seacoasts but no evidence of transport networks or lighting by night and no sounds of electronic transmission. Civilisation had regressed, not unexpectedly.

They chose to inspect Australia first because it was separated from the larger landmasses and because the cameras showed small farming communities and a few townlets. It was decided to send down a Contact Officer to inspect and report back.

The ship could not land. It had been built in space and could live only in space; planetary gravity would have warped its huge but light-bodied structure beyond repair. Exploratory smallcraft could have been despatched, but it was reasoned that a crew of obviously powerful supermen might create an untrusting reserve among the inhabitants, even an unhealthy regard for gods or demons from the sky. A single person, powerfully but unobtrusively armed, would be a suitable ambassador.

They sent a woman, Nugan Johnson, not because she happened to be Australian but because she was a Contact Officer, and it was her rostered turn for duty.

They chose a point in the south of the continent because it was autumn in the hemisphere, and an average daily temperature of twenty-six C would be bearable, and dropped her by tractor beam on the edge of a banana grove owned by Mrs Flighty Jones, who screamed and fled.

2

Flighty, in the English of her day, meant something like *scatterbrained.* Her name was, in fact, Hallo-Mary (a rough – very rough – descendant of Ave Maria), but she was a creature of fits and starts, so much so that the men at the bottling shed made some fun of her before they were convinced that she had seen *something,* and called the Little Mother of the Bottles.

"There was I, counting banana bunches for squeeging into baby pap, when it goes hissss-bump behind me."

"What went hiss-bump?"

"It did."

"What was it?" Little Mother wondered if the question was unfair to Flighty wits.

"I don't know." Having no words, she took refuge in frustrated tears. She had inherited the orchard but not the self-control proper to a proprietary woman.

In front of the men! Little Mother sighed and tried again. "What did it look like? What shape?"

Flighty tried hard. "Like a bag. With legs. And a glass bowl on top. And it bounced. That's what made the bump. And it made a noise."

"What sort of noise?"

"Just a noise." She thought of something else. "You know the pictures on the library wall? In the holy stories part? The ones where the angels go up? Well, like the angels."

Little Mother knew that the pictures did not represent angels, whatever the congregation were told. Hiding trepidation, she sent the nearest man for Top Mother.

Top Mother came, and listened . . . and said, as though visitations were nothing out of the way, "We will examine the thing that hisses and bumps. The men may come with us in case their strength is needed." That provided at least a bodyguard.

The men were indeed a muscular lot, and also a superstitious lot, but they were expected to show courage when the women claimed protection. They picked up whatever knives and mashing clubs lay to hand and tried to look grim. Man-to-man was a bloodwarming event but man-to-whatisit had queasy overtones. They agreed with Little Mother's warning: "There could be danger."

"There might be greater danger later on if we do *not* investigate. Lead the way, Hallo-Mary." A Top Mother did not use nicknames.

Flighty was now thoroughly terrified and no longer sure that she had seen anything, but Top Mother took her arm and pushed her forward. Perhaps it had gone away, perhaps it had bounced up and up . . .

It had not gone anywhere. It had sat down and pushed back its glass bowl and revealed itself, by its cropped hair, as a man.

"A man," murmured Top Mother, who knew that matriarchy was a historical development and not an evolutionary given. She began to think like the politician which at heart she was. A *man* from – from *outside* – could be a social problem.

The men, who were brought up to revere women but often resented them – except during the free-fathering festivals – grinned and winked at each other and wondered what the old girl would do.

The old girl said, "Lukey! Walk up and observe him."

Lukey started off unwillingly, then noticed that three cows grazed unconcernedly not far from the man in a bag and took heart to cross the patch of pasture at the orchard's edge.

At a long arm's length he stood, leaned forward and sniffed. He was forest bred and able to sort out the man in a bag's scents from the norms about him and, being forest bred, his pheromone sense was better than rudimentary. He came so close that Nugan could have touched him and said, "Just another bloody woman!" The stranger should have been a man, a sex hero!

He called back to Top Mother, "It's only a woman with her hair cut short."

They all crowded forward across the pasture. Females were always peaceable – unless you really scratched their pride.

The hiss Flighty had heard had been the bootjets operating to break the force of a too-fast landing by an ineptly handled tractor beam, the bump had been the reality of a contact that wrenched an ankle. Even the bounce was almost real as she hopped for a moment on one leg. The noise was Nugan's voice through a speaker whose last user had left it tuned to baritone range, a hearty, "Shit! Goddam shit!" before she sat down and became aware of a dumpy figure vanishing among columns of what she remembered vaguely as banana palms. Not much of a start for good PR.

She thought first to strip the boot and bind her ankle, then that she should not be caught minus a boot if the runaway brought unfriendly reinforcements. She did not fear the village primitives; though she carried no identifiable weapons, the thick gloves could spit a variety of deaths through levelled fingers. However, she had never killed a civilised organism and had no wish to do so; her business was to prepare a welcome home.

The scents of the air were strange but pleasant, as the orbital analysis had affirmed; she folded the transparent *fishbowl* back into its neck slot. She became aware of animals nearby. Cows. She recognised them from pictures though she had been wholly city bred in an era of gigantic cities. They took no notice of her. Fascinated and unafraid, she absorbed a landscape of grass and tiny flowers in the grass, trees and shrubs and a few vaguely familiar crawling and hopping insects. The only strangeness was the spaciousness stretching infinitely on all sides, a thing that the lush Ecological Decks of *Starfarer* could not mimic, together with the sky like a distant ceiling with wisps of cloud. Might it rain on her? She scarcely remembered rain.

Time passed. It was swelteringly hot but not as hot as autumn in the greenhouse streets.

They came at last, led by a tall woman in a black dress – rather, a robe cut to enhance dignity though it was trimmed off at the knees. She wore a white headdress like something starched and folded in the way of the old nursing tradition and held together by a brooch. She was old, perhaps in her sixties, but she had presence and the dress suggested status.

She clutched another woman by the arm, urging her forward, and Nugan recognised the clothing, like grey denim jeans, that fled through the palms. Grey Denim Jeans pointed and planted herself firmly in a determined no-further pose. Madam In Black gestured to the escort and spoke a few words.

Nugan became aware of the men and made an appreciative sound unbecoming in a middle-aged matron past child-bearing years. These men wore only G-strings and they were *men*. Not big men but shapely, muscular and very male. *Or am I so accustomed to Starfarer crew that any change rings a festival bell? Nugan, behave!*

The man ordered forward came warily and stopped a safe arm's length from her, sniffing. Nugan examined him. *If I were, even looked, twenty years younger* . . . He spoke suddenly in a resentful, blaming tone. The words were strange (of course they must be) yet hauntingly familiar; she thought that part of the sentence was "dam-dam she!"

She kept quiet. Best to observe and wait. The whole party, led by Madam In Black, came across the pasture. They stopped in front of her, fanning out in silent inspection. The men smelled mildly of sweat, but that was almost a pleasure; after thirty years of propinquity, *Starfarer*'s living quarters stank of sweat.

Madam In Black said something in a voice of authority that seemed part of her. It sounded a little like "Oo're yah?" – interrogative with a clipped note to it; the old front-of-the-mouth Australian vowels had vanished in the gulf of years. It should mean, by association, *Who are you?* but in this age might be a generalised, *Where are you from?*, even, *What are you doing here?*

Nugan played the oldest game in language lesson, tapping her chest and saying, "Nugan. I – Nugan."

Madam In Black nodded and tapped her own breast. "Ay Tup-Ma."

"Tupma?"

"Dit – Tup-Ma, Yah Nuggorn?"

"Nugan."

The woman repeated, "Nugan," with a fair approximation of the old vowels and followed with, "Wurriya arta?"

Nugan made a guess at vowel drift and consonant elision and came up with, *Where are you out of?* meaning, Where do you come from?

They must know, she thought, that something new is in the sky. A ship a kilometre long has been circling for weeks with the sun glittering on it at dawn and twilight. They can't have lost all contact with the past; there must be stories of the bare bones of history.

She pointed upwards and said, "From the starship."

The woman nodded as if the statement made perfect sense and said, "Stair-boot."

Nugan found herself fighting sudden tears. *Home, home, HOME has not forgotten us.* Until this moment she had not known what Earth meant to her, swimming in the depths of her shipbound mind. "Yes, stair-boot. We say starship."

The woman repeated, hesitantly, "Stairsheep?" She tried again, reaching for the accent, "Starship! I say it right?"

"Yes, you say it *properly*."

The woman repeated, "Prupperly. Ta for that. It is old-speak. I read some of that but not speak – only small bit."

So not everything had been lost. There were those who had rescued and preserved the past. Nugan said, "You are quite good."

Tup-Ma blushed with obvious pleasure. "Now we go." She waved towards the banana grove.

"I can't." A demonstration was needed. Nugan struggled upright, put the injured foot to the ground and tried for a convincing limp. That proved easy; the pain made her gasp and she sat down hard.

"Ah! You bump!"

"Indeed I bump." She unshackled the right boot and broke the seals before fascinated eyes and withdrew a swelling foot.

"We carry."

We meant two husky males with wrists clasped under her, carrying her through the grove to a large wooden shed where more near-naked men worked at vats and tables. They sat on a table and brought cold water (*How do they cool it? Ice? Doubtful.*) and a thick yellow grease which quite miraculously eased the pain somewhat (*A native pharmacopoeia?*) and stout, unbleached bandages to swathe her foot tightly.

She saw that in other parts of the shed the banana flesh was being mashed into long wooden moulds. Then it was fed into glass cylinders whose ends were capped, again with glass, after a pinch of some noisome-looking fungus was added. (*Preservative? Bacteriophage? Why not?*) A preserving industry, featuring glass rather than metal; such details helped to place the culture.

Tup-Ma called, "Lukey!" and the man came forward to be given a long instruction in which the word *Stair-boot* figured often. He nodded and left the shed at a trot.

"Lukey go – goes – to tell Libary. We carry you there."

"Who is Libary?"

The woman thought and finally produced, "Skuller. Old word, I think."

"Scholar? Books? Learning?"

"Yes, yes, books. Scho-lar. Ta." Ta? Of course – thank you. Fancy the child's word persisting.

"You will eat, please?"

Nugan said quickly, "No, thank you. I have this." She dug out a concentrate pack and swallowed one tablet before the uncomprehending Tup-Ma. She dared not risk local food before setting up the test kit, enzymes and once-harmless proteins could change so much. They brought a litter padded like a mattress and laid her on it. Four pleasantly husky men carried it smoothly, waist-high, swinging gently along a broad path towards low hills, one of which was crowned by a surprisingly large building from which smoke plumes issued.

"Tup-Ma goodbyes you."

"Goodbye, Tup-Ma. And ta."

3

It was a stone building, even larger than it had seemed. But that was no real wonder; the medieval stone masons had built cathedrals far more ornate than this squared-off warehouse of a building. It was weathered dirty grey but was probably yellow sandstone, of which there had been quarries in Victoria. Sandstone is easily cut and shaped even with soft iron tools.

There were windows, but the glass seemed not to be of high quality, and a small doorway before which the bearers set down the litter. A thin man of indeterminate middle age stood there, brown eyes examining her from a dark, clean shaven face. He wore a loose shirt, wide-cut, ballooning shorts and sandals, and he smiled brilliantly at her. He was a full-blooded Aborigine.

He said, "Welcome to the Library, Starwoman," with unexceptionable pronunciation though the accent was of the present century.

She sat up. "The language still lives."

He shook his head. "It is a dead language but scholars speak it, as many of yours spoke Latin. Or did that predate your time? There are many uncertainties."

"Yes, Latin was dead. My name is Nugan."

"I am Libary."

"Library?"

"If you would be pedantic, but the people call me Libary. It is both name and title. I preside." His choice of words, hovering between old-fashioned and donnish, made her feel like a child before a tutor, yet he seemed affable.

He gave an order in the modern idiom and the bearers carried her inside. She gathered an impression of stone walls a metre thick, pierced by sequent doors which formed a temperature lock. The moist heat outside was balanced by an equally hot but dry atmosphere inside. She made the connection at once, having a student's reverence for books. The smoke she had seen was given off by a low-temperature furnace stoked to keep the interior air dry and at a reasonably even temperature. This was more than a scholars' library; it was the past, preserved by those who knew its value.

She was carried past open doorways, catching glimpses of bound volumes behind glass, of a room full of hanging maps and once of a white man at a lectern, touching his book with gloved hands.

She was set down on a couch in a rather bare room furnished mainly by a desk of brilliantly polished wood which carried several jars of coloured inks, pens which she thought had split nibs and a pile of thick, greyish paper. (*Unbleached paper? Pollution free? A psychic prohibition from old time?*)

The light came through windows, but there were oil lamps available with shining parabolic reflectors. And smoke marks on the ceiling. Electricity slept still.

The carriers filed out. Libary sat himself behind the desk. "We have much to say to each other."

Nugan marvelled, "You speak so easily. Do you use the old English all the time?"

"There are several hundred scholars in Libary. Most speak the old tongue. We practise continually."

"In order to read the old books?"

"That, yes." He smiled in a fashion frankly conspirational. "Also it allows private discussion in the presence of the uninstructed."

Politics, no doubt – the eternal game that has never slept in all of history. "In front of Tup-Ma, perhaps?"

"A few technical expressions serve to thwart her understanding. But the Tup-Ma is no woman's fool."

"*The* Tup-Ma? I thought it was her name."

"Her title. Literally, Top Mother. As you would have expressed it, Mother Superior."

"A nun!"

Libary shrugged. "She has no cloister and the world is her convent. Call her priest rather than a nun."

"She has authority?"

"She has great authority." He looked suddenly quizzical. "She is very wise. She sent you to me before you should fall into error."

"Error? You mean, like sin?"

"That also, but I speak of social error. It would be easy. Yours was a day of free thinking and irresponsible doing in a world that could not learn discipline for living. This Australian world is a religious matriarchy. It is fragile when ideas can shatter and dangerous when the women make hard decisions."

It sounded like too many dangers to evaluate at once. Patriarchy and equality she could deal with – in theory – but matriarchy was an unknown quantity in history. He had given his warning and waited silently on her response.

She pretended judiciousness. "That is interesting." He waited, smiling faintly. She said, to gain time, "I would like to remove this travel suit. It is hot."

He nodded, stood, turned away.

"Oh, I'm fully dressed under it. You may watch."

He turned back to her and she pressed the release. The suit split at the seams and crumpled round her feet. She stepped out, removed the gloves with their concealed armament and revealed herself in close-cut shirt and trousers and soft slippers. The damaged ankle hurt less than she had feared.

Libary was impressed but not amazed. "One must expect ingenious invention." He felt the crumpled suit fabric. "Fragile."

She took a small knife from her breast pocket and slit the material, which closed up seamlessly behind the blade. Libary said, "Beyond our capability."

"We could demonstrate – "

"No doubt." His interruption was abrupt, uncivil. "There is little we need." He changed direction. "I think Nugan is of Koori derivation."

"Possibly from Noongoon or Nungar or some such. You might know better than I."

His dark face flashed a smile. "I don't soak up old tribal knowledge while the tribes themselves preserve it in their enclaves."

"Enclaves?"

"We value variety of culture." He hesitated, then added, "Under the matriarchal aegis which covers all."

"All the world."

"Most of it."

That raised questions. "You communicate with the whole world? From space we detected no radio, no electronic signals at all."

"Wires on poles and radiating towers, as in the books? Their time has not come yet."

A queer way of phrasing it. "But you hinted at global communication, even global culture."

"The means are simple. Long ago the world was drawn together by trading vessels; so it is today. Ours are very fast; we use catamaran designs of great efficiency, copied from your books. The past does not offer much but there are simple things we take – things we can make and handle by simple means." He indicated the suit. "A self-healing cloth would require art beyond our talent."

"We could show – " But could they? Quantum chemistry was involved and electro-molecular physics and power generation . . . Simple products were not at all simple.

Libary said, "We would not understand your showing. Among your millions of books, few are of use. Most are unintelligible because of the day of simple explanation was already past in your era. We strain to comprehend what you would find plain texts, and we fail. Chemistry, physics – those disciplines of complex numeration and incomprehensible signs and arbitrary terms – are beyond our understanding."

She began to realise that unintegrated piles of precious but mysterious books are not knowledge.

He said, suddenly harsh, "Understanding will come at its own assimilable pace. You can offer us nothing."

"Surely . . ."

"Nothing! You destroyed a world because you could not control your greed for a thing you called progress but which was no more than a snapping up of all that came to hand or to mind. You destroyed yourselves by inability to control your breeding. You did not ever cry *Hold!* for a decade or a century to unravel the noose of a self-strangling culture. You have nothing to teach. You knew little that mattered when sheer existence was at stake."

Nugan sat still, controlling anger. *You don't know how we fought to stem the tides of population and consumption and pollution; how each success brought with it a welter of unforeseen disasters; how impossible it was to coordinate a world riven by colour, nationality, political creed, religious belief and economic strata.*

Because she had been reared to consult intelligence rather than emotion, she stopped thought in mid-tirade. *Oh, you are right. These were the impossible troubles brought by greed and irresponsible use of a finite world. We begged our own downfall. Yet . . .*

"I think," she said, "you speak with the insolence of a lucky survival. You exist only because we did. Tell me how your virtue saved mankind."

Libary bowed his head slightly in apology. "I regret anger and implied contempt." His eyes met hers again. "But I will not pretend humility. We rebuilt the race. In which year did you leave Earth?"

"In twenty-one eighty-nine. Why?"

"In the last decades before the crumbling. How to express it succinctly? Your world was administered by power groups behind national boundaries, few ruling many, pretending to a mystery termed *democracy* but ruling by decree. Do I read the history rightly?"

"Yes." It was a hard admission. "Well, it was beginning to seem so. Oppression sprang from the need to ration food. We fed fifteen billion only by working land and sea until natural fertility cycles were exhausted, and that only at the cost of eliminating other forms of life. We were afraid when the insects began to disappear . . ."

"Rightly. Without insects, nothing flourishes."

"There was also the need to restrict birth, to deny birth to most of the world. When you take away the right to family from those who have nothing else and punish savagely contravention of the population laws . . ." She shrugged hopelessly.

"You remove the ties that bind, the sense of community, the need to consider any but the self. Only brute force remains."

"Yes."

"And fails as it has always failed."

"Yes. What happened after we left?"

Libary said slowly, "At first, riots. Populations rose against despots, or perhaps against those forced by circumstances into despotism. But ignorant masses cannot control a state; bureaucracies collapsed, supply fell into disarray and starvation set in. Pack leaders – not to be called soldiers – fought for arable territory. Then great fools unleashed biological weaponry – I think that meant toxins and bacteria and viruses, whatever such things may have been – and devastated nations with plague and pestilence. There was a time in the northern hemisphere called by a term I read only as Heart of Winter. Has that meaning for you?"

"A time of darkness and cold and starvation?"

"Yes."

"Nuclear winter. They must have stopped the bombing in the nick of time. It could only have been tried by a madman intent on ruling the ruins."

"We do not know his name – their names – even which country. Few records were kept after that time. No machines, perhaps, and no paper."

"And then?"

"Who knows? Cultural darkness covers two centuries. Then history begins again; knowledge is reborn. Some of your great cities saw the darkness falling and sealed their libraries and museums in hermetic vaults. This building houses the contents of the Central Library of Melbourne; there are others in the world and many yet to be discovered. Knowledge awaits deciphering but there is no hurry. This is, by and large, a happy world."

Sophisticated knowledge was meaningless here. They could not, for instance, create electronic communication until they had a broad base of metallurgy, electrical theory and a suitable mathematics. Text books might as well have been written in cipher.

"And," Libary said, "there were the Ambulant Scholars. They set up farming communities for self support, even in the Dark Age, while they preserved the teachings and even some of the books of their ancestors. They visited each other and established networks around the world. When they set up schools, the new age began."

"Like monks of the earlier Dark Age, fifteen hundred years before."

"So? It has happened before?"

"At least once and with less reason. Tell me about the rise of women to power."

Libary chuckled. "Power? Call it that but it is mostly manipulation. The men don't mind being ruled; they get their own way in most things and women know how to bow with dignity when caught in political error. It is a system of giving and taking wherein women give the decisions and take the blame for their mistakes. The men give them children – under certain rules – and take responsibility for teaching them when maternal rearing is completed."

She made a stab in the dark. "Women established their position by taking control of the birth rate."

"Shrewdly thought, nearly right. They have a mumbo jumbo of herbs and religious observances and fertility periods but in fact it is all contraception, abortion and calculation. Some men believe, more are sceptical, but it results in attractive sexual rituals and occasional carnivals of lust, so nobody minds greatly." He added offhandedly, "Those who cannot restrain their physicality are killed by the women."

That will give Starfarer pause for thought.

"I think," said Libary, "that the idea was conceived by the Ambulant Scholars and preached in religious guise – always a proper approach to basically simple souls who need a creed to cling to. So, you see, the lesson of overpopulation has been learned and put to work."

"This applies across the planet?"

"Not yet, but it will. America is as yet an isolated continent. Our Ambulant Scholars wielded in the end a great deal of respected authority."

"And now call yourselves Librarians?"

His black face split with pleasure. "It is so good to speak with a quick mind."

"Yet a day will come when population will grow again beyond proper maintenance."

"We propose that it shall not. Your machines and factories will arrive in their own good time, but our present interest is in two subjects you never applied usefully to living: psychology and philosophy. Your thinking men and women studied profoundly and made their thoughts

public, but who listened? There is a mountain of the works of those
thinkers to be sifted and winnowed and applied. Psychology is knowledge of the turbulent self; philosophy is knowledge of the ideals of
which that self is capable. Weave these together and there appears a
garment of easy discipline wherein the self is fulfilled and the world
becomes its temple, not just a heap of values for ravishing. We will
solve the problem of population."

Nugan felt, with the uneasiness of someone less than well prepared,
that they would. Their *progress* would lie in directions yet unthought of.

"Now," Libary said, "would you please tell me how you came to
Earth without a transporting craft?"

"I was dropped by tractor beam."

"A – beam?" She had surprised him at last. "A ray of light that
carries a burden?"

"Not light. Monopoles."

"What are those?"

"Do you have magnets? Imagine a magnet with only one end, so
that the attraction goes on in a straight line. It is very powerful. Please
don't ask how it works because I don't know. It is not in my field."

Libary said moodily, "I would not wish to know. Tell me, rather,
what you want here."

Want? Warnings rang in Nugan's head but she could only plough
ahead. "After six hundred years we have come home! And Earth is far
more beautiful than we remember it to be."

His dark eyebrows rose. "Remember? Are you six hundred years
old?"

Explanation would be impossible. She said, despairingly, "Time in
heaven is slower than time on Earth. Our thirty years among the stars
are six centuries of your time. Please don't ask for explanation. It is not
magic; it is just so."

"Magic is unnecessary in a sufficiently wonderful universe. Do you
tell me that you do not understand the working of your everyday
tools?"

"I don't understand the hundredth part. Knowledge is divided
among specialists; nobody knows all of even common things."

Libary considered in silence, then sighed lightly and said, "Leave
that and return to the statement that you have come home. This is not
your home."

"Not the home we left. It has changed."

"Your home has gone away. For ever."

The finality of his tone must have scattered her wits, she thought later; it roused all the homesickness she had held in check and she said quickly, too quickly, "We can rebuild it."

The black face became still, blank. She would have given years of life to recall the stupid words. He said at last, "After all I have told you of resistance to rapid change you propose to redesign our world!"

She denied without thinking, "No! You misunderstand me!" In her mind she pictured herself facing *Starfarer*'s officers, stumbling out an explanation, seeing disbelief that a trained Contact could be such a yammering fool.

"Do I? Can you mean that your people wish to live as members of our society, in conditions they will see as philosophically unrewarding and physically primitive?"

He knew she could not mean any such thing. She tried, rapidly, "A small piece of land, isolated, perhaps an island, a place where we could live on our own terms. Without contact. You would remain – unspoiled."

Insulting, condescending habit of speech, truthful in its meaning, revealing and irrevocable!

"You will live sequestered? Without travelling for curiosity's sake, without plundering resources for your machines, without prying into our world and arguing with it? In that case, why not stay between the stars?"

Only truth remained. "We left Earth to found new colonies. Old Earth seemed beyond rescue; only new Earths could perpetuate a suffocating race."

"So much we know. The books tell it."

Still she tried: "We found no new Earth. We searched light-years of sky for planets suitable for humans. We found the sky full of planets similar to Earth – but only similar. Man's range of habitable conditions is very narrow. We found planets a few degrees too hot for healthy existence or a few degrees too cool to support a terrestrial ecology, others too seismically young or too aridly old, too deficient in oxygen or too explosively rich in hydrogen, too low in carbon dioxide to support a viable plant life or unbearably foul with methane or lacking an ozone layer. Parent stars, even of G-type, flooded surfaces with overloads of ultraviolet radiation, even gamma radiation, or fluctuated in minute but lethal instabilities. We visited forty worlds in thirty years and found not one where we could live. Now you tell me we are not welcome in our own home!"

"I have told you it is not your home. You come to us out of violence and decay; you are conditioned against serenity. You would be only an eruptive force in a world seeking a middle way. You would debate our beliefs, corrupt our young men by offering toys they do not need, tempt the foolish to extend domination over space and time – and in a few years destroy what has taken six centuries to build."

Anger she could have borne but he was reasonable – as a stone wall is reasonable and unbreachable.

"Search!" he said. "Somewhere in such immensity must be what you seek. You were sent out with a mission to propagate mankind, but in thirty years you betray it."

She burst out, "Can't you understand that we *remember* Earth! After thirty years in a steel box we want to come home."

"I do understand. You accepted the steel box; now you refuse the commitment."

She pleaded, "Surely six hundred people are not too many to harbour? There must be small corners – "

He interrupted, "There are small corners innumerable but not for you. Six hundred, you say, but you forget the books with their descriptions of the starships. You forget that we know of the millions of ova carried in the boxes called cryogenic vaults, of how in a generation you would be an army surging out of its small corner to dominate the culture whose careful virtues mean nothing to you. Go back to your ship, Nugan. Tell your people that time has rolled over them, that their home has vanished."

She sat between desperation and fulmination while he summoned the bearers. Slowly she resumed the travel suit.

From the hilltop she saw a world unrolled around her, stirring memory and calling the heart. It should not be lost for a pedantic Aboriginal's obstinacy.

"I will talk with your women!"

"They may be less restrained than I, Nugan. The Tup-Ma's message said you were to be instructed and sent away. My duty is done."

She surrendered to viciousness. "We'll come in spite of you!"

"Then we will wipe you out as a leprous infection."

She laughed, pointed a gloved finger and a patch of ground glowed red, then white. "Wipe us out?"

He told her, "That will not fight the forces of nature we can unleash against you. Set your colony on a hill and we will surround it with bushfires, a weapon your armoury is not equipped to counter. Set it in a valley and we will show you how a flash flood can be created. Force us at your peril."

All her Contact training vanished in the need to assert. "You have not seen the last of us."

He said equably, "I fear that is true. I fear for you, Nugan, and all of yours."

She tongued the switch at mouth level and the helmet sprang up and over her head, its creases smoothing invisibly out. She had a moment's unease at the thought of the Report Committee on *Starfarer,* then she tongued the microphone switch. "Jack!"

"Here, love. So soon?"

"Yes, so damned soon!" She looked once at the steady figure of Libary, watching and impassive, then gave the standard call for return: "Lift me home, Jack."

Hurtling into the lonely sky, she realised what she had said and began silently to weep.

Liquid Sunshine

ALEXANDER KUPRIN
Translated by Leland Fetzer

Alexander Kuprin (1879–1938) is the first Russian writer to incorporate the influence of H. G. Wells, in this 1913 story, and to provide a model for later Russian writers such as Evgeny Zamiatin. Kuprin is also clearly influenced by other literature, including various stories of adventure and shipwreck. (Perhaps, also, Poe's *Narrative of Arthur Gordon Pym.)*

Zamiatin said in his enthusiastic essay on H. G. Wells in 1922, "Of course, science fiction could enter the field of fine literature only in the last decades, when truly fantastic potentialities unfolded before science and technology . . . true science fiction clothed in literary form will be found only at the end of the nineteenth century . . . The petrified life of the old, prerevolutionary Russia produced almost no examples of social fantasies or science fiction, as indeed it could not. Perhaps the only representatives of this genre in the recent history of our literature are Kuprin, with his 'The Liquid Sun,' and Bogdanov . . ."

This is a story that could easily have appeared twenty-five or thirty years later in *Amazing Stories* as a genre story without causing a ripple – and been seen as innovative. It did not, however, appear in English translation until the early 1980s in an academic collection, so it has not been part of the main genre dialogue for decades. It is about the idea of radical transformation of human society through science and technology. Russian and American science fiction share a central fascination with this idea. In the rest of the world, this idea is generally treated ironically, with great suspicion, or as a recipe for disaster.

I, Henry Dibble, turn to the truthful exposition of certain important and extraordinary events in my life with the greatest concern and absolutely understandable hesitation. Much of what I find essential to put to paper will, without doubt, arouse astonishment, doubt, and even disbelief in the future reader of my account. For this I have long been prepared, and I find such an attitude to my memoirs completely plausible and logical. I must myself admit that even to me those years spent in part in travel and in part on the six-thousand-foot summit of the volcano Cayambe in the South American Republic of Ecuador often seem not to have been actual events in my life, but only a strange and fantastic dream or the ravings of a transient cataclysmic madness.

But the absence of four fingers on my left hand, recurring headaches, and the eye ailment which goes by the common name of night blindness, these incontrovertible phenomena compel me to believe that I was in fact a witness to the most astonishing events in world history. And, finally, it is not madness, not a dream, not a delusion, that punctually three times a year from the firm E. Nideston and Son, 451 Regent Street, I receive 400 pounds sterling. This allowance was generously left to me by my teacher and patron, one of the greatest men in all of human history, who perished in the terrible wreck of the Mexican schooner *Gonzalez*.

I completed studies in the Mathematical Department with special studies in Physics and Chemistry at the Royal University in the year . . . That, too, is yet another persistent reminder of my adventures. In addition to the fact that a pulley or a chain took the fingers of my left hand at the time of the catastrophe, in addition to the damage to my optic nerves, etc., as I fell into the sea I received, not knowing when nor how, a sharp blow on the right upper quarter of my skull. That blow left hardly any external sign hut it is strangely reflected in my mind, specifically in my powers of recall. I can remember well words, faces, localities, sounds, and the sequence of events, but I have forgotten forever all numbers and personal names, addresses, telephone numbers, and historical dates; the years, months, and days which marked my personal life have disappeared without a trace, scientific formulae, although I am able to deal with them without difficulty in logical fashion, have fled, and both the names of those I have known and know now have disappeared, and this circumstance is very painful to me. Unfortunately, I did not then maintain a diary, but two or three notebooks which have survived, and a few old letters aid me to a certain degree to orient myself.

Briefly, I completed my studies and received the title Master of Physics two, three, four, or perhaps even five years before the beginning of the twentieth century. Precisely at that time the husband of my elder sister, Maude, a farmer of Norfolk who periodically had loaned me material support and even more important moral support, took ill and died. He firmly believed that I would continue my scientific career at one of the English universities and that in time I would shine as a luminary to cast a ray of glory on his modest family. He was healthy, sanguine, strong as a bull, could drink, write a verse, and box – a lad in the spirit of good old merry England. He died as the result of a stroke one night after consuming one-fourth of a Berkshire mutton roast, which he seasoned with a strong sauce: a bottle of whiskey and two gallons of Scotch light beer.

His predictions and expectations were not fulfilled. I did not join the scientific ranks. Even more, I was not fortunate enough to find the position of a teacher or a tutor in a private or public school; rather, I fell into the vicious, implacable, furious, cold, wearisome world of failure. Oh! who, besides the rare spoiled darlings, has not known and felt on his shoulders this stupid, ridiculous, blind blow of fate? But it abused me for too lengthy a time.

Neither at factories nor at scientific agencies – nowhere could I find a place for myself. Usually I arrived too late: the position was already taken.

In many cases I became convinced that I had fallen into some dark and suspicious conspiracy. Even more often I was paid nothing for two or three months of labor and thrown onto the street like a kitten. One cannot say that I was excessively indecisive, shy, unenterprising, or, on the other hand, sensitive, vain or refractory. No, it was simply that the circumstances of life were against me.

But I was above all an Englishman and I held myself as a gentleman and a representative of the greatest nation in the world. The thought of suicide in this terrible period of my life never came to mind. I fought against the injustice of fate with cold, sober persistence and with the unshakable faith that never, never would an Englishman be a slave. And fate, finally, surrendered in the face of my Anglo-Saxon courage.

I lived then in the most squalid of all the squalid lanes in Bethnal Green, in the God-forsaken East End, dwelling behind a chintz curtain in the home of a dock worker, a coal hauler. I paid him four shillings a month for the place, and in addition I helped his wife with the cooking, taught his three oldest children to read and write, and also scrubbed the kitchen and the backstairs. My hosts always cordially invited me to eat with them, but I had decided not to burden their beggar's budget. I dined, rather, in the dark basement and God knows how many cats', dogs', and horses' lives lay on my black conscience. But my landlord, Mr. John Johnson, requited my natural tact with attentiveness: when there was much work on the East End docks and not enough workmen and the wages reached extraordinary heights, he always managed to find a place for me to load heavy cargoes where with no difficulty I could earn eight or ten shillings in a day. It was unfortunate that this handsome, kind, and religious man became intoxicated every Sunday without fail and when he did so he displayed a great inclination toward fisticuffs.

In addition to my duties as cook and occasional work on the docks, I essayed numerous other ridiculous, onerous, and peculiar professions. I helped clip poodles and cut the tails from fox terriers, clerked in a sausage store when its owner was absent, catalogued old libraries, counted the earnings at horse races, at times gave lessons in mathematics, psychology, fencing, theology, and even dancing, copied off the most tedious reports and infantile stories, watched coach horses when the drivers were eating ham and drinking beer; once, in uniform, I spread rugs and raked the sand between acts in a circus, worked as a sandwich man, and even fought as boxer, a middleweight, translated from German to English and vice versa, composed tombstone inscriptions, and what else did I not do! To be candid, thanks to my inexhaustible energy and temperate habits I was never in particular need. I had a stomach like a camel, I weighed 150 pounds without my clothes, had good hands, slept well and was cheerful in temperament. I had so adjusted to poverty and to its unavoidable deprivations, that occasionally I could not only send a little money to my younger sister, Esther, who had been abandoned in Dublin with her two children by her Irish husband, and actor, a drunkard, a liar, a tramp, and a rake – but I also followed the sciences and public life closely, read newspapers and scholarly journals, bought used books, and belonged to rental libraries. I even managed to make two minor inventions: a very cheap device which would warn a railroad engineer in fog or snow of a closed switch ahead, and an unusual, long-lasting welding flame which burned hydrogen. I must say that I did not enjoy the income from these inventions – others did. But I remained true to science, like a knight to his lady, and I never abandoned the belief that the time would come when my beloved would summon me to her chamber with her bright smile.

That smile shone upon me in the most unexpected and commonplace fashion. One foggy autumn morning my landlord, the good Mr. Johnson, went to a neighboring shop for hot water and milk for his children. He returned with a radiant face, the odor of whiskey on his breath, and a newspaper in his hand. He gave me the newspaper, still damp and smelling of ink, and, pointing out an entry marked with a line from the edge of his dirty nail, exclaimed:

"Look, old man. As easy as I can tell anthracite from coke, I know that these lines are for you, lad."

I read, not without interest, the following announcement:

"The solicitors 'E. Nideston and Son,' 451 Regent Street, seek an individual for an equatorial voyage to a location where he must remain for not less than three years engaged in scientific pursuits. Conditions: age, 22 to 30 years, English citizenship, faultless health, discrete, sober and forbearing, must know one, or yet better, two other European languages (French and German), must be a bachelor, and so far as it is possible, free of family and other ties to his native land. Beginning salary: 400 pounds sterling per year. A university education is desirable, and in particular a gentleman knowing theoretical and applied chemistry and physics has an advantage in obtaining the position. Applicants are to call between nine and ten in the morning." I am able to quote this advertisement with such assurance since it is still preserved among my few papers, although I copied it off in haste and has been subject to the action of sea water.

"Nature has given you long legs, son, and good lungs," Johnson said, approvingly pounding my back. "Start up the engine and full steam ahead. No doubt there will be many more young gentlemen there of irreproachable health and honorable character than at Derby. Anne, make him a sandwich with meat and preserves. Perhaps he will have to wait his turn in line for five hours. Well, I wish you luck, my friend. Onward, brave England!"

I arrived barely in time at Regent Street. Silently I thanked nature for my good legs. As he opened the door the porter with indifferent familiarity said: "Your luck, mister. You got the last chance," and promptly fixed on the outside doors the fateful announcement: "The advertised opening is now closed to applicants."

In the darkened, cramped, and rather dirty reception room – such are almost all the reception rooms belonging to the magicians of the City who deal in millions – were about ten men who had come before me. They sat about the walls on dark, time-polished, soiled wooden benches, above which, at the height of a sitting man's head, the ancient wallpaper displayed a wide, dirty, band. Good God, what a pitiful collection of hungry, ragged men, driven by need, sick and broken, had gathered here, like a parade of monsters! Involuntarily my heart contracted with pity and wounded self-esteem. Sallow faces, averted, malicious, envious, suspicious glances from under lowered brows, trembling hands, tatters, the smell of poverty, cheap tobacco, and fumes of alcohol long since drunk. Some of these young gentlemen were not yet seventeen years of age while others were past fifty. One after another, like pale shades, they drifted into the office and returned from there looking like drowned men only lately removed from the water. I felt both sickened and ashamed to admit to myself that I was infinitely healthier and stronger than all of them taken together.

Finally my turn came. Someone invisible opened the door from the other side and shouted abruptly and disgustedly in an exasperated voice:

"Number eighteen, and Allah be praised, the last!"

I entered the office, nearly as neglected as the reception room, different only that it was papered in peeling checked paper; it had two side chairs, a couch, and two easy chairs on which sat two middle-aged gentlemen of apparently the same medium height, but the elder of the two, in a long coat was slim, swarthy, and seemingly stern, while the other, dressed in a new jacket with silken lapels, was fair, plump, blue-eyed and sat at his ease one leg placed upon the other.

I gave my name and bowed not deeply, but respectfully. Then, seeing that I was not to be offered a seat, I was at the point of taking a place on the couch.

"Wait," said the swarthy one, "First remove your coat and vest. There is a doctor here who will examine you."

I remembered the clause in the advertisement which referred to irreproachable health, and I silently removed my outer garments. The florid stout man lazily freed himself from his chair and placing his arms around me he pressed his ear to my chest.

"Well, at least we have one with clean linen," he said casually.

He listened to my lungs and heart, tapped my spine and chest with his fingers, sat me down and checked the reflexes of my knees, and finally said lazily:

"As fit as a fiddle. He hasn't eaten too well recently, however. But that is nothing and all that is required is two weeks of good food. To his good fortune, I find no traces of exhaustion from over-indulgences in athletics as is common among our young men. In a word, Mr. Nideston, I present you a gentleman, a fortunate, almost perfect example of the healthy Anglo-Saxon race. May I assume that I am no longer needed?"

"You are free, doctor," said the solicitor. "But can you, may I be assured, visit us tomorrow morning, if I require your professional advice?"

"Oh, Mr. Nideston, I am always at your service."

When we were alone, the solicitor sat opposite me and peered intently into my face. He had little sharp eyes the color of a coffee bean with quite yellow whites. Every now and then when he looked directly at you, it seemed as though diminutive sharp and bright needles issued from those tiny blue pupils.

"Let us talk," he said abruptly. "Your name, origins, and place of birth?" I answered him in the same expressionless and laconic fashion.

"Education?"

"The Royal University."

"Subject of study?"

"Department of Mathematics, in particular, Physics."

"Foreign languages?"

"I know German comparatively well. I understand when French is not spoken too rapidly, I can put together a few score essential expressions, and I read it without difficulty."

"Relatives and their social position?"

"Is that of any importance to you, Mr. Nideston?"

"To me? Of supreme unimportance. But I act in the interests of a third party."

I described the situations of my two sisters. During my speech he attentively inspected his nails, and then threw two needles at me from his eyes, asking:

"Do you drink? And how much?"

"Sometimes at dinner I drink a half pint of beer."

"A bachelor?"

"Yes, sir."

"Do you have any intention of commiting that blunder? Of marrying?"

"Oh, no."

"Any present love affairs?"

"No, sir."

"How do you support yourself?"

I answered that question briefly and fairly, omitting, for the sake of brevity, five or six of my latest casual professions.

"So," he said, when I had finished, "do you need money?"

"No. My stomach is full and I am adequately clothed. I always find work. So far as it is possible I follow recent developments in science. I am convinced that sooner or later I will find my opportunity."

"Would you like money in advance? A loan?"

"No, that is not my practice. I don't take money from anyone . . . But we're not finished."

"Your principles are commendable. Perhaps we can come to an agreement. Give me your address and I will inform you, and probably very soon, of our decision. Good-bye."

"Excuse me, Mr. Nideston," I responded. "I have answered all your questions, even the most delicate, with complete candor. May I ask you one question?"

"Please."

"What is the purpose of the journey?"

"Oho! Are you concerned about that?"

"We may assume that I am."

"The purpose of the journey is purely scientific."

"That is not an adequate answer."

"Not adequate?" Mr. Nideston abruptly shouted at me, and his coffee eyes poured out sheaves of needles. "Not adequate? Do you have the insolence to assume that the firm of Nideston and Son now in existence for one hundred and fifty years and respected by all of England's commercial establishments would suggest anything dishonorable or which might compromise you? Or that we would undertake any enterprise without possessing reliable guarantees beforehand that it is unconditionally legal?"

"Oh, sir, I have no doubt of that," I responded in confusion.

"Very well, then," he interrupted me and immediately became tranquil, like a stormy sea spread with oil. "But you see, first of all I am bound by the proviso that you not be informed of any substantial details of the journey until you are aboard the steamship out of Southampton . . ."

"Bound where?" I asked suddenly.

"For the time being I cannot tell you. And secondly, the purpose of your journey (if indeed it comes to pass) is not completely clear even to me."

"Strange," said I.

"Passing strange," the solicitor willingly agreed. "But I may also inform you, if you so desire, that it will be fantastic, grandiose, unprecedented, splendid, and audacious to the point of madness!"

Now it was my turn to say "Hmmm," and this I did with a certain restraint.

"Wait," Mr. Nideston exclaimed with sudden fervor. "You are young. I am twenty-five or thirty years older than you. You are not at all astonished by many of the greatest accomplishments of the human mind, but if, when I was your age, someone had predicted that I would work in the evenings by the light of invisible electricity which flowed through wires or that I would converse with an acquaintance at a distance of eighty miles, that I would see moving, laughing human figures on a screen, that I would send telegraph messages without the benefit of wires, and so on, and so on, then I would have waged my honor, my freedom, my career against one pint of bad London beer that I was confronted with a madman."

"You mean the project involves some new invention or a great discovery?"

"If you wish, yes. But I ask you, do not view me with distrust or suspicion. What would you say, for example, if a great genius were to appeal to your young energy, strength, and knowledge, a genius who, we will assume, is engaged with a problem – to create a pleasing, nutritious, economical food out of the elements found in the air? If you were provided the opportunity to labor for the sake of the future organization and adornment of the earth? To dedicate your talents and spiritual energies to the happiness of future generations? What would you say? Here is an example at hand. Look out the window."

Involuntarily I arose under the spell of his compelling, swift gesture and looked through the clouded glass. There, over the streets, hung a black-rust-gray fog, like dirty cotton from heaven to earth. In it only dimly could be perceived the wavering glow from the street lights. It was eleven o'clock in the morning.

"Yes, yes, look," said Mr. Nideston. "Look carefully. Now assume that a gifted, disinterested man is summoning you to a great project to ameliorate and beautify the earth. He tells you that everything that is on the earth depends on the mind, will, and hands of man. He tells you that if God in his righteous anger has turned his face away from man, then man's measureless mind will come to his own aid. This man will tell you that fogs, disease, climatic extremes, winds, volcanic eruptions – they are all subject to the influence and control of the human will-and that finally the earth could become a paradise and its existence extended by several hundred thousand years. What would you say to that man?"

"But what if he who presents me with this radiant dream is wrong? What if I find myself a dumb plaything in the hands of a monomaniac? A capricious madman?"

Mr. Nideston rose, and, presenting me his hand as a sign of farewell, said firmly:

"No. Aboard the steamship in two or three months from now (if we can come to an agreement) I will inform you of the name of that scientist and the meaning of his great task, and you will remove your hat as a mark of your great reverence for the man and his ideas. But I, unfortunately, Mr. Dibble, am a layman. I am only a solicitor – the guardian and representative of others' interests."

After this interview I had almost no doubt that fate, finally, had grown tired of my fixed inspection of her unbending spine and had decided to show me her mysterious face. Therefore, that same evening with the help of my small savings I produced a banquet of extraordinary luxury, which consisted of a roast, a punch, plum pudding and hot chocolate which was enjoyed in addition to myself by the worthy couple, the elder Johnsons, and, I do not remember exactly – six or seven of the younger Johnsons. My left shoulder was quite blue and out of joint from the friendly pounding of my good landlord who sat next to me on my left.

And I was not wrong. The next evening I received a telegram: "Call at noon tomorrow. 451 Regent Street, Nideston."

I arrived punctually at the appointed time. He was not in his office, but a servant who had been forewarned led me to a small room in a restaurant located around the corner at a distance of two hundred paces. Mr. Nideston was there alone. At first he was not that ebullient, and perhaps even poetic, man who had spoken with me so fervently about the future happiness of mankind two days earlier. No, once more he was that dry and laconic solicitor who on the occasion of our first meeting that morning had so commandingly instructed me to remove my outer clothing and had questioned me like a police inspector.

"Good day. Sit down," he said indicating a chair. "It is my lunch hour, a time I have at my disposal. Although my firm is called 'Nideston and Son' I am in fact a bachelor and a lonely man. And so- would you care to dine? To drink?"

I thanked him and asked for tea and toast. Mr. Nideston ate at leisure, sipped an old port and from time to time transfixed me with the bright needles of his eyes. Finally, he wiped his lips, threw down his napkin, and asked:

"Then, you are agreed?"

"To buy a pig in a poke?" I asked in turn.

"No," he said loudly and angrily. "The previous conditions remain in force. Before your departure to the tropics you will receive as much information as I am empowered to give you. If this is not satisfactory, you may, on your part, refuse to sign the contract and I will pay you a recompense for the time which you have employed in fruitless conversations with me."

I observed him carefully. At that moment he was engaged in an effort to crack two nuts, the right hand enveloping the knuckles of the left. The sharp needles of his eyes were concealed behind the curtain of his brows. And suddenly, as though in a moment of illumination, I perceived all the soul of that man – the strange soul of a formalist and a gambler, the narrow specialist and an extraordinarily expansive temperament, the slave of his counting house traditions and at the same time a secret searcher for adventures, a pettifogger, ready for two pennies to put his opponent in prison for a long sentence, and at the same time an eccentric capable of sacrificing the wealth acquired in dozens of years of unbroken labor for the sake of the shadow of a beautiful idea. This thought passed through me like lightning. And Nideston, suddenly, as though we had been united by some invisible current, opened his eyes, with a great effort crushed the nuts into tiny fragments and smiled at me with an open, childlike, almost mischievous smile.

"When all is said and done, you are risking little, my dear Mr. Dibble. Before you leave for the tropics I will give you several commissions on the continent. These commissions will not require from you any particular scientific knowledge, but they will demand great mechanical accuracy, precision, and foresight. You will need no more than about two months, perhaps a week more or less than that. You are to accept in various European locations certain expensive and very fragile optical glasses as well as several extremely delicate and sensitive physical instruments. I entrust to your care, agility, and skills their packing, delivery to the railroad, and sea and rail transport. You must agree that it would mean nothing to a drunken sailor or porter to throw a crate into the hold and smash into fragments a doubly convex lens over which dozens of men have worked for dozens of years . . ."

"An observatory!" I thought joyfully. "Of course, it's an observatory! What happiness! At last I have my elusive fate by the forelock."

I could see that he had guessed my thoughts and his eyes became yet merrier.

"We will not discuss the remuneration for this, your first, task. We will come to agreement on details, of course, as I can see from your expression. But," and then he suddenly laughed heedlessly, like a child, "I want to turn your attention to a very curious fact. Look, through these fingers have passed ten or twenty thousand curious cases, some of them involving very large sums. Several times I have made a fool of myself, and that in spite of all our subtle casuistic precision and diligence. But, imagine that every time that I have rejected all the tricks of my craft and looked a man straight in the eye, as I am now looking at you, I have never gone wrong and never had cause for repentance. And so?"

His eyes were clear, firm, trusting and affectionate. At that second this little swarthy, wrinkled, yellow-faced man indeed took my heart into his hands and conquered it.

"Good," I said. "I believe you. From this time I am at your disposal."

"Oh, why so fast?" Mr. Nideston said genially. "You have plenty of time. We still have time to drink a bottle of claret together." He pulled the cord for the waiter. "But please put your personal affairs in order, and this evening at eight o'clock you will leave with the tide on board the steamship *The Lion and the Magdalene* to which I will in time deliver your itinerary, drafts on various banks, and money for your personal expenses. My dear young man, I drink to your health and your successes. If only," he suddenly exclaimed with unexpected enthusiasm, "if only you knew how I envy you, my dear Mr. Dibble!"

In order to flatter him and in quite an innocent manner, I responded almost sincerely:

"What's detaining you, my dear Mr. Nideston? I swear that in spirit you are as young as I."

The swarthy solicitor lowered his long delicately modeled nose into his claret cup, was silent for a moment and suddenly said with a sigh of feeling:

"Oh, my dear Mr. Dibble! My office, which has existed nearly from the time of the Plantagenets, the honor of my firm, my ancestors, thousands of ties connecting me with my clients, associates, friends, and enemies . . . I couldn't name it all . . . This means you have no doubts?"

"No."

"Well, let us drink a toast and sing 'Rule, Britannia'!"

And we drank a toast and sang – I almost a boy, yesterday a tramp, and that dry man of business, whose influence extended from the gloom of his dirty office to touch the fates of European powers and business magnates – we sang together in the most improbable and unsteady voices in all the world:

> *"Rule, Britannia!*
> *Britannia, rule the waves!*
> *Britons never, never, never will be slaves!"*

A servant entered, and turning politely to Mr. Nideston, he said:

"Excuse me, sir. I listened to your singing with genuine pleasure. I have heard nothing more pleasing even in the Royal Opera, but next to you in the adjoining room is a meeting of lovers of French medieval music. Perhaps I should not refer to them as gentlemen . . . but they all have very discriminating ears."

"You are no doubt correct," the solicitor answered gently. "And therefore I ask you to accept as a keepsake this round yellow object with the likeness of our good king."

Here is a brief list of the cities and the laboratories which I visited after I crossed the Channel. I copy them out in entirety from my notebook: The Pragemow concern in Paris; Repsold in Hamburg; Zeiss, Schott Brothers, and Schlattf in Jena; in Munich the Frauenhof concern and the Wittschneider Optical Institute and also the Mertz laboratory there; Schick in Berlin, and also Bennech and Basserman. And also, not distant in Potsdam, the superb branch of the Pragemow concern which operates in conjunction with the essential and enlightened support of Dr. E. Hartnack.

The itinerary composed by Mr. Nideston was extraordinarily precise and included train schedules and the addresses of inexpensive but comfortable English hotels. He had drawn it up in his own hand. And here, too, one was aware of his strange and unpredictable character. On the corner of one of the pages he had written in pencil in his angular, firm hand: "If Chance and Co. were real Englishmen they would have not abandoned their concern and it would not be necessary for us to obtain lenses and instruments from the French and Germans with names like Schnurbartbindhalter."

I will admit, not in a spirit of boasting, that everywhere I bore myself with the requisite weight and dignity, because many times in critical moments in my ears I heard Mr. Nideston's terrible goat's voice singing, "Britons never, never, never will be slaves."

But, too, I must say that I cannot complain about any lack of attentiveness and courtesy on the part of the learned scientists and famous technicians whom I met. My letters of recommendation signed with large, black, completely illegible flourishes and reinforced below with Mr. Nideston's precise signature served as a magic wand in my hands which opened all doors and all hearts for me. With unremitting and deep-felt concern I watched the manufacture and polishing of convex and curving lenses and the production of the most delicate, complex and beautiful instruments which gleamed with brass and steel, shining with all their screws, tubing, and machined metal. When in one of the most famous workshops of the globe I was shown an almost complete fifty-inch mirror which had required at least two or three years of final polishing – my heart stood still and my breath caught, so overcome was I with delight and awe at the power of the human mind.

But I was also rendered very uneasy by the persistent curiosity of these serious, learned men who in turn attempted to ascertain the mysterious purpose of my patron whose name I did not know. Sometimes subtly and artfully, sometimes crudely and directly, they attempted to extract from me the details and goal of my journey, the addresses of the firms with which I had business, the type and function of our orders to other workshops, etc., etc. But, firstly, I remembered well Mr. Nideston's very serious warnings about indiscretions; secondly, what could I answer even if I wished to? I myself knew nothing and was feeling my way, as though at night in an unknown forest. I was accepting, after verifying drawings and calculations, some kind of strange optical glasses, metal tubing of various sizes, calculators, small-scale propellors, miniaturized cylinders, shutters, heavy glass retorts of a strange form, pressure gauges, hydraulic presses, a host of electrical devices which I had never seen before, several powerful microscopes, three chronometers and two underwater diving suits with helmets. One thing became obvious to me: the strange enterprise which I served had nothing to do with the construction of an observatory, and on the basis of the objects which I was accepting I found it absolutely impossible to guess the purpose which they were to serve. My only concern was to ensure that they were packed with great care and I constantly devised ingenious devices which protected them from vibrations, concussion, and deformation.

I freed myself from impertinent questions by suddenly falling silent, and not saying a word I would look with stony eyes directly at the face of my interrogator. But one time I was compeled to resort to very persuasive eloquence: a fat, insolent Prussian dared to offer me a bribe of two thousand Marks if I would reveal to him the secret of our enterprise. This happened in Berlin in my own room on the fourth floor of my hotel. I succinctly and sternly informed that stout insolent creature that he spoke with an English gentleman. He neighed like a Percheron, slapped me familiarly on the back and exclaimed:

"Oh, come now, my good man, let's forget these jokes. We both understand what they mean. Do you think that I have not offered you enough? But we, like intelligent men of the world, can come to an agreement, I am sure . . ."

His vulgar tone and crude gestures displeased me inordinately. I opened the great window of my room and pointing below at the pavement I said firmly:

"One word more, and you will not find it necessary to employ the elevator to leave this floor. One, two, three . . ."

Pale, cowed, and enraged, he cursed hoarsely in his harsh Berlin accent, and on his way out slammed the door so hard that the floor of my apartment trembled and objects leaped upon the table.

My last visit on the continent was to Amsterdam. There I was to transmit my letters of recommendation to the two owners of two world famous diamond cutting firms, Maas and Daniels, respectively. They were intelligent, polite, dignified, and sceptical Jews. When I visited them in turn, Daniels first of all said to me slyly: "Of course you have a commission also for Mr. Maas." And Maas, as soon as he read the letter addressed to him, said with a query in his voice, "You have no doubt spoken with Mr. Daniels?"

Both of them displayed the greatest reserve and suspicion in their relations with me; they consulted together, sent off simple and coded telegrams, put to me the most subtle and detailed questions about my personal life, and so on. They both visited me on the day of my departure. A kind of Biblical dignity could be perceived in their words and movements.

"Excuse us, young man, and do not consider it a sign of our distrust that we inform you," said the older and more imposing, Daniels, "that on the route Amsterdam–London all steamships are alive with international thieves of the highest skill. It is true that we hold in strictest confidence the execution of your worthy commission, but who can be assured that one or two of these enterprising, intelligent, at times almost brilliant international knights of commerce will not manage to discover our secret? Therefore, we have not considered it excessive to surround you with an invisible but faithful police guard. You, perhaps, will not even notice them. You know that caution is never unwanted. Will you not agree that we and your associates would be much relieved if that which you transport were under reliable, observant, and ceaseless observation during the entire voyage? This is not a matter of a leather cigarette case, but two objects which cost together approximately one million three hundred thousand francs and which are unique in all the world, and perhaps in all the universe."

I, in the most sincere and concerned tone, hastened to assure the worthy diamond cutter of my complete agreement with his wise and farsighted words. Apparently, my trust inclined him even more in my favor, and he asked in a low voice, in which I detected a quaver, an expression of awe:

"Would you like to see them?"

"If that is convenient, then please," I said, barely able to conceal my curiosity and perplexity.

Both the Jews almost simultaneously, with the expression of priests performing a holy ritual, took out of the side pockets of their long frock coats two small boxes – Daniels' was of oak while that of Maas was of red morocco; they carefully unfastened the gold clasps and lifted the lids. Both boxes were lined in white velvet and at first to me they appeared to be empty. It was only when I had bent close over them and looked closely that I saw two round, convex, totally colorless lenses of extraordinary purity and transparency, which would have been almost invisible except for their delicate, round, precise outlines.

"Astonishing workmanship!" I exclaimed, ecstatically. "Undoubtedly the polishing of glass in this manner must have required much expenditure of time."

"Young man!" said Daniels in a startled whisper. "They are not glass, they are two diamonds. The one from my shop weighs thirty and one-half carats and the diamond of Mr. Maas in all weighs seventy-four carats."

I was so stunned that I lost my usual composure.

"Diamonds? Diamonds cut into spheres? But that's a miracle such as I have never seen or heard. Man has never succeeded in producing anything like them!"

"I have already told you that these objects are unique in all the world," the jeweler reminded me solemnly, "but, excuse me, I am somewhat puzzled by your surprise. Did you not know about them? Had you in fact never heard of them?"

"Never in my life. You know that the enterprise which I serve is a closely guarded secret. Not only I, but also Mr. Nideston, are unacquainted with it in detail. I know only that I am collecting parts and equipment in various locations in Europe for some kind of an enormous project, whose purpose and plan I – a scientist by training – as yet understand nothing."

Daniels looked intently at me with his calm capable eyes, light brown in color, and his Biblical face darkened.

"Yes, that is so," he said slowly and thoughtfully after a brief pause. "Apparently you know nothing more than we, but do I perceive, when I look into your eyes, that even if you were informed of the nature of the enterprise, you would not share your information with us?"

"I have given my word, Mr. Daniels," I said as softly as possible.

"Yes, that is so, that is so. Do not think, young man, that you have come to our city of canals and diamonds completely unknown."

The Jew smiled a thin smile.

"We are even aware of the manner in which you suggested an aerial journey out of your window to a certain individual with commercial connections."

"How could anyone have known of that incident except the two of us involved?" I said, astonished. "Apparently, that German swine could not keep his mouth closed."

The Jew's face became enigmatic. He slowly and significantly passed his hand down his long beard.

"You should know that the German said nothing about his humiliation. But we knew about it the next day. We must! We whose guarded fire-proof vaults contain our own and others' valuables sometimes worth hundreds of millions of francs, must maintain our own intelligence. Yes. And three days later Mr. Nideston also knew of your deed."

"That's going too far!" I exclaimed in confusion.

"You have lost nothing, my young Englishman. Rather you have gained. Do you know how Mr. Nideston responded when he heard of the Berlin incident? He said: 'I knew that Mr. Dibble, an excellent young man, would have done nothing else.' For my part I would like to congratulate Mr. Nideston and his patron on the fact that their interests have fallen into such faithful hands. Although . . . Although . . . Although this disrupts certain of our schemes, our plans, and our hopes."

"Yes," confirmed the taciturn Mr. Maas.

"Yes," repeated quietly the Biblical Mr. Daniels, and once more a sad expression passed over his face. "We were given these diamonds in almost the same form in which you now see them, but their surfaces, as they had only recently been removed from the matrix, were crude and rough. We ground them as patiently and lovingly as though they were a commission from an emperor. To express it more accurately; it was impossible to improve on them. But I, an old man, a craftsman and one of the great gem experts of the world, have long been tortured by one cursed question: who could give such a shape to a diamond? Moreover, look at the diamond – here is a lens – not a crack, not a blemish, not a bubble. This prince of diamonds must have been subjected to the greatest heat and pressure. And I," and here Daniels sighed sadly, "and I must admit that I had counted much on your arrival and your candor."

"Forgive me, but I am in no position . . ."

"That's enough, I understand. But we wish you a pleasant journey."

My ship left Amsterdam that evening. The agents who accompanied me were so skilled at their work that I did not know who among the passengers was my guard. But toward midnight when I wished to sleep and retired to my room, to my surprise I found there a bearded, broad-shouldered stranger whom I had never seen on deck. He stretched out, not on the spare bunk, but on the floor near the door where he spread out a coat and an inflatable rubber pillow and covered himself with a robe. Not without repressed anger I informed him that the entire cabin to its full extent including its cubic content of air belonged to me. But he responded calmly and with a good English accent:

"Do not be disturbed, sir. It is my duty to spend this night near you in the position of a faithful watchdog. May I add that here is a letter and a package from Mr. Daniels."

The old Jew had written briefly and affectionately:

> Do not deny me a small pleasure: take as a souvenir of our meeting this ring I offer you. It is of no great value, but it will serve as an amulet to guard you from danger at sea. The inscription on it is ancient, and may indeed be in the language of the now extinct Incas.
>
> Daniels

In the packet was a ring with a small flat ruby on whose surface were engraved wondrous signs.

Then my "watchdog" locked the cabin, laid a revolver next to him on the floor and seemingly fell instantly asleep.

"Thank you, my dear Mr. Dibble," Mr. Nideston said to me the next day, shaking my hand firmly. "You have excellently fulfilled all your commissions, which were at times difficult enough, employed your time well, and in addition have borne yourself with dignity. Now you may rest for a week and divert yourself as you wish. Sunday morning we shall dine together and then leave for Southampton and on Monday morning you will be at sea aboard *The Southern Cross*, a splendid steamer. Do not forget, may I remind you, to visit my clerk to receive your two months' salary and expenses, and during the next two days I will examine and re-pack all of your baggage. It is dangerous to trust another's hands, and I doubt if there is anyone in London as skilled as I in the packing of delicate objects."

On Sunday I bade farewell to kind Mr. John Johnson and his numerous family, leaving them to the sound of their best wishes for a happy journey. And on Monday morning Mr. Nideston and I were seated in the luxurious stateroom of the huge liner *The Southern Cross* where we drank coffee in expectation of my departure. A fresh breeze blew over the sea and green waves with white caps dashed against the thick glass of the portholes.

"I must inform you, my dear sir, that you will not be traveling alone," said Mr. Nideston. "A certain Mr. de Mon de Rique will be sailing with you. He is an electrician and mechanic with several years of irreproachable experience behind him and I have only the most favorable reports concerning his abilities. I feel no special affection for the lad, but it may well be in this case the voice of my own erroneous and baseless antipathy – an old man's eccentricity. His father was a Frenchman who took English citizenship and his mother was Irish but he himself has the blood of a Gaelic fighting cock in his veins. He is a dandy, handsome in a common sort of way, much taken with himself and his own appearance, and is fond of women's skirts. It was not I who selected him. I acted only in accordance with the instructions issued to me by Lord Charlesbury, your future director and mentor. De Mon de Rique will arrive in twenty or twenty- five minutes with the morning train from Cardiff and we shall speak with him. At any rate I advise you to establish good relations with him. Whether you like it or not you must live three or four years at his side on God-knows-what desert at the equator on the summit of the extinct volcano Cayambe, where you, white men, will be only five or six, while all the others will be Negroes, Mestizos, Indians and others of their ilk. Are you perhaps frightened at such a prospect? Remember, the choice is yours to make. We could at any moment tear up the contract you signed and return together by the eleven o'clock train to London. And I may assure you that this would in no wise reduce the respect and affection I feel for you."

"No, my dear Mr. Nideston, I see myself already on Cayambe," I said with laughter. "I yearn for regular employment, particularly if it involves science, and when I think of it I lick my chops like a starveling in front of a White Chapel sausage shop. I hope that my work will be interesting enough that I will not become bored and involved in petty concerns and personal differences."

"Oh, my dear sir, you will have much beautiful and lofty labor before you complete your scheme. The time has come to be open with you and I will enlighten you on some matters of which I am informed. Lord Charlesbury has been laboring now nine years on a plan of unheard of dimensions. He has decided at any costs to accomplish the transformation of the sun's rays into a gas and what is more – to compress that gas to an extraordinary degree at terribly low temperatures under colossal pressures into liquid form. If God grants him the power of completing his plan, then his discovery will have enormous consequences . . ."

"Enormous!" I repeated softly, subdued and awed by Mr. Nideston's words.

"That is all I know," said the solicitor. "No, I also know from a personal letter from Lord Charlesbury that he is closer than ever to the successful completion of his work and less than ever has any doubts about the rapid solution of his problem. I must tell you, my dear friend, that Lord Charlesbury is one of the great men of science, one of few touched with genius. In addition, he is a genuine aristocrat both in birth and in spirit, an unselfish and self-denying friend of mankind, a patient and considerate teacher, a charming conversationalist and a faithful friend. He is, moreover, the possessor of such attractive spiritual beauty that all hearts are attracted to him . . . But here is your traveling companion coming up the gang plank now," Mr. Nideston said, breaking off his enthusiastic speech. "Take this envelope. You will find in it your steamship tickets, your exact itinerary and money. You will be at sea for sixteen or seventeen days. Tomorrow you will be overcome by depression. For such an occasion I have acquired and deposited in your cabin thirty or so books. And in addition, in your baggage you will find a suitcase with a supply of warm clothing and boots. You did not know that you will be required to live in a mountain region with eternal snows. I attempted to select clothing of your size, but I was so afraid of making an error, that I preferred the larger size to the smaller. Also you will find among your things a small box with seasickness remedies. I do not in fact believe in them, but at any rate . . . do you suffer from seasickness?"

"Yes, but not to a particularly painful degree. And anyway, I have a talisman against all dangers at sea."

I showed him the ruby, Daniels' gift. He examined it carefully, shook his head and said thoughtfully:

"Somewhere I have seen such a stone as that, and it seems with the same inscription. But now I see the Frenchman has noticed us and is coming our way. With all my heart, my dear Dibble, I wish you a happy voyage, good spirits and health . . . Greetings, Mr. de Mon de Rique. May I introduce you: Mr. Dibble, Mr. de Mon de Rique, future colleagues and collaborators."

I personally was not particularly impressed by the dandy. He was tall, slender, effete and sleek, with a kind of grace in his movements, an indolent and flexible strength, such as we see in the great cats. He reminded me first of all of a Levantine with his beautiful velvety dark eyes and small gleaming black mustache, which was carefully trimmed over his classic pink mouth. We exchanged a few insignificant and polite phrases. But at that moment a bell rang above us and a whistle sounded, shaking the deck with its full powerful voice – the ship's whistle.

"Well, now, good-bye, gentlemen," said Mr. Nideston. "With all my heart I hope you will become friends. My greetings to Lord Charlesbury. May you have good weather during your crossing. Until we meet again."

He walked briskly down the gang plank, entered a waiting cab, waved affectionately in our direction for the last time, and without looking back disappeared from our sight. I did not know why, but I felt a kind of sadness, as though when that man disappeared I had lost a true and faithful helper and a moral support.

I remember little that was remarkable in our journey. I will say only that those seventeen days seemed as long to me as 170 years, and they were so monotonous and dreary that now from a distance they seem to me to be one endlessly long day.

De Mon de Rique and I met several times a day at dinner in the salon. We had no other close meetings. He was cooly polite with me and I in turn re-paid him with restrained courtesy, but I constantly felt he was not interested in me personally nor indeed in anyone else in the world. But, on the other hand, when our conversation touched upon our special fields, I was overwhelmed by his knowledge, his audacity, and the originality of his hypotheses, and what was important, by his ability to express his ideas in precise and picturesque language.

I tried to read the books which Mr. Nideston had left for me. Most of them were narrowly scientific works which dealt with the theory of light and optic lenses, observations on high and low temperatures, and the description of experiments on the concentration and liquefaction of gases. There were also several books devoted to the description of remarkable expeditions and two or three books about the equatorial countries of South America. But it was difficult to read because a heavy wind blew constantly and the steamship oscillated in long sliding glides. All the passengers gave their due to seasickness except de Mon de Rique, who in spite of his great height and delicate build conducted himself as well as an old sailor.

Finally, we arrived at Colón in the northern part of the isthmus of Panama. When I disembarked my legs were leaden and would not obey my will. According to Mr. Nideston's instructions we were personally to oversee the trans-shipment of our baggage to the train station and its loading into baggage cars. The most delicate and sensitive instruments we took with ourselves into our compartment. The precious polished diamonds were, of course, in my possession, but – it is now painful to admit this – I not only did not even show them to my companion, I never said a word to him about them.

Our journey henceforth was fatiguing and consequently of little interest. We traveled by railroad from Colón to Panama, from Panama we had two days' journey on the ancient quivering steamship *Gonzalez* to the Bay of Guayaquil, then on horseback and rail to Quito. In Quito, in accordance with Mr. Nideston's instruction we sought out the Equator Hotel where we found a party of guides and packers who were expecting us. We spent the night in the hotel and early in the morning, refreshed, we set off for the mountains. What intelligent, good, charming creatures – the mules. With their bells tinkling steadily, shaking their heads decorated with rings and plumes, carefully stepping on the uneven country roads with their long tumbler-shaped hooves, they calmly proceeded along the rim of the abyss over such defiles that involuntarly you closed your eyes and held to the horn of the high saddle.

We reached the snow about five that evening. The road widened and became level. It was obvious that people of a high civilization had labored over it. The sharp turns were always paralleled with a low stone barrier.

At six o'clock when we had passed through a short tunnel, we suddenly saw residences before us: several low white buildings over which proudly rose a white tower which resembled a Byzantine church spire or an observatory. Still higher into the sky rose iron and brick chimneys. A quarter of an hour later we arrived at our destination.

Out of a door belonging to a house larger and more spacious than the rest emerged to meet us a tall thin old man with a long, irreproachably white beard. He said he was Lord Charlesbury and greeted us with unfeigned kindness. It was hard to know his age from his appearance: fifty or seventy-five. His large, slightly protuberant blue eyes, the eyes of a pure Englishman, were as clear as a lad's, shining and penetrating. The clasp of his hand was firm, warm, and open, and his high broad forehead was notable for its delicate and noble lines. And as I admired his slender beautiful face and responded to his hand-shake it clearly seemed to me that one time long ago I had seen his visage and many times I had heard his name.

"I am infinitely pleased at your arrival," said Lord Charlesbury, climbing up the stairs with us. "Was your journey a pleasant one? And how is the good Mr. Nideston? A remarkable man, is he not? But you can answer all my questions at dinner. Now go refresh yourselves and put yourselves in order. Here is our majordomo, the worthy Sambo," and he indicated a portly old Negro who met us in the foyer. "He will show you to your rooms. We dine punctually at seven, and Sambo will inform you of our remaining schedule."

The worthy Sambo very politely, but without a shadow of servile ingratiation, took us to a small house nearby. Each of us was given three rooms – simple, but at the same time somehow exceptionally comfortable, bright, and cheerful. Our quarters were separated from each other by a stone wall and each had a separate entrance. For some reason I was pleased by this arrangement.

With indescribable pleasure I sank into a huge marble bath (thanks to the rocking of the steamship I had been deprived of this satisfaction, and in the hotels at Colón, Panama and Quito the baths would not have aroused the trust even of my friend John Johnson). But when I luxuriated in the warm water, took a cold shower, shaved, and then dressed with the greatest care I was ridden by the question: why was Lord Charlesbury's face so familiar? And what was it, something almost fabulous, it seemed to me, that I had heard about him? At times in some corner of my consciousness I dimly felt that I could remember something, but then it would disappear, as a light breath disappears from a polished steel surface.

From the window of my study I could see all of this strange settle-ment with its five or six buildings, a stable, a greenhouse with low sooty equipment sheds, a mass of air hoses, with cars drawn over narrow rails by vigorous sleek mules, with high steam cranes which were smoothly carrying through the air steel containers to be filled with coal and oil shale out of a series of dumps. Here and there workers were active, the majority of them half-naked, although the thermometer attached to the outside of my window showed a temperature below freezing, and who were of all colors: white, yellow, bronze, coffee, and gleaming black.

I observed and thought how a flaming will and colossal wealth had been able to transform the barren summit of the extinct volcano into a veritable outpost of civilization with a manufactory, a workshop, and a laboratory, to transport stone, wood and iron to an altitude of eternal snows, to bring water, to construct buildings and machines, to set into motion precious physical instruments, among which the two lenses alone which I had brought cost 1,300,000 francs, to hire dozens of workers and summon highly paid assistants ... Once more there arose clearly in my mind the figure of Lord Charlesbury and suddenly – but wait! enlightenment suddenly came to my memory. I recalled very precisely how fifteen years earlier when I was still a green student at my school all the newspapers for months trumpeted various rumors concerning the disappearance of Lord Charlesbury, the English peer, the only scion of an ancient family, a famous scientist and a million-aire. His photograph was printed everywhere as well as conjectures on the causes of this strange event. Some took it as murder; others asserted that he had fallen under the influence of some malevolent hypnotist who for his evil purposes had removed the nobleman from England, leaving no traces; a third opinion held that the nobleman was in the hands of criminals who were holding him in expectation of a great ransom; a fourth opinion, and the most prescient one, asserted that the scientist had secretly undertaken an expedition to the North Pole.

Shortly later it became known that before his disappearance Lord Charlesbury very advantageously had liquidated all his lands, forests, parks, farms, coal and clay pits, castles, pictures, and other collections for cash, guided by a very acute and farsighted financial sense. But no one knew what had happened to this immense sum of money. When he disappeared there also disappeared, no one knew where, the famous Charlesbury diamonds, which were rightly the pride of all of England. No police, no private investigators were able to illuminate this strange affair. Within two months the press and society had forgotten him, diverted by other earthshaking interests. Only the learned journals which had dedicated many pages to the memory of the lost nobleman long continued to recount in great detail and with respectful deference his major scientific accomplishments in the study of light and heat and in particular in the expansion and contraction of gases, thermostatics, thermometrics, and thermodynamics, light refraction, the theory of lenses, and phosphorescence.

Outside resounded the drawn-out doleful sound of a gong. And then almost immediately someone knocked on my door and then entered a little cheerful Negro lad, as active as a monkey, who, bowing to me with a friendly smile, reported:

"Mister, I have been appointed by Lord Charlesbury to be at your service. Would you, sir, please come to dinner?"

On the table in my sitting room was a small, delicate bouquet of flowers in a porcelain vase. I selected a gardenia and inserted it into the lapel of my dinner-jacket. But just at that moment Mr. de Mon de Rique emerged from his door wearing a modest daisy in the button-hole of his frock coat. I felt a kind of uneasy displeasure sweep over me. And even at that distant time there must have been in me still much shallow juvenile peevishness, because I was very pleased to see that Lord Charlesbury who met us in the salon was not wearing a frock coat but a dinner-jacket as was I.

"Lady Charlesbury will be with us shortly," he said, looking at his watch. "I suggest, gentlemen, that you join me for dinner. During the dinner and afterwards there will be two or three hours of free time to converse about business or whatever. May I add that there is a library, skittles, a billiard room and a smoking room here at your disposal. I ask you to utilize them at your discretion as with everything I possess here. I leave you complete freedom as to breakfast and lunch. And this is true also of dinner. But I know how valuable and fruitful is women's company for young Englishmen and therefore . . ." – he rose and indicated the door through which at that moment entered a slender, young, golden-haired woman escorted by another individual of the female sex, spare and sallow dressed all in black. "And therefore, Lady Charlesbury, I have the honor and the pleasure of introducing to you my future colleagues and, I hope, my friends, Mr. Dibble and Mr. de Mon de Rique."

"Miss Sutton," he said, addressing his wife's faded companion (later I discovered she was a distant relative and companion of Lady Charlesbury), "this is Mr. Dibble and Mr. de Mon de Rique. Please share with them your kindness and attention."

At dinner, which was both simple and refined, Lord Charlesbury revealed himself as a cordial host and a superb conversationalist. He inquired animatedly of political affairs, the latest journalistic and scientific news and the health of one or another public figures. By the way, as strange as it may seem, he appeared to be better informed on these subjects than either of us. In addition, his wine cellar turned out to be above praise.

From time to time I secretly glanced at Lady Charlesbury. She took hardly any part in the conversation, only lifting her dark lashes occasionally in the direction of a speaker. She was much younger, even very much younger, than her husband. Her pale face, untouched by any equatorial tan and distinguished by an unhealthy kind of beauty, was framed by thick golden hair, and she had dark, deep, serious, almost melancholy eyes. And all of her appearance, her attractive, very slim figure in white gauze and delicate white hands with long narrow fingers, was reminiscent of some rare and beautiful, but also perhaps poisonous and exotic flower grown without light in a moist dark conservatory.

But I also noticed that de Mon de Rique, who sat opposite me during the meal, often turned an emotional and meaningful glance from his beautiful eyes on our hostess, a glance which persisted perhaps, a half a second longer than propriety permitted. I found myself disliking him more and more: his soft well-groomed face and hands, his languid sweet eyes, which seemed to conceal something, his confident posture, movements, and tone of voice. In my male opinion he seemed repugnant, but I did not doubt for a moment that he possessed all the marks and attributes of an authentic, life-long, cruel, and indifferent conquerer of women's hearts.

After dinner when everyone had left for the salon and Mr. de Mon de Rique had asked permission to retire to the smoking room, I gave the case with the diamonds to Lord Charlesbury, saying:

"These are from Maas and Daniels in Amsterdam."

"You carried them with you?"

"Yes, sir."

"And you did well. These two stones are more valuable to me than all my laboratory."

He went to his study and returned with an eight-power glass. For a long time he carefully examined the diamonds under an electric lamp, and finally, returning them to the case, he said in a satisfied voice, although not without agitation,

"The polishing is above reproach. They are ideally precise. This evening I will check their curved surfaces with instruments employed to measure lenses. Tomorrow morning, Mr. Dibble, we shall fix them into place. Until ten o'clock I shall be occupied with your comrade, Mr. de Mon de Rique, showing him his future laboratory but at ten I ask you to wait for me in your quarters. I shall come for you. Ah, my dear Mr. Dibble, I feel that together we shall advance our project, one of the greatest enterprises ever undertaken by that noble creature, *Homo sapiens.*"

When he said this his eyes burned with a blue light and his hands stroked the lid of the case. And his wife continued to watch him with her deep, dark, fathomless eyes.

The next morning promptly at ten o'clock my doorbell rang and the smartly dressed Negro boy, bowing deeply, admitted Lord Charlesbury.

"You are ready, I'm pleased to see," said my patron in greeting. "I examined the things you brought yesterday and they all seem to be in excellent order. I thank you for your concern and diligence."

"Three-quarters of that honor, if not more, is due to Mr. Nideston, sir."

"Yes, a fine human being and a true friend," the nobleman said with a gracious smile. "But, now, if there is nothing to hinder you, shall we go to the laboratory?"

The laboratory turned out to be a massive round white building, something like a tower, crowned with the dome which had been the first thing to strike my eye when we emerged from the tunnel.

Wearing our coats we passed through a small anteroom lighted by a single electric lamp and then found ourselves in total darkness. But Lord Charlesbury flipped a switch near me and bright light in a moment flooded a huge round room with a regular hemispherical ceiling some forty feet above the floor. In the midst of the room rose something like a small glass room, which resembled those medical isolation rooms which have lately appeared at university clinics in operating rooms which provide the exceptional cleanliness and disinfected air required during long and complicated operations. From that glass chamber which contained strange equipment such as I had never seen before rose three solid copper cylinders. At a height of about twelve feet both of the cylinders split into three pipes of yet larger diameter; those, in turn, were divided into three and the upper ends of these final massive copper pipes touched the concave surface of the dome. A multitude of pressure gauges and levers, curved and straight steel shafts, valves, wiring, and hydraulic presses completed this extraordinary and, for me, absolutely stunning laboratory. Steep circular staircases, iron columns and beams, narrow catwalks with slender hand rails which crossed high above me, hanging electric lamps, a host of thick pendant fiber hoses and long copper pipes – all of this was wound together, fatiguing the eye and giving the impression of a chaos.

Surmising my state of mind, Lord Charlesbury said calmly:

"When a person for the first time sees what is for him a strange mechanism, such as the workings of a watch or a sewing machine, he at first throws up his hands in despair at their complexity. When I, for the first time, saw the disassembled parts of a bicycle, it seemed to me that even the most ingenious mechanic in the world could not assemble them. But a week later I myself put them together and then disassembled them, astonished at the simplicity of its construction. Please, listen to my explanations patiently. If at first you do not understand, do not hesitate to ask me as many questions as you wish. This will give me only pleasure.

"Thus, there are twenty-seven closely placed openings in the roof. And in these openings are inserted cylinders which you see high above you which emerge into the open air through doubly-concave lenses of great power and exceptional clarity. Perhaps you now understand the scheme. We collect the sun's rays in foci and then, thanks to a whole series of mirrors and optic lenses made according to my plans and calculations, we conduct them, at times concentrating them and at other times dispersing them, through a whole system of pipes until the lowest pipes release concentrated sunlight here under the insulated cover into this very narrow and strong cylinder made of vanadium steel in which there is a whole system of pistons equipped with shutters, something like in a camera, which allow absolutely no light to enter when they are closed. Finally to the free end of this major cylinder with its internal closures I attach in a vacuum a vessel in the shape of a retort in the throat of which there are also several valves. When it is necessary I can open these closures and then insert a threaded stopper into the neck of the retort, unfasten the vessel from the end of the cylinder and then I have a superb means of storing compressed solar emanations."

"This means that Hook and Euler and Young . . . ?"

"Yes," Lord Charlesbury interrupted me. "They, and Fresnel, and Cauchy, and Malus, and Huygens and even the great Arago – they were all wrong when they perceived the phenomenon of light as one of the elements of the earth's atmosphere. I will prove this to you in ten minutes in the most striking fashion. Only the wise old Descartes and the genius of geniuses, the divine Newton, were right. The words of Biot and Brewster have only sustained and confirmed my experiments, but this was only much after I began them. Yes! Now it is clear to me and it will be shortly to you also that sunlight is a dense stream of very small resilient bodies, like tiny balls, which with terrible force and energy move through space, transfixing in their course the mass of the earth's atmosphere . . . But we will talk about theory later. Now, to be methodical, I will demonstrate the procedures which you must perform every day. Let us go outside."

We left the laboratory, climbed a circular staircase almost to the roof of the dome and found ourselves on a bright open gallery which circled the entire spherical roof in a spiral and a half.

"You need not struggle to open in turn all the covers which protect the delicate lenses from dust, snow, hail, and birds," said Lord Charlesbury. "All the more so that even a very strong man could not do that. Simply pull this lever toward yourself, and all twenty-seven shutters will turn their fiber rings in identical circular grooves in a counter-clockwise direction, as though they were all being unscrewed. Now the covers are free of pressure. You will now press that foot pedal. Watch!"

Click! And twenty-seven covers, metal surfaces resounding, instantly opened outward revealing glass sparkling in the sunlight.

"Every morning, Mr. Dibble," the scientist went on, "you are to uncover the lenses and carefully wipe them off with a clean chamois. Observe how this is done."

And he, like an experienced workman, rapidly, carefully, almost affectionately wiped all the glasses with a bit of chamois wrapped in cigarette paper which he brought out of his pocket.

"Now, let us go back down," he went on. "I will show you your other responsibilities."

Below in the laboratory he continued his explanations:

"Then you are 'to catch the sun.' To do this, every day at noon check these two chronometers against the sun. By the way, I checked them myself yesterday. The method is, of course, known to you. Note the time. Take the average time of the two chronometers: 10 hours, 31 minutes, 10 seconds. Here are three curving levers: the largest marks the hour, the middle one is for minutes, the smallest for seconds. Note: I turn the large circle until the hand of the indicator shows ten o'clock. Ready. I place the middle lever a little forward to 36 minutes. So. I move the little lever – that is my own favorite – forward to 50 seconds. Now place this plug in the socket. You can hear how the gears are whining and grinding below you. That is a clock device beginning to move which will rotate the entire laboratory and its dome, instruments, lenses and the two of us to follow the movement of the sun. Observe the chronometers and you will see that we are approaching 10:30. Five seconds more. Now. Can you hear how the clock mechanism has changed its sound? Those are the minute gears beginning to turn. A few seconds more . . . Watch! One minute more! Now there's a new sound, which neatly and precisely is marking off the seconds. That's all. The sun has now been captured. But it's not over yet.

Because of its bulkiness and quite understandable crudity the clock mechanism cannot be especially accurate. Therefore as often as possible check this dial which indicates its movement. Here are the hours, minutes, and seconds; here is the regulator – forward, back. On the basis of the chronometers which are extraordinarily precise you will be able, as often as it is possible, to correct the revolution of the laboratory to a tenth of a second.

"Now we have caught the sun. But that is not all we must do. The light has to pass through a vacuum, otherwise it would become heated and melt all our equipment. And therefore when it is in our closed vessels from which all the air has been pumped the light is almost as cold as when it was passing through the endless regions of space outside the earth's atmosphere. When you look closely you can see a control button for an electromagnetic coil. In each of the cylinders is a stopper around which is a steel band circled by a wire. I press the control button and the current flows into the wire. All the bands are instantly affected and the stoppers leave their seats. Now I pull a bronze lever which starts a vacuum pump, one line of which is connected to each of the cylinders. The finest dust, microscopic flecks of matter, are removed with the air. Look at the gauge F on which is a red line indicating the pressure limit. Listen through an acoustic tube leading into the pump; the hissing has ceased. The gauge now crosses the red line. Disconnect the electricity by pressing the same control button a second time; the steel bands no longer are activated. The stoppers in response to the attraction of the vacuum close tightly in their conic seats. Now the light is passing through an almost absolute vacuum. But that is not adequate for the precision our work requires. We can transform all our laboratory into a giant vacuum chamber; in time we will be working in underwater diving equipment. Air will flow through the fiber pipes and the waste air systematically removed to the outside. In the meantime the air will be pulled out of the laboratory by powerful pumps. Do you understand? You will be in the position of a diver with the only difference being that you will have a container with compressed gas on your back: in case of an accident, the equipment's malfunction, a leak in the hoses, or anything else, open a small valve on your helmet and you will have enough air to breathe for a quarter of an hour. You must only keep your wits about you and you will leave the laboratory fresh and smiling, like a blooming rose.

"We still must check very carefully the installation of the piping. All of the pipes are firmly joined but at places some triple-unions allow an infinitesimal amount of play, two or three millimeters, and this might prove to be a problem. There are thirteen such points and you must check them about three times a day, working downward. Therefore, let us climb these stairs."

We mounted narrow staircases and unsteady platforms to the very top of the dome. The teacher went ahead with a youthful step while I followed, not without effort, because this was new to me. At the union of the first three pipes he showed me a small cover which he opened with one turn of the hand and lifted back so that it was held precisely vertical by springs. Its reverse side was a rigid, silver, finely polished mirror with various incisions and numbers on its edge. Three parallel gold bands, thin, like telescopic hairs, nearly touching each other, cut the smooth surface of the mirror.

"This is a small well through which we covertly follow the flow of the light. The three bands are reflections from three internal mirrors. Combine them into one. No, you do it yourself. Here you see three minute screws to adjust the positions of the lenses. Here is a very strong magnifying glass. Combine the three light bands into one but in such a manner that the total ray of light falls on zero. It is not difficult to do. You will shortly be able to carry it out in one minute."

In fact, the mechanism was very compliant and three minutes later, barely touching the sensitive screws I combined the light bands into one sharp line which was almost painful to look at, and then I introduced it into a narrow incision at zero. Then I closed the cover and screwed it down. I adjusted the remaining twelve control wells alone without Lord Charlesbury's help. Every time I performed this operation it went more smoothly. But by the time we reached the second level of the laboratory my eyes so ached from the bright light that involuntarily the tears streamed down my face.

"Put on goggles. Here they are," said my chief, handing me a case.

But I could not approach the final cylinder which we were to adjust in its location inside the isolation chamber. My eyes would not accept the glare.

"Take some darker glasses," said Lord Charlesbury. "I have them in ten shades. Today we will attach the lenses which you brought yesterday to the main cylinder and then direct observation will be three times as difficult. Good. That's right. Now I am activating an internal piston. I'm opening the valve of a hydraulic pump. I'm also opening a valve with liquid carbon dioxide. Now the temperature inside the cylinder has reached 150 degrees centigrade and the pressure is equal to 20 atmospheres; the latter is indicated by a gauge, the former by a Witkowski thermometer which I have improved. The following is now underway in the cylinder: light is passing through it in a dense vertical stream of blinding brightness approximately the diameter of a pencil. The valve actuated by an electric current is opening and closing its shutter in one one-thousandth of a second. The valve sends the light on through a small, highly convex lens. From there the stream of light emerges yet denser, narrower, and brighter. There are five such valves and lenses in each cylinder. Under the compression of the last, smallest and most powerful piston, a needle-thin stream of light flows into the vessel, passing through three valves in series.

"That is the basis of my liquid sunlight collector," my teacher said triumphantly. "Now, in order that there can be no doubts at all, we will conduct an experiment. Press control button A. You have just stopped the movement of the valve. Lift that bronze lever. Now you have closed the interior covers of the collecting glasses in the building's dome. Turn the red valve as far as it will go, and lower handle C. The pressure is now released and the supply of carbon dioxide cut off. Now you must close the vessel. This is done by ten turns of that small rounded lever. Everything is now complete, my friend. Notice how I disconnect the receiver vessel from the cylinder. See, I have it in my hands now; it weighs no more than twenty pounds. Its internal shutters are controlled by minute screws on the exterior of the cylinder. I am now opening wide the first and largest shutter. Then the intermediate one. The final shutter I will open only one-half a micron. But, first, go and turn off the electric lights."

I obeyed and the room filled with impenetrable darkness.

"Now watch!" I heard Lord Charlesbury's voice from the other end of the laboratory. "I'm opening it!"

An extraordinary golden light, delicate, radiant, transparent, suddenly flooded the room, softly but clearly outlining its walls, gleaming equipment, and the figure of my teacher himself. And, at the same moment, I felt on my face and hands something like a warm breath of air. This phenomenon lasted not more than a second or a second and a half. Then heavy darkness concealed everything from my eyes.

"Lights, please!" exclaimed Lord Charlesbury and once more I saw him emerging from the door of the glass chamber. His face was pale, but illuminated by joy and pride.

"Those were only the first steps, a schoolboy's trials, the first seeds," he said exultantly. "That was not sunlight condensed into a gas, but only a compressed weightless substance. For months I have compressed sunlight in my containers, but not one of them has become heavier by the weight of a human hair. You saw that marvelous, steady, caressing light. Now do you believe in my project?"

"Yes," I answered heatedly, with profound conviction. "I believe in it and I bow before an invention of great genius."

"But let's go on. Still further on! We will lower the temperature inside the cylinder to minus 275 degrees centigrade, to absolute zero. We will raise the hydraulic pressure to thousands, twenty, thirty thousand times the earth's atmosphere. We will replace our eight-inch light collectors with powerful fifty-inch models. We will melt pounds of diamonds by a technique I have developed and pour them into lenses to the specifications we require and place them in our instruments . . . ! Perhaps I will not live to see the time when men will compress the sun's rays into a liquid form, but I believe and I feel that I will compress them to the density of a gas. I only want to see the hand on an electric scale move even one millimeter to the left – and I will be boundlessly happy.

"But time is passing. Let us lunch and then before dinner we will concern ourselves with the installation of our new diamond lenses. Beginning tomorrow we will work together. For a week you will be with me as an ordinary worker, as a simple, obedient helper. A week from now we will exchange roles. The third week I will give you a helper, to whom in my presence you will teach all the procedures with the instruments. Then I will give you complete freedom. I trust you," he said briskly with a captivating, charming smile and reached out to shake my hand.

I remember very well that evening and dinner with Lord Charlesbury. Lady Charlesbury was in a red silk dress and her red mouth against her pale, slightly weary face glowed like a purple flower, like an incandescent ember. De Mon de Rique, whom I saw at dinner for the first time that day, was alert, handsome, and elegant, as I had never seen him either before or afterwards, while I felt enervated and overwhelmed by the flood of impressions I had received during the day. At first I thought that he had spent the day at his customary, simple labors, mostly observations. But it was not I, but Lady Charlesbury who first drew our attention to the fact that the electrician's left hand was bandaged to above the knuckles. De Mon de Rique modestly recounted how he had scraped his hand as he was climbing down a wall with an insufficiently tightened safety belt. That evening he dominated the conversation, but gently and with tact. He told about his journeys to Abyssinia where he prospected for gold in the mountain valleys on the verge of the Sahara, about lion hunting, the races at Epsom, fox hunting in the north of England, and about Oscar Wilde, then becoming fashionable and with whom he was personally acquainted. He had a surprising and probably too rare conversational trait, which, I will add, I have never noticed in anyone else. When he told a story he was extremely abstracted: he never spoke of himself nor in his own voice. But by some mysterious means his personality, remaining in the background, was illuminated, now in mild, now in heroic half-tones.

Now he was looking at Lady Charlesbury much less frequently than she at him. Only from time to time his caressing and languid eyes passed over her from under his long, lowered lashes. But she hardly took her grave and mysterious eyes away from him. Her gaze followed the movements of his hands and head, his mouth and eyes. Strange! That evening she reminded me of a child's toy: a tin fish or a duck with a bit of iron in its mouth which involuntarily, obediently follows after a magnetized stick which compels it from a distance. Frequently in alarm I observed the expression on my host's face. But he was serenely high-spirited and composed.

After dinner when de Mon de Rique asked permission to smoke, Lady Charlesbury herself offered to play billiards with him. They left while the host and I made our way into his study.

"How about a game of chess," he said. "Do you play?"

"Indifferently, but always with pleasure."

"And do you know what else has happened? Let us have a glass of some lively wine."

He pressed a button.

"What is the occasion?" I asked.

"You already have guessed. Because, it seems to me, I have found in you an assistant, and, if fate wills it, someone to carry on my work."

"Oh, sir!"

"One minute. What drink would you prefer?"

"I'm ashamed to admit that I'm no expert in such matters."

"Very well, in such a case I will name four drinks which I love, and a fifth which I detest. Bordeaux wines, port, Scotch ale, and water. But I cannot bear champagne. And, therefore, let us drink Chateau-la-Rose. My dear Sambo," he commanded the butler who stood near, waiting, "a bottle of Chateau-la-Rose."

Lord Charlesbury, to my surprise, played rather poorly. I quickly checkmated his king. After our first game we abandoned play and once more spoke of my morning's impressions.

"Listen, my dear Dibble," said Lord Charlesbury, laying his little, warm and energetic hand on my knuckles. "You have undoubtedly many times heard that one may obtain an authentic and accurate opinion of a man at first glance. I believe that to be a grave error. Many times I have seen men with the faces of convicts, cheats, or perjurors – and by the way, you will meet your assistant in a few days – and they turned out to be honest, faithful in friendship, and attentive, courteous gentlemen. On the other hand, very rarely, a generous, charming face, adorned with gray hair and the flush of age, and honorable speech conceals, as it becomes clear, such a villain that any London hooligan is by comparison an innocent lamb with a pink ribbon round his neck. Now may I ask you to help me to solve a problem? Mr. de Mon de Rique so far has not been involved in any way in the completion of my scientific work. On his mother's side he is distantly related to me. Mr. Nideston, who has known him from childhood, informed me that de Mon de Rique was in a very difficult position (only not in the material sense). I immediately offered him a position which he accepted with a joy that testified to his precarious situation. I have heard tales about him, but I give no credence to rumors and gossip. He made absolutely no impression upon me when first we met. Perhaps this was because I have never met a person such as he. But for some reason it also seems to me that I have met millions of such men. Today I carefully observed him at work. I believe him to be clever, knowing, ingenious and industrious. In addition, he is cultured and can conduct himself well in any society, as it seems to me, and moreover, he is energetic and intelligent. But in one respect I have my doubts. Tell me frankly, dear Mr. Dibble, your opinion of him."

This unexpected and tactless question agitated and distressed me; to tell the truth I did not expect it at all.

"But, sir, I have none. Indeed, I don't know him as well as you and Mr. Nideston. I saw him for the first time on board the steamship *Southern Cross*, and during our journey we met and talked very rarely. And I must tell you that I suffered from seasickness the entire journey. But from our few meetings and conversations I have obtained approximately the same impression as you, sir: knowing, ingenious, energetic, eloquent, well-read and . . . a peculiar and perhaps very rare mixture, very cold-hearted but with a fervent imagination."

"You are right, Mr. Dibble, right. Beautifully said. My dear Mr. Sambo, bring another bottle of wine and then you may go. Thank you. I hardly expected any other evaluation from you. But I will return to my difficulty: should I inform him or not of what you witnessed today?

Just imagine that a year or two will pass, perhaps less, and our dandy, our Adonis, our admirer of women, will suddenly become bored with his life on this God-forsaken volcano. I think that in such a case he would not come to me for my blessing and approval. Simply one beautiful morning he will pack his things and leave. The fact that I would be left without an assistant and a very valuable assistant at that is of secondary importance, but I cannot assure you that after he has arrived in the Old World he will not turn out to be loose-tongued, perhaps very innocently."

"Are you really concerned about this, sir?"

"I tell you frankly – I fear it very much! I am afraid of the notoriety, the publicity, and the invasion of reporters. I am afraid that some influential but talentless scientific reviewer who will base his attitude on a rejection of all new ideas and audacious conjectures will interpret my scheme to the public as a meaningless fantasy, the ravings of a madman. Finally, I am afraid most of all that some hungry upstart, a greedy failure, a talentless ignoramus will misunderstand my idea, and state, as has happened a thousand times, that it is his, thereby belittling, abusing and sullying something I have brought into the world in anguish and joy. Do you understand me, Mr. Dibble?"

"Completely, sir."

"If this happens, then I and my idea will perish. But what does this little 'I' mean when compared to my idea? I am deeply convinced that on the evening when in one of the huge London halls I order the lights extinguished and blind a selected audience of ten thousand with a stream of sunshine which will make flowers open and cause the birds to sing – that evening I will receive a million pounds for my cause. But, a trifle, an accident, an insignificant mistake, as I said, could destroy in a fateful manner the most selfless and grandiose idea. Therefore, I ask your opinion, should I trust Mr. de Mon de Rique or leave him in false and evasive ignorance? This is a dilemma which I cannot avoid without help. On one hand the possibility of a worldwide scandal and failure, and on the other a sure road for arousing a feeling of anger and revenge in a man thanks to my lack of trust in him. And so, Mr. Dibble?"

I wanted to give him the direct answer: "Tomorrow send this Narcissus with all honors back into the world and you can rest in peace." Now I regret deeply that a foolish sense of delicacy prevented me from giving that advice. Instead of saying this, I took on an air of cool correctness and answered:

"I hope you will not be angry with me, sir, if I decline to pass judgment on such a difficult matter."

Lord Charlesbury looked directly at me, shook his head sadly and said with a mirthless smile:

"Let's finish our wine and visit the billiard room. I would like to smoke a cigar."

In the billiard room we saw the following picture. De Mon de Rique was bent over the billiard table telling some lively tale, while Lady Charlesbury, leaning against the mantelpiece, laughed loudly. This struck me more than if I had seen her weeping. Lord Charlesbury inquired into the cause of the merriment, and when de Mon de Rique repeated his story about a certain vain aristocrat who acquired a tame leopard in a desire to pass himself off as an original and then was compelled to sit three hours in his room with the animal because he was so afraid of it, my patron laughed loud and long, like a child . . .

Everything in the world is inter-related in the strangest manner.

That evening in some inscrutable fashion combined the beginnings, the engagement and the tragic denouement of our lives.

The first two days of my existence at Cayambe I remember very well, but as for the rest, the closer they come to the end, the hazier they become. And therefore, with more reason I turn for help to my note-book. The seawater erased the first and last pages and in part the inter-vening pages also. But some of it, with difficulty, I can restore. Thus:

December 11. Today I rode on muleback with Lord Charlesbury into Quito to obtain copper wire. It happened that the subject of the mate-rial support of our project arose (it was not merely the result of my idle curiosity). Lord Charlesbury, who, it seemed to me, had long given me his full confidence, suddenly turned quickly in his saddle to face me and asked unexpectedly:

"You know Mr. Nideston?"

"Certainly, sir."

"A fine man, is he not so?"

"An excellent man."

"And is it not true, in the world, dry and something of a formalist?"

"Yes, sir. But he is also capable of great enthusiasm and even of high emotion."

"You are observant, Mr. Dibble," my mentor answered. "You should know that for fifteen years he has believed in me and my idea as stubbornly as a Mohammedan believes in his Kaaba. You know he is a London solicitor. He not only does not take any pay for my commissions, but long ago he offered to place his own private fortune at my disposal if I so wished. I am deeply convinced that he is the only eccentric left in old England. Therefore let us be of good cheer."

December 12. Today Lord Charlesbury for the first time showed me the force which drives the timing mechanism which turns the laboratory with the sun. It is obvious, simple, and ingenious. Down the slope of the extinct volcano a dressed basalt block weighing thirty-five tons suspended by a steel cable almost as thick as a man's leg moves on almost vertical rails. This weight puts the mechanism into motion. It functions exactly for eight hours and early in the morning an old blind mule raises this counterweight with the help of another cable and a system of blocks without any great effort.

December 20. Today I sat with Lord Charlesbury after dinner in the hothouse sunk in the heady odor of narcissi, pomegranates and tuberoses. Recently my patron has been very withdrawn and his eyes seemingly have begun to lose their beautiful youthful brightness. I take this to be the result of fatigue because we are working very hard now. I am sure that he has guessed nothing about *it*. He suddenly changed the subject of the conversation, as is his wont:

"Our work is the most selfless and honorable on earth. To think about the happiness of one's children or grandchildren is both natural and egotistical. But you and I are thinking of the lives and happiness of humanity so far in the future that they will not know of us nor of our poets, kings, or conquerers, about our language and religion, about our national borders or even the names of our countries. 'Not for those who are near but those who come later!' Isn't that what our most popular philosopher has said? I am willing to give all my strength to this unselfish and pure service to the distant future."

January 3. I went to Quito today to accept a shipment from London. My relationship with Mr. de Mon de Rique has become cold, almost inimical.

February. Today we completed the work of connecting all our piping with the containers of chilling solutions. A combination of ice and salt gives minus 21 degrees centigrade, dry ice and ether – minus 80 degrees, hydrogen – minus 118 degrees, vaporized dry ice – minus 130 degrees, and it seems that we will be able to reduce the atmospheric pressure indefinitely.

April. My assistant continues to arouse my interest. He is some kind of a Slav. A Russian, or a Pole, and, so it seems, an anarchist. He is intelligent and speaks English well, but it seems he prefers not to speak any language at all, but to remain silent. Here is his appearance: he is tall, thin, slightly round-shouldered; his hair is straight and long and falls onto his face in such a manner that his forehead takes the shape of a trapezoid, the narrow end up; he has a tilted nose with great open hairy, but delicate nostrils. His eyes are clear, gray, and boundlessly impertinent. He hears and understands everything that we say about the happiness of future generations and often smiles with a benevolent but contemptuous smile, which reminds me of the expression on the face of a large old bulldog watching a pack of yelping toy terriers. But his attitude toward my mentor – and this I not only know, but feel to the marrow of my bones – is one of boundless adoration. My colleague's attitude, de Mon de Rique's attitude, is quite different. He often speaks to the teacher about the idea of liquid sunshine with such false enthusiasm that I blush for shame and I fear that the technician is mocking our patron. And he is not interested in him at all as a man, and in the most discourteous manner and in the presence of his wife disparages his position as husband and master of the house, although this is unwise and contrary to common sense, the result of his perverted temperament and, perhaps, out of jealousy.

May. Let us hail the names of three talented Poles – Wrublewski, Olszewski, and Witkowski – and the man who completed their work, Dewar. Today we transformed helium into a liquid, and instantly reducing the pressure, reached a temperature of minus 272 degrees centigrade in our major cylinder and the dial on the electric scales for the first time moved, not one, but *five whole millimeters*. Silently, in solitude, I bow before you, my dear preceptor and teacher.

June 26. Apparently de Mon de Rique has come to believe in liquid sunshine – and now without sickening coyness and forced delight. At least today at dinner he made a remarkable statement. He said that in his opinion liquid sunshine would have a brilliant future as an explosive substance in mines or projectiles.

I objected, it is true, rather violently, in German: "You sound like a Prussian lieutenant."

But Lord Charlesbury responded succinctly and in a conciliatory tone: "Our dreams are not of destruction, but of creation."

June 27. I am writing in great agitation, my hands trembling. I worked late this evening in the laboratory, until two o'clock. It was a matter of urgency to install a cooling unit. As I was returning to my quarters the moon shone brightly. I was wearing warm sealskin boots and my footsteps on the frozen path could not be heard. My route lay in shadow. Reaching my door I stopped when I heard voices.

"Come in, Mary dear, for God's sake, come in for only a minute. What are you always afraid of? And don't you always discover that there's no reason to be afraid?"

And then I saw them both in the bright light of the southern moon. He had his arm around her waist, and her head lay passively on his shoulder. Oh, how beautiful they were at that moment!

"But your friend . . ." Lady Charlesbury said timorously.

"What kind of a friend is he?" de Mon de Rique laughed heedlessly. "He's only a boring and sentimental drudge who goes to bed every night at ten o'clock in order to arise at six. Mary, please come in, I beg you."

And both of them, their arms around each other, went onto the porch illuminated by the blue light of the moon and disappeared in an open door.

June 28. Evening. This morning I went to see Mr. de Mon de Rique, refused his proffered hand, would not sit down on the chair he offered and said quietly:

"I must tell you what I think of you, sir. I believe that you, sir, in a situation where we should work together cheerfully and selflessly for the sake of humanity, are conducting yourself in a most unworthy and shameful manner. Last night at two o'clock I saw you when you entered your quarters."

"Were you spying, you scoundrel?" shouted de Mon de Rique, and his eyes gleamed with a violet light, like a cat at night.

"No, I found myself in an impossible situation. I did not speak out, not because I did not want to cause you pain, but because I did not want to harm another person. But this gives me more reason than ever to tell you to your face that you, sir, are a villain and a sneak."

"You will pay for that with your blood with a weapon in your hands," shouted de Mon de Rique, leaping to his feet.

"No," I answered firmly. "First of all, we have no reason to fight except that I called you a villain, but not in the presence of witnesses, and secondly, because I am engaged in a great work of world-wide importance and I do not want to abandon it thanks to your ridiculous bullet until it is completed. Thirdly, would it not be easiest of all for you to pack your bags, mount the first mule available, leave for Quito, and then by your previous route return to hospitable England? Or did you dishonor someone or steal money there, Mr. Scoundrel?"

He leaped to the table and seized a leather whip which lay there.

"I'll kill you like a dog!" he roared.

But I remembered my old boxing skills. Acting quickly, I feinted with my left hand, and then hit him with my right below his chin. He cried out, spun like a top, and blood rushed out of his nose.

I walked out.

June 29. "Why is it that I haven't seen Mr. de Mon de Rique today?" Lord Charlesbury asked unexpectedly.

"It seems he isn't well," I answered, avoiding his eyes.

We were sitting together on the northern slope of the volcano. It was nine in the evening and the moon had not yet risen. Near us stood two porters and my mysterious helper, Peter. Against the quiet dark blue of the sky the slender electric lines, which we had installed that day, could hardly be seen. And on a great heap of stones rested receiver no. 6, firmly braced by basalt boulders, ready any second to open its shutters.

"Prepare the fuse," ordered Lord Charlesbury. "Roll the spool down the hill, I'm too tired and excited; give me your hand, help me down. This is good. And there is no risk of being blinded. Think on it, my dear Dibble, think on it, my dear boy, now the two of us, in the name of glory and the happiness of future mankind, will light all the world with sunshine concentrated in gaseous form. Ready! Light the fuse."

The fiery snake of the lighted fuse ran up the hill and disappeared over the edge of the deep defile in which we sat. Listening carefully I could hear the instantaneous click of contacts closing and the penetrating roar of motors. According to our calculations gaseous sunshine should issue from the containers next to the explosion sites at a rate of approximately six thousand feet per second. At that moment above our heads there was a flash of blinding sunlight, at which the trees below rustled, clouds turned pink in the sky, distant roofs and the windows of houses in Quito gleamed brightly, and the cocks in the village nearby began crowing.

When the light faded as quickly as it had appeared, my teacher pressed the button on a stop watch, turned his flashlight on it, and said:

"It burned for one minute and eleven seconds. This is a genuine triumph, Mr. Dibble. I assure you that within a year we will be able to fill immense reservoirs with heavy liquid golden sunshine, like mercury, and compel it to provide light, heat and drive all our machinery."

When we returned home that night about midnight we discovered that in our absence Lady Charlesbury and Mr. de Mon de Rique in the daylight hours soon after our departure had seemingly gone for a walk but then on mules saddled beforehand had left for the city of Quito below.

Lord Charlesbury remained true to himself. He said without bitterness, but sadly and in pain:

"Why didn't they say anything to me, why this deceit? Didn't I see that they loved each other? I would not have hindered them."

At this point my notes end, and at that they were so damaged by water that I could restore them only with the greatest difficulty and I cannot guarantee their accuracy. Nor can I in the future guarantee the reliability of my memory. But this is always the case: the closer I draw to the final resolution the more confused my recollections become.

For about twenty-five days we worked steadily in the laboratory filling more and more containers with solar gas. During this period we invented ingenious valves for our solar containers. We equipped each of them with a clock mechanism with a simple face, as on an alarm clock. Adjusting the dials of three cylinders we could obtain light over any given period of time, and lengthen the period of its combustion and its intensity from a dim half-hour of glimmer to an instantaneous explosion – depending on the time set. We worked without inspiration, almost unwillingly, but I must admit that this was the most productive time of my stay on Cayambe. But it all ended abruptly, fantastically, and horribly.

Once, early in August, Lord Charlesbury, even more tired and aged than usual, came to visit me in the laboratory; he said to me calmly and with distaste:

"My dear friend, I feel that my death is not far away, and old convictions are making themselves heard. I want to die and be buried in England. I will leave you some money, these buildings, the equipment, the land and this laboratory. The money, on the basis of what I have spent, should be ample for two or three years. You are younger and more active than I and perhaps you will obtain some results for your labors. Our dear Mr. Nideston would give his support at any time. Please think on it."

This man had become dearer to me than my father, mother, brother, wife or sister. And therefore I answered with deep assurance:

"Dear sir, I would not leave you for one minute."

He embraced me and kissed me on my forehead.

The next day he summoned all the workers and paying them two years in advance said that his work on Cayambe had come to an end and that day they were to leave Cayambe for the valley below.

They left carefree and ungrateful, anticipating the sweet proximity of drunkenness and dissipation in the innumerable taverns which swarmed in the city of Quito. Only my assistant, the silent Slav – an Albanian or a Siberian – tarried near the master. "I will stay with you as long as you or I am alive," he said. But Lord Charlesbury looked at him firmly, almost sternly and said:

"I am leaving for Europe, Mr. Peter."

"Then I will go with you."

"But you know what awaits you there, Mr. Peter."

"I know. A rope. But nonetheless I will not abandon you. I have always laughed in my heart at your sentimental concerns for men in the millions of years to come, but when I came to know you better I also learned that the more insignificant is mankind the more precious is man, and therefore I have stayed with you, like an old, homeless, embittered, hungry, and mangy dog turns to the first hand that sincerely caresses it. And therefore I will stay with you. That is all."

With astonishment and deep feeling I turned my eyes to this man whom I had always thought to be incapable of elevated feelings. But my teacher said to him softly and with authority:

"No, you must leave. Right now. I value your friendship and your tireless labors. But I'm leaving for my native land to die and the possibility that you might suffer would only darken my departure from this world. Be a man, Peter. Take this money, embrace me in farewell, and let us part."

I saw how they embraced and how blunt Peter kissed the hand of Lord Charlesbury several times and then left us, not turning back, almost at a run and disappeared around a nearby building.

I looked at my teacher: covering his face with his hands he was weeping . . .

Three days later we left on the old *Gonzalez* from Guayaquil for Panama. The sea was rough, but we had a following wind and to help out the small engine the captain had sails spread. Lord Charlesbury and I never left our cabins. I was seriously concerned about his condition and there were even times when I feared he was losing his mind. I observed him with helpless pity. I was especially troubled by the manner in which he invariably referred after every two or three phrases to container no.216 which we had left behind on Cayambe, and every time he referred to it, he would say through tight lips: "Did I forget, how could I forget?" but then his speech would become melancholy and abstracted.

"Do not think," he said, "that a petty personal tragedy forced me to abandon my work and the persistent searches and inspirations which I have patiently worked out during the course of my conscious life. But circumstances jarred my thoughts. Recently I have much altered my ideas and judgments, but only on a different plane than before. If only you knew how difficult it has been to alter my view of life at the age of sixty-five. I have come to believe, or, more correctly, to feel, that the future of mankind is not worth our concern or our selfless work. Mankind, growing more degenerate every day, is becoming flabbier, more decadent, and hard-hearted. Society is falling under the power of the cruelest despotism in the world – capital. Trusts, manipulating the supply of meat, kerosene, and sugar, are creating a generation of fabulous millionaires and next to them millions of hungry unemployed thieves and murderers. And so it will be forever. And my idea of prolonging the sun's life for the earth will become the property of a handful of villains who will control it or employ my liquid sunshine in shells or bombs of unheard of power . . . No, I do not want that . . . Ah, my God! that container! How could I forget! How could I!" and Lord Charlesbury clapped his hands to his head.

"What troubles you, my dear teacher?" I asked.

"You see, kind Henry, . . . I fear that I have made a small but fateful mistake . . ."

But I heard no more. Suddenly in the east flashed an enormous golden flame. In a moment the sky and the sea were all agleam. Then followed a deafening roar and a burning whirlwind threw me to the deck.

I lost consciousness and revived only when I heard my teacher's voice above me.

"What?" asked Lord Charlesbury. "Are you blind?"

"Yes, I can see nothing, except rainbow-colored circles before my eyes. Was it some kind of a catastrophe, Professor? Why did you do it or allow it to happen? Didn't you foresee it?"

But he softly laid his beautiful little white hand on my shoulder and said in a deep and gentle voice (and from that touch and his confident tone I immediately was calmed):

"Don't you believe me? Wait a moment, close your eyes tightly and cover them with the palm of your right hand, and hold it there until I stop talking or until you catch a glimpse of light; then, before you open your eyes, put on these glasses which I am placing in your left hand. They are very dark. Listen to me. It seems that you have come to know me better in a brief time than anyone else close to me. It was only for your sake, my dear friend, that I did not take on my conscience a cruel and pointless experiment which might have brought death to tens of thousands of people. But what difference would the existence of these dissolute blacks, drunken Indians, and degenerate Spaniards have made? If the Republic of Ecuador with its intrigues, mercenary attitudes and revolutions were instantly transformed into a great door to Hell there would be no loss to science, the arts, or history. I am only a little sorry for my intelligent, patient, and affectionate mules. I will tell you candidly that I would have not hesitated for a second to sacrifice you and millions of lives to the triumph of my idea, if only I were convinced of its significance, but as I said only three minutes ago I have become totally disillusioned about the future generations' ability to love, to be happy and to sacrifice themselves. Do you think I could take revenge on a tiny part of humanity for my great philosophical error? But there is one thing for which I cannot forgive myself: that was a purely technical mistake, a mistake which could have been made by any workman. I am like a craftsman who has worked for twenty years with a complicated machine, and on the next day falls into melancholy over his family affairs, forgets his work, ignores the rhythm of his machine so that a belt parts and kills several unthinking workmen. You see, I have been tormented by the idea that thanks to my forgetfulness for the first time in twenty years I neglected to shut down the controls on container no.216 and left it set at full power. And that realization, like a nightmare, pursued me on board this ship. And I was right. The container exploded and as a result the other storage units also. Once more it was my mistake. Rather than storing such great amounts of liquid sunshine I should have conducted preliminary experiments, it is true at the risk of my life, on the explosive capabilities of compressed light. Now, look in this direction," and he gently but firmly turned my head toward the east. "Remove your hand and then slowly, slowly open your eyes."

At that moment with extraordinary clarity, the way, they say, that occurs in the seconds before death, I saw a smoking red glow to the east, now contracting, now expanding, the steamship's listing deck, waves lashing over the railings, an angry, bloody sea and dark purple clouds in the sky and a beautiful calm face with a gray, silken beard and eyes which shone like mournful stars. A stifling hot wind blew from the shore.

"A fire?" I asked, turning slowly, as though in a dream, to face the south. There, above Cayambe's summit, stood a thick smoky column of fire cut by rapid flashes of lightning.

"No, that is the eruption of our good old volcano. The exploding liquid sunshine has stirred it into life. You must agree that it has enormous power! And to think it was all in vain."

I understood nothing . . . My head was spinning. And then I heard a strange voice near me, both gentle like a mother's voice and commanding like that of a dictator.

"Sit on this bale and do everything faithfully as I tell you. Here is a life belt, put it on and fasten it securely under your arms, but do not restrict your breathing; here is a flask of brandy which you are to place in your left chest pocket along with three bars of chocolate, and here is a waterproof envelope with money and letters. In a moment the *Gonzalez* will be swamped by a terrible wave, such as has rarely been seen since the time of the flood. Lie down on the ship's starboard side. That is so. Place your legs and arms around this railing. Very good. Your head should be behind this steel plate, which will prevent you from becoming deaf from the shock. When you feel the wave hitting the deck, hold your breath for twenty seconds and then throw yourself free, and may God help you! This is all I can wish and advise you. And if you are condemned to die so early and so stupidly . . . I would like to hear you forgive me. I would not say that to any other man, but I know you are an Englishman and a gentleman."

His words, said so calmly and with such dignity, aroused my own sense of self-control. I found enough strength to press his hand and answer calmly:

"You can believe, my dear teacher, that no pleasures in life could replace those happy hours which I spent working with you. I only want to know why you are taking no precautions for yourself?"

I can see him now, holding to a compass box, as the wind blew his clothes and his gray beard, so terrible against the red background of the erupting volcano. That second I noticed with surprise that the unbearably hot shore wind had ceased, but on the contrary a cold, gusty gale blew from the west and our craft nearly lay on its side.

"Oh!" exclaimed Lord Charlesbury indifferently, and waved his arm, "I have nothing to lose. I am alone in this world. I have only one tie, that is you, and you I have put into deadly peril from which you have only one chance in a million to escape. I have a fortune, but I do not know what to do with it," and here his voice expressed a melancholy and gentle irony, "except to disperse it to the poor of County Norfolk and thereby increase the number of parasites and supplicants. I have knowledge, but you can see that it too has failed. I have energy but I have no way to employ it now. Oh, no, I will not commit suicide; if I am not condemned to die this night, I will employ the rest of my life in some garden on a bit of land not far from London. But if death comes," he removed his hat and it was strange to see his blowing hair, tossing beard, and kind, melancholy eyes and to hear his voice resounding like an organ, "but if death comes I shall commit my body and my soul to God, may He forgive the errors of my weak human mind."

"Amen," I said.

He turned his back to the wind and lighted a cigar. His dark figure defined sharply against the purple sky was a fantastic, and magnificent, sight. I could smell the odor of his fine Havana cigar.

"Make ready. There is yet only a minute or two. Are you afraid?"

"No . . . But the crew and the other passengers! . . ."

"While you were unconscious I warned them. Now there is not a sober man nor a lifebelt on the ship. I have no fear for you, for you have the talisman on your finger. I had one, too, but I have lost it. Oh, hold on! Henry! . . .

I turned to the east and froze in horror. Toward our eggshell craft from the east roared an enormous wave as high as the Eiffel tower, black, with a rosy-white, frothing crest. Something crashed, shook . . . and it was as though the whole world fell onto the deck.

I lost consciousness once more and revived only several hours later on a little boat belonging to a fisherman who had rescued me. My damaged left hand was tied in a crude bandage and my head wrapped in rags. A month later, having recovered from my wounds and emotional shock I was on my way back to England.

This history of my strange adventure is complete. I must only add that I live modestly in the quietest part of London, needing nothing, thanks to the generosity of the late Lord Charlesbury. I occupy myself with the sciences and tutoring. Every Sunday Mr. Nideston and I alternate as hosts for dinner. We are bound by close ties of friendship, and our first toast is always to the memory of the great Lord Charlesbury.

H. Dibble

P.S. All the personal names in my tale are not authentic but invented by me for my purposes.

Greenslaves

FRANK HERBERT

Frank Herbert (1920–86) is the author of *Dune* (1965), the single most popular SF novel of the century, according to some published polls of readers. In response to that popularity he wrote a number of sequels in the 1970s and 1980s. Herbert was a journalist (he was proud to show a picture of the Army–McCarthy hearings with himself in the front row) and an articulate public speaker. His first major impact came in the 1950s with his impressive novel *The Dragon in the Sea* (1956), which is an intense psychological examination of a small crew enclosed together in a submarine; it forecast an international oil crisis, and Cold War-style submarine oil theft.

Herbert's fiction is often intellectual and discursive, but he was also concerned with dramatic storytelling. He was particularly fascinated by technology and the idea of progress, yet his stories are always grounded in a political and social awareness that made him especially relevant and popular in the 1960s and '70s.

One of his major themes was the evolution of intelligence, artificial or organic. He was influential in the founding of the ecology movement, which he popularized through works such as *Dune,* this story, and *Hellstrom's Hive* (1973). He was the main speaker advertised at the first Earth Day celebration. "Greenslaves" was later expanded into the novel, *The Green Brain* (1966). As opposed to many stories of this type, it has only gained in pertinence since its original publication. It is a stunning ecological parable set in the rain forest of South America.

He looked pretty much like the bastard offspring of a Guarani Indio and some backwoods farmer's daughter, some *sertanista* who had tried to forget her enslavement to the *encomendero* system by "eating the iron" – which is what they call lovemaking through the grill of a consel gate.

The type-look was almost perfect except when he forgot himself while passing through one of the deeper jungle glades.

His skin tended to shade down to green then, fading him into the background of leaves and vines, giving a strange disembodiment to the mud-gray shirt and ragged trousers, the inevitable frayed straw hat and rawhide sandals soled with pieces cut from worn tires.

Such lapses became less and less frequent the farther he got from the Parana headwaters, the *sertao* hinterland of Goyaz where men with his bang-cut black hair and glittering dark eyes were common.

By the time he reached *bandeirantes* country, he had achieved almost perfect control over the chameleon effect.

But now he was out of the jungle growth and into the brown dirt tracks that separated the parceled farms of the resettlement plan. In his own way, he knew he was approaching the *bandeirante* checkpoints, and with an almost human gesture, he fingered the *cedula de gracias al sacar*, the certificate of white blood, tucked safely beneath his shirt. Now and again, when humans were not near, he practiced speaking aloud the name that had been chosen for him – "Antonio Raposo Tavares."

The sound was a bit stridulate, harsh on the edges, but he knew it would pass. It already had. Goyaz Indios were notorious for the strange inflection of their speech. The farm folk who had given him a roof and fed him the previous night had said as much.

When their questions had become pressing, he had squatted on the doorstep and played his flute, the *qena* of the Andes Indian that he carried in a leather purse hung from his shoulder. He had kept the sound to a conventional non-dangerous pitch. The gesture of the flute was a symbol of the region. When a Guarani put flute to nose and began playing, that was a sign words were ended.

The farm folk had shrugged and retired.

Now, he could see red-brown rooftops ahead and the white crystal shimmering of a *bandeirante* tower with its aircars alighting and departing. The scene held an odd hive-look. He stopped, finding himself momentarily overcome by the touch of instincts that he knew he had to master or fail in the ordeal to come.

He united his mental identity then, thinking, *We are greenslaves subservient to the greater whole.* The thought lent him an air of servility that was like a shield against the stares of the humans trudging past all around him. His kind knew many mannerisms and had learned early that servility was a form of concealment.

Presently, he resumed his plodding course toward the town and the tower.

The dirt track gave way to a two-lane paved market road with its footpaths in the ditches on both sides. This, in turn, curved alongside a four-deck commercial transport highway where even the footpaths were paved. And now there were groundcars and aircars in greater number, and he noted that the flow of people on foot was increasing.

Thus far, he had attracted no dangerous attention. The occasional snickering side-glance from natives of the area could be safely ignored, he knew. Probing stares held peril, and he had detected none. The servility shielded him.

The sun was well along toward mid-morning and the day's heat was beginning to press down on the earth, raising a moist hothouse stink from the dirt beside the pathway, mingling the perspiration odors of humanity around him.

And they were around him now, close and pressing, moving slower and slower as they approached the checkpoint bottleneck. Presently, the forward motion stopped. Progress resolved itself into shuffle and stop, shuffle and stop.

This was the critical test now and there was no avoiding it. He waited with something like an Indian's stoic patience. His breathing had grown deeper to compensate for the heat, and he adjusted it to match that of the people around him, suffering the temperature rise for the sake of blending into his surroundings.

Andes Indians didn't breathe deeply here in the lowlands.

Shuffle and stop.

Shuffle and stop.

He could see the checkpoint now.

Fastidious *bandeirantes* in sealed white cloaks with plastic helmets, gloves, and boots stood in a double row within a shaded brick corridor leading into the town. He could see sunlight hot on the street beyond the corridor and people hurrying away there after passing the gantlet.

The sight of that free area beyond the corridor sent an ache of longing through all the parts of him. The suppression warning flashed out instantly on the heels of that instinctive reaching emotion.

No distraction could be permitted now; he was into the hands of the first *bandeirante*, a hulking blond fellow with pink skin and blue eyes.

"Step along now! Lively now!" the fellow said.

A gloved hand propelled him toward two *bandeirantes* standing on the right side of the line.

"Give this one an extra treatment," the blond giant called. "He's from the upcountry by the look of him"

The other two *bandeirantes* had him now, one jamming a breather mask over his face, the other fitting a plastic bag over him. A tube trailed from the bag out to machinery somewhere in the street beyond the corridor.

"Double shot!" one of the *bandeirantes* called.

Fuming blue gas puffed out the bag around him, and he took a sharp, gasping breath through the mask.

Agony!

The gas drove through every multiple linkage of his being with needles of pain.

We must not weaken, he thought.

But it was a deadly pain, killing. The linkages were beginning to weaken.

"Okay on this one," the bag handler called.

The mask was pulled away. The bag was slipped off. Hands propelled him down the corridor toward the sunlight.

"Lively now! Don't hold up the line."

The stink of the poison gas was all around him. It was a new one – a dissembler. They hadn't prepared him for this poison!

Now, he was into the sunlight and turning down a street lined with fruit stalls, merchants bartering with customers or standing fat and watchful behind their displays.

In his extremity, the fruit beckoned to him with the promise of life-saving sanctuary for a few parts of him, but the integrating totality fought off the lure. He shuffled as fast as he dared, dodging past the customers, through the knots of idlers.

"You like to buy some fresh oranges?"

An oily dark hand thrust two oranges toward his face.

"Fresh oranges from the green country. Never been a bug anywhere near these."

He avoided the hand, although the odor of the oranges came near overpowering him.

Now, he was clear of the stalls, around a corner down a narrow side street. Another corner and he saw far away to his left, the lure of greenery in open country, the free area beyond the town.

He turned toward the green, increasing his speed, measuring out the time still available to him. There was still a chance. Poison clung to his clothing, but fresh air was filtering through the fabric – and the thought of victory was like an antidote.

We can make it yet!

The green drew closer and closer – trees and ferns beside a river bank. He heard the running water. There was a bridge thronging with foot traffic from converging streets.

No help for it: he joined the throng, avoided contact as much as possible. The linkages of his legs and back were beginning to go, and he knew the wrong kind of blow could dislodge whole segments. He was over the bridge without disaster. A dirt track led off the path and down toward the river.

He turned toward it, stumbled against one of two men carrying a pig in a net slung between them. Part of the shell on his right upper leg gave way and he could feel it begin to slip down inside his pants.

The man he had hit took two backward steps, almost dropped the end of the burden.

"Careful!" the man shouted.

The man at the other end of the net said: "Damn drunks."

The pig set up a squirming, squealing distraction.

In this moment, he slipped past them onto the dirt track leading down toward the river. He could see the water down there now, boiling with aeration from the barrier filters.

Behind him, one of the pig carriers said: "I don't think he was drunk, Carlos. His skin felt dry and hot. Maybe he was sick."

The track turned around an embankment of raw dirt dark brown with dampness and dipped toward a tunnel through ferns and bushes. The men with the pig could no longer see him, he knew, and he grabbed at his pants where the part of his leg was slipping, scurried into the green tunnel.

Now, he caught sight of his first mutated bee. It was dead, having entered the barrier vibration area here without any protection against that deadliness. The bee was one of the butterfly type with iridescent yellow and orange wings. It lay in the cup of a green leaf at the center of a shaft of sunlight.

He shuffled past, having recorded the bee's shape and color. They had considered the bees as a possible answer, but there were serious drawbacks to this course. A bee could not reason with humans, that was the key fact. And humans had to listen to reason soon, else all life would end.

There came the sound of someone hurrying down the path behind him, heavy footsteps thudding on the earth.

Pursuit . . . ?

He was reduced to a slow shuffling now and soon it would be only crawling progress, he knew. Eyes searched the greenery around him for a place of concealment. A thin break in the fern wall on his left caught his attention. Tiny human footprints led into it – children. He forced his way through the ferns, found himself on a low narrow path along the embankment. Two toy aircars, red and blue, had been abandoned on the path. His staggering foot pressed them into the dirt.

The path led close to a wall of black dirt festooned with creepers, around a sharp turn and onto the lip of a shallow cave. More toys lay in the green gloom at the cave's mouth.

He knelt, crawled over the toys into the blessed dankness, lay there a moment, waiting.

The pounding footsteps hurried past a few feet below.

Voices reached up to him.

"He was headed toward the river. Think he was going to jump in?"

"Who knows? But I think me for sure he was sick."

"Here; down this way. Somebody's been down this way."

The voices grew indistinct, blended with the bubbling sound of the river.

The men were going on down the path. They had missed his hiding place. But why had they pursued him? He had not seriously injured the one by stumbling against him. Surely, they did not suspect.

Slowly, he steeled himself for what had to be done, brought his specialized parts into play and began burrowing into the earth at the end of the cave. Deeper and deeper he burrowed, thrusting the excess dirt behind and out to make it appear the cave had collapsed.

Ten meters in he went before stopping. His store of energy contained just enough reserve for the next stage. He turned on his back, scattering the dead parts of his legs and back, exposing the queen and her guard cluster to the dirt beneath his chitinous spine. Orifices opened at his thighs, exuded the cocoon foam, the soothing green cover that would harden into a protective shell.

This was victory; the essential parts had survived.

Time was the thing now– – ten and one half days to gather new energy, go through the metamorphosis and disperse. Soon, there would be thousands of him – each with its carefully mimicked clothing and identification papers and appearance of humanity.

Identical – each of them.

There would be other checkpoints, but not as severe; other barriers, lesser ones.

This human copy had proved a good one. They had learned many things from study of their scattered captives and from the odd crew directed by the red-haired human female they'd trapped in the *sertao*. How strange she was: like a queen and not like a queen. It was so difficult to understand human creatures, even when you permitted them limited freedom . . . almost impossible to reason with them. Their slavery to the planet would have to be proved dramatically, perhaps.

The queen stirred near the cool dirt. They had learned new things this time about escaping notice. All of the subsequent colony clusters would share that knowledge. One of them – at least – would get through to the city by the Amazon "River Sea" where the death-for-all originated. One had to get through.

Senhor Gabriel Martinho, prefect of the Mato Grosso Barrier Compact, paced his study, muttering to himself as he passed the tall, narrow window that admitted the evening sunlight. Occasionally, he paused to glare down at his son, Joao, who sat on a tapir-leather sofa beneath one of the tall bookcases that lined the room.

The elder Martinho was a dark wisp of a man, limb thin, with gray hair and cavernous brown eyes above an eagle nose, slit mouth, and boot-toe chin. He wore old style black clothing as befitted his position, his linen white against the black, and with golden cuffstuds glittering as he waved his arms.

"I am an object of ridicule!" he snarled.

Joao, a younger copy of the father, his hair still black and wavy, absorbed the statement in silence. He wore a *bandeirante's* white coverall suit sealed into plastic boots at the calf.

"An object of ridicule!" the elder Martinho repeated.

It began to grow dark in the room, the quick tropic darkness hurried by thunderheads piled along the horizon. The waning daylight carried a hazed blue east. Heat lightning spattered the patch of sky visible through the tall window, sent dazzling electric radiance into the study. Drumming thunder followed. As though that were the signal, the house sensors turned on lights wherever there were humans. Yellow illumination filled the study.

The Prefect stopped in front of his son. "Why does my own son, a *bandeirante*, a jefe of the Irmandades, spout these Carsonite stupidities?"

Joao looked at the floor between his boots. He felt both resentment and shame. To disturb his father this way, that was a hurtful thing, with the elder Martinho's delicate heart. But the old man was so blind!

"Those rabble farmers laughed at me," the elder Martinho said. "I told them we'd increase the green area by ten thousand hectares this month, and they laughed. 'Your own son does not even believe this!' they said. And they told me some of the things you had been saying."

"I am sorry I have caused you distress, Father," Joao said. "The fact that I'm *a bandeirante* . . ." He shrugged. "How else could I have learned the truth about this extermination program?"

His father quivered.

"Joao! Do you sit there and tell me you took a false oath when you formed your Irmandades band?"

"That's not the way it was, Father."

Joao pulled a sprayman's emblem from his breast pocket, fingered it. "I believed it . . . then. We could shape mutated bees to fill every gap in the insect ecology. This I believed. Like the Chinese, I said: 'Only the useful shall live!' But that was several years ago, Father, and since then I have come to realize we don't have a complete understanding of what usefulness means."

"It was a mistake to have you educated in North America," his father said. "That's where you absorbed this Carsonite heresy. It's all well and good for *them* to refuse to join the rest of the world in the Ecological Realignment; they do not have as many million mouths to feed. But my own son!"

Joao spoke defensively: "Out in the red areas you see things, Father. These things are difficult to explain. Plants look healthier out there and the fruit is . . ."

"A purely temporary thing," his father said. "We will shape bees to meet whatever need we find. The destroyers take food from our mouths. It is very simple. They must die and be replaced by creatures which serve a function useful to mankind."

"The birds are dying, Father," Joao said.

"We are saving the birds! We have specimens of every kind in our sanctuaries. We will provide new foods for them to . . ."

"But what happens if our barriers are breached . . . before we can replace the population of natural predators? What happens then?"

The elder Martinho shook a thin finger under his son's nose. "This is nonsense! I will hear no more of it! Do you know what else those *mameluco* farmers said? They said they have seen *bandeirantes* reinfesting the green areas to prolong their jobs! That is what they said. This, too, is nonsense – but it is a natural consequence of defeatist talk just such as I have heard from you tonight. And every setback we suffer adds strength to such charges!"

"Setbacks, Father?"

"I have said it: setbacks!"

Senhor Prefect Martinho turned, paced to his desk and back. Again, he stopped in front of his son, placed hands on hips. "You refer to the Piratininga, of course?"

"You accuse me, Father?"

"Your Irmandades were on that line."

"Not so much as a flea got through us!"

"Yet, a week ago the Piratininga was green. Now, it is crawling. Crawling!"

"I cannot watch every *bandeirante* in the Mato Grosso," Joao protested. "If they . . ."

"The IEO gives us only six months to clean up," the elder Martinho said. He raised his hands, palms up; his face was flushed. "Six months! Then they throw an embargo around all Brazil – the way they have done with North America." He lowered his hands. "Can you imagine the pressures on me? Can you imagine the things I must listen to about the *bandeirantes* and especially about my own son?"

Joao scratched his chin with the sprayman's emblem. The reference to the International Ecological Organization made him think of Dr. Rhin Kelly, the IEO's lovely field director. His mind pictured her as he had last seen her in the A' Chigua nightclub at Bahia – red-haired, green-eyed . . . so lovely and strange. But she had been missing almost six weeks now – somewhere in the *sertao* – and there were those who said she must be dead.

Joao looked at his father. If only the old man weren't so excitable. "You excite yourself needlessly, Father," he said. "The Piratininga was not a full barrier, just a . . ."

"Excite myself!"

The Prefect's nostrils dilated; he bent toward his son. "Already we have gone past two deadlines. We gained an extension when I announced you and the *bandeirantes* of Diogo Alvarez had cleared the Piratininga. How do I explain now that it is reinfested, that we have the work to do over?"

Joao returned the sprayman's emblem to his pocket. It was obvious he'd not be able to reason with his father this night. Frustration sent a nerve quivering along Joao's jaw. The old man had to be told, though; someone had to tell him. And someone of his father's stature had to get back to the Bureau, shake them up there and make *them* listen.

The Prefect returned to his desk, sat down. He picked up an antique crucifix, one that the great Aleihadinho had carved in ivory. He lifted it, obviously seeking to restore his serenity, but his eyes went wide and glaring. Slowly, he returned the crucifix to its position on the desk, keeping his attention on it.

"Joao," he whispered.

It's his heart! Joao thought.

He leaped to his feet, rushed to his father's side. "Father! What is it?"

The elder Martinho pointed, hand trembling.

Through the spiked crown of thorns, across the agonized ivory face, over the straining muscles of the Christ figure crawled an insect. It was the color of the ivory, faintly reminiscent of a beetle in shape, but with a multi-clawed fringe along its wings and thorax, and with furry edging to its abnormally long antennae.

The elder Martinho reached for a roll of papers to smash the insect, but Joao put out a hand restraining him. "Wait. This is a new one. I've never seen anything like it. Give me a handlight. We must follow it, find where it nests."

Senhor Prefect Martinho muttered under his breath, withdrew a small Permalight from a drawer of the desk, handed the light to his son.

Joao peered at the insect, still not using the light. "How strange it is," he said. "See how it exactly matches the tone of the ivory."

The insect stopped, pointed its antennae toward the two men.

"Things have been seen," Joao said. "There are stories. Something like this was found near one of the barrier villages last month. It was inside the green area, on a path beside a river. Two farmers found it while searching for a sick man." Joao looked at his father. "They are very watchful of sickness in the newly green regions, you know. There have been epidemics . . . and that is another thing."

"There is no relationship," his father snapped. "Without insects to carry disease, we will have less illness."

"Perhaps," Joao said, and his tone said he did not believe it.

Joao returned his attention to the insect. "I do not think our ecologists know all they say they do. And I mistrust our Chinese advisors. They speak in such flowery terms of the benefits from eliminating useless insects, but they will not let us go into their green areas and inspect. Excuses. Always excuses. I think they are having troubles they do not wish us to know."

"That's foolishness," the elder Martinho growled, but his tone said this was not a position he cared to defend. "They are honorable men. Their way of life is closer to our socialism than it is to the decadent capitalism of North America. Your trouble is you see them too much through the eyes of those who educated you.

"I'll wager this insect is one of the spontaneous mutations," Joao said. "It is almost as though they appeared according to some plan. Find me something in which I may capture this creature and take it to the laboratory."

The elder Martinho remained standing by his chair. "Where will you say it was found?"

"Right here," Joao said.

"You will not hesitate to expose me to more ridicule?"

"But Father . . ."

"Can't you hear what they will say? In his own home this insect is found. It is a strange new kind. Perhaps he breeds them there to reinfest the green."

"Now *you* are talking nonsense, Father. Mutations are common in a threatened species. And we cannot deny there is threat to insect species – the poisons, the barrier vibrations, the traps. Get me a container, Father. I cannot leave this creature, or I'd get a container myself."

"And you will tell where it was found?"

"I can do nothing else. We must cordon off this area, search it out. This could be . . . an accident . . ."

"Or a deliberate attempt to embarrass me."

Joao took his attention from the insect, studied his father. *That* was a possibility, of course. The Carsonites had friends in many places . . . and some were fanatics who would stoop to any scheme. Still . . .

Decision came to Joao. He returned his attention to the motionless insect. His father had to be told, had to be reasoned with at any cost. Someone whose voice carried authority had to get down to the Capitol and make them listen.

"Our earliest poisons killed off the weak and selected out those insects immune to this threat," Joao said. "Only the immune remained to breed. The poisons we use now . . . some of them do not leave such loopholes and the deadly vibrations at the barriers . . ." He shrugged. "This is a form of beetle, Father. I will show you a thing."

Joao drew a long, thin whistle of shiny metal from his pocket. "There was a time when this called countless beetles to their deaths. I had merely to tune it across their attraction spectrum." He put the whistle to his lips, blew while turning the end of it.

No sound audible to human ears came from the instrument, but the beetle's antennae writhed.

Joao removed the whistle from his mouth.

The antennae stopped writhing.

"It stayed put, you see," Joao said. "And there are indications of malignant intelligence among them. The insects are far from extinction, Father . . . and they are beginning to strike back."

"Malignant intelligence, pah!"

"You must believe me, Father," Joao said. "No one else will listen. They laugh and say we are too long in the jungle. And where is our evidence? And they say such stories could be expected from ignorant farmers but not from *bandeirantes*. You must listen, Father, and believe. It is why I was chosen to come here . . . because you are my father and you might listen to your own son."

"Believe what?" the elder Martinho demanded, and he was the Prefect now, standing erect, glaring coldly at his son.

"In the *sertao* of Goyaz last week," Joao said, "Antonil Lisboa's *bandeirante* lost three men who . . ."

"Accidents."

"They were killed with formic acid and oil of copahu."

"They were careless with their poisons. Men grow careless when they . . ."

"Father! The formic acid was a particularly strong type, but still recognizable as having been . . . or being of a type manufactured by insects. And the men were drenched with it. While the oil of copahu . . ."

"You imply that insects such as this . . ." The Prefect pointed to the motionless creature on the crucifix, ". . . blind creatures such as this . . ."

"They're not blind, Father."

"I did not mean literally blind, but without intelligence," the elder Martinho said. "You cannot be seriously implying that these creatures attacked humans and killed them."

"We have yet to discover precisely how the men were slain," Joao said. "We have only their bodies and the physical evidence at the scene. But there have been other deaths, Father, and men missing and we grow more and more certain that . . ."

He broke off as the beetle crawled off the crucifix onto the desk. Immediately, it darkened to brown, blending with the wood surface.

"Please, Father. Get me a container."

"I will get you a container only if you promise to use discretion in your story of where this creature was found," the Prefect said.

"Father, I . . ."

The beetle leaped off the desk far out into the middle of the room, scuttled to the wall, up the wall, into a crack beside a window.

Joao pressed the switch of the handlight, directed its beam into the hole which had swallowed the strange beetle.

"How long has this hole been here, Father?"

"For years. It was a flaw in the masonry . . . an earthquake, I believe."

Joao turned, crossed to the door in three strides, went through an arched hallway, down a flight of stone steps, through another door and short hall, through a grillwork gate and into the exterior garden. He set the handlight to full intensity, washed its blue glare over the wall beneath the study window.

"Joao, what are you doing?"

"My job, Father," Joao said. He glanced back, saw that the elder Martinho had stopped just outside the gate.

Joao returned his attention to the exterior wall, washed the blue glare of light on the stones beneath the window. He crouched low, running the light along the ground, peering behind each clod, erasing all shadows.

His searching scrutiny passed over the raw earth, turned to the bushes, then the lawn.

Joao heard his father come up behind.

"Do you see it, son?"

"No, Father."

"You should have allowed me to crush it."

From the outer garden that bordered the road and the stone fence, there came a piercing stridulation. It hung on the air in almost tangible waves, making Joao think of the hunting cry of jungle predators. A shiver moved up his spine. He turned toward the driveway where he had parked his airtruck, sent the blue glare of light stabbing there.

He broke off, staring at the lawn. "What is that?"

The ground appeared to be in motion, reaching out toward them like the curling of a wave on a beach. Already, they were cut off from the house. The wave was still some ten paces away, but moving in rapidly.

Joao stood up, clutched his father's arm. He spoke quietly, hoping not to alarm the old man further. "We must get to my truck, Father. We must run across them."

"Them?"

"Those are like the insect we saw inside, father – millions of them. Perhaps they are not beetles, after all. Perhaps they are like army ants. We must make it to the truck. I have equipment and supplies there. We will be safe inside. It is a *bandeirante* truck, Father. You must run with me. I will help you."

They began to run, Joao holding his father's arm, pointing the way with the light.

Let his heart be strong enough, Joao prayed.

They were into the creeping waves of insects then, but the creatures leaped aside, opening a pathway which closed behind the running men.

The white form of the airtruck loomed out of the shadows at the far curve of the driveway about fifteen meters ahead.

"Joao . . . my heart," the elder Martinho gasped.

"You can make it," Joao panted. "Faster!" He almost lifted his father from the ground for the last few paces.

They were at the wide rear door into the truck's lab compartment now. Joao yanked open the door, slapped the light switch, reached for a spray hood and poison gun. He stopped, stared into the yellow-lighted compartment.

Two men sat there – sertao Indians by the look of them, with bright glaring eyes and bang-cut black hair beneath straw hats. They looked to be identical twins – even to the mud-gray clothing and sandals, the leather shoulder bags. The beetle-like insects crawled around them, up the walls, over the instruments and vials.

"What the devil?" Joao blurted.

One of the pair held a qena flute. He gestured with it, spoke in a rasping, oddly inflected voice: "Enter. You will not be harmed if you obey."

Joao felt his father sag, caught the old man in his arms. How light he felt! Joao stepped up into the truck, carrying his father. The elder Martinho breathed in short, painful gasps. His face was a pale blue and sweat stood out on his forehead.

"Joao," he whispered. "Pain . . . my chest."

"Medicine, Father," Joao said. "Where is your medicine?"

"House," the old man said.

"It appears to be dying," one of the Indians rasped.

Still holding his father in his arms, Joao, whirled toward the pair, blazed: "I don't know who you are or why you loosed those bugs here, but my father's dying and needs help. Get out of my way!"

"Obey or both die," said the Indian with the flute.

"He needs his medicine and a doctor," Joao pleaded. He didn't like the way the Indian pointed that flute. The motion suggested the instrument was actually a weapon.

"What part has failed?" asked the other Indian. He stared curiously at Joao's father. The old man's breathing had become shallow and rapid.

"It's his heart," Joao said. "I know you farmers don't think he's acted fast enough for . . ."

"Not farmers," said the one with the flute. "Heart?"

"Pump," said the other.

"Pump." The Indian with the flute stood up from the bench at the front of the lab, gestured down. "Put . . . Father here."

The other one got off the bench, stood aside.

In spite of fear for his father, Joao was caught by the strange look of this pair, the fine, scale-like lines in their skin, the glittering brilliance of their eyes.

"Put Father here," repeated the one with the flute, pointing at the bench. "Help can be . . ."

"Attained," said the other one.

"Attained," said the one with the flute.

Joao focused now on the masses of insects around the walls, the waiting quietude in their ranks. They *were* like the one in the study.

The old man's breathing was now very shallow, very rapid.

He's dying, Joao thought in desperation.

"Help can be attained," repeated the one with the flute. "If you obey, we will not harm."

The Indian lifted his flute, pointed it at Joao like a weapon. "Obey."

There was no mistaking the gesture.

Slowly, Joao advanced, deposited his father gently on the bench.

The other Indian bent over the elder Martinho's head, raised an eyelid. There was a professional directness about the gesture. The Indian pushed gently on the dying man's diaphragm, removed the Prefect's belt, loosened his collar. A stubby brown finger was placed against the artery in the old man's neck.

"Very weak," the Indian rasped.

Joao took another, closer look at this Indian, wondering at the sertao backwoodsman who behaved like a doctor.

"We've got to get him to a hospital," Joao said. "And his medicine in . . ."

"Hospital," the Indian agreed.

"Hospital?" asked the one with the flute.

A low, stridulate hissing came from the other Indian.

"Hospital," said the one with the flute.

That stridulate hissing! Joao stared at the Indian beside the Prefect. The sound had been reminiscent of the weird call that had echoed across the lawn.

The one with the flute poked him, said: "You will go into front and maneuver this . . ."

"Vehicle," said the one beside Joao's father.

"Vehicle," said the one with the flute.

"Hospital?" Joao pleaded.

"Hospital," agreed the one with the flute.

Joao looked once more to his father. The other Indian already was strapping the elder Martinho to the bench in preparation for movement. How competent the man appeared in spite of his backwoods look.

"Obey," said the one with the flute.

Joao opened the door into the front compartment, slipped through, feeling the other one follow. A few drops of rain spattered darkly against the curved windshield. Joao squeezed into the operator's seat, noted how the Indian crouched behind him, flute pointed and ready.

A dart gun of some kind, Joao guessed.

He punched the igniter button on the dash, strapped himself in while waiting for the turbines to build up speed. The Indian still crouched behind him, vulnerable now if the airtruck were spun sharply. Joao flicked the communications switch on the lower left corner of the dash, looked into the tiny screen there giving him a view of the lab compartment. The rear doors were open. He closed them by hydraulic remote. His father was securely strapped to the bench now, Joao noted, but the other Indian was equally secured.

The turbines reached their whining peak. Joao switched on the lights, engaged the hydrostatic drive. The truck lifted six inches, angled upward as Joao increased pump displacement. He turned left onto the street, lifted another two meters to increase speed, headed toward the lights of a boulevard.

The Indian spoke beside his ear: "You will turn toward the mountain over there." A hand came forward, pointing to the right.

The Alejandro Clinic is there in the foothills, Joao thought.

He made the indicated turn down the cross street angling toward the boulevard.

Casually, he gave pump displacement another boost, lifted another meter and increased speed once more. In the same motion, he switched on the intercom to the rear compartment, tuned for the spare amplifier and pickup in the compartment beneath the bench where his father lay.

The pickup, capable of making a dropped pin sound like a cannon, gave forth only a distant hissing and rasping. Joao increased amplification. The instrument should have been transmitting the old man's heartbeats now, sending a noticeable drum-thump into the forward cabin.

There was nothing.

Tears blurred Joao's eyes, and he shook his head to clear them.

My father is dead, he thought. *Killed by these crazy backwoodsmen.*

He noted in the dashscreen that the Indian back there had a hand under the elder Martinho's back. The Indian appeared to be massaging the dead man's back, and a rhythmic rasping matched the motion.

Anger filled Joao. He felt like diving the airtruck into an abutment, dying himself to kill these crazy men.

They were approaching the outskirts of the city, and ring-girders circled off to the left giving access to the boulevard. This was an area of small gardens and cottages protected by over-fly canopies.

Joao lifted the airtruck above the canopies, headed toward the boulevard.

To the clinic, yes, he thought. *But it is too late.*

In that instant, he realized there were no heartbeats at all coming from that rear compartment – only that slow, rhythmic grating, a faint susurration and a cicada-like hum up and down scale.

"To the mountains, there," said the Indian behind him.

Again, the hand came forward to point off to the right.

Joao, with that hand close to his eyes and illuminated by the dash, saw the scale-like parts of a finger shift position slightly. In that shift, he recognized the scale-shapes by their claw fringes.

The beetles!

The finger was composed of linked beetles working in unison!

Joao turned, stared into the *Indian's* eyes, seeing now why they glistened so: they were composed of thousands of tiny facets.

"Hospital, there," the creature beside him said, pointing.

Joao turned back to the controls, fighting to keep from losing composure. They were not Indians . . . they weren't even human. They were insects – some kind of hive-cluster shaped and organized to mimic a man.

The implications of this discovery raced through his mind. How did they support their weight? How did they feed and breathe?

How did they speak?

Everything had to be subordinated to the urgency of getting this information and proof of it back to one of the big labs where the facts could be explored.

Even the death of his father could not be considered now. He had to capture one of these things, get out with it.

He reached overhead, flicked on the command transmitter, set its beacon for a homing call. *Let some of my Irmaos be awake and monitoring their sets*, he prayed.

"More to the right," said the creature behind him.

Again, Joao corrected course.

The moon was high overhead now, illuminating a line of *bandeirante* towers off to the left. The first barrier.

They would be out of the green area soon and into the gray – then, beyond that, another barrier and the great red that stretched out in reaching fingers through the Goyaz and the Mato Grosso. Joao could see scattered lights of Resettlement Plan farms ahead, and darkness beyond.

The airtruck was going faster than he wanted, but Joao dared not slow it. They might become suspicious.

"You must go higher," said the creature behind him.

Joao increased pump displacement, raised the nose. He leveled off at three hundred meters.

More *bandeirante* towers loomed ahead, spaced at closer intervals. Joao picked up the barrier signals on his meters, looked back at the *Indian*. The dissembler vibrations seemed not to affect the creature.

Joao looked out his side window and down. No one would challenge him, he knew. This was a *bandeirante* airtruck headed *into* the red zone . . . and with its transmitter sending out a homing call. The men down there would assume he was a bandleader headed out on a contract after a successful bid – and calling his men to him for the job ahead.

He could see the moon-silvered snake of the São Francisco winding off to his left, and the lesser waterways like threads raveled out of the foothills.

I must find the nest – where we're headed, Joao thought. He wondered if he dared turn on his receiver – but if his men started reporting in . . . No. That could make the creatures suspect; they might take violent counter-action.

My men will realize something is wrong when I don't answer, he thought. *They will follow.*

If any of them hear my call.

Hours droned past.

Nothing but moonlighted jungle sped beneath them now, and the moon was low on the horizon, near setting. This was the deep red region where broadcast poisons had been used at first with disastrous results. This was where the wild mutations had originated. It was here that Rhin Kelly had been reported missing.

This was the region being saved for the final assault, using a mobile barrier line when that line could be made short enough.

Joao armed the emergency charge that would separate the front and rear compartments of the truck when he fired it. The stub wings of the front compartment and its emergency rocket motors could get him back into *bandeirante* country.

With the *specimen* sitting behind him safely subdued, Joao hoped.

He looked up through the canopy, scanned the horizon as far as he could. Was that moonlight glistening on a truck far back to the right? He couldn't be sure.

"How much farther?" Joao asked.

"Ahead," the creature rasped.

Now that he was alert for it, Joao heard the modulated stridulation beneath that voice.

"But how long?" Joao asked. "My father . . ."

"Hospital for . . . the father . . . ahead," said the creature.

It would be dawn soon, Joao realized. He could see the first false line of light along the horizon behind. This night had passed so swiftly. Joao wondered if these creatures had injected some time-distorting drug into him without his knowing. He thought not. He was maintaining himself in the necessities of the moment. There was no time for fatigue or boredom when he had to record every landmark half-visible in the night, sense everything there was to sense about these creatures with him.

How did they coordinate all those separate parts?

Dawn came, revealing the plateau of the Mato Grosso. Joao looked out his windows. This region, he knew, stretched across five degrees of latitude and six degrees of longitude. Once, it had been a region of isolated *fazendas* farmed by independent blacks and by *sertanistos* chained to the *encomendero* plantation system. It was hardwood jungles, narrow rivers with banks overgrown by lush trees and ferns, savannahs, and tangled life.

Even in this age it remained primitive, a fact blamed largely on insects and disease. It was one of the last strongholds of *teeming* insect life, if the International Ecological Organization's reports could be believed.

Supplies for the *bandeirantes* making the assault on this insect stronghold would come by way of São Paulo, by air and by transport on the multi-decked highways, then on antique diesel trains to Itapira, on river runners to Bahus and by airtruck to Registo and Leopoldina on the Araguaya.

This area crawled with insects: wire worms in the roots of the savannahs, grubs digging in the moist black earth, hopping beetles, dart-like angita wasps, chalcis flies, chiggers, sphecidae, braconidae, fierce hornets, white termites, hemipteric crawlers, blood roaches, thrips, ants, lice, mosquitoes, mites, moths, exotic butterflies, mantidae – and countless unnatural mutations of them all.

This would be an expensive fight – unless it were stopped . . . because it already had been lost.

I mustn't think that way, Joao told himself. *Out of respect for my father.*

Maps of the IEO showed this region in varied intensities of red. Around the red ran a ring of gray with pink shading where one or two persistent forms of insect life resisted man's poisons, jelly flames, astringents, sonitoxics – the combination of flamant couroq and supersonics that drove insects from their hiding places into waiting death – and all the mechanical traps and lures in the *bandeirante* arsenal.

A grid map would be placed over this area and each thousand-acre square offered for bid to the independent bands to deinfest.

We bandeirantes *are a kind of ultimate predator,* Joao thought. *It's no wonder these creatures mimic us.*

But how good, really, was the mimicry? he asked himself. And how deadly to the predators?

"There," said the creature behind him, and the multipart hand came forward to point toward a black scarp visible ahead in the gray light of morning.

Joao's foot kicked a trigger on the floor releasing a great cloud of orange dye-fog beneath the truck to mark the ground and forest for a mile around under this spot. As he kicked the trigger, Joao began counting down the five-second delay to the firing of the separation charge.

It came in a roaring blast that Joao knew would smear the creature behind him against the rear bulkhead. He sent the stub wings out, fed power to the rocket motors and back hard around. He saw the detached rear compartment settling slowly earthward above the dye cloud, its fall cushioned as the pumps of the hydrostatic drive automatically compensated.

I will come back, Father, Joao thought. *You will be buried among family and friends.*

He locked the controls, twisted in the seat to see what had happened to his captive.

A gasp escaped Joao's lips.

The rear bulkhead crawled with insects clustered around something white and pulsing. The mud-gray shirt and trousers were torn, but insects already were repairing it, spinning out fibers that meshed and sealed on contact. There was a yellow-like extrusion near the pulsing white, and a dark brown skeleton with familiar articulation.

It looked like a human skeleton – but chitinous.

Before his eyes, the thing was reassembling itself, the long, furry antennae burrowing into the structure and interlocking.

The flute-weapon was not visible, and the thing's leather pouch had been thrown into the rear corner, but its eyes were in place in their brown sockets, staring at him. The mouth was re-forming.

The yellow sac contracted, and a voice issued from the half-formed mouth.

"You must listen," it rasped.

Joao gulped, whirled back to the controls, unlocked them and sent the cab into a wild, spinning turn.

A high-pitched rattling buzz sounded behind him. The noise seemed to pick up every bone in his body and shake it. Something crawled on his neck. He slapped at it, felt it squash.

All Joao could think of was escape. He stared frantically out at the earth beneath, seeing a blotch of white in a savannah off to his right and, in the same instant, recognizing another airtruck banking beside him, the insignia of his own Irmandades band bright on its side.

The white blotch in the savannah was resolving itself into a cluster of tents with an IEO orange and green banner flying beside them.

Joao dove for the tents, praying the other airtruck would follow.

Something stung his cheek. They were in his hair – biting, stinging. He stabbed the braking rockets, aimed for open ground about fifty meters from the tent. Insects were all over the inside of the glass now, blocking his vision. Joao said a silent prayer, hauled back on the control arm, felt the cab mush out, touch ground, skidding and slewing across the savannah. He kicked the canopy release before the cab stopped, broke the seal on his safety harness and launched himself up and out to land sprawling in grass.

He rolled through the grass, feeling the insect bites like fire over every exposed part of his body. Hands grabbed him and he felt a jelly hood splash across his face to protect it. A voice he recognized as Thome of his own band said: "This way, Johnny! Run!" They ran.

He heard a spraygun fire: "Whooosh!"

And again.

And again.

Arms lifted him and he felt a leap.

They landed in a heap and a voice said: "Mother of God! Would you look at that!"

Joao clawed the jelly hood from his face, sat up to stare across the savannah. The grass seethed and boiled with insects around the uptilted cab and the air-truck that had landed beside it.

Joao looked around him, counted seven of his Irmaos with Thome, his chief sprayman, in command.

Beyond them clustered five other people, a red-haired woman slightly in front, half turned to look at the savannah and at him. He recognized the woman immediately: Dr. Rhin Kelly of the IEO. When they had met in the A' Chigua nightclub in Bahia, she had seemed exotic and desirable to Joao. Now, she wore a field uniform instead of gown and jewels, and her eyes held no invitation at all.

"I see a certain poetic justice in this . . . traitors," she said.

Joao lifted himself to his feet, took a cloth proffered by one of his men, wiped off the last of the jelly. He felt hands brushing him, clearing dead insects off his coveralls. The pain of his skin was receding under the medicant jelly, and now he found himself dominated by puzzled questioning as he recognized the mood of the IEO personnel.

They were furious and it was directed at him . . . and at his fellow Irmandades. Joao studied the woman, noting how her green eyes glared at him, the pink flush to her skin.

"Dr. Kelly?" Joao said.

"If it isn't Joao Martinho, jefe of the Irmandades," she said, "the traitor of the Piratininga."

"They are crazy, that is the only thing, I think," said Thome.

"Your pets turned on you, didn't they?" she demanded.

"And wasn't that inevitable?"

"Would you be so kind as to explain," Joao said.

"I don't need to explain," she said. "Let your friends out there explain." She pointed toward the rim of jungle beyond the savannah.

Joao looked where she pointed, saw a line of men in *bandeirante* white standing untouched amidst the leaping, boiling insects in the jungle shadow. He took a pair of binoculars from around the neck of one of his men, focused on the figures. Knowing what to look for made the identification easy.

"Tommy," Joao said.

His chief sprayman, Thome, bent close, rubbing at an insect sting on his swarthy cheek.

In a low voice, Joao explained what the figures at the jungle edge were.

"*Aieeee*," Thome said.

An Irmandade on Joao's left crossed himself.

"What was it we leaped across coming in here?" Joao asked.

"A ditch," Thome said. "It seems to be filled with couroq jelly . . . an insect barrier of some kind."

Joao nodded. He began to have unpleasant suspicions about their position here. He looked at Rhin Kelly. "Dr. Kelly, where are the rest of your people? Surely there are more than five in an IEO field crew."

Her lips compressed, but she remained silent.

"So?" Joao glanced around at the tents, seeing their weathered condition. "And where is your equipment, your trucks and lab huts and jitneys?"

"Funny thing you should ask," she said, but there was uncertainty atop the sneering quality of her voice. "About a kilometer into the trees over there . . ." She nodded to her left. ". . . is a wrecked jungle truck containing most of our . . . equipment, as you call it. The track spools of our truck were eaten away by acid."

"Acid?"

"It smelled like oxalic," said one of her companions, a blond Nordic with a scar beneath his right eye.

"Start from the beginning," Joao said.

"We were cut off here almost six weeks ago," said the blond man. "Something got our radio, our truck – they looked like giant chiggers and they can shoot an acid spray about fifteen meters."

"There's a glass case containing three dead specimens in my lab tent," said Dr. Kelly.

Joao pursued his lips, thinking. "So?"

"I heard part of what you were telling your men there," she said. "Do you expect us to believe that?"

"It is of no importance to me what you believe," Joao said. "How did you get here?"

"We fought our way in here from the truck using *caramuru* cold-fire spray," said the blond man. "We dragged along what supplies we could, dug a trench around our perimeter, poured in the couroq powder, added the jell compound and topped it off with our *copahu* oil . . . and here we sat."

"How many of you?" Joao asked.

"There were fourteen of us," said the man.

Joao rubbed the back of his neck where the insect stings were again beginning to burn. He glanced around at his men, assessing their condition and equipment, counted four spray rifles, saw the men carried spare charge cylinders on slings around their necks.

"The airtruck will take us," he said. "We had better get out of here."

Dr. Kelly looked out to the savannah, said: "I think it has been too late for that since a few seconds after you landed, *bandeirante*. I think in a day or so there'll be a few less traitors around. You're caught in your own trap."

Joao whirled to stare at the airtruck, barked: "Tommy! Vince! Get . . ." He broke off as the airtruck sagged to its left.

"It's only fair to warn you," said Dr. Kelly, "to stay away from the edge of the ditch unless you first spray the opposite side. They can shoot a stream of acid at least fifteen meters . . . and as you can see . . ." She nodded toward the air- truck. ". . . the acid eats metal."

"You're insane," Joao said. "Why didn't you warn us immediately?"

"Warn you?"

Her blond companion said: "Rhin, perhaps we . . ."

"Be quiet, Hogar," she said, and turned back to Joao. "We lost nine men to your playmates." She looked at the small band of Irmandades. "Our lives are little enough to pay now for the extinction of eight of you . . . traitors."

"You *are* insane," Joao said.

"Stop playing innocent, *bandeirante*," she said. "We have seen your companions out there. We have seen the new playmates you bred . . . and we understand that you were too greedy, now your game has gotten out of hand."

"You've not seen my Irmaos doing these things," Joao said. He looked at Thome. "Tommy, keep an eye on these insane ones." He lifted the spray rifle from one of his men, took the man's spare charges, indicated the other three armed men. "You – come with me."

"Johnny, what do you do?" Thome asked.

"Salvage the supplies from the truck," Joao said. He walked toward the ditch nearest the airtruck, laid down a hard mist of foamal beyond the ditch, beckoned the others to follow and leaped the ditch.

Little more than an hour later, with all of them acid-burned – two seriously – the Irmandades retreated back across the ditch. They had salvaged less than a fourth of the equipment in the truck, and this did not include a transmitter.

"It is evident the little devils went first for the communications equipment," Thome said. "How could they tell?"

Joao said: "I do not want to guess." He broke open a first aid box, began treating his men. One had a cheek and shoulder badly splashed with acid. Another was losing flesh off his back.

Dr. Kelly came up, helped him treat the men, but refused to speak, even to answering the simplest question.

Finally, Joao touched up a spot on his own arm, neutralizing the acid and covering the burn with flesh-tape. He gritted his teeth against the pain, stared at Rhin Kelly. "Where are these chigua you found?"

"Go find them yourself!" she snapped.

"You are a blind, unprincipled megalomaniac," Joao said, speaking in an even voice. "Do not push me too far."

Her face went pale and the green eyes blazed.

Joao grabbed her arm, hauled her roughly toward the tents. "Show me these chigua!"

She jerked free of him, threw back her red hair, stared at him defiantly. Joao faced her, looked her up and down with a calculating slowness.

"Go ahead, do violence to me," she said, "I'm sure I couldn't stop you."

"You act like a woman who wants . . . needs violence," Joao said. "Would you like me to turn you over to my men? They're a little tired of your raving."

Her face flamed. "You would not dare!"

"Don't be so melodramatic," he said, "I wouldn't give you the pleasure."

"You insolent . . . you . . ."

Joao showed her a wolfish grin, said: "Nothing you say will make me turn you over to my men!"

"Johnny."

It was Thome calling.

Joao turned, saw Thome talking to the Nordic IEO man who had volunteered information. What had she called him? Hogar.

Thome beckoned.

Joao crossed to the pair, bent close as Thome signaled secrecy.

"The gentleman here says the female doctor was bitten by an insect that got past their barrier's fumes."

"Two weeks ago," Hogar whispered.

"She has not been the same since," Thome said. "We humor her, jefe, no?"

Joao wet his lips with his tongue. He felt suddenly dizzy and too warm.

"The insect that bit her was similar to the ones that were on you," Hogar said, and his voice sounded apologetic.

They are making fun of me! Joao thought.

"I give the orders here!" he snapped.

"Yes, jefe," Thome said. "But you . . ."

"What difference does it make who gives the orders?"

It was Dr. Kelly close behind him.

Joao turned, glared at her. How hateful she looked . . . in spite of her beauty.

"What's the difference?" she demanded. "We'll all be dead in a few days anyway." She stared out across the savannah. "More of your friends have arrived."

Joao looked to the forest shadow, saw more human-like figures arriving. They appeared familiar and he wondered what it was – something at the edge of his mind, but his head hurt. Then he realized they looked like *sertao* Indians, like the pair who had lured him here. There were at least a hundred of them, apparently identical in every visible respect.

More were arriving by the second.

Each of them carried a qena flute.

There was something about the flutes that Joao felt he should remember.

Another figure came advancing through the *Indians*, a thin man in a black suit, his hair shiny silver in the sunlight.

"Father!" Joao gasped.

I'm sick, he thought. *I must be delirious.*

"That looks like the Prefect," Thome said. "Is it not so, Ramon?"

The Irmandade he addressed said: "If it is not the Prefect, it is his twin. Here, Johnny. Look with the glasses."

Joao took the glasses, focused on the figure advancing toward them through the grass. The glasses felt so heavy. They trembled in his hands and the figure coming toward them was blurred.

"I cannot see!" Joao muttered and he almost dropped the glasses.

A hand steadied him, and he realized he was reeling.

In an instant of clarity, he saw that the line of *Indians* had raised their flutes, pointing at the IEO camp. That buzzing-rasping that had shaken his bones in the airtruck cab filled the universe around him. He saw his companions begin to fall.

In the instant before his world went blank, Joao heard his father's voice calling strongly: "Joao! Do not resist! Put down your weapons!"

The trampled grassy earth of the campsite, Joao saw, was coming up to meet his face.

It cannot be my father, Joao thought. *My father is dead and they've copied him . . . mimicry, nothing more.*

Darkness.

There was a dream of being carried, a dream of tears and shouting, a dream of violent protests and defiance and rejection.

He awoke to yellow-orange light and the figure who could not be his father bending over him, thrusting a hand out, saying: "Then examine my hand if you don't believe!"

But Joao's attention was on the face behind his father. It was a giant face, baleful in the strange light, its eyes brilliant and glaring with pupils within pupils. The face turned, and Joao saw it was no more than two centimeters thick. Again, it turned, and the eyes focused on Joao's feet.

Joao forced himself to look down, began trembling violently as he saw he was half enveloped in a foaming green cocoon, that his skin shared some of the same tone.

"Examine my hand!" ordered the old-man figure beside him.

"He has been dreaming." It was a resonant voice that boomed all around him, seemingly coming from beneath the giant face. "He has been dreaming," the voice repeated. "He is not quite awake."

With an abrupt, violent motion, Joao reached out, clutched the proffered hand.

It felt warm . . . human.

For no reason he could explain, tears came to Joao's eyes.

"Am I dreaming?" he whispered. He shook his head to clear away the tears.

"Joao, my son," said his father's voice.

Joao looked up at the familiar face. It *was* his father and no mistake. "But . . . your heart," Joao said.

"My pump," the old man said. "Look." And he pulled his hand away, turned to display where the back of his black suit had been cut away, its edges held by some gummy substance, and a pulsing surface of oily yellow between those cut edges.

Joao saw the hair-fine scale lines, the multiple shapes, and he recoiled.

So it was a copy, another of their tricks.

The old man turned back to face him. "The old pump failed and they gave me a new one," he said. "It shares my blood and lives off me and it'll give me a few more years. What do you think our bright IEO specialists will say about the *usefulness* of that?"

"Is it really you?" Joao demanded.

"All except the pump," said the old man. "They had to give you and some of the others a whole new blood system because of all the corrosive poison that got into you."

Joao lifted his hands, stared at them.

"They know medical tricks we haven't even dreamed about," the old man said. "I haven't been this excited since I was a boy. I can hardly wait to get back and . . . Joao! What is it?"

Joao was thrusting himself up, glaring at the old man. "We're not human anymore if . . . We're not human!"

"Be still, son!" the old man ordered.

"If this is true," Joao protested, "they're in control." He nodded toward the giant face behind his father. "They'll *rule* us!"

He sank back, gasping. "We'll be their slaves."

"Foolishness," rumbled the drum voice.

Joao looked at the giant face, growing aware of the fluorescent insects above it, seeing that the insects clung to the ceiling of a cave, noting finally a patch of night sky and stars where the fluorescent insects ended.

"What is a slave?" rumbled the voice.

Joao looked beneath the face where the voice originated, saw a white mass about four meters across, a pulsing yellow sac protruding from it, insects crawling over it, into fissures along its surface, back to the ground beneath. The face appeared to be held up from that white mass by a dozen of round stalks, their scaled surfaces betraying their nature.

"Your attention is drawn to our way of answering your threat to us," rumbled the voice, and Joao saw that the sound issued from the pulsing yellow sac. "This is our brain. It is vulnerable, very vulnerable, weak, yet strong . . . just as your brain. Now, tell me what is a slave?"

Joao fought down a shiver of revulsion, said: "I'm a slave now; I'm in bondage to you."

"Not true," rumbled the voice. "A slave is one who must produce wealth for another, and there is only one true wealth in all the universe – living time. Are we slaves because we have given your father more time to live?"

Joao looked up to the giant, glittering eyes, thought he detected amusement there.

"The lives of all those with you have been spared or extended as well," drummed the voice. "That makes us your slaves, does it not?"

"What do you take in return?"

"Ah hah!" the voice fairly barked. "Quid pro quo! You are, indeed, our slaves as well. We are tied to each other by a bond of mutual slavery that cannot be broken – never could be."

"It is very simple once you understand it," Joao's father said.

"Understand what?"

"Some of our kind once lived in greenhouses and their cells remembered the experience," rumbled the voice. "You know about greenhouses, of course?" It turned to look out at the cave mouth where dawn was beginning to touch the world with gray. "That out there, that is a greenhouse, too." Again, it looked down at Joao, the giant eyes glaring. "To sustain life, a greenhouse must achieve a delicate balance – enough of this chemical, enough of that one, another substance available when needed. What is poison one day can be sweet food the next."

"What's all this to do with slavery?" Joao demanded.

"Life has developed over millions of years in this greenhouse we call Earth," the voice rumbled. "Sometimes it developed in the poison excrement of other life . . . and then that poison became necessary to it. Without a substance produced by the wire worm, that savannah grass out there would die . . . in time. Without substances produced by . . . insects, your kind of life would die. Sometimes, just a faint trace of the substance is needed, such as the special copper compound produced by the arachnids. Sometimes, the substance must subtly change each time before it can be used by a life-form at the end of the chain. The more different forms of life there are, the more life the greenhouse can support. This is the lesson of the greenhouse. The successful greenhouse must grow many times many forms of life. The more forms of life it has, the healthier it is."

"You're saying we have to stop killing insects," Joao said. "You're saying we have to let you take over."

"We say you must stop killing yourselves," rumbled the voice. "Already, the Chinese are . . . I believe you would call it: *reinfesting* their land. Perhaps they will be in time, perhaps not. Here, it is not too late. There . . . they were fast and thorough . . . and they may need help."

"You . . . give us no proof," Joao said.

"There will be time for proof, later," said the voice. "Now, join your woman friend outside; let the sun work on your skin and the chlorophyll in your blood, and when you come back, tell me if the sun is your slave."

He Who Shapes

ROGER ZELAZNY

Roger Zelazny (1937–95) was among the leading SF writers to emerge in the 1960s. His body of work in that decade was enormously influential, particularly his twelve novellas, of which this is one. With the way paved by the impact of his early stories, his first novel, *This Immortal* (1966) shared the Hugo Award with Frank Herbert's *Dune*. Zelazny became one of the most popular and respected writers of that decade, with five more novels and a collection of novellas by 1970.

At the beginning of the 1970s he launched what was to become his most popular series of books with *Nine Princes in Amber* (1970). With the enormous popularity and financial success of the Amber books, Zelazny lost interest in experimentation with the novel form and limited his most intense aesthetic efforts to occasional short stories and novellas for most of the following twenty-five years. Novels such as *Doorways in the Sand* (1976), *Eye of Cat* (1982), and *A Night in the Lonesome October* (1993) stand out as exceptions. This novella, one of the works upon which his initial fame rests, is a powerful fusion of technology, psychology, and myths of godlike power.

I

Lovely as it was, with the blood and all, Render could sense that it was about to end.

Therefore, each microsecond would be better off as a minute, he decided – and perhaps the temperature should be increased . . .

Somewhere, just at the periphery of everything, the darkness halted its constriction.

Something, like a crescendo of subliminal thunders, was arrested at one raging note. That note was a distillate of shame and pain and fear.

The Forum was stifling.

Caesar cowered outside the frantic circle. His forearm covered his eyes but it could not stop the seeing, not this time.

The senators had no faces and their garments were spattered with blood. All their voices were like the cries of birds. With an inhuman frenzy they plunged their daggers into the fallen figure.

All, that is, but Render.

The pool of blood in which he stood continued to widen. His arm seemed to be rising and falling with a mechanical regularity and his throat might have been shaping birdcries, but he was simultaneously apart from and a part of the scene.

For he was Render, the Shaper.

Crouched, anguished and envious, Caesar wailed his protests.

"You have slain him! You have murdered Marcus Antonius – a blameless, useless fellow!"

Render turned to him and the dagger in his hand was quite enormous and quite gory.

"Aye," said he.

The blade moved from side to side. Caesar, fascinated by the sharpened steel, swayed to the same rhythm.

"Why?" he cried. "Why?"

"Because," answered Render, "he was a far nobler Roman than yourself."

"You lie! It is not so!"

Render shrugged and returned to the stabbing.

"It is not true!" screamed Caesar. "Not true!"

Render turned to him again and waved the dagger. Puppetlike, Caesar mimicked the pendulum of the blade.

"Not true?" smiled Render. "And who are you to question an assassination such as this? You are no one! You detract from the dignity of this occasion! Begone!"

Jerkily, the pink-faced man rose to his feet, his hair half-wispy, half-wetplastered, a disarray of cotton. He turned, moved away, and as he walked, he looked back over his shoulder.

He had moved far from the circle of assassins, but the scene did not diminish in size. It retained an electric clarity. It made him feel even further removed, ever more alone and apart.

Render rounded a previously unnoticed corner and stood before him, a blind beggar.

Caesar grasped the front of his garment.

"Have you an ill omen for me this day?"

"Beware!" jeered Render.

"Yes! Yes!" cried Caesar. " 'Beware!' That is good! Beware what?"

"The ides – "

"Yes? The ides – ?"

" – of Octember."

He released the garment.

"What is that you say? What is Octember?"

"A month."

"You lie! There is no month of Octember!"

"And that is the date noble Caesar need fear – the non-existent time, the never-to-be-calendared occasion."

Render vanished around another sudden corner.

"Wait! Come back!"

Render laughed, and the Forum laughed with him. The birdcries became a chorus of inhuman jeers.

"You mock me!" wept Caesar.

The Forum was an oven, and the perspiration formed like a glassy mask over Caesar's narrow forehead, sharp nose and chinless jaw.

"I want to be assassinated too!" he sobbed. "It isn't fair!"

And Render tore the Forum and the senators and the grinning corpse of Antony to pieces and stuffed them into a black sack – with the unseen movement of a single finger – and last of all went Caesar.

Charles Render sat before the ninety white buttons and the two red ones, not really looking at any of them. His right arm moved, in its soundless sling, across the lap-level surface of the console – pushing some of the buttons, skipping over others, moving on, retracing its path to press the next in the order of the Recall Series.

Sensations throttled, emotions reduced to nothing, Representative Erikson knew the oblivion of the womb.

There was a soft click.

Render's hand had glided to the end of the bottom row of buttons. An act of conscious intent – will, if you like – was required to push the red button.

Render freed his arm and lifted off his crown of Medusa-hair leads and microminiature circuitry. He slid from behind his desk-couch and raised the hood. He walked to the window and transpared it, fingering forth a cigarette.

One minute in the ro-womb, he decided. *No more. This is a crucial one. Hope it doesn't snow till later – those clouds look mean . . .*

It was smooth yellow trellises and high towers, glassy and gray, all smouldering into evening under a shale-colored sky; the city was squared volcanic islands, glowing in the end-of-day light, rumbling deep down under the earth; it was fat, incessant rivers of traffic, rushing.

Render turned away from the window and approached the great egg that lay beside his desk, smooth and glittering. It threw back a reflection that smashed all aquilinity from his nose, turned his eyes to gray saucers, transformed his hair into a light-streaked skyline; his reddish necktie became the wide tongue of a ghoul.

He smiled, reached across the desk. He pressed the second red button.

With a sigh, the egg lost its dazzling opacity and a horizontal crack appeared about its middle. Through the now-transparent shell, Render could see Erikson grimacing, squeezing his eyes tight, fighting against a return to consciousness and the thing it would contain. The upper half of the egg rose vertical to the base, exposing him knobby and pink on half-shell. When his eyes opened he did not look at Render. He rose to his feet and began dressing. Render used this time to check the ro-womb.

He leaned back across his desk and pressed the buttons: temperature control, full range, *check;* exotic sounds – he raised the earphone – *check,* on bells, on buzzes, on violin notes and whistles, on squeals and moans, on traffic noises and the sound of surf; *check,* on the feedback circuit – holding the patient's own voice, trapped earlier in analysis; *check,* on the sound blanket, the moisture spray, the odor banks; *check,* on the couch agitator and the colored lights, the taste stimulants . . .

Render closed the egg and shut off its power. He pushed the unit into the closet, palmed shut the door. The tapes had registered a valid sequence.

"Sit down," he directed Erikson.

The man did so, fidgeting with his collar.

"You have full recall," said Render, "so there is no need for me to summarize what occurred. Nothing can be hidden from me. I was there."

Erikson nodded.

"The significance of the episode should be apparent to you."

Erikson nodded again, finally finding his voice. "But was it valid?" he asked. "I mean, you constructed the dream and you controlled it, all the way. I didn't really *dream* it – in the way I would normally dream. Your ability to make things happen stacks the deck for whatever you're going to say – doesn't it?"

Render shook his head slowly, flicked an ash into the southern hemisphere of his globe-made-ashtray, and met Erikson's eyes.

"It is true that I supplied the format and modified the forms. You, however, filled them with an emotional significance, promoted them to the status of symbols corresponding to your problem. If the dream was not a valid analogue it would not have provoked the reactions it did. It would have been devoid of the anxiety-patterns which were registered on the tapes.

"You have been in analysis for many months now," he continued, "and everything I have learned thus far serves to convince me that your fears of assassination are without any basis in fact."

Erikson glared.

"Then why the hell do I have them?"

"Because," said Render, "you would like very much to be the subject of an assassination."

Erikson smiled then, his composure beginning to return.

"I assure you, doctor, I have never contemplated suicide, nor have I any desire to stop living."

He produced a cigar and applied a flame to it. His hand shook.

"When you came to me this summer," said Render, "you stated that you were in fear of an attempt on your life. You were quite vague as to why anyone should want to kill you – "

"My position! You can't be a Representative as long as I have and make no enemies!"

"Yet," replied Render, "it appears that you have managed it. When you permitted me to discuss this with your detectives I was informed that they could unearth nothing to indicate that your fears might have any real foundation. Nothing."

"They haven't looked far enough – or in the right places. They'll turn up something."

"I'm afraid not."

"Why?"

"Because, I repeat, your feelings are without any objective basis. – Be honest with me. Have you any information whatsoever indicating that someone hates you enough to want to kill you?"

"I receive many threatening letters . . ."

"As do all Representatives – and all of those directed to you during the past year have been investigated and found to be the work of cranks. Can you offer me *one* piece of evidence to substantiate your claims?"

Erikson studied the tip of his cigar.

"I came to you on the advice of a colleague," he said, "came to you to have you poke around inside my mind to find me something of that sort, to give my detectives something to work with – someone I've injured severely perhaps – or some damaging piece of legislation I've dealt with . . ."

" – And I found nothing," said Render, "nothing, that is, but the cause of your discontent. Now, of course, you are afraid to hear it, and you are attempting to divert me from explaining my diagnosis – "

"I am not!"

"Then listen. You can comment afterward if you want, but you've poked and dawdled around here for months, unwilling to accept what I presented to you in a dozen different forms. Now I am going to tell you outright what it is, and you can do what you want about it."

"Fine."

"First," he said, "you would like very much to have an enemy or enemies – "

"Ridiculous!"

" – Because it is the only alternative to having friends – "

"I have lots of friends!"

" – Because nobody wants to be completely ignored, to be an object for whom no one has really strong feelings. Hatred and love are the ultimate forms of human regard. Lacking one, and unable to achieve it, you sought the other. You wanted it so badly that you succeeded in convincing yourself it existed. But there is always a psychic pricetag on these things. Answering a genuine emotional need with a body of desire-surrogates does not produce real satisfaction, but anxiety, discomfort – because in these matters the psyche should be an open system. You did not seek outside yourself for human regard. You were closed off. You created that which you needed from the stuff of your own being. You are a man very much in need of strong relationships with other people."

"Manure!"

"Take it or leave it," said Render. "I suggest you take it."

"I've been paying you half a year to help find out who wants to kill me. Now you sit there and tell me I made the whole thing up to satisfy a desire to have someone hate me."

"Hate you, or love you. That's right."

"It's absurd! I meet so many people that I carry a pocket recorder and a lapel-camera, just so I can recall them all . . ."

"Meeting quantities of people is hardly what I was speaking of. Tell me, *did* that dream sequence have a strong meaning for you?"

Erikson was silent for several tickings of the huge wall-clock.

"Yes," he finally conceded, "it did. But your interpretation of the matter is still absurd. Granting though, just for the sake of argument, that what you say is correct – what would I do to get out of this bind?"

Render leaned back in his chair.

"Rechannel the energies that went into producing the thing. Meet some people as yourself, Joe Erikson, rather than Representative Erikson. Take up something you can do with other people – something non-political, and perhaps somewhat competitive – and make some real friends or enemies, preferably the former. I've encouraged you to do this all along."

"Then tell me something else."

"Gladly."

"Assuming you *are* right, why is it that I am neither liked nor hated, and never have been? I have a responsible position in the Legislature. I meet people all the time. Why am I so neutral a – thing?"

Highly familiar now with Erikson's career, Render had to push aside his true thoughts on the matter, as they were of no operational value. He wanted to cite him Dante's observations concerning the trimmers – those souls who, denied heaven for their lack of virtue, were also denied entrance to hell for a lack of significant vices – in short, the ones who trimmed their sails to move them with every wind of the times, who lacked direction, who were not really concerned toward which ports they were pushed. Such was Erikson's long and colorless career of migrant loyalties, of political reversals.

Render said:

"More and more people find themselves in such circumstances these days. It is due largely to the increasing complexity of society and the depersonalization of the individual into a sociometric unit. Even the act of cathecting toward other persons has grown more forced as a result. There are so many of us these days."

Erikson nodded, and Render smiled inwardly.

Sometimes the gruff line, and then the lecture . . .

"I've got the feeling you could be right," said Erikson. "Sometimes I do feel like what you just described – a unit, something depersonalized . . ."

Render glanced at the clock.

"What you choose to do about it from here is, of course, your own decision to make. I think you'd be wasting your time to remain in analysis any longer. We are now both aware of the cause of your complaint. I can't take you by the hand and show you how to lead your life. I can indicate, I can commiserate – but no more deep probing. Make an appointment as soon as you feel a need to discuss your activities and relate them to my diagnosis."

"I will," nodded Erikson, "and – damn that dream! It got to me. You can make them seem as vivid as waking life – more vivid . . . It may be a long while before I can forget it."

"I hope so."

"Okay, doctor." He rose to his feet, extended a hand. "I'll probably be back in a couple weeks. I'll give this socializing a fair try." He grinned at the word he normally frowned upon. "In fact, I'll start now. May I buy you a drink around the corner, downstairs?"

Render met the moist palm which seemed as weary of the performance as a lead actor in too successful a play. He felt almost sorry as he said, "Thank you, but I have an engagement."

Render helped him on with his coat then, handed him his hat and saw him to the door.

"Well, good night."

"Good night."

As the door closed soundlessly behind him, Render recrossed the dark Astrakhan to his mahogany fortress and flipped his cigarette into the southern hemisphere of a globe ashtray. He leaned back in his chair, hands behind his head, eyes closed.

"Of course it was more real than life," he informed no one in particular, "I shaped it."

Smiling, he reviewed the dream sequence step by step, wishing some of his former instructors could have witnessed it. It had been well-constructed and powerfully executed, as well as being precisely appropriate for the case at hand. But then, he was Render, the Shaper – one of the two hundred or so special analysts whose own psychic makeup permitted them to enter into neurotic patterns without carrying away more than an esthetic gratification from the mimesis of aberrance – a Sane Hatter.

Render stirred his recollections. He had been analyzed himself, analyzed and passed upon as a granite-willed, ultra-stable outsider – tough enough to weather the basilisk gaze of a fixation, walk unscathed amidst the chimarae of perversions, force dark Mother Medusa to close her eyes before the caduceus of his art. His own analysis had not been difficult. Nine years before (it seemed much longer) he had suffered a willing injection of novocain into the most painful area of his spirit. It was after the auto wreck, after the death of Ruth, and of Miranda, their daughter, that he had begun to feel detached. Perhaps he did not want to recover certain empathies; perhaps his own world was now based upon a certain rigidity of feeling. If this was true, he was wise enough in the ways of the mind to realize it, and perhaps he had decided that such a world had its own compensations.

His son Peter was now ten years old. He was attending a school of quality, and he penned his father a letter every week. The letters were becoming progressively literate, showing signs of a precociousness of which Render could not but approve. He would take the boy with him to Europe in the summer.

As for Jill – Jill DeVille (what a luscious, ridiculous name! – he loved her for it) – she was growing if anything, more interesting to him. (He wondered if this was an indication of early middle age.) He was vastly taken by her unmusical nasal voice, her sudden interest in architecture, her concern with the unremovable mole on the right side of her otherwise well-designed nose. He should really call her immediately and go in search of a new restaurant. For some reason though, he did not feel like it.

It had been several weeks since he had visited his club, The Partridge and Scalpel, and he felt a strong desire to eat from an oaken table, alone, in the split-level dining room with the three fireplaces, beneath the artificial torches and the boars' heads like gin ads. So he pushed his perforated membership card into the phone-slot on his desk and there were two buzzes behind the voice- screen.

"Hello, Partridge and Scalpel," said the voice. "May I help you?"

"Charles Render," he said. "I'd like a table in about half an hour."

"How many will there be?"

"Just me."

"Very good, sir. Half an hour, then. – That's 'Render'? – R-e-n-d-er-?"

"Right."

"Thank you."

He broke the connection and rose from his desk. Outside, the day had vanished.

The monoliths and the towers gave forth their own light now. A soft snow, like sugar, was sifting down through the shadows and transforming itself into beads on the windowpane.

Render shrugged into his overcoat, turned off the lights, locked the inner office. There was a note on Mrs. Hedges' blotter.

Miss DeVille called, it said.

He crumpled the note and tossed it into the waste-chute. He would call her tomorrow and say he had been working until late on his lecture.

He switched off the final light, clapped his hat onto his head and passed through the outer door, locking it as he went. The drop took him to the sub-subcellar where his auto was parked.

It was chilly in the sub-sub, and his footsteps seemed loud on the concrete as he passed among the parked vehicles. Beneath the glare of the naked lights, his S-7 Spinner was a sleek gray cocoon from which it seemed turbulent wings might at any moment emerge. The double row of antennae which fanned forward from the slope of its hood added to this feeling. Render thumbed open the door.

He touched the ignition and there was the sound of a lone bee awakening in a great hive. The door swung soundlessly shut as he raised the steering wheel and locked it into place. He spun up the spiral ramp and came to a rolling stop before the big overhead.

As the door rattled upward he lighted his destination screen and turned the knob that shifted the broadcast map. – Left to right, top to bottom, section by section he shifted it, until he located the portion of Carnegie Avenue he desired. He punched out its coordinates and lowered the wheel. The car switched over to monitor and moved out onto the highway marginal. Render lit a cigarette.

Pushing his seat back into the centerspace, he left all the windows transparent. It was pleasant to half-recline and watch the oncoming cars drift past him like swarms of fireflies. He pushed his hat back on his head and stared upward.

He could remember a time when he had loved snow, when it had reminded him of novels by Thomas Mann and music by Scandinavian composers. In his mind now, though, there was another element from which it could never be wholly dissociated. He could visualize so clearly the eddies of milk-white coldness that swirled about his old manual-steer auto, flowing into its fire-charred interior to rewhiten that which had been blackened; so clearly – as though he had walked toward it across a chalky lakebottom – it, the sunken wreck, and he, the diver – unable to open his mouth to speak, for fear of drowning; and he knew, whenever he looked upon falling snow, that somewhere skulls were whitening. But nine years had washed away much of the pain, and he also knew that the night was lovely.

He was sped along the wide, wide roads, shot across high bridges, their surfaces slick and gleaming beneath his lights, was woven through frantic cloverleafs and plunged into a tunnel whose dimly glowing walls blurred by him like a mirage. Finally, he switched the windows to opaque and closed his eyes.

He could not remember whether he had dozed for a moment or not, which meant he probably had. He felt the car slowing, and he moved the seat forward and turned on the windows again. Almost simultaneously, the cut-off buzzer sounded. He raised the steering wheel and pulled into the parking dome, stepped out onto the ramp and left the car to the parking unit, receiving his ticket from that box-headed robot which took its solemn revenge on mankind by sticking forth a cardboard tongue at everyone it served.

As always, the noises were as subdued as the lighting. The place seemed to absorb sound and convert it into warmth, to lull the tongue with aromas strong enough to be tasted, to hypnotize the ear with the vivid crackle of the triple hearths. Render was pleased to see that his favorite table, in the corner off the right of the smaller fireplace, had been held for him. He knew the menu from memory, but he studied it with zeal as he sipped a Manhattan and worked up an order to match his appetite. Shaping sessions always left him ravenously hungry.

"Doctor Render . . . ?"

"Yes?" He looked up.

"Doctor Shallot would like to speak with you," said the waiter.

"I don't know anyone named Shallot," he said. "Are you sure he doesn't want Bender? He's a surgeon from Metro who sometimes eats here . . ."

The waiter shook his head.

"No, sir – 'Render'. See here?" He extended a three-by-five card on which Render's full name was typed in capital letters. "Doctor Shallot has dined here nearly every night for the past two weeks," he explained, "and on each occasion has asked to be notified if you came in."

"Hm?" mused Render. "That's odd. Why didn't he just call me at my office?"

The waiter smiled and made a vague gesture.

"Well, tell him to come on over," he said, gulping his Manhattan, "and bring me another of these."

"Unfortunately, Doctor Shallot is blind," explained the waiter. "It would be easier if you – "

"All right, sure." Render stood up, relinquishing his favorite table with a strong premonition that he would not be returning to it that evening.

"Lead on."

They threaded their way among the diners, heading up to the next level. A familiar face said "hello" from a table set back against the wall, and Render nodded a greeting to a former seminar pupil whose name was Jurgens or Jirkans or something like that.

He moved on, into the smaller dining room wherein only two tables were occupied. No, three. There was one set in the corner at the far end of the darkened bar, partly masked by an ancient suit of armor. The waiter was heading him in that direction.

They stopped before the table and Render stared down into the darkened glasses that had tilted upward as they approached. Doctor Shallot was a woman, somewhere in the vicinity of her early thirties. Her low bronze bangs did not fully conceal the spot of silver which she wore on her forehead like a caste-mark. Render inhaled, and her head jerked slightly as the tip of his cigarette flared. She appeared to be staring straight up into his eyes. It was an uncomfortable feeling, even knowing that all she could distinguish of him was that which her minute photoelectric cell transmitted to her visual cortex over the hair-fine wire implants attached to that oscillator convertor: in short, the glow of his cigarette.

"Doctor Shallot, this is Doctor Render," the waiter was saying.

"Good evening," said Render.

"Good evening," she said. "My name is Eileen and I've wanted very badly to meet you." He thought he detected a slight quaver in her voice. "Will you join me for dinner?"

"My pleasure," he acknowledged, and the waiter drew out the chair.

Render sat down, noting that the woman across from him already had a drink. He reminded the waiter of his second Manhattan.

"Have you ordered yet?" he inquired.

"No."

". . . And two menus – " he started to say, then bit his tongue. "Only one," she smiled.

"Make it none," he amended, and recited the menu. They ordered. Then:

"Do you always do that?"

"What?"

"Carry menus in your head."

"Only a few," he said, "for awkward occasions. What was it you wanted to see – talk to me about?"

"You're a neuroparticipant therapist," she stated, "a Shaper."

"And you are – ?"

" – a resident in psychiatry at State Psych. I have a year remaining."

"You knew Sam Riscomb then."

"Yes, he helped me get my appointment. He was my adviser."

"He was a very good friend of mine. We studied together at Menninger."

She nodded.

"I'd often heard him speak of you – that's one of the reasons I wanted to meet you. He's responsible for encouraging me to go ahead with my plans, despite my handicap."

Render stared at her. She was wearing a dark green dress which appeared to be made of velvet. About three inches to the left of the bodice was a pin which might have been gold. It displayed a red stone in which the outline of a goblet was cast. Or was it really two profiles that were outlined, staring through the stone at one another? It seemed vaguely familiar to him, but he could not place it at the moment. It glittered expensively in the dim light.

Render accepted his drink from the waiter.

"I want to become a neuroparticipant therapist," she told him.

And if she had possessed vision Render would have thought she was staring at him, hoping for some response in his expression. He could not quite calculate what she wanted him to say.

"I commend your choice," he said, "and I respect your ambition." He tried to put his smile into his voice. "It is not an easy thing, of course, not all of the requirements being academic ones."

"I know," she said. "But then, I have been blind since birth and it was not an easy thing to come this far."

"Since birth?" he repeated. "I thought you might have lost your sight recently. You did your undergrad work then, and went on through med school without eyes . . . That's – rather impressive."

"Thank you," she said, "but it isn't. Not really. I heard about the first neuroparticipants – Bartclmetz and the rest – when I was a child, and I decided then that I wanted to be one. My life ever since has been governed by that desire."

"What did you do in the labs?" he inquired. " – Not being able to see a specimen, look through a microscope . . . ? Or all that reading?"

"I hired people to read my assignments to me. I taped everything.

The school understood that I wanted to go into psychiatry and they permitted a special arrangement for labs. I've been guided through the dissection of cadavers by lab assistants, and I've had everything described to me. I can tell things by touch . . . and I have a memory like yours with the menu," she smiled. "'The quality of psychoparticipation phenomena can only be gauged by the therapist himself, at that moment outside of time and space as we normally know it, when he stands in the midst of a world erected from the stuff of another man's dreams, recognizes there the non-Euclidian architecture of aberrance, and then takes his patient by the hand and tours the landscape . . . If he can lead him back to the common earth, then his judgments were sound, his actions valid.'"

"From *Why No Psychometrics in This Place*," reflected Render.

" – by Charles Render, M.D."

"Our dinner is already moving in this direction," he noted, picking up his drink as the speed-cooked meal was pushed toward them in the kitchen-buoy.

"That's one of the reasons I wanted to meet you," she continued, raising her glass as the dishes rattled before her. "I want you to help me become a Shaper."

Her shaded eyes, as vacant as a statue's, sought him again.

"Yours is a completely unique situation," he commented. "There has never been a congenitally blind neuroparticipant – for obvious reasons. I'd have to consider all the aspects of the situation before I could advise you. Let's eat now, though. I'm starved."

"All right. But my blindness does not mean that I have never seen."

He did not ask her what she meant by that, because prime ribs were standing in front of him now and there was a bottle of Chambertin at his elbow. He did pause long enough to notice though, as she raised her left hand from beneath the table, that she wore no rings.

"I wonder if it's still snowing," he commented as they drank their coffee. "It was coming down pretty hard when I pulled into the dome."

"I hope so," she said, "even though it diffuses the light and I can't 'see' anything at all through it. I like to feel it falling about me and blowing against my face."

"How do you get about?"

"My dog, Sigmund – I gave him the night off," she smiled, " – he can guide me anywhere. He's a mutie Shepherd."

"Oh?" Render grew curious. "Can he talk much?"

She nodded.

"That operation wasn't as successful on him as on some of them, though. He has a vocabulary of about four hundred words, but I think it causes him pain to speak. He's quite intelligent. You'll have to meet him sometime."

Render began speculating immediately. He had spoken with such animals at recent medical conferences, and had been startled by their combination of reasoning ability and their devotion to their handlers. Much chromosome tinkering, followed by delicate embryo-surgery, was required to give a dog a brain capacity greater than a chimpanzee's. Several followup operations were necessary to produce vocal abilities. Most such experiments ended in failure, and the dozen or so puppies a year on which they succeeded were valued in the neighborhood of a hundred thousand dollars each. He realized then, as he lit a cigarette and held the light for a moment, that the stone in Miss Shallot's medallion was a genuine ruby. He began to suspect that her admission to a medical school might, in addition to her academic record, have been based upon a sizeable endowment to the college of her choice. Perhaps he was being unfair though, he chided himself.

"Yes," he said, "we might do a paper on canine neuroses. Does he ever refer to his father as 'that son of a female Shepherd'?"

"He never met his father," she said, quite soberly. "He was raised apart from other dogs. His attitude could hardly be typical. I don't think you'll ever learn the functional psychology of the dog from a mutie."

"I imagine you're right," he dismissed it. "More coffee?"

"No, thanks."

Deciding it was time to continue the discussion, he said, "So you want to be a Shaper . . ."

"Yes."

"I hate to be the one to destroy anybody's high ambitions," he told her. "Like poison, I hate it. Unless they have no foundation at all in reality. Then I can be ruthless. So – honestly, frankly, and in all sincerity, I do not see how it could ever be managed. Perhaps you're a fine psychiatrist – but in my opinion, it is a physical and mental impossibility for you ever to become a neuroparticipant. As for my reasons – "

"Wait," she said. "Not here, please. Humor me. I'm tired of this stuffy place – take me somewhere else to talk. I think I might be able to convince you there *is* a way."

"Why not?" he shrugged. "I have plenty of time. Sure – you call it. Where?"

"Blindspin?"

He suppressed an unwilling chuckle at the expression, but she laughed aloud.

"Fine," he said, "but I'm still thirsty."

A bottle of champagne was tallied and he signed the check despite her protests. It arrived in a colorful "Drink While You Drive" basket, and they stood then, and she was tall, but he was taller.

Blindspin.

A single name of a multitude of practices centered about the auto-driven auto. Flashing across the country in the sure hands of an invisible chauffeur, windows all opaque, night dark, sky high, tires assailing the road below like four phantom buzzsaws – and starting from scratch and ending in the same place, and never knowing where you are going or where you have been – it is possible, for a moment, to kindle some feeling of individuality in the coldest brainpan, to produce a momentary awareness of self by virtue of an apartness from all but a sense of motion. This is because movement through darkness is the ultimate abstraction of life itself – at least that's what one of the Vital Comedians said, and everybody in the place laughed.

Actually, now, the phenomenon known as blindspin first became prevalent (as might be suspected) among certain younger members of the community, when monitored highways deprived them of the means to exercise their automobiles in some of the more individualistic ways which had come to be frowned upon by the National Traffic Control Authority. Something had to be done.

It was.

The first, disastrous reaction involved the simple engineering feat of disconnecting the broadcast control unit after one had entered onto a monitored highway. This resulted in the car's vanishing from the ken of the monitor and passing back into the control of its occupants. Jealous as a deity, a monitor will not tolerate that which denies its programmed omniscience: it will thunder and lightning in the Highway Control Station nearest the point of last contact, sending winged seraphs in search of that which has slipped from sight.

Often, however, this was too late in happening, for the roads are many and well-paved. Escape from detection was, at first, relatively easy to achieve.

Other vehicles, though, necessarily behave as if a rebel has no actual existence. Its presence cannot be allowed for.

Boxed-in on a heavily traveled section of roadway, the offender is subject to immediate annihilation in the event of any overall speedup or shift in traffic pattern which involves movement through his theoretically vacant position. This, in the early days of monitor-controls, caused a rapid series of collisions. Monitoring devices later became far more sophisticated, and mechanized cutoffs reduced the collision incidence subsequent to such an action. The quality of the pulpefactions and contusions which did occur, however, remained unaltered.

The next reaction was based on a thing which had been overlooked because it was obvious. The monitors took people where they wanted to go only because people told them they wanted to go there. A person pressing a random series of coordinates, without reference to any map, would either be left with a stalled automobile and a "RECHECK YOUR COORDINATES" light, or would suddenly be whisked away in any direction. The latter possesses a certain romantic appeal in that it offers speed, unexpected sights, and free hands. Also, it is perfectly legal; and it is possible to navigate all over two continents in this manner, if one is possessed of sufficient wherewithal and gluteal stamina.

As is the case in all such matters, the practice diffused upwards through the age brackets. School teachers who only drove on Sundays fell into disrepute as selling points for used autos. Such is the way a world ends, said the entertainer.

End or no, the car designed to move on monitored highways is a mobile efficiency unit, complete with latrine, cupboard, refrigerator compartment and gaming table. It also sleeps two with ease and four with some crowding. On occasion, three can be a real crowd.

Render drove out of the dome and into the marginal aisle. He halted the car.

"Want to jab some coordinates?" he asked.

"You do it. My fingers know too many."

Render punched random buttons. The Spinner moved onto the highway. Render asked speed of the vehicle then, and it moved into the high-acceleration lane.

The Spinner's lights burnt holes in the darkness. The city backed away fast; it was a smouldering bonfire on both sides of the road, stirred by sudden gusts of wind, hidden by white swirlings, obscured by the steady fall of gray ash. Render knew his speed was only about sixty percent of what it would have been on a clear, dry night.

He did not blank the windows, but leaned back and stared out through them. Eileen "looked" ahead into what light there was.

Neither of them said anything for ten or fifteen minutes.

The city shrank to sub-city as they sped on. After a time, short sections of open road began to appear.

"Tell me what it looks like outside," she said.

"Why didn't you ask me to describe your dinner, or the suit of armor beside our table?"

"Because I tasted one and felt the other. This is different."

"There is snow falling outside. Take it away and what you have left is black."

"What else?"

"There is slush on the road. When it starts to freeze, traffic will drop to a crawl unless we outrun this storm. The slush looks like an old, dark syrup, just starting to get sugary on top."

"Anything else?"

"That's it, lady."

"Is it snowing harder or less hard than when we left the club?"

"Harder, I should say."

"Would you pour me a drink?" she asked him.

"Certainly."

They turned their seats inward and Render raised the table. He fetched two glasses from the cupboard.

"Your health," said Render, after he had poured.

"Here's looking at you."

Render downed his drink. She sipped hers. He waited for her next comment. He knew that two cannot play at the Socratic game, and he expected more questions before she said what she wanted to say.

She said: "What is the most beautiful thing you have ever seen?"

Yes, he decided, he had guessed correctly.

He replied without hesitation: "The sinking of Atlantis."

"I was serious."

"So was I."

"Would you care to elaborate?"

"I sank Atlantis," he said, "personally.

"It was about three years ago. And God! it was lovely! It was all ivory towers and golden minarets and silver balconies. There were bridges of opal, and crimson pendants, and a milk-white river flowing between lemon-colored banks. There were jade steeples, and trees as old as the world tickling the bellies of clouds, and ships in the great sea-harbor of Xanadu, as delicately constructed as musical instruments, all swaying with the tides. The twelve princes of the realm held court in the dozen-pillared Colliseum of the Zodiac, to listen to a Greek tenor saxophonist play at sunset.

"The Greek, of course, was a patient of mine – paranoiac. The etiology of the thing is rather complicated, but that's what I wandered into inside his mind. I gave him free rein for a while, and in the end I had to split Atlantis in half and sink it full fathom five. He's playing again and you've doubtless heard his sounds, if you like such sounds at all. He's good. I still see him periodically, but he is no longer the last descendent of the greatest minstrel of Atlantis. He's just a fine, late twentieth-century saxman.

"Sometimes though, as I look back on the apocalypse I worked within his vision of grandeur, I experience a fleeting sense of lost beauty – because, for a single moment, his abnormally intense feelings were my feelings, and he felt that his dream was the most beautiful thing in the world."

He refilled their glasses.

"That wasn't exactly what I meant," she said.

"I know."

"I meant something real."

"It was more real than real, I assure you."

"I don't doubt it, but . . ."

" – But I destroyed the foundation you were laying for your argument. Okay, I apologize. I'll hand it back to you. Here's something that could be real:

"We are moving along the edge of a great bowl of sand," he said. "Into it, the snow is gently drifting. In the spring the snow will melt, the waters will run down into the earth, or be evaporated away by the heat of the sun. Then only the sand will remain. Nothing grows in the sand, except for an occasional cactus. Nothing lives here but snakes, a few birds, insects, burrowing things, and a wandering coyote or two. In the afternoon these things will look for shade. Any place where there's an old fence post or a rock or a skull or a cactus to block out the sun, there you will witness life cowering before the elements. But the colors are beyond belief, and the elements are more lovely, almost, than the things they destroy."

"There is no such place near here," she said.

"If I say it, then there is. Isn't there? I've seen it."

"Yes . . . you're right."

"And it doesn't matter if it's a painting by a woman named O'Keefe, or something right outside our window, does it? If I've seen it?"

"I acknowledge the truth of the diagnosis," she said. "Do you want to speak it for me?"

"No, go ahead."

He refilled the small glasses once more.

"The damage is in my eyes," she told him, "not my brain."

He lit her cigarette.

"I can see with other eyes if I can enter other brains."

He lit his own cigarette.

"Neuroparticipation is based upon the fact that two nervous systems can share the same impulses, the same fantasies . . ."

"*Controlled* fantasies."

"I could perform therapy and at the same time experience genuine visual impressions."

"No," said Render.

"You don't know what it's like to be cut off from a whole area of stimuli! To know that a Mongoloid idiot can experience something you can never know – and that he cannot appreciate it because, like you, he was condemned before birth in a court of biological happenstance, in a place where there is no justice – only fortuity, pure and simple."

"The universe did not invent justice. Man did. Unfortunately, man must reside in the universe."

"I'm not asking the universe to help me – I'm asking you."

"I'm sorry," said Render.

"Why won't you help me?"

"At this moment you are demonstrating my main reason."

"Which is . . . ?"

"Emotion. This thing means far too much to you. When the therapist is in-phase with a patient he is narcoelectrically removed from most of his own bodily sensations. This is necessary – because his mind must be completely absorbed by the task at hand. It is also necessary that his emotions undergo a similar suspension. This, of course, is impossible in the one sense that a person always emotes to some degree. But the therapist's emotions are sublimated into a generalized feeling of exhilaration – or, as in my own case, into an artistic reverie. With you, however, the 'seeing' would be too much. You would be in constant danger of losing control of the dream."

"I disagree with you."

"Of course you do. But the fact remains that you would be dealing, and dealing constantly, with the abnormal. The power of a neurosis is unimaginable to ninety-nine point et cetera percent of the population, because we can never adequately judge the intensity of our own – let alone those of others, when we only see them from the outside. That is why no neuroparticipant will ever undertake to treat a full-blown psychotic. The few pioneers in that area are all themselves in therapy today. It would be like diving into a maelstrom. If the therapist loses the upper hand in an intense session, he becomes the Shaped rather than the Shaper. The synapses respond like a fission reaction when nervous impulses are artificially augmented. The transference effect is almost instantaneous.

"I did an awful lot of skiing five years ago. This is because I was a claustrophobe. I had to run and it took me six months to beat the thing – all because of one tiny lapse that occurred in a measureless fraction of an instant. I had to refer the patient to another therapist. And this was only a minor repercussion. – If you were to go gaga over the scenery, girl, you could wind up in a rest home for life."

She finished her drink and Render refilled the glass. The night raced by. They had left the city far behind them, and the road was open and clear. The darkness eased more and more of itself between the falling flakes. The Spinner picked up speed.

"All right," she admitted, "maybe you're right. Still, though, I think you can help me."

"How?" he asked.

"Accustom me to seeing, so that the images will lose their novelty, the emotions wear off. Accept me as a patient and rid me of my sight-anxiety. Then what you have said so far will cease to apply. I will be able to undertake the training then, and give my full attention to therapy. I'll be able to sublimate the sight-pleasure into something else."

Render wondered.

Perhaps it could be done. It would be a difficult undertaking, though.

It might also make therapeutic history.

No one was really qualified to try it, because no one had ever tried it before.

But Eileen Shallot was a rarity – no, a unique item – for it was likely she was the only person in the world who combined the necessary technical background with the unique problem.

He drained his glass, refilled it, refilled hers.

He was still considering the problem as the "RECOORDINATE" light came on and the car pulled into a cutoff and stood there. He switched off the buzzer and sat there for a long while, thinking.

It was not often that other persons heard him acknowledge his feelings regarding his skill. His colleagues considered him modest.

Offhand, though, it might be noted that he was aware that the day a better neuroparticipant began practicing would be the day that a troubled homo sapien was to be treated by something but immeasurably less than angels.

Two drinks remained. Then he tossed the emptied bottle into the backbin.

"You know something?" he finally said.

"What?"

"It might be worth a try."

He swiveled about then and leaned forward to recoordinate, but she was there first. As he pressed the buttons and the S-7 swung around, she kissed him. Below her dark glasses her cheeks were moist.

II

The suicide bothered him more than it should have, and Mrs. Lambert had called the day before to cancel her appointment. So Render decided to spend the morning being pensive. Accordingly, he entered the office wearing a cigar and a frown.

"Did you see . . . ?" asked Mrs. Hedges.

"Yes." He pitched his coat onto the table that stood in the far corner of the room. He crossed to the window, stared down. "Yes," he repeated, "I was driving by with my windows clear. They were still cleaning up when I passed."

"Did you know him?"

"I don't even know the name yet. How could I?"

"Priss Tully just called me – she's a receptionist for that engineering outfit up on the eighty-sixth. She says it was James Irizarry, an ad designer who had offices down the hall from them – That's a long way to fall. He must have been unconscious when he hit, huh? He bounced off the building. If you open the window and lean out you can see – off to the left there – where . . ."

"Never mind, Bennie. – Your friend have any idea why he did it?"

"Not really. His secretary came running up the hall, screaming. Seems she went in his office to see him about some drawings, just as he was getting up over the sill. There was a note on his board. 'I've had everything I wanted,' it said. 'Why wait around?' Sort of funny, huh? I don't mean *funny* . . ."

"Yeah. – Know anything about his personal affairs?"

"Married. Coupla kids. Good professional rep. Lots of business.

Sober as anybody. – He could afford an office in this building."

"Good Lord!" Render turned. "Have you got a case file there or something?"

"You know," she shrugged her thick shoulders, "I've got friends all over this hive. We always talk when things go slow. Prissy's my sister-in-law, anyhow – "

"You mean that if I dived through this window right now, my current biography would make the rounds in the next five minutes?"

"Probably," she twisted her bright lips into a smile, "give or take a couple. But don't do it today, huh? – You know, it would be kind of anticlimactic, and it wouldn't get the same coverage as a solus.

"Anyhow," she continued, "you're a mind-mixer. You wouldn't do it."

"You're betting against statistics," he observed. "The medical profession, along with attorneys, manages about three times as many as most other work areas."

"Hey!" She looked worried. "Go 'way from my window!

"I'd have to go to work for Dr. Hanson then," she added, "and he's a slob."

He moved to her desk.

"I never know when to take you seriously," she decided.

"I appreciate your concern," he nodded, "indeed I do. As a matter of fact, I have never been statistic-prone – I should have repercussed out of the neuropy game four years ago.

"You'd be a headline, though," she mused. "All those reporters asking me about you . . . Hey, why do they do it, huh?"

"Who?"

"Anybody."

"How should I know, Bennie? I'm only a humble psyche-stirrer. If I could pinpoint a general underlying cause – and then maybe figure a way to anticipate the thing – why, it might even be better than my jumping, for newscopy. But I can't do it, because there is no single, simple reason – I don't think."

"Oh."

"About thirty-five years ago it was the ninth leading cause of death in the United States. Now it's number six for North and South America. I think it's seventh in Europe."

"And nobody will ever really know why Irizarry jumped?"

Render swung a chair backward and seated himself. He knocked an ash into her petite and gleaming tray. She emptied it into the waste-chute, hastily, and coughed a significant cough.

"Oh, one can always speculate," he said, "and one in my profession will. The first thing to consider would be the personality traits which might predispose a man to periods of depression. People who keep their emotions under rigid control, people who are conscientious and rather compulsively concerned with small matters . . ." He knocked another fleck of ash into her tray and watched as she reached out to dump it, then quickly drew her hand back again. He grinned an evil grin. "In short," he finished, "some of the characteristics of people in professions which require individual, rather than group performance – medicine, law, the arts."

She regarded him speculatively.

"Don't worry though," he chuckled, "I'm pleased as hell with life."

"You're kind of down in the mouth this morning."

"Pete called me. He broke his ankle yesterday in gym class. They ought to supervise those things more closely. I'm thinking of changing his school."

"Again?"

"Maybe. I'll see. The headmaster is going to call me this afternoon. I don't like to keep shuffling him, but I do want him to finish school in one piece."

"A kid can't grow up without an accident or two. It's – statistics."

"Statistics aren't the same thing as destiny, Bennie. Everybody makes his own.

"Statistics or destiny?"

"Both, I guess."

"I think that if something's going to happen, it's going to happen."

"I don't. I happen to think that the human will, backed by a sane mind can exercise some measure of control over events. If I didn't think so, I wouldn't be in the racket I'm in."

"The world's a machine – you know – cause, effect. Statistics do imply the prob – "

"The human mind is not a machine, and I do not know cause and effect. Nobody does."

"You have a degree in chemistry, as I recall. You're a scientist, Doc."

"So I'm a Trotskyite deviationist," he smiled, stretching, "and you were once a ballet teacher." He got to his feet and picked up his coat.

"By the way, Miss DeVille called, left a message. She said: 'How about St. Moritz?'"

"Too ritzy," he decided aloud. "It's going to be Davos."

Because the suicide bothered him more than it should have, Render closed the door to his office and turned off the windows and turned on the phonograph. He put on the desk light only.

How has the quality of human life been changed, he wrote, *since the beginnings of the industrial revolution?*

He picked up the paper and reread the sentence. It was the topic he had been asked to discuss that coming Saturday. As was typical in such cases he did not know what to say because he had too much to say, and only an hour to say it in.

He got up and began to pace the office, now filled with Beethoven's Eighth Symphony.

"The power to hurt," he said, snapping on a lapel microphone and activating his recorder, "has evolved in a direct relationship to technological advancement." His imaginary audience grew quiet. He smiled. "Man's potential for working simple mayhem has been multiplied by mass-production; his capacity for injuring the psyche through personal contacts has expanded in an exact ratio to improved communication facilities. But these are all matters of common knowledge, and are not the things I wish to consider tonight. Rather, I should like to discuss what I choose to call autopsychomimesis – the self-generated anxiety complexes which on first scrutiny appear quite similar to classic patterns, but which actually represent radical dispersions of psychic energy. They are peculiar to our times . . ."

He paused to dispose of his cigar and formulate his next words.

"Autopsychomimesis," he thought aloud, "a self-perpetuated imitation complex – almost an attention-getting affair. – A jazzman, for example, who acted hopped-up half the time, even though he had never used an addictive narcotic and only dimly remembered anyone who had – because all the stimulants and tranquilizers of today are quite benign. Like Quixote, he aspired after a legend when his music alone should have been sufficient outlet for his tensions.

"Or my Korean War Orphan, alive today by virtue of the Red Cross and UNICEF and foster parents whom he never met. He wanted a family so badly that he made one up. And what then? – He hated his imaginary father and he loved his imaginary mother quite dearly – for he was a highly intelligent boy, and he too longed after the half-true complexes of tradition. Why?

"Today, everyone is sophisticated enough to understand the time-honored patterns of psychic disturbance. Today, many of the reasons for those disturbances have been removed – not as radically as my now-adult war orphan's, but with as remarkable an effect. We are living in a neurotic past. – Again, why? Because our present times are geared to physical health, security, and well-being. We have abolished hunger, though the backwoods orphan would still rather receive a package of food concentrates from a human being who cares for him than to obtain a warm meal from an automat unit in the middle of the jungle.

"Physical welfare is now every man's right in excess. The reaction to this has occurred in the area of mental health. Thanks to technology, the reasons for many of the old social problems have passed, and along with them went many of the reasons for psychic distress. But between the black of yesterday and the white of tomorrow is the great gray of today, filled with nostalgia and fear of the future, which cannot be expressed on a purely material plane, is now being represented by a willful seeking after historical anxiety-modes . . ."

The phone-box buzzed briefly. Render did not hear it over the Eighth.

"We are afraid of what we do not know," he continued, "and tomorrow is a very great unknown. My own specialized area of psychiatry did not even exist thirty years ago. Science is capable of advancing itself so rapidly now that there is a genuine public uneasiness – I might even say 'distress' – as to the logical outcome: the total mechanization of everything in the world . . ."

He passed near the desk as the phone buzzed again. He switched off his microphone and softened the Eighth.

"Hello?"

"Saint Moritz," she said.

"Davos," he replied firmly.

"Charlie, you are most exasperating!"

"Jill, dear – so are you."

"Shall we discuss it tonight?"

"There is nothing to discuss!"

"You'll pick me up at five, though?"

He hesitated, then:

"Yes, at five. How come the screen is blank?"

"I've had my hair fixed. I'm going to surprise you again."

He suppressed an idiot chuckle, said, "Pleasantly, I hope. Okay, see you then," waited for her "good-bye," and broke the connection.

He transpared the windows, turned off the light on his desk, and looked outside.

Gray again overhead, and many slow flakes of snow – wandering, not being blown about much – moving downward and then losing themselves in the tumult . . .

He also saw, when he opened the window and leaned out, the place off to the left where Irizarry had left his next-to-last mark on the world.

He closed the window and listened to the rest of the symphony. It had been a week since he had gone blindspinning with Eileen. Her appointment was for one o'clock.

He remembered her fingertips brushing over his face, like leaves, or the bodies of insects, learning his appearance in the ancient manner of the blind. The memory was not altogether pleasant. He wondered why.

Far below, a patch of hosed pavement was blank once again; under a thin, fresh shroud of white, it was slippery as glass. A building custodian hurried outside and spread salt on it, before someone slipped and hurt themself.

Sigmund was the myth of Fenris come alive. After Render had instructed Mrs. Hedges, "Show them in," the door had begun to open, was suddenly pushed wider, and a pair of smoky yellow eyes stared in at him. The eyes were set in a strangely misshapen dog-skull.

Sigmund's was not a low canine brow, slanting up slightly from the muzzle; it was a high, shaggy cranium making the eyes appear even more deep-set than they actually were. Render shivered slightly at the size and aspect of that head. The muties he had seen had all been puppies. Sigmund was full-grown, and his gray-black fur had a tendency to bristle, which made him appear somewhat larger than a normal specimen of the breed.

He stared in at Render in a very un-doglike way and made a growling noise which sounded too much like, "Hello, doctor," to have been an accident.

Render nodded and stood.

"Hello, Sigmund," he said. "Come in."

The dog turned his head, sniffing the air of the room – as though deciding whether or not to trust his ward within its confines. Then he returned his stare to Render, dipped his head in an affirmative, and shouldered the door open. Perhaps the entire encounter had taken only one disconcerting second.

Eileen followed him, holding lightly to the double-leashed harness. The dog padded soundlessly across the thick rug – head low, as though he were stalking something. His eyes never left Render's.

"So this is Sigmund . . . ? How are you, Eileen?"

"Fine. – Yes, he wanted very badly to come along, and *I* wanted you to meet him."

Render led her to a chair and seated her. She unsnapped the double guide from the dog's harness and placed it on the floor. Sigmund sat down beside it and continued to stare at Render.

"How is everything at State Psych?"

"Same as always. – May I bum a cigarette, Doctor? I forgot mine."

He placed it between her fingers, furnished a light. She was wearing a dark blue suit and her glasses were flame blue. The silver spot on her forehead reflected the glow of his lighter; she continued to stare at that point in space after he had withdrawn his hand. Her shoulder-length hair appeared a trifle lighter than it had seemed on the night they met; today it was like a fresh-minted copper coin.

Render seated himself on the corner of his desk, drawing up his world-ashtray with his toe.

"You told me before that being blind did not mean that you had never seen. I didn't ask you to explain it then. But I'd like to ask you now."

"I had a neuroparticipation session with Dr. Riscomb," she told him, "before he had his accident. He wanted to accommodate my mind to visual impressions. Unfortunately, there was never a second session."

"I see. What did you do in that session?"

She crossed her ankles and Render noted they were well-turned.

"Colors, mostly. The experience was quite overwhelming."

"How well do you remember them? How long ago was it?"

"About six months ago – and I shall never forget them. I have even dreamed in color patterns since then."

"How often?"

"Several times a week."

"What sort of associations do they carry?"

"Nothing special. They just come into my mind along with other stimuli now – in a pretty haphazard way."

"How?"

"Well, for instance, when you ask me a question it's a sort of yellowish-orangish pattern that I 'see.' Your greeting was a kind of silvery thing. Now that you're just sitting there listening to me, saying nothing, I associate you with a deep, almost violet, blue."

Sigmund shifted his gaze to the desk and stared at the side panel.

Can he hear the recorder spinning inside? wondered Render. *And if he can, can he guess what it is and what it's doing?*

If so, the dog would doubtless tell Eileen – not that she was unaware of what was now an accepted practice – and she might not like being reminded that he considered her case as therapy, rather than a mere mechanical adaptation process. If he thought it would do any good (he smiled inwardly at the notion), he would talk to the dog in private about it.

Inwardly, he shrugged.

"I'll construct a rather elementary fantasy world then," he said finally, "and introduce you to some basic forms today."

She smiled; and Render looked down at the myth who crouched by her side, its tongue a piece of beefsteak hanging over a picket fence.

Is he smiling too?

"Thank you," she said.

Sigmund wagged his tail.

"Well then," Render disposed of his cigarette near Madagascar, "I'll fetch out the 'egg' now and test it. In the meantime," he pressed an unobstrusive button, "perhaps some music would prove relaxing."

She started to reply, but a Wagnerian overture snuffed out the words. Render jammed the button again, and there was a moment of silence during which he said, "Heh heh. Thought Respighi was next."

It took two more pushes for him to locate some Roman pines.

"You could have left him on," she observed. "I'm quite fond of Wagner."

"No thanks," he said, opening the closet, "I'd keep stepping in all those piles of leitmotifs."

The great egg drifted out into the office, soundless as a cloud. Render heard a soft growl behind as he drew it toward the desk. He turned quickly.

Like the shadow of a bird, Sigmund had gotten to his feet, crossed the room, and was already circling the machine and sniffing at it – tail taut, ears flat, teeth bared.

"Easy, Sig," said Render. "It's an Omnichannel Neural T & R Unit. It won't bite or anything like that. It's just a machine, like a car, or a teevee, or a dishwasher. That's what we're going to use today to show Eileen what some things look like."

"Don't like it," rumbled the dog.

"Why?"

Sigmund had no reply, so he stalked back to Eileen and laid his head in her lap.

"Don't like it," he repeated, looking up at her.

"Why?"

"No words," he decided. "We go home now?"

"No," she answered him. "You're going to curl up in the corner and take a nap, and I'm going to curl up in that machine and do the same thing – sort of."

"No good," he said, tail drooping.

"Go on now," she pushed him, "lie down and behave yourself."

He acquiesced, but he whined when Render blanked the windows and touched the button which transformed his desk into the operator's seat.

He whined once more – when the egg, connected now to an outlet, broke in the middle and the top slid back and up, revealing the interior.

Render seated himself. His chair became a contour couch and moved in halfway beneath the console. He sat upright and it moved back again, becoming a chair. He touched a part of the desk and half the ceiling disengaged itself, reshaped itself, and lowered to hover over-head like a huge bell. He stood and moved around to the side of the ro-womb. Respighi spoke of pines and such, and Render disengaged an earphone from beneath the egg and leaned back across his desk. Blocking one ear with his shoulder and pressing the microphone to the other, he played upon the buttons with his free hand. Leagues of surf drowned the tone poem; miles of traffic overrode it; a great clanging bell sent fracture lines running through it; and the feedback said: ". . . Now that you are just sitting there listening to me, saying nothing, I associate you with a deep, almost violet, blue . . ."

He switched to the face mask and monitored, *one* – cinnamon, *two* – leaf mold, *three* – deep reptilian musk . . . and down through thirst, and the tastes of honey and vinegar and salt, and back on up through lilacs and wet concrete, a before-the-storm whiff of ozone, and all the basic olfactory and gustatory cues for morning, afternoon, and evening in the town.

The couch floated normally in its pool of mercury, magnetically stabilized by the walls of the egg. He set the tapes.

The ro-womb was in perfect condition.

"Okay," said Render, turning, "everything checks."

She was just placing her glasses atop her folded garments. She had undressed while Render was testing the machine. He was perturbed by her narrow waist, her large, dark-pointed breasts, her long legs. She was too well-formed for a woman her height, he decided.

He realized though, as he stared at her, that his main annoyance was, of course, the fact that she was his patient.

"Ready here," she said, and he moved to her side.

He took her elbow and guided her to the machine. Her fingers explored its interior. As he helped her enter the unit, he saw that her eyes were a vivid seagreen. Of this, too, he disapproved.

"Comfortable?"

"Yes."

"Okay then, we're set. I'm going to close it now. Sweet dreams." The upper shell dropped slowly. Closed, it grew opaque, then dazzling. Render was staring down at his own distorted reflection.

He moved back in the direction of his desk.

Sigmund was on his feet, blocking the way.

Render reached down to pat his head, but the dog jerked it aside.

"Take me, with," he growled.

"I'm afraid that can't be done, old fellow," said Render. "Besides, we're not really going anywhere. We'll just be dozing, right here, in this room."

The dog did not seem mollified.

"Why?"

Render sighed. An argument with a dog was about the most ludicrous thing he could imagine when sober.

"Sig," he said, "I'm trying to help her learn what things look like. You doubtless do a fine job guiding her around in this world which she cannot see – but she needs to know what it looks like now, and I'm going to show her."

"Then she, will not, need me."

"Of course she will." Render almost laughed. The pathetic thing was here bound so closely to the absurd thing that he could not help it. "I can't restore her sight," he explained. "I'm just going to transfer her some sight-abstractions – sort of lend her my eyes for a short time. Savvy?"

"No," said the dog. "Take mine."

Render turned off the music.

The whole mutie-master relationship might be worth six volumes, he decided, *in German.*

He pointed to the far corner.

"Lie down, over there, like Eileen told you. This isn't going to take long, and when it's all over you're going to leave the same way you came – you leading. Okay?"

Sigmund did not answer, but he turned and moved off to the corner, tail drooping again.

Render seated himself and lowered the hood, the operator's

modified version of the ro-womb. He was alone before the ninety white buttons and the two red ones. The world ended in the blackness beyond the console. He loosened his necktie and unbuttoned his collar.

He removed the helmet from its receptacle and checked its leads. Donning it then, he swung the half-mask up over his lower face and dropped the darksheet down to meet with it. He rested his right arm in the sling, and with a single tapping gesture, he eliminated his patient's consciousness.

A Shaper does not press white buttons consciously. He wills conditions. Then deeply implanted muscular reflexes exert an almost imperceptible pressure against the sensitive arm-sling, which glides into the proper position and encourages an extended finger to move forward. A button is pressed. The sling moves on.

Render felt a tingling at the base of his skull; he smelled fresh-cut grass.

Suddenly he was moving up the great gray alley between the worlds.

After what seemed a long time, Render felt that he was footed on a strange Earth. He could see nothing; it was only a sense of presence that informed him he had arrived. It was the darkest of all the dark nights he had ever known.

He willed that the darkness disperse. Nothing happened.

A part of his mind came awake again, a part he had not realized was sleeping; he recalled whose world he had entered.

He listened for her presence. He heard fear and anticipation.

He willed color. First, red . . .

He felt a correspondence. Then there was an echo.

Everything became red; he inhabited the center of an infinite ruby. Orange. Yellow . . .

He was caught in a piece of amber.

Green now, and he added the exhalations of a sultry sea. Blue, and the coolness of evening.

He stretched his mind then, producing all the colors at once. They came in great swirling plumes.

Then he tore them apart and forced a form upon them.

An incandescent rainbow arced across the black sky.

He fought for browns and grays below him. Self-luminescent, they appeared – in shimmering, shifting patches.

Somewhere, a sense of awe. There was no trace of hysteria though, so he continued with the Shaping.

He managed a horizon, and the blackness drained away beyond it. The sky grew faintly blue, and he ventured a herd of dark clouds.

There was resistance to his efforts at creating distance and depth, so he reinforced the tableau with a very faint sound of surf. A transference from an auditory concept of distance came slowly then, as he pushed the clouds about. Quickly, he threw up a high forest to offset a rising wave of acrophobia.

The panic vanished.

Render focused his attention on tall trees – oaks and pines, poplars and sycamores. He hurled them about like spears, in ragged arrays of greens and browns and yellows, unrolled a thick mat of morning-moist grass, dropped a series of gray boulders and greenish logs at irregular intervals, and tangled and twined the branches overhead, casting a uniform shade throughout the glen.

The effect was staggering. It seemed as if the entire world was shaken with a sob, then silent.

Through the stillness he felt her presence. He had decided it would be best to lay the groundwork quickly, to set up a tangible head-quarters, to prepare a field for operations. He could backtrack later, he could repair and amend the results of the trauma in the sessions yet to come; but this much, at least, was necessary for a beginning.

With a start, he realized that the silence was not a withdrawal. Eileen had made herself immanent in the trees and the grass, the stones and the bushes; she was personalizing their forms, relating them to tactile sensations, sounds, temperatures, aromas.

With a soft breeze, he stirred the branches of the trees. Just beyond the bounds of seeing he worked out the splashing sounds of a brook.

There was a feeling of joy. He shared it.

She was bearing it extremely well, so he decided to extend the scope of the exercise. He let his mind wander among the trees, experiencing a momentary doubling of vision, during which time he saw an enormous hand riding in an aluminum carriage toward a circle of white.

He was beside the brook now and he was seeking her, carefully.

He drifted with the water. He had not yet taken on a form. The splashes became a gurgling as he pushed the brook through shallow places and over rocks. At his insistence, the waters became more articulate.

"Where are you?" asked the brook.

Here! Here!

Here!

. . . *and here!* replied the trees, the bushes, the stones, the grass.

"Choose one," said the brook, as it widened, rounded a mass of rock, then bent its way down a slope, heading toward a blue pool.

I cannot, was the answer from the wind.

"You must." The brook widened and poured into the pool, swirled about the surface, then stilled itself and reflected branches and dark clouds. "Now!"

Very well, echoed the wood, *in a moment.*

The mist rose above the lake and drifted to the bank of the pool.

"Now," tinkled the mist.

Here, then . . .

She had chosen a small willow. It swayed in the wind; it trailed its branches in the water.

"Eileen Shallot," he said, "regard the lake."

The breezes shifted; the willow bent.

It was not difficult for him to recall her face, her body. The tree spun as though rootless. Eileen stood in the midst of a quiet explosion of leaves; she stared, frightened, into the deep blue mirror of Render's mind, the lake.

She covered her face with her hands, but it could not stop the seeing.

"Behold yourself," said Render.

She lowered her hands and peered downward. Then she turned in every direction, slowly; she studied herself. Finally:

"I feel I am quite lovely," she said. "Do I feel so because you want me to, or is it true?"

She looked all about as she spoke, seeking the Shaper.

"It is true," said Render, from everywhere.

"Thank you."

There was a swirl of white and she was wearing a belted garment of damask. The light in the distance brightened almost imperceptibly. A faint touch of pink began at the base of the lowest cloudbank.

"What is happening there?" she asked, facing that direction.

"I am going to show you a sunrise," said Render, "and I shall probably botch it a bit – but then, it's my first professional sunrise under these circumstances."

"Where are *you?*" she asked.

"Everywhere," he replied.

"Please take on a form so that I can see you.

"All right."

"Your natural form."

He willed that he be beside her on the bank, and he was.

Startled by a metallic flash, he looked downward. The world receded for an instant, then grew stable once again. He laughed, and the laugh froze as he thought of something.

He was wearing the suit of armor which had stood beside their table in the Partridge and Scalpel on the night they met.

She reached out and touched it.

"The suit of armor by our table," she acknowledged, running her fingertips over the plates and the junctures. "I associated it with you that night."

". . . And you stuffed me into it just now," he commented. "You're a strong-willed woman."

The armor vanished and he was wearing his gray-brown suit and looseknit bloodclot necktie and a professional expression.

"Behold the real me," he smiled faintly. "Now, to the sunset. I'm going to use all the colors. Watch!"

They seated themselves on the green park bench which had appeared behind them, and Render pointed in the direction he had decided upon as east.

Slowly, the sun worked through its morning attitudes. For the first time in this particular world it shone down like a god, and reflected off the lake, and broke the clouds, and set the landscape to smouldering beneath the mist that arose from the moist wood.

Watching, watching intently, staring directly into the ascending bonfire, Eileen did not move for a long while, nor speak. Render could sense her fascination.

She was staring at the source of all light; it reflected back from the gleaming coin on her brow, like a single drop of blood.

Render said, "That is the sun, and those are clouds," and he clapped his hands and the clouds covered the sun and there was a soft rumble overhead, "and that is thunder," he finished.

The rain fell then, shattering the lake and tickling their faces, making sharp striking sounds on the leaves, then soft tapping sounds, dripping down from the branches overhead, soaking their garments and plastering their hair, running down their necks and falling into their eyes, turning patches of brown earth to mud.

A splash of lightning covered the sky, and a second later there was another peal of thunder.

". . . And this is a summer storm," he lectured. "You see how the rain affects the foliage and ourselves. What you just saw in the sky before the thunderclap was lightning."

". . . Too much," she said. "Let up on it for a moment, please." The rain stopped instantly and the sun broke through the clouds.

"I have the damndest desire for a cigarette," she said, "but I left mine in another world."

As she said it one appeared, already lighted, between her fingers.

"It's going to taste rather flat," said Render strangely. He watched her for a moment, then:

"I didn't give you that cigarette," he noted. "You picked it from my mind."

The smoke laddered and spiraled upward, was swept away.

". . . Which means that, for the second time today, I have underestimated the pull of that vacuum in your mind – in the place where sight ought to be. You are assimilating these new impressions very rapidly. You're even going to the extent of groping after new ones. Be careful. Try to contain that impulse."

"It's like a hunger," she said.

"Perhaps we had best conclude this session now."

Their clothing was dry again. A bird began to sing.

"No, wait! Please! I'll be careful. I want to see more things."

"There is always the next visit," said Render. "But I suppose we can manage one more. Is there something you want very badly to see?"

"Yes. Winter. Snow."

"Okay," smiled the Shaper, "then wrap yourself in that fur-piece . . ."

The afternoon slipped by rapidly after the departure of his patient. Render was in a good mood. He felt emptied and filled again. He had come through the first trial without suffering any repercussions. He decided that he was going to succeed. His satisfaction was greater than his fear. It was with a sense of exhilaration that he returned to working on his speech.

". . . And what is the power to hurt?" he inquired of the microphone.

"We live by pleasure and we live by pain," he answered himself. "Either can frustrate and either can encourage. But while pleasure and pain are rooted in biology, they are conditioned by society: thus are values to be derived. Because of the enormous masses of humanity, hectically changing positions in space every day throughout the cities of the world, there has come into necessary being a series of totally inhuman controls upon these movements. Every day they nibble their way into new areas – driving our cars, flying our planes, interviewing us, diagnosing our diseases – and I cannot even venture a moral judgment upon these intrusions. They have become necessary. Ultimately, they may prove salutary.

"The point I wish to make, however, is that we are often unaware of our own values. We cannot honestly tell what a thing means to us until it is removed from our life-situation. If an object of value ceases to exist, then the psychic energies which were bound up in it are released. We seek after new objects of value in which to invest this – mana, if you like, or libido, if you don't. And no one thing which has vanished during the past three or four or five decades was, in itself, massively significant; and no new thing which came into being during that time is massively malicious toward the people it has replaced or the people it in some manner controls. A society, though, is made up of many things, and when these things are changed too rapidly the results are unpredictable. An intense study of mental illness is often quite revealing as to the nature of the stresses in the society where the illness was made. If anxiety-patterns fall into special groups and classes, then something of the discontent of society can be learned from them. Karl Jung pointed out that when consciousness is repeatedly frustrated in a quest for values, it will turn its search to the unconscious; failing there, it will proceed to quarry its way into the hypothetical collective unconscious. He noted, in the postwar analyses of ex-Nazis, that the longer they searched for something to erect from the ruins of their lives – having lived through a period of classical iconoclasm, and then seen their new ideals topple as well – the longer they searched, the further back they seemed to reach into the collective unconscious of their people. Their dreams themselves came to take on patterns out of the Teutonic mythos.

"This, in a much less dramatic sense, is happening today. There are historical periods when the group tendency for the mind to turn in upon itself, to turn back, is greater than at other times. We are living in such a period of Quixotism, in the original sense of the term. This is because the power to hurt, in our time, is the power to ignore, to baffle-and it is no longer the exclusive property of human beings – "

A buzz interrupted him then. He switched off the recorder, touched the phone-box.

"Charles Render speaking," he told it.

"This is Paul Charter," lisped the box. "I am headmaster at Dilling."

"Yes?"

The picture cleared. Render saw a man whose eyes were set close together beneath a high forehead. The forehead was heavily creased; the mouth twitched as it spoke.

"Well, I want to apologize again for what happened. It was a faulty piece of equipment that caused – "

"Can't you afford proper facilities? Your fees are high enough."

"It was a *new* piece of equipment. It was a factory defect – "

"Wasn't there anybody in charge of the class?"

"Yes, but – "

"Why didn't he inspect the equipment? Why wasn't he on hand to prevent the fall?"

"He *was* on hand, but it happened too fast for him to do anything. As for inspecting the equipment for factory defects, that isn't his job. Look, I'm very sorry. I'm quite fond of your boy. I can assure you nothing like this will ever happen again."

"You're right, there. But that's because I'm picking him up tomorrow morning and enrolling him in a school that exercises proper safety precautions."

Render ended the conversation with a flick of his finger. After several minutes had passed he stood and crossed the room to his small wall safe, which was partly masked, though not concealed, by a shelf of books. It took only a moment for him to open it and withdraw a jewel box containing a cheap necklace and a framed photograph of a man resembling himself, though somewhat younger, and a woman whose upswept hair was dark and whose chin was small, and two youngsters between them – the girl holding the baby in her arms and forcing her bright bored smile on ahead. Render always stared for only a few seconds on such occasions, fondling the necklace, and then he shut the box and locked it away again for many months.

Whump! Whump! went the bass. *Tchg-tchg-tchga-tchg,* the gourds.

The gelatins splayed reds, greens, blues, and God-awful yellows about the amazing metal dancers.

HUMAN? asked the marquee.

ROBOTS? (immediately below).

COME SEE FOR YOURSELF! (across the bottom, cryptically).

So they did.

Render and Jill were sitting at a microscopic table, thankfully set back against a wall, beneath charcoal caricatures of personalities largely unknown (there being so many personalities among the subcultures of a city of fourteen million people). Nose crinkled with pleasure, Jill stared at the present focal point of this particular subculture, occasionally raising her shoulders to ear level to add emphasis to a silent laugh or a small squeal, because the performers were just *too* human – the way the ebon robot ran his fingers along the silver robot's forearm as they parted and passed . . .

Render alternated his attention between Jill and the dancers and a wicked-looking decoction that resembled nothing so much as a small bucket of whiskey sours strewn with seaweed (through which the Kraken might at any moment arise to drag some hapless ship down to its doom).

"Charlie, I think they're really people!"

Render disentangled his gaze from her hair and bouncing earrings.

He studied the dancers down on the floor, somewhat below the table area, surrounded by music.

There *could* be humans within those metal shells. If so, their dance was a thing of extreme skill. Though the manufacture of sufficiently light alloys was no problem, it would be some trick for a dancer to cavort so freely – and for so long a period of time, and with such effortless-seeming ease – within a head-to-toe suit of armor, without so much as a grate or a click or a clank.

Soundless . . .

They glided like two gulls; the larger, the color of polished anthracite, and the other, like a moonbeam falling through a window upon a silk-wrapped manikin.

Even when they touched there was no sound – or if there was, it was wholly masked by the rhythms of the band.

Whump-whump! Tchga-tchg!

Render took another drink.

Slowly, it turned into an apache-dance. Render checked his watch. Too long for normal entertainers, he decided. They must be robots. As he looked up again the black robot hurled the silver robot perhaps ten feet and turned his back on her.

There was no sound of striking metal.

Wonder what a setup like that costs? he mused.

"Charlie! There was no sound! How do they do that?"

"I've no idea," said Render.

The gelatins were yellow again, then red, then blue, then green.

"You'd think it would damage their mechanisms, wouldn't you?"

The white robot crawled back and the other swiveled his wrist around and around, a lighted cigarette between the fingers. There was laughter as he pressed it mechanically to his lipless faceless face. The silver robot confronted him. He turned away again, dropped the cigarette, ground it out slowly, soundlessly, then suddenly turned back to his partner. Would he throw her again? No . . .

Slowly then, like the great-legged birds of the East, they recommenced their movement, slowly, and with many turnings away.

Something deep within Render was amused, but he was too far gone to ask it what was funny. So he went looking for the Kraken in the bottom of the glass instead.

Jill was clutching his biceps then, drawing his attention back to the floor.

As the spotlight tortured the spectrum, the black robot raised the silver one high above his head, slowly, slowly, and then commenced spinning with her in that position – arms outstretched, back arched, legs scissored – very slowly, at first. Then faster.

Suddenly they were whirling with an unbelievable speed, and the gelatins rotated faster and faster.

Render shook his head to clear it.

They were moving so rapidly that they *had* to fall – human or robot. But they didn't. They were a mandala. They were a gray form uniformity. Render looked down.

Then slowing, and slower, slower. Stopped.

The music stopped.

Blackness followed. Applause filled it.

When the lights came on again the two robots were standing statue-like, facing the audience. Very, very slowly, they bowed.

The applause increased.

Then they turned and were gone.

The music came on and the light was clear again. A babble of voices arose. Render slew the Kraken.

"What d'you think of that?" she asked him.

Render made his face serious and said: "Am I a man dreaming I am a robot, or a robot dreaming I am a man?" He grinned, then added: "I don't know."

She punched his shoulder gaily at that and he observed that she was drunk.

"I am not," she protested. "Not much, anyhow. Not as much as you."

"Still, I think you ought to see a doctor about it. Like me. Like now. Let's get out of here and go for a drive."

"Not yet, Charlie. I want to see them once more, huh? Please?"

"If I have another drink I won't be able to see that far."

"Then order a cup of coffee."

"Yaagh!"

"Then order a beer."

"I'll suffer without."

There were people on the dance floor now, but Render's feet felt like lead. He lit a cigarette.

"So you had a dog talk to you today?"

"*Yes*. Something very disconcerting about that . . ."

"Was she pretty?"

"It was a boy dog. And boy, was he ugly!"

"Silly. I mean his mistress."

"You know I never discuss cases, Jill."

"You told me about her being blind and about the dog. All I want to know is if she's pretty."

"Well . . . Yes and no." He bumped her under the table and gestured vaguely. "Well, you know . . ."

"Same thing all the way around," she told the waiter who had appeared suddenly out of an adjacent pool of darkness, nodded, and vanished as abruptly.

"There go my good intentions," sighed Render. "See how you like being examined by a drunken sot, that's all I can say."

"You'll sober up fast, you always do. Hippocratics and all that."

He sniffed, glanced at his watch.

"I have to be in Connecticut tomorrow. Pulling Pete out of that damned school . . ."

She sighed, already tired of the subject.

"I think you worry too much about him. Any kid can bust an ankle. It's part of growing up. I broke my wrist when I was seven. It was an accident. It's not the school's fault, those things some-times happen."

"Like hell," said Render, accepting his dark drink from the dark tray the dark man carried. "If they can't do a good job, I'll find someone who can."

She shrugged.

"You're the boss. All I know is what I read in the papers.

" – And you're still set on Davos, even though you know you meet a better class of people at Saint Moritz?" she added.

"We're going there to ski, remember? I like the runs better at Davos."

"I can't score any tonight, can I?"

He squeezed her hand.

"You always score with me, honey."

And they drank their drinks and smoked their cigarettes and held their hands until the people left the dance floor and filed back to their microscopic tables, and the gelatins spun round and round, tinting clouds of smoke from hell to sunrise and back again, and the bass went *whump!*

Tchga-tchga!

"Oh, Charlie! Here they come again!"

The sky was clear as crystal. The roads were clean. The snow had stopped.

Jill's breathing was the breathing of a sleeper. The S-7 raced across the bridges of the city. If Render sat very still he could convince himself that only his body was drunk; but whenever he moved his head the universe began to dance about him. As it did so, he imagined himself within a dream, and Shaper of it all.

For one instant this was true. He turned the big clock in the sky backward, smiling as he dozed. Another instant and he was awake again, and unsmiling.

The universe had taken revenge for his presumption. For one reknown moment with the helplessness which he had loved beyond helping, it had charged him the price of the lake-bottom vision once again; and as he had moved once more toward the wreck at the bottom of the world – like a swimmer, as unable to speak – he heard, from somewhere high over the Earth, and filtered down to him through the waters above the Earth, the howl of the Fenris Wolf as it prepared to devour the moon; and as this occurred, he knew that the sound was as like to the trump of a judgment as the lady by his side was unlike the moon. Every bit. In all ways. And he was afraid.

III

". . . The plain, the direct, and the blunt. This is Winchester Cathedral," said the guidebook. "With its floor-to-ceiling shafts, like so many huge tree trunks, it achieves a ruthless control over its spaces: the ceilings are flat; each bay, separated by those shafts, is itself a thing of certainty and stability. It seems, indeed, to reflect something of the spirit of William the Conqueror. Its disdain of mere elaboration and its passionate dedication to the love of another world would make it seem, too, an appropriate setting for some tale out of Mallory . . ."

"Observe the scalloped capitals," said the guide. "In their primitive fluting they anticipated what was later to become a common motif . . ."

"Faugh!" said Render – softly though, because he was in a group inside a church.

"Shh!" said Jill (Fotlock – that was her real last name) DeVille.

But Render was impressed as well as distressed.

Hating Jill's hobby, though, had become so much of a reflex with him that he would sooner have taken his rest seated beneath an oriental device which dripped water onto his head than to admit he occasionally enjoyed walking through the arcades and the galleries, the passages and the tunnels, and getting all out of breath climbing up the high twisty stairways of towers.

So he ran his eyes over everything, burned everything down by shutting them, then built the place up again out of the still smouldering ashes of memory, all so that at a later date he would be able to repeat the performance, offering the vision to his one patient who could see only in this manner. This building he disliked less than most. Yes, he would take it back to her.

The camera in his mind photographing the surroundings, Render walked with the others, overcoat over his arm, his fingers anxious to reach after a cigarette. He kept busy ignoring his guide, realizing this to be the nadir of all forms of human protest. As he walked through Winchester he thought of his last two sessions with Eileen Shallot. He recalled his almost unwilling Adam-attitude as he had named all the animals passing before them, led of course by the *one* she had wanted to see, colored fearsome by his own unease. He had felt pleasantly bucolic after boning up on an old Botany text and then proceeding to Shape and name the flowers of the fields.

So far they had stayed out of the cities, far away from the machines. Her emotions were still too powerful at the sight of the simple, carefully introduced objects to risk plunging her into so complicated and chaotic a wilderness yet; he would build her city slowly.

Something passed rapidly, high above the cathedral, uttering a sonic boom. Render took Jill's hand in his for a moment and smiled as she looked up at him. Knowing she verged upon beauty, Jill normally took great pains to achieve it. But today her hair was simply drawn back and knotted behind her head, and her lips and her eyes were pale; and her exposed ears were tiny and white and somewhat pointed.

"Observe the scalloped capitals," he whispered. "In their primitive fluting they anticipated what was later to become a common motif."

"Faugh!" said she.

"Shh!" said a sunburned little woman nearby, whose face seemed to crack and fall back together again as she pursed and unpursed her lips.

Later as they strolled back toward their hotel, Render said, "Okay on Winchester?"

"Okay on Winchester."

"Happy?"

"Happy."

"Good, then we can leave this afternoon."

"All right."

"For Switzerland . . ."

She stopped and toyed with a button on his coat.

"Couldn't we just spend a day or two looking at some old chateaux first? After all, they're just across the channel, and you could be sampling all the local wines while I looked . . ."

"Okay," he said.

She looked up – a trifle surprised.

"What? No argument?" she smiled. "Where is your fighting spirit? – to let me push you around like this?"

She took his arm then and they walked on as he said, "Yesterday, while we were galloping about in the innards of that old castle, I heard a weak moan, and then a voice cried out, 'For the love of God, Montresor!' I think it was my fighting spirit, because I'm certain it was my voice. I've given up *der Geist der stets verneint. Pax vobiscum!* Let us be gone to France. *Alors!*"

"Dear Rendy, it'll only be another day or two . . ."

"Amen," he said, "though my skis that were waxed are already waning."

So they did that, and on the morn of the third day, when she spoke to him of castles in Spain, he reflected aloud that while psychologists drink and only grow angry, psychiatrists have been known to drink, grow angry, and break things. Construing this as a veiled threat aimed at the Wedgewoods she had collected, she acquiesced to his desire to go skiing.

Free! Render almost screamed it.

His heart was pounding inside his head. He leaned hard. He cut to the left. The wind strapped at his face; a shower of ice crystals, like bullets of emery, fled by him, scraped against his cheek.

He was moving. Aye – the world had ended as Weissflujoch, and Dorftali led down and away from this portal.

His feet were two gleaming rivers which raced across the stark, curving plains; they could not be frozen in their course. Downward. He flowed. Away from all the rooms of the world. Away from the stifling lack of intensity, from the day's hundred spoon-fed welfares, from the killing pace of the forced amusements that hacked at the Hydra, leisure; away.

And as he fled down the run he felt a strong desire to look back over his shoulder, as though to see whether the world he had left behind and above had set one fearsome embodiment of itself, like a shadow, to trail along after him, hunt him down and drag him back to a warm and well-lit coffin in the sky, there to be laid to rest with a spike of aluminum driven through his will and a garland of alternating currents smothering his spirit.

"I hate you," he breathed between clenched teeth, and the wind carried the words back; and he laughed then, for he always analyzed his emotions, as a matter of reflex; and he added, "Exit Orestes, mad, pursued by the Furies . . ."

After a time the slope leveled out and he reached the bottom of the run and had to stop.

He smoked one cigarette then and rode back up to the top so that he could come down it again for nontherapeutic reasons.

That night he sat before a fire in the big lodge, feeling its warmth soaking into his tired muscles. Jill massaged his shoulders as he played Rorschach with the flames, and he came upon a blazing goblet which was snatched away from him in the same instant by the sound of his name being spoken somewhere across the Hall of the Nine Hearths.

"Charles Render!" said the voice (only it sounded more like "Sharlz Runder"), and his head instantly jerked in that direction, but his eyes danced with too many afterimages for him to isolate the source of the calling.

"Maurice?" he queried after a moment. "Bartelmetz?"

"Aye," came the reply, and then Render saw the familiar grizzled visage, set neckless and balding above the red and blue shag sweater that was stretched mercilessly about the wine-keg rotundity of the man who now picked his way in their direction, deftly avoiding the strewn crutches and the stacked skis and the people who, like Jill and Render, disdained sitting in chairs.

Render stood, stretching, and shook hands as he came upon them.

"You've put on more weight," Render observed. "That's unhealthy."

"Nonsense, it's all muscle. How have you been, and what are you up to these days?" He looked down at Jill and she smiled back at him.

"This is Miss DeVille," said Render.

"Jill," she acknowledged.

He bowed slightly, finally releasing Render's aching hand.

". . . And this is Professor Maurice Bartelmetz of Vienna," finished Render, "a benighted disciple of all forms of dialectical pessimism, and a very distinguished pioneer in neuroparticipation – although you'd never guess it to look at him. I had the good fortune to be his pupil for over a year."

Bartelmetz nodded and agreed with him, taking in the Schnapsflasche Render brought forth from a small plastic bag, and accepting the collapsible cup which he filled to the brim.

"Ah, you are a good doctor still," he sighed. "You have diagnosed the case in an instant and you make the proper prescription. Nozdrovia!"

"Seven years in a gulp," Render acknowledged, refilling their glasses.

"Then we shall make time more malleable by sipping it."

They seated themselves on the floor, and the fire roared up through the great brick chimney as the logs burned themselves back to branches, to twigs, to thin sticks, ring by yearly ring.

Render replenished the fire.

"I read your last book," said Bartelmetz finally, casually, "about four years ago."

Render reckoned that to be correct.

"Are you doing any research work these days?"

Render poked lazily at the fire.

"Yes," he answered, "sort of."

He glanced at Jill, who was dozing with her cheek against the arm of the huge leather chair that held his emergency bag, the planes of her face all crimson and flickering shadow.

"I've hit upon a rather unusual subject and started with a piece of jobbery I eventually intend to write about."

"Unusual? In what way?"

"Blind from birth, for one thing."

"You're using the ONT&R?"

"Yes. She's going to be a Shaper."

"Verfluchter! – Are you aware of the possible repercussions?"

"Of course."

"You've heard of unlucky Pierre?"

"No."

"Good, then it was successfully hushed. Pierre was a philosophy student at the University of Paris, and was doing a dissertation on the evolution of consciousness. This past summer he decided it would be necessary for him to explore the mind of an ape, for purposes of comparing a moins-nausee mind with his own, I suppose. At any rate, he obtained illegal access to an ONT&R and to the mind of our hairy cousin. It was never ascertained how far along he got in exposing the animal to the stimulibank, but it is to be assumed that such items as would not be immediately trans-subjective between man and ape – traffic sounds and *so weiter* – were what frightened the creature. Pierre is still residing in a padded cell, and all his responses are those of a frightened ape.

"So, while he did not complete his own dissertation," he finished, "he may provide significant material for someone else's."

Render shook his head.

"Quite a story," he said softly, "but I have nothing that dramatic to contend with. I've found an exceedingly stable individual – a psychiatrist, in fact – one who's already spent time in ordinary analysis. She wants to go into neuroparticipation – but the fear of a sight-trauma was what was keeping her out. I've been gradually exposing her to a full range of visual phenomena. When I've finished she should be completely accommodated to sight, so that she can give her full attention to therapy and not be blinded by vision, so to speak. We've already had four sessions."

"And?"

". . . And it's working fine."

"You are certain about it?"

"Yes, as certain as anyone can be in these matters."

"Mm-hm," said Bartelmetz. "Tell me, do you find her excessively strong-willed? By that I mean, say, perhaps an obsessive-compulsive pattern concerning anything to which she's been introduced so far?"

"No."

"Has she ever succeeded in taking over control of the fantasy?"

"No!"

"You lie," he said simply.

Render found a cigarette. After lighting it, he smiled.

"Old father, old artificer," he conceded, "age has not withered your perceptiveness. I may trick me, but never you. – Yes, as a matter of fact, she *is* very difficult to keep under control. She is not satisfied just to see. She wants to Shape things for herself already. It's quite under-standable – both to her and to me – but conscious apprehension and emotional acceptance never do seem to get together on things. She has become dominant on several occasions, but I've succeeded in resuming control almost immediately. After all, I *am* master of the bank."

"Hm," mused Bartelmetz. "Are you familiar with a Buddhist text – *Shankara's Catechism?*"

"I'm afraid not."

"Then I lecture you on it now. It posits – obviously not for thera-peutic purposes – a true ego and a false ego. The true ego is that part of man which is immortal and shall proceed on to nirvana: the soul, if you like. Very good. Well, the false ego, on the other hand, is the normal mind, bound round with the illusions – the consciousness of you and me and everyone we have ever known professionally. Good? – Good. Now, the stuff this false ego is made up of they call skandhas. These include the feelings, the perceptions, the aptitudes, conscious-ness itself, and even the physical form. Very unscientific. Yes. Now they are not the same thing as neuroses, or one of Mr. Ibsen's life-lies, or an hallucination – no, even though they are all wrong, being parts of a false thing to begin with. Each of the five skandhas is a part of the eccentricity that we call identity – then on top come the neuroses and all the other messes which follow after and keep us in business. Okay? – Okay. I give you this lecture because I need a dramatic term for what I will say, because I wish to say something dramatic. View the skandhas as lying at the bottom of the pond; the neuroses, they are ripples on the top of the water; the 'true ego,' if there is one, is buried deep beneath the sand at the bottom. So. The ripples fill up the-the – *zwischenwelt* – between the object and the subject. The skandhas are a part of the subject, basic, unique, the stuff of his being. – So far, you are with me?"

"With many reservations."

"Good. Now I have defined my term somewhat, I will use it. You are fooling around with skandhas, not simple neuroses. You are attempting to adjust this woman's overall conception of herself and of the world. You are using the ONT&R to do it. It is the same thing as fooling with a psychotic or an ape. All may seem to go well, but – at any moment, it is possible you may do something, show her some sight, or some way of seeing which will break in upon her selfhood, break a skandha – and pouf! – it will be like breaking through the bottom of the pond. A whirlpool will result, pulling you – where? I do not want you for a patient, young man, young artificer, so I counsel you not to proceed with this experiment. The ONT&R should not be used in such a manner."

Render flipped his cigarette into the fire and counted on his fingers:

"One," he said, "you are making a mystical mountain out of a pebble. All I am doing is adjusting her consciousness to accept an addi-tional area of perception. Much of it is simple transference work from the other senses – Two, her emotions were quite intense initially because it *did* involve a trauma – but we've passed that stage already. Now it is only a novelty to her. Soon it will be a commonplace – Three, Eileen is a psychiatrist herself; she is educated in these matters and deeply aware of the delicate nature of what we are doing – Four, her sense of identity and her desires, or her skandhas, or whatever you want to call them, are as firm as the Rock of Gibraltar. Do you realize the intense application required for a blind person to obtain the education she has obtained? It took a will of ten-point steel and the emotional control of an ascetic as well – "

" – And if something that strong should break, in a timeless moment of anxiety," smiled Bartelmetz sadly, "may the shades of Sigmund Freud and Karl Jung walk by your side in the valley of darkness.

" – And five," he added suddenly, staring into Render's eyes. "Five," he ticked it off on one finger. "Is she pretty?"

Render looked back into the fire.

"Very clever," sighed Bartelmetz. "I cannot tell whether you are blushing or not, with the rosy glow of the flames upon your face. I fear that you are, though, which would mean that you are aware that you yourself could be the source of the inciting stimulus. I shall burn a candle tonight before a portrait of Adler and pray that he give you the strength to compete successfully in your duel with your patient."

Render looked at Jill, who was still sleeping. He reached out and brushed a lock of her hair back into place.

"Still," said Bartelmetz, "if you do proceed and all goes well, I shall look forward with great interest to the reading of your work. Did I ever tell you that I have treated several Buddhists and never found a 'true ego'?"

Both men laughed.

Like me but not like me, that one on a leash, smelling of fear, small, gray, and unseeing. *Rrowl* and he'll choke on his collar. His head is empty as the oven till. She pushes the button and it makes dinner. Make talk and they never understand, but they are like me. One day I will kill one – why . . . ? Turn here.

"Three steps. Up. Glass doors. Handle to right."

Why? Ahead, drop-shaft. Gardens under, down. Smells nice, there. Grass, wet dirt, trees, and clean air. I see. Birds are recorded though. I see all. I.

"Dropshaft. Four steps."

Down Yes. Want to make loud noises in throat, feel silly. Clean, smooth, many of trees. God . . . She likes sitting on bench chewing leaves smelling smooth air. Can't see them like me. Maybe now, some . . . ? No.

Can't Bad Sigmund me on grass, trees, here. Must hold it. Pity. Best place . . .

"Watch for steps."

Ahead. To right, to left, to right, to left, trees and grass now. Sigmund sees. Walking . . . Doctor with machine gives her his eyes. *Rrowl* and he will not choke. No fearsmell.

Dig deep hole in ground, bury eyes. God is blind. Sigmund to see. Her eyes now filled, and he is afraid of teeth. Will make her to see and take her high up in the sky to see, away. Leave me here, leave Sigmund with none to see, alone. I will dig a deep hole in the ground . . .

It was after ten in the morning when Jill awoke. She did not have to turn her head to know that Render was already gone. He never slept late. She rubbed her eyes, stretched, turned onto her side and raised herself on her elbow. She squinted at the clock on the bedside table, simultaneously reaching for a cigarette and her lighter.

As she inhaled, she realized there was no ashtray. Doubtless Render had moved it to the dresser because he did not approve of smoking in bed. With a sigh that ended in a snort she slid out of the bed and drew on her wrap before the ash grew too long.

She hated getting up, but once she did she would permit the day to begin and continue on without lapse through its orderly progression of events.

"Damn him," she smiled. She had wanted her breakfast in bed, but it was too late now.

Between thoughts as to what she would wear, she observed an alien pair of skis standing in the corner. A sheet of paper was impaled on one. She approached it.

"Join me?" asked the scrawl.

She shook her head in an emphatic negative and felt somewhat sad. She had been on skis twice in her life and she was afraid of them. She felt that she should really try again, after his being a reasonably good sport about the chateaux, but she could not even bear the memory of the unseemly downward rushing – which, on two occasions, had promptly deposited her in a snowbank – without wincing and feeling once again the vertigo that had seized her during the attempts.

So she showered and dressed and went downstairs for breakfast.

All nine fires were already roaring as she passed the big hall and looked inside. Some red-faced skiers were holding their hands up before the blaze of the central hearth. It was not crowded though. The racks held only a few pairs of dripping boots, bright caps hung on pegs, moist skis stood upright in their place beside the door. A few people were seated in the chairs set further back toward the center of the hall, reading papers, smoking, or talking quietly. She saw no one she knew, so she moved on toward the dining room.

As she passed the registration desk the old man who worked there called out her name. She approached him and smiled.

"Letter," he explained, turning to a rack. "Here it is," he announced, handing it to her. "Looks important."

It had been forwarded three times, she noted. It was a bulky brown envelope, and the return address was that of her attorney.

"Thank you."

She moved off to a seat beside the big window that looked out upon a snow garden, a skating rink, and a distant winding trail dotted with figures carrying skis over their shoulders. She squinted against the brightness as she tore open the envelope.

Yes, it was final. Her attorney's note was accompanied by a copy of the divorce decree. She had only recently decided to end her legal relationship to Mr. Fotlock, whose name she had stopped using five years earlier, when they had separated. Now that she had the thing, she wasn't sure exactly what she was going to do with it. It would be a hell of a surprise for dear Rendy, though, she decided. She would have to find a reasonably innocent way of getting the information to him. She withdrew her compact and practiced a "Well?" expression. Well, there would be time for that later, she mused. Not too much later, though . . . Her thirtieth birthday, like a huge black cloud, filled an April but four months distant. Well . . . She touched her quizzical lips with color, dusted more powder over her mole, and locked the expression within her compact for future use.

In the dining room she saw Doctor Bartelmetz, seated before an enormous mound of scrambled eggs, great chains of dark sausages, several heaps of yellow toast, and a half-emptied flask of orange juice. A pot of coffee steamed on the warmer at his elbow. He leaned slightly forward as he ate, wielding his fork like a windmill blade.

"Good morning," she said.

He looked up.

"Miss DeVille – Jill . . . Good morning." He nodded at the chair across from him. "Join me, please."

She did so, and when the waiter approached she nodded and said,

"I'll have the same thing, only about ninety percent less."

She turned back to Bartelmetz.

"Have you seen Charles today?"

"Alas, I have not," he gestured, open-handed, "and I wanted to continue our discussion while his mind was still in the early stages of wakefulness and somewhat malleable. Unfortunately," he took a sip of coffee, "he who sleeps well enters the day somewhere in the middle of its second act."

"Myself, I usually come in around intermission and ask someone for a synopsis," she explained. "So why not continue the discussion with me? – I'm always malleable, and my skandhas are in good shape."

Their eyes met, and he took a bite of toast.

"Aye," he said, at length, "I had guessed as much. Well – good. What do you know of Render's work?"

She adjusted herself in the chair.

"Mm. He being a special specialist in a highly specialized area, I find it difficult to appreciate the few things he does say about it. I'd like to be able to look inside other people's minds sometimes – to see what they're thinking about *me*, of course – but I don't think I could stand staying there very long. Especially," she gave a mock-shudder, "the mind of somebody with – problems. I'm afraid I'd be too sympathetic or too frightened or something. Then, according to what I've read – pow! – like sympathetic magic, it would be my problem.

"Charles never has problems though," she continued, "at least, none that he speaks to me about. Lately I've been wondering, though. That blind girl and her talking dog seem to be too much with him."

"Talking dog?"

"Yes, her seeing-eye dog is one of those surgical mutants."

"How interesting . . . Have you ever met her?"

"Never."

"So," he mused.

"Sometimes a therapist encounters a patient whose problems are so akin to his own that the sessions become extremely mordant," he noted. "It has always been the case with me when I treat a fellow-psychiatrist. Perhaps Charles sees in this situation a parallel to something which has been troubling him personally. I did not administer his personal analysis. I do not know all the ways of his mind, even though he was a pupil of mine for a long while. He was always self-contained, somewhat reticent; he could be quite authoritative on occasion, however. – What are some of the other things which occupy his attention these days?"

"His son Peter is a constant concern. He's changed the boy's school five times in five years.

Her breakfast arrived. She adjusted her napkin and drew her chair closer to the table.

"And he has been reading case histories of suicides recently, and talking about them, and talking about them, and talking about them."

"To what end?"

She shrugged and began eating.

"He never mentioned why," she said, looking up again. "Maybe he's writing something . . ."

Bartelmetz finished his eggs and poured more coffee.

"Are you afraid of this patient of his?" he inquired.

"No . . . Yes," she responded, "I am."

"Why?"

"I am afraid of sympathetic magic," she said, flushing slightly.

"Many things could fall under that heading."

"Many indeed," she acknowledged. And, after a moment, "We are united in our concern for his welfare and in agreement as to what represents the threat. So, may I ask a favor?"

"You may."

"Talk to him again," she said. "Persuade him to drop the case."

He folded his napkin.

"I intend to do that after dinner," he stated, "because I believe in the ritualistic value of rescue-motions. They shall be made."

Dear Father-image,

Yes, the school is fine, my ankle is getting that way, and my class-mates are a congenial lot. No, I am not short on cash, undernourished, or having difficulty fitting into the new curriculum. Okay?

The building I will not describe, as you have already seen the macabre thing. The grounds I cannot describe, as they are currently residing beneath cold white sheets. Brr! I trust yourself to be enjoying the arts wint'rish. I do not share your enthusiasm for summer's opposite, except within picture frames or as an emblem on ice-cream bars.

The ankle inhibits my mobility and my roommate has gone home for the weekend – both of which are really blessings (saith Pangloss), for I now have the opportunity to catch up on some reading. I will do so forthwith.

Prodigally,
Peter

Render reached down to pat the huge head. It accepted the gesture stoically, then turned its gaze up to the Austrian whom Render had asked for a light, as if to say, "Must I endure this indignity?" The man laughed at the expression, snapping shut the engraved lighter on which Render noted the middle initial to be a small 'v.'

"Thank you," he said, and to the dog: "What is your name?"

"Bismark," it growled.

Render smiled.

"You remind me of another of your kind," he told the dog. "One Sigmund, by name, a companion and guide to a blind friend of mine, in America."

"My Bismark is a hunter," said the young man. "There is no quarry that can out think him, neither the deer nor the big cats."

The dog's ears pricked forward and he stared up at Render with proud, blazing eyes.

"We have hunted in Africa and the northern and southwestern parts of America. Central America, too. He never loses the trail. He never gives up. He is a beautiful brute, and his teeth could have been made in Solingen."

"You are indeed fortunate to have such a hunting companion."

"I hunt," growled the dog. "I follow ... Sometimes, I have, the kill ..."

"You would not know of the one called Sigmund then, or the woman he guides – Miss Eileen Shallot?" asked Render.

The man shook his head.

"No, Bismark came to me from Massachusetts, but I was never to the Center personally. I am not acquainted with other mutie handlers."

"I see. Well, thank you for the light. Good afternoon."

"Good afternoon . . ."

"Good, after, noon . . ."

Render strolled on up the narrow street, hands in his pockets. He had excused himself and not said where he was going. This was because he had had no destination in mind. Bartelmetz' second essay at counseling had almost led him to say things he would later regret. It was easier to take a walk than to continue the conversation.

On a sudden impulse he entered a small shop and bought a cuckoo clock which had caught his eye. He felt certain that Bartelmetz would accept the gift in the proper spirit. He smiled and walked on. *And what was that letter to Jill which the desk clerk had made a special trip to their table to deliver at dinnertime?* he wondered. It had been forwarded three times, and its return address was that of a law firm. Jill had not even opened it, but had smiled, overtipped the old man, and tucked it into her purse. He would have to hint subtly as to its contents. His curiosity so aroused, she would be sure to tell him out of pity.

The icy pillars of the sky suddenly seemed to sway before him as a cold wind leaped down out of the north. Render hunched his shoulders and drew his head further below his collar. Clutching the cuckoo clock, he hurried back up the street.

That night the serpent which holds its tail in its mouth belched, the Fenris Wolf made a pass at the moon, the little clock said "cuckoo" and tomorrow came on like Manolete's last bull, shaking the gate of horn with the bellowed promise to tread a river of lions to sand.

Render promised himself he would lay off the gooey fondue.

Later, much later, when they skipped through the skies in a kite-shaped cruiser, Render looked down upon the darkened Earth dreaming its cities full of stars, looked up at the sky where they were all reflected, looked about him at the tape-screens watching all the people who blinked into them, and at the coffee, tea, and mixed drink dispensers who sent their fluids forth to explore the insides of the people they required to push their buttons, then looked across at Jill, whom the old buildings had compelled to walk among their walls – because he knew she felt he should be looking at her then – felt his seat's demand that he convert it into a couch, did so, and slept.

IV

Her office was full of flowers, and she liked exotic perfumes. Sometimes she burned incense.

She liked soaking in overheated pools, walking through falling snow, listening to too much music, played perhaps too loudly, drinking five or six varieties of liqueurs (usually reeking of anise, sometimes touched with wormwood) every evening. Her hands were soft and lightly freckled. Her fingers were long and tapered. She wore no rings.

Her fingers traced and retraced the floral swellings on the side of her chair as she spoke into the recording unit.

". . . Patient's chief complaints on admission were nervousness, insomnia, stomach pains, and a period of depression. Patient has had a record of previous admissions for short periods of time. He had been in this hospital in 1995 for a manic depressive psychosis, depressed type, and he returned here again, 2-3-96. He was in another hospital,

9-20-97. Physical examination revealed a BP of 170/00. He was normally developed and well-nourished on the date of examination, 12-11-98. On this date patient complained of chronic backache, and there was noted some moderate symptoms of alcohol withdrawal. Physical examination further revealed no pathology except that the patient's tendon reflexes were exaggerated but equal. These symptoms were the result of alcohol withdrawal. Upon admission he was shown to be not psychotic, neither delusional nor hallucinated. He was well-oriented as to place, time, and person. His psychological condition was evaluated and he was found to be somewhat grandiose and expansive and more than a little hostile. He was considered a potential trouble-maker. Because of his experience as a cook, he was assigned to work in the kitchen. His general condition then showed definite improvement. He is less tense and is cooperative. Diagnosis: Manic depressive reaction (external precipitating stress unknown). The degree of psychiatric impairment is mild. He is considered competent. To be continued on therapy and hospitalization."

She turned off the recorder then and laughed. The sound frightened her. Laughter is a social phenomenon and she was alone. She played back the recording then, chewing on the corner of her handkerchief while the soft, clipped words were returned to her. She ceased to hear them after the first dozen or so.

When the recorder stopped talking she turned it off. She was alone. She was very alone. She was so damned alone that the little pool of brightness which occurred when she stroked her forehead and faced the window – that little pool of brightness suddenly became the most important thing in the world. She wanted it to be immense. She wanted it to be an ocean of light. Or else she wanted to grow so small herself that the effect would be the same: she wanted to drown in it.

It had been three weeks, yesterday . . .

Too long, she decided, *I should have waited. No! Impossible! But what if he goes as Riscomb went? No! He won't. He would not. Nothing can hurt him. Never. He is all strength and armor. But – but we should have waited till next month to start. Three weeks. . . Sight withdrawal – that's what it is. Are the memories fading? Are they weaker? What does a tree look like? Or a cloud – I can't remember! What is red? What is green? God! It's hysterical! I'm watching and I can't stop it! – Take a pill! A pill!*

Her shoulders began to shake. She did not take a pill though, but bit down harder on the handkerchief until her sharp teeth tore through its fabric.

"Beware," she recited a personal beatitude, "those who hunger and thirst after justice, for we *will* be satisfied.

"And beware the meek," she continued, "for we shall attempt to inherit the Earth.

"And beware . . ."

There was a brief buzz from the phone-box. She put away her handkerchief, composed her face, turned the unit on.

"Hello . . . ?"

"Eileen, I'm back. How've you been?"

"Good, quite well in fact. How was your vacation?"

"Oh, I can't complain. I had it coming for a long time. I guess I deserve it. Listen, I brought some things back to show you – like Winchester Cathedral. You want to come in this week? I can make it any evening."

Tonight. No. I want it too badly. It will set me back if he sees . . .

"How about tomorrow night?" she asked. "Or the one after?"

"Tomorrow will be fine," he said. "Meet you at the P & S, around seven?"

"Yes, that would be pleasant. Same table?"

"Why not? – I'll reserve it."

"All right. I'll see you then."

"Good-bye."

The connection was broken.

Suddenly, then, at that moment, colors swirled again through her head; and she saw trees – oaks and pines, poplars and sycamores – great, and green and brown, and iron-colored; and she saw wads of fleecy clouds, dipped in paintpots, swabbing a pastel sky; and a burning sun, and a small willow tree, and a lake of a deep, almost violet, blue. She folded her torn handkerchief and put it away.

She pushed a button beside her desk and music filled the office: Scriabin. Then she pushed another button and replayed the tape she had dictated, half-listening to each.

Pierre sniffed suspiciously at the food. The attendant moved away from the tray and stepped out into the hall, locking the door behind him. The enormous salad waited on the floor. Pierre approached cautiously, snatched a handful of lettuce, gulped it.

He was afraid.

If only the steel would stop crashing and crashing against steel, somewhere in that dark night . . . If only . . .

Sigmund rose to his feet, yawned, stretched. His hind legs trailed out behind him for a moment, then he snapped to attention and shook himself. She would be coming home soon. Wagging his tail slowly, he glanced up at the human-level clock with the raised numerals, verified his feelings, then crossed the apartment to the teevee. He rose onto his hind legs, rested one paw against the table and used the other to turn on the set.

It was nearly time for the weather report and the roads would be icy.

"I have driven through countrywide graveyards," wrote Render, "vast forests of stone that spread further every day.

"Why does man so zealously guard his dead? Is it because this is the monumentally democratic way of immortalization, the ultimate affirmation of the power to hurt – that is to say, life – and the desire that it continue on forever? Unamuno has suggested that this is the case. If it is, then a greater percentage of the population actively sought immortality last year than ever before in history . . ."

Tch-tchg, tchga-tchg!

"Do you think they're really people?"

"Naw, they're too good."

The evening was starglint and soda over ice. Render wound the S-7 into the cold sub-subcellar, found his parking place, nosed into it.

There was a damp chill that emerged from the concrete to gnaw like rats' teeth at their flesh. Render guided her toward the lift, their breath preceding them in dissolving clouds.

"A bit of a chill in the air," he noted.

She nodded, biting her lip.

Inside the lift, he sighed, unwound his scarf, lit a cigarette.

"Give me one, please," she requested, smelling the tobacco.

He did.

They rose slowly, and Render leaned against the wall, puffing a mixture of smoke and crystallized moisture.

"I met another mutie shep," he recalled, "in Switzerland. Big as Sigmund. A hunter though, and as Prussian as they come," he grinned.

"Sigmund likes to hunt, too," she observed. "Twice every year we go up to the North Woods and I turn him loose. He's gone for days at a time, and he's always quite happy when he returns. Never says what he's done, but he's never hungry. Back when I got him I guessed that he would need vacations from humanity to stay stable. I think I was right."

The lift stopped, the door opened and they walked out into the hall, Render guiding her again.

Inside his office, he poked at the thermostat and warm air sighed through the room. He hung their coats in the inner office and brought the great egg out from its nest behind the wall. He connected it to an outlet and moved to convert his desk into a control panel.

"How long do you think it will take?" she asked, running her finger-tips over the smooth, cold curves of the egg. "The whole thing, I mean. The entire adaptation to seeing."

He wondered.

"I have no idea," he said, "no idea whatsoever, yet. We got off to a good start, but there's still a lot of work to be done. I think I'll be able to make a good guess in another three months."

She nodded wistfully, moved to his desk, explored the controls with finger strokes like ten feathers.

"Careful you don't push any of those."

"I won't. How long do you think it will take me to learn to operate one?"

"Three months to learn it. Six, to actually become proficient enough to use it on anyone, and an additional six under close supervision before you can be trusted on your own. – About a year altogether."

"Uh-huh." She chose a chair.

Render touched the seasons to life, and the phases of day and night, the breath of the country, the city, the elements that raced naked through the skies, and all the dozens of dancing cues he used to build worlds. He smashed the clock of time and tasted the seven or so ages of man.

"Okay," he turned, "everything is ready."

It came quickly, and with a minimum of suggestion on Render's part. One moment there was grayness. Then a dead-white fog. Then it broke itself apart, as though a quick wind had risen, although he neither heard nor felt a wind.

He stood beside the willow tree beside the lake, and she stood half-hidden among the branches and the lattices of shadow. The sun was slanting its way into evening.

"We have come back," she said, stepping out, leaves in her hair. "For a time I was afraid it had never happened, but I see it all again, and I remember now."

"Good," he said. "Behold yourself." And she looked into the lake.

"I have not changed," she said. "I haven't changed . . ."

"No."

"But you have," she continued, looking up at him. "You are taller, and there is something different . . ."

"No," he answered.

"I am mistaken," she said quickly. "I don't understand everything I see yet.

"I will, though."

"Of course."

"What are we going to do?"

"Watch," he instructed her.

Along a flat, no-colored river of road she just then noticed beyond the trees came the car. It came from the farthest quarter of the sky, skipping over the mountains, buzzing down the hills, circling through the glades, and splashing them with the colors of its voice – the gray and the silver of synchronized potency – and the lake shivered from its sounds, and the car stopped a hundred feet away, masked by the shrubberies; and it waited. It was the S-7.

"Come with me," he said, taking her hand. "We're going for a ride."

They walked among the trees and rounded the final cluster of bushes. She touched the sleek cocoon, its antennae, its tires, its windows – and the windows transpared as she did so. She stared through them at the inside of the car, and she nodded.

"It is your Spinner."

"Yes." He held the door for her. "Get in. We'll return to the club. The time is now. The memories are fresh, and they should be reasonably pleasant, or neutral."

"Pleasant," she said, getting in.

He closed the door, then circled the car and entered. She watched as he punched imaginary coordinates. The car leaped ahead and he kept a steady stream of trees flowing by them. He could feel the rising tension, so he did not vary the scenery. She swiveled her seat and studied the interior of the car.

"Yes," she finally said, "I can perceive what everything is."

She stared out the window again. She looked at the rushing trees. Render stared out and looked upon rushing anxiety patterns. He opaqued the windows.

"Good," she said, "thank you. Suddenly it was too much to see – all of it, moving past like a . . ."

"Of course," said Render, maintaining the sensations of forward motion. "I'd anticipated that. You're getting tougher, though."

After a moment, "Relax," he said, "relax now," and somewhere a button was pushed, and she relaxed, and they drove on, and on and on, and finally the car began to slow, and Render said, "Just for one nice, slow glimpse now, look out your window."

She did.

He drew upon every stimulus in the bank which could promote sensations of pleasure and relaxation, and he dropped the city around the car, and the windows became transparent, and she looked out upon the profiles of towers and a block of monolithic apartments, and then she saw three rapid cafeterias, an entertainment palace, a drugstore, a medical center of yellow brick with an aluminum Caduceus set above its archway, and a glassed-in high school, now emptied of its pupils, a fifty-pump gas station, another drugstore, and many more cars, parked or roaring by them, and people, people moving in and out of the doorways and walking before the buildings and getting into the cars and getting out of the cars; and it was summer, and the light of late afternoon filtered down upon the colors of the city and the colors of the garments the people wore as they moved along the boulevard, as they loafed upon the terraces, as they crossed the balconies, leaned on balustrades and windowsills, emerged from a corner kiosk, entered one, stood talking to one another; a woman walking a poodle rounded a corner; rockets went to and fro in the high sky.

The world fell apart then and Render caught the pieces.

He maintained an absolute blackness, blanketing every sensation but that of their movement forward.

After a time a dim light occurred, and they were still seated in the Spinner, windows blanked again, and the air as they breathed it became a soothing unguent.

"Lord," she said, "the world is so filled. Did I really see all of that?"

"I wasn't going to do that tonight, but you wanted me to. You seemed ready."

"Yes," she said, and the windows became transparent again. She turned away quickly.

"It's gone," he said. "I only wanted to give you a glimpse."

She looked, and it was dark outside now, and they were crossing over a high bridge. They were moving slowly. There was no other traffic. Below them were the Flats, where an occasional smelter flared like a tiny, drowsing volcano, spitting showers of orange sparks skyward; and there were many stars: they glistened on the breathing water that went beneath the bridge; they silhouetted by pinprick the skyline that hovered dimly below its surface. The slanting struts of the bridge marched steadily by.

"You have done it," she said, "and I thank you." Then: "Who are you, really?" (He must have wanted her to ask that.)

"I am Render," he laughed. And they wound their way through a dark, now-vacant city, coming at last to their club and entering the great parking dome.

Inside, he scrutinized all her feelings, ready to banish the world at a moment's notice. He did not feel he would have to, though.

They left the car, moved ahead. They passed into the club, which he had decided would not be crowded tonight. They were shown to their table at the foot of the bar in the small room with the suit of armor, and they sat down and ordered the same meal over again.

"No," he said, looking down, "it belongs over there."

The suit of armor appeared once again beside the table, and he was once again inside his gray suit and black tie and silver tie clasp shaped like a tree limb.

They laughed.

"I'm just not the type to wear a tin suit, so I wish you'd stop seeing me that way."

"I'm sorry," she smiled. "I don't know how I did that, or why."

"I do, and I decline the nomination. Also, I caution you once again. You are conscious of the fact that this is all an illusion. I had to do it that way for you to get the full benefit of the thing. For most of my patients though, it is the real item while they are experiencing it. It makes a counter-trauma or a symbolic sequence even more powerful. You are aware of the parameters of the game, however, and whether you want it or not this gives you a different sort of control over it than I normally have to deal with. Please be careful."

"I'm sorry. I didn't mean to."

"I know. Here comes the meal we just had."

"Ugh! It looks dreadful! Did we eat all that stuff?"

"Yes," he chuckled. "That's a knife, that's a fork, that's a spoon. That's roast beef, and those are mashed potatoes, those are peas, that's butter . . ."

"Goodness! I don't feel so well."

". . . And those are the salads, and those are the salad dressings. This is a brook trout – mm! These are French fried potatoes. This is a bottle of wine. Hmm – let's see – Romanee-Conti, since I'm not paying for it – and a bottle of Yquem for the trou – Hey!"

The room was wavering.

He bared the table, he banished the restaurant. They were back in the glade. Through the transparent fabric of the world he watched a hand moving along a panel. Buttons were being pushed. The world grew substantial again. Their emptied table was set beside the lake now, and it was still night-time and summer, and the tablecloth was very white under the glow of the giant moon that hung overhead.

"That was stupid of me," he said. "Awfully stupid. I should have introduced them one at a time. The actual sight of basic, oral stimuli can be very distressing to a person seeing them for the first time. I got so wrapped up in the Shaping that I forgot the patient, which is just dandy! I apologize."

"I'm okay now. Really I am."

He summoned a cool breeze from the lake.

". . . And that is the moon," he added lamely.

She nodded, and she was wearing a tiny moon in the center of her forehead; it glowed like the one above them, and her hair and dress were all of silver.

The bottle of Romanee-Conti stood on the table, and two glasses.

"Where did that come from?"

She shrugged. He poured out a glassful.

"It may taste kind of flat," he said.

"It doesn't. Here – " She passed it to him.

As he sipped it he realized it had a taste – a *fruite* such as might be quashed from the grapes grown in the Isles of the Blest, a smooth, muscular *charnu*, and a *capiteux* centrifuged from the fumes of a field of burning poppies. With a start, he knew that his hand must be traversing the route of the perceptions, symphonizing the sensual cues of a transference and a counter-transference which had come upon him all unaware, there beside the lake.

"So it does," he noted, "and now it is time we returned."

"So soon? I haven't seen the cathedral yet . . ."

"So soon."

He willed the world to end, and it did.

"It is cold out there," she said as she dressed, "and dark."

"I know. I'll mix us something to drink while I clear the unit."

"Fine."

He glanced at the tapes and shook his head. He crossed to his bar cabinet.

"It's not exactly Romanee-Conti," he observed, reaching for a bottle.

"So what? I don't mind."

Neither did he, at that moment. So he cleared the unit, they drank their drinks, he helped her into her coat and they left.

As they rode the lift down to the sub-sub he willed the world to end again, but it didn't.

Dad,

I hobbled from school to taxi and taxi to spaceport, for the local Air Force Exhibit – Outward, it was called. (Okay; I exaggerated the hobble. It got me extra attention though.) The whole bit was aimed at seducing young manhood into a five-year hitch, as I saw it. But it worked. I wanna join up. I wanna go Out There. Think they'll take me when I'm old enuf? I mean take me Out – not some crummy desk job. Think so?

I do.

There was this damn lite colonel ('scuse the French) who saw this kid lurching around and pressing his nose 'gainst the big windowpanes, and he decided to give him the subliminal sell. Great! He pushed me through the gallery and showed me all the pitchers of AF triumphs, from Moonbase to Marsport. He lectured me on the Great Traditions of the Service, and marched me into a flic room where the Corps had good clean fun on tape, wrestling one another in null-G "where it's all skill and no brawn," and making tinted water sculpture-work way in the middle of the air and doing dismounted drill on the skin of a cruiser. Oh joy!

Seriously though, I'd like to be there when they hit the Outer Five – and On Out. Not because of the bogus balonus in the throwaways, and suchlike crud, but because I think someone of sensibility should be along to chronicle the thing in the proper way. You know, raw frontier observer. Francis Parkman. Mary Austin, like that. So I decided I'm going.

The AF boy with the chicken stuff on his shoulders wasn't in the least way patronizing, gods be praised. We stood on the balcony and watched ships lift off and he told me to go forth and study real hard and I might be riding them someday. I did not bother to tell him that I'm hardly intellectually deficient and that I'll have my B.A. before I'm old enough to do anything with it, even join his Corps. I just watched the ships lift off and said, "Ten years from now I'll be looking down, not up." Then he told me how hard his own training had been, so I did not ask howcum he got stuck with a lousy dirt-side assignment like this one. Glad I didn't, now I think on it. He looked more like one of their ads than one of their real people. Hope I never look like an ad.

Thank you for the monies and the warm sox and Mozart's String Quintets, which I'm hearing right now. I wanna put in my bid for

Luna instead of Europe next summer. Maybe . . . ? Possibly . . . ? Contingently . . . ? Huh? – If I can smash that new test you're designing for me . . . ? Anyhow, please think about it.

Your son,
Pete

"Hello. State Psychiatric Institute."

"I'd like to make an appointment for an examination."

"Just a moment. I'll connect you with the Appointment Desk."

"Hello. Appointment Desk."

"I'd like to make an appointment for an examination."

"Just a moment . . . What sort of examination."

"I want to see Doctor Shallot, Eileen Shallot. As soon as possible."

"Just a moment. I'll have to check her schedule . . . Could you make it at two o'clock next Tuesday?"

"That would be just fine."

"What is the name, please?"

"DeVille. Jill DeVille."

"All right, Miss DeVille. That's two o'clock, Tuesday."

"Thank you."

The man walked beside the highway. Cars passed along the highway. The cars in the high-acceleration lane blurred by.

Traffic was light.

It was 10:30 in the morning, and cold.

The man's fur-lined collar was turned up, his hands were in his pockets, and he leaned into the wind. Beyond the fence, the road was clean and dry.

The morning sun was buried in clouds. In the dirty light, the man could see the tree a quarter mile ahead.

His pace did not change. His eyes did not leave the tree. The small stones clicked and crunched beneath his shoes.

When he reached the tree he took off his jacket and folded it neatly.

He placed it upon the ground and climbed the tree.

As he moved out onto the limb which extended over the fence, he looked to see that no traffic was approaching. Then he seized the branch with both hands, lowered himself, hung a moment, and dropped onto the highway.

It was a hundred yards wide, the eastbound half of the highway.

He glanced west, saw there was still no traffic coming his way, then began to walk toward the center island. He knew he would never reach it. At this time of day the cars were moving at approximately one hundred sixty miles an hour in the high-acceleration lane. He walked on.

A car passed behind him. He did not look back. If the windows were opaqued, as was usually the case, then the occupants were unaware he had crossed their path. They would hear of it later and examine the front end of their vehicle for possible sign of such an encounter.

A car passed in front of him. Its windows were clear. A glimpse of two faces, their mouths made into O's, was presented to him, then torn from his sight. His own face remained without expression. His pace did not change. Two more cars rushed by, windows darkened. He had crossed perhaps twenty yards of highway.

Twenty-five . . .

Something in the wind, or beneath his feet, told him it was coming. He did not look.

Something in the corner of his eye assured him it was coming. His gait did not alter.

Cecil Green had the windows transpared because he liked it that way. His left hand was inside her blouse and her skirt was piled up on her lap, and his right hand was resting on the lever which would lower the seats. Then she pulled away, making a noise down inside her throat.

His head snapped to the left.

He saw the walking man

He saw the profile which never turned to face him fully. He saw that the man's gait did not alter.

Then he did not see the man.

There was a slight jar, and the windshield began cleaning itself. Cecil Green raced on.

He opaqued the windows.

"How . . . ?" he asked after she was in his arms again, and sobbing.

"The monitor didn't pick him up."

"He must not have touched the fence . . ."

"He must have been out of his mind!"

"Still, he could have picked an easier way."

It could have been any face . . . Mine?

Frightened, Cecil lowered the seats.

Charles Render was writing the "Necropolis" chapter for *The Missing Link Is Man*, which was to be his first book in over four years. Since his return he had set aside every Tuesday and Thursday afternoon to work on it, isolating himself in his office, filling pages with a chaotic longhand.

"There are many varieties of death, as opposed to dying . . ." he was writing, just as the intercom buzzed briefly, then long, then briefly again.

"Yes?" he asked it, pushing down on the switch.

"You have a visitor," and there was a short intake of breath between "a" and "visitor."

He slipped a small aerosol into his side pocket, then rose and crossed the office.

He opened the door and looked out.

"Doctor . . . Help . . ."

Render took three steps, then dropped to one knee.

"What's the matter?"

"Come – she is . . . sick," he growled.

"Sick? How? What's wrong?"

"Don't know. You come."

Render stared into the unhuman eyes.

"What kind of sick?" he insisted.

"Don't know," repeated the dog. "Won't talk. Sits. I . . . feel, she is sick."

"How did you get here?"

"Drove. Know the Co, or, din, ates . . . Left car, outside."

"I'll call her right now." Render turned.

"No good. Won't answer."

He was right.

Render returned to his inner office for his coat and medkit. He glanced out the window and saw where her car was parked, far below, just inside the entrance to the marginal, where the monitor had released it into manual control. If no one assumed that control a car was automatically parked in neutral. The other vehicles were passed around it.

So simple even a dog can drive one, he reflected. *Better get downstairs before a cruiser comes along. It's probably reported itself stopped there already. Maybe not, though. Might still have a few minutes grace.*

He glanced at the huge clock.

"Okay, Sig," he called out. "Let's go."

They took the lift to the ground floor, left by way of the front entrance and hurried to the car.

Its engine was still idling.

Render opened the passengerside door and Sigmund leaped in. He

squeezed by him into the driver's seat then, but the dog was already
pushing the primary coordinates and the address tabs with his paw.

Looks like I'm in the wrong seat.

He lit a cigarette as the car swept ahead into a U-underpass. It
emerged on the opposite marginal, sat poised a moment, then joined
the traffic flow. The dog directed the car into the high-acceleration
lane.

"Oh," said the dog, "oh."

Render felt like patting his head at that moment, but he looked at
him, saw that his teeth were bared, and decided against it.

"When did she start acting peculiar?" he asked.

"Came home from work. Did not eat. Would not answer me when
I talked. Just sits."

"Has she ever been like this before?"

"No."

*What could have precipitated it? – But maybe she just had a bad day. After all,
he's only a dog – sort of. – No. He'd know. But what, then?*

"How was she yesterday – and when she left home this morning?"

"Like always."

Render tried calling her again. There was still no answer.

"You did, it," said the dog.

"What do you mean?"

"Eyes. Seeing. You. Machine. Bad."

"No," said Render, and his hand rested on the unit of stun-spray in
his pocket.

"Yes," said the dog, turning to him again. "You will, make her
well . . . ?"

"Of course," said Render.

Sigmund stared ahead again.

Render felt physically exhilarated and mentally sluggish. He sought
the confusion factor. He had had these feelings about the case since
that first session. There was something very unsettling about Eileen
Shallot; a combination of high intelligence and helplessness, of determination and vulnerability, of sensitivity and bitterness.

*Do I find that especially attractive? – No. It's just the counter-transference, damn
it!*

"You smell afraid," said the dog.

"Then color me afraid," said Render, "and turn the page."

They slowed for a series of turns, picked up speed again, slowed
again, picked up speed again. Finally, they were traveling along a
narrow section of roadway through a semi-residential area of town.

The car turned up a side street, proceeded about half a mile further, clicked softly beneath its dashboard, and turned into the parking lot behind a high brick apartment building. The click must have been a special servomech which took over from the point where the monitor released it, because the car crawled across the lot, headed into its transparent parking stall, then stopped. Render turned off the ignition.

Sigmund had already opened the door on his side. Render followed him into the building, and they rode the elevator to the fiftieth floor. The dog dashed on ahead up the hallway, pressed his nose against a plate set low in a doorframe and waited. After a moment, the door swung several inches inward. He pushed it open with his shoulder and entered. Render followed, closing the door behind him.

The apartment was large, its walls pretty much unadorned, its color combinations unnerving. A great library of tapes filled one corner: a monstrous combination-broadcaster stood beside it. There was a wide bowlegged table set in front of the window, and a low couch along the right-hand wall; there was a closed door beside the couch; an archway to the left apparently led to other rooms. Eileen sat in an overstuffed chair in the far corner by the window. Sigmund stood beside the chair.

Render crossed the room and extracted a cigarette from his case. Snapping open his lighter, he held the flame until her head turned in that direction.

"Cigarette?" he asked.

"Charles?"

"Right."

"Yes, thank you. I will."

She held out her hand, accepted the cigarette, put it to her lips.

"Thanks – What are you doing here?"

"Social call. I happened to be in the neighborhood."

"I didn't hear a buzz or a knock."

"You most have been dozing. Sig let me in."

"Yes, I must have." She stretched. "What time is it?"

"It's close to four-thirty."

"I've been home over two hours then . . . Must have been very tired . . ."

"How do you feel now?"

"Fine," she declared. "Care for a cup of coffee?"

"Don't mind if I do."

"A steak to go with it?"

"No, thanks."

"Barcardi in the coffee?"

"Sounds good."

"Excuse me, then. It'll only take a moment."

She went through the door beside the sofa and Render caught a glimpse of a large, shiny, automatic kitchen.

"Well?" he whispered to the dog.

Sigmund shook his head.

"Not same."

Render shook his head.

He deposited his coat on the sofa, folding it carefully about the medkit. He sat beside it and thought.

Did I throw too big a chunk of seeing at once? Is she suffering from depressive side-effects – say, memory repressions, nervous fatigue? Did I upset her sensory-adaptation syndrome somehow? Why have I been proceeding so rapidly anyway? There's no real hurry. Am I so damned eager to write the thing up? – Or am I doing it because she wants me to? Could she be that strong, consciously or unconsciously? Or am I that vulnerable – somehow?

She called him to the kitchen to carry out the tray. He set it on the table and seated himself across from her.

"Good coffee," he said, burning his lips on the cup.

"Smart machine," she stated, facing his voice.

Sigmund stretched out on the carpet next to the table, lowered his head between his forepaws, sighed and closed his eyes.

"I've been wondering," said Render, "whether or not there were any after effects to that last session – like increased synesthesiac experiences, or dreams involving forms, or hallucinations or . . ."

"Yes," she said flatly, "dreams."

"What kind?"

"That last session. I've dreamed it over, and over."

"Beginning to end?"

"No, there's no special order to the events. We're riding through the city, or over the bridge, or sitting at the table, or walking toward the car – just flashes, like that. Vivid ones."

"What sort of feelings accompany these – flashes?"

"I don't know, they're all mixed up."

"What are your feelings now, as you recall them?"

"The same, all mixed up."

"Are you afraid?"

"N-no. I don't think so."

"Do you want to take a vacation from the thing? Do you feel we've been proceeding too rapidly?"

"No. That's not it at all. It's – well, it's like learning to swim. When you finally learn how, why then you swim and you swim and you swim until you're all exhausted. Then you just lie there gasping in air and remembering what it was like, while your friends all hover and chew you out for overexerting yourself – and it's a good feeling, even though you do take a chill and there are pins and needles inside all your muscles. At least, that's the way I do things. I felt that way after the first session and after this last one. First times are always very special times . . . The pins and the needles are gone, though, and I've caught my breath again. Lord, I don't want to stop now! I feel fine."

"Do you usually take a nap in the afternoon?"

The ten red nails of her fingers moved across the tabletop as she stretched.

". . . Tired," she smiled, swallowing a yawn. "Half the staff's on vacation or sick leave and I've been beating my brains out all week. I was about ready to fall on my face when I left work. I feel all right now that I've rested, though."

She picked up her coffee cup with both hands, took a large swallow.

"Uh-huh," he said. "Good. I was a bit worried about you. I'm glad to see there was no reason."

She laughed.

"Worried? You've read Dr. Riscomb's notes on my analysis – and on the ONT&R trial – and you think I'm the sort to worry about? Ha! I have an operationally beneficent neurosis concerning my adequacy as a human being. It focuses my energies, coordinates my efforts toward achievement. It enhances my sense of identity. . ."

"You do have on hell of a memory," he noted "That's almost verbatim."

"Of course."

"You had Sigmund worried today, too."

"Sig? How?"

The dog stirred uneasily, opened one eye.

"Yes," he growled, glaring up at Render. "He needs, a ride, home."

"Have you been driving the car again?"

"Yes."

"After I told you not to?"

"Yes."

"Why?"

"I was a, fraid. You would, not, answer me, when I talked."

"I was *very* tired – and if you ever take the car again, I'm going to have the door fixed so you can't come and go as you please."

"Sorry."

"There's nothing wrong with me."

"I, see."

"You are *never* to do it again."

"Sorry." His eye never left Render; it was like a burning lens.

Render looked away.

"Don't be too hard on the poor fellow," he said. "After all, he thought you were ill and he went for the doctor. Suppose he'd been right? You'd owe him thanks, not a scolding."

Unmollified, Sigmund glared a moment longer and closed his eye.

"He has to be told when he does wrong," she finished.

"I suppose," he said, drinking his coffee. "No harm done, anyhow. Since I'm here, let's talk shop. I'm writing something and I'd like an opinion."

"Great. Give me a footnote?"

"Two or three. – In your opinion, do the general underlying motivations that lead to suicide differ in different periods of history or in different cultures?"

"My well-considered opinion is no, they don't," she said. "Frustrations can lead to depressions or frenzies; and if these are severe enough, they can lead to self-destruction. You ask me about motivations and I think they stay pretty much the same. I feel this is a cross-cultural, cross-temporal aspect of the human condition. I don't think it could be changed without changing the basic nature of man."

"Okay. Check. Now, what of the inciting element?" he asked. "Let man be a constant, his environment is still a variable. If he is placed in an overprotective life-situation, do you feel it would take more or less to depress him – or stimulate him to frenzy – than it would take in a not so protective environment?"

"Hm. Being case-oriented, I'd say it would depend on the man. But I see what you're driving at: a mass predisposition to jump out windows at the drop of a hat – the window even opening itself for you, because you asked it to – the revolt of the bored masses. I don't like the notion. I hope it's wrong."

"So do I, but I was thinking of symbolic suicides too – functional disorders that occur for pretty flimsy reasons."

"Aha! Your lecture last month: autopsychomimesis. I have the tape. Well-told, but I can't agree."

"Neither can I, now. I'm rewriting that whole section – 'Thanatos in Cloud-cuckooland,' I'm calling it. It's really the death-instinct moved nearer the surface."

"If I get you a scalpel and a cadaver, will you cut out the death-instinct and let me touch it?"

"Couldn't," he put the grin into his voice, "it would be all used up in a cadaver. Find me a volunteer though, and he'll prove my case by volunteering."

"Your logic is unassailable," she smiled. "Get us some more coffee, okay?"

Render went to the kitchen, spiked and filled the cups, drank a glass of water and returned to the living room. Eileen had not moved; neither had Sigmund.

"What do you do when you're not busy being a Shaper?" she asked him.

"The same things most people do – eat, drink, sleep, talk, visit friends and not-friends, visit places, read . . ."

"Are you a forgiving man?"

"Sometimes. Why?"

"Then forgive me. I argued with a woman today, a woman named De Ville."

"What about?"

"You – and she accused me of such things it were better my mother had not born me. Are you going to marry her?"

"No, marriage is like alchemy. It served an important purpose once, but I hardly feel it's here to stay."

"Good."

"What did you say to her?"

"I gave her a clinic referral card that said, 'Diagnosis: Bitch. Prescription: Drug therapy and a tight gag.'"

"Oh," said Render, showing interest.

"She tore it up and threw it in my face."

"I wonder why?"

She shrugged, smiled, made a gridwork on the tablecloth.

"'Fathers and elders, I ponder,'" sighed Render, "'what is hell?'"

"'I maintain it is the suffering of being unable to love,'" she finished. "Was Dostoevsky right?"

"I doubt it. I'd put him into group therapy myself. That'd be *real* hell for him – with all those people acting like his characters and enjoying it so."

Render put down his cup and pushed his chair away from the table.

"I suppose you must be going now?"

"I really should," said Render.

"And I can't interest you in food?"

"No."

She stood.

"Okay, I'll get my coat."

"I could drive back myself and just set the car to return."

"No! I'm frightened by the notion of empty cars driving around the city. I'd feel the thing was haunted for the next two and a half weeks.

"Besides," she said, passing through the archway, "you promised me Winchester Cathedral."

"You want to do it today?"

"If you can be persuaded."

As Render stood deciding, Sigmund rose to his feet. He stood directly before him and stared upward into his eyes. He opened his mouth and closed it, several times, but no sounds emerged. Then he turned away and left the room.

"No," Eileen's voice came back, "you will stay here until I return."

Render picked up his coat and put it on, stuffing the medkit into the far pocket.

As they walked up the hall toward the elevator Render thought he heard a very faint and very distant howling sound.

In this place, of all places, Render knew he was the master of all things.

He was at home on those alien worlds, without time, those worlds where flowers copulate and the stars do battle in the heavens, falling at last to the ground, bleeding, like so many split and shattered chalices, and the seas part to reveal stairways leading down, and arms emerge from caverns, waving torches that flame like liquid faces – a midwinter night's nightmare, summer go a-begging, Render knew – for he had visited those worlds on a professional basis for the better part of a decade. With the crooking of a finger he could isolate the sorcerers, bring them to trial for treason against the realm – aye, and he could execute them, could appoint their successors.

Fortunately, this trip was only a courtesy call . . .

He moved forward through the glade, seeking her.

He could feel her awakening presence all about him.

He pushed through the branches, stood beside the lake. It was cold, blue, and bottomless, the lake, reflecting that slender willow which had become the station of her arrival.

"Eileen!"

The willow swayed toward him, swayed away.

"Eileen! Come forth!"

Leaves fell, floated upon the lake, disturbed its mirror-like placidity, distorted the reflections.

"Eileen?"

All the leaves yellowed at once then dropped down into the water. The tree ceased its swaying. There was a strange sound in the darkening sky, like the humming of high wires on a cold day.

Suddenly there was a double file of moons passing through the heavens.

Render selected one, reached up and pressed it. The others vanished as he did so, and the world brightened, the humming went out of the air.

He circled the lake to gain a subjective respite from the rejection-action and his counter to it. He moved up along an aisle of pines toward the place where he wanted the cathedral to occur. Birds sang now in the trees. The wind came softly by him. He felt her presence quite strongly.

"Here, Eileen. Here."

She walked beside him then, green silk, hair of bronze, eyes of molten emerald; she wore an emerald in her forehead. She walked in green slippers over the pine needles, saying: "What happened?"

"You were afraid."

"Why?"

"Perhaps you fear the cathedral. Are you a witch?" he smiled.

"Yes, but it's my day off."

He laughed, and he took her arm, and they rounded an island of foliage, and there was the cathedral reconstructed on a grassy rise, pushing its way above them and above the trees, climbing into the middle air, breathing out organ notes, reflecting a stray ray of sunlight from a plane of glass.

"Hold tight to the world," he said. "Here comes the guided tour." They moved forward and entered.

"'. . . With its floor-to-ceiling shafts, like so many huge tree trunks, it achieves a ruthless control over its spaces,'" he said. " – Got that from the guidebook. This is the north transept . . .''

"'Greensleeves,'" she said, "the organ is playing 'Greensleeves.'"

"So it is. You can't blame me for that though. – Observe the scalloped capitals – "

"I want to go nearer to the music."

"Very well. This way then."

Render felt that something was wrong. He could not put his finger on it.

Everything retained its solidity . . .

Something passed rapidly then, high above the cathedral, uttering a sonic boom. Render smiled at that, remembering now; it was like a slip of the tongue: for a moment he had confused Eileen with Jill – yes, that was what had happened.

Why, then . . .

A burst of white was the altar. He had never seen it before, anywhere. All the walls were dark and cold about them. Candles flickered in corners and high niches. The organ chorded thunder under invisible hands.

Render knew that something was wrong.

He turned to Eileen Shallot, whose hat was a green cone towering up into the darkness, trailing wisps of green veiling. Her throat was in shadow, but . . .

"That necklace – Where?"

"I don't know," she smiled.

The goblet she held radiated a rosy light. It was reflected from her emerald. It washed him like a draft of cool air.

"Drink?" she asked.

"Stand still," he ordered.

He willed the walls to fall down. They swam in shadow.

"Stand still!" he repeated urgently. "Don't do anything. Try not even to think.

"Fall down!" he cried. And the walls were blasted in all directions and the roof was flung over the top of the world, and they stood amid ruins lighted by a single taper. The night was black as pitch.

"Why did you do that?" she asked, still holding the goblet out toward him.

"Don't think. Don't think anything," he said. "Relax. You are very tired. As that candle flickers and wanes so does your consciousness. You can barely keep awake. You can hardly stay on your feet. Your eyes are closing. There is nothing to see here anyway."

He willed the candle to go out. It continued to burn.

"I'm not tired. Please have a drink."

He heard organ music through the night. A different tune, one he did not recognize at first.

"I need your cooperation."

"All right. Anything."

"Look! The moon!" he pointed

She looked upward and the moon appeared from behind an inky cloud.

". . . And another, and another."

Moons, like strung pearls, proceeded across the blackness.

"The last one will be red," he stated.

It was.

He reached out then with his right index finger, slid his arm sideways along his field of vision, then tried to touch the red moon.

His arm ached, it burned. He could not move it.

"Wake up!" he screamed.

The red moon vanished, and the white ones.

"Please take a drink."

He dashed the goblet from her hand and turned away. When he turned back she was still holding it before him.

"A drink?"

He turned and fled into the night.

It was like running through a waist-high snowdrift. It was wrong. He was compounding the error by running – he was minimizing his strength, maximizing hers. It was sapping his energies, draining him.

He stood still in the midst of the blackness.

"The world around me moves," he said. "I am its center."

"Please have a drink," she said, and he was standing in the glade beside their table set beside the lake. The lake was black and the moon was silver, and high, and out of his reach. A single candle flickered on the table, making her hair as silver as her dress. She wore the moon on her brow. A bottle of Romanee-Conti stood on the white cloth beside a wide-brimmed wine glass. It was filled to overflowing, that glass, and rosy beads clung to its lip. He was very thirsty, and she was lovelier than anyone he had ever seen before, and her necklace sparkled, and the breeze came cool off the lake, and there was something – something he should remember . . .

He took a step toward her and his armor clinked lightly as he moved. He reached toward the glass and his right arm stiffened with pain and fell back to his side.

"You are wounded!"

Slowly, he turned his head. The blood flowed from the open wound in his biceps and ran down his arm and dripped from his fingertips. His armor had been breached. He forced himself to look away.

"Drink this, love. It will heal you."

She stood.

Beggars in Spain

NANCY KRESS

Nancy Kress (1948–) entered science fiction in the early 1980s but flowered by the early 90s. Kress's early novels were genre fantasy, but her short fiction, which gained her initial recognition, was SF, collected in *Trinity and Other Stories* (1985). Her most ambitious work, in which it became clear that she was determined to develop both character and science in her fiction, began with the novel *An Alien Light* (1988), and then *Brain Rose* (1990). Meanwhile, she continued to write an impressive body of short fiction, much of it collected in *The Aliens of Earth* (1993). With the publication of her Beggars novels *(Beggars in Spain* [1993], *Beggars and Choosers* [1994], and *Beggars Ride* [1996]), and in the techno-thriller *Oaths and Miracles* (1996), she showed the full strength of her powers.

Kress, as much as any SF writer today, is an heir to the tradition of H. G. Wells. Nowhere in her work is this more evident than in "Beggars in Spain" and the novels that have grown out of it. With this story, she began her magnum opus. In this story she deals with human and social evolution, with class and economic issues, and with ordinary characters, as Wells did in "A Story of the Days to Come."

With energy and sleepless vigilance go forward and give us victories.
  – Abraham Lincoln, to Maj. Gen. Joseph Hooker, 1863

I

They sat stiffly on his antique Eames chairs, two people who didn't want to be here, or one person who didn't want to and one who resented the other's reluctance. Dr. Ong had seen this before. Within two minutes he was sure: the woman was the silently furious resister. She would lose. The man would pay for it later, in little ways, for a long time.

"I presume you've performed the necessary credit checks already," Roger Camden said pleasantly. "So let's get right on to details, shall we, Doctor?"

"Certainly," Ong said. "Why don't we start by your telling me all the genetic modifications you're interested in for the baby."

The woman shifted suddenly on her chair. She was in her late twenties – clearly a second wife – but already had a faded look, as if keeping up with Roger Camden was wearing her out. Ong could easily believe that. Mrs. Camden's hair was brown, her eyes were brown, her skin had a brown tinge that might have been pretty if her cheeks had had any color. She wore a brown coat, neither fashionable nor cheap, and shoes that looked vaguely orthopedic. Ong glanced at his records for her name: Elizabeth. He would bet people forgot it often.

Next to her, Roger Camden radiated nervous vitality, a man in late middle-age whose bullet-shaped head did not match his careful haircut and Italian-silk business suit. Ong did not need to consult his file to recall anything about Camden. A caricature of the bullet-shaped head had been the leading graphic of yesterday's on-line edition of the *Wall Street Journal:* Camden had led a major coup in cross-border data-atoll investment. Ong was not sure what cross-border data-atoll investment was.

"A girl," Elizabeth Camden said. Ong hadn't expected her to speak first. Her voice was another surprise: upper-class British. "Blond. Green eyes. Tall. Slender."

Ong smiled. "Appearance factors are the easiest to achieve, as I'm sure you already know. But all we can do about 'slenderness' is give her a genetic disposition in that direction. How you feed the child will naturally – "

"Yes, yes," Roger Camden said, "that's obvious. Now: intelligence. *High* intelligence. And a sense of daring."

"I'm sorry, Mr. Camden – personality factors are not yet under-stood well enough to allow genet – "

"Just testing," Camden said, with a smile that Ong thought was probably supposed to be lighthearted.

Elizabeth Camden said, "Musical ability."

"Again, Mrs. Camden, a disposition to be musical is all we can guarantee."

"Good enough," Camden said. "The full array of corrections for any potential gene-linked health problem, of course."

"Of course," Dr. Ong said. Neither client spoke. So far theirs was a fairly modest list, given Camden's money; most clients had to be argued out of contradictory genetic tendencies, alteration overload, or unrealistic expectations. Ong waited. Tension prickled in the room like heat.

"And," Camden said, "no need to sleep."

Elizabeth Camden jerked her head sideways to look out the window.

Ong picked a paper magnet off his desk. He made his voice pleasant. "May I ask how you learned whether that genetic-modification program exists?"

Camden grinned. "You're not denying it exists. I give you full credit for that, Doctor."

Ong held onto his temper. "May I ask how you learned whether the program exists?"

Camden reached into an inner pocket of his suit. The silk crinkled and pulled; body and suit came from different social classes. Camden was, Ong remembered, a Yagaiist, a personal friend of Kenzo Yagai himself. Camden handed Ong hard copy: program specifications.

"Don't bother hunting down the security leak in your data banks, Doctor – you won't find it. But if it's any consolation, neither will anybody else. Now." He leaned suddenly forward. His tone changed. "I know that you've created twenty children so far who don't need to sleep at all. That so far nineteen are healthy, intelligent, and psychologically normal. In fact, better than normal – they're all unusually precocious. The oldest is already four years old and can read in two languages. I know you're thinking of offering this genetic modification on the open market in a few years. All I want is a chance to buy it for my daughter *now*. At whatever price you name."

Ong stood. "I can't possibly discuss this with you unilaterally, Mr. Camden. Neither the theft of our data – "

"Which wasn't a theft – your system developed a spontaneous bubble regurgitation into a public gate, have a hell of a time proving otherwise – "

" – *nor* the offer to purchase this particular genetic modification lies in my sole area of authority. Both have to be discussed with the Institute's board of directors."

"By all means, by all means. When can I talk to them, too?"

"You?"

Camden, still seated, looked at him. It occurred to Ong that there were few men who could look so confident eighteen inches below eye level. "Certainly. I'd like the chance to present my offer to whoever has the actual authority to accept it. That's only good business."

"This isn't solely a business transaction, Mr. Camden."

"It isn't solely pure scientific research, either," Camden retorted. "You're a for-profit corporation here. *With* certain tax breaks available only to firms meeting certain fair-practice laws."

For a minute Ong couldn't think what Camden meant. "Fair-practice laws . . ."

". . . are designed to protect minorities who are suppliers. I know, it hasn't ever been tested in the case of customers, except for redlining in Y-energy installations. But it could be tested, Dr. Ong. Minorities are entitled to the same product offerings as nonminorities. I know the Institute would not welcome a court case, Doctor. None of your twenty genetic beta-test families is either black or Jewish."

"A court . . . but you're not black or Jewish!"

"I'm a different minority. Polish-American. The name was Kaminisky." Camden finally stood. And smiled warmly. "Look, it is preposterous. You know that, and I know that, and we both know what a grand time journalists would have with it anyway. And you know that I don't want to sue you with a preposterous case, just to use the threat of premature and adverse publicity to get what I want. I don't want to make threats at all, believe me I don't. I just want this marvelous advancement you've come up with for my daughter." His face changed, to an expression Ong wouldn't have believed possible on those particular features: wistfulness. "Doctor – do you know how much more I could have accomplished if I hadn't had to *sleep* all my life?"

Elizabeth Camden said harshly, "You hardly sleep now."

Camden looked down at her as if he had forgotten she was there. "Well, no, my dear, not now. But when I was young . . . college, I might have been able to finish college and still support . . . well. None of that matters now. What matters, Doctor, is that you and I and your board come to an agreement."

"Mr. Camden, please leave my office now."

"You mean before you lose your temper at my presumptuousness?

You wouldn't be the first. I'll expect to have a meeting set up by the end of next week, whenever and wherever you say, of course. Just let my personal secretary, Diane Clavers, know the details. Anytime that's best for you."

Ong did not accompany them to the door. Pressure throbbed behind his temples. In the doorway Elizabeth Camden turned. "What happened to the twentieth one?"

"What?"

"The twentieth baby. My husband said nineteen of them are healthy and normal. What happened to the twentieth?"

The pressure grew stronger, hotter. Ong knew that he should not answer; that Camden probably already knew the answer even if his wife didn't; that he, Ong, was going to answer anyway; that he would regret the lack of self-control, bitterly, later.

"The twentieth baby is dead. His parents turned out to be unstable. They separated during the pregnancy, and his mother could not bear the twenty-four-hour crying of a baby who never sleeps."

Elizabeth Camden's eyes widened. "She killed it?"

"By mistake," Camden said shortly. "Shook the little thing too hard." He frowned at Ong. "Nurses, doctor. In shifts. You should have picked only parents wealthy enough to afford nurses in shifts."

"That's horrible!" Mrs. Camden burst out, and Ong could not tell if she meant the child's death, the lack of nurses, or the Institute's carelessness. Ong closed his eyes.

When they had gone, he took ten milligrams of cyclobenzaprine-III. For his back – it was solely for his back. The old injury hurting again. Afterward he stood for a long time at the window, still holding the paper magnet, feeling the pressure recede from his temples, feeling himself calm down. Below him Lake Michigan lapped peacefully at the shore; the police had driven away the homeless in another raid just last night, and they hadn't yet had time to return. Only their debris remained, thrown into the bushes of the lakeshore park: tattered blankets, newspapers, plastic bags like pathetic trampled standards. It was illegal to sleep in the park, illegal to enter it without a resident's permit, illegal to be homeless and without a residence. As Ong watched, uniformed park attendants began methodically spearing newspapers and shoving them into clean self-propelled receptacles.

Ong picked up the phone to call the president of Biotech Institute's board of directors.

Four men and three women sat around the polished mahogany table of the conference room. *Doctor, lawyer, Indian chief* thought Susan Melling, looking from Ong to Sullivan to Camden. She smiled. Ong caught the smile and looked frosty. Pompous ass. Judy Sullivan, the Institute lawyer, turned to speak in a low voice to Camden's lawyer, a thin, nervous man with the look of being owned. The owner, Roger Camden, the Indian chief himself, was the happiest-looking person in the room. The lethal little man – what did it take to become that rich, starting from nothing? She, Susan, would certainly never know – radiated excitement. He beamed, he glowed, so unlike the usual parents-to-be that Susan was intrigued. Usually the prospective daddies and mommies – specially the daddies – sat there looking as if they were at a corporate merger. Camden looked as if he were at a birthday party.

Which, of course, he was. Susan grinned at him and was pleased when he grinned back. Wolfish, but with a sort of delight that could only be called innocent – what would he be like in bed? Ong frowned majestically and rose to speak.

"Ladies and gentlemen, I think we're ready to start. Perhaps introductions are in order. Mr. Roger Camden, Mrs. Camden are, of course, our clients. Mr. John Jaworski, Mr. Camden's lawyer. Mr. Camden, this is Judith Sullivan, the Institute's head of legal; Samuel Krenshaw, representing Institute director Dr. Brad Marsteiner, who unfortunately couldn't be here today; and Dr. Susan Melling, who developed the genetic modification affecting sleep. A few legal points of interest to both parties – "

"Forget the contracts for a minute," Camden interrupted. "Let's talk about the sleep thing. I'd like to ask a few questions."

Susan said, "What would you like to know?" Camden's eyes were very blue in his blunt-featured face; he wasn't what she had expected. Mrs. Camden, who apparently lacked both a first name and a lawyer, since Jaworski had been introduced as her husband's but not hers, looked either sullen or scared; it was difficult to tell which.

Ong said sourly, "Then perhaps we should start with a short presentation by Dr. Melling."

Susan would have preferred a Q&A, to see what Camden would ask. But she had annoyed Ong enough for one session. Obediently she rose.

"Let me start with a brief description of sleep. Researchers have known for a long time that there are actually three kinds of sleep. One is 'slow-wave sleep,' characterized on an EEC by delta waves. One is 'rapid-eye-movement sleep' or REM sleep, which is much lighter sleep and contains most dreaming. Together, these two make up 'core sleep.' The third type of sleep is 'optional sleep,' so-called because people seem to get along without it with no ill effects, and some short sleepers don't do it at all, sleeping naturally only three or four hours a night."

"That's me," Camden said. "I trained myself into it. Couldn't everybody do that?"

Apparently they were going to have a Q&A after all. "No. The actual sleep mechanism has some flexibility, but not the same amount for every person. The raphe nuclei on the brain stem – "

Ong said, "I don't think we need that level of detail, Susan. Let's stick to basics."

Camden said, "The raphe nuclei regulate the balance among neurotransmitters and peptides that lead to a pressure to sleep, don't they?"

Susan couldn't help it; she grinned. Camden, the laser-sharp ruthless financier, sat trying to look solemn, a third-grader waiting to have his homework praised. Ong looked sour. Mrs. Camden looked away, out the window.

"Yes, that's correct, Mr. Camden. You've done your research."

Camden said, "This is my *daughter*," and Susan caught her breath. When was the last time she had heard that note of reverence in anyone's voice? But no one in the room seemed to notice.

"Well, then," Susan said, "you already know that the reason people sleep is because a pressure to sleep builds up in the brain. Over the last twenty years, research has determined that's the *only* reason. Neither slow-wave sleep nor REM sleep serves functions that can't be carried on while the body and brain are awake. A lot goes on during sleep, but it can go on awake just as well, if other hormonal adjustments are made.

"Sleep once served an important evolutionary function. Once Clem Pre-mammal was done filling his stomach and squirting his sperm around, sleep kept him immobile and away from predators. Sleep was an aid to survival. But now it's a leftover mechanism, like the appendix. It switches on every night, but the need is gone. So we turn off the switch at its source, in the genes."

Ong winced. He hated it when she oversimplified like that. Or maybe it was the lightheartedness he hated. If Marsteiner were making this presentation, there'd be no Clem Pre-mammal.

Camden said, "What about the need to dream?"

"Not necessary. A leftover bombardment of the cortex to keep it on semialert in case a predator attacked during sleep. Wakefulness does that better."

"Why not have wakefulness instead, then? From the start of the evolution?"

He was testing her. Susan gave him a full, lavish smile, enjoying his brass. "I told you. Safety from predators. But when a modern predator attacks – say, a cross-border data-atoll investor – it's safer to be awake."

Camden shot at her, "What about the high percentage of REM sleep in fetuses and babies?"

"Still an evolutionary hangover. Cerebrum develops perfectly well without it."

"What about neural repair during slow-wave sleep?"

"That does go on. But it can go on during wakefulness, if the DNA is programmed to do so. No loss of neural efficiency, as far as we know."

"What about the release of human growth enzyme in such large concentrations during slow-wave sleep?"

Susan looked at him admiringly. "Goes on without the sleep. Genetic adjustments tie it to other changes in the pineal gland."

"What about the – "

"The *side effects*?" Mrs. Camden said. Her mouth turned down. "What about the bloody side effects?"

Susan turned to Elizabeth Camden. She had forgotten she was there. The younger woman stared at Susan, mouth still turned down at the corners.

"I'm glad you asked that, Mrs. Camden. Because there *are* side effects." Susan paused; she was enjoying herself. "Compared to their age mates, the nonsleep children – who have *not* had IQ genetic manipulation – are more intelligent, better at problem-solving, and more joyous."

Camden took out a cigarette. The archaic, filthy habit surprised Susan. Then she saw that it was deliberate: Roger Camden drawing attention to an ostentatious display to draw attention away from what he was feeling. His cigarette lighter was gold, monogrammed, innocently gaudy.

"Let me explain," Susan said. "REM sleep bombards the cerebral cortex with random neural firings from the brainstem; dreaming occurs because the poor besieged cortex tries so hard to make sense of the activated images and memories. It spends a lot of energy doing that. Without that energy expenditure, nonsleep cerebrums save the wear and tear and do better at coordinating real-life input. Thus – greater intelligence and problem-solving.

"Also, doctors have known for sixty years that antidepressants, which lift the mood of depressed patients, also suppress REM sleep entirely. What they have proved in the last ten years is that the reverse is equally true: suppress REM sleep and people don't *get* depressed. The nonsleep kids are cheerful, outgoing . . . *joyous*. There's no other word for it."

"At what cost?" Mrs. Camden said. She held her neck rigid, but the corners of her jaw worked.

"No cost. No negative side effects at all."

"So far," Mrs. Camden shot back.

Susan shrugged. "So far."

"They're only four years old! At the most!"

Ong and Krenshaw were studying her closely. Susan saw the moment the Camden woman realized it; she sank back into her chair, drawing her fur coat around her, her face blank.

Camden did not look at his wife. He blew a cloud of cigarette smoke. "Everything has costs, Dr. Melling."

She liked the way he said her name. "Ordinarily, yes. Especially in genetic modification. But we honestly have not been able to find any here, despite looking." She smiled directly into Camden's eyes. "Is it too much to believe that just once the universe has given us something wholly good, wholly a step forward, wholly beneficial? Without hidden penalties?"

"Not the universe. The intelligence of people like you," Camden said, surprising Susan more than anything that had gone before. His eyes held hers. She felt her chest tighten.

"I think," Dr. Ong said dryly, "that the philosophy of the universe may be beyond our concerns here. Mr. Camden, if you have no further medical questions, perhaps we can return to the legal points Ms. Sullivan and Mr. Jaworski have raised. Thank you, Dr. Melling."

Susan nodded. She didn't look again at Camden. But she knew what he said, how he looked, that he was there.

The house was about what she had expected, a huge mock Tudor on Lake Michigan north of Chicago. The land heavily wooded between the gate and the house, open between the house and the surging water. Patches of snow dotted the dormant grass. Biotech had been working with the Camdens for four months, but this was the first time Susan had driven to their home.

As she walked toward the house, another car drove up behind her. No, a truck, continuing around the curved driveway to a service entry at the side of the house. One man rang the service bell; a second began to unload a plastic-wrapped playpen from the back of the truck. White, with pink and yellow bunnies. Susan briefly closed her eyes.

Camden opened the door himself. She could see the effort not to look worried. "You didn't have to drive out, Susan – I'd have come into the city."

"No, I didn't want you to do that, Roger. Mrs. Camden is here?"

"In the living room." Camden led her into a large room with a stone fireplace. English country-house furniture; prints of dogs or boats, all hung eighteen inches too high: Elizabeth Camden must have done the decorating. She did not rise from her wing chair as Susan entered.

"Let me be concise and fast," Susan said. "I don't want to make this any more drawn out for you than I have to. We have all the amniocentesis, ultrasound, and Langston test results. The fetus is fine, developing normally for two weeks, no problems with the implant on the uterus wall. But a complication has developed."

"What?" Camden said. He took out a cigarette, looked at his wife, put it back unlit.

Susan said quietly, "Mrs. Camden, by sheer chance both your ovaries released eggs last month. We removed one for the gene surgery. By more sheer chance the second fertilized and implanted. You're carrying two fetuses."

Elizabeth Camden grew still. "Twins?"

"No," Susan said. Then she realized what she had said. "I mean, yes. They're twins, but nonidentical. Only one has been genetically altered. The other will be no more similar to her than any two siblings. It's a so-called 'normal' baby. And I know you didn't want a so-called normal baby."

Camden said, "No. I didn't."

Elizabeth Camden said, "I did."

Camden shot her a fierce look that Susan couldn't read. He took out the cigarette again, lit it. His face was in profile to Susan, thinking intently; she doubted he knew the cigarette was there or that he was lighting it. "Is the baby being affected by the other one's being there?"

"No," Susan said. "No, of course not. They're just . . . coexisting."

"Can you abort it?"

"Not without risk of aborting both of them. Removing the unaltered fetus might cause changes in the uterus lining that could lead to a spontaneous miscarriage of the other." She drew a deep breath. "There's that option, of course. We can start the whole process over again. But, as I told you at the time, you were very lucky to have the in vitro fertilization take on only the second try. Some couples take eight or ten tries. If we started all over, the process could be a lengthy one."

Camden said, "Is the presence of this second fetus harming my daughter? Taking away nutrients or anything? Or will it change anything for her later on in the pregnancy?"

"No. Except that there is a chance of premature birth. Two fetuses take up a lot more room in the womb, and if it gets too crowded birth can be premature. But the – "

"How premature? Enough to threaten survival?"

"Most probably not."

Camden went on smoking. A man appeared at the door. "Sir, London calling. James Kendall for Mr. Yagai."

"I'll take it." Camden rose. Susan watched him study his wife's face. When he spoke, it was to her. "All right, Elizabeth. All right." He left the room.

For a long moment the two women sat in silence. Susan was aware of disappointment; this was not the Camden she had expected to see. She became aware of Elizabeth Camden watching her with amusement.

"Oh, yes, Doctor. He's like that."

Susan said nothing.

"Completely overbearing. But not this time." She laughed softly, with excitement. "Two. Do you . . . do you know what sex the other one is?"

"Both fetuses are female."

"I wanted a girl, you know. And now I'll have one."

"Then you'll go ahead with the pregnancy."

"Oh, yes. Thank you for coming, Doctor."

She was dismissed. No one saw her out. But as she was getting into her car, Camden rushed out of the house, coatless. "Susan! I wanted to thank you. For coming all the way out here to tell us yourself."

"You already thanked me."

"Yes. Well. You're sure the second fetus is no threat to my daughter?"

Susan said deliberately, "Nor is the genetically altered fetus a threat to the naturally conceived one."

He smiled. His voice was low and wistful. "And you think that should matter to me just as much. But it doesn't. And why should I fake what I feel? Especially to you?"

Susan opened her car door. She wasn't ready for this, or she had changed her mind, or something. But then Camden leaned over to close the door, and his manner held no trace of flirtatiousness, no smarmy ingratiation. "I better order a second playpen."

"Yes."

"And a second car seat."

"Yes."

"But not a second night-shift nurse."

"That's up to you.

"And you." Abruptly he leaned over and kissed her, a kiss so polite and respectful that Susan was shocked. Neither lust nor conquest would have shocked her; this did. Camden didn't give her a chance to react; he closed the car door and turned back toward the house. Susan drove toward the gate, her hands shaky on the wheel until amusement replaced shock: it *had* been a deliberately distant, respectful kiss, an engineered enigma. And nothing else could have guaranteed so well that there would have to be another.

She wondered what the Camdens would name their daughters.

Dr. Ong strode the hospital corridor, which had been dimmed to half-light. From the nurse's station in Maternity a nurse stepped forward as if to stop him – it was the middle of the night, long past visiting hours – got a good look at his face, and faded back into her station. Around a corner was the viewing glass to the nursery. To Ong's annoyance, Susan Melling stood pressed against the glass. To his further annoyance, she was crying.

Ong realized that he had never liked the woman. Maybe not any women. Even those with superior minds could not seem to refrain from being made damn fools by their emotions.

"Look," Susan said, laughing a little, swiping at her face. "Doctor – *look*."

Behind the glass Roger Camden, gowned and masked, was holding up a baby in a white undershirt and pink blanket. Camden's blue eyes – theatrically blue; a man really should not have such garish eyes – glowed. The baby had a head covered with blond fuzz, wide eyes, pink skin. Camden's eyes above the mask said that no other child had ever had these attributes.

Ong said, "An uncomplicated birth?"

"Yes," Susan Melling sobbed. "Perfectly straightforward. Elizabeth is fine. She's asleep. Isn't she beautiful? He has the most adventurous spirit I've ever known." She wiped her nose on her sleeve; Ong realized that she was drunk. "Did I ever tell you that I was engaged once? Fifteen years ago, in med school? I broke it off because he grew to seem so ordinary, so boring. Oh, God, I shouldn't be telling you all this I'm sorry I'm sorry."

Ong moved away from her. Behind the glass Roger Camden laid the baby in a small wheeled crib. The nameplate said BABY GIRL CAMDEN #1 5.9 POUNDS. A night nurse watched indulgently.

Ong did not wait to see Camden emerge from the nursery or to hear Susan Melling say to him whatever she was going to say. Ong went to have the OB paged. Melling's report was not, under the circumstances, to be trusted. A perfect, unprecedented chance to record every detail of gene alteration with a nonaltered control, and Melling was more interested in her own sloppy emotions. Ong would obviously have to do the report himself, after talking to the OB. He was hungry for every detail. And not just about the pink-cheeked baby in Camden's arms. He wanted to know everything about the birth of the child in the other glass-sided crib: BABY GIRL CAMDEN #2 5.1 POUNDS. The dark-haired baby with the mottled red features, lying scrunched down in her pink blanket, asleep.

II

Leisha's earliest memory was of flowing lines that were not there. She knew they were not there because when she reached out her fist to touch them, her fist was empty. Later she realized that the flowing lines were light: sunshine slanting in bars between curtains in her room, between the wooden blinds in the dining room, between the crisscross lattices in the conservatory. The day she realized the golden flow was light she laughed out loud with the sheer joy of discovery, and Daddy turned from putting flowers in pots and smiled at her.

The whole house was full of light. Light bounded off the lake, streamed across the high white ceilings, puddled on the shining wooden floors. She and Alice moved continually through light, and sometimes Leisha would stop and tip back her head and let it flow over her face. She could feel it, like water.

The best light, of course, was in the conservatory. That's where Daddy liked to be when he was home from making money. Daddy potted plants and watered trees, humming, and Leisha and Alice ran between the wooden tables of flowers with their wonderful earthy smells, running from the dark side of the conservatory where the big purple flowers grew to the sunshine side with sprays of yellow flowers, running back and forth, in and out of the light. "Growth," Daddy said to her. "Flowers all fulfilling their promise. Alice, be careful! You almost knocked over that orchid." Alice, obedient, would stop running for a while. Daddy never told Leisha to stop running.

After a while the light would go away. Alice and Leisha would have their baths, and then Alice would get quiet, or cranky. She wouldn't play nice with Leisha, even when Leisha let her choose the game or even have all the best dolls. Then Nanny would take Alice to "bed," and Leisha would talk with Daddy some more until Daddy said he had to work in his study with the papers that made money. Leisha always felt a moment of regret that he had to go do that, but the moment never lasted very long, because Mamselle would arrive and start Leisha's lessons, which she liked. Learning things was so interesting! She could already sing twenty songs and write all the letters in the alphabet and count to fifty. And by the time lessons were done, the light had come back, and it was time for breakfast.

Breakfast was the only time Leisha didn't like. Daddy had gone to the office, and Leisha and Alice had breakfast with Mommy in the big dining room. Mommy sat in a red robe, which Leisha liked, and she didn't smell funny or talk funny the way she would later in the day, but, still, breakfast wasn't fun. Mommy always started with the Question.

"Alice, sweetheart, how did you sleep?"

"Fine, Mommy."

"Did you have any nice dreams?"

For a long time Alice said no. Then one day she said, "I dreamed about a horse. I was riding him." Mommy clapped her hands and kissed Alice and gave her an extra sticky bun. After that Alice always had a dream to tell Mommy.

Once Leisha said, "I had a dream, too. I dreamed light was coming in the window and it wrapped all around me like a blanket and then it kissed me on my eyes."

Mommy put down her coffee cup so hard that coffee sloshed out of it. "Don't lie to me, Leisha. You did not have a dream."

"Yes, I did," Leisha said.

"Only children who sleep can have dreams. Don't lie to me. You did not have a dream."

"Yes, I did! I did!" Leisha shouted. She could see it, almost: the light streaming in the window and wrapping around her like a golden blanket.

"I will not tolerate a child who is a liar. Do you hear me, Leisha – I won't tolerate it!"

"You're a liar!" Leisha shouted, knowing the words weren't true, hating herself because they weren't true but hating Mommy more, and that was wrong, too, and there sat Alice stiff and frozen with her eyes wide. Alice was scared and it was Leisha's fault.

Mommy called sharply, "Nanny! Nanny! Take Leisha to her room at once. She can't sit with civilized people if she can't refrain from telling lies."

Leisha started to cry. Nanny carried her out of the room. Leisha hadn't even had her breakfast. But she didn't care about that; all she could see while she cried was Alice's eyes, scared like that, reflecting broken bits of light.

But Leisha didn't cry long. Nanny read her a story and then played Data Jump with her, and then Alice came up and Nanny drove them both into Chicago to the zoo, where there were wonderful animals to see, animals Leisha could not have dreamed – nor Alice *either*. And by the time they came back Mommy had gone to her room, and Leisha knew that she would stay there with the glasses of funny-smelling stuff the rest of the day, and Leisha would not have to see her.

But that night she went to her mother's room.

"I have to go to the bathroom," she told Mamselle. Mamselle said, "Do you need any help?" maybe because Alice still needed help in the bathroom. But Leisha didn't, and she thanked Mamselle. Then she sat on the toilet for a minute even though nothing came, so that what she had told Mamselle wouldn't be a lie.

Leisha tiptoed down the hall. She went first into Alice's room. A little light in a wall socket burned near the "crib." There was no crib in Leisha's room. Leisha looked at her sister through the bars. Alice lay on her side with her eyes closed. The lids of the eyes fluttered quickly, like curtains blowing in the wind. Alice's chin and neck looked loose.

Leisha closed the door very carefully and went to her parents' room.

They didn't "sleep" in a crib but in a huge enormous "bed," with enough room between them for more people. Mommy's eyelids weren't fluttering; she lay on her back making a hrrr-hrrr sound through her nose. The funny smell was strong on her. Leisha backed away and tiptoed over to Daddy. He looked like Alice, except that his neck and chin looked even looser, folds of skin collapsed like the tent that had fallen down in the backyard. It scared Leisha to see him like that. Then Daddy's eyes flew open so suddenly that Leisha screamed.

Daddy rolled out of bed and picked her up, looking quickly at Mommy. But she didn't move. Daddy was wearing only his underpants. He carried Leisha out into the hall, where Mamselle came rushing up saying, "Oh, sir. I'm sorry, she just said she was going to the bathroom –"

"It's all right," Daddy said. "I'll take her with me."

"No!" Leisha screamed, because Daddy was only in his underpants and his neck had looked all funny and the room smelled bad because of Mommy. But Daddy carried her into the conservatory, set her down on a bench, wrapped himself in a piece of green plastic that was supposed to cover up plants, and sat down next to her.

"Now, what happened, Leisha? What were you doing?"

Leisha didn't answer.

"You were looking at people sleeping, weren't you?" Daddy said, and because his voice was softer Leisha mumbled, "Yes." She immediately felt better; it felt good not to lie.

"You were looking at people sleeping because you don't sleep and you were curious, weren't you? Like Curious George in your book?"

"Yes," Leisha said. "I thought you said you made money in your study all night!"

Daddy smiled. "Not all night. Some of it. But then I sleep, although not very much." He took Leisha on his lap. "I don't need much sleep, so I get a lot more done at night than most people. Different people need different amounts of sleep. And a few, a very few, are like you. You don't need any."

"Why not?"

"Because you're special. Better than other people. Before you were born, I had some doctors help make you that way."

"Why?"

"So you could do anything you want to and make manifest your own individuality."

Leisha twisted in his arms to stare at him; the words meant nothing. Daddy reached over and touched a single flower growing on a tall potted tree. The flower had thick white petals like the cream he put in coffee, and the center was a light pink.

"See, Leisha – this tree made this flower. Because it *can*. Only this tree can make this kind of wonderful flower. That plant hanging up there can't, and those can't either. Only this tree. Therefore the most important thing in the world for this tree to do is grow this flower. The flower is the tree's individuality – that means just *it*, and nothing else-made manifest. Nothing else matters."

"I don't understand, Daddy."

"You will. Someday."

"But I want to understand *now*," Leisha said, and Daddy laughed with pure delight and hugged her. The hug felt good, but Leisha still wanted to understand.

"When you make money, is that your indiv . . . that thing?"

"Yes," Daddy said happily.

"Then nobody else can make money? Like only that tree can make that flower?"

"Nobody else can make it just the ways I do."

"What do you do with the money?"

"I buy things for you. This house, your dresses, Mamselle to teach you, the car to ride in."

"What does the tree do with the flower?"

"Glories in it," Daddy said, which made no sense. "Excellence is what counts, Leisha. Excellence supported by individual effort. And that's *all* that counts."

"I'm cold, Daddy."

"Then I better bring you back to Mamselle."

Leisha didn't move. She touched the flower with one finger. "I want to sleep, Daddy."

"No, you don't, sweetheart. Sleep is just lost time, wasted life. It's a little death."

"Alice sleeps."

"Alice isn't like you."

"Alice isn't special?"

"No. You are."

"Why didn't you make Alice special, too?"

"Alice made herself. I didn't have a chance to make her special."

The whole thing was too hard. Leisha stopped stroking the flower and slipped off Daddy's lap. He smiled at her. "My little questioner. When you grow up, you'll find your own excellence, and it will be a new order, a specialness the world hasn't ever seen before. You might even be like Kenzo Yagai. He made the Yagai generator that powers the world."

"Daddy, you look funny wrapped in the flower plastic." Leisha laughed. Daddy did, too. But then she said, "When I grow up, I'll make my specialness find a way to make Alice special, too," and Daddy stopped laughing.

He took her back to Mamselle, who taught her to write her name, which was so exciting she forgot about the puzzling talk with Daddy. There were six letters, all different, and together they were *her name*. Leisha wrote it over and over, laughing, and Mamselle laughed, too. But later, in the morning, Leisha thought again about the talk with Daddy. She thought of it often, turning the unfamiliar words over in and over in her mind like small hard stones, but the part she thought about most wasn't a word. It was the frown on Daddy's face when she told him she would use her specialness to make Alice special, too.

Every week Dr. Melling came to see Leisha and Alice, sometimes alone, sometimes with other people. Leisha and Alice both liked Dr. Melling, who laughed a lot and whose eyes were bright and warm. Often Daddy was there, too. Dr. Melling played games with them, first with Alice and Leisha separately and then together. She took their pictures and weighed them. She made them lie down on a table and stuck little metal things to their temples, which sounded scary but wasn't because there were so many machines to watch, all making interesting noises, while you were lying there. Dr. Melling was as good at answering questions as Daddy. Once Leisha said, "Is Dr. Melling a special person? Like Kenzo Yagai?" And Daddy laughed and glanced at Dr. Melling and said, "Oh, yes, indeed."

When Leisha was five, she and Alice started school. Daddy's driver took them every day into Chicago. They were in different rooms, which disappointed Leisha. The kids in Leisha's room were all older. But from the first day she adored school, with its fascinating science equipment and electronic drawers full of math puzzlers and other children to find countries on the map with. In half a year she had been moved to yet a different room, where the kids were still older, but they were nonetheless nice to her. Leisha started to learn Japanese. She loved drawing the beautiful characters on thick white paper. "The Sauley School was a good choice," Daddy said.

But Alice didn't like the Sauley School. She wanted to go to school on the same yellow bus as cook's daughter. She cried and threw her paints on the floor at the Sauley School. Then Mommy came out of her room – Leisha hadn't seen her for a few weeks, although she knew Alice had – and threw some candlesticks from the mantelpiece on the floor. The candlesticks, which were china, broke. Leisha ran to pick up the pieces while Mommy and Daddy screamed at each other in the hall by the big staircase.

"She's my daughter, too. And I say she can go!"

"You don't have the right to say anything about it! A weepy drunk, the most rotten role model possible for both of them . . . and I thought I was getting a fine English aristocrat."

"You got what you paid for. Nothing! Not that you ever needed anything from me or anybody else."

"Stop it!" Leisha cried. "Stop it!" and there was silence in the hall. Leisha cut her fingers on the china; blood streamed onto the rug.

Daddy rushed in and picked her up. "Stop it," Leisha sobbed, and didn't understand when Daddy said quietly, "*You* stop it, Leisha. Nothing *they* do should touch you at all. You have to be at least that strong."

Leisha buried her head in Daddy's shoulder. Alice transferred to Carl Sandburg Elementary School, riding there on the yellow school bus with cook's daughter.

A few weeks later Daddy told them that Mommy was going away for a few weeks to a hospital, to stop drinking so much. When Mommy came out, he said, she was going to live somewhere else for a while. She and Daddy were not happy. Leisha and Alice would stay with Daddy, and they would visit Mommy sometimes. He told them this very carefully, finding the right words for truth. Truth was very important, Leisha already knew. Truth was being true to your self, your specialness. Your individuality. An individual respected facts, and so always told the truth.

Mommy, Daddy did not say but Leisha knew, did not respect facts.

"I don't want Mommy to go away," Alice said. She started to cry. Leisha thought Daddy would pick Alice up, but he didn't. He just stood there looking at them both.

Leisha put her arms around Alice. "It's all right, Alice. It's all right! We'll make it all right! I'll play with you all the time we're not in school so you don't miss Mommy."

Alice clung to Leisha. Leisha turned her head so she didn't have to see Daddy's face.

III

Kenzo Yagai was coming to the United States to lecture. The title of his talk, which he would give in New York, Los Angeles, Chicago, and Washington, with a repeat in Washington as a special address to Congress, was "The Further Political Implications of Inexpensive Power." Leisha Camden, eleven years old, was going to have a private introduction after the Chicago talk, arranged by her father.

She had studied the theory of cold fusion at school, and her Global Studies teacher had traced the changes in the world resulting from Yagai's patented, low-cost applications of what had, until him, been unworkable theory. The rising prosperity of the Third World, the last death throes of the old communist systems, the decline of the oil states, the renewed economic power of the United States. Her study group had written a news script, filmed with the school's professional-quality equipment, about how a 1985 American family lived with expensive energy costs and a belief in tax-supported help, while a 2019 family lived with cheap energy and a belief in the contract as the basis of civilization. Parts of her own research puzzled Leisha.

"Japan thinks Kenzo Yagai was a traitor to his own country," she said to Daddy at supper.

"No," Camden said. "*Some* Japanese think that. Watch out for generalizations, Leisha. Yagai patented and marketed Y-energy first in the United States because here there were at least the dying embers of individual enterprise. Because of his invention, our entire country has slowly swung back toward an individual meritocracy, and Japan has slowly been forced to follow."

"Your father held that belief all along," Susan said. "Eat your peas, Leisha." Leisha ate her peas. Susan and Daddy had only been married less than a year; it still felt a little strange to have her there. But nice. Daddy said Susan was a valuable addition to their household: intelligent, motivated, and cheerful. Like Leisha herself.

"Remember, Leisha," Camden said. "A man's worth to society and to himself doesn't rest on what he thinks other people should do or be or feel, but on himself. On what he can actually do, and do well. People trade what they do well, and everyone benefits. The basic tool of civilization is the contract. Contracts are voluntary and mutually beneficial. As opposed to coercion which is wrong."

"The strong have no right to take anything from the weak by force," Susan said. "Alice, eat your peas, too, honey."

"Nor the weak to take anything by force from the strong," Camden said. "That's the basis of what you'll hear Kenzo Yagai discuss tonight, Leisha."

Alice said, "I don't like peas."

Camden said, "Your body does. They're good for you."

Alice smiled. Leisha felt her heart lift; Alice didn't smile much at dinner anymore. "My body doesn't have a contract with the peas."

Camden said, a little impatiently, "Yes, it does. Your body benefits from them. Now eat."

Alice's smile vanished. Leisha looked down at her plate. Suddenly she saw a way out. "No, Daddy, look – Alice's body benefits, but the peas don't. It's not a mutually beneficial consideration – so there's no contract. Alice is right!"

Camden let out a shout of laughter. To Susan he said, "Eleven years old . . . *eleven.*" Even Alice smiled, and Leisha waved her spoon triumphantly, light glinting off the bowl and dancing silver on the opposite wall.

But, even so, Alice did not want to go hear Kenzo Yagai. She was going to sleep over at her friend Julie's house; they were going to curl their hair together. More surprisingly, Susan wasn't coming, either. She and Daddy looked at each other a little funny at the front door, Leisha thought, but Leisha was too excited to think about this. She was going to hear *Kenzo Yagai*.

Yagai was a small man, dark and slim. Leisha liked his accent. She liked, too, something about him that took her awhile to name. "Daddy," she whispered in the half-darkness of the auditorium, "he's a joyful man."

Daddy hugged her in the darkness.

Yagai spoke about spirituality and economics. "A man's spirituality – which is only his dignity as a man – rests on his own efforts. Dignity and worth are not automatically conferred by aristocratic birth – we have only to look at history to see that. Dignity and worth are not automatically conferred by inherited wealth – a great heir may be a thief, a wastrel, cruel, an exploiter, a person who leaves the world much poorer than he found it. Nor are dignity and worth automatically conferred by existence itself – a mass murderer exists, but is of negative worth to his society and possesses no dignity in his lust to kill.

"No, the only dignity, the only spirituality, rests on what a man can achieve with his own efforts. To rob a man of the chance to achieve, and to trade what he achieves with others, is to rob him of his spiritual dignity as a man. This is why communism has failed in our time. *All* coercion – all force to take from a man his own efforts to achieve – causes spiritual damage and weakens a society. Conscription, theft, fraud, violence, welfare, lack of legislative representation – *all* rob a man of his chance to choose, to achieve on his own, to trade the results of his achievement with others. Coercion is a cheat. It produces nothing new. Only freedom – the freedom to achieve, the freedom to trade freely the results of achievement – creates the environment proper to the dignity and spirituality of man."

Leisha applauded so hard her hands hurt. Going backstage with Daddy, she thought she could hardly breathe. Kenzo Yagai!

But backstage was more crowded than she had expected. There were cameras everywhere. Daddy said, "Mr. Yagai, may I present my daughter Leisha," and the cameras moved in close and fast – on *her*. A Japanese man whispered something in Kenzo Yagai's ear, and he looked more closely at Leisha. "Ah, yes."

"Look over here, Leisha," someone called, and she did. A robot camera zoomed so close to her face that Leisha stepped back, startled. Daddy spoke very sharply to someone, then to someone else. The cameras didn't move. A woman suddenly knelt in front of Leisha and thrust a microphone at her. "What does it feel like to never sleep, Leisha?"

"What?"

Someone laughed. The laugh was not kind. "Breeding geniuses . . ."

Leisha felt a hand on her shoulder. Kenzo Yagai gripped her very firmly, pulled her away from the cameras. Immediately, as if by magic, a line of Japanese men formed behind Yagai, parting only to let Daddy through. Behind the line, the three of them moved into a dressing room, and Kenzo Yagai shut the door.

"You must not let them bother you, Leisha," he said in his wonderful accent. "Not ever. There is an old Oriental proverb: 'The dogs bark, but the caravan moves on.' You must never let your individual caravan be slowed by the barking of rude or envious dogs."

"I won't," Leisha breathed, not sure yet what the words really meant, knowing there was time later to sort them out, to talk about them with Daddy. For now she was dazzled by Kenzo Yagai, the actual man himself, who was changing the world without force, without guns, with trading his special individual efforts. "We study your philosophy at my school, Mr. Yagai."

Kenzo Yagai looked at Daddy. Daddy said, "A private school. But Leisha's sister also studies it, although cursorily, in the public system. Slowly, Kenzo, but it comes. It comes." Leisha noticed that he did not say why Alice was not here tonight with them.

Back home, Leisha sat in her room for hours, thinking over everything that had happened. When Alice came home from Julie's the next morning, Leisha rushed toward her. But Alice seemed angry about something.

"Alice – what is it?"

"Don't you think I have enough to put up with at school already?" Alice shouted. "Everybody knows, but at least when you stayed quiet it didn't matter too much. They'd stopped teasing me. Why did you have to do it?"

"Do what?" Leisha said, bewildered.

Alice threw something at her: a hard-copy morning paper, on newsprint flimsier than the Camden system used. The paper dropped open at Leisha's feet. She stared at her own picture, three columns wide, with Kenzo Yagai. The headline said, YAGAI AND THE FUTURE:

ROOM FOR THE REST OF US? Y-ENERGY INVENTOR CONFERS WITH "SLEEP-FREE" DAUGHTER OF MEGA-FINANCIER ROGER CAMDEN.

Alice kicked the paper. "It was on TV last night, too – on TV. I work hard not to look stuck-up or creepy, and you go and do this! Now Julie probably won't even invite me to her slumber party next week." She rushed up the broad curving stairs toward her room.

Leisha looked down at the paper. She heard Kenzo Yagai's voice in her head: "The dogs bark, but the caravan moves on." She looked at the empty stairs. Aloud she said, "Alice – your hair looks really pretty curled like that."

IV

"I want to meet the rest of them," Leisha said. "Why have you kept them from me this long?"

"I haven't kept them from you at all," Camden said. "Not offering is not the same as denial. Why shouldn't you be the one to do the asking? You're the one who now wants it."

Leisha looked at him. She was fifteen, in her last year at the Sauley School. "Why didn't you offer?"

"Why should I?"

"I don't know," Leisha said. "But you gave me everything else."

"Including the freedom to ask for what you want."

Leisha looked for the contradiction and found it. "Most things that you provided for my education I didn't ask for, because I didn't know enough to ask and you, as the adult, did. But you've never offered the opportunity for me to meet any of the other sleepless mutants – "

"Don't use that word," Camden said sharply.

" – so either you must think it was not essential to my education or else you had another motive for not wanting me to meet them."

"Wrong," Camden said. "There's a third possibility. That I think meeting them is essential to your education, that I do not want you to, but this issue provided a chance to further the education of your self-initiative by waiting for *you* to ask."

"All right," Leisha said, a little defiantly; there seemed to be a lot of defiance between them lately, for no good reason. She squared her shoulders. Her new breasts thrust forward. "I'm asking. How many of the Sleepless are there, who are they, and where are they?"

Camden said, "If you're using that term – 'the Sleepless' – you've already done some reading on your own. So you probably know that there are 1,082 of you so far in the United States, a few more in foreign countries, most of them in major metropolitan areas. Seventy-nine are in Chicago, most of them still small children. Only nineteen anywhere are older than you."

Leisha didn't deny reading any of this. Camden leaned forward in his study chair to peer at her. Leisha wondered if he needed glasses. His hair was completely gray now, sparse and stiff, like lonely broom-straws. The *Wall Street Journal* listed him among the hundred richest men in America; *Women's Wear Daily* pointed out that he was the only billionaire in the country who did not move in the society of inter-national parties, charity balls, and personal jets. Camden's jet ferried him to business meetings around the world, to the chairmanship of the Yagai Economics Institute, and to very little else. Over the years he had grown richer, more reclusive, and more cerebral. Leisha felt a rush of her old affection.

She threw herself sideways into a leather chair, her long slim legs dangling over the arm. Absently she scratched a mosquito bite on her thigh. "Well, then, I'd like to meet Richard Keller." He lived in Chicago and was the beta-test Sleepless closest to her own age. He was seventeen.

"Why ask me? Why not just go?"

Leisha thought there was a note of impatience in his voice. He liked her to explore things first, then report on them to him later. Both parts were important.

Leisha laughed. "You know what, Daddy? You're predictable."

Camden laughed, too. In the middle of the laugh Susan came in.

"He certainly is not. Roger, what about that meeting in Buenos Aires Thursday? Is it on or off?" When he didn't answer, her voice grew shriller. "Roger? I'm talking to you!"

Leisha averted her eyes. Two years ago Susan had finally left genetic research to run Camden's house and schedule; before that she had tried hard to do both. Since she had left Biotech, it seemed to Leisha, Susan had changed. Her voice was tighter. She was more insistent that cook and the gardener follow her directions exactly, without deviation. Her blond braids had become stiff sculptured waves of platinum.

"It's on," Roger said.

"Well, thanks for at least answering. Am I going?"

"If you like."

"I like."

Susan left the room. Leisha rose and stretched. Her long legs rose on tiptoe. It felt good to reach, to stretch, to feel sunlight from the wide windows wash over her face. She smiled at her father and found him watching her with an unexpected expression.

"Leisha – "

"What?"

"See Keller. But be careful."

"Of what?"

But Camden wouldn't answer.

The voice on the phone had been noncommittal. "Leisha Camden? Yes, I know who you are. Three o'clock on Thursday?" The house was modest, a thirty-year-old Colonial on a quiet suburban street where small children on bicycles could be watched from the front window. Few roofs had more than one Y-energy cell. The trees, huge old sugar maples, were beautiful.

"Come in," Richard Keller said.

He was no taller than she, stocky, with a bad case of acne. Probably no genetic alterations except sleep, Leisha guessed. He had thick dark hair, a low forehead, and bushy black brows. Before he closed the door Leisha saw him stare at her car and driver, parked in the driveway next to a rusty ten-speed bike.

"I can't drive yet," she said. "I'm still fifteen."

"It's easy to learn," Keller said. "So, you want to tell me why you're here?"

Leisha liked his directness. "To meet some other Sleepless."

"You mean you never have? Not any of us?"

"You mean the rest of you know each other?" She hadn't expected that.

"Come to my room, Leisha."

She followed him to the back of the house. No one else seemed to be home. His room was large and airy, filled with computers and filing cabinets. A rowing machine sat in one corner. It looked like a shabbier version of the room of any bright classmate at the Sauley School, except there was more space without a bed. She walked over to the computer screen.

"Hey – you working on Boesc equations?"

"On an application of them."

"To what?"

"Fish migration patterns."

Leisha smiled. "Yeah – that would work. I never thought of that."

Keller seemed not to know what to do with her smile. He looked at the wall, then at her chin. "You interested in Gaea patterns? In the environment?"

"Well, no," Leisha confessed. "Not particularly. I'm going to study politics at Harvard. Prelaw. But of course we had Gaea patterns at school."

Keller's gaze finally came unstuck from her face. He ran a hand through his dark hair. "Sit down, if you want."

Leisha sat, looking appreciatively at the wall posters, shifting green on blue, like ocean currents. "I like those. Did you program them yourself?"

"You're not at all what I pictured," Keller said.

"How did you picture me?"

He didn't hesitate. "Stuck-up. Superior. Shallow, despite your IQ."

She was more hurt than she had expected to be.

Keller blurted, "You're the only one of the Sleepless who's really rich. But you already know that."

"No, I don't. I've never checked."

He took the chair beside her, stretching his stocky legs straight in front of him, in a slouch that had nothing to do with relaxation. "It makes sense, really. Rich people don't have their children genetically modified to be superior – they think any offspring of theirs is already superior. By their values. And poor people can't afford it. We Sleepless are upper-middle class, no more. Children of professors, scientists, people who value brains and time."

"My father values brains and time," Leisha said. "He's the biggest supporter of Kenzo Yagai."

"Oh, Leisha, do you think I don't already know that? Are you flashing me or what?"

Leisha said with great deliberateness, "I'm *talking* to you." But the next minute she could feel the hurt break through on her face.

"I'm sorry," Keller muttered. He shot off his chair and paced to the computer, back. "I *am* sorry. But I don't . . . I don't understand what you're doing here."

"I'm lonely," Leisha said, astonished at herself. She looked up at him. "It's true. I'm lonely. I am. I have friends and Daddy and Alice – but no one really knows, really understands – what? I don't know what I'm saying."

Keller smiled. The smile changed his whole face, opened up its dark planes to the light. "I do. Oh, do I. What do you do when they say, 'I had such a dream last night!'?"

"Yes!" Leisha said. "But that's even really minor – it's when *I* say,

'I'll look that up for you tonight,' and they get that funny look on their face that means 'She'll do it while I'm asleep.'"

"But that's even really minor," Keller said. "It's when you're playing basketball in the gym after supper and then you go to the diner for food and then you say, 'Let's have a walk by the lake,' and they say, 'I'm really tired. I'm going home to bed now.'"

"But that's really minor," Leisha said, jumping up. "It's when you really are absorbed by the movie and then you get the point and it's so goddamn beautiful you leap up and say, 'Yes! Yes!' and Susan says, 'Leisha, really – you'd think nobody but you ever enjoyed anything before.'"

"Who's Susan?" Keller said.

The mood was broken. But not really; Leisha could say "my step-mother" without much discomfort over what Susan had promised to be and what she had become. Keller stood inches from her, smiling that joyous smile, understanding, and suddenly relief washed over Leisha so strong that she walked straight into him and put her arms around his neck, tightening them only when she felt his startled jerk. She started to sob – she, Leisha, who never cried.

"Hey," Richard said. "Hey."

"Brilliant," Leisha said, laughing. "Brilliant remark."

She could feel his embarrassed smile. "Wanta see my fish migration curves instead?"

"No," Leisha sobbed, and he went on holding her, patting her back awkwardly, telling her without words that she was home.

Camden waited up for her, although it was past midnight. He had been smoking heavily. Through the blue air he said quietly,

"Did you have a good time, Leisha?"

"Yes."

"I'm glad," he said, and put out his last cigarette and climbed the stairs – slowly, stiffly; he was nearly seventy now – to bed.

They went everywhere together for nearly a year: swimming, dancing, to the museums, the theater, the library. Richard introduced her to the others, a group of twelve kids between fourteen and nineteen, all of them intelligent and eager. All Sleepless.

Leisha learned.

Tony's parents, like her own, had divorced. But Tony, fourteen, lived with his mother, who had not particularly wanted a Sleepless child, while his father, who had, acquired a red hovercar and a young girlfriend who designed ergonomic chairs in Paris. Tony was not allowed to tell anyone – relatives, schoolmates – that he was Sleepless. "They'll think you're a freak," his mother said, eyes averted from her son's face. The one time Tony disobeyed her and told a friend that he never slept, his mother beat him. Then she moved the family to a new neighborhood. He was nine years old.

Jeanine, almost as long-legged and slim as Leisha, was training for the Olympics in ice skating. She practiced twelve hours a day, hours no Sleeper still in high school could ever have. So far the newspapers had not picked up the story. Jeanine was afraid that if they did they would somehow not let her compete.

Jack, like Leisha, would start college in September. Unlike Leisha, he had already started his career. The practice of law had to wait for law school; the practice of investment required only money. Jack didn't have much, but his precise financial analyses parlayed $600 saved from summer jobs to $3,000 through stock-market investing, then to $10,000, and then he had enough to qualify for information-fund speculation. Jack was fifteen, not old enough to make legal investments; the transactions were all in the name of Kevin Baker, the oldest of the Sleepless, who lived in Austin. Jack told Leisha, "When I hit eighty-four percent profit over two consecutive quarters, the data analysts logged onto me. They were just sniffing. Well, that's their job, even when the overall amounts are actually small. It's the patterns they care about. If they take the trouble to cross-reference data banks and come up with the fact that Kevin is a Sleepless, will they try to stop us from investing somehow?"

"That's paranoid," Leisha said.

"No, it's not," Jeanine said. "Leisha, you don't *know*."

"You mean because I've been protected by my father's money and caring," Leisha said. No one grimaced; all of them confronted ideas openly, without shadowy allusions. Without dreams.

"Yes," Jeanine said. "Your father sounds terrific. And he raised you to think that achievement should not be fettered – Jesus Christ, he's a Yagaiist. Well, good. We're glad for you." She said it without sarcasm. Leisha nodded. "But the world isn't always like that. They hate us."

"That's too strong," Carol said. "Not hate."

"Well, maybe," Jeanine said. "But they're different from us. We're better, and they naturally resent that."

"I don't see what's natural about it," Tony said. "Why shouldn't it be just as natural to admire what's better? We do. Does any one of us resent Kenzo Yagai for his genius? Or Nelson Wade, the physicist? Or Catherine Raduski?"

"We don't resent them because we *are* better," Richard said. "Q.E.D."

"What we should do is have our own society," Tony said. "Why should we allow their regulations to restrict our natural, honest achievements? Why should Jeanine be barred from skating against them and Jack from investing on their same terms just because we're Sleepless? Some of them are brighter than others of them. Some have greater persistence. Well, we have greater concentration, more biochemical stability, and more time. All men are not created equal."

"Be fair, Tony – no one has been barred from anything yet," Jeanine said.

"But we will be."

"*Wait.*" Leisha said. She was deeply troubled by the conversation. "I mean, yes, in many ways we're better. But you quoted out of context, Tony. The Declaration of Independence doesn't say all men are created equal in ability. It's talking about rights and power – it means that all are created equal *under the law*. We have no more right to a separate society or to being free of society's restrictions than anyone else does. There's no other way to freely trade one's efforts, unless the same contractual rules apply to all."

"Spoken like a true Yagaiist," Richard said, squeezing her hand.

"That's enough intellectual discussion for me," Carol said, laughing. "We've been at this for hours. We're at the beach, for Chrissake. Who wants to swim with me?"

"I do," Jeanine said. "Come on, Jack."

All of them rose, brushing sand off their suits, discarding sunglasses. Richard pulled Leisha to her feet. But just before they ran into the water, Tony put his skinny hand on her arm. "One more question, Leisha. Just to think about. If we achieve better than most other people, and we trade with the Sleepers when it's mutually beneficial, making no distinction there between the strong and the weak – what obligation do we have to those so weak they don't have anything to trade with us? We're already going to give more than we get – do we have to do it when we get nothing at all? Do we have to take care of their deformed and handicapped and sick and lazy and shiftless with the products of our work?"

"Do the Sleepers have to?" Leisha countered.

"Kenzo Yagai would say no. He's a Sleeper."

"He would say they would receive the benefits of contractual trade even if they aren't direct parties to the contract. The whole world is better fed and healthier because of Y-energy."

"Come on," Jeanine yelled. "Leisha, they're dunking me. Jack, you stop that. Leisha, help me!"

Leisha laughed. Just before she grabbed for Jeanine, she caught the look on Richard's face, on Tony's: Richard frankly lustful, Tony angry. At her. But why? What had she done, except argue in favor of dignity and trade?

Then Jack threw water on her, and Carol pushed Jack into the warm spray, and Richard was there with his arms around her, laughing.

When she got the water out of her eyes, Tony was gone.

Midnight. "Okay," Carol said. "Who's first?"

The six teenagers in the bramble clearing looked at each other. A Y-lamp, kept on low for atmosphere, cast weird shadows across their faces and over their bare legs. Around the clearing Roger Camden's trees stood thick and dark, a wall between them and the closest of the estate's outbuildings. It was very hot. August air hung heavy, sullen. They had voted against bringing an air-conditioned Y-field because this was a return to the primitive, the dangerous; let it be primitive.

Six pairs of eyes stared at the glass in Carol's hand.

"Come *on*," she said. "Who wants to drink up?" Her voice was jaunty, theatrically hard. "It was difficult enough to get this."

"How *did* you get it?" said Richard, the group member – except for Tony – with the least influential family contacts, the least money. "In a drinkable form like that?"

"My cousin Brian is a pharmaceutical supplier to the Biotech Institute. He's curious." Nods around the circle; except for Leisha, they were Sleepless precisely because they had relatives somehow connected to Biotech. And everyone was curious. The glass held inter-leukin-l, an immune-system booster, one of many substances that as a side effect induced the brain to swift and deep sleep.

Leisha stared at the glass. A warm feeling crept through her lower belly, not unlike the feeling when she and Richard made love.

Tony said, "Give it to me!"

Carol did. "Remember – you only need a little sip."

Tony raised the glass to his mouth, stopped, looked at them over the rim with his fierce eyes. He drank.

Carol took back the glass. They all watched Tony. Within a minute he lay on the rough ground; within two, his eyes closed in sleep.

It wasn't like seeing parents sleep, siblings, friends. It was Tony.

They looked away, didn't meet each other's eyes. Leisha felt the warmth between her legs tug and tingle, faintly obscene.

When it was her turn, she drank slowly, then passed the glass to Jeanine. Her head turned heavy, as if it were being stuffed with damp rags. The trees at the edge of the clearing blurred. The portable lamp blurred, too – it wasn't bright and clean anymore but squishy, blobby; if she touched it, it would smear. Then darkness swooped over her brain, taking it away: *taking away her mind*. "Daddy!" She tried to call, to clutch for him, but then the darkness obliterated her.

Afterward they all had headaches. Dragging themselves back through the woods in the thin morning light was torture, compounded by an odd shame. They didn't touch each other. Leisha walked as far away from Richard as she could. It was a whole day before the throbbing left the base of her skull or the nausea her stomach.

There had not even been any dreams.

"I want you to come with me tonight," Leisha said, for the tenth or twelfth time. "We both leave for college in just two days; this is the last chance. I really want you to meet Richard."

Alice lay on her stomach across her bed. Her hair, brown and lusterless, fell around her face. She wore an expensive yellow jump suit, silk by Ann Patterson, which rucked up in wrinkles around her knees.

"Why? What do you care if I meet Richard or not?"

"Because you're my sister," Leisha said. She knew better than to say "my twin." Nothing got Alice angry faster.

"I don't want to." The next moment Alice's face changed. "Oh, I'm sorry, Leisha – I didn't mean to sound so snotty. But . . . but I don't want to."

"It won't be all of them. Just Richard. And just for an hour or so. Then you can come back here and pack for Northwestern."

"I'm not going to Northwestern."

Leisha stared at her.

Alice said, "I'm pregnant."

Leisha sat on the bed. Alice rolled onto her back, brushed the hair out of her eyes, and laughed. Leisha's ears closed against the sound. "Look at you," Alice said. "You'd think it was *you* who was pregnant. But you never would be, would you, Leisha? Not until it was the proper time. Not you."

"How?" Leisha said. "We both had our caps put in . . ."

"I had the cap removed," Alice said.

"You wanted to get pregnant?"

"Damn flash I did. And there's not a thing Daddy can do about it. Except, of course, cut off all credit completely, but I don't think he'll do that, do you?" She laughed again. "Even to me?"

"But, Alice . . . why? Not just to anger Daddy."

"No," Alice said. "Although you would think of that, wouldn't you? Because I want something to love. Something of my *own*. Something that has nothing to do with this house."

Leisha thought of her and Alice running through the conservatory, years ago, her and Alice darting in and out of the sunlight. "It hasn't been so bad growing up in this house."

"Leisha, you're stupid. I don't know how anyone so smart can be so stupid. Get out of my room! Get out!"

"But, Alice . . . *a baby* . . ."

"Get out!" Alice shrieked. "Go to Harvard. Go be successful. Just get out!"

Leisha jerked off the bed. "Gladly! You're irrational, Alice. You don't think ahead; you don't plan a *baby* . . ." But she could never sustain anger. It dribbled away, leaving her mind empty. She looked at Alice, who suddenly put out her arms. Leisha went into them.

"You're the baby," Alice said wonderingly. "You *are*. You're so . . . I don't know what. You're a baby."

Leisha said nothing. Alice's arms felt warm, felt whole, felt like two children running in and out of sunlight. "I'll help you, Alice. If Daddy won't."

Alice abruptly pushed her away. "I don't need your help."

Alice stood. Leisha rubbed her empty arms, fingertips scraping across opposite elbows. Alice kicked the empty, open trunk in which she was supposed to pack for Northwestern and then abruptly smiled, a smile that made Leisha look away. She braced herself for more abuse. But what Alice said, very softly, was, "Have a good time at Harvard."

V

She loved it.

From the first sight of Massachusetts Hall, older than the United States by a half century, Leisha felt something that had been missing in Chicago: Age. Roots. Tradition. She touched the bricks of Widener Library, the glass cases in the Peabody Museum, as if they were the grail. She had never been particularly sensitive to myth or drama; the anguish of Juliet seemed to her artificial, that of Willy Loman merely wasteful. Only King Arthur, struggling to create a better social order, had interested her. But now, walking under the huge autumn trees, she suddenly caught a glimpse of a force that could span generations, fortunes left to endow learning and achievement the benefactors would never see, individual effort spanning and shaping centuries to come. She stopped and looked at the sky through the leaves, at the buildings solid with purpose. At such moments she thought of Camden, bending the will of an entire genetic-research institute to create her in the image he wanted.

Within a month she had forgotten all such mega-musings.

The workload was incredible, even for her. The Sauley School had encouraged individual exploration at her own pace; Harvard knew what it wanted from her, at its pace. In the last twenty years, under the academic leadership of a man who in his youth had watched Japanese economic domination with dismay, Harvard had become the controversial leader of a return to hard-edged learning of facts, theories, applications, problem solving, intellectual efficiency. The school accepted one out of every two hundred applications from around the world. The daughter of England's Prime Minister had flunked out her first year and been sent home.

Leisha had a single room in a new dormitory, the dorm because she had spent so many years isolated in Chicago and was hungry for people, the single so she would not disturb anyone else when she worked all night. Her second day, a boy from down the hall sauntered in and perched on the edge of her desk.

"So you're Leisha Camden."

"Yes."

"Sixteen years old."

"Almost seventeen."

"Going to outperform us all, I understand, without even trying."

Leisha's smile faded. The boy stared at her from under lowered downy brows. He was smiling, his eyes sharp. From Richard and Tony and the others, Leisha had learned to recognize the anger that presented itself as contempt.

"Yes," Leisha said coolly. "I am."

"Are you sure? With your pretty little-girl hair and your mutant little-girl brain?"

"Oh, leave her alone, Hannaway," said another voice. A tall blond boy, so thin his ribs looked like ripples in brown sand, stood in jeans and bare feet, drying his wet hair. "Don't you ever get tired of walking around being an asshole?"

"Do you?" Hannaway said. He heaved himself off the desk and started toward the door. The blond moved out of his way. Leisha moved into it.

"The reason I'm going to do better than you," she said evenly, "is because I have certain advantages you don't. Including sleeplessness. And then after I 'outperform' you I'll be glad to help you study for your tests so that you can pass, too."

The blond, drying his ears, laughed. But Hannaway stood still, and into his eyes came an expression that made Leisha back away. He pushed past her and stormed out.

"Nice going, Camden," the blond said. "He deserved that."

"But I meant it," Leisha said. "I will help him study."

The blond lowered his towel and stared. "You did, didn't you? You meant it."

"Yes! Why does everybody keep questioning that?"

"Well," the boy said, "*I* don't. You can help me if I get into trouble." Suddenly he smiled. "But I won't."

"Why not?"

"Because I'm just as good at anything as you are, Leisha Camden." She studied him. "You're not one of us. Not Sleepless."

"Don't have to be. I know what I can do. Do, be, create, trade."

She said, delighted, "You're a Yagaiist!"

"Of course." He held out his hand. "Stewart Sutter. How about a fishburger in the Yard?"

"Great," Leisha said. They walked out together, talking excitedly.

When people stared at her she tried not to notice. She was here. At Harvard. With space ahead of her, time to learn, and with people like Stewart Sutter who accepted and challenged her.

All the hours he was awake.

She became totally absorbed in her classwork. Roger Camden drove up once, walking the campus with her, listening, smiling. He was more at home than Leisha would have expected: he knew Stewart Sutter's father, Kate Addams's grandfather. They talked about Harvard, business, Harvard, the Yagai Economics Institute, Harvard. "How's Alice?" Leisha asked once, but Camden said that he didn't know; she had moved out and did not want to see him. He made her an allowance through his attorney. While he said this, his face remained serene.

Leisha went to the Homecoming Ball with Stewart, who was also majoring in prelaw but was two years ahead of Leisha. She took a weekend trip to Paris with Kate Addams and two other girlfriends, taking the Concorde III. She had a fight with Stewart over whether the metaphor of superconductivity could apply to Yagaiism, a stupid fight they both knew was stupid but had anyway, and afterward they became lovers. After the fumbling sexual explorations with Richard, Stewart was deft, experienced, smiling faintly as he taught her how to have an orgasm both by herself and with him. Leisha was dazzled.

"It's so *joyful,*" she said, and Stewart looked at her with a tenderness she knew was part disturbance but didn't know why.

At mid-semester she had the highest grades in the freshman class. She got every answer right on every single question on her midterms. She and Stewart went out for a beer to celebrate, and when they came back Leisha's room had been destroyed. The computer was smashed, the data banks wiped, hard copies and books smoldering in a metal wastebasket. Her clothes were ripped to pieces, her desk and bureau hacked apart. The only thing untouched, pristine, was the bed.

Stewart said, "There's no way this could have been done in silence. Everyone on the floor – hell, on the floor *below* – had to know. Someone will talk to the police." No one did. Leisha sat on the edge of the bed, dazed, and looked at the remnants of her homecoming gown. The next day Dave Hannaway gave her a long, wide smile.

Camden flew east again, taut with rage. He rented her an apartment in Cambridge with E-lock security and a bodyguard named Toshio. After he left Leisha fired the bodyguard but kept the apartment. It gave her and Stewart more privacy, which they used to endlessly discuss the situation. It was Leisha who argued that it was an aberration, an immaturity.

"There have always been haters, Stewart. Hate Jews, hate blacks, hate immigrants, hate Yagaiists who have more initiative and dignity than you do. I'm just the latest object of hatred. It's not new, it's not remarkable. It doesn't mean any basic kind of schism between the Sleepless and Sleepers."

Stewart sat up in bed and reached for the sandwiches on the night stand. "Doesn't it? Leisha, you're a different kind of person entirely. More evolutionarily fit, not only to survive but to prevail. Those other 'objects of hatred' you cite except Yagaiists – they were all powerless in their societies. They occupied *inferior* positions. You, on the other hand – all three Sleepless in Harvard Law are on the *Law Review.* All of them. Kevin Baker, your oldest, has already founded a successful bio-interface software firm and is making money, a lot of it. Every Sleepless is making superb grades, none have psychological problems, all are healthy – and most of you aren't even adults yet. How much hatred do you think you're going to encounter once you hit the big-stakes world of finance and business and scarce endowed chairs and national politics?"

"Give me a sandwich," Leisha said. "Here's my evidence you're wrong: you yourself. Kenzo Yagai. Kate Addams. Professor Lane. My father. Every Sleeper who inhabits the world of fair trade, mutually beneficial contracts. And that's most of you, or at least most of you who are worth considering. You believe that competition among the most capable leads to the most beneficial trades for everyone, strong and weak. Sleepless are making real and concrete contributions to society, in a lot of fields. That has to outweigh the discomfort we cause. We're *valuable* to you. You know that."

Stewart brushed crumbs off the sheets. "Yes. I do. Yagaiists do."

"Yagaiists run the business and financial and academic worlds. Or they will. In a meritocracy, they *should*. You underestimate the majority of people, Stew. Ethics aren't confined to the ones out front."

"I hope you're right," Stewart said. "Because, you know, I'm in love with you."

Leisha put down her sandwich.

"Joy," Stewart mumbled into her breasts. "You are joy."

When Leisha went home for Thanksgiving, she told Richard about Stewart. He listened tight-lipped.

"A Sleeper."

"A *person*," Leisha said. "A good, intelligent, achieving person."

"Do you know what your good intelligent achieving Sleepers have done, Leisha? Jeanine has been barred from Olympic skating. 'Genetic alteration, analogous to steroid abuse to create an unsportsmanlike advantage.' Chris Devereaux's left Stanford. They trashed his laboratory, destroyed two years' work in memory-formation proteins. Kevin Baker's software company is fighting a nasty advertising campaign, all underground, of course, about kids using software designed by 'nonhuman minds.' Corruption, mental slavery, satanic influences: the whole bag of witch-hunt tricks. Wake up, Leisha!"

They both heard his words. Moments dragged by. Richard stood like a boxer, forward on the balls of his feet, teeth clenched. Finally he said, very quietly, "Do you love him?"

"Yes," Leisha said. "I'm sorry."

"Your choice," Richard said coldly. "What do you do while he's asleep? Watch?"

"You make it sound like a perversion!"

Richard said nothing. Leisha drew a deep breath. She spoke rapidly but calmly, a controlled rush: "While Stewart is asleep I work. The same as you do. Richard – don't do this. I didn't mean to hurt you. And I don't want to lose the group. I believe the Sleepers are the same species as we are – are you going to punish me for that? Are you going to *add* to the hatred? Are you going to tell me that I can't belong to a wider world that includes all honest, worthwhile people whether they sleep or not? Are you going to tell me that the most important division is by genetics and not by economic spirituality? Are you going to force me into an artificial choice, 'us' or 'them'?"

Richard picked up a bracelet. Leisha recognized it: she had given it to him in the summer. His voice was quiet. "No. It's not a choice." He played with the gold links a minute, then looked up at her. "Not yet."

By spring break, Camden walked more slowly. He took medicine for his blood pressure, his heart. He and Susan, he told Leisha, were getting a divorce. "She changed, Leisha, after I married her. You saw that. She was independent and productive and happy, and then after a few years she stopped all that and became a shrew. A whining shrew." He shook his head in genuine bewilderment. "You saw the change."

Leisha had. A memory came to her: Susan leading her and Alice in "games" that were actually controlled cerebral-performance tests. Susan's braids dancing around her sparkling eyes. Alice had loved Susan, then, as much as Leisha had.

"Dad, I want Alice's address."

"I told you up at Harvard, I don't have it," Camden said. He shifted in his chair, the impatient gesture of a body that never expected to wear out. In January Kenzo Yagai had died of pancreatic cancer; Camden had taken the news hard. "I make her allowance through an attorney. By her choice."

"Then I want the address of the attorney."

The attorney, however, refused to tell Leisha where Alice was. "She doesn't want to be found, Ms. Camden. She wanted a complete break."

"Not from me," Leisha said.

"Yes," the attorney said, and something flickered behind his eyes, something she had last seen in Dave Hannaway's face.

She flew to Austin before returning to Boston, making her a day late for classes. Kevin Baker saw her instantly, canceling a meeting with IBM. She told him what she needed, and he set his best datanet people on it, without telling them why. Within two hours she had Alice's address from the attorney's electronic files. It was the first time, she realized, that she had ever turned to one of the Sleepless for help, and it had been given instantly. Without trade.

Alice was in Pennsylvania. The next weekend Leisha rented a hovercar and driver – she had learned to drive, but only groundcars as yet – and went to High Ridge, in the Appalachian Mountains.

It was an isolated hamlet, twenty-five miles from the nearest hospital. Alice lived with a man named Ed, a silent carpenter twenty years older than she, in a cabin in the woods. The cabin had water and electricity but no news net. In the early spring light the earth was raw and bare, slashed with icy gullies. Alice and Ed apparently worked at nothing. Alice was eight months pregnant.

"I didn't want you here," she said to Leisha. "So why are you?"

"Because you're my sister."

"God, look at you. Is that what they're wearing at Harvard? Boots like that? When did you become fashionable, Leisha? You were always too busy being intellectual to care."

"What's this all about, Alice? Why here? What are you doing?"

"Living," Alice said. "Away from dear Daddy, away from Chicago, away from drunken broken Susan – did you know she drinks? Just like Mom. He does that to people. But not to me. I got out. I wonder if you ever will."

"Got out? To *this*?"

"I'm happy," Alice said angrily. "Isn't that what it's supposed to be about? Isn't that the aim of your great Kenzo Yagai – happiness through individual effort?"

Leisha thought of saying that Alice was making no efforts that she could see. She didn't say it. A chicken ran through the yard of the cabin. Behind, the Appalachian Mountains rose in layers of blue haze. Leisha thought what this place must have been like in winter: cut off from the world where people strived toward goals, learned, changed.

"I'm glad you're happy, Alice."

"Are you?"

"Yes."

"Then I'm glad, too," Alice said, almost defiantly. The next moment she abruptly hugged Leisha, fiercely, the huge hard mound of her belly crushed between them. Alice's hair smelled sweet, like fresh grass in sunlight.

"I'll come see you again, Alice."

"Don't," Alice said.

VI

SLEEPLESS MUTIE BEGS FOR REVERSAL OF GENE TAMPERING, screamed the headline in the Food Mart. "PLEASE LET ME SLEEP LIKE REAL PEOPLE!" CHILD PLEADS.

Leisha typed in her credit number and pressed the news kiosk for a printout, although ordinarily she ignored the electronic tabloids. The headline went on circling the kiosk. A Food Mart employee stopped stacking boxes on shelves and watched her. Bruce, Leisha's bodyguard, watched the employee.

She was twenty-two, in her final year at Harvard Law, editor of the *Law Review*, ranked first in her class. The next three were Jonathan Cocchiara, Len Carter, and Martha Wentz. All Sleepless.

In her apartment she skimmed the printout. Then she accessed the Groupnet run from Austin. The files had more news stories about the child, with comments from other Sleepless, but before she could call them up Kevin Baker came online himself, on voice.

"Leisha. I'm glad you called. I was going to call you."

"What's the situation with this Stella Bevington, Kev? Has anybody checked it out?"

"Randy Davies. He's from Chicago, but I don't think you've met him; he's still in high school. He's in Park Ridge; Stella's in Skokie. Her parents wouldn't talk to him – were pretty abusive, in fact – but he got to see Stella face-to-face anyway. It doesn't look like an abuse case, just the usual stupidity: parents wanted a genius child, scrimped and saved, and now they can't handle that she is one. They scream at her to sleep, get emotionally abusive when she contradicts them, but so far no violence."

"Is the emotional abuse actionable?"

"I don't think we want to move on it yet. Two of us will keep in close touch with Stella – she does have a modem, and she hasn't told her parents about the net – and Randy will drive out weekly."

Leisha bit her lip. "A tabloid shitpiece said she's seven years old."

"Yes."

"Maybe she shouldn't be left there. I'm an Illinois resident, I can file an abuse grievance from here if Candy's got too much in her briefcase . . ." *Seven years old.*

"No. Let it sit awhile. Stella will probably be all right. You know that."

She did. Nearly all of the Sleepless stayed "all right," no matter how much opposition came from the stupid segment of society. And it was only the stupid segment, Leisha argued – a small if vocal minority. Most people could, and would, adjust to the growing presence of the Sleepless, when it became clear that that presence included not only growing power but growing benefits to the country as a whole.

Kevin Baker, now twenty-six, had made a fortune in microchips so revolutionary that artificial intelligence, once a debated dream, was yearly closer to reality. Carolyn Rizzolo had won the Pulitzer Prize in drama for her play *Morning Light*. She was twenty-four. Jeremy Robinson had done significant work in superconductivity applications while still a graduate student at Stanford. William Thaine, *Law Review* editor when Leisha first came to Harvard, was now in private practice. He had never lost a case. He was twenty-six, and the cases were becoming important. His clients valued his ability more than his age.

But not everyone reacted that way.

Kevin Baker and Richard Keller had started the datanet that bound the Sleepless into a tight group, constantly aware of each other's personal fights. Leisha Camden financed the legal battles, the educational costs of Sleepless whose parents were unable to meet them, the support of children in emotionally bad situations. Rhonda Lavelier got herself licensed as a foster mother in California, and whenever possible the Group maneuvered to have small Sleepless who were removed from their homes assigned to Rhonda. The Group now had three ABA lawyers; within the next year they would gain four more, licensed to practice in five different states.

The one time they had not been able to remove an abused Sleepless child legally, they kidnapped him.

Timmy DeMarzo, four years old. Leisha had been opposed to the action. She had argued the case morally and pragmatically – to her they were the same thing – thus: if they believed in their society, in its fundamental laws and in their ability to belong to it as free-trading productive individuals, they must remain bound by the society's contractual laws. The Sleepless were, for the most part, Yagaiists. They should already know this. And if the FBI caught them, the courts and press would crucify them.

They were not caught.

Timmy DeMarzo – not even old enough to call for help on the datanet; they had learned of the situation through the automatic police-record scan Kevin maintained through his company – was stolen from his own backyard in Wichita. He had lived the last year in an isolated trailer in North Dakota; no place was too isolated for a modem. He was cared for by a legally irreproachable foster mother who had lived there all her life. The foster mother was second cousin to a Sleepless, a broad cheerful woman with a much better brain than her appearance indicated. She was a Yagaiist. No record of the child's existence appeared in any data bank: not the IRS's, not any school's, not even the local grocery store's computerized checkout slips. Food specifically for the child was shipped in monthly on a truck owned by a Sleepless in State College, Pennsylvania. Ten of the Group knew about the kidnapping, out of the total 3,428 born in the United States. Of that total, 2,691 were part of the Group via the net. Another 701 were as yet too young to use a modem. Only 36 Sleepless, for whatever reason, were not part of the Group.

The kidnapping had been arranged by Tony Indivino.

"It's Tony I wanted to talk to you about," Kevin said to Leisha. "He's started again. This time he means it. He's buying land."

She folded the tabloid very small and laid it carefully on the table. "Where?"

"Allegheny Mountains. In southern New York State. A lot of land. He's putting in the roads now. In the spring, the first buildings."

"Jennifer Sharifi still financing it?" She was the American-born daughter of an Arab prince who had wanted a Sleepless child. The prince was dead, and Jennifer, dark-eyed and multilingual, was richer than Leisha would one day be.

"Yes. He's starting to get a following, Leisha."

"I know."

"Call him."

"I will. Keep me informed about Stella."

She worked until midnight at the *Law Review*, then until four a.m. preparing her classes. From four to five she handled legal matters for the Group. At five a.m. she called Tony, still in Chicago. He had finished high school, done one semester at Northwestern, and at Christmas vacation he had finally exploded at his mother for forcing him to live as a Sleeper. The explosion, it seemed to Leisha, had never ended.

"Tony? Leisha."

"The answer is yes, yes, no, and go to hell."

Leisha gritted her teeth. "Fine. Now tell me the questions."

"Are you really serious about the Sleepless withdrawing into their own self-sufficient society? Is Jennifer Sharifi willing to finance a project the size of building a small city? Don't you think that's a cheat of all that can be accomplished by patient integration of the Group into the mainstream? And what about the contradictions of living in an armed restricted city and still trading with the Outside?"

"I would never tell *you* to go to hell."

"Hooray for you," Tony said. After a moment he added, "I'm sorry. That sounds like one of *them*."

"It's wrong for us, Tony."

"Thanks for not saying I couldn't pull it off."

She wondered if he could. "We're not a separate species, Tony."

"Tell that to the Sleepers."

"You exaggerate. There are haters out there, there are *always* haters, but to give up . . ."

"We're not giving up. Whatever we create can be freely traded: software, hardware, novels, information, theories, legal counsel. We can travel in and out. But we'll have a safe place to return *to*. Without the leeches who think we owe them blood because we're better than they are."

"It isn't a matter of owing."

"Really?" Tony said. "Let's have this out, Leisha. All the way. You're a Yagaiist – what do you believe in?"

"Tony . . ."

"Do *it*," Tony said, and in his voice she heard the fourteen-year-old Richard had introduced her to. Simultaneously, she saw her father's face: not as he was now, since the bypass, but as he had been when she was a little girl, holding her on his lap to explain that she was special.

"I believe in voluntary trade that is mutually beneficial. That spiritual dignity comes from supporting one's life through one's own efforts, and trading the results of those efforts in mutual cooperation throughout the society. That the symbol of this is the contract. And that we need each other for the fullest, most beneficial trade."

"Fine," Tony bit off. "Now what about the beggars in Spain?"

"The what?"

"You walk down a street in a poor country like Spain and you see a beggar. Do you give him a dollar?"

"Probably."

"Why? He's trading nothing with you. He has nothing to trade."

"I know. Out of kindness. Compassion."

"You see six beggars. Do you give them all a dollar?"

"Probably," Leisha said.

"You would. You see a hundred beggars and you haven't got Leisha Camden's money – do you give them each a dollar?"

"No."

"Why not?"

Leisha reached for patience. Few people could make her want to cut off a comm link; Tony was one of them. "Too draining on my own resources. My life has first claim on the resources I earn."

"All right. Now consider this. At Biotech Institute – where you and I began, dear pseudo sister – Dr. Melling has just yesterday – "

"*Who?*"

"Dr. Susan Melling. Oh, God, I completely forgot – she used to be married to your father!"

"I lost track of her," Leisha said. "I didn't realize she'd gone back to research. Alice once said . . . never mind. What's going on at Biotech?"

"Two crucial items, just released. Carla Dutcher has had first-month fetal genetic analysis. Sleeplessness is a dominant gene. The next generation of the Group won't sleep, either."

"We all knew that," Leisha said. Carla Dutcher was the world's first pregnant Sleepless. Her husband was a Sleeper. "The whole world expected that."

"But the press will have a windfall with it anyway. Just watch. 'Muties Breed!' 'New Race Set to Dominate Next Generation of Children!'"

Leisha didn't deny it. "And the second item?"

"It's sad, Leisha. We've just had our first death."

Her stomach tightened. "Who?"

"Bernie Kuhn. Seattle." She didn't know him. "A car accident. It looks pretty straightforward – he lost control on a steep curve when his brakes failed. He had only been driving a few months. He was seventeen. But the significance here is that his parents have donated his brain and body to Biotech, in conjunction with the pathology department at the Chicago Medical School. They're going to take him apart to get the first good look at what prolonged sleeplessness does to the body and brain."

"They should," Leisha said. "That poor kid. But what are you so afraid they'll find?"

"I don't know. I'm not a doctor. But whatever it is, if the haters can use it against us, they will."

"You're paranoid, Tony."

"Impossible. The Sleepless have personalities calmer and more reality-oriented than the norm. Don't you read the literature?"

"Tony – "

"What if you walk down that street in Spain and a hundred beggars each want a dollar and you say no and they have nothing to trade you, but they're so rotten with anger about what you have that they knock you down and grab it and then beat you out of sheer envy and despair?"

Leisha didn't answer.

"Are you going to say that's not a human scenario, Leisha? That it never happens?"

"It happens," Leisha said evenly. "But not all that often."

"Bullshit. Read more history. Read more *newspapers*. But the point is: what do you owe the beggars then? What does a good Yagaiist who believes in mutually beneficial contracts do with people who have nothing to trade and can only take?"

"You're not – "

"*What*, Leisha? In the most objective terms you can manage, what do we owe the grasping and nonproductive needy?"

"What I said originally. Kindness. Compassion."

"Even if they don't trade it back? Why?"

"Because . . ." She stopped.

"Why? Why do law-abiding and productive human beings owe anything to those who neither produce very much nor abide by laws? What philosophical or economic or spiritual justification is there for owing them anything? Be as honest as I know you are."

Leisha put her head between her knees. The question gaped beneath her, but she didn't try to evade it. "I don't know. I just know we do."

"Why?"

She didn't answer. After a moment Tony did. The intellectual challenge was gone from his voice. He said, almost tenderly, "Come down in the spring and see the site for Sanctuary. The buildings will be going up then."

"No," Leisha said.

"I'd like you to."

"No. Armed retreat is not the way."

Tony said, "The beggars are getting nastier, Leisha. As the Sleepless grow richer. And I don't mean in money."

"Tony – " she said, and stopped. She couldn't think what to say.

"Don't walk too many streets armed with just the memory of Kenzo Yagai."

In March, a bitterly cold March of winds whipping down the Charles River, Richard Keller came to Cambridge. Leisha had not seen him for four years. He didn't send her word on the Groupnet that he was coming. She hurried up the walk to her townhouse, muffled to the eyes in a red wool scarf against the snowy cold, and he stood there blocking the doorway. Behind Leisha, her bodyguard tensed.

"Richard! Bruce, it's all right; this is an old friend."

"Hello, Leisha."

He was heavier, sturdier looking, with a breadth of shoulder she didn't recognize. But the face was Richard's, older but unchanged: dark low brows, unruly dark hair. He had grown a beard.

"You look beautiful," he said.

She handed him a cup of coffee. "Are you here on business?" From the Groupnet she knew that he had finished his master's and had done outstanding work in marine biology in the Caribbean but had left that a year ago and disappeared from the net.

"No. Pleasure." He smiled suddenly, the old smile that opened up his dark face. "I almost forgot about that for a long time. Contentment, yes, we're all good at the contentment that comes from sustained work, but pleasure? Whim? Caprice? When was the last time you did something silly, Leisha?"

She smiled. "I ate cotton candy in the shower."

"Really? Why?"

"To see if it would dissolve in gooey pink patterns."

"Did it?"

"Yes. Lovely ones."

"And that was your last silly thing? When was it?"

"Last summer," Leisha said, and laughed.

"Well, mine is sooner than that. It's now. I'm in Boston for no other reason than the spontaneous pleasure of seeing you."

Leisha stopped laughing. "That's an intense tone for a spontaneous pleasure, Richard."

"Yup," he said, intensely. She laughed again. He didn't.

"I've been in India, Leisha. And China and Africa. Thinking, mostly. Watching. First I traveled like a Sleeper, attracting no attention. Then I set out to meet the Sleepless in India and China. There are a few, you know, whose parents were willing to come here for the operation. They pretty much are accepted and left alone. I tried to figure out why desperately poor countries – by our standards, anyway; over there Y-energy is mostly available only in big cities – don't have any trouble accepting the superiority of Sleepless, whereas Americans, with more prosperity than any time in history, build in resentment more and more."

Leisha said, "Did you figure it out?"

"No. But I figured out something else, watching all those communes and villages and kampongs. We are too individualistic."

Disappointment swept Leisha. She saw her father's face: *Excellence is what counts, Leisha. Excellence supported by individual effort* . . . She reached for Richard's cup. "More coffee?"

He caught her wrist and looked up into her face. "Don't misunderstand me, Leisha. I'm not talking about work. We are too much individuals in the rest of our lives. Too emotionally rational. Too much alone. Isolation kills more than the free flow of ideas. It kills joy."

He didn't let go of her wrist. She looked down into his eyes, into depths she hadn't seen before: it was the feeling of looking into a mine shaft, both giddy and frightening, knowing that at the bottom might be gold or darkness. Or both.

Richard said softly, "Stewart?"

"Over long ago. An undergraduate thing." Her voice didn't sound like her own.

"Kevin?"

"No, never – we're just friends."

"I wasn't sure. Anyone?"

"No."

He let go of her wrist. Leisha peered at him timidly. He suddenly laughed. "Joy, Leisha." An echo sounded in her mind, but she couldn't place it and then it was gone and she laughed, too, a laugh airy and frothy as pink cotton candy in summer.

"Come home, Leisha. He's had another heart attack."

Susan Melling's voice on the phone was tired. Leisha said, "How bad?"

"The doctors aren't sure. Or say they're not sure. He wants to see you. Can you leave your studies?"

It was May, the last push toward her finals. The *Law Review* proofs were behind schedule. Richard had started a new business, marine consulting to Boston fishermen plagued with sudden inexplicable shifts in ocean currents, and was working twenty hours a day. "I'll come," Leisha said.

Chicago was colder than Boston. The trees were half budded. On Lake Michigan, filling the huge east windows of her father's house, whitecaps tossed up cold spray. Leisha saw that Susan was living in the house: her brushes on Camden's dresser, her journals on the credenza in the foyer.

"Leisha," Camden said. He looked old. Gray skin, sunken cheeks, the fretful and bewildered look of men who accepted potency like air, indivisible from their lives. In the corner of the room, on a small eighteenth-century slipper chair, sat a short, stocky woman with brown braids.

"*Alice.*"

"Hello, Leisha."

"*Alice.* I've looked for you . . ." The wrong thing to say. Leisha had looked but not very hard, deterred by the knowledge that Alice had not wanted to be found. "How are you?"

"I'm fine," Alice said. She seemed remote, gentle, unlike the angry Alice of six years ago in the raw Pennsylvania hills. Camden moved painfully on the bed. He looked at Leisha with eyes that, she saw, were undimmed in their blue brightness.

"I asked Alice to come. And Susan. Susan came a while ago. I'm dying, Leisha."

No one contradicted him. Leisha, knowing his respect for facts, remained silent. Love hurt her chest.

"John Jaworski has my will. None of you can break it. But I wanted to tell you myself what's in it. The last few years I've been selling, liquidating. Most of my holdings are accessible now. I've left a tenth to Alice, a tenth to Susan, a tenth to Elizabeth, and the rest to you, Leisha, because you're the only one with the individual ability to use the money to its full potential for achievement."

Leisha looked wildly at Alice, who gazed back with her strange remote calm. "Elizabeth? My . . . mother? Is alive?"

"Yes," Camden said.

"You told me she was dead! Years and years ago."

"Yes. I thought it was better for you that way. She didn't like what you were, was jealous of what you could become. And she had nothing to give you. She would only have caused you emotional harm."

Beggars in Spain . . .

"That was wrong, Dad. You were *wrong*. She's my *mother* . . ." She couldn't finish the sentence.

Camden didn't flinch. "I don't think I was. But you're an adult now. You can see her if you wish."

He went on looking at her from his bright, sunken eyes, while around Leisha the air heaved and snapped. Her father had lied to her. Susan watched her closely, a small smile on her lips. Was she glad to see Camden fall in his daughter's estimation? Had she all along been that jealous of their relationship, of Leisha . . .

She was thinking like Tony.

The thought steadied her a little. But she went on staring at Camden, who went on staring implacably back, unbudged, a man positive even on his deathbed that he was right.

Alice's hand was on her elbow, Alice's voice so soft that no one but Leisha could hear. "He's done now, Leisha. And after a while you'll be all right."

Alice had left her son in California with her husband of two years, Beck Watrous, a building contractor she had met while waitressing in a resort on the Artificial Islands. Beck had adopted Jordan, Alice's son.

"Before Beck there was a real bad time," Alice said in her remote voice. "You know, when I was carrying Jordan I actually used to dream that he would be Sleepless? Like you. Every night I'd dream that, and every morning I'd wake up and have morning sickness with a baby that was only going to be a stupid nothing like me. I stayed with Ed – in Pennsylvania, remember? You came to see me there once – for two more years. When he beat me, I was glad. I wished Daddy could see. At least Ed was touching me."

Leisha made a sound in her throat.

"I finally left because I was afraid for Jordan. I went to California, did nothing but eat for a year. I got up to a hundred and ninety pounds." Alice was, Leisha estimated, five-foot-four. "Then I came home to see Mother."

"You didn't tell me," Leisha said. "You knew she was alive and you didn't tell me."

"She's in a drying-out tank half the time," Alice said, with brutal simplicity. "She wouldn't see you if you wanted to. But she saw me, and she fell slobbering all over me as her 'real' daughter, and she threw up on my dress. And I backed away from her and looked at the dress and knew it *should* be thrown up on, it was so ugly. Deliberately ugly. She started screaming how Dad had ruined her life, ruined mine, all for *you*. And do you know what I did?"

"What?" Leisha said. Her voice was shaky.

"I flew home, burned all my clothes, got a job, started college, lost fifty pounds, and put Jordan in play therapy."

The sisters sat silent. Beyond the window the lake was dark, unlit by moon or stars. It was Leisha who suddenly shook, and Alice who patted her shoulder.

"Tell me . . ." Leisha couldn't think what she wanted to be told, except that she wanted to hear Alice's voice in the gloom, Alice's voice as it was now, gentle and remote, without damage anymore from the damaging fact of Leisha's existence. Her very existence as damage. ". . . tell me about Jordan. He's five now? What's he like?"

Alice turned her head to look levelly into Leisha's eyes. "He's a happy, ordinary little boy. Completely ordinary."

Camden died a week later. After the funeral, Leisha tried to see her mother at the Brookfield Drug and Alcohol Abuse Center. Elizabeth Camden, she was told, saw no one except her only child, Alice Camden Watrous.

Susan Melling, dressed in black, drove Leisha to the airport. Susan talked deftly, determinedly, about Leisha's studies, about Harvard, about the *Review*. Leisha answered in monosyllables, but Susan persisted, asking questions, quietly insisting on answers: When would Leisha take her bar exams? Where was she interviewing for jobs? Gradually Leisha began to lose the numbness she had felt since her father's casket was lowered into the ground. She realized that Susan's persistent questioning was a kindness.

"He sacrificed a lot of people," Leisha said suddenly.

"Not me," Susan said. She pulled the car into the airport parking lot. "Only for a while there, when I gave up my work to do his. Roger didn't respect sacrifice much."

"Was he wrong?" Leisha said. The question came out with a kind of desperation she hadn't intended.

Susan smiled sadly. "No. He wasn't wrong. I should never have left my research. It took me a long time to come back to myself after that."

He does that to people, Leisha heard inside her head. Susan? Or Alice? She couldn't, for once, remember clearly. She saw her father in the old conservatory, potting and repotting the dramatic exotic flowers he had loved.

She was tired. It was muscle fatigue from stress, she knew, twenty minutes of rest would restore her. Her eyes burned from unaccustomed tears. She leaned her head back against the car seat and closed them.

Susan pulled the car into the airport parking lot and turned off the ignition. "There's something I want to tell you Leisha."

Leisha opened her eyes. "About the will?"

Susan smiled tightly. "No. You really don't have any problems with how he divided the estate, do you? It seems to you reasonable. But that's not it. The research team from Biotech and Chicago Medical has finished its analysis of Bernie Kuhn's brain."

Leisha turned to face Susan. She was startled by the complexity of Susan's expression. Determination, and satisfaction, and anger, and something else Leisha could not name.

Susan said, "We're going to publish next week, in the *New England Journal of Medicine*. Security has been unbelievably restricted – no leaks to the popular press. But I want to tell you now, myself, what we found. So you'll be prepared."

"Go on," Leisha said. Her chest felt tight.

"Do you remember when you and the other Sleepless kids took interleukin-1 to see what sleep was like? When you were sixteen?"

"How did you know about that?"

"You kids were watched a lot more closely than you think. Remember the headache you got?"

"Yes." She and Richard and Tony and Carol and Jeanine . . . after her rejection by the Olympic Committee, Jeanine had never skated again. She was a kindergarten teacher in Butte, Montana.

"Interleukin-1 is what I want to talk about. At least, partly. It's one of a whole group of substances that boost the immune system. They stimulate the production of antibodies, the activity of white blood cells, and a host of other immunoenhancements. Normal people have surges of IL-1 released during the slow-wave phases of sleep. That means that they – we – are getting boosts to the immune system during sleep. One of the questions we researchers asked ourselves twenty-eight years ago was: will Sleepless kids who don't get those surges of IL-1 get sick more often?"

"I've never been sick," Leisha said.

"Yes, you have. Chicken pox and three minor colds by the end of your fourth year," Susan said precisely. "But in general you were all a very healthy lot. So we researchers were left with the alternative theory of sleep-driven immunoenhancement: that the burst of immune activity existed as a counterpart to a greater vulnerability of the body in sleep to disease, probably in some way connected to the fluctuations in body temperature during REM sleep. In other words, sleep *caused* the immune vulnerability that endogenous pyrogens like IL-1 counteract. Sleep was the problem; immune-system enhancements were the solution. Without sleep, there would be no problem. Are you following this?"

"Yes."

"Of course you are. Stupid question." Susan brushed her hair off her face. It was going gray at the temples. There was a tiny brown age spot beneath her right ear.

"Over the years we collected thousands – maybe hundreds of thousands – of Single Photon Emission Tomography scans of you and the other kids' brains, plus endless EEGs, samples of cerebrospinal fluid, and all the rest of it. But we couldn't really see inside your brains, really know what's going on in there. Until Bernie Kuhn hit that embankment."

"Susan," Leisha said, "give it to me straight. Without more buildup."

"You're not going to age."

"What?"

"Oh, cosmetically, yes. Gray hair, wrinkles, sags. But the absence of sleep peptides and all the rest of it affects the immune and tissue-restoration systems in ways we don't understand. Bernie Kuhn had a perfect liver. Perfect lungs, perfect heart, perfect lymph nodes, perfect pancreas, perfect medulla oblongata. Not just healthy or young – *perfect*. There's a tissue-regeneration enhancement that clearly derives from the operation of the immune system but is radically different from anything we ever suspected. Organs show no wear and tear – not even the minimal amount expected in a seventeen-year-old. They just repair themselves, perfectly, on and on . . . and on."

"For how long?" Leisha whispered.

"Who the hell knows? Bernie Kuhn was young – maybe there's some compensatory mechanism that cuts in at some point and you'll all just collapse, like an entire fucking gallery of Dorian Grays. But I don't think so. Neither do I think it can go on forever, no tissue regeneration can do that. But a long, long time."

Leisha stared at the blurred reflections in the car windshield. She saw her father's face against the blue satin of his casket, banked with white roses. His heart, unregenerated, had given out.

Susan said, "The future is all speculative at this point. We know that the peptide structures that build up the pressure to sleep in normal people resemble the components of bacterial cell walls. Maybe there's a connection between sleep and pathogen receptivity. We don't know. But ignorance never stopped the tabloids. I wanted to prepare you because you're going to get called supermen, *Homo perfectus*, who all knows what. Immortal."

The two women sat in silence. Finally Leisha said, "I'm going to tell the others. On our datanet. Don't worry about the security. Kevin Baker designed Groupnet; nobody knows anything we don't want them to."

"You're that well organized already?"

"Yes."

Susan's mouth worked. She looked away from Leisha. "We better go in. You'll miss your flight."

"Susan . . ."

"What?"

"Thank you."

"You're welcome," Susan said, and in her voice Leisha heard the thing she had seen before in Susan's expression and not been able to name: it was longing.

Tissue regeneration. A long, long time, sang the blood in Leisha's ears on the flight to Boston. *Tissue regeneration*. And, eventually: *immortal*. No, not that, she told herself severely. Not that. The blood didn't listen.

"You sure smile a lot," said the man next to her in first class, a business traveler who had not recognized Leisha. "You coming from a big party in Chicago?"

"No. From a funeral."

The man looked shocked, then disgusted. Leisha looked out the window at the ground far below. Rivers like microcircuits, fields like neat index cards. And on the horizon fluffy white clouds like masses of exotic flowers, blooms in a conservatory filled with light.

The letter was no thicker than any hard-copy mail, but hard-copy mail addressed by hand to either of them was so rare that Richard was nervous. "It might be explosive." Leisha looked at the letter on their hall credenza. MS. LIESHA CAMDEN. Block letters, misspelled.

"It looks like a child's writing," she said.

Richard stood with head lowered, legs braced apart. But his expression was only weary. "Perhaps deliberately like a child's. You'd be more open to a child's writing, they might have figured."

"'They'? Richard, are we getting that paranoid?"

He didn't flinch from the question. "Yes. For the time being."

A week earlier the *New England Journal of Medicine* had published Susan's careful, sober article. An hour later the broadcast and datanet news had exploded in speculation, drama, outrage, and fear. Leisha and Richard, along with all the Sleepless on the Groupnet, had tracked and charted each of four components, looking for a dominant reaction: speculation ("The Sleepless may live for centuries, and this might lead to the following events . . ."); drama ("If a Sleepless marries only Sleepers, he may have lifetime enough for a dozen brides – and several dozen children, a bewildering blended family . . ."); outrage

("Tampering with the law of nature has only brought among us unnatural so-called people who will live with the unfair advantage of time: time to accumulate more kin, more power, more property than the rest of us could ever know . . ."); and fear ("How soon before the Super-race takes over?").

"They're all fear, of one kind or another," Carolyn Rizzolo finally said, and the Groupnet stopped their differentiated tracking.

Leisha was taking the final exams of her last year of law school. Each day comments followed her to the campus, along the corridors, and in the classroom; each day she forgot them in the grueling exam sessions, all students reduced to the same status of petitioner to the great university. Afterward, temporarily drained, she walked silently back home to Richard and the Groupnet, aware of the looks of people on the street, aware of her bodyguard, Bruce, striding between her and them.

"It will calm down," Leisha said. Richard didn't answer.

The town of Salt Springs, Texas, passed a local ordinance that no Sleepless could obtain a liquor license, on the grounds that civil rights statutes were built on the "all men were created equal" clause of the Declaration of Independence and Sleepless clearly were not covered. There were no Sleepless within a hundred miles of Salt Springs, and no one had applied for a new liquor license there for the past ten years, but the story was picked up by United Press and by Datanet News, and within twenty-four hours heated editorials appeared, on both sides of the issue, across the nation.

More local ordinances appeared. In Pollux, Pennsylvania, the Sleepless could be denied apartment rental on the grounds that their prolonged wakefulness would increase both wear and tear on the landlord's property and utility bills. In Cranston Estates, California, Sleepless were barred from operating twenty-four-hour businesses: "unfair competition." Iroquois County, New York, barred them from serving on county juries, arguing that a jury containing Sleepless, with their skewed idea of time, did not constitute "a jury of one's peers."

"All those statutes will be thrown out in superior courts," Leisha said. "But, God, the waste of money and docket time to do it!" A part of her mind noticed that her tone as she said this was Roger Camden's.

The state of Georgia, in which some sex acts between consenting adults were still a crime, made sex between a Sleepless and a Sleeper a third-degree felony, classing it with bestiality.

Kevin Baker had designed software that scanned the newsnets at high speed, flagged all stories involving discrimination or attacks on Sleepless,

and categorized them by type. The files were available on Groupnet.
Leisha read through them, then called Kevin. "Can't you create a
parallel program to flag defenses of us? We're getting a skewed picture."

"You're right," Kevin said, a little startled. "I didn't think of it."

"Think of it," Leisha said, grimly. Richard, watching her, said
nothing.

She was most upset by the stories about Sleepless children. Shunned
at school, verbal abuse by siblings, attacks by neighborhood bullies,
confused resentment from parents who had wanted an exceptional
child but had not bargained on one who might live centuries. The
school board of Cold River, Iowa, voted to bar Sleepless children from
conventional classrooms because their rapid learning "created feelings
of inadequacy in others, interfering with their education." The board
made funds available for Sleepless to have tutors at home. There were
no volunteers among the teaching staff. Leisha started spending as
much time on Groupnet with the kids, talking to them all night long,
as she did studying for her bar exams, scheduled for July.

Stella Bevington stopped using her modem.

Kevin's second program catalogued editorials urging fairness
toward Sleepless. The school board of Denver set aside funds for a
program in which gifted children, including the Sleepless, could use
their talents and build teamwork through tutoring even younger
children. Rive Beau, Louisiana, elected Sleepless Danielle du Cherney
to the city council, although Danielle was twenty-two and technically
too young to qualify. The prestigious medical research firm of Halley-
Hall gave much publicity to their hiring of Christopher Amren, a
Sleepless with a Ph.D. in cellular physics.

Dora Clarq, a Sleepless in Dallas, opened a letter addressed to her,
and a plastic explosive blew off her arm.

Leisha and Richard stared at the envelope on the hall credenza. The
paper was thick, cream-colored, but not expensive: the kind of paper
made of bulky newsprint dyed the shade of vellum. There was no
return address. Richard called Liz Bishop, a Sleepless who was
majoring in criminal justice in Michigan. He had never spoken with
her before – neither had Leisha – but she came on Groupnet immediately and told them how to open it, or she could fly up and do it if they
preferred. Richard and Leisha followed her directions for remote deto-
nation in the basement of the townhouse. Nothing blew up. When the
letter was open, they took it out and read it:

Dear Ms. Camden,

   You been pretty good to me and I'm sorry to do this but I quit. They are making it pretty hot for me at the union not officially but you know how it is. If I was you I wouldn't go to the union for another bodyguard I'd try to find one privately. But be careful. Again I'm sorry but I have to live too.

Bruce

   "I don't know whether to laugh or cry," Leisha said. "The two of us getting all this equipment, spending hours on this set-up so an explosive won't detonate . . ."

   "It's not as if I at least had a whole lot else to do," Richard said. Since the wave of anti-Sleepless sentiment, all but two of his marine-consultant clients, vulnerable to the marketplace and thus to public opinion, had canceled their accounts.

   Groupnet, still up on Leisha's terminal, shrilled in emergency over-ride. Leisha got there first. It was Tony.

   "Leisha. I'll need your legal help, if you'll give it. They're trying to fight me on Sanctuary. Please fly down here."

Sanctuary was raw brown gashes in the late-spring earth. It was situated in the Allegheny Mountains of southern New York State, old hills rounded by age and covered with pine and hickory. A superb road led from the closest town, Belmont, to Sanctuary. Low, maintenance-free buildings, whose design was plain but graceful, stood in various stages of completion. Jennifer Sharifi, looking strained, met Leisha and Richard. "Tony wants to talk to you, but first he asked me to show you both around."

   "What's wrong?" Leisha asked quietly. She had never met Jennifer before, but no Sleepless looked like that – pinched, spent, *weary* – unless the stress level was enormous.

   Jennifer didn't try to evade the question. "Later. First look at Sanctuary. Tony respects your opinion enormously, Leisha; he wants you to see everything."

   The dormitories each held fifty, with communal rooms for cooking, dining, relaxing, and bathing, and a warren of separate offices and studios and labs for work. "We're calling them 'dorms' anyway, despite the etymology," Jennifer said, trying to smile. Leisha glanced at Richard. The smile was a failure.

   She was impressed, despite herself, with the completeness of Tony's plans for lives that would be both communal and intensely private.

There was a gym, a small hospital – "By the end of next year, we'll have eighteen AMA-certified doctors, you know, and four are thinking of coming here" – a day-care facility, a school, an intensive-crop farm. "Most of our food will come in from the outside, of course. So will most people's jobs, although they'll do as much of them as possible from here, over datanets. We're not cutting ourselves off from the world – only creating a safe place from which to trade with it." Leisha didn't answer.

Apart from the power facilities, self-supported Y-energy, she was most impressed with the human planning. Tony had Sleepless interested from virtually every field they would need both to care for themselves and to deal with the outside world. "Lawyers and accountants come first," Jennifer said. "That's our first line of defense in safeguarding ourselves. Tony recognizes that most modern battles for power are fought in the courtroom and boardroom."

But not all. Last, Jennifer showed them the plans for physical defense. She explained them with a mixture of defiance and pride: every effort had been made to stop attackers without hurting them. Electronic surveillance completely circled the 10 square miles Jennifer had purchased – some *counties* were smaller than that, Leisha thought, dazed. When breached, a force field a half-mile within the E-gate activated, delivering electric shocks to anyone on foot – "But only on the *outside* of the field. We don't want any of our kids hurt." Unmanned penetration by vehicles or robots was identified by a system that located all moving metal above a certain mass within Sanctuary. Any moving metal that did not carry a special signaling device designed by Donna Pospula, a Sleepless who had patented important electronic components, was suspect.

"Of course, we're not set up for an air attack or an outright army assault," Jennifer said. "But we don't expect that. Only the haters in self-motivated hate." Her voice sagged.

Leisha touched the hard copy of the security plans with one finger. They troubled her. "If we can't integrate ourselves into the world . . . free trade should imply free movement."

"Yeah. Well," Jennifer said, such an uncharacteristic Sleepless remark – both cynical and inarticulate – that Leisha looked up. "I have something to tell you, Leisha."

"What?"

"Tony isn't here."

"Where is he?"

"In Allegheny County Jail. It's true we're having zoning battles about Sanctuary – zoning! In this isolated spot. But this is something else, something that just happened this morning. Tony's been arrested for the kidnapping of Timmy DeMarzo."

The room wavered. "FBI?"

"Yes."

"How . . . how did they find out?"

"Some agent eventually cracked the case. They didn't tell us how. Tony needs a lawyer, Leisha. Dana Monteiro has already agreed, but Tony wants you."

"Jennifer – I don't even take the bar exams until July."

"He says he'll wait. Dana will act as his lawyer in the meantime. Will you pass the bar?"

"Of course. But I already have a job lined up with Morehouse, Kennedy & Anderson in New York – " She stopped. Richard was looking at her hard, Jennifer gazing down at the floor. Leisha said quietly, "What will he plead?"

"Guilty," Jennifer said. "With – what is it called legally? – extenuating circumstances."

Leisha nodded. She had been afraid Tony would want to plead not guilty: more lies, subterfuge, ugly politics. Her mind ran swiftly over extenuating circumstances, precedents, tests to precedents . . . They could use *Clements v. Voy* . . .

"Dana is at the jail now," Jennifer said. "Will you drive in with me?"

"Yes."

In Belmont, the county seat, they were not allowed to see Tony. Dana Monteiro, as his attorney, could go in and out freely. Leisha, not officially an attorney at all, could go nowhere. This was told them by a man in the D.A.'s office whose face stayed immobile while he spoke to them and who spat on the ground behind their shoes when they turned to leave, even though this left him with a smear of spittle on his courthouse floor.

Richard and Leisha drove their rental car to the airport for the flight back to Boston. On the way Richard told Leisha he was leaving her. He was moving to Sanctuary, now, even before it was functional, to help with the planning and building.

She stayed most of the time in her townhouse, studying ferociously for the bar exams or checking on the Sleepless children through Groupnet. She had not hired another bodyguard to replace Bruce, which made her reluctant to go outside very much; the reluctance in turn made her angry with herself. Once or twice a day she scanned Kevin's electronic news clippings.

There were signs of hope. The *New York Times* ran an editorial, widely reprinted on the electronic news services:

PROSPERITY AND HATRED: A LOGIC CURVE WE'D RATHER NOT SEE

The United States has never been a country that much values calm, logic, rationality. We have, as a people, tended to label these things "cold." We have, as a people, tended to admire feeling and action: we exalt in our stories and our memorials; not the creation of the Constitution but its defense at Iwo Jima; not the intellectual achievements of a Stephen Hawking but the heroic passion of a Charles Lindbergh; not the inventors of the monorails and computers that unite us but the composers of the angry songs of rebellion that divide us.

A peculiar aspect of this phenomenon is that it grows stronger in times of prosperity. The better off our citizenry the greater their contempt for the calm reasoning that got them there, and the more passionate their indulgence in emotion. Consider, in the last century the gaudy excesses of the Roaring Twenties and the antiestablishment contempt of the sixties. Consider, in our own century the unprecedented prosperity brought about by Y-energy – and then consider that Kenzo Yagai, except to his followers, was seen as a greedy and bloodless logician, while our national adulation goes to neonihilist writer Stephen Castelli, to "feelie" actress Brenda Foss, and to daredevil gravity-well diver Jim Morse Luter.

But most of all, as you ponder this phenomenon in your Y-energy houses, consider the current outpouring of irrational feeling directed at the "Sleepless" since the publication of the joint findings of the Biotech Institute and the Chicago Medical School concerning Sleepless tissue regeneration.

Most of the Sleepless are intelligent. Most of them are calm, if you define that much-maligned word to mean directing one's energies into solving problems rather than to emoting about them. (Even Pulitzer Prize winner Carolyn Rizzolo gave us a stunning play of ideas, not of passions run amok.) All of them show a natural bent toward achievement, a bent given a decided boost by the one-third more time in their days to achieve in. Their achievements lie, for the most part, in logical fields rather than emotional ones: Computers. Law. Finance. Physics. Medical research. They are rational, orderly, calm, intelligent, cheerful, young, and possibly very long-lived.

And, in our United States of unprecedented prosperity, increasingly hated.

Does the hatred that we have seen flower so fully over the last few months really grow, as many claim, from the "unfair advantage" the Sleepless have over the rest of us in securing jobs, promotions, money, success? Is it really envy over the Sleepless' good fortune? Or does it come from something more pernicious, rooted in our tradition of shoot-from-the-hip American action: hatred of the logical, the calm, the considered? Hatred in fact of the superior mind?

If so, perhaps we should think deeply about the founders of this country: Jefferson, Washington, Paine, Adams – inhabitants of the Age of Reason, all. These men created our orderly and balanced system of laws precisely to protect the property and achievements created by the individual efforts of balanced and rational minds. The Sleepless may be our severest internal test yet of our own sober belief in law and order. No, the Sleepless were not "created equal," but our attitudes toward them should be examined with a care equal to our soberest jurisprudence. We may not like what we learn about our own motives, but our credibility as a people may depend on the rationality and intelligence of the examination.

Both have been in short supply in the public reaction to last month's research findings.

Law is not theater. Before we write laws reflecting gaudy and dramatic feelings, we must be very sure we understand the difference.

Leisha hugged herself, gazing in delight at the screen, smiling. She called the *New York Times:* who had written the editorial? The receptionist, cordial when she answered the phone, grew brusque. The *Times* was not releasing that information, "prior to internal investigation."

It could not dampen her mood. She whirled around the apartment, after days of sitting at her desk or screen. Delight demanded physical action. She washed dishes, picked up books. There were gaps in the furniture patterns where Richard had taken pieces that belonged to him; a little quieter now, she moved the furniture to close the gaps.

Susan Melling called to tell her about the *Times* editorial; they talked warmly for a few minutes. When Susan hung up, the phone rang again.

"Leisha? Your voice still sounds the same. This is Stewart Sutter."

"Stewart." She had not seen him for years. Their romance had lasted two years and then dissolved, not from any painful issue so much as from the press of both their studies. Standing by the comm terminal, hearing his voice, Leisha suddenly felt again his hands on her breasts in the cramped dormitory bed: all those years before she had found a good use for a bed. The phantom hands became Richard's hands, and a sudden pain pierced her.

"Listen," Stewart said. "I'm calling because there's some information I think you should know. You take your bar exams next week, right? And then you have a tentative job with Morehouse, Kennedy & Anderson."

"How do you know all that, Stewart?"

"Men's-room gossip. Well, not as bad as that. But the New York legal community – that part of it, anyway – is smaller than you think. And you're a pretty visible figure."

"Yes," Leisha said neutrally.

"Nobody has the slightest doubt you'll be called to the bar. But there is some doubt about the job with Morehouse, Kennedy. You've got two senior partners, Alan Morehouse and Seth Brown, who have changed their minds since this . . . flap. 'Adverse publicity for the firm,' 'turning law into a circus,' blah blah blah. You know the drill. But you've also got two powerful champions, Ann Carlyle and Michael Kennedy, the old man himself. He's quite a mind. Anyway, I wanted you to know all this so you can recognize exactly what the situation is and know whom to count on in the in-fighting."

"Thank you," Leisha said. "Stew . . . why do you care if I get it or not? Why should it matter to you?"

There was a silence on the other end of the phone. Then Stewart said, very low, "We're not all noodleheads out here, Leisha. Justice does still matter to some of us. So does achievement."

Light rose in her, a bubble of buoyant light.

Stewart said, "You have a lot of support here for that stupid zoning fight over Sanctuary, too. You might not realize that, but you do. What the parks commission crowd is trying to pull is . . . but they're just being used as fronts. You know that. Anyway, when it gets as far as the courts, you'll have all the help you need."

"Sanctuary isn't my doing. At all."

"No? Well, I meant the plural you."

"Thank you. I mean that. How are you doing?"

"Fine. I'm a daddy now."

"Really! Boy or girl?"

"Girl. A beautiful little bitch, drives me crazy. I'd like you to meet my wife sometime, Leisha."

"I'd like that," Leisha said.

She spent the rest of the night studying for her bar exams. The bubble stayed with her. She recognized exactly what it was: joy.

It was going to be all right. The contract, unwritten, between her and her society – Kenzo Yagai's society, Roger Camden's society – would hold. With dissent and strife and, yes, some hatred: she suddenly thought of Tony's beggars in Spain, furious at the strong because they themselves were not. Yes. But it would hold.

She believed that.

She did.

VII

Leisha took her bar exams in July. They did not seem hard to her. Afterward three classmates, two men and a woman, made a fakely casual point of talking to Leisha until she had climbed safely into a taxi whose driver obviously did not recognize her, or stop signs. The three were all Sleepers. A pair of undergraduates, clean-shaven blond men with the long faces and pointless arrogance of rich stupidity, eyed Leisha and sneered. Leisha's female classmate sneered back.

Leisha had a flight to Chicago the next morning. Alice was going to join her there. They had to clean out the big house on the lake, dispose of Roger's personal property, put the house on the market. Leisha had had no time to do it earlier.

She remembered her father in the conservatory, wearing an ancient flat-topped hat he had picked up somewhere, potting orchids and jasmine and passion flowers.

When the doorbell rang she was startled: she almost never had visitors. Eagerly, she turned on the outside camera – maybe it was Jonathan or Martha, back in Boston to surprise her, to celebrate – why hadn't she thought before about some sort of celebration?

Richard stood gazing up at the camera. He had been crying.

She tore open the door. Richard made no move to come in. Leisha saw that what the camera had registered as grief was actually something else: tears of rage.

"Tony's dead."

Leisha put out her hand, blindly. Richard did not take it.

"They killed him in prison. Not the authorities – the other prisoners. In the recreation yard. Murderers, rapists, looters, scum of the earth – and they thought they had the right to kill *him* because he was different."

Now Richard did grab her arm, so hard that something, some bone, shifted beneath the flesh and pressed on a nerve. "Not just different –

better. Because he was better, because we all are, we goddamn just
don't stand up and shout it out of some misplaced feeling for *their*
feelings . . . God!"

Leisha pulled her arm free and rubbed it, numb, staring at Richard's
contorted face.

"They beat him to death with a lead pipe. No one even knows how
they got a lead pipe. They beat him on the back of the head and they
rolled him over and – "

"Don't!" Leisha said. It came out a whimper.

Richard looked at her. Despite his shouting, his violent grip on her
arm, Leisha had the confused impression that this was the first time he
had actually seen her. She went on rubbing her arm, staring at him in
terror.

He said quietly, "I've come to take you to Sanctuary, Leisha. Dan
Walcott and Vernon Bulriss are in the car outside. The three of us will
carry you out, if necessary. But you're coming. You see that, don't
you? You're not safe here, with your high profile and your spectacular
looks – you're a natural target if anyone is. Do we have to force you?
Or do you finally see for yourself that we have no choice – the bastards
have left us no choice – except Sanctuary?"

Leisha closed her eyes. Tony, at fourteen, at the beach. Tony, his
eyes ferocious and alight, the first to reach out his hand for the glass of
Interleukin-l. Beggars in Spain.

"I'll come."

She had never known such anger. It scared her, coming in bouts
throughout the long night, receding but always returning again.
Richard held her in his arms, sitting with their backs against the wall
of her library, and his holding made no difference at all. In the living
room Dan and Vernon talked in low voices.

Sometimes the anger erupted in shouting, and Leisha heard herself
and thought, *I don't know you*. Sometimes it became crying, sometimes
talking about Tony, about all of them. Not the shouting nor the crying
nor the talking, eased her at all.

Planning did, a little. In a cold dry voice she didn't recognize, Leisha
told Richard about the trip to close the house in Chicago. She had to go;
Alice was already there. If Richard and Dan and Vernon put Leisha on
the plane, and Alice met her at the other end with union bodyguards, she
should be safe enough. Then she would change her return ticket from
Boston to Belmont and drive with Richard to Sanctuary.

"People are already arriving," Richard said. "Jennifer Sharifi is organizing it, greasing the Sleeper suppliers with so much money they can't resist. What about this townhouse here, Leisha? Your furniture and terminal and clothes?"

Leisha looked around her familiar office. Law books lined the walls, red and green and brown, although most of the same information was on-line. A coffee cup rested on a printout on the desk. Beside it was the receipt she had requested from the taxi driver this afternoon, a giddy souvenir of the day she had passed her bar exams; she had thought of having it framed. Above the desk was a holographic portrait of Kenzo Yagai.

"Let it rot," Leisha said.

Richard's arm tightened around her.

"I've never seen you like this," Alice said, subdued. "It's more than just clearing out the house, isn't it?"

"Let's get on with it," Leisha said. She yanked a suit from her father's closet. "Do you want any of this stuff for your husband?"

"It wouldn't fit."

"The hats?"

"No," Alice said. "Leisha – what is it?"

"Let's just *do* it!" She yanked all the clothes from Camden's closet, piled them on the floor, scrawled FOR VOLUNTEER AGENCY on a piece of paper, and dropped it on top of the pile. Silently, Alice started adding clothes from the dresser, which already bore a taped paper scrawled ESTATE AUCTION.

The curtains were already down throughout the house; Alice had done that yesterday. She had also rolled up the rugs. Sunset glared redly on the bare wooden floors.

"What about your old room?" Leisha said "what do you want there?"

"I've already tagged it," Alice said. "A mover will come Thursday."

"Fine. What else?"

"The conservatory. Sanderson has been watering everything, but he didn't really know what needed how much, so some of the plants are – "

"Fire Sanderson," Leisha said curtly. "The exotics can die. Or have them sent to a hospital, if you'd rather. Just watch out for the ones that are poisonous. Come on, let's do the library."

Alice sat slowly on a rolled-up rug in the middle of Camden's bedroom. She had cut her hair; Leisha thought it looked ugly, jagged brown spikes around her broad face. She had also gained more weight. She was starting to look like their mother.

Alice said, "Do you remember the night I told you I was pregnant? Just before you left for Harvard?"

"Let's do the library."

"Do you?" Alice said. "For God's sake, can't you just once listen to someone else, Leisha? Do you have to be so much like Daddy every single minute?"

"I'm not like Daddy!"

"The hell you're not. You're exactly what he made you. But that's not the point. Do you remember that night?"

Leisha walked over the rug and out the door. Alice simply sat. After a minute Leisha walked back in. "I remember."

"You were near tears," Alice said implacably. Her voice was quiet. "I don't even remember exactly why. Maybe because I wasn't going to college after all. But I put my arms around you, and for the first time in years – years, Leisha – I felt you really were my sister. Despite all of it – the roaming the halls all night and the show-off arguments with Daddy and the special school and the artificially long legs and golden hair – all that crap. You seemed to need me to hold you. You seemed to need me. You seemed to *need*."

"What are you saying?" Leisha demanded. "That you can only be close to someone if they're in trouble and need you? That you can only be a sister if I was in some kind of pain, open sores running? Is that the bond between you Sleepers? 'Protect me while I'm unconscious, I'm just as crippled as you are'?"

"No," Alice said. "I'm saying that *you* could be a sister only if you were in some kind of pain."

Leisha stared at her. "You're stupid, Alice."

Alice said calmly, "I know that. Compared to you, I am. I know that."

Leisha jerked her head angrily. She felt ashamed of what she had just said, and yet it was true, and they both knew it was true, and anger still lay in her like a dark void, formless and hot. It was the formless part that was the worst. Without shape, there could be no action; without action, the anger went on burning her, choking her.

Alice said, "When I was twelve, Susan gave me a dress for our birthday. You were away somewhere, on one of those overnight field trips your fancy progressive school did all the time. The dress was silk, pale blue, with antique lace – very beautiful. I was thrilled, not only because it was beautiful but because Susan had gotten it for me and gotten software for you. The dress was mine. Was, I thought, *me*." In the gathering gloom Leisha could barely make out her broad, plain features. "The first time I wore it a boy said, 'Stole your sister's dress, Alice? Snitched it while she was *sleeping*?' Then he laughed like crazy, the way they always did.

"I threw the dress away. I didn't even explain to Susan, although I think she would have understood. Whatever was yours was yours, and whatever wasn't yours was yours, too. That's the way Daddy set it up. The way he hard-wired it into our genes."

"You, too?" Leisha said. "You're no different from the other envious beggars?"

Alice stood up from the rug. She did it slowly, leisurely, brushing dust off the back of her wrinkled skirt, smoothing the print fabric. Then she walked over and hit Leisha in the mouth.

"Now do you see me as real?" Alice asked quietly.

Leisha put her hand to her mouth. She felt blood. The phone rang, Camden's unlisted personal line. Alice walked over, picked it up, listened, and held it calmly out to Leisha. "It's for you."

Numb, Leisha took it.

"Leisha? This is Kevin. Listen; something's happened. Stella Bevington called me, on the phone, not Groupnet; I think her parents took away her modem. I picked up the phone and she screamed, 'This is Stella! They're hitting me, he's drunk – ' and then the line went dead. Randy's gone to Sanctuary – hell, they've *all* gone. You're closest to her; she's still in Skokie. You better get there fast. Have you got bodyguards you trust?"

"Yes," Leisha said, although she hadn't. The anger – finally – took form. "I can handle it."

"I don't know how you'll get her out of there," Kevin said. "They'll recognize you, they know she called somebody, they might even have knocked her out . . ."

"I'll handle it," Leisha said.

"Handle what?" Alice said.

Leisha faced her. Even though she knew she shouldn't, she said, "What your people do. To one of ours. A seven-year-old kid who's getting beaten up by her parents because she's Sleepless – because she's *better* than you are – " She ran down the stairs and out to the rental car she had driven from the airport.

Alice ran right down with her. "Not your car, Leisha. They can trace a rental car just like that. My car."

Leisha screamed. "If you think you're – "

Alice yanked open the door of her battered Toyota, a model so old the Y-energy cones weren't even concealed but hung like drooping jowls on either side. She shoved Leisha into the passenger seat, slammed the door, and rammed herself behind the wheel. Her hands were steady. "Where?"

Blackness swooped over Leisha. She put her head down, as far between her knees as the cramped Toyota would allow. Two – no, three – days since she had eaten. Since the night before the bar exams. The faintness receded, swept over her again as soon as she raised her head.

She told Alice the address in Skokie.

"Stay way in the back," Alice said. "And there's a scarf in the glove compartment – put it on. Low, to hide as much of your face as possible."

Alice had stopped the car along Highway 42. Leisha said. "This isn't – "

"It's a union quick-guard place. We have to look like we have some protection, Leisha. We don't need to tell him anything. I'll hurry."

She was out in three minutes with a huge man in a cheap dark suit. He squeezed into the front seat beside Alice and said nothing at all. Alice did not introduce him.

The house was small, a little shabby, with lights on downstairs, none upstairs. The first stars shone in the north, away from Chicago. Alice said to the guard, "Get out of the car and stand here by the car door – no, more in the light – and don't do anything unless I'm attacked in some way." The man nodded. Alice started up the walk. Leisha scrambled out of the backseat and caught her sister two-thirds of the way to the plastic front door.

"Alice, what the hell are you doing? *I* have to – "

"Keep your voice down," Alice said, glancing at thc guard. "Leisha, *think*. You'll be recognized. Here, near Chicago, with a Sleepless daughter – these people have looked at your picture in magazines for years. They've watched long-range holovids of you. They know you. They know you're going to be a lawyer. Me they've never seen. I'm nobody."

"Alice – "

"For Chrissake, get back in the car!" Alice hissed, and pounded on the front door.

Leisha drew off the walk, into the shadow of a willow tree. A man opened the door. His face was completely blank.

Alice said, "Child Protection Agency. We got a call from a little girl, this number. Let me in."

"There's no little girl here."

"This is an emergency, priority one," Alice said. "Child Protection Act 186. Let me in!"

The man, still blank-faced, glanced at the huge figure by the car. "You got a search warrant?"

"I don't need one in a priority-one child emergency. If you don't let me in, you're going to have legal snarls like you never bargained for."

Leisha clamped her lips together. No one would believe that; it was legal gobbledygook . . . Her lip throbbed where Alice had hit her.

The man stood aside to let Alice enter.

The guard started forward. Leisha hesitated, then let him. He entered with Alice.

Leisha waited, alone, in the dark.

In three minutes they were out, the guard carrying a child. Alice's broad face gleamed pale in the porch light. Leisha sprang forward, opened the car door, and helped the guard ease the child inside. The guard was frowning, a slow puzzled frown shot with wariness.

Alice said, "Here. This is an extra hundred dollars. To get back to the city by yourself."

"Hey . . ." the guard said, but he took the money. He stood looking after them as Alice pulled away.

"He'll go straight to the police," Leisha said despairingly. "He has to, or risk his union membership."

"I know," Alice said. "But by that time we'll be out of the car."

"Where?"

"At the hospital," Alice said.

"Alice, we can't – " Leisha didn't finish. She turned to the backseat. "Stella? Are you conscious?"

"Yes," said the small voice.

Leisha groped until her fingers found the rear-seat illuminator. Stella lay stretched out on the backseat, her face distorted with pain. She cradled her left arm in her right. A single bruise colored her face, above the left eye.

"You're Leisha Camden," the child said, and started to cry.

"Her arm's broken," Alice said.

"Honey, can you . . ." Leisha's throat felt thick; she had trouble getting the words out ". . . can you hold on till we get you to a doctor?"

"Yes," Stella said. "Just don't take me back there!"

"We won't," Leisha said. "Ever." She glanced at Alice and saw Tony's face.

Alice said, "There's a community hospital about ten miles south of here."

"How do you know that?"

"I was there once. Drug overdose," Alice said briefly. She drove hunched over the wheel, with the face of someone thinking furiously. Leisha thought, too, trying to see a way around the legal charge of kidnapping. They probably couldn't say the child came willingly: Stella would undoubtedly cooperate, but at her age and in her condition she was probably *non sui juris*, her word would have no legal weight . . .

"Alice, we can't even get her into the hospital without insurance information. Verifiable on-line."

"Listen," Alice said, not to Leisha but over her shoulder, toward the backseat. "Here's what we're going to do, Stella. I'm going to tell them you're my daughter and you fell off a big rock you were climbing while we stopped for a snack at a roadside picnic area. We're driving from California to Philadelphia to see your grandmother. Your name is Jordan Watrous and you're five years old. Got that, honey?"

"I'm seven," Stella said. "Almost eight."

"You're a very large five. Your birthday is March twenty-third. Can you do this, Stella?"

"Yes," the little girl said. Her voice was stronger.

Leisha stared at Alice. "Can *you* do this?"

"Of course I can," Alice said. "I'm Roger Camden's daughter."

Alice half carried, half supported Stella into the emergency room of the small community hospital. Leisha watched from the car: the short stocky woman, the child's thin body with the twisted arm. Then she drove Alice's car to the farthest corner of the parking lot, under the dubious cover of a skimpy maple, and locked it. She tied the scarf more securely around her face.

Alice's license plate number, and her name, would be in every police and rental-car databank by now. The medical banks were slower; often they uploaded from local precincts only once a day, resenting the governmental interference in what was still, despite a half century of battle, a private-sector enterprise. Alice and Stella would probably be all right in the hospital. Probably. But Alice could not rent another car.

Leisha could.

But the data file that would flash to rental agencies on Alice Camden Watrous might or might not include that she was Leisha Camden's twin.

Leisha looked at the rows of cars in the lot. A flashy luxury Chrysler, an Ikeda van, a row of middle-class Toyotas and Mercedes, a vintage

'99 Cadillac – she could imagine the owner's face if that were missing – ten or twelve cheap runabouts, a hovercar with the uniformed driver asleep at the wheel. And a battered farm truck.

Leisha walked over to the truck. A man sat at the wheel, smoking. She thought of her father.

"Hello," Leisha said.

The man rolled down his window but didn't answer. He had greasy brown hair.

"See that hovercar over there?" Leisha said. She made her voice sound young, high. The man glanced at it indifferently; from this angle you couldn't see that the driver was asleep. "That's my bodyguard. He thinks I'm in the hospital, the way my father told me to, getting this lip looked at." She could feel her mouth swollen from Alice's blow.

"So?"

Leisha stamped her foot. "So I don't want to be inside. He's a shit and so's Daddy. I want out. I'll give you four thousand bank credits for your truck. Cash."

The man's eyes widened. He tossed away his cigarette, looked again at the hovercar. The driver's shoulders were broad, and the car was within easy screaming distance.

"All nice and legal," Leisha said, and tried to smirk. Her knees felt watery.

"Let me see the cash."

Leisha backed away from the truck, to where he could not reach her. She took the money from her arm clip. She was used to carrying a lot of cash; there had always been Bruce, or someone like Bruce. There had always been safety.

"Get out of the truck on the other side," Leisha said, "and lock the door behind you. Leave the keys on the seat, where I can see them from here. Then I'll put the money on the roof where you can see it."

The man laughed, a sound like gravel pouring. "Regular little Dabney Engh, aren't you? Is that what they teach you society debs at your fancy schools?"

Leisha had no idea who Dabney Engh was. She waited, watching the man try to think of a way to cheat her, and tried to hide her contempt. She thought of Tony.

"All right," he said, and slid out of the truck.

"Lock the door!"

He grinned, opened the door again, locked it. Leisha put the money on the roof, yanked open the driver's door, clambered in, locked the door, and powered up the window. The man laughed. She put the key into the ignition, started the truck, and drove toward the street. Her hands trembled.

She drove slowly around the block twice. When she came back, the man was gone, and the driver of the hovercar was still asleep. She had wondered if the man would wake him, out of sheer malice, but he had not. She parked the truck and waited.

An hour and a half later Alice and a nurse wheeled Stella out of the emergency entrance. Leisha leaped out of the truck and yelled, "Coming, Alice!" waving both her arms. It was too dark to see Alice's expression; Leisha could only hope that Alice showed no dismay at the battered truck, that she had not told the nurse to expect a red car.

Alice said, "This is Julie Bergadon, a friend that I called while you were setting Jordan's arm." The nurse nodded, uninterested. The two women helped Stella into the high truck cab; there was no backseat. Stella had a cast on her arm and looked drugged.

"How?" Alice said as they drove off.

Leisha didn't answer. She was watching a police hovercar land at the other end of the parking lot. Two officers got out and strode purposefully toward Alice's locked car under the skimpy maple.

"My God," Alice said. For the first time she sounded frightened.

"They won't trace us," Leisha said. "Not to this truck. Count on it."

"Leisha." Alice's voice spiked with fear. "Stella's *asleep*."

Leisha glanced at the child, slumped against Alice's shoulder. "No, she's not. She's unconscious from painkillers."

"Is that all right? Normal? For . . . her?"

"We can black out. We can even experience substance-induced sleep." Tony and she and Richard and Jeanine in the midnight woods . . . "Didn't you know that, Alice?"

"No."

"We don't know very much about each other, do we?"

They drove south in silence. Finally Alice said, "Where are we going to take her, Leisha?"

"I don't know. Any one of the Sleepless would be the first place the police would check – "

"You can't risk it. Not the way things are," Alice said. She sounded weary. "But all my friends are in California. I don't think we could drive this rust bucket that far before getting stopped."

"It wouldn't make it anyway."

"What should we do?"

"Let me think."

At an expressway exit stood a pay phone. It wouldn't be data shielded, as Groupnet was. Would Kevin's open line be tapped? Probably.

There was no doubt the Sanctuary line would be.

Sanctuary. All of them going there or already there, Kevin had said. Holed up, trying to pull the worn Allegheny Mountains around them like a safe little den. Except for the children like Stella, who could not.

Where? With whom?

Leisha closed her eyes. The Sleepless were out; the police would find Stella within hours. Susan Melling? But she had been Alice's all-too-visible stepmother and was co-beneficiary of Camden's will; they would question her almost immediately. It couldn't be anyone traceable to Alice. It could only be a Sleeper that Leisha knew, and trusted, and why should anyone at all fit that description? Why should she risk so much on anyone who did? She stood a long time in the dark phone kiosk. Then she walked to the truck. Alice was asleep, her head thrown back against the seat. A tiny line of drool ran down her chin. Her face was white and drained in the bad light from the kiosk. Leisha walked back to the phone.

"Stewart? Stewart Sutter?"

"Yes?"

"This is Leisha Camden. Something has happened." She told the story tersely, in bald sentences. Stewart did not interrupt.

"Leisha – " Stewart said, and stopped.

"I need help, Stewart." "*I'll help you, Alice.*" "*I don't need your help.*" A wind whistled over the dark field beside the kiosk, and Leisha shivered. She heard in the wind the thin keen of a beggar. In the wind, in her own voice.

"All right," Stewart said, "this is what we'll do. I have a cousin in Ripley, New York, just over the state line from Pennsylvania on the route you'll be driving east. It has to be in New York; I'm licensed in New York. Take the little girl there. I'll call my cousin and tell her you're coming. She's an elderly woman, was quite an activist in her youth; her name is Janet Patterson. The town is – "

"What makes you so sure she'll get involved? She could go to jail. And so could you."

"She's been in jail so many times you wouldn't believe it. Political protests going all the way back to Vietnam. But no one's going to jail. I'm now your attorney of record, I'm privileged. I'm going to get Stella declared a ward of the state. That shouldn't be too hard with the hospital records you established in Skokie. Then she can he transferred to a foster home in New York; I know just the place, people who are fair and kind. Then Alice – "

"She's resident in Illinois. You can't – "

"Yes, I can. Since those research findings about the Sleepless life span have come out, legislators have been railroaded by stupid constituents scared or jealous or just plain angry. The result is a body of so-called 'law' riddled with contradictions, absurdities, and loopholes. None of it will stand in the long run – or at least I hope not – but in the meantime it can all be exploited. I can use it to create the most goddamn convoluted case for Stella that anybody ever saw, and in the meantime she won't be returned home. But that won't work for Alice – she'll need an attorney licensed in Illinois."

"We have one," Leisha said. "Candace Holt."

"No, not a Sleepless. Trust me on this, Leisha. I'll find somebody good. There's a man in – are you crying?"

"No," Leisha said, crying.

"Ah, God," Stewart said. "Bastards. I'm sorry all this happened, Leisha."

"Don't be," Leisha said.

When she had directions to Stewart's cousin, she walked back to the truck. Alice was still asleep, Stella still unconscious. Leisha closed the truck door as quietly as possible. The engine balked and roared, but Alice didn't wake. There was a crowd of people with them in the narrow and darkened cab: Stewart Sutter, Tony Indivino, Susan Melling, Kenzo Yagai, Roger Camden.

To Stewart Sutter she said, You called to inform me about the situation at Morehouse, Kennedy. You are risking your career and your cousin for Stella. And you stand to gain nothing. Like Susan telling me in advance about Bernie Kuhn's brain. Susan, who lost her life to Daddy's dream and regained it by her own strength. A contract without consideration for each side is not a contract: every first-year student knows that.

To Kenzo Yagai she said, Trade isn't always linear. You missed that. If Stewart gives me something, and I give Stella something, and ten years from now Stella is a different person because of that and gives something to someone else as yet unknown – it's an ecology. An *ecology* of trade, yes, each niche needed, even if they're not contractually bound. Does a horse need a fish? *Yes.*

To Tony she said, Yes, there are beggars in Spain who trade nothing, give nothing, do nothing. But there are *more* than beggars in Spain. Withdraw from the beggars, you withdraw from the whole damn country. And you withdraw from the possibility of the ecology of help. That's what Alice wanted, all those years ago in her bedroom. Pregnant, scared, angry, jealous, she wanted to help *me,* and I wouldn't let her because I didn't need it. But I do now. And she did then. Beggars need to help as well as be helped.

And, finally, there was only Daddy left. She could *see* him, bright-eyed, holding thick-leaved exotic flowers in his strong hands. To Camden she said, You were wrong. Alice is special. Oh, Daddy – the specialness of Alice! You were *wrong*.

As soon as she thought this, lightness filled her. Not the buoyant bubble of joy, not the hard clarity of examination, but something else: sunshine, soft through the conservatory glass, where two children ran in and out. She suddenly felt light herself, not buoyant but translucent, a medium for the sunshine to pass clear through, on its way to some-where else.

She drove the sleeping woman and the wounded child through the night, east, toward the state line.

Rumfuddle

JACK VANCE

John Holbrook Vance (1916–   ) is one of the premier stylists of science fiction, popular world-wide and influential on other writers for six decades. His book *The Dying Earth* (1950), set in a fantastically distant future, is one of the classics of genre science fiction. It is also one of those genre-stretching works that blur the borders between science fiction and fantasy, in the manner of the *Weird Tales* writers of the 1920s and '30s. He has written award-winning mysteries under his full name, and as Ellery Queen (many of the later novels of Queen were written by SF writers such as Theodore Sturgeon, Avram Davidson, and Vance). He is a huge man, a lover of hot jazz and writing, but also a carpenter by trade who was still, in the 1980s, building and rebuilding his own house.

Vance found his writing voice early and hit his stride in the 1950s. Since then he has produced a continuing stream of exquisite work, much of it brilliant. Critics often praise his intricacies and ironies, his subtle wit, his settings and atmospherics. Yet his characters are usually motivated by common passions, no matter how nicely expressed, and his plots are clever. He is still writing distinctive novels of fantasy and SF and winning genre awards in the mid-1990s. He is most often at his best in the novel form, but this piece is one of his later novellas, pure Vance compressed and distilled.

I

From *Memoirs and Reflections,* by Alan Robertson:

Often I hear myself declared humanity's preeminent benefactor, though the jocular occasionally raise a claim in favor of the original serpent. After all circumspection I really cannot dispute the judgment. My place in history is secure; my name will persist as if it were printed indelibly across the sky. All of which I find absurd but understandable. For I have given wealth beyond calculation. I have expunged deprivation, famine, over-population, territorial constriction: All the first-order causes of contention have vanished. My gifts go freely and carry with them my personal joy, but as a reasonable man (and for lack of other restrictive agency), I feel that I cannot relinquish all control, for when has the human animal ever been celebrated for abnegation and self-discipline?

We now enter an era of plenty and a time of new concerns. The old evils are gone: we must resolutely prohibit a flamboyant and perhaps unnatural set of new vices.

The three girls gulped down breakfast, assembled their homework, and departed noisily for school.

Elizabeth poured coffee for herself and Gilbert. He thought she seemed pensive and moody. Presently she said, "It's so beautiful here . . . We're very lucky, Gilbert."

"I never forget it."

Elizabeth sipped her coffee and mused a moment, following some vagrant train of thought. She said, "I never liked growing up. I always felt strange – different from the other girls. I really don't know why."

"It's no mystery. Everyone for a fact is different."

"Perhaps . . . But Uncle Peter and Aunt Emma always acted as if I were more different than usual. I remember a hundred little signals. And yet I was such an ordinary little girl . . . Do you remember when you were little?"

"Not very well." Gilbert Duray looked out the window he himself had glazed, across green slopes and down to the placid water his daughters had named the Silver River. The Sounding Sea was thirty miles south; behind the house stood the first trees of the Robber Woods.

Duray considered his past. "Bob owned a ranch in Arizona during the 1870s: one of his fads. The Apaches killed my father and mother. Bob took me to the ranch, and then when I was three he brought me to Alan's house in San Francisco, and that's where I was brought up."

Elizabeth sighed. "Alan must have been wonderful. Uncle Peter was so grim. Aunt Emma never told me anything. Literally, not anything! They never cared the slightest bit for me, one way or the other . . . I wonder why Bob brought the subject up – about the Indians and your mother and father being scalped and all . . . He's such a strange man."

"Was Bob here?"

"He looked in a few minutes yesterday to remind us of his Rumfuddle. I told him I didn't want to leave the girls. He said to bring them along."

"Hah!"

"I told him I didn't want to go to his damn Rumfuddle with or without the girls. In the first place, I don't want to see Uncle Peter, who's sure to be there . . ."

II

From *Memoirs and Reflections:*

I insisted then and I insist now that our dear old Mother Earth, so soiled and toil-worn, never be neglected. Since I pay the piper (in a manner of speaking), I call the tune, and to my secret amusement I am heeded most briskly the world around, in the manner of bellboys, jumping to the command of an irascible old gentleman who is known to be a good tipper. No one dares to defy me. My whims become actualities; my plans progress.

Paris, Vienna, San Francisco, St. Petersburg, Venice, London, Dublin, surely will persist, gradually to become idealized essences of their former selves, as wine in due course becomes the soul of the grape. What of the old vitality? The shouts and curses, the neighborhood quarrels, the raucous music, the vulgarity? Gone, all gone! (But easy of reference at any of the cognates.) Old Earth is to be a gentle, kindly world, rich in treasures and artifacts, a world of old places – old inns, old roads, old forests, old palaces – where folk come to wander and dream, to experience the best of the past without suffering the worst

Material abundance can now be taken for granted: Our resources are infinite. Metal, timber, soil, rock, water, air: free for anyone's taking. A single commodity remains in finite supply: human toil.

Gilbert Duray, the informally adopted grandson of Alan Robertson, worked on the Urban Removal Program. Six hours a day, four days a week, he guided a trashing machine across deserted Cuperinto, destroying tract houses, service stations, and supermarkets. Knobs and toggles controlled a steel hammer at the end of a hundred-foot boom; with a twitch of the finger, Duray toppled powerpoles, exploded picture windows, smashed siding and stucco, exploded picture windows, smashed siding and stucco, pulverized concrete. A disposal rig crawled fifty feet behind. The detritus was clawed upon a conveyor belt, carried to a twenty-foot orifice, and dumped with a rush and a rumble into the Apathetic Ocean. Aluminum siding, asphalt shingles, corrugated fiber-glass, TVs and barbecues, Swedish Modern furniture, Book-of-the-Month selections, concrete patio-tiles, finally the sidewalk and street itself: all to the bottom of the Apathetic Ocean. Only the trees remained, a strange eclectic forest stretching as far as the eye could reach: liquidambar and Scotch pine; Chinese pistachio, Atlas cedar, and ginkgo; white birch and Norway maple.

At one o'clock Howard Wirtz emerged from the caboose, as they called the small locker room at the rear of the machine. Wirtz had homesteaded a Miocene world; Duray, with a wife and three children, had preferred the milder environment of a contemporary semicognate: the popular Type A world on which man had never evolved.

Duray gave Wirtz the work schedule. "More or less like yesterday — straight out Persimmon to Walden, then right a block and back."

Wirtz, a dour and laconic man, acknowledged the information with a jerk of the head. On his Miocene world he lived alone, in a house-boat on a mountain lake. He harvested wild rice, mushrooms, and berries; he shot geese, ground-fowl, deer, young bison, and had once informed Duray that after his five-year work-time he might just retire to his lake and never appear on Earth again, except maybe to buy clothes and ammunition. "Nothing here I want, nothing at all."

Duray had given a derisive snort. "And what will you do with all your time?"

"Hunt, fish, eat, and sleep, maybe sit on the front deck."

"Nothing else?"

"I just might learn to fiddle. Nearest neighbor is fifteen million years away."

"You can't be too careful, I suppose."

Duray descended to the ground and looked over his day's work: a quarter-mile swath of desolation. Duray, who allowed his subconscious few extravagances, nevertheless felt a twinge for the old times, which, for all their disadvantages, at least had been lively. Voices, bicycle bells, the barking of dogs, the slamming of doors, still echoed along Persimmon Avenue. The former inhabitants presumably preferred their new homes. The self-sufficient had taken private worlds; the more gregarious lived in communities on worlds of every description: as early as the Carboniferous, as current as the Type A. A few had even returned to the now-uncrowded cities. An exciting era to live in: a time of flux. Duray, thirty-four years old, remembered no other way of life; the old existence, as exemplified by Persimmon Avenue, seemed antique, cramped, constricted.

He had a word with the operator of the trashing machine; returning to the caboose, Duray paused to look through the orifice across the Apathetic Ocean. A squall hung black above the southern horizon, toward which a trail of broken lumber drifted, ultimately to wash up on some unknown pre-Cambrian shore. There never would be an inspector sailing forth to protest; the world knew no life other than mollusks and algae, and all the trash of Earth would never fill its submarine gorges. Duray tossed a rock through the gap and watched the alien water splash up and subside. Then he turned away and entered the caboose.

Along the back wall were four doors. The second from the left was marked "G. DURAY." He unlocked the door, pulled it open, and stopped short, staring in astonishment at the blank back wall. He lifted the transparent plastic flap that functioned as an air-seal and brought out the collapsed metal ring that had been the flange surrounding his passway. The inner surface was bare metal; looking through, he saw only the interior of the caboose.

A long minute passed. Duray stood staring at the useless ribbon as if hypnotized, trying to grasp the implications of the situation. To his knowledge no passway had ever failed, unless it had been purposefully closed. Who would play him such a spiteful trick? Certainly not Elizabeth. She detested practical jokes and if anything, like Duray himself, was perhaps a trifle too intense and literal-minded. He jumped down from the caboose and strode off across Cupertino Forest: a sturdy, heavy-shouldered man of about average stature. His features were rough and uncompromising; his brown hair was cut crisply short; his eyes glowed golden-brown and exerted an arresting force. Straight, heavy eyebrows crossed his long, thin nose like the bar of a T; his mouth, compressed against some strong inner urgency, formed a lower horizontal bar. All in all, not a man to be trifled with, or so it would seem.

He trudged through the haunted grove, preoccupied by the strange and inconvenient event that had befallen him. What had happened to the passway? Unless Elizabeth had invited friends out to Home, as they called their world, she was alone, with the three girls at school . . . Duray came out upon Stevens Creek Road. A farmer's pickup truck halted at his signal and took him into San Jose, now little more than a country town.

At the transit center he dropped a coin in the turnstile and entered the lobby. Four portals designated "LOCAL," "CALIFORNIA," "NORTH AMERICA," and "WORLD" opened in the walls, each portal leading to a hub on Utilis.*

Duray passed into the "California" hub, found the "Oakland" portal, returned to the Oakland Transit Center on Earth, passed back through the "Local" portal to the "Oakland" hub on Utilis, and returned to Earth through the "Montclair West" portal to a depot only a quarter mile from Thornhill School,† to which Duray walked.

In the office Duray identified himself to the clerk and requested the presence of his daughter Dolly.

The clerk sent forth a messenger who, after an interval, returned alone. "Dolly Duray isn't at school."

Duray was surprised; Dolly had been in good health and had set off to school as usual. He said, "Either Joan or Ellen will do as well."

The messenger again went forth and again returned. "Neither one is in their classrooms, Mr. Duray. All three of your children are absent."

"I can't understand it," said Duray, now fretful. "All three set off to school this morning."

"Let me ask Miss Haig. I've just come on duty." The clerk spoke into a telephone, listened, then turned back to Duray. "The girls went home at ten o'clock. Mrs. Duray called for them and took them back through the passway."

*Utilis: a world cognate to Paleocene Earth, where, by Alan Robertson's decree, all the industries, institutions, warehouses, tanks, dumps, and commercial offices of old Earth were now located. The name Utilis, so it had been remarked, accurately captured the flavor of Alan Robertson's pedantic, quaint, and idealistic personality.
†Alan Robertson had proposed another specialized world, to be known as Tutelar, where the children of all the settled worlds should receive their education in a vast array of pedagogical facilities. To his hurt surprise, he encountered a storm of wrathful opposition from parents. His scheme was termed mechanistic, vast, dehumanizing, repulsive. What better world for schooling than old Earth itself? Here was the source of all tradition; let Earth become Tutelar! So insisted the parents, and Alan Robertson had no choice but to agree.

"Did she give any reason whatever?"

"Miss Haig says no; Mrs. Duray just told her she needed the girls at home."

Duray stifled a sigh of baffled irritation. "Could you take me to their locker? I'll use their passway to get home."

"That's contrary to school regulations, Mr. Duray. You'll understand, I'm sure."

"I can identify myself quite definitely," said Duray. "Mr. Carr knows me well. As a matter of fact, my passway collapsed, and I came here to get home."

"Why don't you speak to Mr. Carr?"

"I'd like to do so."

Duray was conducted into the principal's office, where he explained his predicament. Mr. Carr expressed sympathy and made no difficulty about taking Duray to the children's passway.

They went to a hall at the back of the school and found the locker numbered 382. "Here we are," said Carr. "I'm afraid that you'll find it a tight fit." He unlocked the metal door with his master key and threw it open. Duray looked inside and saw only the black metal at the back of the locker. The passway, like his own, had been closed.

Duray drew back and for a moment could find no words.

Carr spoke in a voice of polite amazement. "How very perplexing! I don't believe I've ever seen anything like it before! Surely the girls wouldn't play such a silly prank!"

"They know better than to touch the passway," Duray said gruffly. "Are you sure that this is the right locker?"

Carr indicated the card on the outside of the locker, where three names had been typed: "DOROTHY DURAY, JOAN DURAY, ELLEN DURAY." "No mistake," said Carr, "and I'm afraid that I can't help you any further. Are you in common residency?"

"It's our private homestead."

Carr nodded with lips judiciously pursed, to suggest that insistence upon so much privacy seemed eccentric. He gave a deprecatory little chuckle. "I suppose if you isolate yourself to such an extent, you more or less must expect a series of emergencies."

"To the contrary," Duray said crisply. "Our life is uneventful, because there's no one to bother us. We love the wild animals, the quiet, the fresh air. We wouldn't have it any differently."

Carr smiled a dry smile. "Mr. Robertson has certainly altered the lives of us all. I understand that he is your grandfather?"

"I was raised in his household. I'm his nephew's foster son. The blood relationship isn't all that close."

III

From *Memoirs and Reflections:*

I early became interested in magnetic fluxes and their control. After taking my degree, I worked exclusively in this field, studying all varieties of magnetic envelopes and developing controls over their formation. For many years my horizons were thus limited, and I lived a placid existence.

Two contemporary developments forced me down from my "ivory castle." First: the fearful overcrowding of the planet and the prospect of worse to come. Cancer already was an affliction of the past; head diseases were under control; I feared that in another ten years immortality might be a practical reality for many of us, with a consequent augmentation of population pressure.

Secondly, the theoretical work done upon "black holes" and "white holes" suggested that matter compacted in a "black hole" broke through a barrier to spew forth from a "white hole" in another universe. I calculated pressures and considered the self-focusing magnetic sheaths, cones, and whorls with which I was experimenting. Through their innate properties these entities constricted themselves to apexes of a cross section indistinguishable from a geometric point. What if two or more cones (I asked myself) could be arranged in contra position to produce an equilibrium? In this condition charged particles must be accelerated to near light-speed and at the mutual focus constricted and impinged together. The pressures thus created, though of small scale, would be far in excess of those characteristic of the "black holes": to unknown effect.

I can now report that the mathematics of the multiple focus are a most improbable thicket, and the useful service I enforced upon what I must call a set of absurd contradictions is one of my secrets. I know that thousands of scientists, at home and abroad, are attempting to duplicate my work; they are welcome to the effort. None will succeed. Why do I speak so positively? This is my other secret.

Duray marched back to the Montclair West depot in a state of angry puzzlement. There were four passways to Home, of which two were closed. The third was located in his San Francisco locker: the "front door," so to speak. The last and the original orifice was cased, filed, and indexed in Alan Robertson's vault.

Duray tried to deal with the problem in rational terms. The girls would never tamper with the passways. As for Elizabeth, no more than the girls would she consider such an act. At least Duray could imagine no reason that would so urge or impel her. Elizabeth, like himself, a foster child, was a beautiful, passionate woman, tall, dark-haired, with lustrous dark eyes and a wide mouth that tended to curve in an endearingly crooked grin. She was also responsible, loyal, careful, industrious; she loved her family and Riverview Manor. The theory of erotic intrigue seemed to Duray as incredible as the fact of the closed passways. Though for a fact, Elizabeth was prone to wayward and incomprehensible moods. Suppose Elizabeth had received a visitor who for some sane or insane purpose had forced her to close the passway? . . . Duray shook his head in frustration, like a harassed bull. The matter no doubt had some simple cause. Or on the other hand, Duray reflected, the cause might be complex and intricate. The thought, by some obscure connection, brought before him the image of his nominal foster father, Alan Robertson's nephew, Bob Robertson. Duray gave his head a nod of gloomy asseveration, as if to confirm a fact he long ago should have suspected. He went to the phone booth and called Bob Robertson's apartment in San Francisco. The screen glowed white and an instant later displayed Bob Robertson's alert, clean, and handsome face. "Good afternoon, Gil. Glad you called; I've been anxious to get in touch with you."

Duray became warier than ever. "How so?"

"Nothing serious, or so I hope. I dropped by your locker to leave off some books that I promised Elizabeth, and I noticed through the glass that your passway is closed. Collapsed. Useless."

"Strange," said Duray. "Very strange indeed. I can't understand it. Can you?"

"No . . . not really."

Duray thought he detected a subtlety of intonation. His eyes narrowed in concentration. "The passway at my rig was closed. The passway at the girls' school was closed. Now you tell me that the downtown passway is closed."

Bob Robertson grinned. "That's a pretty broad hint, I would say. Did you and Elizabeth have a row?"

"No."

Bob Robertson rubbed his long aristocratic chin. "A mystery. There's probably some very ordinary explanation."

"Or some very extraordinary explanation."

"True. Nowadays a person can't rule out anything. By the way, tomorrow night is the Rumfuddle, and I expect both you and Elizabeth to be on hand."

"As I recall," said Duray, "I've already declined the invitation." The Rumfuddlers were a group of Bob's cronies. Duray suspected that their activities were not altogether wholesome. "Excuse me; I've got to find an open passway, or Elizabeth and the kids are marooned."

"Try Alan," said Bob. "He'll have the original in his vault."

Duray gave a curt nod. "I don't like to bother him, but that's my last hope."

"Let me know what happens," said Bob Robertson. "And if you're at loose ends, don't forget the Rumfuddle tomorrow night. I mentioned the matter to Elizabeth, and she said she'd be sure to attend."

"Indeed. And when did you consult Elizabeth?"

"A day or so ago. Don't look so damnably gothic, my boy."

"I'm wondering if there's a connection between your invitation and the closed passways. I happen to know that Elizabeth doesn't care for your parties."

Bob Robertson laughed with easy good grace. "Reflect a moment. Two events occur. I invite you and wife Elizabeth to the Rumfuddle. This is event one. Your passways close up, which is event two. By a feat of structured absurdity you equate the two and blame me. Now is that fair?"

"You call it 'structured absurdity,'" said Duray. "I call it instinct."

Bob Robertson laughed again. "You'll have to do better than that. Consult Alan, and if for some reason he can't help you, come to the Rumfuddle. We'll rack our brains and either solve your problem or come up with new and better ones." He gave a cheery nod, and before Duray could roar an angry expostulation, the screen faded.

Duray stood glowering at the screen, convinced that Bob Robertson knew much more about the closed passways than he admitted. Duray went to sit on a bench . . . If Elizabeth had closed him away from Home, her reasons must have been compelling indeed. But unless she intended to isolate herself permanently from Earth, she would leave at least one passway ajar, and this must be the master orifice in Alan Robertson's vault.

Duray rose to his feet, somewhat heavily, and stood a moment, head bent and shoulders hunched. He gave a surly grunt and returned to the phone booth, where he called a number known to not more than a dozen persons.

The screen glowed white while the person at the other end of the line scrutinized his face . . . The screen cleared, revealing a round pale face from which pale blue eyes stared forth with a passionless intensity.

"Hello, Ernest," said Duray. "Is Alan busy at the moment?"

"I don't think he's doing anything particular – except resting."

Ernest gave the last two words a meaningful emphasis. "I've got some problems," said Duray. "What's the best way to get in touch with him?"

"You'd better come up here. The code is changed. It's MHF now."

"I'll be there in a few minutes."

Back in the "California" hub on Utilis, Duray went into a side chamber lined with private lockers, numbered and variously marked with symbols, names, colored flags, or not marked at all. Duray went to Locker 122, and, ignoring the keyhole, set the code lock to the letters MHF. The door opened; Duray stepped into the locker and through the passway to the High Sierra headquarters of Alan Robertson.

IV

From *Memoirs and Reflections:*

If one basic axiom controls the cosmos, it must be this:

In a situation of infinity every possible condition occurs, not once, but an infinite number of times.

There is no mathematical nor logical limit to the number of dimensions. Our perceptions assure us of three only, but many indications suggest otherwise: parapsychic occurrences of a hundred varieties, the "white holes," the seemingly finite state of our own universe, which, by corollary, asserts the existence of others.

Hence, when I stepped behind the lead slab and first touched the button, I felt confident of success; failure would have surprised me!

But (and here lay my misgivings) what sort of success might I achieve?

Suppose I opened a hole into the interplanetary vacuum?

The chances of this were very good indeed; I surrounded the machine in a strong membrane to prevent the air of Earth from rushing off into the void.

Suppose I discovered a condition totally beyond imagination?

My imagination yielded no safeguards.

I proceeded to press the button.

Duray stepped out into a grotto under damp granite walls. Sunlight poured into the opening from a dark-blue sky. This was Alan Robertson's link to the outside world; like many other persons, he disliked a passway opening directly into his home. A path led fifty yards across bare granite mountainside to the lodge. To the west spread a great vista of diminishing ridges, valleys, and hazy blue air; to the east rose a pair of granite crags, with snow caught in the saddle between. Alan Robertson's lodge was built just below the timberline, beside a small lake fringed with tall dark firs. The lodge was built of rounded granite stones, with a wooden porch across the front; at each end rose a massive chimney.

Duray had visited the lodge on many occasions; as a boy he had scaled both of the crags behind the house, to look wonderingly off across the stillness, which on old Earth had a poignant breathing quality different from the uninhabited solitudes of worlds such as Home.

Ernest came to the door: a middle-aged man with an ingenuous face, small white hands, and soft, damp, mouse-colored hair. Ernest disliked the lodge, the wilderness, and solitude in general; he nevertheless would have suffered tortures before relinquishing his post as subaltern to Alan Robertson. Ernest and Duray were almost antipodal in outlook. Ernest thought Duray brusque, indelicate, a trifle coarse, and probably not disinclined to violence as an argumentative adjunct. Duray considered Ernest, when he thought of him at all, as the kind of man who takes two bites out of a cherry. Ernest had never married; he showed no interest in women, and Duray, as a boy, had often fretted at Ernest's overcautious restrictions.

In particular Ernest resented Duray's free and easy access to Alan Robertson. The power to restrict or admit those countless persons who demanded Alan Robertson's attention was Ernest's most cherished perquisite, and Duray denied him the use of it by simply ignoring Ernest and all his regulations. Ernest had never complained to Alan Robertson for fear of discovering that Duray's influence exceeded his own. A wary truce existed between the two, each conceding the other his privileges.

Ernest performed a polite greeting and admitted Duray into the lodge. Duray looked around the interior, which had not changed during his lifetime: varnished plank floors with red, black, and white Navaho rugs, massive pine furniture with leather cushions, a few shelves of books, a half-dozen pewter mugs on the mantle over the big fireplace – a room almost ostentatiously bare of souvenirs and mementos. Duray turned back to Ernest: "Whereabouts is Alan?"

"On his boat."

"With guests?"

"No," said Ernest, with a faint sniff of disapproval. "He's alone, quite alone."

"How long has he been gone?"

"He just went through an hour ago. I doubt if he's left the dock yet. What is your problem, if I may ask?"

"The passways to my world are closed. All three. There's only one left, in the vault."

Ernest arched his flexible eyebrows. "Who closed them?"

"I don't know. Elizabeth and the girls are alone, so far as I know."

"Extraordinary," said Ernest in a flat metallic voice. "Well, then, come along." He led the way down a hall to a back room. With his hand on the knob, Ernest paused and looked back over his shoulder. "Did you mention the matter to anyone? Robert, for instance?"

"Yes," said Duray curtly, "I did. Why do you ask?"

Ernest hesitated a fraction of a second. "No particular reason. Robert occasionally has a somewhat misplaced sense of humor, he and his Rumfuddlers." He spoke the word with a hiss of distaste.

Duray said nothing of his own suspicions. Ernest opened the door; they entered a large room illuminated by a skylight. The only furnishing was a rug on the varnished floor. Into each wall opened four doors. Ernest went to one of these doors, pulled it open, and made a resigned gesture. "You'll probably find Alan at the dock."

Duray looked into the interior of a rude hut with palm-frond walls, resting on a platform of poles. Through the doorway he saw a path leading under sunlit green foliage toward a strip of white beach. Surf sparkled below a layer of dark-blue ocean and a glimpse of the sky. Duray hesitated, rendered wary by the events of the morning. Anyone and everyone was suspect, even Ernest, who now gave a quiet sniff of contemptuous amusement. Through the foliage Duray glimpsed a spread of sail; he stepped through the passway.

V

From *Memoirs and Reflections:*

Man is a creature whose evolutionary environment has been the open air. His nerves, muscles, and senses have developed across three million years in intimate contiguity with natural earth, crude stone, live wood, wind, and rain. Now this creature is suddenly – on the geologic scale, instantaneously – shifted to an unnatural environment of metal and glass, plastic and plywood, to which his psychic substrata lack all compatibility. The wonder is not that we have so much mental instability but so little. Add to this the weird noises, electrical pleasures, bizarre colors, synthetic foods, abstract entertainments! We should congratulate ourselves on our durability.

I bring this matter up because, with my little device – so simple, so easy so flexible – I have vastly augmented the load upon our poor primeval brain, and for a fact many persons find the instant transition from one locale to another unsettling, and even actively unpleasant.

Duray stood on the porch of the cabin, under a vivid green canopy of sunlit foliage. The air was soft and warm and smelled of moist vegetation. He stood listening. The mutter of the surf came to his ears and from a far distance a single birdcall.

Duray stepped down to the ground and followed the path under tall palm trees to a riverbank. A few yards downstream, beside a rough pier of poles and planks, floated a white-and-blue ketch, sails hoisted and distended to a gentle breeze. On the deck stood Alan Robertson, on the point of casting off the mooring lines. Duray hailed him; Alan Robertson turned in surprise and vexation, which vanished when he recognized Duray. "Hello, Gil, glad you're here! For a moment I thought it might be someone to bother me. Jump aboard; you're just in time for a sail."

Duray somberly joined Alan Robertson on the boat. "I'm afraid I am here to bother you."

"Oh?" Alan Robertson raised his eyebrows in instant solicitude. He was a man of no great height, thin, nervously active. Wisps of rumpled white hair fell over his forehead; mild blue eyes inspected Duray with concern, all thoughts of sailing forgotten. "What in the world has happened?"

"I wish I knew. If it were something I could handle myself, I wouldn't bother you."

"Don't worry about me; there's all the time in the world for sailing. Now tell me what's happened."

"I can't get through to Home. All the passways are closed off. Why and how I have no idea. Elizabeth and the girls are out there alone; at least I think they're *out there*."

Alan Robertson rubbed his chin. "What an odd business! I can certainly understand your agitation . . . You think Elizabeth closed the passways?"

"It's unreasonable – but there's no one else."

Alan Robertson turned Duray a shrewd, kindly glance. "No little family upsets? Nothing to cause her despair and anguish?"

"Absolutely nothing. I've tried to reason things out, but I draw a blank. I thought that maybe someone – a man had gone through to visit her and decided to take over, but if this were the case, why did she come to the school for the girls? That possibility is out. A secret love affair? Possible but so damn unlikely. Since she wants to keep me off the planet, her only motive could be to protect me or herself or the girls from danger of some sort. Again this means that another person is concerned in the matter. Who? How? Why? I spoke to Bob. He claims to know nothing about the situation, but he wants me to come to his damned Rumfuddle, and he hints very strongly that Elizabeth will be on hand. I can't prove a thing against Bob, but I suspect him. He's always had a taste for odd jokes."

Alan Robertson gave a lugubrious nod. "I won't deny that." He sat down in the cockpit and stared off across the water. "Bob has a complicated sense of humor, but he'd hardly close you away from your world . . . I hardly think that your family is in actual danger, but of course we can't take chances. The possibility exists that Bob is not responsible, that something uglier is afoot." He jumped to his feet. "Our obvious first step is to use the master orifice in the vault." He looked a shade regretfully toward the ocean. "My little sail can wait . . . A lovely world this: not fully cognate with Earth – a cousin, so to speak. The fauna and flora are roughly contemporary except for man. The hominids have never developed."

The two men returned up the path, Alan Robertson chatting light-heartedly:

"Thousands and thousands of worlds I've visited, and looked into even more, but do you know I've never hit upon a good system of classification. There are exact cognates – of course we're never sure exactly *how* exact they are. These cases are relatively simple but then the problems begin . . . Bah! I don't think about such things anymore. I know that when I keep all the determinates at zero, the cognates appear. Overintellectualizing is the bane of this and every other era. Show me a man who deals only with abstraction, and I'll show you the dead futile end of evolution." Alan Robertson chuckled. "If I could control the machine tightly enough to produce real cognates, our troubles would be over . . . Much confusion, of course. I might step through into the cognate world immediately as a true cognate Alan Robertson steps through into our world, with net effect of zero. An amazing business, really; I never tire of it . . ."

They returned to the transit room of the mountain lodge. Ernest appeared almost instantly. Duray suspected he had been watching through the passway.

Alan Robertson said briskly, "We'll be busy for an hour or two, Ernest. Gilbert is having difficulties, and we've got to set things straight."

Ernest nodded somewhat grudgingly, or so it seemed to Duray. "The progress report on the Ohio Plan has arrived. Nothing particularly urgent."

"Thank you, Ernest, I'll see to it later. Come along, Gilbert; let's get to the bottom of this affair." They went to door No.1 and passed through to the Utilis hub. Alan Robertson led the way to a small green door with a three-dial coded lock, which he opened with a flourish. "Very well, in we go." He carefully locked the door behind them, and they walked the length of a short hall. "A shame that I must be so cautious," said Alan Robertson. "You'd be astonished at the outrageous requests otherwise sensible people make of me. I sometimes become exasperated . . . Well, it's understandable, I suppose."

At the end of the hall Alan Robertson worked the locking dials of a red door. "This way, Gilbert; you've been through before." They stepped through a passway into a hall that opened into a circular concrete chamber fifty feet in diameter, located, so Duray knew, deep under the Mad Dog Mountains of the Mojave Desert. Eight halls extended away into the rock; each hall communicated with twelve aisles. The center of the chamber was occupied by a circular desk twenty feet in diameter; here six clerks in white smocks worked at computers and collating machines. In accordance with their instructions they gave Alan Robertson neither recognition nor greeting.

Alan Robertson went up to the desk, at which signal the chief clerk, a solemn young man bald as an egg, came forward. "Good afternoon, sir."

"Good afternoon, Harry. Find me the index for 'Gilbert Duray,' on my personal list."

The clerk bowed smartly. He went to an instrument and ran his fingers over a bank of keys; the instrument ejected a card that Harry handed to Alan Robertson. "There you are, sir."

Alan Robertson showed the card to Duray, who saw the code: "4:8:10/6:13:29."

"That's your world," said Alan Robertson. "We'll soon learn how the land lies. This way, to Radiant four." He led the way down the hall, turned into the aisle numbered "8," and proceeded to Stack 10. "Shelf six," said Alan Robertson. He checked the card. "Drawer thirteen . . . here we are." He drew forth the drawer and ran his fingers along the tabs. "Item twenty-nine. This should be Home." He brought forth a metal frame four inches square and held it up to his eyes. He frowned in disbelief. "We don't have anything here either." He turned to Duray a glance of dismay. "This is a serious situation!"

"It's no more than I expected," said Duray tonelessly.

"All this demands some careful thought." Alan Robertson clicked his tongue in vexation. "Tst, tst, tst." He examined the identification plaque at the top of the frame. "Four: eight: ten/six: thirteen: twenty-nine," he read. "There seems to be no question of error." He squinted carefully at the numbers, hesitated, then slowly replaced the frame. On second thought he took the frame forth once more. "Come along, Gilbert," said Alan Robertson. "We'll have a cup of coffee and think this matter out."

The two returned to the central chamber, where Alan Robertson gave the empty frame into the custody of Harry the clerk. "Check the records, if you please," said Alan Robertson. "I want to know how many passways were pinched off the master."

Harry manipulated the buttons of his computer. "Three only, Mr. Robertson."

"Three passways and the master – four in all?"

"That's right, sir."

"Thank you, Harry."

VI

From *Memoirs and Reflections:*

I recognized the possibility of many cruel abuses, but the good so outweighed the bad that I thrust aside all thought of secrecy and exclusivity. I consider myself not Alan Robertson but, like Prometheus, an archetype of Man, and my discovery must serve all men.

But caution, caution, caution!

I sorted out my ideas. I myself coveted the amplitude of a private, personal world; such a yearning was not ignoble, I decided. Why should not everyone have the same if he so desired, since the supply was limitless? Think of it! The wealth and beauty of an entire world: mountains and plains, forests and flowers, ocean cliffs and crashing seas, winds and clouds – all beyond value, yet worth no more than a few seconds of effort and a few watts of energy.

I became troubled by a new idea. Would everyone desert old Earth and leave it a vile junk-heap? I found the concepts intolerable . . . I exchange access to a world for three to six years of remedial toil, depending upon occupancy.

A lounge overlooked the central chamber. Alan Robertson gestured Duray to a seat and drew two mugs of coffee from a dispenser. Settling in a chair, he turned his eyes up to the ceiling. "We must collect our thoughts. The circumstances are somewhat unusual; still, I have lived with unusual circumstances for almost fifty years.

"So then: the situation. We have verified that there are only four passways to Home. These four passways are closed, though we must accept Bob's word in regard to your downtown locker. If this is truly the case, if Elizabeth and the girls are still on Home, you will never see them again."

"Bob is mixed up in this business. I could swear to nothing, but – "

Alan Robertson held up his hand. "I will talk to Bob; this is the obvious first step." He rose to his feet and went to the telephone in the corner of the lounge. Duray joined him. Alan spoke into the screen. "Get me Robert Robertson's apartment in San Francisco."

The screen glowed white. Bob's voice came from the speaker. "Sorry, I'm not at home. I have gone out to my world Fancy, and I cannot be reached. Call back in a week, unless your business is urgent, in which case call back in a month."

"Mmph," said Alan Robertson, returning to his seat. "Bob is sometimes a trifle too flippant. A man with an under-extended intellect . . ." He drummed his fingers on the arm of his chair. "Tomorrow night is his party? What does he call it? A Rumfuddle?"

"Some such nonsense. Why does he want me? I'm a dead dog; I'd rather be home building a fence."

"Perhaps you had better plan to attend the party."

"That means, submit to his extortion."

"Do you want to see your wife and family again?"

"Naturally. But whatever he has in mind won't be for my benefit, or Elizabeth's."

"You're probably right there. I've heard one or two unsavory tales regarding the Rumfuddlers . . . The fact remains that the passways are closed. All four of them."

Duray's voice became harsh. "Can't you open a new orifice for us?"

Alan Robertson gave his head a sad shake. "I can tune the machine very finely. I can code accurately for the 'Home' class of worlds and as closely as necessary approximate a particular world-state. But at each setting, no matter how fine the tuning, we encounter an infinite number of worlds. In practice, inaccuracies in the machine, backlash, the gross size of electrons, the very difference between one electron and another, make it difficult to tune with absolute precision. So even if we tuned exactly to the 'Home' class, the probability of opening into your particular Home is one of an infinite number: in short, negligible."

Duray stared off across the chamber. "Is it possible that space once entered might tend to open more easily a second time?"

Alan Robertson smiled. "As to that, I can't say. I suspect not, but I really know so little. I see no reason why it should be so."

"If we can open into a world precisely cognate, I can at least learn why the passways are closed."

Alan Robertson sat up in his chair. "Here is a valid point. Perhaps we can accomplish something in this regard." He glanced humorously sidewise at Duray. "On the other hand – consider this situation. We create access into a 'Home' almost exactly cognate to your own – so nearly identical that the difference is not readily apparent. You find there an Elizabeth, a Dolly, a Joan, and an Ellen indistinguishable from your own, and a Gilbert marooned on Earth. You might even convince yourself that this is your very own Home."

"I'd know the difference," said Duray shortly, but Alan Robertson seemed not to hear.

"Think of it! An infinite number of Homes isolated from Earth, an infinite number of Elizabeths, Dollys, Joans, and Ellens marooned, an infinite number of Gilbert Durays trying to regain access . . . The sum effect might be a wholesale reshuffling of families, with everyone more or less good-natured about the situation. I wonder if this could be Bob's idea of a joke to share with his Rumfuddlers."

Duray looked sharply at Alan Robertson, wondering whether the man was serious. "It doesn't sound funny and I wouldn't be very good-natured."

"Of course not," said Alan Robertson hastily. "An afterthought – in rather poor taste, I'm afraid."

"In any event, Bob hinted that Elizabeth would be at the damned

Rumfuddle. If that's the case, she must have closed the passways from this side."

"A possibility," Alan Robertson conceded, "but unreasonable. Why should she seal you away from Home?"

"I don't know, but I'd like to find out."

Alan Robertson slapped his hands down upon his shanks and jumped to his feet, only to pause once more. "You're sure you want to look into these cognates? You might see things you wouldn't like."

"So long as I know the truth, I don't care whether I like it or not."

"So be it."

The machine occupied a room behind the balcony. Alan Robertson surveyed the device with pride and affection. "This is the fourth model, and probably optimum; at least I don't see any place for significant improvement. I use a hundred and sixty-seven rods converging upon the center of the reactor sphere. Each rod produces a quotum of energy and is susceptible to several types of adjustment to cope with the very large number of possible states. The number of particles to pack the universe full is on the order of ten raised to the power of sixty; the possible permutations these particles would number is two raised to the power of ten raised to the power of sixty. The universe, of course, is built of many different particles, which makes the final number of possible, or let us say, thinkable states a number like two raised to the power of ten raised to the power of sixty, all times x, where x is the number of particles under consideration. A large, unmanageable number, which we need not consider, because the conditions we deal with – the possible variations of planet Earth – are far fewer."

"Still a very large number," said Duray.

"Indeed yes. But again the sheer unmanageable bulk is swept away by a self-normalizing property of the machine. In what I call floating neutral, the machine reaches the closest cognate – which is to say, that infinite class of perfect cognates. In practice, because of infinitesimal inaccuracies, 'floating neutral' reaches cognates more or less imperfect, perhaps by no more than the shape of a single grain of sand. Still, 'floating neutral' provides a natural base, and by adjusting the controls, we reach cycles at an ever greater departure from base. In practice I search out a good cycle and strike a large number of passways, as many as a hundred thousand. So now to our business." He went to a porthole at the side. "Your code number, what was it now?"

Duray brought forth the card and read the numbers: "Four: eight:ten/six:thirteen:twenty-nine."

"Very good. I give the code to the computer, which searches the files and automatically adjusts the machine. Now then, step over here; the process releases dangerous radiation."

The two stood behind lead slabs. Alan Robertson touched a button; watching through a periscope, Duray saw a spark of purple light and heard a small groaning, gasping sound seeming to come from the air itself.

Alan Robertson stepped forth and walked to the machine. In the delivery tray rested an extensible ring. He picked up the ring and looked through the hole. "This seems to be right." He handed the ring to Duray. "Do you see anything you recognize?"

Duray put the ring to his eye. "That's Home."

"Very good. Do you want me to come with you?"

Duray considered. "The time is now?"

"Yes. This is a time-neutral setting."

"I think I'll go alone."

Alan Robertson nodded. "Whatever you like. Return as soon as you can, so I'll know you're safe."

Duray frowned at him sidewise. "Why shouldn't I be safe? No one is there but my family."

"Not *your* family. The family of a cognate Gilbert Duray. The family may not be absolutely identical. The cognate Duray may not be identical. You can't be sure exactly what you will find – so be careful."

VII

From *Memoirs and Reflections:*

When I think of my machine and my little forays in and out of infinity, an idea keeps recurring to me which is so rather terrible that I close it out of my mind, and I will not even mention it here.

Duray stepped out upon the soil of Home and stood praising the familiar landscape. A vast meadow drenched in sunlight rolled down to wide Silver River. Above the opposite shore rose a line of low bluffs, with copses of trees in the hollows. To the left, the landscape seemed to extend indefinitely and at last become indistinct in the blue haze of distance. To the right, the Robber Woods ended a quarter mile from where Duray stood. On a flat beside the forest, on the bank of a small stream, stood a house of stone and timber: a sight that seemed to

Duray the most beautiful one he had ever seen. Polished glass windows sparkled in the sunlight; banks of geraniums glowed green and red. From the chimney rose a wisp of smoke.

The air smelled cool and sweet but seemed – so Duray imagined – to carry a strange tang, different – so he imagined – from the meadow-scent of his own Home. Duray started forward, then halted. The world was his own, yet not his own. If he had been conscious of the fact, would he have recognized the strangeness? Nearby rose an outcrop of weathered gray field-rock: a rounded mossy pad on which he had sat only two days before, contemplating the building of a dock. He walked over and looked down at the stone. Here he had sat; here were the impressions of his heels in the soil; here was the pattern of moss from which he had absently scratched a fragment. Duray bent close. The moss was whole. The man who had sat here, the cognate Duray, had not scratched at the moss. So then: The world was perceptibly different from his own.

Duray was relieved and yet vaguely disturbed. If the world had been the exact simulacrum of his own, he might have been subjected to unmanageable emotions – which still might be the case. He walked toward the house, along the path that led down to the river. He stepped up to the porch. On a deck chair was a book: *Down There: A Study of Satanism*, by J. K. Huysmans. Elizabeth's tastes were eclectic. Duray had not previously seen the book; was it perhaps that that Bob Robertson had put through the parcel delivery?

Duray went into the house. Elizabeth stood across the room. She had evidently watched him coming up the path. She said nothing; her face showed no expression.

Duray halted, somewhat at a loss as to how to address this familiar-strange woman. "Good afternoon," he said at last.

Elizabeth allowed a wisp of a smile to show. "Hello, Gilbert."

At least, thought Duray, on cognate worlds the same language was spoken. He studied Elizabeth. Lacking prior knowledge, would he have perceived her to be someone different from his own Elizabeth? Both were beautiful women: tall and slender, with curling black shoulder-length hair, worn without artifice. Their skin was pale, with a dusky undertone; their mouths were wide, passionate, stubborn. Duray knew his Elizabeth to be a woman of explicable moods, and this Elizabeth was doubtless no different – yet somehow a difference existed that Duray could not define, deriving perhaps from the strangeness of her atoms, the stuff of a different universe. He wondered if she sensed the same difference in him.

He asked, "Did you close off the passways?"

Elizabeth nodded, without change of expression.

"Why?"

"I thought it the best thing to do," said Elizabeth in a soft voice.

"That's no answer."

"I suppose not. How did you get here?"

"Alan made an opening."

Elizabeth raised her eyebrows. "I thought that was impossible."

"True. This is a different world to my own. Another Gilbert Duray built this house. I'm not your husband."

Elizabeth's mouth dropped in astonishment. She swayed back a step and put her hand up to her neck: a mannerism Duray could not recall in his own Elizabeth. The sense of strangeness came ever more strongly upon him. He felt an intruder. Elizabeth was watching him with a wide-eyed fascination. She said in a hurried mutter: "I wish you'd leave, go back to your own world; do!"

"If you've closed off all the passways, you'll be isolated," growled Duray. "Marooned, probably forever."

"Whatever I do," said Elizabeth, "it's not your affair."

"It is my affair, if only for the sake of the girls. I won't allow them to live and die alone out here."

"The girls aren't here," said Elizabeth in a flat voice. "They are where neither you nor any other Gilbert Duray will find them. So now go back to your own world, and leave me in whatever peace my soul allows me."

Duray stood glowering at the fiercely beautiful woman. He had never heard his own Elizabeth speak so wildly. He wondered if on his own world another Gilbert Duray similarly confronted his own Elizabeth, and as he analyzed his feelings toward this woman before him, he felt a throb of annoyance. A curious situation. He said in a quiet voice, "Very well. You and my own Elizabeth have decided to isolate yourselves. I can't imagine your reasons."

Elizabeth gave a wild laugh. "They're real enough."

"They may be real now, but ten years from now or forty years from now they may seem unreal. I can't give you access to your own Earth, but if you wish, you can use the –

Elizabeth turned away and went to look out over the passway to the Earth from which I'd just come,

– and you need never see me again."

Duray spoke to her back. "We've never had secrets between us, you and I – or I mean, Elizabeth and I. Why now? Are you in love with some other man?"

Elizabeth gave a snort of sardonic amusement. "Certainly not . . . I'm disgusted with the entire human race."

"Which presumably includes me."

"It does indeed, and myself as well."

"And you won't tell me why?"

Elizabeth, still looking out the window, wordlessly shook her head.

"Very well," said Duray in a cold voice. "Will you tell me where you've sent the girls? They're mine as much as yours, remember."

"These particular girls aren't yours at all."

"That may be, but the effect is the same."

Elizabeth said tonelessly: "If you want to find your own particular girls, you'd better find your own particular Elizabeth and ask her. I can only speak for myself . . . To tell you the truth, I don't like being part of a composite person, and I don't intend to act like one. I'm just me. You're you, a stranger, whom I've never seen before in my life. So I wish you'd leave."

Duray strode from the house, out into the sunlight. He looked once around the wide landscape, then gave his head a surely shake and marched off along the path.

VIII

From *Memoirs and Reflections:*

The past is exposed for our scrutiny; we can wander the epochs like lords through a garden, serene in our purview. We argue with the noble sages, refuting their laborious concepts, should we be so unkind. Remember (at least) two things. First: The more distant from now, the less precise our conjunctures, the less our ability to strike to any given instant. We can break in upon yesterday at a stipulated second; during the Eocene, plus or minus ten years is the limit of our accuracy; as for the Cretaceous or earlier, an impingement with three hundred years of a given date can be considered satisfactory. Secondly: The past we broach is never our own past but at best the past of a cognate world, so that any illumination cast upon historical problems is questionable and perhaps deceptive. We cannot plumb the future; the process involves a negative flow of energy which is inherently impractical. An instrument constructed of antimatter has been jocularly recommended but would yield no benefit to us. The future, thankfully remains forever shrouded.

"Aha, you're back!" exclaimed Alan Robertson. "What did you learn?"

Duray described the encounter with Elizabeth. "She makes no excuse for what she's done; she shows hostility, which doesn't seem real, especially since I can't imagine a reason for it."

Alan Robertson had no comment to make.

"The woman isn't my wife, but their motivations must be the same. I can't think of one sensible explanation for conduct so strange, let alone two."

"Elizabeth seemed normal this morning?" asked Alan Robertson.

"I noticed nothing unusual."

Alan Robertson went to the control panel of his machine. He looked over his shoulder at Duray. "What time do you leave for work?"

"About nine."

Alan Robertson set one dial and turned two others until a ball of green light balanced, wavering, precisely halfway along a glass tube. He signaled Duray behind the lead slab and touched the button. From the center of the machine came the impact of 167 colliding nodules of force and the groan of rending dimensional fabric.

Alan Robertson brought forth the new passway. "The time is morning. You'll have to decide for yourself how to handle the situation. You can try to watch without being seen; you can say that you have paperwork to catch up on, that Elizabeth should ignore you and go about her normal routine, while you unobtrusively see what happens."

Duray frowned. "Presumably for each of these worlds there is a Gilbert Duray who finds himself in my fix. Suppose each tries to slip inconspicuously into someone else's world to learn what is happening. Suppose each Elizabeth catches him in the act and furiously accuses the man she believes to be her husband of spying on her – this in itself might be the source of Elizabeth's anger."

"Well, be as discreet as you can. Presumably you'll be several hours, so I'll go back to the boat and putter about. Locker five in my private hub yonder; I'll leave the door open."

Once again Duray stood on the hillside above the river, with the rambling stone house built by still another Gilbert Duray two hundred yards along the slope. From the height of the sun, Duray judged local time to be about nine o'clock – somewhat earlier than necessary. From the chimney of the stone house rose a wisp of smoke; Elizabeth had built a fire in the kitchen fireplace. Duray stood reflecting. This morning in his own house Elizabeth had built no fire. She had been on the point of striking a match and then had decided that the morning was already warm. Duray waited ten minutes, to make sure that the local Gilbert Duray had departed, then set forth toward the house. He paused by the big flat stone to inspect the pattern of moss. The crevice seemed narrower than he remembered, and the moss was dry and discolored. Duray took a deep breath. The air, rich with the odor of grasses and herbs, again seemed to carry an odd, unfamiliar scent. Duray proceeded slowly to the house, uncertain whether, after all, he was engaged in a sensible course of action.

He approached the house. The front door was open. Elizabeth came to look out at him in surprise. "That was a quick day's work!"

Duray said lamely, "The rig is down for repairs. I thought I'd catch up on some paper work. You go ahead with whatever you were doing."

Elizabeth looked at him curiously. "I wasn't doing anything in particular."

He followed Elizabeth into the house. She wore soft black slacks and an old gray jacket; Duray tried to remember what his own Elizabeth had worn, but the garments had been so familiar that he could summon no recollection.

Elizabeth poured coffee into a pair of stoneware mugs, and Duray took a seat at the kitchen table, trying to decide how this Elizabeth differed from his own – if she did. This Elizabeth seemed more subdued and meditative; her mouth might have been a trifle softer. "Why are you looking at me so strangely?" she asked suddenly.

Duray laughed. "I was merely thinking what a beautiful girl you are."

Elizabeth came to sit in his lap and kissed him, and Duray's blood began to flow warm. He restrained himself; this was not his wife; he wanted no complications. And if he yielded to temptations of the moment, might not another Gilbert Duray visiting his own Elizabeth do the same . . . He scowled.

Elizabeth, finding no surge of ardor, went to sit in the chair opposite. For a moment she sipped her coffee in silence. Then she said, "Just as soon as you left, Bob called through."

"Oh?" Duray was at once attentive. "What did he want?"

"That foolish party of his – the Rubble-menders or some such thing. He wants us to come."

"I've already told him no three times."

"I told him no again. His parties are always so peculiar. He said he wanted us to come for a very special reason, but he wouldn't tell me the reason. I told him, 'Thank you but no.'"

Duray looked around the room. "Did he leave any books?"

"No. Why should he leave me books?"

"I wish I knew."

"Gilbert," said Elizabeth, "you're acting rather oddly."

"Yes, I suppose I am." For a fact Duray's mind was whirling. Suppose now he went to the school passway, brought the girls home from school, then closed off all the passways, so that once again he had an Elizabeth and three daughters, more or less his own; then the conditions he had encountered would be satisfied. And another Gilbert Duray, now happily destroying the tract houses of Cupertino, would find himself bereft . . . Duray recalled the hostile conduct of the previous Elizabeth. The passways in that particular world had certainly not been closed off by an intruding Duray . . . A startling possibility came to his mind. Suppose a Duray had come to the house and, succumbing to temptation, had closed off all passways except that one communicating with his own world; suppose then that Elizabeth, discovering the imposture, had killed him . . . The theory had a grim plausibility and totally extinguished whatever inclination Duray might have had for making the world his home.

Elizabeth said, "Gilbert, why are you looking at me with that strange expression?"

Duray managed a feeble grin. "I guess I'm just in a bad mood this morning. Don't mind me. I'll go make out my report." He went into the wide cool living room, at once familiar and strange, and brought out the work-records of the other Gilbert Duray . . . He studied the handwriting: like his own, firm and decisive, but in some indefinable way different – perhaps a trifle more harsh and angular. The three Elizabeths were not identical, nor were the Gilbert Durays.

An hour passed. Elizabeth occupied herself in the kitchen; Duray pretended to write a report.

A bell sounded. "Somebody at the passway," said Elizabeth.

Duray said, "I'll take care of it."

He went to the passage room, stepped through the passway, looked through the peephole – into the large, bland sun-tanned face of Bob Robertson.

Duray opened the door. For a moment he and Bob Robertson confronted each other. Bob Robertson's eyes narrowed. "Why, hello, Gilbert. What are you doing home?"

Duray pointed to the parcel Bob Robertson carried. "What do you have there?"

"Oh, these?" Bob Robertson looked down at the parcel as if he had forgotten it. "Just some books for Elizabeth."

Duray found it hard to control his voice. "You're up to some mischief, you and your Rumfuddlers. Listen, Bob. Keep away from me and Elizabeth. Don't call here, and don't bring around any books. Is this definite enough?"

Bob raised his sun-bleached eyebrows. "Very definite, very explicit. But why the sudden rage? I'm just friendly old Uncle Bob."

"I don't care what you call yourself; stay away from us."

"Just as you like, of course. But do you mind explaining this sudden decree of banishment?"

"The reason is simple enough. We want to be left alone."

Bob made a gesture of mock despair. "All this over a simple invitation to a simple little party, which I'd really like you to come to."

"Don't expect us. We won't be there."

Bob's face suddenly went pink. "You're coming a very high horse over me, my lad, and it's a poor policy. You might just get hauled up with a jerk. Matters aren't all the way you think they are."

"I don't care a rap one way or another," said Duray. "Good-bye." He closed the locker door and backed through the passway. He returned into the living room.

Elizabeth called from the kitchen. "Who was it, dear?"

"Bob Robertson, with some books."

"Books? Why books?"

"I didn't trouble to find out. I told him to stay away. After this, if he's at the passway, don't open it."

Elizabeth looked at him intently. "Gil – you're so strange today! There's something about you that almost scares me."

"Your imagination is working too hard."

"Why should Bob trouble to bring me books? What sort of books? Did you see?"

"Demonology. Black magic. That sort of thing."

"Mmf. Interesting – but not all *that* interesting . . . I wonder if a world like ours, where no one has ever lived, would have things like goblins and ghosts?"

"I suspect not," said Duray. He looked toward the door. There was nothing more to be accomplished here, and it was time to return to his own Earth. He wondered how to make a graceful departure. And what would occur when the Gilbert Duray now working his rig came home?

Duray said, "Elizabeth, sit down in this chair here."

Elizabeth slowly slid into the chair at the kitchen table and watched him with a puzzled gaze.

"This may come as a shock," he said. "I am Gilbert Duray, but not your personal Gilbert Duray. I'm his cognate."

Elizabeth's eyes widened to lustrous dark pools.

Duray said, "On my own world Bob Robertson caused me and my Elizabeth trouble. I came here to find out what he had done and why and to stop him from doing it again."

Elizabeth asked, "What has he done?"

"I still don't know. He probably won't bother you again. You can tell your personal Gilbert Duray whatever you think best, or even complain to Alan."

"I'm bewildered by all this!"

"No more so than I." He went to the door. "I've got to leave now. Goodbye."

Elizabeth jumped to her feet and came impulsively forward. "Don't say goodbye. It was such a lonesome sound, coming from you . . . It's like my own Gilbert saying good-bye."

"There's nothing else to do. Certainly I can't follow my inclinations and move in with you. What good are two Gilberts? Who'd get to sit at the head of the table?"

"We could have a round table," said Elizabeth. "Room for six or seven. I like my Gilberts."

"Your Gilberts like their Elizabeths." Duray sighed and said, "I'd better go now."

Elizabeth held out her hand. "Good-bye, cognate Gilbert."

IX

From *Memoirs and Reflections:*

The Oriental world-view differs from our own – specifically my own – in many respects, and I was early confronted with a whole set of dilemmas. I reflected upon Asiatic apathy and its obverse, despotism; warlords and brain-laundries: indifference to disease, filth, and suffering; sacred apes and irresponsible fecundity.

I also took note of my resolve to use my machine in the service of all men.

In the end I decided to make the "mistake" of many before me; I proceeded to impose my own ethical point of view upon the Oriental lifestyle.

Since this was precisely what was expected of me, since I would have been regarded as a fool and a mooncalf had I done otherwise, since the rewards of cooperation far exceeded the gratifications of obduracy and scorn, my programs are a wonderful success, at least to the moment of writing.

Duray walked along the riverbank toward Alan Robertson's boat. A breeze sent twinkling cat's-paws across the water and bellied the sails that Alan Robertson had raised to air; the boat tugged at the mooring lines.

Alan Robertson, wearing white shorts and a white hat with a loose, flapping brim, looked up from the eye he had been splicing at the end of a halyard. "Aha, Gil! You're back. Come aboard and have a bottle of beer."

Duray seated himself in the shade of the sail and drank half the beer at a gulp. "I still don't know what's going on – except that one way or another Bob is responsible. He came while I was there. I told him to clear out. He didn't like it."

Alan Robertson heaved a melancholy sigh. "I realize that Bob has the capacity for mischief."

"I still can't understand how he persuaded Elizabeth to close the passways. He brought out some books, but what effect could they have?"

Alan Robertson was instantly interested. "What were the books?"

"Something about satanism, black magic; I couldn't tell you much else."

"Indeed, indeed!" muttered Alan Robertson. "Is Elizabeth interested in the subject?"

"I don't think so. She's afraid of such things."

"Rightly so. Well, well, that's disturbing." Alan Robertson cleared his throat and made a delicate gesture, as if beseeching Duray to geniality and tolerance. "Still, you mustn't be too irritated with Bob. He's prone to his little mischiefs, but – "

"'Little mischiefs'!" roared Duray. "Like locking me out of my home and marooning my wife and children? That's going beyond mischief!"

Alan Robertson smiled. "Here, have another beer; cool off a bit. Let's reflect. First, the probabilities. I doubt if Bob has really marooned Elizabeth and the girls or caused Elizabeth to do so."

"Then why are all the passways broken?"

"That's susceptible to explanation. He has access to the vaults; he might have substituted a blank for your master orifice. There's one possibility, at least."

Duray could hardly speak for rage. At last he cried out: "He has no right to do this!"

"Quite right, in the largest sense. I suspect that he only wants to induce you to his Rumfuddle."

"And I don't want to go, expecially when he's trying to put pressure on me."

"You're a stubborn man, Gil. The easy way, of course, would be to relax and look in on the occasion. You might even enjoy yourself."

Duray glared at Alan Robertson. "Are you suggesting that I attend the affair?"

"Well – no. I merely proposed a possible course of action."

Duray drank more beer and glowered out across the river. Alan Robertson said, "In a day or so, when this business is clarified, I think that we – all of us – should go off on a lazy cruise, out there among the islands. Nothing to worry us, no bothers, no upsets. The girls would love such a cruise."

Duray grunted. "I'd like to see them again before I plan any cruises. What goes on at these Rumfuddler events?"

"I've never attended. The members laugh and joke and eat and drink and gossip about the worlds they've visited and show each other movies: that sort of thing. Why don't we look in on last year's party? I'd be interested myself."

Duray hesitated. "What do you have in mind?"

"We'll set the dials to a year-old cognate to Bob's world, Fancy, and see precisely what goes on. What do you say?"

"I suppose it can't do any harm," said Duray grudgingly.

Alan Robertson rose to his feet. "Help me get these sails in."

X

From *Memoirs and Reflections*:

The problems that long have harassed historians have now been resolved. Who were the Cro-Magnons; where did they evolve? Who were the Etruscans? Where were the legendary cities of the proto-Sumerians before they migrated to Mesopotamia? Why the identity between the ideographs of Easter Island and Mohenjo Daro? All these fascinating questions have now been settled and reveal to us the full scope of our early history. We have preserved the library at old Alexandria from the Mohammedans and the Inca codices from the Christians. The Guanches of the Canaries, the Ainu of Hokkaido, the Mandans of Missouri, the blond Kaffirs of Bhutan: All are now known to us. We can chart the development of every language syllable by syllable, from the earliest formulation to the present. We have identified the Hellenic heroes, and I myself have searched the haunted forests of the ancient North and, in their own stone keeps, met face to face those mighty men who generated the Norse myths.

Standing before his machine, Alan Robertson spoke in a voice of humorous self-deprecation. "I'm not as trusting and forthright as I would like to be; in fact I sometimes feel shame for my petty subterfuges, and now I speak in reference to Bob. We all have our small faults, and Bob certainly does not lack his share. His imagination is perhaps his greatest curse: He is easily bored and sometimes tends to overreach himself. So while I deny him nothing, I also make sure that I am in a position to counsel or even remonstrate, if need be. Whenever I open a passway to one of his formulae, I unobtrusively strike a duplicate which I keep in my private file. We will find no difficulty in visiting a cognate to Fancy."

Duray and Alan Robertson stood in the dusk, at the end of a pale white beach. Behind them rose a low basalt cliff. To their right, the ocean reflected the afterglow and a glitter from the waning moon; to the left, palms stood black against the sky. A hundred yards along the beach dozens of fairy lamps had been strung between the trees to illuminate a long table laden with fruit, confections, punch in crystal bowls. Around the table stood several dozen men and women in animated conversation; music and the sounds of gaiety came down the beach to Duray and Alan Robertson.

"We're in good time," said Alan Robertson. He reflected a moment. "No doubt we'd be quite welcome; still, it's probably best to remain inconspicuous. We'll just stroll unobtrusively down the beach, in the shadow of the trees. Be careful not to stumble or fall, and no matter what you see or hear, do nothing! Discretion is essential; we want no awkward confrontations."

Keeping to the shade of the foliage, the two approached the merry group. Fifty yards distant, Alan Robertson held up his hand to signal a halt. "This is as close as we need approach; most of the people you know, or more accurately, their cognates. For instance, there is Royal Hart, and there is James Parham and Elizabeth's aunt, Emma Bathurst, and her uncle Peter and Maude Granger and no end of other folk."

"They all seem very gay."

"Yes, this is an important occasion for them. You and I are surly outsiders who can't understand the fun."

"Is this all they do, eat and drink and talk?"

"I think not," said Alan Robertson. "Notice yonder. Bob seems to be preparing a projection screen. Too bad that we can't move just a bit closer." Alan Robertson peered through the shadows. "But we'd better take no chances; if we were discovered, everyone would be embarrassed."

They watched in silence. Presently Bob Robertson went to the projection equipment and touched a button. The screen became alive with vibrating rings of red and blue. Conversations halted; the group turned toward the screen. Bob Robertson spoke, but his words were inaudible to the two who watched from the darkness. Bob Robertson gestured to the screen, where now appeared the view of a small country town, as if seen from an airplane. Surrounding was flat farm country, a land of wide horizons; Duray assumed the location to be somewhere in the Middle West. The picture changed to show the local high school, with students sitting on the steps. The scene shifted to the football field, on the day of a game – a very important game, to judge from the conduct of the spectators. The local team was introduced; one by one the boys ran out on the field to stand blinking into the autumn sunlight; then they ran off to the pregame huddle.

The game began; Bob Robertson stood by the screen in the capacity of an expert commentator, pointing to one or another of the players, analyzing the play. The game proceeded, to the manifest pleasure of the Rumfuddlers. At half time the bands marched and counter-marched, then play resumed. Duray became bored and made fretful comments to Alan Robertson, who only said: "Yes, yes; probably so" and "My word, the agility of that halfback!" and "Have you noticed the precision of the line-play? Very good indeed!" At last the final quarter ended; the victorious team stood under a sign reading:

THE SHOWALTER TORNADOES

CHAMPIONS OF TEXAS

1951

The players came forward to accept trophies; there was a last picture of the team as a whole, standing proud and victorious; then the screen burst out into a red and gold starburst and went blank. The Rumfuddlers rose to their feet and congratulated Bob Robertson, who laughed modestly and went to the table for a goblet of punch.

Duray said disgustedly, "Is this one of Bob's famous parties? Why does he make such a tremendous occasion of the affair? I expected some sort of debauch."

Alan Robertson said, "Yes, from our standpoint at least, the proceedings seem somewhat uninteresting. Well, if your curiosity is satisfied, shall we return?"

"Whenever you like."

Once again in the lounge under the Mad Dog Mountains, Alan Robertson said:

"So now and at last we've seen one of Bob's famous Rumfuddles. Are you still determined not to attend the occasion of tomorrow night?"

Duray scowled. "If I have to go to reclaim my family, I'll do so. But I just might lose my temper before the evening is over."

"Bob has gone too far," Alan Robertson declared. "I agree with you there. As for what we saw tonight, I admit to a degree of puzzlement."

"Only a degree? Do you understand it at all?"

Alan Robertson shook his head with a somewhat cryptic smile. "Speculation is pointless. I suppose you'll spend the night with me at the lodge?"

"I might as well," grumbled Duray. "I don't have anywhere else to go."

Alan Robertson clapped him on the back. "Good lad. We'll put some steaks on the fire and turn our problems loose for the night."

XI

From *Memoirs and Reflections*:

When I first put the Mark I machine into operation, I suffered great fears. What did I know of the forces that I might release? . . . With all adjustments at dead neutral, I punched a passway into a cognate Earth. This was simple enough – in fact, almost anticlimactic . . . Little by little I learned to control my wonderful toy; our own world and all its past phases became familiar to me. What of other worlds? I am sure that in due course we will move instantaneously from world to world, from galaxy to galaxy using a special space-traveling hub on Utilis. At the moment I am candidly afraid to punch through passways at blind random. What if I opened into the interior of a sun? Or into the center of a black hole? Or into an antimatter universe? I would certainly destroy myself and the machine and conceivably Earth itself.

Still, the potentialities are too entrancing to be ignored. With painstaking precautions and a dozen protective devices, I will attempt to find my way to new worlds, and for the first time interstellar travel will be a reality.

Alan Robertson and Duray sat in the bright morning sunlight beside the flinty-blue lake. They had brought their breakfast out to the table and now sat drinking coffee. Alan Robertson made cheerful conversation for the two of them. "These last few years have been easier on me; I've relegated a great deal of responsibility. Ernest and Henry know my policies as well as I do, if not better; and they're never frivolous or inconsistent." Alan Robertson chuckled. "I've worked two miracles: first, my machine, and second, keeping the business as simple as it is. I refuse to keep regular hours; I won't make appointments; I don't keep records; I pay no taxes; I exert great political and social influence, but only informally; I simply refuse to be bothered with administrative detail, and consequently I find myself able to enjoy life."

"It's a wonder some religious fanatic hasn't assassinated you," said Duray sourly.

"No mystery there! I've given them all their private worlds, with my best regards, and they have no energy left for violence! And as you know, I walk with a very low silhouette. My friends hardly recognize me on the street." Alan Robertson waved his hand. "No doubt you're more concerned with your immediate quandary. Have you come to a decision regarding the Rumfuddle?"

"I don't have any choice," Duray muttered. "I'd prefer to wring Bob's neck. If I could account for Elizabeth's conduct, I'd feel more comfortable. She's not even remotely interested in black magic. Why did Bob bring her books on satanism?"

"Well – the subject is inherently fascinating," Alan Robertson suggested, without conviction. "The name Satan derives from the Hebrew word for 'adversary'; it never applied to a real individual. 'Zeus,' of course, was an Aryan chieftain of about 3500 B.C., while 'Woden' lived somewhat later. He was actually 'Othinn,' a shaman of enormous personal force who did things with his mind that I can't do with the machine . . . But again I'm rambling."

Duray gave a silent shrug.

"Well, then, you'll be going to the Rumfuddle," said Alan Robertson, "by and large the best course, whatever the consequences.

"I believe that you know more than you're telling me."

Alan Robertson smiled and shook his head. "I've lived with too much uncertainty among my cognate and near-cognate worlds. Nothing is sure; surprises are everywhere. I think the best plan is to fulfill Bob's requirements. Then if Elizabeth is indeed on hand, you can discuss the event with her."

"What of you? Will you be coming?"

"I am of two minds. Would you prefer that I came?"

"Yes," said Duray. "You have more control over Bob than I do."

"Don't exaggerate my influence! He is a strong man, for all his idleness. Confidentially, I'm delighted that he occupies himself with games rather than . . ." Alan Robertson hesitated.

"Rather than what?"

"Than that his imagination should prompt him to less innocent games. Perhaps I have been overingenuous in this connection. We can only wait and see."

XII

From *Memoirs and Reflections:*

If the past is a house of many chambers, then the present is the most recent coat of paint.

At four o'clock Duray and Alan Robertson left the lodge and passed through Utilis to the San Francisco depot. Duray had changed into a somber dark suit; Alan Robertson wore a more informal costume: blue jacket and pale-gray trousers. They went to Bob Robertson's locker, to find a panel with the sign "NOT HOME! FOR THE RUMFUDDLE GO TO ROGER WAILLE'S LOCKER RC 3-96, AND PASS THROUGH TO EKSHAYAN!"

The two went on to Locker RC 3-96, where a sign read: "RUMFUDDLERS: PASS! ALL OTHERS: AWAY!"

Duray shrugged contemptuously, and parting the curtain, looked through the passway into a rustic lobby of natural wood, painted in black, red, yellow, blue, and white floral designs. An open door revealed an expanse of open land and water glistening in the afternoon sunlight. Duray and Alan Robertson passed through, crossed the foyer, and looked out upon a vast, slow river flowing from north to south. A rolling plain spread eastward away and over the horizon. The western bank of the river was indistinct in the afternoon glitter. A path led north to a tall house of eccentric architecture. A dozen domes and cupolas stood against the sky; gables and ridges created a hundred unexpected angles. The walls showed a fish-scale texture of hand-hewn shingles; spiral columns supported the second- and third-story entablatures, where wolves and bears, carved in vigorous curves and masses, snarled, fought, howled, and danced. On the side overlooking the river a pergola clothed with vines cast a dappled shade; here sat the Rumfuddlers.

Alan Robertson looked at the house, up and down the river, across the plain. "From the architecture, the vegetation, the height of the sun, the characteristic haze, I assume the river to be either the Don or the Volga, and yonder the steppes. From the absence of habitation, boats, and artifacts, I would guess the time to be early historic – perhaps 2,000 or 3,000 B.C., a colorful era. The inhabitants of the steppes are nomads; Scyths to the east, Celts to the west, and to the north the homeland of the Germanic and Scandinavian tribes; and yonder the mansion of Roger Waille, and very interesting, too, after the extra-vagant fashion of the Russian baroque. And, my word! I believe I see an ox on the spit! We may even enjoy our little visit!"

"You do as you like," muttered Duray. "I'd just as soon eat at home."

Alan Robertson pursed his lips. "I understand your point of view, of course, but perhaps we should relax a bit. The scene is majestic; the house is delightfully picturesque, the roast beef is undoubtedly delicious; perhaps we should meet the situation on its own terms."

Duray could find no adequate reply and kept his opinions to himself.

"Well, then," said Alan Robertson, "equability is the word. So now let's see what Bob and Roger have up their sleeves." He set off along the path to the house, with Duray sauntering morosely a step or two behind.

Under the pergola a man jumped to his feet and flourished his hand; Duray recognized the tall, spare form of Bob Robertson. "Just in time," Bob called jocosely. "Not to early, not too late. We're glad you could make it."

"Yes, we found we could accept your invitation after all," said Alan Robertson. "Let me see, do I know anyone here? Roger, hello! . . . And

William . . . Ah! the lovely Dora Gorski! . . . Cypriano . . ." He looked around the circle of faces, waving to his acquaintants.

Bob clapped Duray on the shoulder. "Really pleased you could come! What'll you drink? The locals distill a liquor out of fermented mare's milk, but I don't recommend it."

"I'm not here to drink," said Duray. "Where's Elizabeth?"

The corners of Bob's wide mouth twitched. "Come now, old man; let's not be grim. This is the Rumfuddle! A time for joy and self-renewal! Go dance about a bit! Cavort! Pour a bottle of champagne over your head! Sport with the girls!"

Duray looked into the blue eyes for a long second. He strained to keep his voice even. "Where is Elizabeth?"

"Somewhere about the place. A charming girl, your Elizabeth! We're delighted to have you both!"

Duray swung away. He walked to the dark and handsome Roger Waille. "Would you be good enough to take me to my wife?"

Waille raised his eyebrows as if puzzled by Duray's tone of voice. "She is primping and gossiping. If necessary I suppose I could pull her away for a moment or two."

Duray began to feel ridiculous, as if he had been locked away from his world, subjected to harrassments and doubts, and made the butt of some obscure joke. "It's necessary," he said. "We're leaving."

"But you've just arrived!"

"I know."

Waille gave a shrug of amused perplexity and turned away toward the house. Duray followed. They went through a tall, narrow doorway into an entry-hall paneled with a beautiful brown-gold wood that Duray automatically identified as chestnut. Four high panes of tawny glass turned to the west filled the room with a smoky half-melancholy light. Oak settees, upholstered in leather, faced each other across a black, brown, and gray rug. Taborets stood at each side of the settees, and each supported an ornate golden candelabra in the form of conventionalized stag's heads. Waille indicated these last. "Striking, aren't they? The Scythians made them for me. I paid them in iron knives. They think I'm a great magician; and for a fact, I am." He reached into the air and plucked forth an orange, which he tossed upon a settee. "Here's Elizabeth now, and the other maenads as well."

Into the chamber came Elizabeth, with three other young women whom Duray vaguely recalled having met before. At the sight of Duray, Elizabeth stopped short. She essayed a smile and said in a light, strained voice, "Hello, Gil. You're here after all." She laughed nervously and, Duray felt, unnaturally. "Yes, of course you're here. I didn't think you'd come."

Duray glanced toward the other women, who stood with Waille, watching half expectantly. Duray said, "I'd like to speak to you alone."

"Excuse us," said Waille. "We'll go on outside."

They departed. Elizabeth looked longingly after them and fidgeted with the buttons of her jacket.

"Where are the children?" Duray demanded curtly.

"Upstairs, getting dressed." She looked down at her own costume, the festival raiment of a Transylvanian peasant girl: a green skirt embroidered with red and blue flowers, a white blouse, a black velvet vest, glossy black boots.

Duray felt his temper slipping; his voice was strained and fretful. "I don't understand anything of this. Why did you close the passways?"

Elizabeth attempted a flippant smile. "I was bored with routine."

"Oh? Why didn't you mention it to me yesterday morning? You didn't need to close the passways."

"Gilbert, please. Let's not discuss it."

Duray stood back, tongue-tied with astonishment. "Very well," he said at last. "We won't discuss it. You go up and get the girls. We're going home."

Elizabeth shook her head. In a neutral voice she said, "It's impossible. There's only one passway open. I don't have it."

"Who does? Bob?"

"I guess so; I'm not really sure."

"How did he get it? There were only four, and all four were closed."

"It's simple enough. He moved the downtown passway from our locker to another and left a blank in its place."

"And who closed off the other three?"

"I did."

"Why?"

"Because Bob told me to. I don't want to talk about it. I'm sick to death of the whole business." And she half whispered: "I don't know what I'm going to do with myself."

"I know what I'm going to do," said Duray. He turned toward the door.

Elizabeth held up her hands and clenched her fists against her breast. "Don't make trouble – please! He'll close our last passway!"

"Is that why you're afraid of him? If so – don't be. Alan wouldn't allow it."

Elizabeth's face began to crumple. She pushed past Duray and walked quickly out upon the terrace. Duray followed, baffled and furious. He looked back and forth across the terrace. Bob was not to be seen. Elizabeth had gone to Alan Robertson; she spoke in a hushed, urgent voice. Duray went to join them. Elizabeth became silent and turned away, avoiding Duray's gaze.

Alan Robertson spoke in a voice of easy geniality. "Isn't this a lovely spot? Look how the setting sun shines on the river!"

Roger Waille came by rolling a cart with ice, goblets, and a dozen bottles. He said: "Of all the places on all the Earths, this is my favorite. I call it Ekshayan, which is the Scythian name for this district."

A woman asked, "Isn't it cold and bleak in the winter?"

"Frightful!" said Waille. "The blizzards howl down from the north; then they stop, and the land is absolutely still. The days are short, and the sun comes up red as a poppy. The wolves slink out of the forests, and at dusk they circle the house. When a full moon shines, they howl like banshees, or maybe the banshees are howling! I sit beside the fireplace, entranced."

"It occurs to me," said Manfred Funk, "that each person, selecting a site for his home, reveals a great deal about himself. Even on old Earth, a man's home was ordinarily a symbolic simulacrum of the man himself; now, with every option available, a person's house is himself."

"This is very true," said Alan Robertson, "and certainly Roger need not fear that he has revealed any discreditable aspects of himself by showing us his rather grotesque home on the lonely steppes of prehistoric Russia."

Roger Waille laughed. "The grotesque house isn't me; I merely felt that it fitted its setting . . . Here, Duray, you're not drinking. That's chilled vodka; you can mix it or drink it straight in the time-tested manner."

"Nothing for me, thanks."

"Just as you like. Excuse me; I'm wanted elsewhere." Waille moved away, rolling the cart. Elizabeth leaned as if she wanted to follow him, then remained beside Alan Robertson, looking thoughtfully over the river.

Duray spoke to Alan Robertson as if she were not there. "Elizabeth refuses to leave. Bob has hypnotized her."

"That's not true," said Elizabeth softly.

"Somehow, one way or another, he's forced her to stay. She won't tell me why."

"I want the passway back," said Elizabeth. But her voice was muffled and uncertain.

Alan Robertson cleared his throat. "I hardly know what to say. It's a very awkward situation. None of us wants to create a disturbance – "

"There you're wrong," said Duray.

Alan Robertson ignored the remark. "I'll have a word with Bob after the party. In the meantime I don't see why we shouldn't enjoy the company of our friends, and that wonderful roast ox! Who is that turning the spit? I know him from somewhere."

Duray could hardly speak for outrage. "After what he's done to us?"

"He's gone too far, much too far," Alan Robertson agreed. "Still, he's a flamboyant, feckless sort, and I doubt if he understands the full inconvenience he's caused you."

"He understands well enough. He just doesn't care."

"Perhaps so," said Alan Robertson sadly. "I had always hoped – but that's neither here nor there. I still feel that we should act with restraint. It's much easier not to do than to undo."

Elizabeth abruptly crossed the terrace and went to the front door of the tall house, where her three daughters had appeared – Dolly, twelve; Joan, ten; Ellen, eight – all wearing green, white, and black peasant frocks and glossy black boots. Duray thought they made a delightful picture. He followed Elizabeth across the terrace.

"It's Daddy," screamed Ellen, and threw herself in his arms. The other two, not to be outdone, did likewise.

"We thought you weren't coming to the party," cried Dolly. "I'm glad you did, though."

"So'm I."

"So'm I."

"I'm glad I came, too, if only to see you in these pretty costumes. Let's go see Grandpa Alan." He took them across the terrace, and after a moment's hesitation, Elizabeth followed. Duray became aware that everyone had stopped talking to look at him and his family, with, so it seemed, an extraordinary, even avid, curiosity, as if in expectation of some entertaining extravagance of conduct. Duray began to burn with emotion. Once, long ago, while crossing a street in downtown San Francisco, he had been struck by an automobile, suffering a broken leg and a fractured clavicle. Almost as soon as he had been knocked down, pedestrians came pushing to stare down at him, and Duray, looking up in pain and shock, had seen only the ring of white faces and intent eyes, greedy as flies around a puddle of blood. In hysterical fury he had staggered to his feet, striking out into every face within reaching distance, men and women alike. He hated them more than the man who had run him down: the ghouls who had come to enjoy his pain. Had he the miraculous power, he would have crushed them into a screaming bale of detestable flesh and hurled the bundle twenty miles out into the Pacific Ocean . . .

Some faint shadow of this emotion affected him now, but today he would provide them no unnatural pleasure. He turned a single glance of cool contempt around the group, then took his three eager-faced daughters to a bench at the back of the terrace. Elizabeth followed, moving like a mechanical object. She seated herself at the end of the bench and looked off across the river. Duray stared heavily back at the Rumfuddlers, compelling them to shift their gazes to where the ox roasted over a great bed of coals. A young man in a white jacket turned the spit; another basted the meat with a long-handled brush. A pair of Orientals carried out a carving table; another brought a carving set; a fourth wheeled out a cart laden with salads, round crusty loaves, trays of cheese and herrings. A fifth man, dressed as a Transylvanian gypsy, came from the house with a violin. He went to the corner of the terrace and began to play melancholy music of the steppes.

Bob Robertson and Roger Waille inspected the ox, a magnificent sight indeed. Duray attempted a stony detachment, but his nose was under no such strictures; the odor of the roast meat, garlic, and herbs tantalized him unmercifully. Bob Robertson returned to the terrace and held up his hands for attention; the fiddler put down his instrument. "Control your appetites; there'll still be a few minutes, during which we can discuss our next Rumfuddle. Our clever colleague Bernard Ulman recommends a hostelry in the Adirondacks: the Sapphire Lake Lodge. The hotel was built in 1902, to the highest standards of Edwardian comfort. The clientele is derived from the business community of New York. The cuisine is kosher; the management maintains an atmosphere of congenial gentility; the current date is 1930. Bernard has furnished photographs. Roger, if you please."

Waille drew back a curtain to reveal a screen. He manipulated the projection machine, and the hotel was displayed on the screen: a rambling, half-timbered structure overlooking several acres of park and a smooth lake.

"Thank you, Roger. I believe that we also have a photograph of the staff."

On the screen appeared a stiffly posed group of about thirty men and women, all smiling with various degrees of affability. The Rumfuddlers were amused; some among them tittered.

"Bernard gives a very favorable report as to the cuisine, the amenities, and the charm of the general area. Am I right, Bernard?"

"In every detail," declared Bernard Ulman. "The management is attentive and efficient; the clientele is well-established."

"Very good," said Bob Robertson. "Unless someone has a more entertaining idea, we will hold our next Rumfuddle at the Sapphire Lake Lodge. And now I believe that the roast beef should be ready – done to a turn, as the expression goes."

"Quite right," said Roger Waille. "Tom, as always, has done an excellent job at the spit."

The ox was lifted to the table. The carver set to work with a will. Duray went to speak to Alan Robertson, who blinked uneasily at his approach. Duray asked, "Do you understand the reason for these parties? Are you in on the joke?"

Alan Robertson spoke in a precise manner: "I certainly am not 'in on the joke,' as you put it." He hesitated, then said: "The Rumfuddlers will never again intrude upon your life or that of your family. I am sure of this. Bob became overexuberant; he exercised poor judgment, and I intend to have a quiet word with him. In fact, we have already exchanged certain opinions. At the moment your best interests will be served by detachment and unconcern."

Duray spoke with sinister politeness: "You feel, then, that I and my family should bear the brunt of Bob's jokes?"

"This is a harsh view of the situation, but my answer must be Yes."

"I'm not so sure. My relationship with Elizabeth is no longer the same. Bob has done this to me."

"To quote an old apothegm: 'Least said, soonest mended.'"

Duray changed the subject. "When Waille showed the photograph of the hotel staff, I thought some of the faces were familiar. Before I could be quite sure, the picture was gone."

Alan Robertson nodded unhappily. "Let's not develop the subject, Gilbert. Instead – "

"I'm into the situation too far," said Duray. "I want to know the truth."

"Very well, then," said Alan Robertson hollowly, "your instincts are accurate. The management of the Sapphire Lake Lodge, in cognate circumstances, has achieved an unsavory reputation. As you have guessed, they comprise the leadership of the National Socialist party during 1938 or thereabouts. The manager, of course, is Hitler, the desk clerk is Goebbels, the headwaiter is Göring, the bellboys are Himmler and Hess, and so on down the line. They are, of course, not aware of the activities of their cognates of other worlds. The hotel's clientele is for the most part Jewish, which brings a macabre humor to the situation."

"Undeniably," said Duray. "What of that Rumfuddlers party that we looked in on?"

"You refer to the high-school football team? The 1951 Texas champions, as I recall." Alan Robertson grinned. "And well they should be. Bob identified the players for me. Are you interested in the lineup?"

"Very much so."

Alan Robertson drew a sheet of paper from his pocket. "I believe – yes, this is it." He handed the sheet to Duray who saw a schematic lineup:

LE	LT	LG	C	RG	RT	RE
Achilles	Charle-magne	Hercules	Goliath	Samson	Richard the Lion-hearted	Billy the Kid

	LHB	Q Machiavelli	RHB	
	Sir Galahad		Geronimo	

FB
Cuchulain

Duray returned the paper. "You approve of this?"

"I had best put it like this," said Alan Robertson, a trifle uneasily. "One day, chatting with Bob, I remarked that much travail could be spared the human race if the more notorious evildoers were early in their lives shifted to environments which afforded them constructive outlets for their energies. I speculated that having the competence to make such changes, it was perhaps our duty to do so. Bob became interested in the concept and formed his group, the Rumfuddlers, to serve the function I had suggested. In all candor I believe that Bob and his friends have been attracted more by the possibility of entertainment than by altruism, but the effect has been the same."

"The football players aren't evildoers," said Duray. "Sir Galahad, Charlemagne, Samson, Richard the Lion-hearted . . ."

"Exactly true," said Alan Robertson, "and I made this point to Bob. He asserted that all were brawlers and bullyboys, with the possible exception of Sir Galahad; that Charlemagne, for example, had conquered much territory to no particular achievement; that Achilles, a national hero to the Greeks, was a cruel enemy to the Trojans; and so forth. His justifications are somewhat specious perhaps . . . Still, these young men are better employed making touchdowns than breaking heads."

After a pause Duray asked: "How are these matters arranged?"

"I'm not entirely sure. I believe that by one means or another, the desired babies are exchanged with others of similar appearance. The child so obtained is reared in appropriate circumstances."

"The jokes seem elaborate and rather tedious."

"Precisely!" Alan Robertson declared. "Can you think of a better method to keep someone like Bob out of mischief?"

"Certainly," said Duray. "Fear of the consequences." He scowled across the terrace. Bob had stopped to speak to Elizabeth. She and the three girls rose to their feet.

Duray strode across the terrace. "What's going on?"

"Nothing of consequence," said Bob. "Elizabeth and the girls are going to help serve the guests." He glanced toward the serving table, then turned back to Duray. "Would you help with the carving?"

Duray's arm moved of its own volition. His fist caught Bob on the angle of the jaw and sent him reeling back into one of the white-coated Orientals, who carried a tray of food. The two fell into an untidy heap. The Rumfuddlers were shocked and amused and watched with attention.

Bob rose to his feet gracefully enough and gave a hand to the Oriental. Looking toward Duray, Bob shook his head ruefully. Meeting his glance, Duray noted a pale blue glint; then Bob once more became bland and debonair.

Elizabeth spoke in a low despairing voice: "Why couldn't you have done as he asked? It would have all been so simple."

"Elizabeth may well be right," said Alan Robertson.

"Why should she be right?" demanded Duray. "We are his victims! You've allowed him a taste of mischief, and now you can't control him!"

"Not true!" declared Alan Robertson. "I intend to impose rigorous curbs upon the Rumfuddlers, and I will be obeyed."

"The damage is done, so far as I am concerned," said Duray bitterly. "Come along, Elizabeth, we're going Home."

"We can't go Home. Bob has the passway."

Alan Robertson drew a deep sigh and came to a decision. He crossed to where Bob stood with a goblet of wine in one hand, massaging his jaw with the other. Alan Robertson spoke to Bob politely but with authority. Bob was slow in making a reply. Alan Robertson spoke again, sharply. Bob only shrugged. Alan Robertson waited a moment, then returned to Duray, Elizabeth, and the three children.

"The passway is at his San Francisco apartment," said Alan Robertson in a measured voice. "He will give it back to you after the party. He doesn't choose to go for it now."

Bob once more commanded the attention of the Rumfuddlers. "By popular request we replay the record of our last but one Rumfuddle, contrived by one of our most distinguished, diligent, and ingenious Rumfuddlers, Manfred Funk. The locale is the Red Barn, a roadhouse twelve miles west of Urbana, Illinois; the time is the late summer of 1926; the occasion is a Charleston dancing contest. The music is provided by the legendary Wolverines, and you will hear the fabulous cornet of Leon Bismarck Beiderbecke." Bob gave a wry smile, as if the music were not to his personal taste. "This was one of our most rewarding occasions, and here it is again."

The screen showed the interior of a dance-hall, crowded with excited young men and women. At the back of the stage sat the Wolverines, wearing tuxedos; to the front stood the contestants: eight dapper young men and eight pretty girls in short skirts. An announcer stepped forward and spoke to the crowd through a megaphone: "Contestants are numbered one through eight! Please, no encourage-ment from the audience. The prize is this magnificent trophy and fifty dollars cash; the presentation will be made by last year's winner, Boozy Horman. Remember, on the first number we eliminate four con-testants, on the second number, two; and after the third number we select our winter. So then: Bix and the Wolverines and 'Sensation Rag'!"

From the band came music; from the contestants, agitated motion.

Duray asked, "Who are these people?"

Alan Robertson replied in an even voice: "The young men are locals and not important. But notice the girls: No doubt you find them attractive. You are not alone. They are Helen of Troy, Deirdre, Marie Antoinette, Cleopatra, Salome, Lady Godiva, Nefertiti, and Mata Hari."

Duray gave a dour grunt. The music halted; judging applause from the audience, the announcer eliminated Marie Antoinette, Cleopatra, Deirdre, Mata Hari, and their respective partners. The Wolverines played "Fidgety Feet"; the four remaining contestants danced with verve and dedication, but Helen and Nefertiti were eliminated. The

Wolverines played "Tiger Rag." Salome and Lady Godiva and their young men performed with amazing zeal. After carefully appraising the volume of applause, the announcer gave his judgment to Lady Godiva and her partner. Large on the screen appeared a close-up view of the two happy faces; in an excess of triumphant joy they hugged and kissed each other. The screen went dim; after the vivacity of the Red Barn the terrace above the Don seemed drab and insipid.

The Rumfuddlers shifted in their seats. Some uttered exclamations to assert their gaiety; others stared out across the vast empty face of the river.

Duray glanced toward Elizabeth; she was gone. Now he saw her circulating among the guests with three other young women, pouring wine from Scythian decanters.

"It makes a pretty picture, does it not?" said a calm voice. Duray turned to find Bob standing behind him; his mouth twisted in an easy half-smile, but his eye glinted pale blue.

Duray turned away. Alan Robertson said, "This is not at all a pleasant situation, Bob, and in fact completely lacks charm."

"Perhaps at future Rumfuddles, when my face feels better, the charm will emerge . . . Excuse me; I see that I must enliven the meeting." He stepped forward. "We have a final pastiche: oddments and improvisations, vignettes and glimpses, each in its own way entertaining and instructive. Roger, start the mechanism, if you please."

Roger Waille hesitated and glanced sidelong toward Alan Robertson.

"The item number is sixty-two, Roger," said Bob in a calm voice. Roger Waille delayed another instant, then shrugged and went to the projection machine.

"The material is new," said Bob, "hence I will supply a commentary. First we have an episode in the life of Richard Wagner, the dogmatic and occasionally irascible composer. This year is 1843; the place is Dresden. Wagner sets forth on a summer night to attend a new opera, *Der Sanger Krieg*, by an unknown composer. He alights from his carriage before the ball; he enters; he seats himself in his loge. Notice the dignity of his posture, the authority of his gestures! The music begins. Listen!" From the projector came the sound of music. "It is the overture," stated Bob. "But notice Wagner: Why is he stupefied? Why is he overcome with wonder? He listens to the music as if he has never heard it before. And in fact he hasn't; he has only just yesterday set down a few preliminary notes for this particular opus, which he planned to call *Tannhäuser*; today, magically, he hears it in its final form. Wagner will walk home slowly tonight, and perhaps in his abstraction he will kick the dog Schmutzi . . . Now to a different scene: St. Petersburg in the year 1880 and the stables in back of the Winter Palace. The ivory and gilt carriage rolls forth to convey the czar and the czarina to a reception at the British Embassy. Notice the drivers: stern, well-groomed, intent at their business. Marx's beard is well-trimmed; Lenin's goatee is not so pronounced. A groom comes to watch the carriage roll away. He has a kindly twinkle in his eye, does Stalin." The screen went dim once more, then brightened to show a city street lined with automobile showrooms and used-car lots. "This is one of Shawn Henderson's projects. The four used-car lots are operated by men who in other circumstances were religious notables: prophets and so forth. That alert, keen-featured man in front of Quality Motors, for instance, is Mohammed. Shawn is conducting a careful survey, and at our next Rumfuddle he will report upon his dealings with these four famous figures."

Alan Robertson stepped forward, somewhat diffidently. He cleared his throat. "I don't like to play the part of spoilsport, but I'm afraid I have no choice. There will be no further Rumfuddles. Our original goals have been neglected, and I note far too many episodes of purposeless frivolity and even cruelty. You may wonder at what seems a sudden decision, but I have been considering the matter for several days. The Rumfuddles have taken a turn in an unwholesome direction and conceivably might become a grotesque new vice, which, of course, is far from our original ideal. I'm sure that every sensible person, after a few moments' reflection, will agree that now is the time to stop. Next week you may return to me all passways except those to worlds where you maintain residence."

The Rumfuddlers sat murmuring together. Some turned resentful glances toward Alan Robertson; others served themselves more bread and meat. Bob came over to join Alan and Duray. He spoke in an easy manner. "I must say that your admonitions arrive with all the delicacy of a lightning bolt. I can picture Jehovah smiting the fallen angels in a similar style."

Alan Robertson smiled. "Now, then, Bob, you're talking nonsense. The situations aren't at all similar. Jehovah struck out in fury; I impose my restriction in all goodwill in order that we can once again turn our energies to constructive ends."

Bob threw back his head and laughed. "But the Rumfuddlers have lost the habit of work. We only want to amuse ourselves, and after all, what is so noxious in our activities?"

"The trend is menacing, Bob." Alan Robertson's voice was reasonable. "Unpleasant elements are creeping into your fun, so stealthily that you yourself are unaware of them. For instance, why torment poor Wagner? Surely there was gratuitous cruelty, and only to provide you a few instants of amusement. And since the subject is in the air, I heartily deplore your treatment of Gilbert and Elizabeth. You have brought them both an extraordinary inconvenience, and in Elizabeth's case, actual suffering. Gilbert got something of his own back, and the balance is about even."

"Gilbert is far too impulsive," said Bob. "Self-willed and egocentric, as he always has been."

Alan held up his hand. "There is no need to go further into the subject, Bob. I suggest that you say no more."

"Just as you like, though the matter, considered as practical rehabilitation, isn't irrelevant. We can amply justify the work of the Rumfuddlers."

Duray asked quietly, "Just how do you mean, Bob?"

Alan Robertson made a peremptory sound, but Duray said, "Let him say what he likes and make an end to it. He plans to do so anyway."

There was a moment of silence. Bob looked across the terrace to where the three Orientals were transferring the remains of the beef to a service cart.

"Well?" Alan Robertson asked softly. "Have you made your choice?"

Bob held out his hands in ostensible bewilderment. "I don't understand you! I want only to vindicate myself and the Rumfuddlers. I think we have done splendidly. Today we have allowed Torquemada to roast a dead ox instead of a living heretic; Marquis de Sade has fulfilled his obscure urges by caressing seared flesh with a basting brush, and did you notice the zest with which Ivan the Terrible hacked up the carcass? Nero, who has real talent, played his violin. Attila, Genghis Khan, and Mao Tse-tung efficiently served the guests. Wine was poured by Messalina, Lucrezia Borgia, Delilah, and Gilbert's charming wife, Elizabeth. Only Gilbert failed to demonstrate his rehabilitation, but at least he provided us a touching and memorable picture: Gilles de Rais, Elizabeth Báthory, and their three virgin daughters. It was sufficient. In every case we have shown that rehabilitation is not an empty word."

"Not in every case," said Alan Robertson, "specifically that of your own."

Bob looked at him askance. "I don't follow you."

"No less than Gilbert are you ignorant of your background. I will now reveal the circumstances so that you may understand something of yourself and try to curb the tendencies which have made your cognate an exemplar of cruelty, stealth, and treachery."

Bob laughed: a brittle sound like cracking ice. "I admit to a horrified interest."

"I took you from a forest a thousand miles north of this very spot while I traced the phylogeny of the Norse gods. Your name was Loki. For reasons which are not now important I brought you back to San Francisco, and there you grew to maturity."

"So I am Loki."

"No. You are Bob Robertson, just as this is Gilbert Duray, and here is his wife, Elizabeth. Loki, Gilles de Rais, Elizabeth Báthory: These names applied to human material which has not functioned quite as well. Gilles de Rais, judging from all evidence, suffered from a brain tumor; he fell into his peculiar vices after a long and honorable career. The case of Princess Elizabeth Báthory is less clear, but one might suspect syphilis and consequent cerebral lesions."

"And what of poor Loki?" inquired Bob with exaggerated pathos.

"Loki seemed to suffer from nothing except a case of old-fashioned meanness.

Bob seemed concerned. "So that these qualities apply to me?"

"You are not necessarily identical to your cognate. Still, I advise you to take careful stock of yourself, and so far as I am concerned, you had best regard yourself as on probation."

"Just as you say." Bob looked over Alan Robertson's shoulder. "Excuse me; you've spoiled the party, and everybody is leaving. I want a word with Roger."

Duray moved to stand in his way, but Bob shouldered him aside and strode across the terrace, with Duray glowering at his back.

Elizabeth said in a mournful voice, "I hope we're at the end of all this."

Duray growled. "You should never have listened to him."

"I didn't listen; I read about it in one of Bob's books; I saw your picture; I couldn't – "

Alan Robertson intervened. "Don't harass poor Elizabeth; I consider her both sensible and brave; she did the best she could."

Bob returned. "Everything taken care of," he said cheerfully. "All except one or two details."

"The first of these is the return of the passway. Gilbert and Elizabeth – not to mention Dolly, Joan, and Ellen – are anxious to return to Home."

"They can stay here with you," said Bob. "That's probably the best solution."

"I don't plan to stay here," said Alan Robertson in mild wonder. "We are leaving at once."

"You must change your plans," said Bob. "I have finally become bored with your reproaches. Roger doesn't particularly care to leave his home, but he agrees that now is the time to make a final disposal of the matter."

Alan Robertson frowned in displeasure. "The joke is in very poor taste, Bob."

Roger Waille came from the house, his face somewhat glum. "They're all closed. Only the main gate is open."

Alan Robertson said to Gilbert: "I think that we will leave Bob and Roger to their Rumfuddle fantasies. When he returns to his senses, we'll get your passway. Come along, then, Elizabeth! Girls!"

"Alan," said Bob gently, "you're staying here. Forever. I'm taking over the machine."

Alan Robertson asked mildly: "How do you propose to restrain me? By force?"

"You can stay here alive or dead; take your choice."

"You have weapons, then?"

"I certainly do." Bob displayed a pistol. "There are also the servants. None have brain tumors or syphilis; they're all just plain bad."

Roger said in an awkward voice, "Let's go and get it over."

Alan Robertson's voice took on a harsh edge. "You seriously plan to maroon us here, without food?"

"Consider yourself marooned."

"I'm afraid that I must punish you, Bob, and Roger as well."

Bob laughed gaily. "You yourself are suffering from brain disease – megalomania. You haven't the power to punish anyone."

"I still control the machine, Bob."

"The machine isn't here. So now – "

Alan Robertson turned and looked around the landscape, with a frowning air of expectation. "Let me see. I'd probably come down from the main gate; Gilbert and a group from behind the house. Yes, here we are."

Down the path from the main portal, walking jauntily, came two Alan Robertsons with six men armed with rifles and gas grenades. Simultaneously from behind the house appeared two Gilbert Durays and six more men, similarly armed.

Bob stared in wonder. "Who are these people?"

"Cognates," said Alan, smiling. "I told you I controlled the machine, and so do all my cognates. As soon as Gilbert and I return to our Earth, we must similarly set forth and in our turn do our part on other worlds cognate to this . . . Roger, be good enough to summon your servants. We will take them back to Earth. You and Bob must remain here."

Waille gasped in distress. "Forever?"

"You deserve nothing better," said Alan Robertson. "Bob perhaps deserves worse." He turned to the cognate Alan Robertsons. "What of Gilbert's passway?"

Both replied, "It's in Bob's San Francisco apartment, in a box on the mantelpiece."

"Very good," said Alan Robertson. "We will now depart. Good-bye, Bob. Good-bye, Roger. I am sorry that our association ended on this rather unpleasant basis."

"Wait!" cried Roger. "Take me back with you!"

"Good-bye," said Alan Robertson. "Come along then, Elizabeth. Girls! Run on ahead!"

XIII

Elizabeth and the children had returned to Home; Alan Robertson and Duray sat in the lounge above the machine. "Our first step," said Alan Robertson, "is to dissolve our obligation. There are, of course, an infinite number of Rumfuddles at Ekshayans and an infinite number of Alans and Gilberts. If we visited a single Rumfuddle, we would, by the laws of probability, miss a certain number of the emergency situations. The total number of permutations, assuring that an infinite number of Alans and Gilberts makes a random choice among an infinite number of Ekshayans, is infinity raised to the infinite power. What percentage of this number yields blanks for any given Ekshayan, I haven't calculated. If we visited Ekshayans until we had by our own efforts rescued at least one Gilbert and Alan set, we might be forced to scour fifty or a hundred worlds or more. Or we might achieve our rescue on the first visit. The wisest course, I believe, is for you and I to visit, say, twenty Ekshayans. If each of the Alan and Gilbert sets does the same, then the chances for any particular Alan and Gilbert to be abandoned are one in twenty times nineteen times eighteen times seventeen, et cetera. Even then I think I will arrange that an operator check another five or ten thousand worlds to gather up that one lone chance . . ."